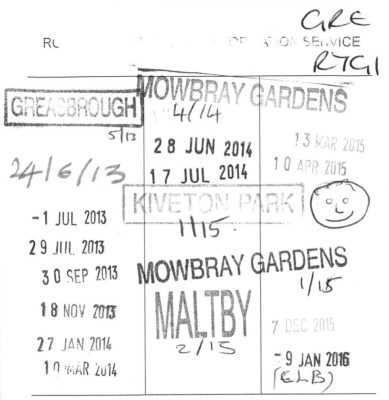

This book must be returned by the date specified at the time of issue as the DATE DUE FOR RETURN.
The loan may be extended (personally, by post, telephone or online) for a further period if the book is not required by another reader, by quoting the above number / author / title.

Enquiries: 01709 336774

www.rotherham.gov.uk/libraries

Lizzie Enfield is a journalist and regular contributor to national newspapers and magazines. She is married with three children and lives in Brighton.

UNCOUPLED

Holly has always been in control of her life, juggling her job in London, with being a mother to Chloe and Jake and wife to Mark, who she loves and still fancies — even after seventeen years of marriage. So when she emerges unharmed from a train crash, which leaves several dead and many more injured, Holly is determined to carry on as normal and not to become a victim. But she can't forget the younger man who comforted her in the chaos of the crash, and when she sees him again on her daily commute up to town, there's a flash of something between them. Is it recognition? Curiosity? Or is there something more? And what of Anne-Marie, another 'survivor'? Just what is her story?

LIZZIE ENFIELD

UNCOUPLED

Complete and Unabridged

CHARNWOOD
Leicester

First published in Great Britain in 2012 by
Headline Review
An imprint of Headline Publishing Group
London

First Charnwood Edition
published 2013
by arrangement with
Headline Publishing Group
London

British Library CIP Data

Enfield, Lizzie.
  Uncoupled.
  1. Large type books.
  I. Title
  823.9'2–dc23

  ISBN 978–1–4448–1443–9

Published by
F. A. Thorpe (Publishing)
Anstey, Leicestershire

Set by Words & Graphics Ltd.
Anstey, Leicestershire
Printed and bound in Great Britain by
T. J. International Ltd., Padstow, Cornwall

This book is printed on acid-free paper

To Chrissie, Kitty and Lucas
(you shouldn't be reading this yet)

1

BBC Radio 4
12 April
9 a.m.
The news is read by Charlotte Green.
We are getting very early reports of a train crash on the Brighton to London line. Part of the Southern train appears to have derailed inside the Balcombe tunnel between Haywards Heath and Gatwick Airport. Passengers on board say the vehicle was going into the tunnel, when there was a loud crash and it jolted to a halt.

Emergency services are on the way to the scene . . .

★   ★   ★

Holly knew that by staying with her he was putting himself at risk. But, as he held her in the darkness, she didn't want him to let go. He squeezed her hand, as if he knew what she was thinking, and said, 'It'll be OK.'

It was eerily quiet in the tunnel and Holly suspected he was as scared as she was. The initial cries of surprise, when the train had lurched from standstill and ricocheted off the walls on to its side, had quickly given way to a quieter sense of shock and then a unanimous flurry of activity.

'We ought to get out,' several voices had said at once.

1

'We'll need to break the windows,' a chorus of others responded.

Then there was the sound of windows breaking and people scrambling up over the upturned floor of the carriage, desperate to escape.

No one actually said, 'Do you think it was a bomb?' or 'There could be another.'

And, with a perverse sense of logic, Holly thought that as long as she didn't say it either then it might make it untrue.

But that didn't stop her from being terrified, especially when people began to struggle up from wherever they'd been thrown and edge themselves towards the broken carriage windows. Then she realised that she was trapped beneath the twisted metal of her seat and couldn't move.

'We need to get out,' a soft voice said somewhere near her.

In the weak light, emanating from mobile phones and laptop screens, Holly could just about make out the outline of the young man who'd been sitting opposite her.

'I can't move,' she told him, surprising herself by sounding remarkably calm and matter-of-fact. 'I don't think I'm hurt but I can't get out from under the seat.'

He bent down to investigate and felt for her in the semi-darkness, brushing her torso with his hands without apology.

'It's twisted.' He tried to move the seat but it was firmly lodged against the wall of the carriage and over Holly's prone body.

Holly saw him turn and look towards the other passengers who were now climbing through the broken windows.

'Please don't leave me,' she heard herself say, although she wished she hadn't.

He ought to get out too, whoever he was. He might have a wife and family of his own who needed him more than she did. But he was already settling down beside her, reaching out for her hand and taking hold of it.

*   *   *

Holly felt strangely detached from what was going on, as if she was watching it happen to someone else. She urged herself to think of Mark and the children, to try to see their faces and hear their chatter. She was physically unable to do anything, but at least she could stay focused on the people she needed to get out for.

As if he too was thinking the same thing, he began asking questions.

'Are you married?'

'Yes.' Holly felt the reassuring warmth of his hand in hers. 'And I've got two children.'

'Tell me about them,' he said.

Holly wished he'd been more specific, asked her what her name was or how long she'd been married or what she did or how old she was. His question was too general.

'Mark, my husband . . . ' She considered this, thinking it was important to describe him accurately now. 'He's kind and clever and funny and good looking. And he's very compelling. If

3

you met him, you would like him. Everybody does.'

Holly never prayed but she hoped hard now that Mark knew this was how she thought of him. He'd been a bit down recently, his energy diminished, and slightly less himself. She knew he was worried about work but hadn't asked if anything else was bothering him.

'And the children?' he asked, squeezing her hand again. 'Are they boys or girls?'

'A girl and a boy,' she said. 'They are both gorgeous.'

Saying this helped her sense them more keenly.

Chloe seemed to be emerging from the moody phase of adolescence, beautiful, clever and enjoying Holly's company again, while Jake still filled her with wonder every time she looked at him. Even though his beautiful fresh face was peppered with spots and his hair was beginning to smell of wet PE kit, he still seemed impossibly perfect.

Chloe had been in the shower when she'd left the house and Holly had shouted goodbye through the sound of running water, but her daughter hadn't answered.

'Bye, Jakey,' Holly had said, trying to force something muttered out of him, when he left for school.

A group of his friends had called and when Holly opened the door and Jake had snuck past, his adolescent body language screamed: Don't try to kiss or hug me in front of my friends!

'I didn't say goodbye properly to any of them

4

this morning,' she said, as if confessing this to a stranger would ease the burden of not having done so.

'We'll be out of here soon enough,' he tried to reassure her, but she could hear the fear in his voice.

Holly thought of her late grandmother, Mary, whose mantra had been: 'Never leave the house without saying goodbye properly, you never know when you might be hit by a bus.'

Mary had been Irish and her life was governed by superstitions. She was for ever crossing herself, calling upon various saints or shouting, 'Get those shoes off the table, before something terrible occurs!'

The saying goodbye properly was founded on a terrible reality. Her husband Bob had been knocked down and killed by a 5A bus, as he went to buy a paper. It had happened on the same morning Mary had turned on him in an uncharacteristic fit of anger when he'd asked, innocently enough, 'What's it like out? Will I need a coat?'

'How do I know if you need your coat or not? Are you not old enough to decide for yourself?' she had shouted at him across the breakfast table. 'I've enough children without you wanting to become one of them yourself.'

'I'm sure he was fretting about it and not concentrating,' Mary said later, referring to the moment when Bob stepped into the path of the oncoming double-decker. 'Perhaps that's why he wasn't looking properly.'

Mary came to live with them, shortly after her

5

husband's death. So Holly spent the last years of her teenage life unable to leave the house without an elaborate ritual of goodbyes. It had made her anxious at the time, never leaving to go to school without being reminded she might meet an untimely end.

As an adult, she'd happily shut the door on her family and gone wherever she was going without saying any fond farewells first.

But now, as her grandmother's face swam into the forefront of her mind, Holly wished she'd opened the door of the bathroom and said goodbye to Chloe through the steam of the shower, and that, instead of respecting Jake's pre-pubescent angst, she'd ruffled his hair as he left for school.

To Mark her goodbye had been a slightly mocking, 'Are you going to wear that hat to work?'

She'd said it in a tone that people who have been married for a long time reserve for each other. It wasn't outright rude but it implied that she didn't think it suited him. Twenty years ago Holly thought Mark utterly gorgeous, no matter what he put on or took off.

'Mark bought a hat at the weekend,' Holly told the man with her now.

'Yes?' He sounded unsure how to react to this.

'The children liked it but I didn't really.'

It was a grey pork-pie style with blue-spotted ribbon trim. A very pretty girl had been selling them in an outside stall in the North Laine. Holly thought Mark had stopped to look at the hats so that he could get a better look at the pretty girl and had been surprised when he had begun trying them on.

'How much was it?' she asked him as they continued their walk through the North Laine to the seafront.

'It was only eight pounds,' he said, and Holly presumed he'd thought this a price worth paying not to have the pretty girl think him a time-waster.

He had put the hat on when they'd got home.

'I love it.' Chloe had run her finger around the ribbon. 'Is it vintage? Can I borrow it?'

'You look like one of the Specials,' Jake had said, and Mark had done a little ska dance in the sitting room.

'When have you come across the Specials?' Holly asked.

'Chloe bought a vinyl album in the market.'

'But we don't have anything to play records on.'

'I know,' Chloe interjected. 'I want to get a turntable for my birthday. They're cool.'

'We should go to a gig sometime, Hol,' Mark had said, singing the first few lines of *Too Much Too Young* and taking her hands so she had to join him in the sitting room dance.

Chloe had laughed but Jake had rolled his eyes in embarrassment and then done an impression of his parents' generation's dance routines.

'This is how middle-aged people dance.' He had stood up and, with his feet firmly rooted to the floor, twisted slightly at the waist and moved his arms a fraction. 'And then, when they get drunk, they do this!'

Jake had raised one leg off the floor, continued the slight twisting of the waist and begun rotating the lifted foot around in the same direction.

It was a good impression and they'd all laughed.

'It was worth eight pounds, just for that,' Holly had said, when Mark took the hat off.

Later, when she was brushing her teeth and she'd looked at Mark, lying naked in the bath, his hair plastered against the sides of his face, she had wondered if he was becoming sensitive about his receding hair line and the tiny coin-shaped patch of baldness which was new to the top of his head.

She'd bent over the side of the bath and kissed him and he'd slipped his hand under her dressing gown and stroked her breast, saying, 'I'll be out in a minute.'

Holly tried to keep hold of that moment now, and the evening which preceded it, not think about what might happen next.

'You should go,' she said, suddenly resolute that she shouldn't rob this stranger of his chance to get out of danger and near-stifling darkness.

'Is there anybody in here?' a voice rang out through the carriage.

'Here!' he called back. 'There's a woman over here. Her leg's trapped under the luggage rack and she can't get out.'

'It's OK now, love.' The voice came closer. 'We'll try and get you moved as soon as possible. Are you hurt, sir?'

Torches flashed through the carriage and

Holly saw clearly again the face of the man who'd been sitting opposite her before it all happened.

He was bending towards her, and kissing her on the forehead.

'Good luck,' he whispered.

'Thank you.' Holly heard her own voice say this quietly. As she let go of his hand he disappeared into a blur of fluorescent jackets.

2

People asked Holly afterwards if her life had flashed before her and she said, 'No, not exactly.'

She had suddenly recalled certain scenes from her life so vividly that they seemed almost real, like the last time the family had been on holiday in Cornwall. She wondered afterwards if she'd thought of this because they were going again to the same part of the country in a week's time. By recalling the past in such detail, she was probably subconsciously trying to cling to the future.

★ ★ ★

'Dad bought a wetsuit!' Chloe and Jake looked flushed and healthy from the two hours they'd spent chasing waves. They were beside themselves with laughter at Mark's new buy.

Holly had no idea why this was so funny but their laugher was infectious and she began giggling too, as she waited to find out what the joke was.

'Where is Dad now?' she asked them, as they queued to buy hot chocolate at the café next to the surf-hire shop. 'Does he want a drink too?'

'He's waiting in the car.' This was enough to start Chloe off again.

'He won't be joining us,' Jake snorted. 'He said we can have the drinks in the car. He wants to go straight back to the cottage.'

'Yes,' Chloe spluttered. 'He wants to go straight back!'

It was early May and Holly had the tail end of a cold and had not wanted to go in the sea, with or without a wetsuit. So Mark had spent the last couple of hours body-boarding on the beach at Polzeath, while Holly had walked across the cliffs to Daymer Bay and back. She'd hoped they'd all have a drink or lunch in the café together and wondered why he was so anxious to get back.

Perhaps he was cold, she thought. The children were rosy with exertion but when she'd kissed them their cheeks were freezing.

'Two hot chocolates, please, and a cup of tea,' she said, when she reached the front of the queue. 'And should I get something for Dad? Did he say?'

'Why don't you get him a hot chocolate and I'll have two if he doesn't want it?' Jake suggested hopefully, and looked surprised when Holly said that was a good idea.

They walked the short distance across the sand to where Mark was waiting in the car. He was sitting on a towel, still wearing his wetsuit. He looked up and smiled when Holly knocked on the window with the lid of the cup.

'Hot chocolate?' she asked as he wound the window down.

'Thank you, gorgeous.' He took it from her and winked.

'Chloe and Jake can't tell me for laughing how you came to buy a wetsuit,' she said, before walking round to the passenger seat and getting

11

in. 'I take it it's the one you are modelling right now?'

'Does my paunch look big in it?' Mark asked, sitting up straighter and breathing in as she sat next to him.

Holly glanced down at his stomach. Wetsuits flattered only the very shapely. For all that they held bits of you in, they seemed to dislodge other bits and made you bulge in places where you hadn't previously. Mark now had a strange tyre slightly higher than where his, only recently acquired, excess flesh usually protruded.

'You've hardly got a paunch.' She leaned over and ran her hand across the black material of the wetsuit. She hadn't thought she had a thing for clammy Neoprene but felt slightly turned on by the feel of Mark's belly beneath it. If the children had not been climbing into the back of the car, she would have been tempted to undo the zip and stick her hand beneath it.

'I've got enough of a paunch that I may never be able to get out of this bloody thing.' Mark glanced over his shoulder at Chloe and Jake. 'You might have to cut me out of it when we get home, Holly.'

'That's why he bought it,' Chloe said triumphantly, doing up her seatbelt. 'It took him about half an hour to get it on, and when we'd finished he said he couldn't face trying to get out of it on the beach . . . '

'So he told the guys at the shop he wanted to buy it and wear it home!' Jake finished off the story for her.

'Really?' Holly looked at Mark.

12

'Really.' He looked sideways at her and shrugged. 'Thirty quid to save myself the embarrassment of being a fat bloke on a beach, trying to get out of a wetsuit. I need to lose some weight. I've had too many business lunches this year.'

'You look good to me.' Holly reached her hand over the gear stick and rubbed his stomach beneath the suit material again. It was true he had put on a bit of weight recently, but she thought it suited him. He was tall enough to carry off a bit of extra flesh around his midriff and, perversely, she found the flaw made him more attractive to her anyway. It was as if the slight imperfection of middle-aged spread and the few grey hairs that were appearing in his otherwise full head of dark hair gave him a kind of vulnerability which had previously been lacking.

Mark had always seemed too physically perfect to her. He was tall and dark and lean, but with a kindness to his face that softened his otherwise almost intimidating good looks. The stretches and scars of childbirth and the tell-tale signs of middle age had left a definite impression on Holly herself and, in moments of self-doubt, she felt inferior by comparison. So Mark's tiny bit of extra belly and his obvious embarrassment about it made her feel less vulnerable herself and more protective towards him.

'It was that trip to Finland that did it,' he said, starting the engine of the car. 'They fed us every five minutes.'

'Only when they weren't whipping you,' Chloe

13

sang from the back of the car.

'Birching.' Mark grinned over his shoulder at her. 'There's a difference, you know.'

'It's all part and parcel of selling whisky to the Finns,' Holly said. 'Or so I'm told.'

'It's true.' Mark began reversing out of the parking space. 'Most of the business on that trip was conducted in the sauna or the snow, with a little light birching in between. I still have the scars to show for it.'

'Don't I know it!' Holly grinned.

Mark's business partner, Chris, had corroborated his version of discussing whisky sales in the sauna, before being led naked into the snow and handed twigs for tapping away impurities.

'I started tapping Mark and wondering how we would ever face each other in the office again,' Chris had told her, 'when Iivarim, who was six foot six and had the most enormous balls I've ever seen, said we weren't doing it hard enough and took over!'

'I've never been so scared in a professional capacity,' Mark had told Holly, as she rubbed Sudocrem on to the welt marks. 'But it was worth it. They're going to start selling Red Ptarmigan in several Finnish hotel chains.'

'Did they get a good deal?' Holly asked as Mark winced when she came across a wound that looked slightly raw.

'Yes. As you can see, they put me under pressure, Holly,' he laughed back and then inhaled sharply as her hands moved down his back.

'The wetsuit wasn't the only humiliation I've

14

been subjected to today,' Mark said as he drove between the lines of cars parked on the beach. Their boots served as changing rooms for hard-core surfers, all of whom, Holly noted and hoped Mark hadn't, seemed to be peeling off wetsuits with ease and revealing perfectly honed torsos.

'You know that deli in St James' Street at home?' Mark looked ahead.

'Yes?' Holly caught sight of a man who had taken off his wetsuit and was wearing nothing underneath it. 'Wow!'

'What?' Mark glanced in the surfer's direction but he'd stepped around the side of a camper van.

'Nothing.' Holly smiled to herself. 'You were saying about the deli in St James' Street?'

'Yes. There's a very pretty girl who works in there. We had a conversation about Cornwall once and I told her we often went to Polzeath and went surfing.' Mark paused as he checked the traffic before pulling on the road. 'She looked suitably impressed when I said it.'

'Do you mean you gave her the impression you were like someone out of *Endless Summer*?' Holly eyed him quizzically.

'Not quite, but maybe one of the penguins in *Surf's Up*.' Mark shrugged.

'How does she come into your humiliating day?' Holly asked.

'We got one really good wave that took us right to the shore and as I was floundering around in the shallows, trying to get up and looking like a beached whale, I heard this voice say, 'Aren't you from Brighton?'' Mark pulled out into the road. 'I looked up to see this vision in a wetsuit, with a proper standing up surfboard tucked under her arm, looking at me as if to say, 'I never believed you could really surf'.'

'I'm sure she was looking at you as if to say, 'Wow, he looks hot in that wetsuit!'' Holly laughed.

'Err Mum, pl-ease,' Jake and Chloe had chorused from the back seat.

They'd have pl-eased some more if they hadn't gone downstairs to make more hot chocolate and slump in front of the television the moment they got back to the holiday cottage.

It had a huge wet room just by the front door and Mark had gone in there to try to get out of his new wetsuit and take a shower.

'Can you help me undo the bloody thing?' he'd called to Holly, as the kids disappeared downstairs, and after she'd managed slowly to unroll the suit as far as his waist, she'd found middle-aged spread wasn't the only bulge that was making it difficult to get off.

'That's not helping.'

She'd looked up at Mark and he'd looked at her and said, 'You're looking a bit salty after your walk, Holly. Why don't you have a shower too?'

I watched the news, because I couldn't think what else to do. I'd cried all afternoon, after I got the call. Then, when I was exhausted from the tears, I cleaned the kitchen; scrubbed it from top to bottom. I had to do something and cleaning has a certain reassuring rhythm and effect.

'Call someone,' Julia had said, when she left. 'Do you want me to call someone? You shouldn't be on your own.'

'No,' I snapped at her, partly because it wasn't her place to call anyone. It wasn't her who had lost her husband and I couldn't bear her concern. It seemed to make it worse, Julia thinking she might help if she called someone else to come and be with me. I didn't want to give her the satisfaction of saying, 'I made sure she had someone with her, just in case.' I wanted her to worry about me.

Besides, I couldn't think who else to call. I don't have that many friends here. Julia had to go and pick up her children from school and nursery; Toby and Gemma, her perfect off-spring, one dark like her ex-husband and one blonde, like herself.

'Blessed,' my mother would have said, of her children, if she were still alive to see them. 'She's blessed with two beautiful children.'

My mother was only blessed with the one. 'A

17

gift from God,' she used to tell me and anyone else who cared to listen. She was forty-four when I was born. Mum thought she couldn't have children. She'd resigned herself to a life without them and then suddenly 'a gift from God'.

Geoff and I hadn't been blessed either but I didn't want to think about that, not today. It was too much, on top of everything else. I'd lost my husband and with him my chance to have a child.

Julia, Toby and Gemma would be the perfect family, except that Andrew, her ex, left her not long after Gemma was born.

'He said it wasn't what he wanted,' she told me once, when I was having coffee in her kitchen. She threw out her arm in a broad sweep as she said it, as if it was the kitchen and the dining room and the lounge beyond that Andrew hadn't wanted, rather than Julia and the children and the domesticity.

'Do you think you'll ever get back together again?' I asked her once, over another coffee. That seemed to be the extent of our friendship really, the odd coffee, but in the absence of any others, I valued that. I thought of her as my best friend, at this stage of my life, because really there weren't any others.

I thought Andrew might regret it later, that one rash moment, triggered by something probably insignificant that made him decide to leave behind his life to date. I know my mother regretted not being at home with me when I was a teenager, even though she said she couldn't help the way she felt at the time.

18

'I should have been there for you then,' she said to me, when I visited her in hospital the week before she died.

'I was OK, Mum,' I said, lying to protect her. There was no point her knowing then how much I had hated the new life her absence forced upon me. And it was behind me now. I had Geoff and I was looking forward, not back.

Now I found myself looking backward again, to my time with him, because I couldn't bring myself to think forward, to the time without him.

So I put on BBC News 24 and watched their coverage of the crash, giving it my full time and attention, hoping maybe I'd catch a glimpse of Geoff, see him again in the moments while he was still mine. It seemed possible while I was watching. I almost believed that, if I caught sight of him on the television, then perhaps I'd be able to turn the clock back and make it all go away.

But I didn't see Geoff. By the time I turned the television on, the emergency services had been there for several hours and the reporter was saying that they were still working to free people stuck in the wreckage.

Then they cut to footage, filmed earlier, showing ambulance workers carrying a woman on a stretcher away from the mouth of the tunnel. There was a close-up of her face and I thought I recognised her from the train.

I've definitely seen her before. She's a striking-looking woman, with dark hair and dark eyes, not young but beautiful. I was sure as I watched her being carried on the stretcher that

19

I'd sat opposite her a few weeks ago and she had smiled when I sat down, acknowledging my presence with an openness that a lot of commuters don't have.

They didn't say, on the news, what had happened to her or whether she was seriously injured or not, but when I saw her face she looked haunted, as if she'd seen something she wished she had never seen.

I recognised the look immediately, because it was the same look my mother wore when she'd realised exactly what we'd been a part of: a look that sets you apart from the rest of the world. The look of someone who has witnessed something they wish they'd never had to.

The woman on the news had been trapped in that tunnel God knows how long. Minutes? Hours? The reporter didn't say. But however long it was, it must have been long enough for her to question whether she'd ever get out. I wondered then, as I looked at her moving off the screen into a waiting ambulance, if she'd seen Geoff.

Had he passed her in the carriage, and had she smiled at him when he noticed her while looking for a seat?

The TV camera cut back to the mouth of the tunnel, where the back end of the train was being slowly pulled back, and the reporter was saying it might take days to clear the wreckage from the line, but it would take everyone caught up in the accident much longer to get their lives back on track.

I felt as if he was talking directly to me, as if he

20

knew that without Geoff I had no idea how I was going to carry on. There are only so many times you can keep on picking up the pieces and carrying on. I didn't know if I could do it again, but I knew that in a few weeks' time, when people stopped being sympathetic and understanding and asking how I was, that was what I was going to have to do.

And so was she, the woman on the stretcher. She was going to have to carry on too.

3

BBC Radio 4
14 April
4 p.m.
The news is read by Corrie Corfield.
Another person has died in hospital following a train crash in Sussex earlier this week. Greg Simpson was travelling in one of the carriages of the commuter train, which came uncoupled and was hit by another train in the Balcombe tunnel near Haywards Heath. His death brings the total number killed to five. Several others involved in the crash are still being treated for their injuries, though none are thought to be life-threatening. The line between Haywards Heath and Gatwick Airport remains closed while accident investigators try to find out how the carriages from the Brighton train became detached . . .

*   *   *

'Your mother's here.' Mark didn't usually curtain twitch when either of Holly's parents was expected, but today he seemed eager for her mum to arrive. 'She's never going to get the car in that space.'

'Don't watch her.' Holly could hear a car moving backwards and forwards, snail-like. 'You'll put her off. She hates parking at the best of times.'

22

'I'll put the kettle on,' Mark said.

He'd been doing this more or less constantly for the past two days. Holly wished she'd been able to go straight back to work, but people kept saying it was too soon: Mark, the counsellor he'd arranged for her to see tomorrow, the paramedics who had checked her over after she was cut free from the train, and her mother when she'd spoken to her on the phone.

'It feels odd, us both being at home with the children at school and nothing to do,' Holly kept saying to Mark, who had taken time off to look after her.

'Do you want a cup of tea?' was his usual reply.

Holly was glad of her mother's visit. Susan didn't really do fussing, a fact Jake became aware of when he was about five years old and she had looked after him for the day.

'If I fall over,' he told Holly on her return from wherever it was she had been, 'you stop whatever you are doing and say, 'Oh, dear, darling, are you all right?' But Granny just carries on whatever she is doing and says, 'Bad luck!''

Holly suspected that if Susan mentioned the train crash at all it would be obliquely: 'How are you, really?' rather than just 'How are you?' or 'Have you been eating properly?'

She wondered what her mother would make of the fact she was booked to see a counsellor tomorrow. Neither of her parents believed in going over things.

'In my day,' her father, Patrick, would say if the subject arose, 'people just built the Burma railway and got on with it.'

Holly realised she was more like her parents than she had previously thought.

Even as Mark was phoning the counsellor to book an appointment, she was thinking that she didn't need it.

'I was lucky to get out alive and unhurt, when so many others were not,' she told him. 'I'd rather go back to work or do something than sit around talking about it.'

'It's too soon,' he had said. 'And anyway, it's only a few days. We're going on holiday on Friday. Shall I put the kettle on?'

The Easter holidays began on Friday and they were going to Cornwall again. The memory of their last holiday there, which had seemed so vivid to Holly on the train, now seemed distant. Holly felt as if that holiday had been taken by someone else, not the person who in a couple of days would be packing up the car and driving five hours to Polzeath with her husband and rapidly growing children.

The doorbell rang with a brisk 'ping', which suggested her mother was the caller. Susan was always keen not to disturb anyone or put them out. Rather than ringing the bell with the insistence of someone who wanted to come in, she brushed it with her fingertips, as if she might go away again, if no one heard.

'I'll pop in quickly on my way back from the funeral,' she had told Holly on the phone, with the emphasis on popping. She wasn't one to outstay her welcome.

'I'm sorry about Hugh,' Holly had said.

'Where is the funeral being held?'

'Forest Row,' Susan replied. 'I'll see you on Wednesday then.'

Her parents' lives seemed to be punctuated by funerals at the moment. Patrick was five years older than Susan, but friends of both of them seemed to keep passing on. They read the Obituaries every day after lunch and usually found someone they had known buried in the column inches.

'Darling.' Her mother stood on the doorstep, taking Holly in as if she expected to see some sign of physical change. 'How are you, really?'

'Hello, Mum.' Holly held the door wide open. 'I'm fine. How was it?'

'Oh, well, you know how these things are,' Susan replied, neither of them asking and neither of them answering the questions they wanted to ask and answer. 'I was quite glad to be able to get away.'

She put her bag down and hugged Holly, closer and for slightly longer than was normal. Holly suspected this might be her mother's only reference to what had happened.

'Susan, I didn't hear you arrive.' Mark appeared in the hallway now, lying. 'Did you manage to park all right?'

'It took me a while to find a space,' she replied. 'I'm in the street around the corner.'

'Oh.' Mark's voice registered surprise mixed with a hint of knowingness, as if he'd suspected all along that she would never be able to get into the space he'd watched her navigating.

He stepped forward now and kissed his mother-in-law.

'Would you like a drink, Susan?' he asked. 'Or a cup of tea? I've just boiled the kettle.'

'I'd love a cup of tea.' She was more appreciative of Mark's offer than Holly. 'I've been wanting one all afternoon. There was tea at the funeral but not enough cups to go round.'

'It was good of you to come on and see us.' Mark was boiling the kettle again and clattering around with cups. 'You've had rather a lot of driving today.'

'I wanted to come and see you all,' she said, looking around. 'Where are the children?'

'Jake's in his room, I think, I'll call him in a minute,' Mark told her. 'And Chloe isn't back from school yet. They'll be pleased to see you. It's a shame Patrick couldn't come too.'

'I know and he sends his love,' Susan addressed this to Holly, 'but he promised to stay and help Jean clear up afterwards. He helped her a lot with the arrangements, so I think he wants to see the thing through. It was terrible the way Hugh died. He had a stroke while they were on holiday in Petra.'

'Yes, Holly told me,' Mark said. 'It must have made it all seem much worse, being away from home.'

'I wish I could have come, Mum,' Holly said. 'I liked Hugh.'

Her parents had known Hugh and his wife Jean long before Holly and her sister Fay were born. They had moved around a lot and ended up living in Northampton, but often went to stay for long weekends with their old friends in Sussex.

'I liked him too,' Susan acknowledged. 'But there was no need for you to come too. Fay was there.'

'Jean is Fay's godmother,' Holly said as if explaining to Mark why her sister's presence at the funeral was deemed more necessary than hers.

'I can't remember meeting either of them,' Mark said, bringing a teapot over to the table where Susan and Holly were now sitting. 'Did they come to our wedding?'

'No,' Susan smiled thankfully at the sight of the tea. 'They were Patrick's friends really.'

'Were they?' Holly had never heard her mother describe them this way before.

She thought of most of her parents' friends as being her mother's primarily and that on social occasions her father, often grudgingly, simply tagged along. Patrick used to have a few colleagues he would mention from time to time, but not friends.

'Patrick was at university with Jean,' her mother said, pulling the teapot across the table and pouring herself a cup. 'He's known her since they were twenty, long before she met Hugh.'

'So were there many people you knew at the funeral?' Mark put a tin of biscuits on to the table.

'There were a few, but Patrick seemed to know quite a lot. I left him there, with old university friends, reminiscing.'

She rolled the last word around her tongue as if it were slightly distasteful to her.

'So, darling,' she changed the subject, 'you've

27

been through the wars. How are you?'

'I'll go and see what Jake is up to,' Mark said, getting up. 'He can't have heard you come in.'

'I'm OK, Mum,' Holly said, adding a 'really' before her mother could say one with a question mark attached.

'But you've had such a shock. It must have been awful for you.' Susan paused, looking for the right words. 'Terrifying.'

'I was scared at the time, Mum,' Holly admitted. 'And frustrated. It seemed ridiculous that I wasn't hurt, but I couldn't get out and I was worried about what might happen next.'

'I heard about the crash on the news,' her mother told her. 'But I told myself there were so many trains going up and down to London that it was unlikely to be yours.'

'You never think something like that is going to happen to you, do you?' Holly replied. 'And now, I feel already as if it didn't.'

'What do you mean?' Susan asked.

'Like I said, I was scared at the time. But now I realise how lucky I've been. There were people killed, and I haven't even got a scratch to show for it.' Holly glanced down at her legs which were slightly bruised beneath the jeans she was wearing. 'I was very lucky. It could have been worse, but it wasn't.'

'Hi, Gran.' Jake ambled in and over to where they were sitting, taking a biscuit from the tin with one hand as he bent over and lightly kissed his grandmother. 'I didn't hear you come in.'

'Gosh, look how tall you are!' Jake had had another growth spurt recently but the rest of his body was on catch up. He kept putting on inches upwards but never out, rendering him well and truly lanky. 'Were you plugged into some piece of equipment in your room?'

Susan and Patrick were perpetually bemused by the technology of the twenty-first century. At home they had a television, a 'wireless' and a 'gramophone record player'.

Holly had once bought them an iPod and dock for Christmas, planning to convert their records into sound files and load it for them, but even the sight of the box had reduced her mother to tears.

'I know it seems terribly ungrateful,' she had sobbed, 'but I really don't want to have to use it. Can you take it back?'

'I was on my Xbox.' Jake sat down at the table.

'Is that a reality TV programme?' Susan asked.

'No, it's a games console,' Jake told her.

'Hugh and Jean's daughter lives in France,' Susan told them all. 'She's got a five-year-old boy who hardly speaks any English. I thought it must be hard for them, not being able to communicate with him, but now I don't often know what my own grandchildren are talking about either!'

'I'll show you, if you like,' Jake said. 'I've got a Monopoly game on it.'

'Thank you, Jake.' Susan smiled at him. 'But I ought to get going really. I don't like driving in the dark.'

'When will Dad get back?' Holly asked, as her mother drained her tea.

'Actually, he was going to stay over with Jean.'

Her mother looked away as she said this. 'Her daughter's going back to France tonight and she didn't want to be alone in the house.'

'Oh.' Holly wasn't sure what else to say.

'Look after yourself, darling.' Susan stood up and gave her a hug. 'Such a shock.'

'I'm OK, Mum,' Holly told her again.

'Life goes on, I suppose,' Susan said.

Her mother had always been stoical, but as Holly looked at her now, she thought she saw tears starting to form in her eyes.

'Life goes on,' she repeated, blinking them away.

4

BBC Radio 4
3 May
7 a.m.
The news is read by Charlotte Green.
Salvage teams have finished clearing the wreckage of a train from the Balcombe tunnel, in Sussex, and the line has reopened.

The carriages were stuck in the tunnel, when they became detached from the rest of the train and were then hit by another, travelling on the route between London and Brighton.

Five people were killed and scores of others were injured in the incident.

An investigation has been launched into the cause of the uncoupling . . .

* * *

It *was* him. Holly was sure of it. He was sitting across the aisle a few rows ahead of her, facing in the direction the train was moving. Holly couldn't see his face but she recognised the slight wave of his mousey-blond hair and the way his shoulders hunched as he bent over a laptop.

Holly had hoped she'd encounter him again, at some point, but she hadn't expected it to be so soon, or for her stomach to flip like it did when she looked across the carriage and set eyes on him.

She studied the back of his neck where a recent haircut exposed a white line above a level of sun tan. He raised his hand and ran it through the thick crown of hair down to the newly styled nape, as if he could sense he was being watched. Holly saw he was wearing a wedding ring. Perhaps he was newly married.

She wondered if there was a word for how she felt now. She could only liken it to the way she had felt when she first set eyes on Chloe after she was born. It was not as intense, but it was the unexpectedness of feeling anything at all for someone you knew so little about.

It was a relief, as well as a surprise, when she clapped eyes on her newborn daughter and was overwhelmed by an all-consuming something for her.

It hadn't been love, not at first. But there had been a connection, and the initial fear had been replaced by a sense of wonder at what their joint futures might hold.

As Holly looked across the crowded railway carriage she felt a mixture of anticipation and relief coupled with a strange sense of recognition, not just of his profile from this angle, but of him. Even though she knew almost nothing about him.

Perhaps, she thought to herself, there is a German word to describe what I'm feeling, like *schadenfreude* or *ersatz* or that Finnish word that Mark kept telling her meant leaving one last biscuit on the plate. It was the sort of thing he knew and liked to tell anyone who cared to listen.

'The French have a word for singing and crying at the same time,' he would say. '*Chantepleurer*. We don't have a word for that.'

'That's because English people don't do it,' Holly had replied. 'There's probably also a word in French for smoking Gauloises while wandering around your apartment, after having sex with your lover in the afternoon.'

Mark had laughed, a little oddly.

'It's *Latterkrampe* — the Norwegian word for convulsive laughter,' he informed her.

'Oh, I see. I thought you were spluttering because you suddenly felt guilty at the mention of an afternoon lover!' Holly had joked.

'*Freir Bunuelos*, darling.' Mark used one of his favourite Spanish expressions for 'get lost'.

'And fry doughnuts to you to!' Holly had replied, kissing him to show no offence had been taken.

She thought of Chloe again now, and how when her daughter had looked up at her for the first time she'd realised that they already knew each other, because for the past nine months they'd been sharing the same body. She felt as if she knew *him* because of the time they'd spent together.

The fat man sitting next to her shifted in his seat, nudging Holly back to the present.

The train was always busy at this time in the morning but she'd got on early enough at Brighton to find a window seat, facing forward, in the middle of the train. This, she told herself, was a safe seat.

Holly had taken her newspaper from her bag

and tried to muster interest in a by-election for a hitherto Tory safe seat in London. She'd meant to bring her book, which might have absorbed her more than column inches of newsprint, but had forgotten it.

She blamed Mark for this. He'd been fussing so much that she'd just wanted to get out of the house. In her haste she'd forgotten half the stuff she would normally have taken to London.

By the time she'd read how Labour thought they had a real chance of winning this particular election, the train had reached Haywards Heath and a man she was sure fell into the clinically obese category was inching down the aisle towards her.

Please don't sit here, she had thought to herself, knowing that he would. She was one of the few people on the train who actually fitted into the allocated seat space. The carriages were new but the measurements had obviously been drawn up by an anorexic dwarf.

There was a spare seat opposite but the newcomer had shifted his weight towards her now, and signalled his intent to sit next to her with a slight nod of the head. Holly reasoned that her instinctive recoiling was not because she was fattist, but rather slightly claustrophobic. The blubbery slab of thigh, which had overlapped on to her side of the seat, felt warm and sweaty and she felt the panic beginning to rise inside her.

She'd given the fat man a big smile, hoping this gave the impression that she welcomed his bulky presence. Then she'd felt her stomach lurch as she'd noticed the back of *his* head, bending over a laptop a few seats up the aisle.

Holly crossed her legs but kicked a woman who had just taken the seat opposite as she did so.

'Sorry,' she said.

The woman was filing her nails. Holly didn't think a train was the place for this. It was too personal, like brushing your teeth or shaving your legs, but the woman obviously thought the carriage as good a space as any to get ready for the day ahead. She put her file in a small make-up bag on her lap, took out a compact, snapped it open and began applying blusher to her cheeks with a brush.

This isn't a bathroom, you know! Holly wanted to snap, but she knew she'd be directing her irritation at the wrong person.

She smiled at the woman, in apology for what she'd been thinking and the woman smiled back and took out a small compact from the make-up bag and began applying eye shadow. Holly noticed that her eyes looked slightly red, as if she'd been crying or maybe not sleeping properly. Had she been on that train, too, and was this her first day back? Holly wondered. Perhaps she'd been up all night, worrying about getting on it this morning, and that was why she looked tired.

Holly smiled at her again and the woman smiled back, a more decided smile this time, the kind you wore when you were putting on a brave face. Perhaps she was feeling some of what Holly was feeling. Holly relaxed a little now that she no longer felt annoyance towards this woman but instead a strange rapport.

She was still annoyed, though, with Mark for insisting on coming with her to the station and trying to keep her buoyant with jokes that she'd heard too often before.

He obviously thought his presence would be reassuring, but it had the opposite effect. His forced humour made it difficult for her to focus on staying calm. She knew she was being ungracious, but she couldn't help it.

If he makes the Hastings-and-or-where? joke, Holly had thought to herself, as a disembodied voice began announcing the arrival of a train on platform seven, I might just hit him.

Holly usually tolerated Mark making the same jokes over and over again. Every time she asked if they should go next door, meaning from the kitchen to the living room, and he answered 'Hadn't we better ask the neighbours if they mind?' she would smile indulgently. Mark had no idea she actually found the joke extremely irritating.

Today she was having trouble masking this irritation.

'The train on platform seven,' said the announcer, 'is the 8.58 service to Hastings, calling at . . . '

'You don't have to wait,' Holly had said abruptly to Mark. 'You'll be late for work.'

'Only a few minutes.' He failed to pick up on the fact she didn't want him there. 'I'd rather be here.'

'Bexhill-on-Sea, St Leonard's Warrior Square . . . '

36

the announcer had been reeling out station names during their brief exchange ' . . . Hastings and Ore.'

Ore, once a small village, was now a large suburb of Hastings.

'And or where?' said Mark, on cue and as expected.

'I *knew* you were going to say that,' Holly snapped.

'Can't teach an old dog new . . . ' he began but stopped, realising she was annoyed. 'Sorry.'

'What for?' Holly scanned the departures board, hoping the London Victoria platform would appear and she could get away from him.

'I don't know.' It was true, Mark obviously didn't know but he was sorry anyway. That was typical of him, understanding, even when he didn't quite understand. And he *didn't* understand what she was feeling right now. Holly didn't really understand herself. She just wanted to get on with things, the first one being boarding the train.

'Platform four,' she said as the indicator flicked round to reveal that the train that had been standing at the platform for the past ten minutes was indeed the train everyone thought it was.

'Will you be OK?' Mark asked, tentatively, aware now he might be saying the wrong thing.

'I think so.' Holly was apprehensive but she knew she had to get on the train; delaying the moment wouldn't make it any easier. 'Goodbye.'

She turned to kiss him, hoping this would serve as an apology. 'See you tonight,' she said, turning towards the ticket barrier. 'Thanks for coming with me.'

'Holly . . . ' he called after her.

She didn't answer, but looked over her shoulder as she fumbled her ticket into the barrier.

Mark shrugged and smiled.

Holly smiled back and waved the ticket at him before placing it between her teeth and making her way on to the platform.

Now, on the train, she felt bad, realising how her irritation with her husband contrasted with what she felt on seeing 'the man'. He hadn't seen her. He was too engrossed in whatever he was doing on his laptop.

Holly's phone rang, with the embarrassing ringtone that Chloe had put in for her. She answered it quickly, before the recognisable strains of Paulo Nutini disturbed everyone in the carriage. She knew it would be Mark, even before she saw his name and number on the caller display.

'Hi,' she answered quietly, not wishing to draw any more attention to herself.

'Hi.' Mark sounded concerned by her quietness. 'Are you OK?'

'Yes, I'm fine.'

You don't have to keep checking up on me, she wanted to say, but knew it would be churlish.

'We've just gone past Gatwick Airport,' she added, as if this might interest him.

'Is the train busy?' Mark asked.

'It's not too bad,' she answered, wanting him to hang up soon.

'Not squashed up with a sixteen-stoner then?' Mark joked.

Holly hoped the fat man could not hear him.

'I'm in a quiet carriage,' she lied. 'I ought to go.'

'Ok, I just wanted to make sure you were all right,' Mark said. 'I love you.'

'You too,' said Holly. She wasn't going to say 'I love you too' in a crowded train carriage on a Monday morning. Anyone within earshot would probably guess what she was 'you too-ing' to anyway, if they were taking any notice of her conversation.

Holly glanced around her as she said it and saw the man was no longer looking at his laptop but straight at her.

He smiled when she glanced in his direction, a half-smile that Holly was unsure whether to interpret as a gesture of recognition. She held his gaze and he smiled again. This time definitely in acknowledgement, she hoped, of what had passed between them. She looked away, busied herself with putting her phone away, and when she dared to look in his direction again he was back on his computer.

Was that it? Holly wondered. After everything, would a quick smile one morning be all that ever passed between them again?

5

'I saw you flirting with the Home Secretary!' said a voice behind her as Holly stepped into the lifts of Broadcasting House.

'Oh, God! Was *that* who it was?' She turned round to find Dimitri, a fellow producer of *Antennae*, entering the lift behind her.

Seconds before, after she'd pressed the button to call it, a man in a suit had emerged, someone she'd recognised but could not quite place.

'Oh, hello,' Holly had said to him, finding that increasingly her memory was failing her when it came to names and faces — a sure sign of middle age.

'Hello,' the man had replied, and smiled before heading out of the building.

'Like you didn't know who he was!' Dimitri was saying now as he moved closer to kiss her in a friendly 'welcome back' way that acknowledged her temporary absence.

'Well, I wasn't *sure* who he was,' she replied. 'But I never pass up the chance to flirt with a man in a lift.'

Holly was strangely reassured that already she was having this type of banter with her colleague. She'd felt as if she had been away for ages when she'd first walked though the doors of Broadcasting House.

She expected the receptionist to look up and ask how she was or the security guard to remark on her slightly prolonged absence. Neither of these things happened.

The only reminder that she had been in a train crash was the card, which she felt for in her pocket.

★   ★   ★

He'd been waiting for her on the platform, when she got off the train.

'Hi,' he'd said. 'I don't know if you'll remember me . . .'

'I do.' Holly wondered how he thought she could forget. 'Of course I do. I didn't know if you'd be back.'

'Afraid so.' He'd smiled reassuringly, as if to say that everything was all right. Here he was on the train, living proof of that.

'I'm glad,' Holly said thoughtfully. 'I wanted to see you again.'

She paused to fumble with her ticket and push it through the barrier before turning to face him again. 'I don't even know your name.'

'Daniel,' he'd said, smiling and extending his hand. She shook it and smiled back.

'Holly,' she offered.

'Nice to see you again, Holly,' he'd said, still holding her hand and looking at her in a way that was at odds with the normality of his 'nice to see you again'.

For a moment Holly felt transported back to the last time she had seen Daniel, and she shivered slightly. As if sensing this he dropped her hand and took a card out of his pocket.

'I have to dash,' he'd said, pressing it into her hand. 'We should talk, though. Are you getting the tube?'

Holly shook her head. She wasn't quite ready to but she wasn't going to tell Daniel that.

'I usually walk,' she lied. If she'd left enough time or the weather was particularly nice, she did sometimes walk. And if she walked fast it didn't take much longer than getting the Underground.

'Oh.' Daniel had looked at her as if he knew this wasn't true, but understood. 'Well, I'll see you again some time, won't I?'

'Yes.' Holly slowed her pace, allowing him to put some distance between them, and looked at the card again.

★   ★   ★

'You look well,' Dimitri smiled at her now. 'You've aged, of course! But you look well.'

It was actually only three weeks that she'd been off work. She had planned to spend the last two of them in Cornwall with Mark and the children, but they'd come home early to escape the perpetual rain.

'The weather's generally nice at Easter.' Mark had tried to stay optimistic even as it rained hard for the fifth day running.

'Can't we just go home?' Chloe and Jake had asked hopefully.

In the event they did, though Mark tried to keep up the pretence that they were still on holiday by arranging local outings.

Holly knew he was doing his best to make up

for the fact they could not afford to go abroad this year, but she wished he'd realise the kids would be perfectly happy to stay at home and have unrestricted internet access.

'It's good to have you back, Holly,' Dimitri said. 'How are you? Apart from having developed a bit of thing for the Home Secretary, that is.'

'I'm not sure he's really my type.' This much was true. Holly had what her children described as 'beard phobia'. She denied this, saying merely that she preferred her chins clean shaven, but Chloe and Jake insisted she was petrified of them.

'What about that man on *Masterchef*?' Jake would say if ever the subject came up. 'You didn't want him to win just because he had a beard.'

'I couldn't stomach the thought of all that hair so near the food,' Holly had protested. 'It's not the beard *per se*.'

'You are a beardist,' Chloe added, 'and a moustachist,' pleased to have two 'ists' to add to their growing list of things they believed Holly was prejudiced against. If they'd been here now they'd have backed her up about the Home Secretary definitely not being her type.

'So you say,' Dimitri went on. 'But I saw the way you were looking at him.'

Holly laughed.

She liked Dimitri. He was fun. He was in his early thirties but retained a certain cheeky boyish charm. A lot of men his age were full of their own self-importance, especially at the BBC, but Dimitri, though very good at his job, gave the impression of only being there for the pleasure of the office banter. He was an Alpha-male who gave the outward impression of being an Omega, if there was such a thing.

'Talking of which,' he added, 'a very pretty producer has been filling in for you while you were away.'

'Well, I'm very sorry for coming back then,' Holly said, thinking her temporary replacement would have been deployed elsewhere.

'Actually,' Dimitri corrected this impression, 'she's going to stay. Sarah got the job on *Woman's Hour*. Starts this week. So it's the old team plus the gorgeous Rebecca.'

The old team consisted of Katherine Murray, the programme's editor, Natalie the assistant editor, and a team of three producers: Holly, Dimitri and Sarah, who had now been replaced by the gorgeous Rebecca. They all worked on *Antennae*, a programme broadcast on BBC Radio 4. Their remit was to pick up on anything which might be of interest to listeners and was not specifically covered in any of the other programmes.

'So essentially,' Holly would tell her friends, 'it's a mish-mash of stuff that doesn't really fit anywhere else, or whatever we can come up with when there's a hole in the programme to fill.'

Antennae was presented by James Darling, the BBC's roving news correspondent.

James Darling's voice was his calling card. It was deep but soft and had a slightly hypnotic quality. Holly had heard him on the radio frequently before he came to present the programme, and from his voice had imagined a cross between George Clooney and Sean Connery; someone dark and tall. She'd imagined height and physical presence were prerequisites for anyone with a deep, brooding voice. She was not sure that she'd hidden her disappointment well enough when Natalie, who had known Darling since they'd worked together at Radio Hull twenty years ago, had introduced her.

In the flesh he was small. He couldn't be more than five foot seven, and without much of a frame to carry excess flesh he appeared rather overweight. He had obviously once been blond but had now lost most of the hair on his head and, as if to compensate, sported a large wiry beard.

He had, as they say, a perfect face for radio.

Dimitri Georgiades, by contrast, had a perfect face for life. He was tall, dark, olive skinned, hazel eyed — striking by anyone's standards. He was also very well spoken. Holly suspected he had been to an English public school but, with a name like Georgiades, imagined his parents were Greek.

They took the lift together to the sixth floor where a very pretty young woman was keying a security code into the doors that led to *Antennae*'s offices.

'The gorgeous Rebecca,' Dimitri whispered to Holly in a loud stage whisper, which Rebecca clearly heard.

She spun round, smiling.

'Hello,' she said to Dimitri, her tone of voice suggesting she found him equally gorgeous. 'Hi,'

45

she said to Holly, more tentatively.

'Hi. I'm Holly.'

'Oh! Right.' Rebecca became instantly friendlier. 'Hi, I'm Rebecca. Nice to meet you. Great that you're back.'

A slight look of panic crossed her face, as if it occurred to her that she shouldn't have mentioned the fact Holly had been away.

'Nice to be back,' Holly said, wondering if others would keep reminding her why she'd been away with the things they said or didn't say.

She inwardly cursed Rebecca for the look on her face, which served as a reminder of the exact thing she was trying not to think about.

'I suppose I'd better report to Katherine before I do anything else,' Holly said briskly, to show she meant business.

She walked down the narrow corridor between the open-plan parts of the office to the editor's office. She peered though the glass walls and could see Katherine's immaculate dark bob bent over a stack of paperwork. 'Holly!' she cried, seeing her and opening the door. 'How lovely! Come in. Have a seat. It's great to have you back.'

This, Holly suspected, was a lie. Katherine didn't really like women, especially ones who had children and took maternity leave and holidays plus time off when they'd been in a train crash. She was of the generation who didn't have it all and were expected not to allow anything from their private lives to interfere with their work.

Holly had worked at BBC Radio 4 for nearly

eighteen years; full-time at first, then part-time when the children were young. She'd started full-time again the previous September, prompted partly by the fact that Mark's business wasn't bringing in much and they needed the extra money.

'How are you?' Katherine said, wheeling a chair away from the wall for Holly to sit on.

'I'm pretty good.' She gave the response she knew was wanted, which was also fairly accurate.

'Good,' said Katherine. She seemed relieved. 'So you'll be able to cope with everything?'

Holly nodded.

'Excellent.' Katherine was already turning her chair back to face her desk, signalling their brief exchange was at an end. 'The morning meeting is at nine-thirty upstairs in the mezzanine. See you there.'

'OK. I'll go and get a coffee first then. See you in a bit,' she said to her boss's back and walked out of the office and straight into Natalie.

'Holly Holt!' Natalie said, smiling and dropping her bag where she stood in order to give Holly the biggest and most welcoming hug. 'I am *so* pleased that you're back. You look fantastic. Come into my office, I want to hear how you are.'

Katherine looked up as this exchange took place. 'Were you coming to see me?' she asked, looking slightly peeved.

'No,' Natalie replied. 'Well, yes, but it can wait. See you at the morning meeting.'

She closed the door of Katherine's office and showed Holly into her own opposite.

'It's really good to see you,' Natalie said. 'It felt like longer than three weeks that you were off. Everyone here seems to be getting younger and younger ... except Katherine, who is getting older and more bitter by the day.'

Holly laughed.

'Dimitri told me I looked older,' she said.

'Untactful cheeky monkey!' Natalie replied. 'Tea?'

She pushed a polystyrene cup across the table. 'I bought two cups just in case you got here early — oh, and desk!'

Natalie pointed at a desk on the other side of the room from hers. 'No more open-planning it amongst the twenty-somethings. You'll have to put up with me.'

'Really? How come?' Holly rather liked the camaraderie of the open-plan bit of the office.

'Rebecca was at your desk while you were away and Katherine decided she should stay put,' Natalie told her.

'Great.' Holly tried to sound a bit more upbeat about sharing an office with Natalie.

In fact, it unsettled her. She'd wanted everything to be the same; to have her surroundings mask the fact that something in her had changed. And besides, she liked the company of the twenty-somethings.

Natalie was in her early forties, only a couple of years younger than Holly, but they were both well aware that they were both considered oldies who led dull boring lives with their husbands and children. Natalie had young twins.

'And,' she added, 'I think it pissed Katherine

off, my having an office to myself. I think she thinks I do fuck all all day and now you will be able to keep me on my toes.'

'It'll be great,' Holly said, trying to emphasise the great.

She had first met Natalie when they were both in their twenties and worked briefly at Radio Northampton. Later Holly moved to Brighton and Natalie to Hull. Then, they'd spent a brief period on *Woman's Hour* together before Holly switched to a part-time job in Central Planning. When she'd started working full-time again, it was on *Antennae* and she was glad to be back with Natalie.

Holly knew her well enough to be relaxed around her, and Natalie now had children too so they could compare notes on trying to have it all.

'How was the train journey?' Natalie asked, as Holly sat down at her new desk. 'Was that the first time you've been on one since . . . '

'I had a few practice runs with Mark.' Holly flipped the lid of the plastic cup and took a sip of the tepid liquid. 'We came back from holiday a bit early and he decided we'd keep up the holiday spirit by going on day trips to coastal retirement towns. We had lunch in Eastbourne, Littlehampton and Worthing last week.'

'The glamorous life you lead!' Natalie feigned envy. 'And was it OK? On the train?'

'I think Mark thought I'd be terrified of ever going on one again but actually it feels strangely normal. It's almost as if I've done my train crash now, so I'm pretty unlikely to be in another one.' Holly paused, wondering how much to tell

Natalie about the journey. 'In fact, there was a man on the train . . . '

'Bloody hell, quick work,' Natalie interjected. 'First day back and you meet a man on the way to work. Who is he?'

'Daniel Harrison,' Holly told her.

This was the name on the card he had given her as they disembarked from the train and walked towards the ticket barrier. Daniel Harrison, Systems Analyst. And there were details of his office addresses and phone numbers. She'd stared at it as she walked through Green Park, as if by absorbing the stark typeface she would somehow be able to glean more details from it.

'And?' Natalie was looking at her expectantly.

'And what?' Holly wasn't stalling.

'Who is he? This Daniel Harrison?'

'He was on the train when the accident happened.' Holly suddenly found saying this out loud took her back to the scene of the crash and she didn't want to go there. Not now. 'He stayed with me until the fire brigade arrived.'

'Oh, I see,' Natalie adopted a slightly hushed reverential tone which annoyed Holly more than it should have. 'So, are you going to see him again?'

'I don't know,' Holly said, putting her hand in her pocket to feel Daniel Harrison's card again. It made her feel safe just touching it, representing as it did the man who had assured her that everything would be all right. 'I expect I'll bump into him again at some point.'

I've started to write things down again. The counsellor I saw before, after Mum went into hospital, told me it might be useful at the time.

'It might help you clarify your feelings,' she had said to me, during one of the sessions, and it did in a way. Any rate, I preferred writing things down to talking to her. That's why I stopped the sessions — that and Lisa telling everyone at school that I was a nutter too.

'Anne-Marie is seeing a shrink,' she told our friends, challenging me to deny it. 'Aren't you?'

'She's not a shrink, she's a counsellor,' I protested.

'Same difference,' Lisa had said, smirking, and even though it had helped, having someone to talk to, I stopped going. But I kept on writing the diary the counsellor encouraged me to begin. I still have them all, somewhere in the attic, with other stuff from Mum and Dad's house.

And now I've started another. I started this diary on the day of the crash, because I wanted to talk about it and the one person I really wanted to talk to was Geoff and he was no longer there. So I started writing instead.

I thought about the counsellor I'd seen as a teenager, too. She was nice. Helen, I think her name was. I did like talking to her and I often wished I hadn't stopped going. I still told her things, in the months and years that followed, but the conversations were only ever imagined, in my head, and then I moved on and forgot about her.

Now, I've started thinking about her again and I found myself telling a vacant chair in the living room that I'd started writing a diary. I imagined Helen was in the chair, listening, trying to understand.

'That's good,' she said. 'You won't feel like this for ever but it will help if you articulate your thoughts, rather than bottling them up.'

I wonder what she'd think if I was talking to her now, if she'd remember the conversations we had after my mother went into the psychiatric hospital, which made people realise that what we'd seen that day wasn't just a bad memory, it was something much more.

If she were here now, would she bring it up again? Or would she just ask me about Geoff and how I was coping; whether there was anyone else I could talk to about what had happened — friends, for example, or family?

She wouldn't know that my mum and dad had both died a few years ago, my mother from cancer and my father from heart failure.

'They just said it was old age,' I imagined telling her. It didn't seem relevant which particular bits of my parents' bodies had packed up or why. They knew death was coming eventually and preferred dying of old age to anything more medically accurate.

'And friends?' she might ask.

Would she already know about Julia, by this point in the session?

'Apart from Julia, I don't really know that many people where we live,' I would tell her. 'We only moved in the last year, from London, and we both commuted a lot of the time. So we didn't really have much chance to meet anyone new.'

We'd never have met Julia if it hadn't been for the postman leaving her mailorder shoes in our porch by mistake. She insisted I come in for coffee when I took them round. And then Geoff insisted she come in to ours for coffee when she stopped to chat to him, as he was weeding the front garden.

'I'm the shoe lady,' she had said, by way of introduction, but I hadn't told Geoff about the shoes so he'd had no idea what she was on about. To be honest, if I had told him he'd probably have forgotten and been none the wiser. So she'd explained and something in her rendition of the postman mistakenly taking her parcel to number sixty-eight instead of one hundred and sixty-eight had made Geoff laugh and he'd insisted she come and have coffee with us.

'What about your old friends from London?' the counsellor might ask. 'Or university? Or before even?'

But she would already know about my oldest friend, Lisa Woodward. Even if she'd forgotten, it would be in my notes.

'My best friend from university, Laura, went back to New Zealand.' I would fill Helen in on the years since she last saw me. 'And we seem to have lost touch.'

'Why was that?' she'd ask.

And I would probably say something about time and distance. But really I think now that it was because we'd become linked by something other than being outsiders and we both wanted to forget that.

She felt she'd escaped the earthquake by being in the UK and she didn't think she deserved to. Her parents were devastated by the loss of her younger sister, so she felt she had to go back. I told her before she left about my mother, about what had happened to us. I thought it might help her, but she didn't really want to know.

'What's happened in New Zealand is different,' she'd said.

We emailed regularly at first when she went back, and I still think of her as a good friend even though we've lost touch.

I've thought about calling Laura several times over the past few weeks, but the time never seems right. She's eleven hours ahead in New Zealand and, whenever I think I'd like to talk to her, I realise it would be the middle of the night there.

And then I wonder what I would say to her anyway when she picked up the phone.

It would be a bit of a shock for her, hearing from me after all this time and then me telling her about Geoff.

But now that I was thinking about her, it struck me that that was who the woman I'd seen on the news reminded me of. I'd thought she seemed familiar because I'd seen her on the train, but now that I've been thinking about

Laura, I realise she also reminds me of her. Maybe that's why I felt compelled to talk to her when I saw her on the train this morning.

I didn't realise it was her when I sat down. She was reading a newspaper and I couldn't see her face properly, but then she put it down and I knew it was the same person. She looked nervous and I wondered if it was her first day back at work too.

I wanted to tell her that I'd seen her on the news and ask if she was OK. I don't know if it was because she reminded me of Laura or because of the way she smiled, but I had a feeling that I might be able to tell her about Geoff. Not immediately, of course, but at some point.

Her phone rang and she looked away while she took the call. I tried to catch her eye and smile again but she was looking across the carriage at someone. She had that look on her face again, the same look she had when I saw her on the news.

I waited for her to get off the train and I walked down the platform behind her. I imagined I might say hello or something, once we'd gone through the barriers.

But there was a man already there, waiting for her.

I couldn't really go up to her then, not with him there.

I wanted to tell her that I knew she'd been alone in the tunnel, and that I knew what it felt to be involved in something like that and to feel utterly alone. But I couldn't tell her because she was talking to him.

6

Mark was making dinner when Holly got home that evening and, when Mark cooked, it was to demonstrate his abilities rather than to satisfy his family's hunger. He liked to use two or three TV cookbooks at a time, creating a main dish and at least two accompaniments. These never seemed to be ready simultaneously and only ever well past the point when everyone was hungry.

They did usually look and taste good but Holly could have done without the aesthetics and the painstakingly sourced ingredients. She would have preferred something on the table when she got home, rather than several hours later.

Mark also liked to use every single kitchen implement and pan they possessed. So, having waited several hours to eat, it would then take several hours to clear up afterwards. Holly thought this clattering of pans was the twenty-first-century equivalent to the hunter-gatherer's big kill. It was as if, by producing several options to eat, and using twenty different knives in the process, Mark was saying, 'Look what a man I am. I ripped a chicken carcass apart with my bare hands, beheaded butternut squash and had garlic cloves begging for mercy, just to bring you this meal.'

'Hello,' she said, trying not to think about the

56

clear-up operation afterwards, as she surveyed the kitchen. There were already three different empty but dirty baking trays cluttering up the dining table.

'Hi.' Mark's tone had all the triumph of a man who had just headed up a mammoth hunt. 'Rack of lamb, with Moroccan parsnip mash and roasted vegetables, followed by almond oranges.'

'That sounds wonderful,' said Holly, wondering if cavewomen had felt the same feeling of dread when their menfolk triumphantly dragged back the carcass of a mammal. Were they hugely relieved that they would eat for months to come or secretly peeved that the cave would be full of drying skins, bloodied rocks and male triumphalism for the foreseeable future?

'How was your day?' said Mark, wiping his hands on an already bloodied tea towel.

Holly made a mental note to stick it in the washing machine, as soon his back was turned, and before they all got salmonella.

'It was fine,' she said, kissing him.

'Were they all pleased to have you back then?' He poured a large glass of wine and handed it to her. He had his concerned expression on.

'Yes.' Holly didn't think there was any point in telling him that her absence had barely been noted.

'And the train?' Mark looked at her closely as he asked this.

'It was fine,' she said again. 'I was a little nervous when I first got on, but as soon as it started crawling up the track, I felt OK.'

'Really?' Mark was adding wine to a pan of

something that was bubbling on the stove, but still watching her.

'Yes, really.'

Holly hadn't said this to anyone, not even the counsellor, but she suspected that a small part of Mark wanted her to be more traumatised by the train crash than she was, so that he could step up and look after her.

He'd told her he was terrified when he heard the news that morning that she might have been killed. And he was fearful, after she was cut free from the wreckage, that it would leave her nervous and reluctant to start commuting again. He didn't seem prepared for the fact that she felt as if she'd had a lucky escape and was carrying on as if nothing had happened.

Holly couldn't help thinking that rather than being relieved that she was OK, he'd found himself robbed of the opportunity to show he was still an Alpha-male.

★   ★   ★

'The Iceman cometh!' was how Mark had introduced himself to Holly, twenty years ago.

Lydia, a friend Holly then worked with, had decided to throw a party in the garden of her ground-floor flat, because the weather had been unusually hot. She'd invited a lot of people but done little else. Among the things she hadn't done was clearing her fridge. So, when people began arriving with wine and beer, there was nowhere for it to go where it would stay chilled.

Cue Mark who, as Holly arrived, walked up

the steps to the front door behind her, shouldering a dustbin full of ice.

'Lydia's fridge is full of rotting meat!' he had said, as if by way of explanation after the Iceman comment. Then he put out his free hand to shake hers. 'I'm Mark.'

Holly immediately liked his openness and the casual way in which he was carrying what must undoubtedly have been a heavy load. And he was good looking too, tanned and dark-haired with eyes that looked almost black.

'Holly,' she said, taking his hand, which was cold from the ice. 'Bloody hell, you're freezing!'

'Cold hands, warm heart.' Mark had shrugged in acknowledgement of the cliché and the fact that he couldn't come up with anything better. 'Hurry up, Lydia,' he'd added as they waited for the door to be answered, and Holly had wondered if he was her boyfriend and if so why he didn't have a key.

'Were your parents *Breakfast at Tiffany's* fans?' he asked, putting down the bin and looking at Holly as if he needed to take her in properly.

'Yes.' Holly had indeed been named after Holly Golightly because her mother had watched the film, starring Audrey Hepburn, nearly every afternoon in the last few months of her pregnancy. If anyone ever thought to ask about her name, they usually asked if she was born at Christmas. Mark was possibly the first person who had instantly made the right connection.

'How did you know?' she asked, looking at him with renewed admiration.

'I thought you looked like Audrey Hepburn when I saw you walking down the road,' he'd replied. 'And then when you said your name was Holly, it seemed to fit.'

'Oh, thank you.' She wasn't usually good at taking compliments, but even though she'd only exchanged a few words with him so far she already felt relaxed enough in Mark's company to accept this one.

'How do you know Lydia?' she'd asked as he rapped on the door again.

'I live in the flat upstairs.' He'd nodded towards a wooden Venetian blind above the door, which was suddenly flung open by Mandy, another work colleague.

'Hi, Holly!' She had stopped to take in Mark. 'Hello, Holly's friend . . .'

Holly had expected Mark to say something about them only having just met, but he simply smiled and said, 'Hello, another of Holly's friends. I'll talk to you in a minute, but first I need to get this bucket of ice out the back.'

There had been something so masculine and confident about Mark back then. It was this, as much as his dark handsome looks, which captivated Holly, first at the party and then during the subsequent months when he swept her along with his conviction that they must swim in the sea . . . walk on Beachy Head . . . watch the sunrise over the downs . . . move in together and eventually get married.

It wasn't that he was domineering or forceful in any way; rather there was something about him which was so self-assured and compelling that Holly found it hard to resist whatever he happened to suggest.

'Shall I get you another drink and then we can find somewhere to sit and talk properly?' he had asked her a few hours into the party as Holly made her way to Lydia's kitchen, hoping she might bump into him en route.

They'd chatted briefly to begin with, then Lydia had pulled her away to meet her old university roommate.

'Actually, I was going to see if I could make myself a cup of tea.' Holly smiled, sensing it was a bit middle-aged of her to be wanting a cuppa just as a party got into full swing.

But she'd had enough to drink for the time being and it was getting cold in the garden. She felt as if she needed something to warm her up.

'It's pretty crowded in there.' Mark gestured towards the kitchen. 'Why don't you come up to my flat and I'll make you a cup?'

'OK,' Holly had replied, even though her natural instinct would not have been to disappear from a party with a man she'd only just met.

She had the strange sensation, as they walked out of Lydia's flat and up the stairs, of having known him for some time. There was the usual nervous anticipation, but this meeting felt right.

'Sorry, it's a bit of a mess,' Mark said as he opened the door to his flat and indicated the living room. 'I've been away for a few days and haven't got round to clearing up.'

Holly looked through the door to the living room. It *was* a mess. There were newspapers and magazines strewn across the floor, clothes slung across the backs of chairs, and half-empty coffee cups and plates on just about every surface.

'Where've you been?' she asked, alluding to the days away and wondering if he'd been with anyone. Despite the mess, she did like the fact that Mark's living room appeared to be entirely free from any feminine influence. She hoped he lived on his own and did not have a girlfriend.

'My flatmate never tidies up,' Mark said, pulling clothes off a large leather armchair and gesturing for her to sit in it. 'Tim. Big guy with a beard. He was at the party too. Did you talk to him?'

'No.' Holly sank into the chair. She'd seen a man who fitted that description and hoped he wouldn't be coming home any time soon. She wanted more time with Mark, on his own.

'Paris.' He carried on tidying. 'In answer to your earlier question.'

'That's nice.' Holly couldn't help but feel disappointed. Paris was not the sort of city he'd be likely to have visited on his own.

'For work,' Mark told her, as if he could tell what she was thinking. He already seemed to have scooped all the clothes into a pile that he was putting on a stool, and picked up a large tray from the floor together with some dirty crockery. The room already looked a whole lot better.

'What do you do?' Holly had asked, and Mark had told her that he worked for the marketing department of a big American conglomerate, and though it was dull at times it was good experience. Ultimately he wanted to set up on his own.

'Are you a reporter or a producer?' he asked her as he brought a pint-sized mug of tea and a plate of biscuits in from the kitchen. He'd obviously talked to Lydia about the local radio station where they both worked.

'Reporter,' Holly had said, accepting the tea and looking around her at the walls, which were hung with several paintings of windswept coastlines. 'I like these. Are they of Cornwall?'

'Yes.' Mark had smiled as if pleased she'd recognised the scenes. 'My dad painted them.'

'Is he an artist?' Holly had been impressed.

'No, a local government officer. Or at least he was.' Mark paused. 'He died a few years ago, from bowel cancer.'

Mark must have been in his mid-twenties then. She suspected his father's death had come too early.

'I'm sorry. How old was he?'

'Sixty. I was at university, doing my finals. They didn't find the cancer until it had spread so there wasn't much he could do, but he gave up his job and did as much painting as he could before he died. He loved painting.'

'And he was very good.' Holly looked at the paintings again. 'Is that Sennen Cove?'

'Yes.' Mark glanced up at the painting. 'Do you know it?'

'We used to go there when I was a child, for family holidays,' Holly told him. 'I love Cornwall but I haven't been for years.'

'We'll have to go,' Mark said, sipping his own

tea, as if what he suggested was the most natural thing in the world, despite the fact that they had only just met. He didn't seem cocky to Holly, just accepting of the fact that there was something between them. And not, like most men of his age, afraid of that.

'So, Reporter Holly,' he had said. 'Are you going to stay in local radio for a while or will you be disappearing off to London before we've had time to go to Cornwall or anywhere else?'

'I like my job here,' she had told him. 'But I suppose eventually London will be the next step.'

★   ★   ★

She'd been right. Not long after they were married, she began commuting to London to work for BBC Radio 4 and Mark had set up his own marketing and PR company. Business boomed and when Holly had Chloe she went back to work part-time, to keep her hand in.

But then Mark's successful company began to struggle, slowly at first.

'I've lost two holiday company contracts,' he told her one evening when she'd asked why he seemed a bit down. 'Bookings are slow after 9/11 and they can't afford to use me any more. People are still nervous of flying, even though it's the safest form of transport.'

'I can understand why,' Holly had said, watching as he poured them both a large glass of wine. 'The world no longer seems safe.'

The twin towers had come down on their son Jake's first day at infant school.

It was a warm sunny day in Brighton and Holly had picked him up and brought him home for lunch. She put the television on so that he could watch *Teletubbies* before they went to get Chloe from school. Instead of being greeted by the cheery 'eh-oh' of Tinky Winky they saw the image of a plane hitting one of the towers, being repeated over and again.

Jake had thought the spectacle wonderful and almost immediately began building Lego towers and Lego aeroplanes with which he could destroy them, but Holly had felt as if something had been taken away from her personally, even though they were not directly affected.

'I think it was because it was Jake's first day at school,' she had said to Mark a few weeks later when he told her he'd lost the contracts. 'It should have been a day that was full of promise, but instead it seemed as if something had been taken away from us all.'

'Sorry, Hol, now I'm making you morose,' Mark had said, upbeat again, pulling her to him and kissing her. 'I didn't mean to, and I'm not really worried about these contracts. If people aren't going abroad they'll holiday at home, so perhaps I'll get something local to replace them.'

Holly had smiled, admiring his eternal optimism, but latterly she'd discovered it wasn't eternal after all.

'Best Homes has gone bust.' He had been despondent when he'd told her this news several months before. 'Another victim of the credit crunch. They owed us a few thousand. We'll never see it now.'

'Shit.' Holly knew that Best Homes was Mark's last remaining big client although he'd put in a bid for a job with a new chain of bars. 'Have you heard anything about the tender for Cosy Corner?'

'We didn't get it,' he'd said, refusing to meet her eyes as he spoke. 'It went to a new company which has just been set up by a couple of twenty-somethings.'

That was when Holly first noticed that the energy and drive that always used to keep Mark going were diminishing.

'I could go back to work full-time, now that Jake's at secondary school,' she had said, expecting him to say, as he always did, that she didn't need to.

'Do you think you could?' He'd glanced down with a look of defeat as he spoke.

'I'll speak to Personnel,' Holly had replied, trying to sound upbeat herself. 'I'd like to. It might mean I could work on a programme again, and I'd prefer that. I'm bored in Central Planning, but most of the part-time jobs are there.'

Holly knew there was a bit of Mark that still wanted to be the main breadwinner. The part of him that shouldered the bin full of ice with such ease would have liked to provide for all his family's needs.

He didn't like the fact he got home from work before Holly and was forced to fill the time with knife-wielding in the kitchen. He'd lost some of that initial sense of purpose she'd first found so attractive in him. He was no longer so confident and compelling.

And, although he'd never said it in so many words, Holly knew Mark hated the fact that he had not been the one to talk her through the minutes before the fire crews arrived to cut her free from the wreckage of the train crash.

So when he asked now how her train journey had been, she couldn't quite bring herself to tell him that Daniel Harrison, the man who had been there with her at the crash, was also on it.

7

'Hi, Mum!' Holly heard Jake shouting from the sitting room in his newly deepened voice.

It still took her by surprise every time he opened his mouth — this new husky-sounding Jake, with his downy top lip, thicker hair and ever-increasing height. He had only just turned thirteen but already her little boy seemed to be disappearing before her eyes, to be replaced by a continuously growing young man.

'Hello, Jakey!' she said, going into the sitting room and finding him lying prone across the floor, apparently contemplating the ceiling. He'd obviously heard her come in but couldn't be bothered to move.

Jake grimaced as she was about to bend down and kiss him, something he still, thankfully, allowed her to do as long as his friends weren't looking. He put up his hand in warning.

'Ed's here.' He indicated the sofa, where a floppy-haired friend was also lying in a languid pose.

'All right, Holly?' Ed's sing-song, higher voice asked.

'Yes, good thanks, Ed.' Holly marvelled at the number of hours her son could spend doing nothing companionably with one of his friends.

Chloe was constantly talking, texting, listing to music or posting photos of herself and her friends on Facebook. She was more like her father. Mark had never been able just to be somewhere without doing anything.

In the days immediately after the train crash, Holly had found it easier to be with Jake than anyone else in the family. He never asked her to talk or tell him how she was feeling, he'd just be in the same space as her, a reassuring presence.

'Are you two inspecting the ceiling for cobwebs?' she asked now, knowing that she wouldn't be able to stare at it for long without noticing some corner that needed dusting or a crack that warranted a builder.

There was an alarming-looking one over the bay window. When they'd moved in it was on Holly and Mark's list of things to do something about, but after about six months of painting and decorating during evenings and weekends they had lost enthusiasm for home improvements.

'Are we going to get a new fireplace put in?' Mark had asked one autumn evening when the sitting room was feeling chilly.

'It would be nice,' Holly had replied. 'But I don't think I can face sharing the house with builders any more.'

'I thought you had a bit of crush on Vaclav?' Mark had teased her, referring to the Czech who had helped convert the attic.

'Familiarity breeds contempt,' Holly had said, putting her hand on Mark's knee.

'Thank you very much!' He'd looked mock-affronted.

'I meant Vaclav, not you!'

The house was in a quiet residential part of Brighton. Holly hadn't liked it at first. Looking out of the windows at the other large Edwardian red-brick houses opposite, she'd felt it could be in any city.

'I miss the sea views,' she told people. 'We could see the sea from our bedroom in the old house. And there were always lots of drunks around. It felt more like Brighton.'

'You can see the sea, if you're prepared to risk breaking your neck,' Mark said, demonstrating that if you stood on a ledge in the attic and stuck your entire torso out of the window and leaned, you could catch sight of a strip of silvery grey. 'And if it's drunks you miss, we can always open another bottle of wine ourselves!'

'Ed's not staying for dinner,' Jake said, looking up. 'His dad's coming soon.'

'That's lucky,' Holly said. 'Because Dad's cooking, so it probably won't be ready until midnight anyway.'

'We're just waiting for him,' Ed volunteered, as if this explained the torpor in the living room. 'Did you have a good day at work?'

'Yes, thank you, Ed.' Holly smiled at the innocence of his question. Ed was endearingly polite. Jake and he had been friends since infant school, and even aged five he'd always thanked her for 'delicious fish fingers' or 'a really fun day'.

'How was yours?' she asked both boys, but the ceiling appeared to be absorbing all their thoughts and energy and neither of them answered.

'Where's Chloe?' she asked this time, noticing that her laptop was not on the desk by the

French windows and wondering if her daughter had it.

'I think she's in her room with Ruaridh,' Jake said.

Ruaridh was a close friend of her daughter's. Holly was beginning to wonder just how close. They'd met when they started secondary school and always been friends, but lately they seemed never to be apart.

Holly thought Chloe was looking particularly beautiful at the moment. Her awkward adolescent skin had cleared, and she was now all long limbs, shiny hair and very engaging smile. Holly wouldn't be at all surprised if Ruaridh had stopped thinking of her simply as a friend.

He was one of six children. His parents were Irish Catholics, which Holly supposed accounted for the six of them.

Mark almost always referred to Ruaridh as 'Scrabble Boy'. This was a joke he made nearly every time Ruaridh's name came up. The first time he had spelled it out for them, Mark had said Irish names must have been created during a game of Scrabble.

'Rory?' he'd said in his best Irish accent. 'How should we spell that?' Then proceeded to act out an imaginary scenario in which a family sat around a table pulling Scrabble letters randomly from a bag and deciding that that was how their names should be spelled.

'Niamh. Shall we spell that N-E-E-V-E?' Mark had lilted, before answering himself, 'No. I've got an 'm' and an 'h'. We need to fit those in too.'

71

Holly had worried Ruaridh would think him horribly patronising, but he seemed to think it was funny.

'I'm here,' said Chloe, breaking into Holly's thoughts as she padded down the stairs.

'Hello.' Holly turned and bit back the temptation to ask if she'd worn that strip of material masquerading as a skirt to school today. 'Hello, Ruaridh.'

'Hello, Mrs Constantine.' Ruaridh grinned.

He had recently taken to calling Holly this, although she never actually used her married name. Holly's maiden name was Holt and she thought it suited her better. Constantine, the name of a Roman Emperor, suited Mark perfectly.

Holly suspected that Ruaridh was being ironic. This was one of Chloe's favourite current pastimes. She frequently used irony to explain why she was doing something that could be construed as childish. Like lining up all the soft toys she'd had as a child on the end of her bed, or creating sculptures out of Lego. It was as if she didn't quite want to relinquish her childhood but was embarrassed about playing with childish things. So she would explain, if anything was commented on, that it was ironic.

That would cue Mark to make his ironic joke.

'Ironic is getting your newly ironed shirt crumpled when you try to fold the ironing board.'

Holly sighed inwardly, thinking of her husband's tired jokes.

'How was school?' she asked Chloe.

'Fine.' Her standard response to most questions.

'Did you get your test results?' Holly had managed to extract the information from her earlier in the week that she was having a Spanish test.

'Yeah.'

'And?' Holly waited for a bit more information. 'What did you get?'

'I got a level six.'

This didn't really mean anything to Holly. The whole school system seemed to be structured towards making all pupils think they were doing fine, even if they weren't. And it seemed to exclude parents from knowing if their offspring were doing anything at all.

Chloe would be taking her GCSEs the following year and Holly had no idea if she was going to pass them with flying colours or fail miserably.

'Is that good?' she asked.

'It's the average level expected.' Chloe seemed satisfied with her marks.

Holly thought she ought to aspire to better than average. She'd said as much at one of the rare parents evenings their school held. The teacher had looked at her in disbelief, as if wanting your child to do better was outrageous.

'Well done,' she said, wondering if her words sounded as hollow as they felt. 'That's really good, Chloe. By the way, have you got my laptop?'

'It's in my room.' Chloe seemed to distance herself from any involvement with the laptop, trying to make out it had somehow got there by itself. 'Do you want it?'

'I might need to send an email before dinner. Are you staying for dinner, Ruaridh?'

'No, I need to go home.'

Holly jumped as the doorbell rang.

'That'll be my dad.' Ed had suddenly sprung into action and was twitching back the living room curtain to see who was outside. He slipped on his shoes.

'Thanks for the . . . ' he said to Holly, and smiled, realising that the extent of their hospitality had been to allow him to lie on the sofa undisturbed.

'Any time, Ed!' She gave him a half-wave. 'Are you going to say goodbye, Jake?'

By this she meant get up and go to the door with him.

'I already have,' he replied, unmoving.

'Here it is.' Chloe had been up to her room and come down again with the laptop. She plonked it on the desk. 'Shall I leave it on?'

'Yes, please,' Holly said.

'I'm off too.' Ruaridh waved vaguely in everyone's direction and headed for the door.

'When's dinner? I'm starving,' Chloe asked.

'Me, too. Ravenous!' Jake had always liked hyperbole. 'Can I get a sandwich?'

'It might spoil your dinner,' Holly said, knowing this was unlikely. Jake seemed to be eating as much as the rest of the family put together these days, without it making much of a dent in his appetite.

'Dad says it's going to be at least half an hour.'

Chloe came out of the kitchen, scowling.

'Go on then, Jakey.' Holly directed her son to get himself something to stave off impending death by hunger. 'I'm just going to email someone before dinner.'

'I'm going back to my room then,' said Chloe as Holly sat at the desk and tapped a key to wake the computer.

'Can you not call me Jakey when there are other people here?' he said from across the room.

'Sorry.' Holly knew he didn't like being called this in front of friends, but found it hard to kick the habit.

'It's embarrassing,' Jake muttered as he left the room.

Holly was glad to have the room to herself, as she needed space to think exactly what she was going to write.

Dear Daniel, she began, putting his card back in her bag after writing the email address. *I'm glad I met you on the train today. I wasn't sure if you travelled regularly. I also wondered who you were! It was my first day back at work today and I felt very reassured to see you there. Who knows if I would have been on the train today if you hadn't been where you were and done what you did then? Perhaps we can talk sometime.*

She began reading it to herself but was startled to find Jake standing behind her.

'I've brought your wine in.' He was holding the glass in one hand and a doorstep of a sandwich in the other. 'Shall I put it next to the sofa?'

75

'Yes, thank you,' she replied, hastily adding *Very best, Holly*, and pressing the Send button. 'I'm done here.'

Holly moved to sit next to her son.

She took a sip of wine as Jake stretched out and put his feet in her lap, balancing his plate on his stomach. He was still a very tactile and affectionate boy in private, despite the onslaught of puberty.

'How was it back at work?' he asked. The question when he voiced it didn't seem as loaded as when Mark had. 'Did the sanctimonious bitch give you hell?'

Holly laughed.

'Don't call my beloved boss that,' she said, squeezing his foot.

'That's what you call her.' Jake had heard her referring to Katherine in less than glowing terms once too often to be able to resist joining in.

'Yes, but I have to call her names as a way of releasing the pressure built up by working for her.' Holly watched him putting nearly an entire sandwich into his mouth. 'Don't eat so quickly. You'll get indigestion.'

Jake's mouth was too full to protest, so he made a noise which was accompanied by a ping from the other side of the room. This indicated Holly had an email.

She had to resist an unusually strong desire to jump up and open it as Mark came into the room announcing that dinner was ready, with a flourish of the oven gloves.

8

'There she is.' Dimitri nodded towards a sofa in the lobby of Broadcasting House. Holly's mother was leafing through a magazine.

'Oh, yes.' Holly could see Susan now. 'How did you know it was my mother?'

'She looks just like you,' he said, crossing towards her.

'Hello!' Holly greeted her mother.

'Darling.' Susan looked up and began gathering her things. 'How are you?'

'Good, thanks.' Holly kissed her.

Dimitiri had told Holly he was popping out to buy a sandwich but appeared to be waiting for an introduction. She did the honours.

'Nice to meet you, Mrs Holt. I knew you were Holly's mother as soon as I saw you. Either that or her sister. You look just like her,' Dimitri said, shaking Susan's hand and holding it for rather longer than was necessary.

Is there no one he doesn't flirt with? Holly thought to herself.

'Oh, call me me Susan, please,' she said, smiling in a way which Holly could only think to describe as coquettish. 'Nice to meet you too, Dimitri. Have you been working on *Antennae* long?'

'It feels like that sometimes,' he replied. 'But only about a year. Do you listen to the programme ever?'

'No, she doesn't,' Holly answered for her. 'They tuned in once, decided James Darling was too full of himself and never listened again.'

'That's not entirely true,' her mother protested, embarrassed in front of one of Holly's colleagues by how little interest she took in what her daughter did for a living.

'Very wise. He is full of himself,' Dimitri responded.

'Shall we go?' Holly said to her mother.

'Holly says you're taking her out to lunch,' Dimitri said, failing to take his cue to leave. 'Are you going anywhere nice?'

'We're going to John Lewis. I want to buy a computer and I need Holly's help,' Susan said, revealing the purpose of her trip to London.

'Oh, really? Do you know what sort of thing you're looking for?' He sounded like a salesman, Holly thought.

'She has absolutely no idea,' Holly answered for Susan again, slightly embarrassed by the way she was so obviously flirting back with her colleague.

They had walked through the doors of Broadcasting House and were outside on the pavement now.

'We're going this way,' Holly said.

'And I'm heading in the opposite direction,' Dimitri replied, taking the hint now. 'See you later, Holly. Very nice to meet you, Susan.'

She stared after him as he turned into Mortimer Street. 'What an exceedingly nice young man. I'm surprised you've never mentioned him before.'

'I'm sure I have,' Holly replied. 'Let's cross, shall we?'

They walked down Margaret Street to the back entrance of John Lewis. It was her mother's favourite shop, and working so near meant Holly often met her there for lunch when she was up looking for socks or sheets or something.

Both Susan and Patrick were computer averse, and called Holly quite often to ask if she could look up something on the internet for them, because even the prospect of going down to their local library and being shown by the kindly librarian how to navigate in cyberspace filled them with dread.

'The place is full of mice,' Patrick had said when Holly suggested this. 'It terrifies me.'

'I did try to use one,' Susan had admitted, 'but I couldn't get it to work. The pointer thing kept disappearing altogether.'

Holly's sister Fay had once suggested getting them both a laptop as a joint present.

'You'd better ask them first,' Holly had told her, thinking back to the Christmas iPod that she'd had to take back untouched.

'They said it was a very kind thought but they'd absolutely hate it!' Fay had reported back, after asking them.

So it was a total surprise to Holly when her mother had announced she was coming to London to buy herself a computer from John Lewis.

'What on earth has brought about this transformation?' Holly asked her now, as they stood outside the lifts.

'Oh, I just felt as if I was getting a bit left behind. Lots of our friends have email addresses and I suppose it's a good way of keeping in touch with the ones who are still alive.' Susan said, before adding, 'Your father's even bought himself a mobile phone.'

'Has he?' Holly exclaimed. She found this hard to believe. She had lent him hers once when her parents had been to stay. Patrick had set off on a long walk, and Holly had given him the phone in case he got lost. It took her about an hour to show him how to make a call if he did. Then, when it got late and the rest of the family were staring to worry about him, she called but found the phone switched off.

'I didn't want to waste the battery,' her father had said when he eventually got back, unperturbed that they had been anxious on his behalf.

'What's he going to do with a mobile phone?' Holly asked her mother now.

'I'm not entirely sure,' Susan replied. 'And I've tried calling him on it a couple of times but he never seems to answer.'

'Perhaps you could get a phone of your own and then you could text him?' Holly suggested.

'Oh, I don't imagine he'll want me bothering him when he's busy,' Susan said as they stepped into the lift. 'Which floor was it?'

'Fifth,' Holly said, feeling slightly uneasy about whatever it was her father was busy with.

Holly noticed for the second time that day that her mother seemed to light up when there was a young man about.

Dean, according to his nametag, had asked if he could help.

'I want to buy a computer.' Susan smiled at him.

Dean led her to the laptop section and Holly trailed after them feeling like a spare part.

She smiled at a woman who was browsing digital radios. She looked familiar but Holly could not place her. She thought it was probably someone from the BBC.

'What is it you want to use it for?' Dean was asking Susan.

'I'm sure once I have it, I might want to do all sorts of things,' she told him, with an air that suggested she might even be able to. Holly doubted this.

'But initially I just want to stay in touch with friends . . . maybe even make new ones.'

Holly could see why her mother wanted to stay in touch with friends, especially as those she had kept dying, but she wondered where this sudden urge to make new ones had come from.

'I'm not very technically competent, though,' Susan was telling Dean, who had already assumed this and began giving her a rough guide to the desktop.

'Why won't the arrow move?' Susan asked, exasperated, when he tried to show her how easy it was to shop online.

'That's the hardest part,' Dean said gently, and it wasn't long before she was clicking her way through online stores.

'It's a bit like returning library books.' She smiled gleefully, having managed to add some passion fruit to a virtual supermarket basket.

Half an hour later, she was marching Holly to the in-store café, with a netbook tucked under her arm.

'I'll ask Fay to help me set it all up. She's coming over with V and the girls at the weekend,' Susan said, settling down with a slice of quiche and plate of salad.

Vanessa or V was Fay's partner and the natural mother of their children, Kate and Lucy. Peter, a close gay friend of them both, was the father.

Holly and Fay's parents, especially their father, found it hard to accept this domestic set up completely. They did their best to give the impression that they found everything perfectly normal, but the effect was comic rather than genuine.

'Dad said he liked the new décor in Lucy's bedroom,' Fay had told Holly after a visit. 'He described it as: 'What we used to be able to call gay!' Then Mum tried to make up for the gaffe by telling V she'd made a lovely job of painting the walls and how clever she was to 'do all the man's jobs as well'.'

'Have you spoken to Fay recently?' Susan asked now.

'Not since we got back from holiday,' Holly told her.

Her sister had called, concerned, after the train crash but hadn't been in touch again since.

'She said she was going to call you,' Susan said. 'I think she's coming up to London next week. She said she would try to meet up with you.'

'I'll email her,' Holly promised, taking a spoonful of soup. 'I suppose I'll be able to email you soon, too, once you've got it all set up. Will you get a joint email with Dad?'

Holly and Mark had their own separate work email addresses but at home they shared one.

'No, I don't think so.' Susan sounded appalled at the very suggestion. 'Anyway I don't suppose Patrick will have time to get to grips with it.'

Holly wondered again what Patrick was so busy doing but something stopped her from asking. She took another mouthful of soup instead.

'So how are you, Holly?' her mother asked. 'Really?'

'Fine.' Holly trotted out her standard response. 'And the children are well and Mark's fine too.'

'And how has it been going back to work?' Her mother looked at her more closely now. 'How are you finding the train journey?'

'It's OK, Mum,' Holly said truthfully. 'I was a bit nervous at first, but once I was on it was fine.'

'It must be strange though,' Susan persisted. 'I mean, are some of the people who were injured still travelling on the train?'

'I haven't noticed anyone,' Holly said truthfully. She'd not encountered anyone with any visible signs of having been hurt when the train crashed.

But it was still early days. She presumed the people who had been seriously injured would not be back for a few weeks yet, if at all.

'And have you seen . . . ' Susan paused and began toying with the salad on her plate, as if unsure whether to ask or not. 'The man who stayed with you, when it all happened?'

'I've bumped into him a couple of times,' Holly said, and looked at her watch, as her mother put a sizeable piece of quiche into her mouth.

'I ought to be getting back to work soon, Mum.' She had finished her soup, and although she didn't need to get back to work immediately, found herself not wanting to talk to her mother about Daniel Harrison — or to tell her that she was having a drink with him that evening.

'OK. Sorry, darling. I don't want to hold you up.' Susan had now finished her quiche. 'I might stay and have a cup of coffee but you go on back to work. I don't want to make you late.'

'It was lovely to see you anyway.' Holly kissed her mother goodbye. 'Good luck with the laptop. And send my love to Dad.'

'I expect he'll let you know his mobile number. Then you can text him yourself,' Susan replied. 'And tell that nice Greek chap my mission was successful, won't you?'

I saw the woman from the train again today, out of context, and I couldn't place her at first. I went to John Lewis in my lunch hour to buy a digital radio. The house is too quiet without Geoff. It's as if the silence in every room is a reminder that he's gone.

I wanted to get a decent radio. A cheap one would have made him seem easily replaceable, and it's not easy, not easy at all. I still switch off the alarm every morning and turn over to ask if he wants a cup of tea. I walk though the door at the end of the day and shout 'Hello', expecting someone to reply. I wanted something to fill that awful silence of the no reply.

I was looking at a Roberts leather-covered radio, a modern version of the one my parents used to have, when I looked up and there she was. I recognised her but I couldn't think where I knew her from, and then I realised and smiled. She smiled back, as if she knew exactly who I was. And I thought that I could have talked to her then, said something, introduced myself, told her I knew what had happened to her, but she was with an older woman.

The assistant was showing them laptops. I kept looking over, thinking she might catch my eye and smile again. But she didn't. She seemed wrapped up in the discussions they were having. So I just watched them from behind the stack of radios.

I thought the older woman was probably her mother and that made me feel resentful. I know that's unreasonable. I should be pleased that she has someone who is there for her. But when I first saw her on the news, she looked so alone and I thought she might be someone who could understand what I was going through. I thought maybe we could be there for each other.

Now, I am discovering she has people all around her; first that man on the train and now her mother. I told myself not to be silly; not to be cross with her. It's not her fault that I have no one, is it?

I keep imagining that I'm talking to the counsellor again, mentally explaining to her why I might be feeling a certain way.

'I think I felt resentful because I was already thinking about my mother,' I ran the imagined conversation in my head afterwards. 'Because I bought an exact replica of the radio my parents used to have in their front room and because I was in a department store.'

That always makes me think about my mother. For years, I never went into a department store and my mother stayed away from them until she died. But I realised I was letting events dictate my actions and decided to take control. I think Helen, the counsellor, must have told me that I needed to 'take control'. I don't think I would have put it like that myself, but it did gradually begin to dawn on me that avoiding department stores for the rest of my life was pointless.

'Do you want to tell me about what happened?' Helen asked me when I first started going to see her.

'It was because I needed a new coat,' I told her. 'We got there early because my mother thought there would be a queue, what with it being a closing down sale and that.'

And then I ran though the story about the crowd building up, so that by the time the store was due to open its doors, people were pushing against us and I felt myself being crushed against those around me. I was ten at the time, small for my age, so my face was being pressed into coat tails and I found it hard to breathe.

There was a small wall by the steps that led up to the shop doors and my mother managed to lift me up and place me on it, so that I was above the crowd which still appeared to be growing and pushing forward with an intensity that made the people at the front start to panic.

'You ought to open the doors,' my mother said to the security guard. 'I know it's not time, but someone might get hurt. All these people and nowhere for them to go.'

She smiled when she said this, as if it was just a suggestion. But the people around her became more agitated and began chanting, 'Open the doors. Open the doors!' And because they were chanting, the pushing seemed to get worse and the security guard, who my mother told me afterwards 'couldn't have been more than eighteen', looked unsure what to do.

'Stand back a bit,' he said, and began fumbling with keys. 'The doors open outwards.'

And those were the last words he ever spoke. We didn't know that at the time. We never knew when we surged inside the store and took the escalators up to the children's clothing section, that he'd lost his footing as the crowd began flooding in and over him, trampling him to death in their anxiety to secure cheap goods.

My mother wouldn't let me wear the coat when we heard the news. It was navy blue with silver buttons, a bit too big for me because she wanted it 'to last', but beautiful. I only wore it that once, on the way back home. After she'd switched on the Roberts radio in the living room and found out what had happened she wrapped it up again and put it back in the bag, then put the bag on top of the wardrobe in their bedroom, where she knew I wouldn't be able to reach it.

'It wouldn't be right to wear it,' she said, as I watched her. 'Not now.'

I wonder if my mother would forgive me today for using a department store. 'It's not as if there's a lot of choice,' I would tell her, if she was here to hear. 'The radio shop in the village closed years ago. It's here or the internet.'

'It just doesn't feel right, Anne-Marie,' I can almost hear her replying. 'But I suppose these are exceptional circumstances.'

She'd have tried not to mind that I'd broken her rule because she'd be so worried about me.

Part of me is glad that she's not here, that she doesn't have one more thing to worry about. It's the sort of thing that might push her over the edge again and she was OK, towards the end. She seemed to have stopped thinking about it, stopped blaming herself so much, started nodding when my dad said, 'It wasn't your fault my love. You have to believe that.'

If she was still alive now, I imagine my mother would have asked me to stay, cooked for me, looked after me. I could have really let go and maybe that would have helped. But I'm on my own and the only way I know how to cope is to try and carry on.

Perhaps that's what she's doing too, the woman from the train. Sometimes, even when you have people around, you can't always tell them what's happened, can you? You can't explain.

'I could never really explain to your father what it felt like,' Mum used to say to me. I wonder if this woman I saw today has explained to her own mother how it felt when she was trapped in that tunnel.

Perhaps not. Perhaps she can't. Perhaps she wants to spare her mother's feelings. But she could tell me, if she wanted to, because I would understand what it's like to feel alone, what it's like to worry that no one is looking out for you any more.

I bought the radio and it's on now in the living room, switched to BBC Radio 4, mocking me with idle chatter. I was wrong. It doesn't make the house seem less empty. If anything, it feels more so.

There are three people talking about global warming and I know that if Geoff were here he'd say something about it being a conspiracy. I don't agree with him and it always annoyed me when he started going on about the effects of burning fossil fuels being over-exaggerated. When they were talking about it on the radio I expected him to pipe up with his conspiracy theory. But of course he didn't.

I wanted to cry then, but didn't because if I started I'm not sure when I would stop and I'm tired of crying. There comes a point when you can't even summon up the energy to cry any more and I seem to have reached that point.

So, I got up and switched the radio over to BBC Radio 6. They were playing Arctic Monkeys' 'Don't Sit Down, 'Cause I've Moved Your Chair'.

I thought, Too right, you moved my chair. You pulled it and the rug it was on right out from under my feet.

Then I started to dance.

9

Holly opened the door of the Lebanese brasserie tentatively and was immediately greeted by a waiter.

'I'm meeting someone,' she said, scanning the muted beige-and-grey interior. 'But I don't think he's here yet.'

'Holly.' She felt a hand touch her shoulder lightly and turned to find Daniel coming in the door.

'I've been walking up the road behind you,' he said, smiling at the waiter as if they were fairly familiar with each other. 'I tried to catch up but you walk very fast!'

'It's the only exercise I get, and I've been sitting at a desk all day,' she told him, although she always walked everywhere fast. Thankfully, so did Mark. She was not sure she could have married a dawdler.

'I would have called out but I wasn't sure it was you.' Daniel allowed the waiter to usher them to a small table in the window, with a low armchair set either side.

'This looks nice.' Holly looked around at the sleek curved lines of the restaurant. It reminded her of an ocean liner. 'I've never noticed it before but I must have walked past nearly every day.'

'A friend who's a recovering alcoholic told me about it.' Daniel picked up the wine list and shrugged as if in apology to his absent friend.

'He always orders mint tea, but I could do with a large glass of red wine. How about you?'

'Same,' said Holly, realising she'd felt in need of one ever since saying goodbye to her mother. 'I could definitely do with a drink.'

'What train do you need to get?' Daniel asked. 'Shall we share a half-carafe or do you want something else?'

'Sounds good to me,' said Holly, relaxing back into her chair, knowing that alcohol would soon be coming her way. 'I was going to aim for the seven-fifteen, but if you need to go earlier . . . '

'No.' Daniel was looking towards the bar, trying to catch the waiter's attention. 'I'll get that too.'

★ ★ ★

He had replied immediately to Holly's email, earlier in the week, and suggested they meet in a place he knew close to Victoria station. She was thankful to him for this. She had feared he would suggest simply sitting together on the train and she knew she couldn't talk to him in that setting.

Now she looked at Daniel as he pointed out the wine they wanted to the waiter.

'Do you want any olives?' he asked her. 'Or we could share a mezze plate?'

'Why not?' Holly was peckish and the food looked good. 'I'm getting hungry and it will be hours before I get to eat at home.'

The bowl of soup she'd had with her mother hadn't been very filling.

'No dinner waiting on the table for you back

home then,' said Daniel, and then to the waiter, 'Can we get the mezze plate too, please?'

'It certainly won't be ready.' Holly thought back to the last few nights spent waiting for Mark's offerings to be brought to the table. 'My husband likes to cook. But he likes to take his time.'

'What does he do?' Daniel asked as the waiter returned and began pouring a half-inch of wine into his glass.

He gave a brief cursory swig and nodded, going through the rigmarole of tasting so that the waiter could then pour them both a glass.

Mark had mentioned he might have a drink with some former colleagues after work this evening. 'Networking,' he'd said, and Holly suspected he hoped it might yield more work.

'He's in marketing.' She raised her glass. 'Cheers! And thank you.'

'What for?' said Daniel, clinking her glass.

Holly sat back in her chair and looked at him. She must have seen him on the train hundreds of times before the crash but had never really taken in any detail about him. He was just another familiar face, to be ignored in a crowded carriage or occasionally smile at apologetically as she'd moved around him to get to a seat or reached up to take a bag from the overhead luggage rack. His face was becoming more familiar since she'd seen him again, last week, but this was the first time she'd had the chance to take him in properly.

She'd initially thought he was roughly the same age as her but now she realised he must be at least ten years younger. He was attractive in an irregular way. It was hard to make out whether his salt-and-pepper hair veered towards blond or brown, if his eyes were green or blue. He had the sort of face which she imagined would not photograph particularly well, but which in the flesh was strangely attractive.

'For staying with me,' Holly said, knowing that much was understood between them and didn't really need saying.

'It helped me, having something to do,' Daniel said, stretching his arm across the table and covering her hand briefly with his. The gesture didn't seem flirtatious, it seemed right.

'Daisy was angry with me afterwards,' he went on. 'She'd heard about the crash on the radio and had been trying to call me. When I didn't answer, she thought I might have been killed.'

'That's understandable,' Holly said, presuming Daisy was his wife.

'She was angry that I stayed.' Daniel took another sip of wine. 'She told me I should have got myself out as soon as I could, let the rescue workers deal with everyone else.'

'That's understandable too,' Holly told him. 'I'm not sure how I would have felt if Mark had been on the train and he'd stayed to help someone, rather than getting himself out. It sounds selfish but I wouldn't have wanted him to have risked his life for some stranger.'

'It felt like the right thing to do.' Daniel looked at her. 'I didn't think about whether to stay with you or not. I couldn't have left.'

Holly was sure that if Mark had been in

Daniel's position he would have stayed too.

Soon after she had first met him they'd been lying on the beach one day, dozing off a bedroom-induced lethargy. A boy who couldn't have been more than six had caught their attention as he walked along the groyne out to sea. He was holding his arms out like an aeroplane to balance himself, but wobbling precariously nevertheless.

'He's gone!' Mark said suddenly, jumping up from the towel they were lying on and running towards the beach before Holly had time to ask what had happened.

Then she saw what Mark had already seen. The boy had fallen into the sea, was out of his depth and being pushed under by waves that were rough for the time of year.

Mark swam straight out. He was a strong swimmer but Holly still worried when he dived under the water and disappeared.

He emerged, what seemed a long time later but could only have been seconds, with the boy under one arm and swam back to shore with him.

The boy's mother, whose attention had been focused on her new boyfriend's licking of her nipples, had seen none of this and seemed irritated when Mark brought him to her.

Holly had marvelled at the fact Mark hadn't even stopped to think but had gone straight after the boy. She dreaded to think what might have happened if he hadn't.

When the train was hit, they'd been as much in the dark about what had happened as they had been in the blackness of the tunnel. Only later would it emerge that their portion of the train had come uncoupled and the back been hit by another train.

As the smell of smoke began to filter through the carriage, Holly had wondered if there had been some sort of terrorist attack. She'd thought then, as people rushed to get out of the wreckage, that perhaps there would be another, nearer explosion. Daniel must have thought the same, and yet he'd stayed with her.

Holly pulled the elastic band she wore around her wrist so that, pinged against her skin just hard enough, it would distract her from thinking about what had happened. It was a trick she'd heard mentioned somewhere, she wasn't sure where, and it seemed to work. If anyone commented on the band, she'd say she was keeping it for Jake who was growing a rubber-band ball.

'I'm so grateful that you stayed,' she said, looking directly at Daniel. 'Things might have been different if you hadn't.'

'The fire crews would have got to you anyway.' He shrugged off his part in it all.

'I know,' Holly said. 'But I'd have been on my own.'

Daniel poured some more wine into her glass. 'Staying with you made me feel as if I'd at least done something.'

The waiter returned to the table, bearing a plate of mezze which he set in the middle.

Holly smiled in thanks.

'Everyone keeps telling me I need to talk,

ought to see a counsellor, and that I need to deal with what happened . . . but it doesn't feel right to keep going over things, because I'm OK,' she told him. 'Counselling should be for people who were injured . . . '

Holly paused and Daniel said what she was thinking out loud.

'Or the relatives of the people who died.' He took a deep-fried aubergine from the plate between them.

'I went back to work immediately, even though it meant getting a bus from Gatwick to East Croydon,' he said. 'Daisy kept saying I needed time to get over the shock and the trauma, but I just wanted to get on with things.'

'Me too.' Holly took an aubergine herself. 'It's funny how people always seem to think it odd if you do, though. My husband's father died when he was at university. He had a football match that day. Everyone told him he should pull out but Mark played in it because he said he needed to do something.'

'Did he win?' Daniel asked.

'I don't know.' Holly considered this. 'I never actually asked. He told me about it when Harold Shipman was convicted. Apparently he went running after his mother died and all the pundits said this pointed to him being a serial killer.'

'Is your husband a serial killer yet?' Daniel raised his eyebrows.

Holly laughed again. She liked him.

'The wife is always the last to know,' she said. 'Or is that with adultery?'

'Probably both.' Daniel smiled. 'Does he keep himself to himself?'

'I'm not with you?' Holly looked at him questioningly.

'Serial killers,' Daniel said, and then explained further. 'On the news, they always say they kept themselves to themselves. If your husband is gregarious, you'll probably be OK.'

'Well, he's fairly sociable,' Holly told him, and then reverted to the conversation they'd been having before Harold Shipman somehow came into it.

'Have you talked to anyone?' she asked. 'About the crash, I mean?'

'No.' Daniel shook his head. 'You?'

'My husband made an appointment for me with a counsellor,' she said. 'I went, to shut him up, but I felt fraudulent. I hadn't got any scars to show.'

The counsellor had urged Holly to go over exactly what had happened that day. But she hadn't wanted to talk to him about it, or to Mark when he'd asked her gently what it had been like. The only person she thought she might be able to talk to was the man whose name she hadn't known until last week. The man who was sitting opposite her now, making her laugh for what felt the first time in ages.

'Is Daisy your wife?' Holly asked.

'Yes.' Daniel looked a his wedding ring as if to confirm the fact to himself.

'Children?' Holly asked, knowing the question was slightly impudent but wanting to get a fuller picture of him.

'We've been trying.' Daniel appeared not to mind the question. 'But none yet.'

Holly wondered how long they'd been trying for and whether other people had started trying for babies since the accident. She knew the birth rate had soared after 9/11, as people felt the need to take life-affirming action after such large numbers had died. Or perhaps it was just that they valued their own lives more and needed to get on with them, stop putting off families or marriage or whatever it was they'd been waiting for the right moment to begin. After 9/11 Holly had felt a strong desire to have another baby herself, but Mark had resisted and once Jake settled into school she found herself enjoying the extra time she had.

But the train crash seemed to have had the opposite effect on her, making her feel slightly detached from the life that she had and less willing to embrace it.

Daniel looked at his watch.

'We should get going,' he said. 'If we're still aiming for the seven-fifteen?'

'OK.' Holly reached for her bag, getting up slowly, in no particular hurry to get home.

They walked the short distance to the station together and Holly wondered if Daniel always walked slowly or if he was dawdling because she was.

'*Pagad*,' she said to herself, a word which Mark had told her was a Filipino expression, meaning to walk slowly so that a slow walker could keep up.

It implied, Mark had told her, that the person

slowing their pace was considerate. She glanced at Daniel now, knowing this much already, and smiled to herself. The slight anxiety she had felt about meeting him had disappeared. She hoped she'd see more of him.

10

The blinds of the office Holly now shared with Natalie were still drawn and when she tried the handle it was locked. She took her key from her bag and was just putting it in the lock when the door swung open from the inside. Holly fell forward slightly and stumbled into the office and the arms of James Darling.

'Oh, sorry, I thought the door was locked.' She backed off a bit and stepped past James towards Natalie, who was leaning against her desk. 'Hi, Natalie. James.'

Holly was probably the only person on the programme who didn't call James 'Darling'. It felt too forward given that she didn't particularly like him, plus she suspected that, having had at least fifty years of people calling him Darling, he was probably getting a bit sick of it. He must have heard all the jokes a million times, if not more.

As if to underline her thoughts, Natalie piped up a well-worn line.

'Move over, Darling,' she said, noticing that James appeared temporarily frozen and was blocking Holly's access to her desk.

'Oh, sorry, Holly.' He stood aside.

Holly sat in her chair and swivelled round to face both of them.

Natalie was still leaning against her desk with an air of nonchalance. James looked as if he was

101

not quite sure what to do with himself.

'So, have I interrupted something?' Holly presumed they'd been discussing some of the items under consideration for this week's programme.

'No.' James's negative came only a split second before Natalie's.

'No,' she said, picking up a sheaf of papers from her desk. 'We were about to go through a couple of possible interviews for this Friday, that's all.'

Natalie had known James Darling for longer than anyone else on the programme. They'd worked in local radio together and then in the Broadcasting House newsroom in their twenties.

In Holly's opinion Natalie was cleverer, sharper and more intuitive than James, but he had had the more glittering career. James had become a correspondent and spent his thirties reporting from Rome, Berlin, Prague and Kiev before returning to take up the new position of breaking news correspondent. Natalie had stayed in London, become a news producer and then moved into programme production.

'What's on the cards then?' he asked, nodding towards the sheaf of papers Natalie was shuffling in front of her.

'You're not going to like this but Katherine is very keen on it.' Natalie had the job of running though all the potential items in the programme with James early in the week. She had a knack for bringing him round to things he didn't like at first. They worked well together, possibly because of the longevity of their relationship.

Natalie shifted up the desk a little, allowing James to rest his backside against it, next to hers, and read the piece of A4 she was holding.

'Global warming linked to snails?' he asked, nudging her conspiratorially as he did.

Holly couldn't help finding James Darling physically repellent. She found the way he peered through his ridiculous big square glasses rather creepy. Plus, he was slightly sweaty and his stripy shirt was stretched too tight around his spreading middle. If he wasn't careful he would end up like the fat man on the train whom she had deliberately avoided this morning.

★　★　★

Holly felt she had skipped a generation, and instead of turning into her mother was turning into her grandmother and becoming superstitious about all sorts of things. One was keeping Daniel Harrison's card in her bag whenever she took the train, treating it as a lucky charm to protect her against any future dangers. Another was trying to sit in the same place; window seat, facing forward, not too near the doors and in the middle of the train. Although the train crash had been a completely random occurrence and it was luck that saw her come out of it alive and in one piece, she also knew that if she'd been sitting further back she could have been injured or worse. So she'd stuck to the same carriage and the same seat as much as possible, since then.

The very overweight man appeared to be doing the same.

He'd sat next to her three times this week already and it wasn't only the way he seemed to spread over from his side of the seat and into hers that annoyed her. It was his personal habits too.

He'd had a cold and would shift around in their joint seat as he fumbled to get tissues from his pocket; tissues which, after a great deal of blowing, he deposited on his lap. Holly was sure she would come down with whatever virus he had. By mid-week the cold appeared to have affected his breathing and, although there were fewer dirty tissues around, her thoughts were disturbed by the heavy rasping of his breath.

So this morning Holly decided she'd had enough and sat in another carriage, further up the train.

There was a leaflet on the seat she found, giving details of the Balcombe tunnel survivors group's meeting. Holly skimmed the agenda. ALL WELCOME was written across the bottom in large bold letters as if, Holly thought, to emphasise that even people like her, with nothing to show for having been on the train that day, could attend.

If you were not a victim then you were a survivor.

Holly folded the leaflet and put it on the half-table by the window. She wasn't going to be either.

'Do you mind if I sit here?' said a voice she recognised.

She looked up and saw Daniel, smiling but looking hesitant.

'Of course not.' She smiled back at him.

'You looked as if you didn't want to be disturbed.' He sat down and put his cup of coffee by the leaflet on her table. 'I won't talk all the way to London or anything.'

He eased himself out of his coat and hung it over the armrest.

'I don't mind if you do,' Holly replied. Then, joking, 'I might not listen, but I won't mind.'

Daniel shrugged a quiet acceptance of the joke.

'You don't usually sit in this carriage?' he said questioningly.

'No,' she told him. 'I usually sit further back. I was getting into the habit of sitting in the same place but I thought I'd try to make a change.'

'I try to avoid the part of the train we were sitting in,' Daniel said.

'I was doing the opposite,' Holly told him.

'Why?' He reached across her to pick up his coffee cup.

'A sort of silly superstition.' She watched as he flicked the plastic lid off and took a sip. 'I got out in one piece, sitting in that particular carriage. I told myself I'd probably be OK there if anything happened again.'

'I try to sit anywhere but where we were,' Daniel said, licking a line of milky froth from his upper lip. 'Your routine makes more sense, though.'

'I don't know if any of it makes any sense,' Holly said, reaching for the leaflet which she had been trying to ignore. 'Have you seen this? Will you go?'

'I'm not sure,' he said, studying it. 'Will you?'

'I don't know,' Holly replied. 'It probably doesn't make sense but I think I'd feel a bit fraudulent.'

'It makes perfect sense.' Daniel handed the leaflet back to her. 'Sometimes I feel saying I was on the train when it crashed is a bit like saying I was on the roller coaster on the Palace Pier when in fact I was only on the bumper cars. I might have been in the same place, but I didn't have the same experience as others.'

Holly laughed.

'We had the same experience,' she said.

'I know.' Daniel briefly caught her eye and then looked away. 'We could go together? And leave if we don't feel comfortable?'

He'd stopped talking and shifted in his seat slightly, allowing a woman who had got on the train at Hawyards Heath to sit in the seat opposite them.

Holly recognised her as the woman she'd seen applying make-up on her first day back at work. She smiled and the woman smiled in return, as if she recognised her too. Today her make-up was fully applied and she sat still and stared out of the window for the rest of the journey.

Holly began reading her newspaper and Daniel took out his laptop and opened it, their conversation ended by the slightly uncomfortable presence of a third person in their quadrangle of seats.

*   *   *

Natalie obviously did feel comfortable with James Darling firmly planted in their office, his backside taking up most of her desk.

'That's all we've got for now,' she said, picking up a few more documents from her desk. 'Plus the ones we've already talked about.'

James put his hand out to take them from her, without looking up, and Natalie put the wad of papers in it, and then forced his fingers closed with her hand.

That made him look up and smile.

Uggh! Holly thought.

'By the way,' Natalie added, 'did you hear Liam Hicks has been having an affair with the singer from Ecstatic?'

Liam Hicks was a TV news reporter. He'd worked with Natalie and James in the radio newsroom but was always destined for television. He looked like a film star. Tall, dark, penetrating green eyes, six o'clock shadow — the works!

'Isn't he married?' Holly asked.

'Yes, to Maria Goulding.' Darling reeled off the name of another TV reporter. Maria was brilliant; clever, incisive and dogged. Her reports had won her numerous awards, but compared to her handsome husband she was mousey and unprepossessing-looking.

'Honestly!' Holly felt exasperated by the cliché of the affair. 'He's married to a very bright woman and yet he goes off with a beautiful airhead.'

'She is *very* beautiful,' James said, as if this justified Liam Hicks' dalliance.

'It must be a terrible curse, having a

good-looking husband,' Natalie said.

Holly laughed out loud.

'What?' Natalie and James said together.

'Well, you sound as if you don't think you have a good-looking husband.' Holly watched Natalie's half-smile as she realised what she'd said. 'Or me, for that matter.'

'Oh, well. You know what I mean.' Natalie shrugged. 'Mark is gorgeous, of course.'

'And so is Guy,' Holly prompted, wondering if Natalie really thought Mark was gorgeous or if she was just being polite.

Holly seemed to have stopped seeing Mark as the almost unbelievably good-looking man she had thought he was for so long, but did others still view him like that?

'Cue my exit,' James said, standing up. 'I'll leave you to discuss the various merits of your husbands. See you later.'

'So,' Natalie rolled her chair over to Holly's desk and sat down, 'talking of which, how was the tall, dark and handsome stranger?'

Holly wondered what she was talking about and then realised it must be her drink with Daniel Harrison.

'Quite small and sandy-haired. He works with computers,' Holly told her, trying to give Natalie the impression that Daniel was ordinary. She didn't want her to probe any further.

'How disappointing,' she said. 'I'd imagined he would be like Dimitri.'

'Not like Dimitri at all,' she told Natalie. 'But nice. He was very nice.'

'Nice?' Natalie was unimpressed. 'This cup of

108

coffee is very nice. What was he *like*?'

'I'm not sure how to describe him,' Holly said slowly. She felt protective of Daniel Harrison. She owed him that much. Natalie said nothing, sensing her mood.

'We only had a quick drink really.' Holly eased up a little towards her friend. 'But I felt as if I knew him quite well.'

'How so?' Natalie asked.

'It was a bit like meeting an old school friend,' she tried to explain. 'Someone you knew quite well, but haven't seen for years.'

'A bit like James Darling then?' Natalie nodded towards the outer office where he was presumably now hovering somewhere.

They were interrupted by a knock at the door.

Sharon, Katherine's PA, peered cautiously around the office, as if she expected someone else to be there.

'Katherine says can we have a meeting in fifteen minutes, in her office?'

'Yes,' Natalie answered for both of them. 'We'll be there.'

The interruption meant Holly never answered her question. In her mind she had formed a reply. No, he's nothing like James Darling. He's not like anyone I've ever met before. He's not like anyone I would usually be friends with, and yet I feel completely at ease with him and compelled to see more of him.

She kept these thoughts to herself.

11

There was a time when Holly would have been pleased that Mark had taken it upon himself to clean the fridge. But when she got home from work and found its entire contents strewn across the floor, she was annoyed — and not just because it meant she had to step across bags of frozen vegetables to get into the kitchen.

No, Holly was annoyed that Mark had nothing better to do. 'Be careful what you wish for,' she said quietly to herself, thinking how it used to drive her mad that he never attempted the household jobs. He had always been too busy, dealing with clients or bits of work that had to be tackled there and then.

'Hi.' Mark was crouching down, examining the contents of the bottom drawer of the freezer. 'How was your day?'

'Fine.' Holly had long since given up filling him in on the details. 'What are you doing?'

'A lot of this stuff is past its sell-by-date,' Mark explained, brandishing a packet of frozen fish fingers in one hand to illustrate his point.

'Does it matter?' Holly asked. She had always been of the mind that sell-by-dates were manipulation by supermarkets, designed to make you chuck out perfectly good food and buy more, rather than to protect you from salmonella. 'This looks OK.'

She picked up a packet of soft cheese, which

Mark had consigned to the kitchen table. Holly suspected the table was a staging post between the fridge and the bin. She looked at the packaging and then sniffed the cheese. It was a few days past its sell-by-date but it looked and smelled fine.

'You can't be too careful,' he said, taking the cheese from her and extending his foot to open the aluminium pedal bin.

'Well, it seems like a waste to me,' Holly said, doubly annoyed now that Mark was fussing around in the kitchen and also that what appeared to be perfectly good cheese was being chucked out.

Holly knew that she and Mark did not qualify as hard up, but with two teenage children to feed and a mortgage to pay, they weren't so flush that they didn't have to be careful. She felt, perhaps irrationally, that as she was the one bringing in most of the money at the moment, she should be the one who decided if it was spent on replacing items they might well have been able to eat.

'Blimey, look at this!' Mark appeared not to notice Holly's irritation and carried on rejecting packets of food. 'This bacon's going green.'

He held it up to show her before chucking it. 'And this butter looks a bit rancid, although the sell-by-date says it's still OK.'

Holly thought to herself, meanly, that it was not the food but Mark who was getting past his sell-by-date. Again, there was a time when she might have said this to him in jest and Mark would have laughed at the joke. Now she was not sure how he would take such a comment.

'Hi, Mum,' Chloe came down the stairs with Ruaridh in tow.

'Evening, Mrs Constantine,' he said.

'Evening, Mr O'Connor,' Holly replied. 'Hello, Chloe love. How was school today?'

'Good and bad.' She shot a sidelong glance at Ruaridh, as if seeking his corroboration that the day had had its ups and downs. 'I've got a couple of notes for you.'

She handed Holly a piece of paper and an envelope and Holly tried to clear a small space on the kitchen table. She sat down and opened the envelope.

''Dear Mr and Mrs Constantine,'' Holly read out loud so Mark, who was included in the addressees, could hear what it was about.

''It has come to our attention,'' she carried on reading, ''that CHLOE CONSTANTINE . . .'' her name had been inserted into what must have been a standard letter in bold capitals '' . . . has been coming to school wearing a skirt which does not meet the school uniform criteria.''

Holly looked at Chloe. There was a tiny thin black strip, visible just below the end of her school jumper. It certainly didn't resemble a skirt.

'Did you wear that to school?' Holly asked. 'I've never even seen that skirt before. It looks like a boob tube you've stuck on your bum!'

'Everyone does,' Chloe replied. 'It's a long vest.'

She lifted her jumper and shirt to reveal that what was masquerading as a skirt was indeed just a long vest.

'Well, this letter says,' Holly speed-read the rest of the note, 'that you will now have to buy a regulation school skirt and wear that to school, which is a nuisance, Chloe, because I gave you money to buy a skirt you could wear to school only a few weeks ago.'

'We don't have to get one.' Chloe shrugged. 'Everyone gets sent that letter. They won't take any notice if I don't get a school skirt.'

'I think she looks nice,' Mark said, deciding to add his opinion.

'We're not allowed to wear skirts,' Ruaridh chipped in. 'Which is sex discrimination.'

'Would you want to wear a skirt to school, Ruaridh?' Holly said, looking up at him questioningly.

'I wouldn't want to wear one, personally,' he laughed. 'But there might be boys who do. So it's still sex discrimination. We could probably take the school to the European Court of Human Rights.'

'I wish you luck with that,' Holly told him.

'Ugh, what's this?' Chloe had picked up a tub of mouldy spread, which Mark had unearthed from the back of the fridge.

'Some sort of vegan pâté.' Holly glanced at the label. 'I bought it when that friend of yours who doesn't eat dairy came to stay.'

'Freya,' Chloe told her.

'Do you remember when you used to think virgins didn't eat dairy products?' Mark asked, landing a load more yoghurt pots on the table.

'Did I?' Chloe obviously didn't.

'You got virgins and vegans confused,' he

113

explained, as she peeled the lid off one of the yoghurt pots and began licking it.

'Well, Chloe obviously eats dairy,' Ruaridh commented, and Holly looked up from the other letter she was reading and wondered what exactly Ruaridh meant by that.

She decided to ignore the comment and carried on reading the next letter from school.

'Botswana?' The letter was about a proposed school trip which would take place next summer, after Chloe had finished her GCSE's. It cost a fortune.

'I can't believe they are planning a school trip to Botswana!' Holly exclaimed, looking at Mark who was now putting things back in the fridge. 'That's a gap-year destination, not somewhere you go on a school trip. It costs fifteen hundred pounds! I can't imagine they'll have any takers.'

'I *really* want to go, Mum,' Chloe said. 'They showed us a film today of a trip from another year. It looked amazing.'

'I'm sure it did.' Holly hadn't imagined Chloe really thought she would be able to go. 'But we can't afford it, love. Can we, Mark?'

She looked to him to back her up but he appeared not to be listening.

'Do we still want these magnets?' He had closed the door of the fridge and was indicating the random magnetic words that had been on the door since Chloe and Jake were little. Holly had bought them to help them learn to read.

'It's much harder being a parent these days,' Holly remembered her mother saying, at the time. 'We never had to put magnets on fridges to get you to read!'

Or fork out for school trips to Botswana, Holly thought to herself now. The furthest she had ever been on a school trip was a day trip to the Isle of Wight.

'I don't care. Throw them away if you want,' Holly said to Mark. 'Did you hear *any* of what's just been said?'

'About Chloe's skirt?' He had obviously not been listening to the latter part of the conversation.

'No, about the school trip,' Ruaridh interjected.

'Are you wanting to go, Ruaridh?' Holly wondered if this was why Chloe was keen to go.

'No way would I be allowed,' he replied, and Holly realised this was true. If Ruaridh wanted to go on a school trip to Botswana, then the O'Connors might have to let all six of their children follow and she didn't imagine they could afford that.

'There's a meeting in the hall next week,' Chloe persisted. 'For parents to find out more about it. Why don't you go to that?'

'We could do that, I suppose.' Mark now appeared to be joining in this conversation. 'Couldn't we?'

'Maybe. Where's Jake?' Holly wanted Chloe and Ruaridh to leave them now to discuss the trip alone. Not that they could suddenly find an extra £1500 from anywhere.

'I think he's in his room.' Chloe took her cue. 'Shall we tell him you're home?'

'Yes, tell him to come down in a bit.' Holly smiled at Chloe, hoping she wouldn't be too disappointed to miss out on the trip.

'We could go to the meeting and see what we think.' Mark was reading the letter from school over Holly's shoulder.

'But have you seen the price?' She nodded towards the bottom of the page. 'Is there any point in going when we can't afford it anyway?'

'We could see,' he replied, and Holly wondered what he might have in mind.

'Anyway,' she continued, 'I'm not sure I can go. There's another meeting that evening that I said I might go to.'

'Oh, yes?' Mark walked around the table and opened the fridge again. She presumed, this time, it was in preparation for dinner.

'It's about the train crash,' Holly began, rooting in her bag, partly to try to find the leaflet about the meeting but also because she wanted to avoid eye contact with Mark.

She found the leaflet and put it folded on the table then went to get herself a glass of water while Mark read it. She hadn't realised that Daniel's card had fallen on to the table when she took it out.

'Who is Daniel Harrison?' Mark had picked it up and was reading the details.

'He's . . . ' Holly paused, not quite sure what to say, feeling guilty for still not having told Mark about him yet. 'He's the man who stayed with me, when the train crashed.'

'Oh, I see,' Mark said, although he clearly didn't. 'When did you see him again?'

116

'He was on the train today,' she lied, knowing that if she told him she'd met Daniel her first day back, he'd want to know why she hadn't told him. Holly wasn't sure herself. There was nothing to hide from Mark, but for some reason she'd wanted to keep her meeting with Daniel to herself.

'And you spoke to him?' Mark said.

'We had a quick chat on the platform at Victoria.' Holly was now telling Mark what had happened when she'd first met Daniel again. 'And he gave me his card, but he was rushing to work.'

'Will he be at this meeting?' Mark asked now, picking up the leaflet.

'I don't know.' Holly felt uncomfortable being cross-questioned.

'Do you want to go?' Mark asked.

'I think so.' Holly turned on the tap. She could feel her husband looking at her, even though she had her back to him.

'I didn't think you were keen to . . . ' Mark paused, as if searching for the right words ' . . . go over things.'

'I just thought I might pop in and see what it was like,' Holly said, filling her glass and drinking from it.

'I could come with you.' Mark had moved over to where she was standing now and put his arm around her. She wanted to shrug him off but had no reason. He was only being thoughtful.

'No,' she said, a bit too abruptly. 'It's not worth your coming all the way up. I might change my mind and I probably won't stay long anyway. I don't want to be too late home.'

'Stay if you want to,' Mark said, taking his arm away. 'It might be helpful.'

Holly suspected he wanted her to go to the meeting for the same reason he had wanted her to see the counsellor again. He thought she needed to talk about what had happened.

'Maybe you could go to the school meeting and report back?' Holly suggested, not wanting to talk about the survivors meeting any more in case Mark guessed that her real reason for going was because she wanted to see Daniel again and the meeting gave her an excuse.

When I got on the train today, she was sitting with him again — the man who was waiting for her at the ticket barrier. I wondered, briefly, if they were married but I don't think they are. They weren't sitting together the first time I saw her on the train, after the accident, although it's often hard to find two seats together. I rarely managed to find one next to Geoff on the occasions we both caught the same train.

But they don't look like a couple. He's much younger than her. And she's beautiful, I think, while he is quite ordinary in comparison — almost geeky looking. They don't look right together, yet they seem easy in each other's company, as if they know each other well.

They both looked up when I paused, wondering whether to sit in the vacant seat opposite. She smiled, as if she recognised me, so I sat down, wondering if she would acknowledge me further. But that was it, a brief smile when I sat down.

They'd been looking at a leaflet, which she then folded and put in her bag. There was another on my seat and I unfolded it and began reading, like a mirror opposite, about a meeting for survivors of the crash.

I wanted to ask if they were planning on going. It would have seemed perfectly normal to ask but by the time I'd plucked up the courage, a newspaper hid her and his face was obscured by a laptop screen — a barrier between us.

I wondered then what my mother would have thought about this meeting with its promise of information about where to get help with compensation claims and trauma. Nobody ever offered my mum help and she didn't seem to realise she needed it either. The sleepless nights, the flashbacks, and the inability to talk to my father about it . . . she thought that was all normal and would get better in time. It was only when she found herself standing in the bathroom with a bottle of Paracetamol, intending to swallow them all, that she went to the doctor.

She said she thought then he might give her some sleeping pills or 'something to take the edge off it'. She never thought she'd be admitted to hospital; never envisaged that without her there my father would find himself unable to cope with his only daughter and send me to live with friends; never realised that her not being there made me start clinging desperately to anyone who was, as if sheer force of will would stop them disappearing too.

I thought if I loved Geoff enough he'd always be there for me, and then it all started to fall apart; first the announcement on the radio, then the waiting for further news, and finally the sickening realisation that he wasn't coming back.

I looked across the space between our seats again and wondered if the woman sitting opposite had seen Geoff on the train that day. I decided then that I'd go to the meeting. Perhaps I'd be able to introduce myself to her there, if she went too, or others who'd been on the train that day. Perhaps there'd be other meetings and a survivors group would give me the sense of purpose which I lacked without Geoff to look after.

'It could get difficult if you start talking to people who were on the train,' the voice of Helen, my former counsellor, suddenly said in my head. 'Do you see yourself as a survivor?' she added.

'Yes,' I told her, in defiance of anything she might say.

I do see myself as a survivor. That's just exactly what I'm doing right now — surviving. I'm not really living at the moment, just going through the motions, because losing Geoff is the worst thing that has ever happened to me; worse than seeing my mother in the psychiatric ward, and worse than being sent to live with Lisa, and even worse than losing the baby.

12

Dimitri and Rebecca were hidden by the screen that surrounded her desk so Holly couldn't see them, but she heard Dimitri say, 'Stop, someone's coming.'

Then Rebecca stood up and peered over the edge of the screen.

'Oh, hi, Holly.' Did her greeting sound slightly guilty?

'Hello-o?' Holly elongated the word slightly, to sound questioning and imply that she knew something was going on.

'Morning, Hol!' Dimitri was grinning, as if he realised the game was up, whatever the game was. 'You look very glamorous this morning. Is that a new coat?'

'No.' Holly gave him a firm look to indicate that compliments were not going to put her off the scent of whatever it was she was on to.

She secretly admired Dimitri's persistent flirtatiousness. Twenty years ago she might have thought it slightly creepy — the way he never passed up an opportunity to compliment a woman if there was one in the vicinity. Now that she was older and not often on the receiving end of compliments, she liked the way he was with women.

'I've been wearing this coat every day for the past fortnight,' she said, looking at him squarely, taking in his dark good looks but feeling rather school-marmish as she did so. She imagined he came from the sort of family where you'd be letting the side down if you didn't try it on with women as a matter of course.

'How was your journey?' Rebecca asked innocently, then coloured slightly as if remembering that, with Holly, the question could be construed as loaded.

'It was fine.' She suspected Rebecca was only asking to deflect her attention from whatever it was the two of them had been doing.

'Close the page,' Rebecca hissed. It was supposed to be a whisper, audible only to Daniel, but it came out much louder.

There was something about the way Dimitri was looking at her, the resigned shrug of his shoulders, that seemed to invite Holly to ask more.

'What are you two up to?' She accepted the hint of an invitation.

'Christopher Perrin is coming in this afternoon.' Dimitri smiled, and moved his head slightly, indicating she should come round to their side of the desk.

'I know.' Holly had arranged for him to come in.

Christopher Perrin was an un-typical historian. In his mid-forties, he was good looking and energetic and, after making a series of television documentaries in which he bounded his way through the ruins of Ancient Mesopotamia, Damascus and Georgia, had become a household name.

The press were won over by his looks and

123

energy, and their interest in him was further aroused when he married cookery writer and TV chef Rosa Martinez. She was Spanish and extremely beautiful. If you were cynical you might have thought it was her accent and cleavage that made her programmes popular, especially with men who had no intention of creating tapas in their own home.

Mark was one of those men.

'I think I might watch Rosa Martinez this evening,' he would say to Holly. 'She's doing Cantabrian cooking tonight.'

'Really?' Holly would reply. 'I wonder what she'll be wearing?'

'I won't notice.' And Mark would grin, knowing that Holly knew full well that he would.

She'd bought him Rosa's cookery book for his last birthday.

'You are a very good wife,' Mark had said, opening it and looking appreciatively at the photographs. 'Buying me porn for my birthday!'

The food was only foreground interest, the focus was always Rosa.

'I know,' Holly had laughed. 'I thought about getting you Nigel Slater but I guessed you might prefer this.'

'You guessed right!' Mark said. 'Shall I keep it by our bed?'

Holly had found the book a few weeks later by Jake's bed and presumed he shared Mark's admiration of Rosa's perfectly rounded breasts. She thought about taking it downstairs and then decided she would rather Jake thought about Rosa under his duvet than some shaven porn star he might have access to via the internet.

James Darling was also a fan of Ms Martinez. 'I met his wife once at a festival. She is a fascinating woman.' He had become all animation when, earlier in the week, Holly had suggested an interview with Christopher Perrin.

'Research notes for Darling.' Dimitri said now, touching her arm briefly as she joined them in front of the computer screen.

He and Rebecca had pulled up several images from the internet. They were of Rosa Martinez: bending revealingly over plates of steaming food, licking sauce off a spoon suggestively, and peering out seductively over mountains of vegetables.

Holly laughed.

'What are you going to do with them?' she asked, looking from Dimitri to Rebecca as they exchanged a look.

'Actually, don't tell me.' She decided to leave them to it. 'Is James in yet?'

'He was in earlier,' Rebecca confirmed. 'But he's gone out to record something at the British Museum with Natalie.'

'Oh, yes.' Holly vaguely remembered her friend saying something about being out in the morning.

She unlocked the door of her office and ignored Natalie's phone, which was ringing. She'd let it go to voicemail. This instructed people to call Holly if they needed to talk about the programme urgently.

This caller obviously did as, by the time she had taken her coat off and hung it up, her phone was ringing, too.

'Hello. Holly Holt speaking,' she said, pulling the phone across the desk so she could sit down.

'Hi, Holly, it's Guy,' Natalie's husband identified himself. 'I'm trying to get hold of Nat, do you know where she is?'

'I think she's out recording something.' Holly settled back in her chair. 'Can I help?'

'Only if you can pass yourself off as Al and Kirsty's mum.'

Guy MacDonald was a reluctant house husband. He'd started his working life as a freelance travel writer and photographer, and spent a lot of time filing copy from far-flung locations.

Natalie had met him on a press trip to the Greek Islands.

She told Holly that when she wrote her piece, she had raved about the crisp white sheets and nautical decor of her cabin, but in reality she had never actually slept there. Over the next few years she'd been increasingly absent from her own bed, using all her annual leave to join Guy wherever he was.

Now they were married, had two children, and Guy was a stay-at-home husband.

'Guy's work dried up during the credit crunch,' Natalie always said when explaining their arrangement. 'And I have a full-time job so it makes sense for him to look after the children rather than pay a nanny.'

Holly wondered whether Natalie would have stayed at home and looked after the twins if Guy's work hadn't dried up. She doubted it. Natalie loved her job and loathed domesticity.

Guy adored the children but Holly suspected he resented being with them all the time.

'Apparently she's at the British Museum with James,' Holly said to Guy now, switching her computer on as she spoke.

'She never mentioned it,' he said, sounding pissed off. 'Do you know when she'll be back?'

'Not sure.' Holly flicked through her emails as she spoke. 'She said something about it last night, but I wasn't listening properly.'

'Maybe she said something to me.' Guy sounded doubtful.

'Do you want me to give her a message?' Holly reached for a pen in readiness. 'Or you could try her on her mobile.'

'I already did,' Guy said. 'It was switched off.'

'They were probably recording. Is it important?' Holly didn't have anything terribly important to do herself but felt she ought to be getting on.

'Al's doing some sort of performance at school today,' Guy told her.

'He thinks Natalie promised she would come. I told him she was working but he seemed adamant. So I just thought I'd ask, in case she was planning to sneak off work and come and see it.'

'Well, if I speak to her before you do, I'll tell her you called.'

Holly thought it unlikely that Natalie would be able to get out of the office today but she sensed the frustration in Guy's voice, as if Natalie's not going would be an issue in the MacDonald household.

* ★ ★

Natalie announced her arrival back at work by storming into their office, muttering about infantile behaviour.

'Have you seen what they've done?' she fumed. 'We've only got half an hour before Christopher Perrin arrives. What if James wants to chat to him in his office before we go to the studio?'

'Hang on a minute.' Holly wished Natalie were a bit less volatile sometimes. 'Who's done what?'

'Those bloody immature children!' She spat out the last word. 'Dimitri and Rebecca. Go and have a look at Darling's office for yourself.'

Holly shrugged and stood up. She was curious and didn't really want to be sharing the same air space as a fuming Natalie.

Whatever it was that had made her so cross had clearly had the opposite effect on James Darling.

Holly bumped into him as she made her way down the corridor to his office. He was roaring with laughter.

'Holly,' he cried, 'have you seen my office? It's fucking hilarious! Do you know who the decorators are?'

'Of what?' Holly thought she would decide whether to reveal her suspicions about the decorators once she had seen whatever it was they had done.

James turned round and she followed him to his office where he opened the door with a triumphant, 'Dah-dah!'

Rebecca and Dimitri had been hard at work. They had printed out all the pictures of Christopher Perrin's glamorous wife on sheets of A4 paper, and then plastered them around James Darling's office.

Rosa Martinez was everywhere: smiling coyly from the noticeboard, running her tongue over her top lip from the screen of Darling's computer, icing fairy cakes on his desk, and pouting and preening all over the walls.

It was childish but very funny, and James Darling clearly saw the joke. Holly laughed but also shared Natalie's misgivings about what Christopher Perrin might think.

'I'm going down to reception now to wait for Perrin,' James told her. He obviously felt he had the crisis under control. 'I'll go straight to the studio when he arrives. Will you tell Natalie to meet me there?'

'Sure,' Holly said, and went back to their office.

★　★　★

Natalie was still angry.

'It is quite funny,' Holly ventured.

'It's pathetic,' Natalie snapped. 'They're like a couple of schoolkids.'

'By the way,' Holly decided to change the subject, 'Guy called.'

'Bloody hell, that's all I need.' Natalie's response left Holly wondering if subject changing had been such a good idea after all.

She was about to tell her he'd called to remind her that Al was in some sort of performance at school when the door opened and James Darling stuck his head round.

'Nat,' he said, 'I need you.'

Natalie flounced out of the office after him.

'You're not the only one,' Holly said to their departing backs.

13

'Can you spare any change?'

Three men were sitting drinking from beer cans on the corner of the road when Holly and Daniel emerged from the building in which the survivors group meeting had been held.

'Sorry, don't have any,' Holly mumbled out of habit.

'No worries, love.' One of them raised his beer can as if he was about to toast her meanness. 'Next time we see you, we'll have credit-card facilities.'

Holly laughed, stopped and took out her purse.

'Let's see,' she said to herself as she looked inside and discovered she had been telling the truth. She didn't have any change. A fiver was the smallest denomination she had but she felt she couldn't very well not give them anything now.

'Don't spend it all at once.' Holly handed the money to the man who'd made the credit-card remark.

'Thank you, gorgeous.' He looked surprised but grateful. 'Thank you.'

'We're going to have a loyalty card as well,' one of the others said.

Holly looked at him. He didn't look much older than Jake. She was glad now she'd given them the money. She didn't want to think about the reasons they might be there, but she knew they weren't likely to be good.

'So, next time you come, we'll stamp it for you,' the young boy said. 'Six stamps and you get . . . '

He paused and looked around, as if wondering what he could offer. His dog sat quietly next to him.

'To stroke the dog?' His tone was questioning, as if Holly needed to agree to his proposition.

'Thank you,' she said. She looked at him and smiled before walking on.

'There was something about the young one . . . ' Holly looked at Daniel, wondering if he'd looked at the three men properly. 'He didn't seem much older than my son.'

'He was certainly young.' Daniel glanced back over his shoulder.

'I suppose I just felt a bit empty, after that meeting. It was all so official and businesslike.' Holly tried to explain why she'd been suddenly moved to give the man money.

'I know what you mean,' Daniel agreed. 'It felt like a planning application meeting or something, but I suppose most of the people there were only . . . '

Holly looked up at him, wondering if he was thinking the same as her.

'Like us?' she asked him. 'Not really hurt or anything.'

'I suppose the people who were really badly hurt are still recovering,' Daniel said, echoing what a man in a wheelchair had said to Holly at the meeting.

She had stood back to let him manoeuvre himself into a space and had taken in the fact he only had one leg; the other was missing from just below the knee.

'Shark attack,' the man said, in a loud cheery voice, as if he had known what she had been thinking.

'Really?' Holly presumed he was referring to his leg.

'No.' The man smiled. 'I got gangrene while I was backpacking in Indonesia, but I get bored of telling that story so I try to vary it a little. Sometimes I tell people I lost it in Vietnam, although I'm not quite old enough to have been there.'

Holly was not quite sure how to take this piece of information. It seemed in poor taste, especially given the nature of the meeting. 'I thought that maybe you'd lost it when . . . '

'In the train crash?' the American said. 'If I had, I'd still be in hospital recovering now. There's not likely to be anyone here today who was seriously hurt. Call me a sceptic but I'm pretty sure that's the only reason there's a Railtrack rep here today. He knows he won't have to face anyone who was really badly affected.'

Holly had laughed and relaxed a bit.

★   ★   ★

'Excuse me,' she heard a voice saying behind them now, as they walked up the road towards the station.

Holly turned round and saw the woman she now thought of as the make-up woman. She'd noticed her at the meeting too.

'Sorry to interrupt,' she said to them, 'but I think I saw you both at the meeting, didn't I?'

'Yes,' Daniel replied.

'Yes, you were there too, weren't you?' Holly tried to be a bit more forthcoming.

'I was. I'm Anne-Marie by the way,' she introduced herself. 'Are you heading to the station now?'

She walked with them to Victoria, telling them about herself as they went. Daniel and Holly were less forthcoming and she didn't ask what had brought them to the meeting.

★   ★   ★

'Do you want to try a Marmite chocolate bar?' A woman with long blond hair was handing out free samples in the middle of the station concourse.

'No, thanks,' Holly and Daniel both said in unison.

'Not a Marmite fan then?' he asked. 'I hate it.'

'I love it.' Holly smiled as she realised they fulfilled the Marmite you-either-love-it-or-hate-it USP. 'What about you, Anne-Marie?'

'What?' She didn't appear to have been listening.

'Marmite. Do you love it or hate it?'

'Oh, I don't mind really,' Anne-Marie replied.

'I'm just going to buy a paper.' Holly paused outside W H Smith. 'You go on and find a seat.'

'I'll wait.' There was still ten minutes before the train was due to leave and Daniel didn't seem anxious to be on board just yet.

'I think I'll go on,' Anne Marie said. 'It was nice to meet you both properly.'

'You too,' said Holly.

Daniel appeared to be examining the latest P. D. James on a bookstand, and said nothing.

'Well,' Anne-Marie hovered as if she expected them to be a little more forthcoming, 'I'll give you my card, shall I? It has my numbers on?'

'Thank you,' Daniel said, taking one of his own from his pocket and trading it.

They both looked at Holly.

'I don't have a card,' she said. 'I'll give you my number though. I'll write it on the back of Daniel's.'

She took out a pen and scrawled her direct line in the office. She didn't want to give her mobile number.

The train crash had skewed the natural order of things. Under normal circumstances commuters didn't speak to each other. Holly couldn't remember ever having seen Anne-Marie before the crash. But now she knew something about her, it was impossible not to talk to her if Anne-Marie wanted her to.

'You'd better be quick,' Daniel said, as she stood watching Anne-Marie take out her ticket and pass it though the machine.

'Oh . . . yes.' Holly wondered what he would say if she told him she didn't really want a paper but had simply not wanted to sit with Anne-Marie. Would he think her heartless and

135

unsympathetic, after what they'd just been told?

Mark would have understood her reasons. They had more to do with safeguarding her own privacy on the train than being completely unsympathetic.

'I like our friends and everything,' he often said. 'But do they have to come to dinner?' Or, 'If we clear out the spare room, there is a very real danger than someone might come and stay!'

Mark was sociable, but he liked his own space too.

'Actually, Holly,' Daniel was shuffling his feet slightly, 'do you have to go home right now? Are you expected back?'

'Sort of.' She wondered what the alternative was. 'I mean, I told Mark I was going to this meeting and would be late. I wasn't sure what time it would end.'

'Do you want a quick drink somewhere first?' Daniel was looking at the floor as he said this, as if he wasn't quite sure if the suggestion was appropriate and couldn't quite meet her eye as he asked. 'It's just . . . I feel as if . . . '

'Yes,' Holly cut in. 'I could get the train an hour later.'

*   *   *

She found a quiet table in the corner of the pub while Daniel went to the bar and bought himself a pint and glass of wine for her. She texted Mark while she waited.

Meeting still going on. Can't leave easily. Will call when on train.

She told herself she would tell him later she had stopped for a drink with Daniel.

'White wine.' He put a glass down in front of her.

'That's an enormous glass.' Holly was going to have to gulp it down. 'Are you sure it's not a vase?'

'Oh, that's what the flowers were doing in it!' Daniel smiled and took a sip from his own glass. 'I needed a large drink and I reckoned you probably did too. The flowers were past their best anyway.'

'Thank you.' Holly picked it up. 'So, what did you think?'

'I was a bit anxious when we got there and the chairs were all laid out in a circle.' Daniel said exactly what Holly had decided when they'd walked into the room where the meeting was to be held. 'I thought it might be like an AA meeting and we'd all have to stand up and introduce ourselves and explain what we were doing there.'

She nodded. 'I think I'd have left if that had been the case. Although do you think Anne-Marie might have wanted that?'

'Maybe.' Daniel considered this. 'The way she spoke to us . . . It was almost as if she had come to the meeting to tell someone what happened.'

'Yes,' Holly agreed. 'I've seen her on the train before a few times and she almost invited conversation then, not quite but almost. She smiled as if she wanted to talk but knew that she couldn't.'

* * *

'What made you decide to come?' Holly had asked Anne-Marie as they walked to the station from the meeting.

'I lost my husband in the crash,' she had said quietly.

'Oh. I'm sorry . . . ' Holly was at a loss for what to say next. 'What was his name?'

She wondered if she would remember it from the reports that followed the accident. Five people had been killed. Holly hadn't known any of them or even recognised the pictures they'd printed in the papers.

Anne-Marie appeared lost in thought and didn't answer immediately.

'We'd been married for a while,' she said finally. 'We wanted to start a family.'

* * *

'She seems to be coping remarkably well,' Holly said to Daniel now. 'I can't imagine that I'd be able to carry on so calmly if something like that had happened to Mark.'

'No.' Daniel took another sip of his pint, as if to fortify himself before his next question. 'Can I ask you something, Holly?'

She hated that question. It always preceded something difficult or embarrassing and, when someone asked it, she was always torn between saying 'Do you have to?' and curiosity about what it might be they wanted to ask.

Curiosity usually won out.

'What is it?' she asked Daniel.

'Well, it's not really any of my business.' He looked down as he said this. 'I don't know you well enough to ask, but does your husband . . . Does Mark . . . ? How have you been getting on since it happened?'

Holly didn't want to be disloyal to Mark. She knew she should say he'd been really supportive, was trying to look after her and had done everything he could to make things easier for her. And she should keep quiet about the fact that his solicitousness annoyed her and she didn't want to talk to him about the crash.

'It's just that,' Daniel spoke into her silence, 'things seem to have been a bit difficult between Daisy and me.'

'Same,' Holly conceded. 'With Mark, I mean. He's really looked after me and everything, but it's as if . . . '

She paused.

'The fact that Mark wasn't there seems to have created a barrier between us. Does that make sense?'

'Yes, Holly,' Daniel said, looking at her directly for the first time that evening. 'I know exactly what you mean.'

14

It took Holly a moment to realise the man walking up their road just ahead of her was Mark.

If he hadn't been wearing his hat, she might have walked past him. He was walking slowly, which was out of character.

Holly remembered when they had been to view their house after it came on the market. Mark had spotted the FOR SALE sign one day when he came back from work, even though Holly didn't like the area. But they'd been talking about moving somewhere bigger.

Mark had walked up the street, slowly taking in all the houses, not just the one they were going to see.

'It's the sort of street we could live in for ever,' he'd said to her then. 'I'm just taking it all in.'

The house had been owned by a vicar, whose wife had died and children had left home.

'I shall be moving somewhere smaller,' he had told them.

The viewing had been a bit like an interview and Holly had the feeling that the man wanted it to go to people he approved of.

'Will you be mother?' he had asked her after setting a tea tray down on a table in the sitting room and inviting them to sit.

She had obediently poured the tea and settled back to drink hers while Mark had charmed the vicar by being himself.

'Oh, that's you, isn't it?' he had pointed out, examining a black-and-white photo of a cricket team which hung on the wall. 'Who did you play for? I used to play for Twineham and Wineham, but then the family came along.'

And later, on, spotting a book about a yacht voyage that nearly ended in tragedy, 'Do you sail as well? I don't but I read that book. I loved it.'

The vicar, if he hadn't been delicately picking up crumbs from a floral china plate, would have been eating out of Mark's hand.

They offered a little under the asking price and their offer was accepted immediately.

'He wanted it to go to a nice family,' the estate agent had told them. 'And he said he liked you.'

'Obviously the well-read, cricket-playing family man with a wife who would be mother, went down well then,' Holly had said to Mark as they opened a bottle of wine that evening and allowed themselves a tiny celebration.

'I reckon he's a bit of a dark horse,' Mark had said. 'Cheers, Mother!'

'Why do you say that?' Holly had asked, thinking he had seemed a typical vicar to her, right down to the horn-rimmed spectacles and his fastidiousness with the tea.

'I don't know. There was just something about him . . . ' Mark had said, and been proved right when they moved into the house and found a stash of exceedingly hard-core pornography and some women's underwear tucked at the back of a shelf in one of the cupboards.

'I wonder how the pervy vicar is doing?' Mark

141

used to wonder out loud, a lot, until Holly asked him to stop.

'It makes me feel as if he is still here, watching us,' she told him once when they'd just gone to bed and sex was obviously on the agenda. 'You're putting me right off what we're about to do.'

'We don't want that,' Mark had said, kissing her and dropping the pervy vicar from his repertoire of anecdotes.

★   ★   ★

'Mark?' Holly called out now, not quite sure if she wanted him to stop and allow her to catch up with him or whether she wanted the last couple of minutes of her journey home to herself.

'Hello.' He turned and waved. 'How was it?'

'What?' Holly asked, thinking back to her drink with Daniel and wondering how Mark could possibly know about it.

'Your meeting,' he said,

'Oh, well, it was rather boring actually.' Holly looked past him, not wanting to meet his concerned expression. 'Where have you been?'

At this time of night it wasn't unusual for him to walk up the hill to the off licence, but there were no giveaway bottles of wine about his person.

'I went to the presentation at Chloe's school,' he reminded her, as they approached their house. 'About the trip to Botswana.'

'Oh, yes,' Holly said, unlocking the door.

She wished he hadn't been to that meeting. It would only raise Chloe's hopes about going on the trip and, as they could not afford it, it seemed pointless to do so.

'Hello!' Holly called once she was inside.

There was no answer but she could see Jake and Ed, sitting at her desk looking at her laptop.

'Hello,' she said again.

'Oh, hi.' Jake did not look round.

'Hello.' Ed was a little more forthcoming. 'We're doing a homework project together.'

'I said I'd run him home after dinner,' Mark said. 'Chloe's made something.'

'Good.' Holly was hungry and knew if Chloe was cooking something it was likely to be pasta and ready soon. 'What's the project?'

'What?' Jake appeared to have heard but not understood her question.

'The homework.' She gestured towards the computer screen. 'What are you working on?'

'Oh, something for PHSE,' Ed answered for him. 'We probably don't need to do it. Mr Stone is never actually in. He just gets supply teachers to give out homework sheets on his behalf.'

'He must be in sometimes,' Holly said.

'Hardly ever.' Jake appeared to be less engrossed in the homework than he had been when she came in, and swivelled round in his chair to face her.

'There's a sign in his room that's printed and laminated. It says, 'Mr Stone is unwell and will not be in today.' He obviously doesn't expect to be in much, if he has a special sign.'

Holly smiled to herself. Jake was becoming

more like his father as he got older. She could see him retelling this anecdote about the teacher with the laminated absent sign, refining it as he told it again and again, adding or subtracting details depending on the response they got. She wondered if she would ever start to find him annoying.

'Oh, by the way,' he said. 'V called. I said you'd call her later.'

'Hi, Mum.' Chloe came out of the kitchen, wearing as apron which was covered in flour. 'Where's Dad?'

'He was right behind me.' Holly wondered what she was cooking. 'He must have gone upstairs.'

'Did he say anything about the trip?' Chloe asked as Mark appeared at the top of the landing and began coming down.

'It certainly looks fantastic.' Mark smiled at his daughter.

'But we can't afford it,' Holly cut in, hating herself for being the killjoy but irritated with Mark for not being firm.

'We'll talk about it after supper.' He addressed this remark to Holly. 'Is it nearly ready?'

'Just waiting for the rolls to cook,' Chloe said, and then to Holly, 'I've made an Irish stew and soda bread rolls. It's a recipe from *Masterchef.*'

'Wow!' Holly was impressed.

'It'll only be about five minutes.' Chloe seemed to have guessed that she was hungry.

'Great.' Holly smiled.

'Do you want to sit down and I'll get you a drink?' Mark asked her.

They were still hovering in the doorway to the sitting room. The boys had shut the laptop and were trying to get past.

'Going to my room,' muttered Jake.

'OK,' Holly said, wondering if Mark would guess that she'd already had one. She didn't want to drink too much on an empty stomach.

'And then you can tell me a bit about the meeting,' he said as Holly sat down and he left the room.

★   ★   ★

Holly was just finishing stacking the dishwasher when Mark got back from taking Ed home.

'Will you talk to Dad about the trip when he gets back?' Chloe had asked after he'd left.

'I will, Chloe,' Holly said. 'But to be honest, darling, even if he says it's the most fantastic trip in the world and thinks you should go on it, I really don't know where we are going to find that sort of money. I'm sorry, but that's the way it is.'

''S'allright,' Chloe mumbled and left the room.

Holly wasn't sure if she was angry or just disappointed.

Jake had stayed and helped her clear the table in companionable silence. She was thankful for both the help and the silence.

'Chloe's gone up to her room,' she told Mark when he came back. 'I think she's leaving us to talk about the school trip, although I've told her we can't afford it.'

'I've been thinking about that.' Mark, who had

not drunk with dinner as he was driving Ed home, now poured himself a glass of wine. 'Want another?'

Holly shook her head and put the kettle on.

'How was your meeting?' Mark asked, conversationally, as if he'd just remembered and was asking her out of politeness.

'It was a bit weird, really,' Holly sighed. She didn't want to talk to him about it. 'Quite low-key. There wasn't anyone there who'd been seriously injured.'

'That's good,' he said.

'Why?'

'It might have been difficult.' He paused. 'For you, I mean. Were there any relatives there?'

'I don't think so.' Holly didn't want to tell him about Anne-Marie. She thought he might worry about the effect the encounter might have on her.

And she didn't want to tell him about her drink with Daniel. Not just yet anyway.

'So what were you thinking about the trip?' Holly asked, as she poured boiling water into a cup.

'I've been thinking about giving my office up,' he said.

'What?' Holly turned abruptly, and splashed herself with boiling water. 'But then you will have nowhere to work,' she said, running her hand under the cold tap.

'I could work from home.' He was fiddling with something on the side, refusing to make eye contact with her. 'The lease on the office runs out in August and I don't really need the space any more. If I wasn't paying rent every month, we could use some of that money to pay for this trip, if that's what Chloe wants to do.'

'But if you don't have an office to work from, you won't be making any money,' Holly protested.

Mark rented a small office in a block near the seafront. A few years ago he'd downsized from a large office in the same block when work started to dry up and he began shedding staff.

Holly thought giving up the office was tantamount to giving up even trying to get more work.

'I could work from home,' he said again.

'How long have you been thinking about this?' Holly thought he sounded defeatist.

'A little while.' Mark was vague. 'I know it's not ideal, but if work picked up I could rent another place. In the meantime we'd have a bit more money from what I would save.'

'I don't know,' Holly said, feeling irrationally angry towards him. He seemed to her to be throwing in the towel, relinquishing all responsibility for earning to her.

She wasn't sure if she could take it.

' ' . . . *I Nearly Died*' is on, Dad.' Jake wandered into the kitchen, oblivious to the tension in the air. 'You know, that programme I was telling you about? Are you going to watch it?'

'I'll be in in a minute,' Mark said, as Jake ambled out again. 'It's a new programme with that Scottish comic we like. You know?'

Holly thought he was asking her permission to

go and join Jake and felt too drained after her day to carry on the discussion they'd begun about his office.

'You'd best go and watch it then.' She sounded, to herself, as if she was talking to a naughty child.

Mark could obviously detect the displeasure in her voice.

'Why don't you come and watch it too?' he entreated.

'In a minute. I'll just finish making my tea.'

Today was the first time I've actually said it out loud to someone I didn't know: someone who hadn't already guessed, when Geoff didn't come home, what had happened.

It felt something of a relief, as if by saying it gives me licence to ask what it was like to have been on the train when it was hit, and if I know, maybe it will help me understand.

I need to tread carefully, I know that, but I think Holly might be able to talk to me about it.

I know her name now because I did go to the survivors group meeting.

It felt strange and businesslike. Someone talked about compensation claims and what was being done to improve safety. There were a few questions, but the atmosphere felt like an ordinary work meeting. They could have been talking about pitching for a new contract. No one behaved as if they were discussing a momentous event, which changed people's lives.

The only reference made to the fact that it might have was when one of the speakers said that there was information about counselling and dealing with post-traumatic stress on the website, and leaflets at the back of the hall.

No one ever offered my mother or me counselling until it was too late. No one ever seemed to think that we might be affected in any way by what we'd been involved in.

149

Mum told me she felt responsible because she'd suggested to the security guard that he might open the doors. She told me that she could see his anxious young face, looking up at her, wondering what the right thing to do was, and later she couldn't bear to think that it might have been the last one he ever looked at properly.

I keep hearing her saying that to me now and wondering whose faces all the people killed in the tunnel had seen before it went dark; whose expressions of boredom or insouciance would be the last things they ever noted.

I'd expected someone in the meeting to get angry or emotional but it was all very restrained. Perhaps everyone feels as I do; that they need to stay in control or they might go completely to pieces.

I screamed at the radio the other day — really screamed, like a madwoman, and afterwards I felt ashamed and hoped the neighbours weren't in and hadn't heard me through the walls.

I was working from home and I had it on as background noise. I wasn't really listening but I knew they were talking about cooking. One of the women was talking about less used vegetables; things like beetroot and artichokes and radishes. She was saying, 'It's very important to use these vegetables so that they don't get forgotten.'

She stressed the words very important and there was something in her tone of voice that really got to me. She sounded as if she meant it, that it really was very important, and if we didn't realise that we were somehow stupid.

And that's when I started shouting, 'It's not important. It's not important at all! You need to know that. You need to realise what's important before it's too late . . . before you lose it!'

Then I picked up the cup of coffee I was drinking and hurled it at the radio, but it missed and hit a photograph of Geoff and me on our wedding day, and the glass shattered, and that's when I knew I had two choices.

I could have slumped down on the floor with the broken pieces of glass and looked at the pictures and let it all out, but I didn't.

I took a deep breath and went and got the dustpan and brush from the kitchen, and I swept it all up and put it in the bin, even the photograph.

I thought perhaps if Geoff weren't sitting there on the bookcase looking at me, it would be easier.

Then I concentrated very hard on finishing the report I was writing.

I told Helen my imaginary counsellor about that and she said, 'It's OK to cry. You need an outlet for your emotions.'

But I'm not like that. I can't let it all out. I need to keep going.

I sense that Holly is like me in that respect.

She never said anything at the meeting, nor did Daniel, the man I've seen her with. They both looked as if they weren't sure if they should really be there, which was exactly how I felt.

I caught up with them walking to the station afterwards.

That's when I said it.

Holly asked, 'What made you decide to come to the meeting?'

And I took a deep breath and told her.

'I lost my husband that day,' I said. And even though they must have expected someone to say something like that at the meeting, they both looked shocked.

They didn't seem to know what to say or how to respond.

'What was his name?' Holly asked, after a while.

I thought that was a strange question to ask. She said it as if I'd been talking about a new baby or something, but I didn't mind. People don't know what to say, not at first. Nobody knew what to say to me after I lost the baby. They couldn't even ask its name, and when Mum was in hospital people just seemed to pretend that nothing was happening, that it was perfectly normal for her to be away and me to be living with Lisa and her family.

'Which hospital?' some people would occasionally ask, but then, when they realised it was the psychiatric one, they'd look awkward and say something about how it must be nice for me to be staying with Lisa and her family.

I never told them that Lisa didn't want me there; that my presence in her home had ruined our friendship, turned it from an easy teenage alliance into something altogether more claustrophobic.

I know from experience that people need time to absorb shocking information and work out their response to it.

I realised Holly needed time before she could really talk to me. That's why I went on ahead once we got to the station.

She stopped at the newsagent's to buy a paper but I said I wanted to find a seat. I don't know if she and Daniel made that train. I didn't see them later but we exchanged numbers. So now I know their names and I'm sure we'll meet up and get to talk properly.

I talked to Holly in my head on the way home.

'Geoff was in the fourth carriage,' I told her in my imagined conversation, although I didn't know this for sure. 'Where were you sitting, Holly?'

15

'I used to want to be an architect,' Fay told Holly, pausing to look at one of the photographs on the walls of the RIBA restaurant.

The Royal Institute of British Architects was just up the road from Broadcasting House and Holly thought the restaurant would be a good place to take her elder sister.

'Did you? I never knew that.' Fay was always guaranteed to tell Holly something she didn't know. They were only two and half years apart in age but her sister was always coming up with things which Holly either never knew or had forgotten. If Holly questioned them, Fay pulled rank and told her she must have been too young to remember.

'It was when I was going through my Lego phase,' Fay said, as she looked around, taking in the patterned marble and wood floors and vast floor-to-ceiling windows. 'I wish I had been now. Hanging out here beats the inside of a police station!'

'How old were you then?' Holly asked, wondering if it was warm enough to sit on the roof terrace.

'Six or seven, I suppose. We had a huge box that some friend of Dad's gave me. I was always making towering edifices.'

'I can see the attraction.' Holly decided against going outside but found a table by the window. 'I don't remember playing with Lego as a child but I used to love helping Jake make fire stations and airports. He used to want a job at Legoland, but now he wants to work with computers. What changed your mind?'

Fay was a forensic psychologist for Reading police.

'I'm not sure,' she answered, looking at the glass-etched doors of the restaurant. 'Though I do remember Dad saying it was a man's job. Perhaps I could have been the next Richard Rogers.'

'I don't suppose Dad thinks working with rapists and murderers is women's work either,' Holly commented.

This was how their parents described Fay's job.

While Patrick and Susan weren't very good at disguising the fact that they were not entirely happy that Fay was a lesbian, neither could they seem to help wondering if they were somehow to blame.

'Patrick thinks it's his fault because we didn't have a boy, so he taught her to play cricket and climb trees,' their mother had once said.

'Do you think the fact Fay works with so many rapists has put her off men?' was another often-asked question.

'Fay says she always knew she was gay,' Holly had told them both on many occasions, wishing they could try harder to accept her sister for what she was.

'You used to want to be a cheese-maker when you grew up,' Fay said to her now.

'Did I? How very Pythonesque.' Again, Holly had no recollection of this and wondered if it was true or a story Fay had made up to amuse her friends. 'Is that because I wanted to be blessed?'

'No, it was because you liked cheese,' Fay told her. 'Mum only ever bought Cheddar but some friends, I think it might have been Hugh and Jean, always brought lots of 'exotic' cheese when they came to stay. I thought they were disgusting but you loved them and were fascinated that they all began as milk.'

'Really?' Holly picked up the menu and looked at it.

'Anyway,' Fay added, 'you were blessed. You always led a charmed life.'

This was a frequent refrain of hers and Holly had learned to let it pass without comment. Whether it was because their parents found it hard to accept Fay's sexuality and career choice, or because of something else, she had decided that she was the second-best sibling in their eyes.

'Fay definitely thinks that I am their favourite,' Holly told Mark once when they were discussing her parents' attitude to their daughters. 'But I don't think that's true. She was always the clever one, the achiever. I think they are really proud of her, they just don't know how to show it.'

'She says it was because you were in intensive care when you were born,' Mark had replied.

Holly was two months premature and spent the first weeks of her life in a specialist baby unit.

'Fay says she was always expected to achieve

156

things when she was little, but you just had to stay alive and your mum and dad were delighted,' he explained. 'I guess there may be some truth in that.'

Holly considered this. She didn't think her parents favoured either of them, but if Fay thought that they did she had to be sympathetic to her feelings.

'Shall we order?' she asked her sister now.

* * *

'So what brings you to London?' Holly asked, as they waited for their food.

'I had a meeting with someone at the Met about a case,' Fay told her. 'I dealt with something similar a few years back. I can't really go into details, though.'

'You *can* tell me about the case you've already worked on.' Holly was used to her sister being secretive about her work, but she knew it wasn't always necessary.

'It wasn't very nice.' Fay leaned back, waiting while a waitress brought them cutlery and their drinks.

'It was a man who killed one of his children. He smothered him with a pillow while the child slept. But he wasn't really fit to stand trial.'

Holly pictured her own children sleeping. This was when she loved them most. They always looked so beautiful and peaceful that, even though they now closed their bedroom doors firmly at night, she couldn't resist pushing them open and watching them while they slept.

157

Chloe still slept with her hands up beside her head, as she had done when she was a baby, but Jake invariably had his hands down the front of his pyjamas. She knew he wouldn't forgive her if he knew she looked at him, but he was still only thirteen, still her boy.

'Why did he do it?' Holly asked Fay.

'It was very sad,' she answered. 'They had two boys and he had taken them to a festival. There was a crush near one of the main stages and the younger boy was trampled to death.'

'Oh, yes, I remember that.' Holly had heard the story in the news. 'But I don't think I heard anything else about the boy's father.'

'He was devastated obviously,' Fay told her. 'And he felt guilty because he'd been with them when it happened. He got this idea that it wasn't fair the younger one had died.'

'Is that why he killed the other?' Holly was horrified.

'Yes, but he really didn't know what he was doing,' Fay told her. 'The CPS wanted to bring a murder charge but he wasn't fit to stand trial.'

'Poor man,' Holly mused. 'And his poor wife. Are they still together?'

'I don't know,' Fay said. 'I shouldn't think so. People often split up when one of them has been through a major ordeal anyway. They often don't seem to understand each other any more.'

'One venison steak and one fillet of sea bass.' The waitress was back.

'The fish is for me,' Fay told her.

'Thank you,' Holly said, glad of the food and the chance to change the topic of conversation.

'Have you seen Mum and Dad recently?' she asked.

'We went over there last weekend actually,' Fay replied. 'It was a bit odd, though.'

'How so?' Holly began cutting her steak.

'Well, we thought we were going because it had been Lucy's birthday in the week. Mum asked us for lunch and we thought she wanted to see Lucy and give her her present but when we got there she never mentioned it,' Fay told her.

'Shit!' Holly paused, her fork halfway to her mouth. 'I forgot too. I'm really sorry.'

'You've got good reason. I told Lucy that. She doesn't mind.'

'No, I don't,' Holly protested. 'I'm her aunt. I shouldn't have forgotten. I was going to get her something from that shop in the North Laine that we went to when you last came down, but I forgot all about it. I don't have a good reason at all.'

'You've been in a train crash,' Fay said in a tone which Holly couldn't help thinking was patronising.

'And lived to tell the tale,' she replied dismissively. 'Tell her I'm really sorry. I'll make sure I get something in the post to her this weekend.'

'You don't have to,' Fay said again.

'I do and I want to,' Holly said firmly. 'Anyway, what else was odd about lunch with Mum and Dad?'

'Well, Dad wasn't there for starters,' Fay said, flaking fish off the bone with her fish fork.

'For starters, Dad wasn't there at all?' Holly

quibbled. 'Or Dad wasn't there for starters?'

'What are you on about?' Fay adopted her big sister tone. It infuriated Holly still, even though they were both grown women.

'I mean, was the first thing that was odd the fact that Dad was not there? Or was Dad absent when you ate your starter but did he turn up for the main meal?' Holly spelled it out.

'He wasn't there at all,' Fay answered. 'And we didn't have a starter. We had roast chicken, and vegetables for V.'

V was a vegetarian but their parents never acknowledged this and served her only whatever vegetables they were having anyway.

She generally had to stomach potatoes cooked with meat if she wasn't to go hungry.

'What, no 'nut cutlet'?' Holly used the expression her mother used to describe any vegetarian food. 'Where was Dad then?'

'He'd gone to help Jean Hayward sort though Hugh's old clothes,' Fay told her. 'Mum said Jean couldn't face it on her own.'

'I suppose her daughter can't come back from France to help.' Holly couldn't imagine their father sorting through old clothes with anyone, let alone the widow of an old friend. 'It's a long way for Dad to drive on his own, though, and I'm surprised Mum didn't go to help.'

'That's the other thing,' Fay said. 'Mum seems totally preoccupied with learning to use her laptop. She spent most of the time we were there asking Lucy to show her how to set up a Facebook account.'

'Really?' Holly wouldn't have been surprised if

Susan had decided to take the computer back. 'She did say something about keeping in touch with old friends. I don't suppose many of them are on Facebook though.'

'There were a few,' Fay told her. 'And she kept going on about making new ones too.'

'Oh, yes, she mentioned that to me. Perhaps she's having some sort of mid-life crisis.'

'Only if she's going to live to one hundred and forty,' Fay retorted.

'OK, well, a seven-eighths life crisis or something!' Holly joked. 'Three-quarter life crisis probably. Mum shows no signs of flagging.'

'No, but Dad seems older.' Fay looked concerned.

'He is older,' Holly pointed out. Patrick was five years older than Susan, although he seemed to have very little energy these days and his hearing was going, making him sometimes appear much older.

'I know.' Fay nodded. 'But he suddenly seems older and more frail somehow, and their friends seem to keep dying. I wonder if Mum has started worrying about him going and being left on her own. Perhaps he's ill and she's not telling us.'

'Maybe,' Holly said, feeling suddenly tired.

She'd been looking forward to seeing her sister but the meeting was bringing her down somehow. She kept thinking about the man who'd killed his child and was cross with herself for forgetting her niece's birthday. Now Fay had suggested something else for her to worry about.

'Mum has always been more sociable,' she said. 'Maybe she just wants to get out a bit more while Dad sits at home doing the crossword.'

'Maybe.' Fay did not sound convinced.

'Look, it *is* Lord Rogers.' Holly nodded to a corner of the restaurant. She felt cheered by a bit of celebrity spotting. 'Isn't it?'

16

'Let's all go for a walk on the beach and have lunch somewhere,' Mark suggested at breakfast on Sunday.

Holly wondered if this was his attempt at foreplay. They hadn't had sex for a while, certainly not since the train crash. It hadn't become an issue yet, but Holly suspected it would soon.

Mark usually slept in a t-shirt and boxers but the previous evening, he'd taken all his clothes off before coming to bed and immediately slid his hand under her t-shirt. Holly had feigned sleep and Mark had got up again and gone to the bathroom. She suspected he'd sorted himself out while he was there.

'It would be nice to spend some time together,' he said now, pushing the button down on the toaster. 'We've hardly seen you this week.'

It *was* a nice idea. Working late and a couple of train delays meant Holly had been home late on several occasions in the last week. She had thought that on Saturday she might see a bit of the children, but Chloe had gone out with Ruaridh and Jake seemed to spend the entire day hunched over the computer.

'Do we have to come?' Chloe protested. She looked sidelong at Jake who was staring at the back of a cereal packet. He failed to notice his sister's none-too-subtle stare.

'It'll be nice.' Holly tried to make it sound more inviting. 'We could look at some of the stalls by the West Pier and have lunch outside. It's warm enough.'

'I was going to go into town with Megan today.' Chloe sat next to her brother and nudged him in irritation as she did so.

'I've hardly seen you all week,' Holly said, wondering if Chloe was pissed off that the Botswana trip had not been mentioned again. 'You could arrange to meet Megan afterwards.'

'Yeah.' Jake gave the impression of someone about to join in the discussion but then went back to the back of the cereal packet.

'Yeah, what?' Chloe challenged him.

'What?' Jake had only recently taken on this adolescent torpor in the mornings. It was funny to watch. He really seemed to have no idea what was going on around him.

'What are you saying yeah to?' Chloe took the cereal packet from under his nose and poured some into her bowl.

'Going for a walk with Mum.' Jake lowered his gaze from where the box had been to his cereal bowl. 'It'll be nice.'

'That's settled then.' Mark rubbed his hands together, as if he had just concluded a major business deal. It was something he did a lot around the home and, again, something Holly found increasingly irritating. It was as if there was an indirect correlation between the number of triumphs he was not having at work and the number of things he considered to be achievements elsewhere.

'That's done then!' he'd say, slapping his palms as if he'd just secured a new client, rather than changed a light bulb. Or 'Job well done!' when he'd hung the washing out. The fact that he'd hung it folded in half, so it would not dry, and Holly had had to take it down and hang it properly, seemed to escape him.

There'd been an item on the radio that morning, which she and Mark had listened to as they lay in bed, making the most of not having to get up. It was about men doing nothing around the house, not even the traditional DIY.

'That's true,' Holly had commented.

'I do things around the house.' Mark had immediately jumped to his own defence. 'I cleaned the filter on the washing machine last week.'

'OK.' Holly conceded this. 'But when was the last time you dusted the sitting room?'

'It doesn't need dusting, does it?' Mark had asked, in a show of innocence.

'Somebody needs to rebrand household chores,' Holly said, trying hard not to rise to his bait. 'If they called dusting 'minute particle extraction' and there was a tool with a motor to do it with, men would be quite happy to blitz the house.'

'And I changed the light bulb in the bathroom last night.' Mark obviously still thought he did his fair share.

'Well, if I listed every single thing I had done in the house this week, we'd still be in bed at lunchtime,' Holly said, under her breath but loud enough for Mark to hear, as she pushed the

165

duvet off and got up.

The conversation had obviously irked him and after breakfast he decided to wash the kitchen floor.

It was self-defeating.

'Has someone been painting in here?' he asked the rest of the family, as he tried to get a white mark off the tiles.

'That's from when we had the room painted after we moved in,' Holly told him.

'I've not noticed it before.'

'Really?' This didn't surprise her. They'd only lived in the house for five years.

★   ★   ★

'Slow down a bit,' Holly said to Mark, who was powering down the seafront. 'Chloe's not with us. She's probably dawdling by one of the stalls.'

Holly had just spotted Daniel, walking ahead of them, accompanied by a woman with a white-blond bob. She hadn't anticipated Mark meeting Daniel like this and didn't want him to. She wasn't ready for it. But Mark seemed keen to work up an appetite, or perhaps he was just walking too fast to discourage further discussion about his plans to give up his office. Holly had broached the subject tentatively in the morning but he had ignored her.

'No, she's up ahead.' Mark pointed. Chloe was wearing a dress that was noticeable for its bright turquoise colour and incredible shortness.

'Is that actually a dress?' Holly had asked her as they got ready to leave.

'It's a t-shirt but it's long enough to be a dress,' Chloe replied, as Holly registed that it barely covered her knickers.

It made her easy to spot and Holly could now see her, drawing level with Daniel.

'Chloe!' Mark shouted, so loud that several people stopped to look round, as if forgetting that they were not actually called that.

Holly still looked about her when anyone shouted 'Mum', even if she knew Chloe and Daniel were both at school. It was a reflex you never seemed to grow out of.

When Jake was younger, he'd realised that calling 'Mum' in a park, shopping centre or other crowded place was not particularly selective, and if he lost sight of her he used to shout 'Holly Holt!' so that she alone would react. He wouldn't call out to her in public now. That would be far too embarrassing.

Daniel was amongst those who'd reacted to Mark's shout. He turned, immediately catching sight of Holly, and looked unsure what to do as her family advanced towards him.

'Hello!' Holly feigned surprise, even though she had known he was there.

'Wait for us or we'll lose you,' Mark was saying to Chloe. Then he realised that Holly was talking to someone else.

'Hi.' Daniel took in the four of them.

Time for introductions.

'Mark, this is Daniel,' Holly said, noting the way her husband tensed slightly. 'Daniel, Mark,' she continued. 'And this is Jake and Chloe.'

'Nice to meet you all.' Daniel shook the hand

Mark had extended and smiled vaguely at the children.

'This is Daisy,' he said, as the blonde woman slipped her arm though his.

She was extraordinarily pretty which, for some reason, Holly had not anticipated. Her white-blond hair looked natural and fell in an almost perfect bob around her face, which was small with two huge blue eyes, taking Holly in.

'Hi,' she said. 'Daniel's told me about you.'

Holly thought she detected a note of warning in her voice but the accompanying smile was friendly enough.

'You too,' Holly lied. Daniel had told her very little about Daisy and she'd expected someone different.

Daisy was wearing a close fitting t-shirt and tracksuit bottoms. She looked fit for purpose, as if she had just finished some gravity-defying yoga poses rather than slipped on some clothes that were comfortable.

'Good to meet you, Daniel,' Mark said. 'Enjoying the sunshine?'

'Yes. It's nice to get down to the sea,' he replied. 'Sometimes I go for weeks without seeing it.'

'Long hours?' Mark asked.

'Sometimes,' Daniel told him.

There was a pause. The small talk appeared to have run dry and Holly hoped they would mutter things about getting on and go their separate ways. But Mark seemed keen to interrogate Daniel and his wife further.

'What line of work are you in?' he asked.

Holly squirmed. She thought Mark sounded

pompous but the question was one that men always seemed to ask almost immediately.

She often wondered what she would say if she didn't have a job to the frequently asked 'And what do you do?'

'I'm a systems analyst.' Daniel didn't ask what Mark did in return, but he had already moved on, to focus on the beautiful Daisy.

'What about you, Daisy?' Mark was doing his charming thing. 'What profession are you in?'

'None,' she said, exhibiting signs of the nervousness Holly thought she'd feel if she didn't work at all.

'Really?' Mark sounded extremely surprised. 'That's unusual.'

Holly couldn't believe quite how rude he was being, failing to mask his astonishment that in this day and age a woman should not have a career.

'I've trained as a fitness instructor.' Daisy appeared flustered. 'But I'm not working much at the moment.'

'Oh, I see.' Mark started laughing and they all looked on, wondering what it was that he found so funny about the exchange.

'I'm so sorry, Daisy,' he said, putting his arm over-familiarly on her shoulder. 'I misunderstood.'

Further explanation was needed.

'When you said none,' Mark wiped the tears of laughter now forming in the corners of his eyes, 'I thought you meant you were a nun!'

Now they all laughed, although Holly felt cross.

'I thought you were far too pretty to be a nun.' Mark seemed bolstered by the laughter his faux-pas had generated.

Daisy accepted the compliment, smiling, and turned the huge pools of her eyes on him.

'Julie Andrews was a pretty nun.' Jake spoke for the first time. 'In *The Sound of Music*.'

'We were all going to have lunch at the Terraces,' Mark said. The misunderstanding seemed to have relaxed him. 'Why don't you two join us?'

'I'm not sure . . . ' Daniel looked at Holly.

'Daniel and Daisy probably want some time on their own together,' Holly said. 'Though of course it would be lovely if you did want to join us.'

'It's very kind but . . . ' Daniel began, then Daisy interjected.

'We'd love to,' she said. 'Wouldn't we, Dan?'

He didn't answer.

'Lunch on us then,' Mark said, oblivious to the fact that both Jake and Chloe were looking at them both pleadingly, obviously not wanting to spend lunch with people they'd never met before.

'Think of it as a small thank you, Daniel,' Mark was saying. 'For what you did for Holly.'

She hoped Mark wouldn't bring up the subject of the train crash over lunch. It wasn't the right time or place. The two men were now walking slightly ahead and she could hear Mark saying, ' . . . draw a line under things.'

It was as if he thought buying Daniel lunch would somehow make what he had done and Holly's friendship with him go away. She smiled uneasily at Daisy, who was walking beside her and Jake, knowing that it wouldn't.

17

'What do you fancy then?' said Natalie, picking up the plastic-coated menu and peering at it.

'James Cracknell for starters!' Holly had just encountered the former Olympic rower going into the lifts of Broadcasting House as she came out.

A bit of side dancing had gone on, as he and Holly had mirrored each other's getting-out-of-the-way steps and stayed in each other's way, until he had finally taken a ninety-degree turn and held out his arm, gesturing for her to pass.

She smiled a 'thank you' at him and was almost certain he'd winked at her in return.

'In the flesh he is almost unbearably gorgeous,' she said to Natalie. 'You couldn't really look at him for too long.'

'Or what?' Natalie handed the menu over to her. 'I'm having the goat's cheese salad.'

'I don't know. You'd tingle so much that you might explode or something!' Holly had already decided what she wanted to eat but she ran her eyes over the menu anyway, as if it was expected of her.

'You must be having some sort of pre-menopausal hormone rush,' Natalie said, trying to catch the waiter's eye as he walked past, but he was busying himself cleaning another table and refused to be drawn into taking orders.

Holly wondered if there was a small amount of

truth in what Natalie was saying. She did seem to keep finding herself semi-attracted to all sorts of people, but put it down to finding Mark increasingly less alluring.

It was as if there was some sort of quadratic equation at play where y = a x b/c, with y being a level of attraction, a being another person, b your partner and c his current desirability status.

'By the way,' Natalie added, looking at the waiter, who reluctantly came over and pulled a pad from his belt loop, 'who were you talking to on the phone before we came out?'

The waiter's presence meant Holly didn't have to answer Natalie's question. She'd been talking to Anne-Marie who'd called 'to say hello'.

Holly couldn't think who she was at first and then remembered that she was the woman they'd met at the survivors meeting. She'd asked what train Holly usually caught and if they might meet up some time. Holly had been vague in her 'Yes. Why not?' reply. She wasn't sure if she wanted to meet up with her, but it felt callous not to.

'I'd like a goat's cheese salad and a Diet Coke,' Natalie told the reluctant waiter.

'And I'll have the aubergine and mozzarella panini and a glass of water,' Holly said.

'Still or sparkling?' The waiter didn't look up as he scribbled in his pad.

'Just tap water.' Holly smiled pleasantly as he scowled at her response. 'You'd think half the waiters in London only got paid if they manage to flog a couple of bottles of mineral water with every meal,' she said to Natalie, when he'd gone, but her friend was focusing on two people sitting in the corner of the café.

'Isn't that Rebecca and Dimitri?' she asked.

'Oh, yes.' Holly twisted round to look.

'Do you think they're having an affair?' Natalie was still looking in their direction.

'No.' Holly hadn't really ever considered this before. 'I think they're just having lunch.'

'But they're very flirtatious with each other,' Natalie persisted. 'And they spend a lot of time together.'

'Well, Dimitri is very flirtatious with everyone.' Holly stated a fact. 'And he lives with his girlfriend and Rebecca is always going on about her boyfriend, so from where I'm sitting they're just colleagues who get on well.'

'They obviously fancy each other.' Natalie was still looking at them. 'They should do something about it, if they're going to, before they get married and have kids.'

'I'm sure they're perfectly happy as they are.' Holly resisted the urge to turn and look at them again. She wondered if Daniel and Daisy were happy.

★   ★   ★

'I'm sorry if Mark forced you to have lunch with us,' Holly had said as she sat down next to Daniel on the train that morning. 'I'm sure you wanted a quiet lunch with Daisy.'

Holly had thought about pretending she hadn't seen him when she spotted Daniel sitting by a window. He'd half-waved as she walked past his carriage and she wasn't sure if he was trying

173

to attract her attention or simply acknowledging her. She suspected he might have had enough of her.

But she wanted a debrief after the weekend's seafront encounter.

'It was nice.' Daniel looked up at her. 'It was good to meet your husband and your children. They're great.'

'They're OK, when they're not moody,' Holly said.

'Well, they weren't moody yesterday.' Daniel smiled. 'Daisy said they were lovely kids.'

'They were very taken with her too.' Holly resisted adding 'all' to include Mark in the being very taken with her category. 'She's very beautiful.'

'Yes.' Daniel nodded. 'She always has been.'

'Have you known her long then?' Holly was curious as to how Daniel had met Daisy. They were so different; what her mother would have called 'an unlikely couple'.

'Since school.' He bent down to move his bag towards him when a man came to sit opposite. 'We were at the same secondary school.'

'Wow, you've been together since then?' Holly was impressed. It was unusual for people to stay together from such a young age. Sex and experimenting with other people usually got in the way.

'No,' Daniel corrected her. 'We weren't together at school. I knew who Daisy was. Everyone did. She was gorgeous and very popular. But I don't think she ever noticed me.'

'So how did you meet?' Holly found she could

easily picture Daisy as young and blonde, sporty and surrounded by admirers of both sexes. She couldn't quite imagine the quieter, mousier Daniel attracting her attention.

'There was a summer holiday,' he told her. 'Nearly everyone was going on a school trip to Norway. It was a camp after GCSEs. It was optional but virtually everyone went.'

'I know the sort of thing.' Holly thought again about the Botswana trip.

A tent in Norway was more like it.

'I was supposed to go, but I fell off a wall and broke my leg the day before.' Daniel paused as if wondering how to phrase what came next. 'Daisy was supposed to go too, but her parents had caught her in bed with a boy at the weekend and banned her from going.'

'So you were the only ones left?' Holly wanted him to tell her the full story.

'Well, not quite the only ones, but we grew up in a fairly small village.' Daniel paused, remembering. 'I was sitting by the cricket pitch one day with my leg in plaster and she came and sat next to me, tapped my cast and asked if that was why I hadn't gone to Norway.'

'You had a lucky break then.' Holly only realised she'd made a very poor joke when the words were out.

'I guess so.' Daniel was polite enough to smile, at least. 'I don't think she would ever have looked at me twice if I hadn't been virtually the only person left for her to hang out with.'

'I'm sure that's not true,' Holly said, looking past him to his reflection in the window. He wasn't immediately striking but he definitely grew on you.

The train had just stopped at Haywards Heath when she suddenly saw Anne-Marie, walking down the aisle looking for a seat, reflected in the window.

'Oh, hello,' she said, stopping where they were sitting.

'Hi.' Holly smiled and Daniel turned and said, 'Hello.'

There were no empty seats where they were and she moved on a couple of rows and sat down, not within earshot but close enough for Holly to feel that she was in their space.

'It's funny that Daisy and I both have names from American classics,' she said to Daniel, recalling something Mark had said the day before.

'She is my idea of what Daisy Buchanan should have looked like. I didn't like the woman who played her in the film.' Mark had obviously been very struck by Daisy.

Daniel looked blank.

'I was named after Holly Golightly in *Breakfast at Tiffany's*,' Holly explained.

'I don't really read novels.' As he said this, Holly realised she had never seen him take out a book on the train.

'You must have seen the film?' Perhaps he hadn't. Would she have consigned every bit of it to memory if her mother hadn't been such a fan? 'And *The Great Gatsby*.'

'Not seen either of them.' He smiled. 'Which one is Daisy in?'

'*The Great Gatsby*,' Holly said. 'She's very attractive and fought over by men.'

'Sounds like Daisy,' Daniel had replied.

★　★　★

'Mark has decided to run the Brighton marathon,' Holly told Natalie as they waited for their food. 'Did I tell you he was thinking about it?'

'Last I heard, he was thinking of getting a sports car,' Natalie answered. 'Or was it a motorbike?'

'Both. He went off the sports car idea when he found out how much it would cost to insure,' Holly told her friend. 'And I think I put him off getting a bike by taking the piss out of his friend Tim.'

'Does he have one then?' Natalie asked.

'Yes. A great steaming beast of a machine, which he rides very slowly, with a couple of other middle-aged men on similar bikes, down to the café at Roedean where they drink tea!' Holly raised her eyebrows.

'Is that the café that was in *Quadrophenia*?' Natalie's knowledge of Brighton was taken mainly from films.

'One of them, yes.' Holly nodded. 'I don't suppose Ace Face asked for sweetener in his tea!'

Natalie laughed.

'So has Mark started training?'

'No.' Holly pulled a face. 'He hasn't actually run anywhere in years, but he keeps talking about it. And I looked at his internet history the other day and he'd been looking at shoes, so he must be serious.'

'Well, at least it will keep him busy.' Natalie moved back in her seat as the waiter returned with a Coke and a very small glass of tap water — a begrudging amount if ever Holly had seen one. 'Guy's driving me mad at the moment. He's really lethargic and never does anything that actually needs doing.'

'Neither does Mark,' Holly sympathised.

'All Guy's sentences at the moment seem to begin with, 'I know I ought to know this but . . . ' And then he asks where we keep the vacuum cleaner.'

'Mark's the same,' Holly agreed. 'Last night the washing machine finished its cycle, just as we were about to have dinner. He spent about ten minutes looking in the oven and fiddling with the timer to make it stop beeping. He had no idea it was the washing machine making the noise!'

The occasional lunch and coffee with Natalie was one of the few opportunities Holly got these days to air family grievances. She'd had to stop going to her book group when she started working full-time again, and missed the company of the other women.

'They never actually discuss the book,' Mark used to say of the group. 'They just drink a lot and bitch about their husbands.'

Men didn't seem to understand that women needed to vent their frustrations.

'I wish Guy had more get up and go,' Natalie sighed, as the waiter placed a plate of leaves and glistening white cheese in front of her. 'I like men who are good at their jobs. There's something sexy about that. Like . . . '

'Like James Darling?' Holly asked, wondering if this was why her sentence trailed off.

'Not necessarily.' Natalie took a mouthful of salad. 'Like Mark. I've heard you saying you catch yourself looking at him with fresh eyes when you've been to his office and seen him fielding phone calls and getting into a project.'

'That happens less and less at the moment.' Holly had told Natalie that Mark's business hadn't been doing so well since the credit crunch. 'He's talking about giving up the office altogether. I'm more likely to see him at home, trying to make himself appear useful without much success. Hence the marathon running, I think.'

'Well, I suppose running is better than zooming about in a sports car with a woman half his age. Can I pinch a tiny bit of your bread?' Natalie tore off a corner of Holly's sandwich and began to mop up oil from her plate with it.

'Yes, I suppose so,' said Holly.

Last night, Mark had said, casually, as if it were of no real importance, that perhaps *he* should have a couple of personal training sessions and get some advice on running. No prizes, thought Holly, for guessing who he had in mind to be the personal trainer.

18

Daniel always appeared to be half smiling, as if he were enjoying some private joke. He had earphones in and was staring out of the window so he didn't see Holly until she was all but sitting down next to him.

She mouthed 'Hello' as her presence caused him to look up. He took his earphones out and smiled a whole smile.

'Hello,' he replied, as if surprised. It was a much earlier train than either of them usually caught and he obviously had not expected to see her on it.

'Am I disturbing you?' Holly was still hovering, not quite sure whether to sit down or not.

'No.' Daniel patted the seat and she sat down, glad to have bumped into him unexpectedly.

'So are you skiving as well?'

It was early in the week and Holly had put in all the calls she could to possible guests for this week's programme, had a meeting and spoken at length to James Darling. Dimitri and Rebecca were liaising with reporters. There was very little left for her actually to do, so she'd decided to leave work early.

It was only three o'clock.

'Not exactly.' Daniel suddenly looked a little thrown by her presence, as if the initial pleasure he'd felt on seeing her were being gradually wiped out by having to explain what he was doing.

'Well, it's nice to see you anyway.' Holly wriggled out of her coat, thinking the action would show she was moving on from her earlier question and there was no need for him to explain.

She felt pleased to see Daniel, which contrasted with her hope that Mark would not be at home when she got back. He'd hinted in the morning that he might go for a run after work.

'If dogs are colour-blind,' Jake had been listening to something on the radio about canine eyesight, 'how do guide dogs get people over pedestrian crossings?'

'I've no idea.' Holly had been trying to get something to eat before leaving for the station.

'They wait for a gap in the traffic.' Mark knew the answer to Jake's question. 'Then they cross.'

'Right.' Jake had appeared satisfied with the answer.

'That's why they don't have greyhounds for the blind,' Mark had joked. 'Although they could be guide dogs for very busy people.'

'What?' Jake had appeared confused.

'Because they run so fast,' Mark explained his joke. 'Their charges might not be able to keep up, and get run over.'

'Poor taste,' Holly had muttered.

'Talking of which,' he had said, ignoring her comment, 'I might go for a bit of a run myself this evening.'

'Fine.' Holly finished her cereal and put the

181

bowl in the dishwasher. 'Good luck.'

She'd wondered if he'd ordered the running shoes he'd been looking at on the internet and was reminded of this now when a man wearing no shoes at all wandered into the carriage.

'Is this train going to Brighton?' he asked, picking up a newspaper that had been left on the seats opposite.

'Yes.' Holly tried not to stare at his bare feet.

'Anywhere else?' he asked.

'I'm sorry?' She was not quite sure what he was asking.

'Does it go anywhere else apart from Brighton?' He looked around the carriage as if it might hold the answer to his questions.

'It stops at East Croydon,' Daniel said. 'And I think it stops at Haywards Heath as well. Where did you want to go?'

'I haven't decided.' The man smiled and walked on down the corridor.

'How strange,' Holly said.

'Completely different people at a different time of day,' Daniel observed, obliquely referencing the fact that they were both going home early.

'I was at an unusual loose end at work,' Holly explained. 'So I decided to knock off early.'

'I've got a doctor's appointment . . . ' Daniel was interrupted by the train announcer, telling them that the train would indeed be calling at both East Croydon and Haywards Heath. 'That gives our friend three destinations to choose from then.'

Holly laughed and wondered if Daniel's

appointment was related to the crash. She'd not been sleeping very well lately and Mark had been urging her to go to the doctor. She'd assured him she didn't need to.

'Nothing serious, I hope,' she said. It was the sort of ubiquitous line you used when people said they had a hospital appointment.

'Maybe.' Daniel looked briefly around the carriage as the train pulled out of the station. He seemed to be checking that they were alone and that what he said would not be overheard by others.

Shoeless Man appeared to have gone and they seemed to be the only people in the immediate cluster of seats.

'I'm not ill or anything.' Daniel shifted awkwardly and looked out of the window before turning back to her. 'It's a bit delicate.'

'You don't have to tell me,' she said. 'It's none of my business, obviously.'

'I'd like to, though,' Daniel caught her eye directly and she returned his gaze. 'I haven't really talked to anyone about it and I feel as if I need to.'

'OK.' Holly fixed her attention on him.

'Daisy and I . . . ' He paused as if unsure how to go on and scanned the carriage again. 'We've been trying to have a baby for a while, but it doesn't seem to be happening.'

'Oh.' This was not what Holly had been expecting. 'Well, it sometimes takes a while.'

'How long did it take you?' Daniel asked, shrugging as if to acknowledge that it was a somewhat personal question.

'Well, no time at all actually,' she laughed. 'But it takes most people a bit longer. I wasn't really ready to have a baby, but friends had said it had taken them a year or so to get pregnant so I thought we could start trying and it happened first time. It was rather a shock.'

'Weren't you pleased?' Daniel asked.

'Not exactly, no.' Holly still felt slightly guilty about saying this. She obviously didn't regret having Chloe, not for a minute, it was just at the time, she'd thought she'd have another couple of years working, get herself more established on the career ladder.

'I was twenty-eight when I had Chloe. It seemed an odd age,' Holly tried to explain to him. 'Everyone in my antenatal group was either sixteen or thirty-five. None of my friends had started having babies at the time. I felt a bit out on a limb.'

She remembered Natalie had barely been able to mask her horror when told the 'good' news.

'But you've only just been made a producer,' she'd said, echoing the thought that Holly was keeping to herself. It didn't feel like a good time to have a baby as far as her career was concerned, though after Chloe was born her career was the last thing on her mind.

'I didn't really feel ready,' Holly told Daniel. 'It sounds ridiculous because you ought to know what's going to happen if you start trying to have a baby, but it took me completely by surprise.'

'But you don't regret it?' he asked.

'Oh, God, no. It was the best thing that ever happened to me,' Holly said truthfully. 'All I'm saying is, maybe it's not such a bad thing, if it takes a while. It gives you more time to get used to the idea.'

'I've always wanted to have children,' Daniel told her. 'And Daisy has too. Her mother died when she was doing her A-levels. Maybe if you lose a parent when you are young, it makes you want to have children of your own sooner rather than later.'

Holly noted that having a parent die relatively young was something Daisy had in common with Mark. She wondered if they would talk about it in the training session he said he had booked with her.

'How old is she?' This was a good opportunity to find out exactly how old Daniel was too.

'She's twenty-five.' That was even younger than Holly had thought. Nearly twenty years younger than she was. Daniel looked younger than her but Holly didn't notice the age gap when she talked to him. Now that he'd said his wife was twenty-five, she suddenly felt ridiculously old.

'That's no age.' She smiled ruefully. 'There's still plenty of time.'

'I know. But it puts pressure on . . . ' Daniel stopped talking and looked out of the window. Holly wasn't sure whether to ask him to go on but he did so unprompted.

'Do you remember I told you things had been a bit strained between us since . . . '

Holly nodded. Neither of them liked referring to the crash directly.

'To be honest, they were already a bit strained

because of the baby thing.'

'So have you had tests?' Holly wasn't sure if she should have asked the question but the conversation had already taken a personal turn.

'That's what the appointment is about today,' he told her.

'I'm sure it will happen,' Holly reassured him. 'You're both still so young.'

'I think Daisy finds it difficult because she doesn't have a career.' Daniel looked out of the window again and carried on talking. 'Daisy's clever. She was going to go to university and do law, but after her mother died she decided to wait, then she got a job and we got together and it never happened.'

'She could go now,' Holly ventured.

'It would be difficult,' Daniel said. 'Maybe one day, but for the moment she's . . . '

'In limbo?' Holly could well imagine the frustration Daisy must feel if she was bright but going nowhere. And then, having decided to have children young, nothing was happening.

'I guess.' Daniel considered this.

'What about you?' Holly asked. 'Do you want to be a father?'

'Of course. I've always wanted kids,' he told her. 'I'd be gutted if we couldn't have them.'

Holly remembered Mark's reaction when she'd said she was pregnant with Chloe. She'd been so ambivalent about it herself that she'd wanted him to be delighted for both of them. But his reaction had been one of mustered up enthusiasm rather than pure genuine joy.

'I always thought I would have a family,'

Daniel went on. 'Everything is in place. I've got a lovely wife, a good job. I can provide for them. I just can't have them . . .'

Holly said nothing. The one thing Mark had been pleased about, when she'd first got pregnant, was that it confirmed his virility.

'First time!' he'd say, with the smile of a Cheshire cat if people asked if they'd been trying long.

The fact that he could get his wife pregnant, just like that, seemed to please him more than the fact that another human being was on the way. It was another manifestation of the fact that twentieth-century man was still a caveman at heart.

It had been just as important to Mark to get her pregnant naturally, she now realised, as it had been for him to provide for the baby she had been carrying too.

'You don't have to go back to work,' he kept saying after Chloe was born and Holly couldn't bear to be parted from her. 'I can earn enough to keep us afloat.'

Daniel had echoed those sentiments when he'd talked about having a good job and being able to provide for a family.

She wondered how he would react if the tables were turned and Daisy became the main breadwinner.

Holly was beginning to realise that Mark hated this new facet of their relationship as much as he probably would have hated having to go through IVF.

'The next station is Brighton,' the train

announcer interrupted her thoughts. 'Please ensure you have all your bags and belongings with you when you leave the train.'

Daniel stood up and pulled his briefcase off the overhead luggage rack.

'Between ourselves?' he said, taking his coat off the peg next to the seat.

'Of course.' Holly began putting her coat on.

'I'll have to run,' he said as the train drew into the station.

'Sure.' Holly was in no great hurry and realised he probably needed to separate himself from her to get in the right frame of mind for his doctor's appointment.

'I might see you later in the week.' Daniel leaned towards her and kissed her.

It was kiss on the cheek, a perfectly natural goodbye, but somehow it felt different, perhaps because it came after the conversation they had just had.

'I hope so,' she said.

19

Holly had paused by Rebecca's desk on her way to the meeting, then, as she was busy doing something on her computer, felt bound to wait for her.

'Facebook?' she said conversationally, catching sight of various photographs set alongside a few lines of text.

'Just checking my boyfriend's wall.' Rebecca shut the page and got up from her seat. 'OK, I'm ready.'

'Why do you do that?' Holly was only half-heartedly on Facebook. She had no details or picture on her profile and it mockingly reminded her whenever she did go on that she had only five friends and three of them were her own family.

'I want to see who he's been talking to,' Rebecca said matter-of-factly as they made their way towards the lift. 'Make sure none of his ex-girlfriends has been in touch with him.'

'Doesn't he mind you checking up on him like that?' Holly asked. 'Don't you trust him?'

'I check my wife's page.' James Darling had obviously been behind them long enough to overhear their conversation. 'Don't you ever look to see what hubby's been up to?'

'No.' Holly balked at the word 'hubby'. 'I don't think he ever uses Facebook anyway.'

'You should have a look.' Darling pressed the button for the third floor.

'How was your day?' Daniel was asking Holly now as they managed to bag a double seat before the train began filling up.

'Fairly unproductive.' She shrugged. 'We had a programme-planning meeting, which involves a lot of going round in circles.'

'Isn't that what all meetings are like?' Daniel grinned. 'I hate them.'

'So have you been . . . ' Holly paused because she had absolutely no idea what a systems analyst might do on a day-to-day basis ' . . . analysing systems?'

'Yes, I have.' Daniel laughed, bending down to pick his bag off the floor as a man came to sit opposite them. 'I've been doing a job for one of the big ticketing agencies, actually.'

'The ones that sell theatre tickets?' Holly asked.

'And for sports events and music gigs — that sort of thing.' Daniel moved his legs in as another commuter paused, then thought better of commandeering the free seat opposite and moved on. 'What was your meeting about?'

'We seemed to end up talking about Facebook for rather a lot of it,' Holly said, thinking back to the conversation she'd started with Rebecca earlier in the day.

'Do you mind if I sit here?' Her thoughts were interrupted by the arrival of Anne-Marie.

Holly hadn't contacted her since the night of the meeting and hadn't thought to ask Daniel if he had.

'No!' Holly's voice was loud and abrupt. She'd intended her response to be friendly but thought the way it had come out sounded a little hostile.

'I mean, no,' she said again, more softly.

Anne-Marie hesitated as if the level of the first response was an indicator she was not actually welcome.

Her moment of hesitation cost her the seat, as another woman muttered a brief 'excuse me' and sat in it.

'I'd best go and find somewhere else then,' Anne-Marie said, and disappeared before they had time to ask her how she was.

'That was odd,' Holly mused. 'I wonder why she didn't just sit down.'

'You told her not to.' Daniel's voice had an edge to it that Holly hadn't heard before. He was looking at her curiously too.

'I didn't,' Holly protested. 'I told her she could sit here.'

'She asked if she could sit there,' Daniel persisted. 'And you said, 'No!''

'No,' Holly insisted. 'She said, 'Do you *mind* if I sit here?' and I said 'No', as in, 'No, I don't mind. Be my guest. Have the seat.''

'I'm pretty sure she just asked if she could sit there.' Daniel looked uncomfortable.

Holly began to feel that way too.

'Oh, God, did she?' She felt mortified. 'Are you sure?'

'Pretty sure,' he said quietly.

'Oh, no.' Holly was no longer sure exactly what Anne-Marie had said. 'I'd better go and find her. I'll leave my stuff with you.' She wanted

Daniel to offer her some guidance as to what she should do next.

'OK,' he said gently, as if he'd forgiven her for the rudeness he'd thought her capable of only minutes earlier. Then he touched her arm reassuringly as she stood up. 'Unless you want me to come with you?'

'No.' Holly thought she'd find it easier to talk to Anne-Marie on her own. 'But thanks.'

Holly got up and caught Daniel's eye as she did so. She couldn't quite interpret the look he gave her as he momentarily held her gaze. But it was definitely a look. Holly turned away and began walking in the direction Anne-Marie had gone.

She hadn't found a seat and was standing in the corridor between carriages.

'I wanted to apologise.' Holly came straight to the point. 'I must have seemed incredibly rude.'

Anne-Marie muttered, 'No.'

'It sounds ridiculous.' Holly wondered whether she would be believed or not. 'But I thought you asked if I *minded* if you sat opposite, so I said no, but Daniel said you just asked if you *could* sit opposite, so my answer should have been yes.'

Anne-Marie looked thoughtful and then she began laughing.

'The world is full of misunderstandings.' She smiled now.

'I suppose so.' Holly smiled back, slightly relieved. 'I hope I didn't upset you?'

'No, not really,' Anne-Marie said. 'I was a bit put out but I thought you must have your reasons.'

'Why don't you come and sit with us now?' Holly suggested. 'You can have my seat. It would be nice to talk. And I'm sorry I haven't got back to you, since you called. Things have been busy.'

'I'm OK,' Anne-Marie replied. 'Someone will get off at East Croydon and I'll take their seat. You are settled with Daniel. Another time.'

'Maybe tomorrow then?' Holly asked. 'Is this your usual train?'

'No, I usually only work in London on Wednesdays. The rest of the time I'm based in Haywards Heath,' she said.

'Oh, I see.' Holly supposed this explained why she hadn't noticed her before. 'I don't know why, I just presumed you commuted daily.'

'My husband used to,' Anne-Marie said, as if she felt the need to explain how he came to be on the train when it crashed. 'He was a regular.'

'Well, maybe next week then?' Holly suggested. 'You've got our numbers, haven't you? And we've got yours.'

She felt slightly self-conscious referring to herself and Daniel as 'we' and their respective numbers as 'ours'. 'Why don't you let us know which train you'll be on and we can try and sit together then?'

★　★　★

'All sorted?' Daniel asked when she returned to her seat.

'I think so.' Holly sat down. 'I said we might try and meet up with her next week. She only comes up on Wednesday, apparently. She said it

193

was her husband who was the regular commuter.'

'Oh. I wonder if I ever saw him,' Daniel said.

The train stopped in a tunnel and Holly looked past him at his reflection in the window. She wished they would get going again and shifted nervously in her seat, unable for the moment to get the thought of Anne-Marie's husband and what had happened in the tunnel out of her head. She concentrated on her breathing and tried to think of something else.

'Well, I'm glad you sorted things out.' Daniel smiled at her and put his hand on her arm, as if he could tell what she was thinking.

'So am I.' Holly decided to revert back to the conversation they'd been having before Anne-Marie arrived.

'We might be doing something in the programme about Facebook stalking,' she told Daniel. 'People tracking down their ex's movements through their Facebook pages. Are you on Facebook?'

'No,' Daniel surprised her by saying. She thought that working with computers, he would be. 'And I'm not a stalker either. Daisy is, though.'

'A stalker?' Holly asked, half-joking.

'No,' Daniel said. 'On Facebook. She seems to use it a lot.'

Holly didn't tell him that this much she already knew.

When she'd got back to her office, after the morning meeting, Natalie had not been anxious to get on with any work.

'Are you gong to have a look at Mark's Facebook site then?' she'd asked.

'I wasn't going to, no.' Holly swivelled her chair round.

'Aren't you the tiniest bit curious to see who he's friends with? Guy has hundreds of women friends. Lots of them ex-girlfriends or people he briefly dated.' Natalie paused. 'I'm sure Mark doesn't, though. I mean, you two have been together for longer than we have — less of a past to keep up with.'

'It doesn't seem right.' Holly had scruples. 'It's like going through someone's text messages.'

'Don't you do that either?' Natalie appeared flabbergasted. 'Holly, you are far too trusting.'

'I'm not sure that's true.' She considered this. 'But everything is open to misinterpretation, isn't it? I mean, even fairly innocent text messages can be misunderstood. I've probably got some texts that could be easily misinterpreted.'

'Have you?' Natalie sounded doubtful so Holly began scrolling through her phone.

'Here's one.'

Where are you, Holly? the text read. *I'm at the hotel waiting for you but you are nowhere to be seen. Are you standing me up? Darling x*

'You see, if you didn't know that James was called Darling and that I was supposed to meet him at the Cadogan Hotel to interview that American author, you might well wonder what that was all about.' She handed the phone to Natalie.

'Where were you?' Natalie asked, sounding as

if she too was pissed off with Holly for not having turned up on time.

'It was the day of the train crash.' Holly adopted a jokey tone. 'I was stuck in a tunnel and there was no mobile reception.'

'Oh.' Natalie was momentarily flummoxed but she swiftly regained her composure.

'As I'm the one producing this item about Facebook stalking,' she said, 'wouldn't you like to help me with my research by checking out Mark's site?'

'Ok, you win.' Holly logged into her Facebook site and was greeted by an invitation to join a group called Totally Pointless and news feed informing her that Jake had just downloaded the latest Gorillaz single and the sad fact that she only had four friends.

'I thought I had five,' she told Natalie. 'I'm sure Chloe was one of them.'

'She must have defriended you,' Natalie said, cheerily. 'Teenage girls don't want their mothers knowing what they are up to.'

'Can she do that?' Holly was not at all sure how Facebook worked.

'Easily,' Natalie told her. 'You've got a friend request though. Who's Anne-Marie Roberts?'

'She's another commuter,' Holly replied, slightly surprised at this request. She was about to confirm Anne-Marie as a friend. It seemed rude not to, although Holly wasn't sure she wanted to.

'Are we going to look at Mark or not?' Natalie asked, distracting her from replying to Anne-Marie.

Holly typed his name and was directed to his page.

'Take a look at his wall,' Natalie instructed, as Holly peered at the photographs of glamorous-looking women who had suddenly appeared alongside three-line comments.

Hey, Mark, said a Marilyn lookalike who called herself Celeste. *Great to bump into you yesterday. Let's do lunch.*

Glad that we are friends now, Mark, said a brunette, Vanessa, who Natalie pointed out tactfully was practically kissing the camera. *Must definitely have a drink when you are next in London.*

'Bloody hell! Who are all these women?' Holly had never heard Mark mention Celeste or Vanessa.

'Probably just work colleagues,' Natalie reassured her. 'I'm sure it's just all what would be normal office flirting, but posting it in public makes it look somehow worse.'

'I guess.' Holly had been distracted by another post on Mark's wall.

Looking forward to seeing you the weekend after next and hopefully get a chance to talk about how things are.

'Bloody hell,' Holly said. 'Doesn't she realise that these conversations aren't private but everyone can see what you write on someone's wall?'

'Why?' asked Natalie, looking at the post Holly was reading. 'Who is Susan Holt? Is that your mother?'

'Yessss,' Holly hissed. 'I can't believe she is

197

talking to Mark on Facebook. It's weird.'

'I think it's funny,' Natalie laughed. 'You never use it but your seventy-something mother does.'

'It's a bit unnerving,' Holly said, clicking on her mother's profile and finding she had 23 friends.

Jake, Mark and Chloe were among them, so was Lucy, but V was not and neither was she. Holly wondered why her mother hadn't sent her a friend request and who some of the friends she had never heard of were. She was about to close the page when she noticed something.

'That's odd.'

'What?' Natalie was looking over her shoulder, taking in the information as Holly was slowly digesting.

'Who is Daisy Harrison?' Natalie asked, looking at the recent activity post, which told them that Mark and Daisy were now friends.

'She's Daniel's wife,' Holly told her.

'Daniel as in Daniel your knight in shining armour?' Natalie asked.

'Daniel from the train, yes.' Holly ignored her description of him.

'He's not even my Facebook friend.'

'No one is your Facebook friend,' Natalie pointed out.

'I suppose not,' Holly agreed. Nevertheless there was something about Mark and Daisy's virtual friendship that unsettled her.

I wonder if Lisa ever realised just how much she hurt me. I can still remember that day at school as if it were yesterday. I'd walked there with her in the morning, because by then I'd been staying with her family for nearly three weeks.

'You're like one of the family,' Mrs Granger, her mother, had remarked at breakfast, when I'd asked if I might have another piece of toast. 'No need to ask, darling. Just help yourself.'

I think it was that that annoyed Lisa more than the 24-hour, bedroom-sharing contact, which was getting on her nerves. She didn't want me overstepping the mark, getting too close to her family, not when I had one of my own, albeit one which at that moment was unable to cope with life throwing up unexpected turns of events.

We had separate lessons but usually met for lunch in the canteen, with the rest of our loosely fluctuating group of friends. There was a spare seat at the table where Lisa was already sitting as I arrived, but when I went over with my tray, she said, 'Melanie is sitting there.'

I looked around and couldn't see Melanie.

'She'll be here in a minute,' Lisa insisted, but Melanie never showed.

I asked her later, when we were doing homework on Lisa's dining room table, why she hadn't let me sit with her at lunch, and she lowered her voice to make sure her mother, who was making us hot chocolate in the kitchen, didn't hear.

'Just because your mum's in the loony bin doesn't mean I still have to be your friend.'

I never replied because Mrs Granger came in then, with two steaming mugs of hot chocolate.

'I got some of that squirty cream today.' She beamed at us through the steam. 'I hope you like it, Anne-Marie?'

I nodded, still smarting from Lisa's earlier comment, and then she asked me if I'd got the notes we needed for Geography.

'Do you have that sheet on earthquakes?' she asked, as if nothing had happened, and I began to wonder if she had really said it.

We carried on much as before but it wasn't the same. I never felt close to her after that, and when Mum came out of hospital and I went back home, we hardly saw each other at all.

'People who don't need friends always have lots,' my mother said, after asking me why I didn't see so much of Lisa any more.

I'd told her she'd found new friends in a different crowd and didn't seem to need me. I, by comparison, needed friends but was starting to find it increasingly hard to make them.

I still do . . . need friends, that is . . . and I still seem to find it difficult to make them.

Today was a case in point.

When I got on the train this morning, I found myself looking around for two seats, thinking Geoff was with me. We used to go up together on the days when I worked in London. Not always: sometimes he had an earlier meeting or might have stayed overnight somewhere on business, but usually, if he were home, we'd go up together. As I was casting around for seats I almost believed that he was there, just for a brief moment, before the reality came flooding back to me, making me want to go back to the door of the carriage, get off and return home.

Then I spotted Holly sitting further down and I thought, If she can keep getting on, day in and day out, after what happened to her, then so can I.

She didn't see me. She was on her own, reading the paper. I wondered if she'd got my friend request on Facebook. I looked at her page, after the meeting, once I knew her name. She obviously doesn't use it very often. She only had a handful of friends and they looked to be her family. Three of them had the same name, although it was different from hers — but that's not unusual these days.

It made me wonder what I should do about my name now. I hadn't thought about it but it suddenly struck me that it will be odd going through the rest of my life, with Geoff's name but without him. At the same time, I want to keep it because that's one part of him that I can keep. If I still have his name, then something of him is still mine.

I checked to see if Holly had responded to my friend request, when I got to the office, but she hadn't and that's when I decided to unfriend Geoff.

Whenever I log on, there he is, smiling at me from a beach in Corfu at the top of my short list of friends. It was a holiday we had last year, and if I'm honest with myself it wasn't that great. Geoff was preoccupied with work and spent more time with his BlackBerry than he did with me. The picture was taken after a day when I forced him to leave his phone behind and go on a boat trip, and he relaxed a little.

It was easy to lose him. One click of the 'Remove from Friends' button and he was gone. I wish it were as easy to get him out of my mind.

When I unfriended Geoff, I had a momentary feeling of power. I've felt pretty powerless since it all happened but removing him from my Facebook friends made me feel momentarily in control of my life.

So now I have one fewer friend and I keep thinking that sooner or later Holly will respond to my request or call me. But then I saw her on the train again, after work, and she seemed almost hostile.

She was sitting with him again, Daniel, whoever he is, and there was a free seat opposite.

I asked if I could sit there and Holly said no.

I was too stunned to reply. It was like Lisa in the canteen again. I'd thought there was a kind of recognition between us. I'd thought that's why Holly had smiled when I first saw her, before I'd introduced myself. I'd thought she could tell that we'd both been through something similar.

I couldn't think what to say so I just walked on down the train and stood in the corridor, wondering why she was behaving like that. Why is it that women who I think of as my friends can treat me so badly? I thought Holly would be different.

Then she appeared in the corridor and explained there'd been a misunderstanding. It was silly really. It made me laugh because it was so silly, and I laughed again later because I felt almost happy. She'd asked if I'd like to have a drink some time soon. And now, for the first time since it happened, I feel as if I have something to look forward to.

20

'Anyone fancy a coffee at my place?' James Darling asked.

Holly knew he lived in Buckinghamshire in a large-sounding house called Tudor something or other.

She'd occasionally sent books or DVDs there that he needed to read or watch to prepare for the programme. She had imagined a large black-and-white edifice bought on the proceeds of the ridiculous advance he'd secured for his book. *Pretentious, Moi? A History of Perception from The Emperor's New Clothes to Tracey Emin's Bed* had sold well, though Holly had yet to meet anyone who had actually read it.

'What place?' she asked, wondering if Natalie, Dimitri and herself were expected to jump on the Metropolitan line and head out to the suburbs to take up his offer; or whether he was referring to a coffee bar he frequented so often that he claimed it as his own.

'My flat,' Darling replied, as if Holly should have known. 'It's just round the corner in Covent Garden.'

'Oh.' She had no knowledge of the flat.

There was no reason she should. James Darling's living arrangements were his own affair. A lot of the BBC presenters and correspondents did rent a pied-à-terre near work, as their hours often prevented them from getting home. Holly had imagined he would want to get back to his wife and children.

'It's in Wild Court.' Natalie's dismissive tone suggested she thought Holly would have known this.

'Well, I ought to be getting back really,' she said.

'Me too.' Dimitri wasn't letting on if he already knew Darling had a flat in the centre of town, but he didn't appear to want to go back to it.

The four of them had just been to the press night of *Je ne Sais Quoi!*, a French-Canadian variety show featuring a controversial double-amputee trampolining act. The act was good, incredible in fact, but his inclusion had sparked 'freak show' accusations. These would be discussed on *Antennae* later in the week.

'We'll say goodbye then,' said James, making no attempt at changing their minds. 'You're up for a coffee, aren't you, Nat?'

'Sure,' she concurred. 'Are you both heading towards Victoria?'

'I am,' Dimitri replied. 'Are you getting the tube, Holly?'

She nodded. She'd been on the tube now a couple of times when she'd been running late. She hadn't particularly liked it, but she hadn't panicked either.

'So,' Dimitri asked, as they began walking towards the Embankment, 'you weren't tempted by a peek at Darling's pad and some euphemistic coffee?'

'Is coffee always euphemistic?' Holly asked,

turning and seeing Darling briefly put his arm around Natalie's shoulders.

'Usually is at this time of night,' Dimitri replied. 'I mean, if I suggested you got off your train at Clapham Junction and came back to my place for a coffee, what would you say?'

'I'd say I don't drink coffee,' said Holly, laughing at the very idea of the godlike Dimitri suggesting she come back to his place

'Don't you?' Dimitri didn't sound particularly surprised. 'That fits.'

'How?' Holly wondered what part of her gave the impression that she didn't drink coffee, apart from the fact that she didn't. 'I drink tea,' she added, as if her dislike of coffee needed some sort of qualification.

'Tea is never euphemistic,' Dimitri said, smiling at her in a way which Holly suspected was indulgent.

'Never?' said Holly. 'Even if there are Digestives on offer as well?'

'I suppose dunking could be a bit of a double-entendre,' he conceded, as they walked down the steps to the platform of the tube. 'But still, 'Would you like to come back to my place for a cuppa?' doesn't have quite the same ring as 'Shall we end the evening off with coffee?''

'What about Horlicks?' Holly wondered. 'Could that be construed as an invitation to do anything other than fall asleep?'

Dimitri shook his head. 'I doubt it.'

'I could do with a cup of tea now.' Holly checked her watch as the underground train arrived and they took seats alongside each other;

she was wondering if there was time for her to buy a cup at the station before her train was due to leave.

'There you go!' Dimitri winked at her.

'What do you mean, 'There you go'?' Holly asked, noting the peculiar Englishness of the expression and how it could be used to underline a whole range of things.

'You and the not drinking coffee thing,' he said. 'It fits. You're safe.'

'What do you mean, I'm safe?' She had the feeling this was not exactly a compliment.

'Well, you know . . . ' Dimitri obviously hoped he could leave it at this. 'You know', like 'there you go', could be conversational full stops but Holly put on an 'I'm waiting' expression until he elaborated.

'Well, you're married. You're Holly,' he said, as if this were an explanation in itself. 'Very married.'

'Is there such a thing as 'very married'?' she queried. 'Surely you are either married or not.'

'Some people are more married than others,' Dimitri answered. 'I don't think James Darling's wife need worry if you had taken up his invitation to have 'coffee'.'

He made quotation marks in the air with his fingers as he said this.

'Well, obviously.' Holly inwardly balked at the thought. 'But I could be up for euphemistic coffee with someone else.'

'Are you?'

'No.' She was failing completely to make

Dimitri think she might have another side to her. 'But I could be.'

Safe indeed, she thought to herself, as the tube pulled into Victoria.

It was true, she was safe, but she would like to have given the impression that she was perhaps a little less so. Everyone around her seemed to have very specific views about her. Dimitri thought she was safe. Mark thought she was privately traumatised. The only person who seemed to assume nothing was Daniel.

'Whereas with Natalie . . . ' Dimitri said as they got on to the escalator.

'Natalie what?' Holly felt a twinge of jealousy as she anticipated Dimitri saying that he thought Natalie was a bit of a dark horse.

'Nothing.' Dimitri had obviously thought better of whatever it was he was going to say.

'Natalie and James are old friends.' She stressed the 'friends' as they went through the barriers and on to the station concourse.

'If you say so.' Dimitri raised his eyebrows slightly.

'They are,' Holly insisted. 'I've known Natalie for years and she's worked with Darling for ages.'

'The 23.06 to Brighton, platform eighteen,' Dimitri read the departure board. 'Which also stops at Clapham Junction. I will escort you as far as there.'

'Why, thank you.' Holly smiled as they walked together to the other side of the station and passed through the barriers on to the platform.

'Are you going to get your tea then?' asked Dimitri, nodding towards the Costa coffee stall at the end of the platform.

'Have I got time?' Holly checked her watch again.

Dimitri nodded and she joined the queue, realising only as she did so that the person in front of her was Daniel.

'Hello,' she said, wondering why he was on this late train.

'Hello-o.' Daniel elongated the O slightly, as if he too was surprised to find her here at this hour. 'Can I get you a drink, as I'm here?'

'She wants a cup of tea,' said Dimitri, making his presence known.

'I would like a cup of tea.' Holly frowned at Dimitri. 'This is Dimitri, who I work with.'

'Anything?' Daniel asked him.

'No, thanks,' Dimitri said, and Daniel asked for a tea for Holly.

★   ★   ★

'We've been to a variety show on the South Bank,' Holly told Daniel once they were on the train. She felt the need to explain why she was with Dimitri and exactly when he would be leaving them too. 'Dimitri is going to Clapham Junction.'

'Oh, right.' Daniel looked slightly relieved. 'Was it good?'

'It was,' Dimitri confirmed. 'We're going to be talking about it on the programme later this week.'

Daniel nodded.

'But I imagine Natalie and Darling may have

sewn up exactly what angle the discussion will take over 'coffee'.' He made the finger sign again. Holly shot him a warning glance.

'There's a guy with no legs doing a trampolining act in it,' she told Daniel. 'Although he was so good that you stopped noticing that he didn't have any legs.'

'Which is the point,' Dimitri said, standing up when the train slowed as it neared Clapham Junction.

'Nice to meet you.' He nodded to Daniel. 'See you tomorrow, Holly.'

'Yes, see you tomorrow.' She smiled at him.

'Unless . . . ' Dimitri turned, as he was about to get off ' . . . you fancy a coffee?'

'I don't drink coffee, as you know.' She laughed and felt flattered by the attention, despite knowing he was taking the piss.

'What's all that about?' asked Daniel.

Holly shook her head after Dimitri knocked on the window and mimed a coffee-drinking action through it.

'Office gossip.' She shrugged, not wanting to go into details. 'About some of our colleagues.'

'Why all the thing about coffee?' Daniel looked out of the window at Dimitri's departing back.

'One of the women I work with has just gone back to the presenter's flat, for a coffee.' Holly wondered if this would satisfy him.

She was tempted to explain how they'd discussed euphemisms and Dimitri had described her as safe. But she decided not to because, it began to dawn on her, she didn't want Daniel to think of her that way.

21

'Bloody hell, who left those there?' Holly muttered as she tripped and nearly lost her balance coming down the stairs on her way to the kitchen.

She realised who had left them there, when she realised what they were; Mark's fairly new, but already dirty and smelly running shoes. He seemed to be taking running seriously. He'd been several times now and had a session with Daisy.

It was not yet 9 o'clock on Saturday morning. Holly had wondered where he was when she woke an hour earlier and found their bed empty. The space where he should have been was cold, as if long since vacated. Any thoughts about his whereabouts had quickly been replaced by making the most of his absence. There was no one snoring or pulling the bedclothes away from her, no half-hearted foreplay (Saturday morning had once been their preferred time to have sex). So Holly had an opportunity to enjoy a lie in and think her own thoughts, without anyone asking what they were.

'I nearly broke my neck falling over your trainers,' she said blearily as she went into the kitchen, hoping to make herself a cup of tea and head back to bed.

'Good morning!' Mark sounded ridiculously up for this time in the day and ignored her rather grouchy greeting. 'Sleep well?'

'Have you been running?' Holly asked.

It was a rhetorical question; the trainers and the sweat-infused t-shirt gave her the answer.

'Four miles.' Mark beamed, obviously hoping she would share in his sense of achievement.

'That's great.' Holly tried to sound enthusiastic. 'You really are taking running the marathon seriously.'

She had expected him to lose interest after a few jogs around the park.

'I need to build up distance gradually,' Mark said, with the air of a seasoned pro. 'And try to improve my times as well.'

This was not the talk of someone who was about to give up.

'Where did you go?' asked a voice which sounded much lovelier and softer than Holly felt.

She looked over at the table and noticed Chloe, behind a cereal packet, looking all fresh haired and gorgeous as she poured milk on the supermarket-brand cornflakes.

'Hello, love.' Holly hoped the pronounced change in her tone when she addressed their daughter was not as noticeable to Mark as it sounded to her. 'You're up early.'

'Yeah, I'm going out.' Chloe took a mouthful of cereal.

'Already?' Holly wondered where she was off to, so early on a Saturday morning, but doubted her daughter would tell her if she asked.

Chloe nodded and Mark saved her from further interrogation by filling them in on the details of his run.

'I ran up to the golf course, round Hollingbury Fort then back via your school, Chloe.' He paused momentarily and Holly was pretty sure deliberately too, to give his next words more dramatic effect. 'Four miles!'

'Wow, that's pretty impressive.' His utterance had had the right effect on Chloe. 'You've only been running a couple of weeks.'

Holly was going to say nothing but her daughter prompted her as she filled the kettle up.

'That's good, isn't it, Mum?'

'Did you actually go through Chloe's school?' Holly decided not to play up to his mid-life posturing. 'Isn't it locked at the weekend?'

'I went round.' Mark was looking slightly disappointed that his morning feat of endurance had provoked so little reaction from his wife.

'You can cut across the playing fields at the moment,' Chloe volunteered. 'Someone's pulled down a section of the fence on Surrenden Road.'

'Don't take offence,' Mark quipped.

Holly groaned inwardly as she filled the kettle up, only apparently it was outwardly as Chloe, usually the first to point up 'terrible Dad jokes', accused her of being unfair.

'That was funny, Mum.' Her daughter was giving her an angry look as she brought her now-empty cereal bowl over to the dishwasher.

'It was funny the first time.' Holly wondered why Chloe was suddenly being so defensive of Mark. 'But I've heard it before, quite a lot.'

'Yeah well . . . ' Chloe's voice trailed off as she put her spoon in the cutlery rack. 'You could laugh sometimes, just to be polite.'

Holly was about to say something about not needing to be polite when you'd been married for sixteen years, but she stopped herself. It unnerved her that her fifteen-year-old daughter appeared to be giving her marriage guidance advice. Holly had thought the subtle putdowns or simply her lack of reaction to Mark went largely unnoticed, but this was obviously not the case.

Chloe was right. She ought to make more of an effort with Mark, for Chloe and Jake's sake, if not for his.

'Do you want a croissant?' She hoped this would suffice as a peace offering.

'No, thanks,' Chloe said.

Holly switched the radio on as she busied herself with the croissants.

A husband and wife were talking about how they had met. They'd been on a climbing expedition in the Himalayas and the man had fallen and broken his leg. The weather was closing in and they needed to get down the mountain but he was slowing up the rest of the party so the woman had volunteered to stay with him, dig a snow hole for the night and start the descent again the following day. She was a doctor and had made a makeshift cast for his leg.

In the event the weather had not cleared and they'd been stuck there for several days.

'I knew that she would always stick by me,' the man was telling the radio interviewer. 'Because she stuck by me then.'

'That's really sweet,' Chloe commented, but Mark seemed cross.

'Most people would do that if they found themselves in those circumstances,' he growled. 'But not everyone does.'

'I have to go.' Chloe got up from the breakfast table.

'Do you know where she's off to?' Holly asked as their daughter breezed out of the kitchen.

'Somewhere with Scrabble Boy, I think,' Mark said.

Holly made a concerted effort to laugh now at the Scrabble Boy reference.

'Do you want a croissant?' she repeated. 'You must be hungry after a four-mile run.'

'Yes, please.' Mark hovered in the middle of the kitchen as Holly took some croissants out of a paper bag and stuck them on a baking tray. 'Oh, great — crescent ones. The best.'

'Is there a difference?' She lit the oven and stuck the tray in it. 'I mean, apart from the shape?'

'Straight ones are made with margarine, but the crescent-shaped ones are butter.' Mark was full of random information, some of it interesting. He was a one-man pub quiz trivia resource, always willing to point out that a banana plant was a shrub and not in fact a tree, and that there were three landlocked countries beginning with B on the African continent.

'Really, I never knew that?' This particular piece of information Holly did find interesting. 'It had never even occurred to me that there might be a reason for the difference in shape.'

'They are like women,' Mark said. 'Straight ones are margarine but curvy ones are butter.'

215

Holly, who was on the curvy side, had no idea what he meant. But as the mood seemed to have turned light and buttery, she wondered if it might be some sort of verbal foreplay.

'Well, I am going to take my tea and buttery croissant back to bed,' she told her husband. 'Do you want to come?'

She wondered what would happen if he did.

'I don't think so.' There was an edge to Mark's voice, which Holly was not quite sure how to translate. 'I'm kind of up now.' He gestured towards his t-shirt and tracksuit bottoms as if the wearing of them made it impossible for him to go back to bed. 'And I was going to have a look at the guttering this morning. It's been driving me mad, dripping every time it rains.'

'OK.' Holly knew his reluctance to follow her upstairs was partly her fault. She hadn't done much recently to prop up his flagging self-esteem, but Chloe's earlier dig had nudged her and she was trying to make amends.

'Why don't you get a man to fix the gutter?' she suggested.

'I am a man,' Mark snapped.

'I know.' Holly was slightly taken aback. 'I just meant you could get an odd job man and not have to spend your weekend dealing with it.'

'It won't take me long.' Mark was adamant. 'And I am perfectly capable of doing it myself.'

'I know,' she said, on the defensive now. 'I just thought it might be easier to get someone in.'

'I'm perfectly capable of clearing the gutter and fixing it too, if necessary.' Mark had his hands on his hips, as if squaring up for a fight. 'I know you seem to think I'm not up to much these days, Holly, but I'm doing my best.'

'I don't know what you mean,' she faltered.

She did know what he meant. She had been treating him, not exactly badly, but dismissively. She wondered how things could seem to change so quickly. This time last year she would have described herself and Mark as happy. Now she wasn't so sure. They weren't unhappy but they were definitely coming unstuck.

'Oh, I think you do,' he said bitterly, and made towards the back door. 'I'm going to get the ladder out of the shed. You take your croissant upstairs and leave mine in the oven. I'll have it when I've finished being a man.'

22

Natalie appeared unusually anxious to be away from work.

'I need to leave by five-thirty today.' She looked at the clock on the wall of the meeting room. 'So, are we finished here?'

'I think so.' Katherine began gathering various bits of paper, which seemed to signal the weekly ideas meeting was at an end. 'Going anywhere nice?'

'What?' Natalie seemed unable to think why she might be going anywhere nice. Then she realised that as far as workaholic Katherine was concerned, leaving early implied something worth leaving early for.

'Me? Oh, no, just home.' Natalie's answer had the predictable effect of causing Katherine to raise her eyebrows ever so slightly. The reaction would have been barely discernible to a passer by but those who worked with her on a daily basis were attuned to her indications of displeasure.

Natalie ignored her and picked up her things to leave, providing a cue for the rest of the team to do the same.

Holly wondered if Natalie had taken the recent discussion about house husbands person-ally.

It had arisen when Dimitri had suggested they interview Claire Jacobs, a detective novelist, whose books aimed at teenagers were now topping the bestseller lists.

'I don't think so,' Katherine had dismissed the idea. 'We'll leave that to *Front Row*.'

And that would have been it, if Darling had not mentioned that he'd met Claire Jacobs at a literary festival once.

'She's a bit of a witch,' he'd said.

'A bitch or a witch?' Dimitri had asked.

'Well, both,' James had told them. 'She was laying into her poor husband in his absence as if he were a complete no hoper.'

'What does her husband do?' Holly had asked.

'Well, that was her gripe,' Darling said. 'He looks after their children while she writes her bestsellers, but she seems to resent him for it.'

Holly said nothing more because she found herself sympathising with Claire Jacobs. She wondered how many women really were content with role reversal, and how many, even if they worked, would rather their partners were also eagerly pursuing their careers.

She looked up and caught Natalie's eye but looked away as Rebecca spoke up.

'I read that house husbands are five times as likely to have affairs as other men.'

'And how likely are other men to have affairs?' Dimitri had asked, winking at her as he spoke.

'I don't remember.' Rebecca smiled to herself.

★ ★ ★

'Dimitri, can I have a word?' Katherine stopped him as he headed for the door. 'It won't take a minute.'

'Wonder what that's about?' Rebecca mused as the rest of them headed towards the lift.

'Probably just making sure he doesn't try to leave before it's dark,' Darling said, raising his eyebrows in an expression no one could possibly miss. 'What are you heading home for, Natalie? Anything nice?'

'No,' she giggled. 'Twins' bath and bedtime. Guy has started going to the gym on Wednesday evenings and it's more trouble than it's worth making him miss it.'

'Fuck! That reminds me . . . ' Darling's expletive caused eyebrows to be raised a third time in as many minutes by an elderly man who emerged from the lift as it arrived and the doors opened.

'Reminds you of what?' Natalie asked, as they all piled in.

'I'm supposed to get home early too,' he replied, pushing the button for the sixth floor.

Now it was Rebecca's turn to raise her eyebrows. She caught Holly's eye across the lift and moved them in a gesture that was clear enough. It implied, Natalie has to leave early, Darling has to leave early, what do we make of that then?

Holly suspected Darling had seen her face in the mirror at the back of the lift.

'Mila has a sculpting class to go to,' he said, as if in answer to Rebecca's unasked question.

'I didn't know she sculpted,' Holly said, realising she knew very little about Darling's wife other than the odd thing he threw into the general discussion, which was usually something to do with her attitude to childcare.

'Well, it's a relatively new thing,' said Darling as the lift doors opened and they began dispersing. 'She used to do a bit of stone carving but this is working with bronze or something . . . '

He reached the door of his office and began unlocking it.

'See you tomorrow then.' Natalie touched his arm briefly as she walked past, causing him to turn.

'Yes, have fun in the bath,' he said, responding to her touch by putting his hand on her shoulder and running it down her arm as far as her elbow.

'I doubt it.' Natalie smiled as she moved on towards the office she and Holly shared.

'I didn't know Mila sculpted,' Holly said, following her in.

'Yeah, she's an artist.' Natalie was beginning to gather up stuff, ready to go home. 'Or, at least, she was. She doesn't really do anything any more.'

'She does if she's going to sculpting classes.' Holly thought Natalie was being slightly dismissive of Darling's wife.

'I mean professionally,' Natalie said. 'At one stage she used to sell quite a lot of stuff. That's how they met. Have you seen my phone?'

'It's on your desk,' Holly pointed. 'How did they meet?'

'Oh, yes.' Natalie put the phone in her bag. 'They met at one of Mila's exhibitions, at a gallery in Cork Street. James was a business reporter at the time and he was doing a piece on investing in art. Mila was the hot young next big thing.'

'Really?' Holly was impressed. It was strange, she thought, how easily women were reclassified once they became mothers. She had never heard James refer to Mila as anything other than a wife and mother, and yet she must have been . . . no, she corrected her thoughts, still was . . . a talented artist. 'That's really impressive.'

'Well, she doesn't do anything any more.' Natalie put Mila firmly back in her box.

'I don't suppose she has a lot of time,' Holly said. 'What with the boys and . . . '

'And what?' Natalie asked.

'And James not being around much.' Holly wondered if her friend would jump to his defence. 'I imagine his career comes first and Mila gets left with most of the childcare.'

'Their children are at school.' Natalie put the emphasis on 'are', as if these few hours a day left Mila more than enough time to get her career back on track. 'And she does write a bit. For art-history journals or something.'

'She can't have much time left to do her own work then,' Holly mused. 'Kids take up an awful lot of time when they're young.'

'I do know that,' Natalie said crossly. 'I have got two of my own, in case you'd forgotten.'

'Of course not.' Holly tried to inject some warmth into her voice while she thought to herself that Natalie didn't really know.

Natalie checked her watch, which, it occurred to Holly, was not something she often did. She hardly ever rushed to pick the twins up from nursery or get back before bedtime. She left most of that to Guy.

'I ought to be going.' She sat on the edge of her desk, showing no sign of following up her statement.

'So Guy's started going to the gym?' Holly tried to send her on her way. Her sympathies for the moment were with him. She remembered what it was like to have been at home with children all day.

Natalie nodded. 'Yes, they all seem to be at it. He started going a few weeks ago. Apparently there was some sort of deal at our local health club. I don't suppose it will last, though.'

'Why not?'

'Well, Guy keeps having these bursts of enthusiasm for various projects, but they never seem to amount to much.'

'I guess he doesn't have that much time,' Holly remarked.

'Don't start defending him. The twins go to nursery. He does fuck all a lot of the time, as far as I can tell.'

Holly decided to say nothing.

'What about Mark?' Natalie asked.

'What about him?' She didn't feel entirely comfortable talking to Natalie about Mark's current lack of direction.

'Is he still an aspiring marathon man?' Natalie asked, picking up her bag and standing up.

'He is actually. He seems to keep disappearing for the odd hour and arriving back hot and sweaty.'

'From running?' Natalie asked. Now it was her

turn to raise her eyebrows.

'Well, if it's not running, it's something he does in running shoes and shorts,' Holly told her.

'Middle-aged men used to sleep with dumb blondes.' Natalie smiled. 'Now they cosy up with dumb bells instead.'

'A good headline.' Holly could see it in *Men's Health* or one of the other magazines, which catered for middle-aged men's obsession with their bodies.

'I suppose it's better than having an affair.' Natalie appeared to concede Guy's entitlement to an evening in the gym and finally began to walk towards the door.

It was opened from the outside, before she had the chance to do it herself.

'Are we off then?' Holly heard Darling's voice, and then, as she shut the door, Natalie's reply.

'Yes. Let's go, shall we?'

23

'Excuse me.' Susan had just yawned.

'Are we boring you, Gran?' Chloe asked.

'Of course not.' Susan straightened her back as if this would re-energise her. 'I just had a bit of a late night last night.'

Holly's mother and father were 'doing the rounds', spending a few days visiting friends and relatives on the South Coast before returning home to Northampton.

First stop was lunch with Holly and family, then on for a night in Chichester. The following day would be spent with an old colleague of Patrick's he insisted he had never liked, but whose wife Susan claimed as a good friend. Then they'd have a night with Fay, in Reading.

Holly knew these visits were arranged by her mother. Her father, given the choice, would happily stay at home and never see anyone at all. Patrick was five years older than Susan but sometimes it seemed liked fifteen. He seemed to get very tired and had little appetite for keeping up with old friends, never mind making new ones.

Holly looked at him closely now, as he sat at the dinner table, and wondered if he was OK or if her sister was right and he was ill. He looked quite normal to her.

'What were you doing last night?' Jake was spinning his knife around on the table while they waited for Holly to dish out their lunch.

'She went to the theatre with her new chums,' Patrick said, and Holly noticed that he reached out his hand instinctively to stop Jake playing with his cutlery. Then, as if he'd remembered this was not his child, he put it back on his lap.

'I've joined a theatre club.' Susan beamed at them all as they sat around the table. 'They do block bookings for shows, so we get discounts for whatever's on at the Playhouse and every now and then we go on a trip to London. We went to see a Japanese play with subtitles at the South Bank last night.'

'No wonder you're tired,' Jake said. 'A Japanese play would send anyone to sleep.'

'Your grandmother is tired because she got on the wrong train home,' Patrick said quietly.

'We misread the platform number.' Susan shrugged, implying that it was easy enough to do. 'Ended up getting on a train to Cambridge and having to change.'

'Do you remember when Mark went to a meeting in the wrong country?' Holly put a steaming dish of chicken casserole down at the end of the table.

'Did he?' Susan sounded surprised, although Holly was sure they must have heard this story before. At one time it had been a favourite mealtime anecdote of Mark's.

'You tell it, Mark.' She smiled at her husband, anticipating that he would relish the chance to tell one of his funnier stories.

'I'm sure they've heard it before.' He looked reluctant. 'Jake, don't do that.'

Jake had picked his fork up and was holding it to his eye, staring through the steam from the casserole at Chloe. It was a habit he'd started when he was about three and had never seemed to grow out of. Whenever there was anything that produced steam on the table, he was instantly compelled to pick up his fork and look at his sister through it.

'Yes. Stop it, Jake, you retard.' It infuriated Chloe, which was probably one of the reasons he found it hard to give up.

'Chloe!' Her grandmother instantly admonished her for her use of the word 'retard'. She'd become aware of political correctness in her later years. Patrick was mystified by the twenty-first century and its new use of language and still said things like 'Is he a queer?' and referred to black men as 'coloured chaps'.

'I don't think we've heard about your meeting in the wrong country,' Susan switched the subject back again.

'It was a long time ago.' Mark sounded slightly irritated now and got up to take some wine out of the fridge.

'It's really funny.' Chloe encouraged him to tell the story too.

'You tell them then, if everyone wants to hear it.' Mark sounded distinctly surly. Holly hoped her parents hadn't noticed.

'Dad and Chris were going to a meeting in Stockholm,' Chloe started. 'You know, Chris who he used to work with?'

'Yes, we remember,' Susan spoke for them both, although Holly suspected her father would have no memory of Chris.

He had joined Mark a year after he'd first set up his own marketing and PR Company. The work was coming in thick and fast and Mark could not cope with it all on his own. They'd soon taken on another permanent member of staff, Fiona, and contracted a couple of freelancers as business boomed.

A few years after that, Chris had left to set up his own company, taking Fiona with him and marrying her while he was at it. Mark had been gracious about letting them go but didn't mention Chris or what he was up to much these days. Holly wondered if his company was doing well and if he and Fiona were still together.

'They got a taxi from the airport and when they got to the headquarters of the company, where their meeting was, it was dead quiet and there was just one man sitting at the reception desk,' Chloe told them.

'Oh, yeah!' Jake suddenly seemed to have remembered this story too.

'They said they'd come to meet with the managing director.' Chloe paused slightly before delivering the punchline. 'And the reception guy said, 'But he is in Copenhagen!''

'They'd flown to Stockholm instead of Copenhagen,' Jake added, for the benefit of anyone who'd missed this.

'We were always flying back and forth between Sweden and Demark at the time,' Mark said defensively. 'More wine, Patrick?'

'Oh yes, please.' Patrick moved his glass a fraction across the table.

'I suppose that must have happened a lot.'

'Never,' Holly interjected. 'You asked the man on reception that, didn't you, Mark?'

She paused but he said nothing. So she continued, doing her best to put on a Scandinavian accent.

'I have worked here for fifty years and never before has this happened!'

They all laughed, except Mark. It was a good story and, in the days when he used to tell it at dinner parties, he'd done so to greater comic effect than either Chloe and Holly could muster. Today he appeared to be embarrassed by the incident.

'That was in the days before *Yuppienalle*,' Mark commented, trying to interest them all in something else.

'What?' Chloe and Jake asked in unison.

'Mobile phones,' Mark said. 'Or 'yuppie teddies', as the Swedes used to call them, because they were like security blankets for yuppies, when they first came out.'

Patrick laughed.

'This is lovely.' Holly's mother sensed the subject needed changing and switched it to the food. 'What's the sauce with the chicken?'

'Tomatoes, olives, chilies and capers,' Holly told her. 'It's a Jamie Oliver recipe.'

'I got it off the internet, Gran,' Chloe told her. 'You could look it up. It's on jamieoliver. com.'

'Oh, yeah. How's your laptop, Gran?' Jake was suddenly interested in the conversation.

'I don't know how I ever managed without it, Jake,' she said. 'There's so much you can find out so easily, and of course I can find out what you're up to by looking at Facebook.'

Holly was surprised that Chloe and Jake had accepted their gran as a friend. She had thought they would not want her to see some of the posts they put up, especially Chloe. But this generation seemed content to live their whole life in the glare of the internet and not be particularly bothered by who saw them living it. Secrets for them were virtual impossibilities.

'What have you discovered about Jake that you didn't already know?' Holly asked Susan now, but Mark cut in before she had time to answer.

'Holly never goes on Facebook, Susan. She thinks it's a waste of time.'

Holly decided not to tell him that she had been on earlier in the week and was likely to go on again soon to find out if he'd maintained Facebook contact with Daisy. Or anyone else for that matter.

'You haven't been tempted to join the digital age then, Granddad?' Jake was asking Patrick.

'He does have a mobile.' Patrick appeared not to have heard Jake, his hearing was getting worse, and so Susan answered for him. 'But he never seems to use it.'

'Really?' Jake raised his voice. 'Have you got a mobile, Granddad?'

'A yuppie teddy!' Patrick replied. 'Yes, I have. You'll be able to call me if I get lost again.'

He was referring to his long walk when they'd tried to call him on Holly's phone.

'I've tried that,' Susan said. 'When he's been out and I've been wondering where he's got to.

He never answers, though.'

'Delicious!' Patrick said, bringing the subject back to the food.

'You have a Jamie Oliver restaurant in Brighton, don't you?' Susan asked. 'Have you been?'

'Yes, when it first opened. But we haven't been for a long time,' Holly told her. 'It was nice, though.'

'And I was reading about a very good vegetarian restaurant in the paper. Terra something or other.'

'Terre à Terre?' Holly said. 'I used to go a lot when I worked at Radio Sussex, but I haven't been recently. I'm told it's very good.'

'It's always very busy — apparently,' Chloe said.

'We should try that, Patrick,' Susan said enthusiastically. From where Holly was sitting, at the other end of the table, she couldn't be entirely sure but she thought she heard her father mutter, 'Must we?'

'It's really hard to get a table.' For some reason, Chloe seemed to want to steer them clear of the restaurant. 'You're better off going somewhere else.'

'Quite right,' Patrick said.

Holly suspected he was having trouble hearing everything that was being said but wanted to join in.

'So, Mark,' Patrick cleared his throat slightly, 'how's business going?'

'It's quite tough at the moment. Difficult times and all that,' Mark said quietly, trying to keep the conversation just between the two of them. 'But I might have a new client. An off licence in Kemptown.'

'That sounds interesting,' Patrick said politely.

Holly wondered if her father remembered that, in the not-so-distant past, Mark's company had had a contract with one of the world's major drinks distributors. They'd decided to do their marketing in-house a few years ago. Holly sensed that while the off licence in Kemptown was work that he needed, it also served as a reminder to Mark of his more illustrious client. She didn't tell her parents that he was thinking of giving up his office and working on Sean's account from the table they were sitting around now.

'No more karaoke in Taiwan then?' Patrick said, proving that he did enjoy and remember Mark's anecdotes.

'Karaoke in Taiwan?' Jake obviously didn't remember this one.

'I used to go on a lot of business trips to Taiwan,' Mark said, apparently happy to dust down this story for the benefit of the assembled company.

'It was when you were much younger, Jake. The Taiwanese were very civilised by day, but at night, when we did research trips to various bars and clubs, they were a different breed.'

'Research?' Chloe interjected.

'Yes, Chloe,' Mark continued. 'It was a hard job but someone had to do it. Anyway, my Taiwanese colleagues used to drink me under the table and I found it hard to keep up.'

'I find that hard to believe,' Jake said.

'It was rude to refuse a drink.' Mark ignored his son. 'But there were always karaoke machines everywhere. If I went to wait my turn to perform, then I could have a bit of a break from whisky. Taiwan is the only place where I have found myself jumping up and queueing to sing 'I Will Survive' to a room full of businessmen!'

They all laughed.

'That's funny,' Holly said, hoping to make up for having brought up the 'meeting in the wrong country' scenario earlier.

'Holly never actually laughs any more.' Mark said. His tone was even but she suspected that had her parents not been present, he might have injected some bitterness into it. 'She just says if she thinks things are funny.'

Holly was about to protest but realised that there was some truth in what he said. She laughed at other people's jokes, but she didn't seem to find Mark funny any more. She wondered if this was just because she'd heard most of his stories before and knew his humour so well that she could predict where he was going with new ones, or if it was part of the general malaise in their marriage.

'Susan and I had lunch in a public house last week.' As a rule, Holly's father didn't like abbreviations, even ones as common as 'pub'. 'And when I asked for the menu, they gave me one for all the drinks they stocked behind the bar. We were hoping for some food, but we had to go to the restaurant for that.'

'They've started doing that in quite a few

places,' Mark told him.

'I had a quick look and one of the things they sold was whisky from the Corkney Islands!' Patrick said.

'That's funny,' Mark said, without seeming to realise he was doing what he'd just accused Holly of. 'It sounds like an island where they sent East End evacuees during the war!'

Holly laughed out loud and got up to clear the empty plates.

'Did you know Dad is going to run a marathon?' Jake asked his grandmother as Holly scraped the plates and put them in the dishwasher.

'Really? How very impressive,' Susan said.

'Well, I've only just started training. We'll see if I make it. But it's good to have a goal.'

Holly took out a strawberry pavlova from the fridge.

'What is it?' Jake asked as she put it on the table. He never wanted to try anything unless he knew exactly what it was.

'Pavlova.'

'Aren't you supposed to ring a bell before bringing it out?' quipped Mark.

'What?' Jake asked. Holly knew he'd heard the Pavlov's dog quip many times before. Mark said the thing about ringing a bell first every time they had it.

'That looks lovely,' her mother said, admiring the pudding. Then, as if it warranted an announcement, she made one.

'We have some news,' she said, looking slightly nervously at Patrick as she said this.

Holly sat down again. A slight feeling of panic came over her. She hoped neither of them was ill. Perhaps Fay had been right and there was something up with Patrick.

'You don't have to look so worried,' her mother said.

'I . . .' Holly was not quite sure what to say so she waited for her mother's news.

'I'm going to Thailand for four months,' Susan announced.

'Oh,' Holly said. 'That sounds lovely. When will you go?'

'I was planning to leave in September. Or late August, so that I'm back in December. I don't really want to leave Patrick on his own for Christmas.'

That took Holly aback, not least because Susan sounded as if she were talking about leaving a dog behind rather than her husband of forty-plus years.

'Oh,' she said again. 'Dad's not going with you then?'

'Not really my sort of thing,' Patrick said. His tone didn't give away what he felt about his wife going off on her own.

'I suppose not.' Holly was not sure exactly how to interpret this piece of information. She stuck a knife into the pavlova and wondered if her mother sometimes found her father as difficult to be with as she was finding Mark.

'But won't you be lonely, Dad?' she asked. 'And how will you manage?'

Her father hadn't cooked anything more elaborate than a boiled egg in the past forty years, and he couldn't survive on boiled eggs for four months.

'Oh, I'm sure people will rally round and cook for him,' Susan said, in a voice which hinted that she thought this conversation was at an end.

24

'Here she is now!' James Darling looked up from Holly's desk and told whoever he was talking to on her phone that she'd just arrived at work. 'She's just walked through the door. She looks a bit wet.'

Holly made a face and mouthed, 'Who is it?' as she took off her coat and pushed rain-soaked hair off her face.

'It's your sister Fay,' he told her, and then continued the conversation he appeared to be having quite happily with Holly's elder sibling. 'She's just de-robing, Fay. Her coat is off. Her sweater is coming off . . . Holly, stop, I can't take any more!'

Holly raised her eyebrows at Natalie who was watching Darling as he chatted to her sister. She had a plate on her lap and was picking croissant crumbs from it and putting them in her mouth.

'Give it to me!' Holly said, putting her hand out to take the phone. She didn't trust Darling not to start asking Fay all sorts of things about what she'd been like when she was little.

'Nice talking to you, Fay,' James said, holding up a finger in a 'one minute' gesture to Holly. 'Your little sister wants to take over now . . . You too. 'Bye.'

Holly took the phone and motioned to James to get off her chair too. He made a great play of the effort involved, before finally standing up and going to sit on Natalie's desk.

'Oh, and your husband called too,' he mouthed as Holly picked up the phone. 'Can you call him?'

She nodded and began talking to her sister.

'Hello, Fay?' Holly's tone was questioning because it was unusual for Fay to call during office hours. Her job was not the sort that allowed her to take or make personal calls at work. 'How are you?' Holly asked. 'Did you get on OK with Mum and Dad?'

'Who was that who answered the phone?' Fay asked now, ignoring her question about their parents.

'Oh, that was James Darling. He presents the programme.' Holly looked over to where Darling sat perched on Natalie's desk. He was fiddling with her bag and, she suspected, still half-listening to her conversation with her sister.

Natalie had her back to Holly but she appeared to sense her glance in their direction and tapped James on the leg.

'Let's go and get more coffee,' she whispered, nodding her head in Holly's direction. She obviously thought she could do with some privacy.

'Sure,' James slid off the desk, brushing briefly against Natalie as he did so.

If he'd behaved like that with Holly, she would have considered it an invasion of her space. Natalie didn't seem to mind or even notice.

'He's got a lovely voice,' Fay said. 'Very deep and masculine.'

Holly checked herself. She'd been about to say

238

something along the lines of 'I didn't think you went in for deep masculine voices', but realised this was just the sort of thing her parents might say.

'Yes,' she replied, and paused until the door clicked firmly behind Darling and Natalie. 'It's completely at odds with the rest of his appearance.'

'Really?' Fay sounded surprised. 'He sounds as if he might look like George Clooney.'

'That is the beauty of radio,' Holly told her. 'In fact, he looks like a paler, balder, bespectacled and bearded Tom Cruise.'

'Not a very flattering picture,' Fay said.

'Quite accurate though,' Holly continued. 'Sometimes we get listeners writing in asking for signed photos of him and I worry they may stop listening when they find out what he actually looks like.'

'Do Radio Four listeners really write in for signed photos?' Fay commented.

'You'd be surprised,' Holly said. 'Do you remember Uncle George?'

George was their mother's brother-in-law. He had died when they were in their twenties and their aunt had remarried a car salesman, and left the pub in Dorset which they had run together.

'What about him?' Fay asked.

'Oh, I was just reminded of him telling me one day how he always used to close the pub and then listen to *Woman's Hour*,' Holly told her sister.

'Well, I certainly wouldn't have had him down as a *Woman's Hour* man,' Fay commented.

'Nor me.' Holly had thought it completely out of character. 'But then he told me he used to watch Jenni Murray when she presented the news on BBC South and was rather taken with her looks — and in particular her bust.'

'Bust' was not the word Uncle George had used, Holly realised, continuing. 'When she left BBC South he followed her career with great interest. And ended up hardly ever missing an episode of *Woman's Hour*!'

'That's so sexist,' Fay said, as Holly had anticipated she would.

'I know,' Holly agreed, 'but it just goes to show that not everyone is listening to Radio Four for the content.'

'S'pose not,' Fay agreed. 'Anyway, I didn't call to talk about radio presenters.'

'No, I thought not if you're calling from work,' Holly said. 'Did you want to talk about Mum and Dad?'

She wondered what Fay had made of the news that their mother planned to spend several months in Thailand on her own.

'No, why?' Fay sounded as if she could think of no reason why she would want to talk about their parents.

'I presume Mum told you she was off travelling?' Holly flicked her computer on as she chatted to her sister.

'Oh, yes, that,' Fay said, as if it was of no importance.

'Don't you think it's a bit odd?' Holly asked her, typing her login with one finger.

'No, not really. She just wants to do her own

thing for bit,' Fay replied. 'They *are* worried about you, though. They asked me to talk to you.'

'Why are they worried about me?' Holly said, feeling defensive. She was used to them worrying about Fay. 'I cooked a nice lunch.'

'Yes, of course you did.' Both sisters knew their mother judged them largely on the basis of what they produced at mealtimes. Accordingly they did their best when their parents visited. 'It's not your culinary skills they're worried about. It's you and Mark.'

'They don't need to worry about us.' Holly hoped Fay hadn't picked up the slight defensiveness that had crept into her voice. She tried to inject a bit of light-heartedness into it. 'Dad ought to be worrying about Mum going off to Thailand, and Mum should worry about how Dad will cope if he's left on his own.'

'Seriously,' Fay said. 'Apparently Mark had a chat with Dad after dinner, when he was showing him how to send an email.'

'Really?' Holly recalled Mark telling Patrick he would show him, so that he could communicate with Susan while she was away.

'Yes,' her sister said. 'Mark told Dad he was worried about you. He said you're working really long hours and you don't talk to him any more.'

'I do talk to him,' Holly said, knowing this wasn't entirely true. She hadn't had a proper talk with her husband for a long time. But they passed the time of day.

'What did Dad say?' she asked.

'He probably asked how many days emails

took to get there,' Fay joked. 'You know what he's like. He doesn't like to talk about anything remotely personal.'

'I know.' Holly recalled another phone conversation with her sister following the weekend she had told their parents she was gay.

Fay had told her, 'I went into the sitting room and said to Dad as a precursor to my news, 'We don't really talk, do we, Dad?' And he said, 'No,' and left the room!'

Fay had then had to force her parents to sit down and listen to what she had to say.

'Mum said you looked tired as well,' she said to Holly now.

'I am tired,' Holly told her. 'It's tiring going up and down to London nearly every day. And I'm not sleeping very well at the moment. I think it's the light mornings.'

'Or you might be suffering from post-traumatic stress?' The psychologist in her sister reared her head.

'From having Mum and Dad to lunch?' Holly joked.

'No, you know what I mean.' Fay had adopted her serious elder sister tone. 'After the crash. I know you *say* you are fine and you've been carrying on, but sometimes these things affect you in different ways; like not sleeping, and not being able to have functioning relationships.'

'I have functioning relationships all over the place.' Holly began to feel angry.

'OK, fine.' Fay sounded unconvinced. 'But if Mark's worried about you, perhaps you need to reassure him. It would probably do you good to talk to someone, Holly. Though I realise that someone is probably not your interfering older sister.'

'Sorry,' Holly said, realising Fay probably didn't want to have this conversation any more than she did. 'I didn't mean to snap. It just annoys me that people assume anything slightly wrong must be down to the fact I was in a train crash. Mark's not been easy to live with since his business started having problems, you know.'

'I realise that,' Fay said sympathetically. 'I know it can't be easy for you, being the main breadwinner and doing all the family stuff as well. I don't suppose Mark does all the things you used to do when you were at home?'

'Of course not.' Holly sometimes envied her sister, living with another woman. They were the only people she knew who actually shared domestic chores equally. 'But he thinks he does.'

'It might be worth giving the counselling another go,' Fay said gently.

'It won't help make Mark do the washing up,' Holly joked, but Fay didn't react. 'Did Dad say he thought I should have counselling?'

'No, of course not!' her sister laughed. They both knew this was an unlikely scenario.

'Dad thought you seemed fine,' she conceded. 'He was just passing on Mark's concerns. To be honest . . . '

'What?' Holly challenged her to be just that.

'I thought maybe you could do with talking to someone outside the family about what happened. And about what's going on at home too.'

'There is someone I talk to,' Holly said, and

wondered if the family grapevine had heard via Mark that she'd been meeting up with Daniel.

★ ★ ★

Holly remembered when she'd finished talking to Fay that she needed to call Mark too. She wasn't sure if he would have gone into his office or still be at home so she tried him on his mobile.

'Hello.' Mark sounded breathless when he picked up.

'Hello. It's me,' she identified herself.

'Yes?' Mark sounded distracted.

'Are you OK?' she asked.

'Yes, I'm just on my way somewhere. Was there something you wanted?'

'You called me earlier,' Holly told him. 'Darling said you wanted me to call you back.'

'Oh, yes.' Mark cleared his throat and Holly wondered if his slight breathlessness was because he was out running. 'Only to say that Fay called. She said she'd try you at work.'

'I've spoken to her,' Holly told him, wondering why he didn't tell her he was out running, if he was. Perhaps he thought she'd be pissed off that he wasn't at work.

'Everything OK?' Mark asked her.

'Yes. Fine.' This conversation didn't seem to be going anywhere.

'Good.' Mark sounded very distant now. 'See you later then.'

25

'I'm glad you arrived first.' Daniel was already nursing a pint at a table in the corner when Holly arrived at The Shakespeare's Head.

He stood up and kissed her and she was immediately glad that they'd decided to have a drink here and not just try to talk awkwardly on the train.

'Anne-Marie is coming then?' Holly asked.

'Yes. She said she might be a few minutes late. Can I get you a drink?' Daniel half stood up.

'You're all right,' Holly said, sitting down with her back to the entrance. 'I'll wait for Anne-Marie to arrive and then get us both one.'

'This feels a bit odd, doesn't it?' Daniel said what Holly was thinking. 'Arranging to meet someone we hardly know. All the rules of commuting have suddenly gone out of the window.'

'Yes, I know what you mean.' Holly lowered her voice. 'I feel desperately sorry for Anne-Marie, but at the same time I'm not really sure that I want to get involved. Does that sound selfish?'

'No.' Daniel leaned forward and touched her arm. She thought it was a gesture of understanding, then realised he was nodding his head towards the door, alerting her to Anne-Marie's arrival.

'Hello.' She approached their table and pulled

the spare seat back. 'I hope I'm not too late?'

'No,' Holly said, giving what she hoped was a welcoming smile. 'I've only just got here, though Daniel is on his third pint.'

He grinned, and Anne-Marie looked confused.

'I'm joking,' Holly said, wondering if every encounter with Anne-Marie was going to be riddled with such misunderstandings. She stood up. 'But you and I do need to do some catching up. What would you like to drink?'

'It still seems quite early to be drinking.' Anne-Marie looked a little hesitant. 'I'll have a small glass of white wine, please.'

Holly went to the bar, leaving Daniel to the small talk. When she came back he was saying something about ensuring computer systems met needs. Anne-Marie must have asked what he did.

'There you are.' Holly put the glass on a beer mat in front of Anne-Marie and sat down next to Daniel. 'Cheers!'

'Cheers!' they all chorused, and then there was a moment of awkward silence.

'So . . . ' began Holly, although she had not yet thought of anything to say. Anne-Marie was also saying 'So' at the same time.

They both stopped and did a bit of 'you first'-ing. Anne-Marie was more insistent and Holly had to go first.

'What made you decide to go to the meeting?' she came up with. She hadn't intended to ask this but couldn't think of anything else. 'Had you been to any others?'

'No.' Anne-Marie didn't seem put out by her probing. 'That was the first. I might go to the next one perhaps, if you are? I'd heard there were a couple of other meetings not long after . . . I didn't think I should go to them, because I wasn't actually on the train myself . . . '

Her voice trailed off.

'That was my first too,' Holly said. 'I felt a bit of a fraud because I wasn't hurt or anything. Daniel thought the same.'

She stopped, thinking she should let him speak for himself. He'd previously implied he felt that, but she didn't really know if this was the case.

'Are you both married?' Anne-Marie asked, looking from Holly to Daniel.

In other circumstances, the question might have seemed out of place but, as they knew they were only meeting now because of the accident in which Anne-Marie had lost her husband, it seemed perfectly natural.

Holly, however, felt slightly guilty answering in the affirmative. It felt indecent to flaunt the fact they both had spouses when Anne-Marie no longer had hers.

'Yes,' she said, tentatively.

'Yes,' Daniel answered, at the same time, with more conviction.

'How long?' Anne-Marie asked.

'Five years,' he said.

'Sixteen years,' Holly said, wondering if that must seem like an eternity to Daniel.

'I thought when I saw you both at the meeting that you might be married to each other,' Anne-Marie said. 'And when I saw you sitting on the train.'

'I'm far too old,' Holly said quickly, feeling embarrassed and wondering if Daniel felt the same.

'So how do you know each other?'

'We met on the train,' he said, looking at Holly as if he needed her permission to say exactly how they'd come to know each other.

'We were sitting in the same carriage when the train stopped in the tunnel that day.' Holly didn't want to tell Anne-Marie what had happened but didn't really see how she could avoid it. 'I got trapped when the carriage turned over. Daniel stayed with me until the fire crews arrived.'

She didn't like being forced to recall the exact moment when the carriage was hit by the other train and the ensuing chaos.

She could feel it now, the terror she had experienced when she realised that people were trying to clamber out of the carriage and she was stuck.

'Can anyone hear me?' she remembered asking, and wondering why she didn't just yell, 'Help!'

'Are you OK?' Daniel had asked.

She hadn't been able to move. She didn't feel hurt but her leg was stuck underneath something. Her whole being was screaming at her to get out, and she couldn't, and if she didn't she had no idea what might happen.

'Where are you?' Daniel's voice had asked again, and she'd sensed a hand moving in the darkness and finding hers.

It had seemed like hours that they'd stayed like that, time in which Holly wondered at the selflessness of this man. She'd thought of Mark and Chloe and Jake and how much she wanted to see them again. He must be thinking the same about somebody, she'd thought. He must be as desperate to get out as I am, but she'd held on to him and he hadn't left.

Holly took a long sip of wine now and stared at the table. She felt upset with Anne-Marie for having made her go back to that moment, and in retaliation decided to ask her a direct question.

'Where was your husband? Was he on the same train as us, or the one that hit us?' Her voice sounded harsh as she said it. She wasn't sure why she was so cross.

'I'm not sure exactly.' Anne-Marie sounded upset.

'How long were you married?' Daniel asked.

Holly couldn't look at him when he asked this. She didn't want him to be angry with her for asking the question she had, but when she did look up he caught her eye and smiled, as if he understood.

'Three years,' Anne-Marie said quietly. 'I thought we'd be together for ever.'

I tried to find out a bit more about Holly and Daniel before I went to meet them this evening. I Googled them both, but very little came up. Daniel was simply listed on his company's website as a systems analyst. Holly is credited with producing programmes for the BBC, but there was nothing else out there, so I tried Facebook again.

She still hadn't responded to my friend request, but I'm not going to let this bother me. She obviously hardly ever uses the site. I looked at the rest of her friends and am sure they are her family.

Jake, who must be her son, had pictures of himself with her on what looks like a family holiday. In one they are walking along a cliff top, waving at the camera. In another they are sitting with their arms around each other beside a barbecue. And there were some of Holly with her daughter Chloe, paddling in the sea. They have their arms raised and look as if they might be dancing.

Chloe's page had the locked symbol and the thing saying she only shares some profile information with people who are not friends, but Mark's was full of stuff.

Mark Constantine — he must be her husband — has 292 friends. His family include Chloe and Jake Constantine, though strangely not Holly.

Perhaps I am wrong about him being her husband, but I don't think so. He's into French cinema, likes stand-up comedy and Belgian fruit beers. It's amazing what you can find out if people will let you, and Mark Constantine will let you.

Mark's recently been to the Old Market Arts Centre in Hove and the Komedia and had lunch at the Red Roaster Coffee House. I made a note of this. I thought I might go into Brighton at the weekend. I don't really know what to do with myself at weekends any more. So I thought I might do a bit of shopping and have lunch somewhere; try to be normal. I might try the Red Roaster. It's good to have a recommendation.

A lot of Mark's friends are women. I wondered if Holly knows or minds, and then I wondered if Mark knew how much time she seems to spend with this Daniel and why.

They were already in the pub when I arrived, looking quite cosy, so I asked them, when we'd all got a drink, 'Are you both married?'

I wanted to know the answer but also to remind them that, if they are, they already have someone. They don't need each other. They don't.

He looks nice, Holly's husband, Mark Constantine. She's lucky to have him and I don't want her to lose sight of that. I think that if we become friends then I must make sure I remind her of the importance of appreciating the person you are with, making sure they know how you feel about them, before it's too late.

Holly answered 'yes', but she said it in a way that made her sound as if she wasn't quite sure.

So I asked her how long and she said 'sixteen years', and I thought that was a long time, the sort of time after which you start taking things for granted.

So I decided to tell her, to warn her, how things looked from the outside.

'I thought when I saw you both at the meeting that you might be married to each other. And when I saw you sitting on the train.'

Holly said something about her being too old. But they both looked awkward, as if maybe they had something to hide.

Then she asked me about Geoff and there was something steely about her tone, as if she was deflecting attention from herself rather than asking me because she actually wanted to know how long we'd been together.

I thought back briefly to when I'd first met Geoff, the day my mother died.

My father had already been dead a couple of years and the realisation that I was now on my own in the world hadn't quite dawned. So it was with almost perfect timing that Geoff walked into my life within hours of my mother leaving it.

I'd been carrying on in a surprisingly normal way. I'd left the hospice, after sitting with Mum, holding her hand and listening to her struggling to breathe, until she stopped struggling and her hand began to go cold. And then I'd gone home, knowing that the next few weeks would be a round of sorting and organising, and that busying myself with funeral arrangements and sorting my parents' house would delay the grief for a while.

I hadn't counted on the kindness of strangers.

I'd stopped off at the supermarket on my way home. I'd spent so much time at the hospice that I hardly had any food left. As I was walking out of the revolving doors with several bags on each arm, someone tapped me on the shoulder and I turned round and there was Geoff.

I didn't hear what he'd said at first but when I did it all came out. I burst into tears and, within minutes, they were huge, vast, heaving sobs.

'Do you want my Nectar points?' was what he'd said. 'I don't collect them. Do you want mine?'

He had a soft lilting accent, which I couldn't quite place, and he looked at me expectantly as if he wanted me to have them. And that was what got me going.

'Thank you.' I tried to choke back the tears but I couldn't, and the man who was simply offering me unwanted Nectar points found himself dealing with a woman on the edge.

Geoff didn't seem to find this odd at all.

'Here, let me take your bags,' he said, and he slung them on top of his trolley. 'Then we'll find somewhere to sit down.'

He found a low wall outside the store. We sat on it and he asked my name and what was bothering me.

'Well, Anne-Marie,' he said, after we'd chatted for a while, 'it sounds as if you've had a hell of a few weeks and I would drive you home, but I don't want you getting in a car with a strange man. So I'm going to call you a taxi instead and I'll pay for it. My treat. And I'm going to give you my number. And when you get home, I want you to put this fish pie for one . . .'

He held up the pie, which he'd found in one of my bags.

'I want you to put this in the oven, pour yourself a large glass of wine and text me to let me know how you are.'

He'd fished in his pocket and gave me a card with his name and numbers on.

'And if you think that I might be able to cheer you up, rather than reducing you to tears, you could call me some time and we'll go out for a coffee or something.'

It was an inauspicious start to our relationship, but it was the start.

'Three years,' I told Holly, when she asked how long we'd been married. 'I thought we'd be together for ever,' I told her, and tried to stress the 'ever' to make her understand.

26

The prospect of a new client had put Mark in an exceedingly good mood. There was an energy to the way he was darting about the kitchen which had been lacking in recent months.

'How was your day?' he greeted Holly animatedly, unable to wait for her to settle back into home before sharing his potential good news. 'I might have a new client!'

'Really?' Holly could see from the zestful way he was taking the cork out of a new bottle of wine that he was excited by whoever it was. 'Who?'

'Jimmy Finlay?' He poured wine into the two glasses he had ready and waiting.

'What? The comedian?' Representing a comic would be a new direction for Mark and Jimmy Finlay was extremely popular. 'I love him. He's brilliant. What's he doing? How do you fit in?'

'I know.' They'd both been watching him on . . . *I Nearly Died* only a few days beforehand with Jake, and had found him very funny. 'Apparently he's going to run from Inverness, around the entire coast of Scotland, to raise awareness of heart disease. He wants a big PR campaign, to make sure everyone knows he's doing it.'

'Really?' Holly wondered if she'd got the names muddled up and was thinking of the wrong man. The Jimmy Finlay she was thinking of was a young Scottish comic who didn't look as if he'd be able to run for a bus, let along the entire circumference of Scotland.

'I know what you're thinking.' Mark picked up a glass and handed it to her. 'Cheers!'

'That I've got the wrong Jimmy Finlay?' Holly asked.

'I thought you'd be thinking that Jimmy Finlay is too fat to run anywhere!' he laughed. 'I mean the Jimmy Finlay we were watching on TV the other night.'

'The one that must be at least twenty stone and incredibly unfit,' Holly pointed out.

'The very same.' Mark still seemed excited by the prospect.

Holly feared it might never happen. If Jimmy Finlay ran anywhere in his current state, she thought he would probably have a heart attack ... *I Nearly Died* might suddenly take on a terrible irony. She didn't say this because she didn't want to hear Mark's irony joke.

'And why does he want to run round Scotland?' Holly didn't want to spoil Mark's moment but she couldn't help sounding a note of caution. 'Or think he will be able to?'

'Ah, well, that's the thing,' Mark said, using that peculiar English explain-all phrase.

He moved over to the work surface where he'd begun preparing dinner.

'Steak,' he said, indicating four slabs of meat marinating in something herby-looking.

'Lovely.' Holly still wanted to hear more about Jimmy Finlay.

'Apparently his father died recently of a heart

attack.' Mark took a steak out and began hammering it with the tool designed for the purpose. 'He was only forty-five.'

'That's terrible!' Holly was genuinely shocked, both by the fact that Jimmy Finlay's father had died at such a young age and that Jimmy Finlay had a father who only a few months ago had been the same age as Mark.

'Awful,' he agreed. 'But it's given Jimmy a bit of a wake-up call and he's decided to get fit and do something to highlight the high rate of heart disease in Scotland. He's not planning to start the run until next year so he'll have time to get in shape.'

'As long as he doesn't have a heart attack too.' Holly could suddenly see a carefully orchestrated PR campaign going horribly wrong.

'Well, we'll just have to make sure he doesn't.' Mark had finished bashing steaks and was transferring them to the grill.

'So how might you come to be involved?' Holly brought the conversation back to its starting point.

'Well, that's the thing,' Mark said again, as if this alone explained something. 'He's started going to this gym in London, to try to get fit, and someone Daisy knows works there. He told her about it and Daisy told her that I was in marketing and . . . '

'So have you actually been in touch with him directly?' Holly was slightly confused by all the 'he said, she said' and she was worried that Mark was placing too much hope on a chat that someone else had had in a gym. She imagined someone like Jimmy Finlay already had someone to handle his PR and Mark might simply be clutching at straws.

'Yes,' he said emphatically. 'Daisy got his email address and I emailed him and said I'd be interested in pitching for the campaign, and he emailed back and said he'd looked at my website and knew that I was training for a marathon too, so that was a plus, and he hasn't got anyone else in mind and wants to meet me.'

'That's great.' Holly was pleased that Mark was at least getting to meet Jimmy Finlay and had been so pro-active. He generally made a good impression face to face and Jimmy Finlay would be a good client. If Mark got him, more work was bound to stem from it.

'When are you meeting? Have you set a date?'

'Next Wednesday.' Mark picked up his glass of wine and clinked Holly's. 'Cheers!'

'Cheers,' she said, looking at him. He seemed different in a way she couldn't quite put her finger on. Perhaps it was just that he seemed happy.

Holly knew that Mark had been worried about his lack of work, but she hadn't quite realised the extent of it on him personally.

Now that there was the prospect of something which might excite and stimulate him on the horizon, she could see the old Mark again, the will-do, energised, man of action that she'd first met. She smiled at her own mental description of him.

'What?' Mark was looking at her too.

'What do you mean, what?'

'What are you smiling at?' he asked.

'I am allowed to smile at you if I want to,' Holly said, and smiled again, an over-the-top wide grin.

She expected Mark to return the expression with an equally stupid face, but he put his glass down and walked over to her and kissed her. Holly closed her eyes, savouring the taste of her husband's lips. She realised she hadn't kissed him for ages.

It was nice. But it didn't last long. They were interrupted by the ear-piercing beep of the smoke alarm, in response to the charred steaks which Mark had forgotten were under the grill.

'Bugger!' He pulled away from Holly and took them out.

'Language!' Jake, who had been lying on the sofa, staring at the ceiling in the living room, had been roused from his state of torpor. 'What's for dinner?'

'Steak.' Mark inspected them. 'Well done.'

'Is it ready?' Jake eyed his father suspiciously.

'It was ready about five minutes ago,' Mark replied. 'Can you go and get Chloe? I think she's in her room.'

★   ★   ★

'That was a lovely evening,' Holly said to Mark later as he got into bed.

'Right down to the burned steaks!' He switched off the bedside light.

'I like them well done.' Holly moved towards his side of the bed as he got in. 'It was a pity

Chloe missed dinner.'

'She is spending a lot of time with Ruaridh at the moment.' Mark put his arm tentatively around Holly. 'But he's a nice lad.'

'Yes, I just wish she'd spend a bit more time at home.' Holly wondered how the evening was going to end.

She was tired. They had watched television waiting for Chloe, who had been to the cinema with Ruaridh, to come home. But Mark's upbeat mood had infected Holly too and she'd enjoyed just being with him, without the children. Now he was slipping his hand under the vest she wore to bed.

'We could all benefit from spending a bit more time together,' he said, running his hand across her stomach and pausing as if expecting Holly to push him away or turn over.

'Yes.' She reached out and began to caress her husband, thinking that perhaps they should try and go away for a weekend.

'Daniel said he and Daisy are going to Southwold for a couple of days.' He had mentioned this in passing at some point during the week and Holly wondered if Daisy had also told Mark.

She intended this statement to be a precursor to suggesting they should get away themselves

It had the opposite effect.

'Bloody hell!' Mark sounded angry. He rolled away from her.

'What?' Holly had no idea what had provoked this sudden mood swing.

'I thought we might be going to have sex for

the first time in God knows how long,' he said. 'And then you have to go and mention Daniel.'

'I was just going to suggest that we should go away too.' Holly kept her tone neutral. She didn't think she had anything to apologise for.

'What, with Daniel and Daisy?' Mark's tone was now sarcastic.

'No, of course not,' Holly tried not to rise to the bait.

'Because from where I am standing,' Mark said as he began to get out of bed, 'it seems Daniel can do no wrong and I can do no right.'

Holly said nothing.

She began to formulate a defence in her head. Daniel was a good friend to her, and Mark's insecurities about work had nothing to do with him. She was working all hours and doing everything she could to keep the family afloat. That was why they hadn't had sex in a long time.

Plus, she thought, as she looked at Mark taking his dressing gown from the back of their bedroom door, he had spent much of their evening saying how fantastic Daisy was; how he'd never have got the introduction to Jimmy Finlay without her; how brilliant his personal training sessions with her had been; and how, if the job came off, he might try to get her involved in the campaign.

Holly was about to point this out when he opened the bedroom door.

'I'm going to get a drink,' he said, and left the room.

27

Holly hadn't known what time Mark had come back to bed on Friday night and, when she woke the following morning, the bed beside her was empty, though warm from having been slept in. The radio alarm said it was 8.30 and she wondered if he'd got up to go running.

She was no longer tired, or particularly worried by the altercation they'd had the night before. Looked at with fresh morning eyes, it had been a slight and stupid row. She was glad they had not made it worse by saying more when they were both tired.

She acknowledged to herself now that mentioning Daniel just as they were about to have sex had probably not been a good idea.

Holly got up, took a bathrobe off the back of the bedroom door and went downstairs. Mark was not in the kitchen and his running shoes were not in the hall. She made herself a cup of tea, and set a pot of coffee ready for him when he came back from wherever he was, and switched on the radio. The news was just finishing and a continuity announcer was giving details of the rest of the morning's programmes on BBC Radio 4.

'And on *Excess Baggage* this week,' Holly heard her saying, 'we will be talking about staying in touch on your travels. The humble postcard is a relic of the twentieth century. These days the traveller blogs, emails, Facebooks and texts. Reporter and presenter James Darling, travel writer Mark Johnson, and founder of lastminute.com Martha Lane-Fox, will be joining John McCarthy at nine-thirty . . . '

Holly scooped ground coffee into a cafetière and wondered why Darling was on the programme. It wasn't a likely subject for him to be discussing.

'Hi, Mum,' Chloe interrupted her thoughts.

'Hello,' Holly said, looking at her daughter. Chloe had dark circles under her eyes. 'You must be tired.'

'I'm OK.' Chloe slumped down at the table, her posture suggesting this was not entirely true. 'Are you making coffee?'

'Yes, I was getting a pot ready for when Dad gets back. I think he's gone out running.' Holly took a couple of cups from the cupboard.

'Why is Dad always running?' Jake slunk into the room. 'It's like all he ever does.'

'He needs to train if he's going to run the marathon,' Holly explained, wondering if he'd keep it up if he got the job with Jimmy Finlay.

'He must be tired,' Chloe volunteered. 'I came down to get a drink at three and he was still watching telly.'

'What was he watching?' Jake asked, his interest in the general goings on triggered by the mention of television.

'Well, he wasn't really watching anything,' Chloe told them. 'He'd fallen asleep on the sofa and the TV was still on. I woke him up and told him to go back to bed.'

263

Holly put the cafetière on the table and placed mugs next to it as Chloe continued to talk.

'He had his pyjamas on so he must have decided to watch the news after getting ready for bed. He always does that.'

'Often, yes.' Holly was grateful for her daughter's interpretation of events.

She opened the bread bin and took out some croissants that she'd bought on her way home from the station the previous evening.

'I thought I might go into town later. Does either of you fancy coming?' Holly knew this was a long shot. 'Or joining me for lunch somewhere?'

'Where are you going for lunch?' Chloe's interest appeared to have been stirred.

'The Red Roaster probably,' Holly answered. 'I'm cooking tonight so I'll probably just have a sandwich or something.'

'Oh, right.' Chloe looked relieved and Holly wasn't sure why. 'I'm going to meet Emma in town later so I'll probably get something with her. I don't know why you always go there, Mum. You don't even drink coffee.'

'I like it there,' Holly said.

'I think I'll stay here today.' Jake looked up. 'I've got stuff to do.'

The front door rattled and slammed. Mark panted in, sweat running down his face and his chest still heaving.

'Ten miles this morning,' he gasped, throwing himself down on the easy chair at the side of the kitchen. 'I'm knackered.'

Holly looked at him and tried to suppress an

instinct to recoil as he stretched his sweaty legs across the kitchen floor. At this moment she couldn't quite imagine how she had even entertained the thought of having sex with him the night before. If that was the state Mark was usually in when Daisy spent time with him, there was no chance of her finding him a turn on.

'Do you want something to drink?' she asked, forgetting that the last communication they had had was when he'd stormed out of the bedroom.

'I think I'll take a shower.' Mark ignored her question and began getting up. 'What's everyone up to today?'

No one in the room volunteered anything so Holly answered for them.

'Chloe is off out with Emma, Jake's planning on an exciting day staying in, and I am going into town and thought I might have lunch out. Do you fancy joining me?' She hoped he would say yes and they could wipe clean the slate from the night before.

'I don't think so,' Mark said, but he did smile as he said it, so it wasn't a complete brush off. 'I've got this meeting with Jimmy Finlay on Wednesday and I want to put together a bit of a presentation. I think I'll work on that today.'

'I'll just have lunch on my own then.' Holly found she was saying it to herself as Mark was already leaping upstairs on his way to the shower and Chloe and Jake were edging towards the kitchen door.

Left on her own, she wiped croissant crumbs from the table and put coffee cups in the dishwasher then took her phone from her handbag.

There was a new message in her inbox.

Hi, Holly, it read. *Really good meeting you properly the other day. I might be in Brighton over the weekend and wondered if you fancied meeting again for a coffee or something. Hope you are OK? Anne-Marie.*

Holly was not sure what to reply so she ignored it and instead pressed the Create Message option.

Beautiful day ☺ *What does yours hold? A few chores in town for me. Don't suppose you fancy a quick coffee?*

She pressed the Send button and sent the message to Daniel.

★ ★ ★

Holly looked around for a table, feeling unnerved by having walked straight into Anne-Marie, who'd been leaving the Red Roaster.

'Hi, Holly,' she'd said, as if she had fully expected to see her there.

'Hi.' Holly tried to sound enthusiastic but didn't want to encourage her to stay. 'This isn't your neck of the woods.'

'No,' Anne-Marie replied. 'But I've been doing a bit of shopping and decided to have lunch here. It's a nice café.'

'Yes.' Holly nodded, wondering if she was going to have to ask her to stay for a coffee. 'Look. I'm sorry I did not reply to your text. I

266

had my phone off. I was going to reply, when I sat down.'

'Do you come here a lot?' Anne-Marie asked.

'Sometimes, at the weekends. Mark's office is around the corner and he sometimes comes here if he needs to pop in at the weekend.'

'Oh.' Anne-Marie seemed unsure what to say. 'What does Mark do?'

'He works in marketing,' Holly said, looking over her shoulder to see if she could spot a free table.

If there was one she supposed she should ask Anne-Marie to join her for coffee but the café was busy and none seemed to be free.

'Are you meeting him now?' Anne-Marie asked.

'Possibly.' Holly did not want to tell her she was meeting Daniel. 'It looks busy, though. I might just call him first.'

She took her phone from her bag, which Anne-Marie took as a cue to leave.

'Well, nice to see you, Holly,' she said. 'Maybe see you in the week?'

'Yes, that would be nice.' Holly smiled as Anne-Marie set off towards the Pavilion and scanned the café again for somewhere to sit. 'I'll be in touch.'

'I'm just leaving,' a woman sitting at the table Holly was hovering by with her tray of tea said to her, and began gathering up her stuff.

'Oh, thank you.' Holly smiled at her and put her tray down on the table.

'There you go, darling,' the woman said, picking up a scarf from the back of a chair and winding it around her neck.

Only then did Holly realise that this wasn't a woman at all but the man Mark referred to as the most convincing transvestite in town.

Holly had been meeting Mark for a coffee in town a few years ago and when she'd arrived had found him chatting to a tall blonde.

Quick work, she had thought to herself, since she wasn't more than a few minutes late, hardly long enough for him to have picked up another woman.

'Oh, here she is now,' Mark said to the blonde as Holly approached the table they were both sitting at.

'Nice to meet you, Mark,' the blonde had said, getting up to make way for her.

'Interesting woman,' Mark said to Holly as she sat down, stressing the interesting, as if to underline the fact he'd only been talking to her because of that, not because she was tall and blonde.

'Very interesting, I'm sure,' Holly had said, looking at the departing figure of Mark's erstwhile companion. 'But no woman.'

'What do you mean?' Mark asked.

'A transvestite,' Holly said. 'I've seen him doing cabaret at the Komedia. I think he's called Michael something or other.'

'Are you sure?' Mark had asked. 'If you're right, he's the most convincing transvestite in town!'

They'd seen him a few times since and Mark had gradually become convinced. Strange, Holly thought now, that he was once again giving up his seat in a café for her, albeit this time it was Daniel and not Mark she was meeting.

'Sorry I'm late.' Daniel had arrived now, slightly out of breath, from walking fast. 'Can I get you anything?'

'I've already got tea.' Holly indicated the tray.

'Won't be a minute.' He went to get himself a coffee before sitting in the seat recently vacated by Michael.

'It's nice to see you.' Holly was about to make some remark about meeting on a Saturday. Most of their meetings before had been somehow linked to journeys to and from work. They were treading new ground now and Holly felt it needed alluding to.

'It's good to get out of the house,' he said, sitting down. 'Things haven't been very easy at home.'

'I'm sorry.' Holly gave what she hoped was the right response. There was a slight pause. She didn't feel she could ask him any more and Daniel seemed to be considering whether to continue.

'You know I said we were trying to have a baby?' He looked up as he stirred his coffee.

'Yes.' Holly maintained eye contact but took another sip of her tea. 'You said you were having some tests . . .'

'We got the results.' Daniel picked up a sugar packet and started fiddling with it absent-mindedly. 'And there doesn't seem to be any reason why Daisy is not getting pregnant.'

'That's good.' Holly watched his hands as he twisted the paper.

'That's what I thought, initially,' Daniel told her. 'But the doctor said something about some people being incompatible. He said we are both perfectly capable of conceiving children, but unable to conceive them with each other.'

'Can't they help?' Holly thought this was when IVF was most successful.

'Possibly.' Daniel put the packet down. 'In the end. He told us to give it a while a longer but . . . '

He stopped talking and took a sip of his coffee.

Holly thought he'd probably decided against finishing the sentence he'd begun, but she was wrong.

'There's nothing like a doctor telling you you might be incompatible to put a strain on a relationship.'

'What will you do?' Holly asked, noticing that the usual playful smile around the edges of Daniel's mouth had disappeared and the sparkle in his eyes had given way to something that looked more like tears.

'I don't know, Holly,' he said. 'I'm not sure what to do.'

28

'Isn't it a bit late to go running?' Holly opened the door of the house, expecting everyone to be settling in for the evening, but found Mark in shorts and running shoes doing calf stretches in the hallway.

The running was starting to make him look well, she thought, as she watched him straighten up. From a distance you might think he was in his early thirties, rather than his late forties. He was still a good-looking man. His recent loss of energy and vigour had made him appear to lose some of his sparkle, but today, she thought, he looked almost the same as he had when she'd first met him.

'I like running at this time of night, when the days are long,' he said, stretching his other leg but looking up, as Holly closed the front door. 'And I've arranged to run with Daisy. Plus I'm a bit hyped up and need to work off some excess energy.'

'Why's that?' Holly asked, wondering to herself why he had arranged to run with Daisy at a time when he knew she would be home from work and everyone would want dinner. She knew, too, that she was being unreasonable.

'I had the meeting with Jimmy Finlay today,' he said, as if she might have forgotten.

'I know,' Holly retorted. 'I did leave a message, asking how it went, and I texted.'

'Did you?' Mark sounded surprised. 'What time was that?'

'Early afternoon.' Holly was sure he must have got one of her messages. 'Anyway, how did it go?'

'Really well, actually.' Mark stood up now and grinned. 'He was very funny, very easy company, and we got on well. He wants me to do it!'

'That's fantastic, Mark. Well done!' Holly put her bag down and reached up to kiss him. 'We should celebrate.'

'Thank you,' he said, looking pleased. 'We will, when I get back. I haven't told Daisy yet, and if it wasn't for her there would be no job with Jimmy Finlay. I'd better go.'

He looked at his watch, anxious to get out of the house.

'OK, see you later,' Holly said, feeling that the celebratory moment had been lost.

She closed the door behind him and wondered why, instead of feeling pleased that Mark had some decent work, she felt a bit pissed off and a little suspicious. She hadn't asked him where he was planning to run but wondered if it was along the seafront. It was a lovely evening and the summer sun was low now. The promenade would be busy with people strolling, rollerblading, skateboarding. Other runners, too. She felt suddenly jealous of Mark running with Daisy.

She remembered the one and only time she had been running with her husband, which must have been about twenty years ago. Holly didn't like running, never had. She preferred walking and swimming and used to do yoga, though no longer had the time or, if she was honest, the inclination. She could, she thought wistfully, do with a rather more toned body than the one she currently had.

Mark hadn't attempted marathons in his twenties but he did like to clock up a regular three or four miles before or after work, claiming it enabled him to eat well without putting on weight and stopped him getting tired after sitting at a desk all day.

'You should try it,' he'd said one evening when Holly had come home from work and flopped on the sofa, exhausted from having been in the office all day. 'It'll make you feel much better.'

She had allowed herself to be persuaded.

'We'll have to go very slowly.' She'd smiled at Mark as she laced up a pair of trainers, which she had no business to own. They were a relic from a time when she had thought about going to the gym, but had never got further than the sports store.

That had a been a beautiful evening too, late summer, the sun was setting and Holly had thought, as they ran along the seafront in the direction of the Marina, that her life was just about perfect. She lived in a beautiful town, with a man who seemed to think *she* was just about perfect, and she had a job that she loved. She also started to find she was enjoying the sensation of running, albeit slowing along the front, thinking her thoughts and taking in her surroundings. But that feeling had been temporary. Her legs had started to hurt and her breathing became more laboured and she'd felt hot and disinclined to run much further. So she had turned off the promenade and run down the shingle and flopped on to the pebbles by the shore. Mark had followed, mocking her for being a lightweight, and lain down beside her.

'You were doing well, for a beginner,' he'd teased her.

'I definitely prefer swimming,' Holly had said, propping herself up on her elbows and looking at the sea.

Then she'd surprised herself and Mark. This part of the beach was empty. It was out of town. It was now almost dusk and there was a slight chill in the air. She looked around then stood up and took off her trainers, t-shirt and tracksuit bottoms. She thought about diving into the sea in her bra and knickers, then threw caution and them to the wind and ran in naked. Mark laughed and stood up slowly, watching her swim out to sea. Then he slowly took off his t-shirt and shorts and underwear and joined her in the water, which had felt warmer than either of them anticipated.

*   *   *

'What are you thinking about?' Jake said now, sitting at the kitchen table with the computer, looking at Holly as she stood in the doorway, reminiscing. 'Are you OK, Mum?'

'Nothing.' Holly shook her head to remove the mental image she'd captured. In its place came another of Mark running along the seafront, with Daisy easily keeping pace with him, talking and laughing. She wondered if she would tell him what Daniel had told her on Sunday.

'I didn't see you there, Jakey. What are you up to?' She tried to focus her attention now on her son who had a plate of cheese and crackers on the table beside the computer and was shoving a Ritz with a large slab of Cheddar on it into his mouth.

'You are a *fresser*!' Mark had said to him earlier in the week, coming up with another word pilfered from another language. 'It's Yiddish for someone who eats too quickly.'

'Just talking to Ed on Facebook,' Jake muttered to Holly, through the mouthful. 'There's a message from Gran too. She's in Koh Samui. She says it's cool.'

'Did she actually use the word cool?' Holly couldn't keep up.

'Well, she probably said beautiful or something,' Jake conceded. 'Ed's got a ukulele.'

'We haven't seen him round here for a while,' Holly said, picking up a bit of cheese that had fallen on to the table and putting it in her mouth.

'No, I've been busy,' Jake said, as if it were true. He looked back at the computer screen and began tapping away again.

Holly decided to text Daniel, partly because she now knew Daisy would not be at home when he got there.

She hadn't been in touch since having coffee with him on Saturday.

Haven't seen you last few days. Hope you're OK. Hx

'Who are you texting?' Jake looked up.

'No one.' Holly hoped the answer would satisfy him but they were both distracted by the sound of a key turning in the door.

Chloe came in.

'Hello, love,' Holly called out. 'Where have you been?'

'Hi, Mum,' Chloe said coming into the kitchen. 'I've been round at Ruaridh's. Is Dad back?'

'Back, but gone out again,' Holly told both children. 'He's gone for a run. He needed to work off some excess energy.'

She thought she'd give Chloe and Jake the same reason he'd given her.

'Oh, he had that meeting today, didn't he?' Chloe remembered. 'How did it go?'

'I haven't had time to talk to him properly but really well apparently,' Holly told her. 'He seems to have got the job.'

'Fantastic. That's really good.' Chloe seemed relieved.

'Will he get lots of money?' Jake showed signs of interest.

'I don't know.' Holly didn't. 'It's a charity run, so I don't imagine there will be much money involved. But it should be good for his company. He'll probably get other work off the back of it.'

'That's good,' Chloe said again.

Holly wondered if she thought this might mean she could go on the school trip. She hadn't mentioned it again and Holly didn't know if she'd accepted that it was unlikely she could go or whether she still harboured hopes that she would.

'Have you eaten anything?' she asked Chloe, wondering what to cook.

Jake appeared to have eaten half a pound of cheese but that never dented his appetite, and Mark would no doubt be hungry when he came back from running.

'Not really.' Chloe's answer was ambiguous and Holly noticed that she smelled slightly of fried food. Perhaps she and Ruaridh had been to the chippy.

'Yuk!' Chloe had picked up another piece of cheese that Jake had dropped on to the table and put it in her mouth. 'What is that?' she exclaimed.

'D'oh. Cheese,' Jake told her. 'What's wrong with it?'

'Oh, in that case, nothing.' Chloe smiled and appeared to savour the food in her mouth. 'I thought it was a bit of shortbread when I picked it up, and it tasted all wrong.'

'There ought to be a word for that,' Jake commented. 'Is there, Mum?'

'Is there what?' Holly's phone had just bleeped and she was opening a message from Daniel.

'A word for when you eat something that turns out to be something else,' he said.

'I can't think of it, if there is,' Holly told him. 'It's the sort of thing Dad might know, though. Ask him when he gets back.'

She looked at the text again.

I'm OK. Felt better for talking to you at weekend. Always do.x

Holly smiled to herself and put the phone down.

She wondered if there was a word for the feeling she felt whenever she had contact with Daniel. She couldn't put it into words but she felt reassured, calmer, and less afraid of the world and all its uncertainties.

The way she used to feel when she first met Mark.

29

'It's a way of perceiving things as colours.' Holly was telling Daniel about the programme she had produced that day.

There'd been a discussion about synesthesia, which had prompted a lot of calls from listeners.

'A lot of synesthetes see numbers as colours or emotions.'

'Like a blue mood?' said Daniel. 'Or being green with envy?'

'Yes,' Holly replied. 'Or just going through a yellow phase, which is what one of the guests on the programme said she was going through.'

'What's that then?' He had spotted her through the window of the train and had joined her where she was sitting.

'I couldn't say exactly.' Holly found the subject fascinating, but couldn't quite comprehend the various aspects of it. 'She just said her life had been very yellow lately.'

'I saw Anne-Marie further back,' Daniel said. 'I nearly joined her but I hoped I might find you so I moved further down the train. What colour would you say she is?'

'I don't know.' Holly considered his question. 'Purple maybe?'

'Why do you say that?' He looked at her keenly.

'Because she seems bruised,' Holly said, feeling this was an accurate summary of how she found Anne-Marie.

'A new report claims as many as one in ten people have some form of the condition,' she continued. 'It causes people to perceive certain sensations in another form; like seeing numbers as colours or dates as specific places, or hearing a visual motion — like a flicker.'

'I suppose we all have a certain amount of that,' Daniel observed. 'Like being able to see if someone is unhappy. You'd think you can't, but sometimes you can.'

Holly looked at him, wondering if he was alluding to her or himself.

'The woman going through the yellow phase,' she carried on, 'said her children were green and brown and her husband was grey.'

Holly didn't say to Daniel what she had said earlier to Natalie: that she thought a lot of middle-aged women might describe their husbands that way.

'Your job sounds really interesting,' he said, considering it further. 'It must be so different every day.'

'It is.' Holly knew her job was better than most but could still moan about it at the drop of a hat. 'Although sometimes you feel as if you're just setting up interviews with the same people. They are different, but it can start feeling all a bit samey.'

'I imagine you're very good at it,' he said encouragingly.

'I'm OK.' Holly shrugged. 'Not bad enough to get rid of anyway.'

'No, I bet you *are* good at it,' he emphasised. 'You've got a very warm way with you. I imagine you can bring out the best in the people you have on the programme.'

'That's really down to the presenter,' she said, though she felt uplifted by his comment. 'But thank you.'

Daniel flipped the lid off the cup of coffee he'd brought on to the train and took a sip.

He frowned slightly then looked up at her.

'This coffee's not quite right.' He held the cup towards her for inspection. 'It tastes a bit . . . green!'

Holly looked at the drink, which looked perfectly normal to her, and realised, a beat too late, that Daniel was joking.

She laughed and shoved him slightly.

'I don't know,' she said. 'It looks pretty black to me.'

As she said this, she sensed a presence to her right, which anyone who was not a synesthete would have described as pinstripe.

She turned to find Carl, her friend Hannah's husband, in the aisle beside them.

'Hi, Holly,' he said. 'I thought that was you.'

'Hello,' she said. 'How are you?'

'Good, good.' He paused. 'How are you?'

Carl had readjusted his face slightly to show concern and spoke more quietly than he had at first.

'Fine,' Holly said, knowing what had brought about the change. It still happened a lot, this gradual dawning on people that she had been involved in the crash and therefore had to be treated differently.

'I'm fine,' she said again, to emphasise that she was really OK.

There were no spare seats, and Holly thought Carl would want to keep the conversation brief and find somewhere else to sit. But he didn't move and was looking at Daniel, as if expecting an introduction.

'This is Daniel,' she obliged. 'And this is Carl. You look very smart today,' she said, turning to Daniel and adding, 'Carl usually works from home and wears jeans and a t-shirt.'

'A client meeting,' he explained. He was an architect and, while most of his work was done from the loft of the family home, every now and then had to leave it and go out into the big wide world. 'Chance to take the suit for an outing!'

'I hope it enjoyed it?' Holly joked.

'It had a productive day,' Carl replied. 'But now it wants to find a seat. Nice to see you, Holly.'

'You too.' She half-rose as he half-bent to kiss her. 'Send my love to Hannah. We keep trying to go to the cinema together but never seem to make it.'

'I will tell her that rather nice dress you are wearing wants to see the latest Quentin Tarantino.' Carl smiled. 'We'd both like to see you properly. You and Mark should come for dinner. Nice to meet you.' He nodded in Daniel's direction.

'You too,' Daniel muttered and, when he was out of earshot, 'Who was that?'

'My friend Hannah's husband,' Holly told him. 'And also Chloe's friend Emma's dad. We met when the girls were at junior school together.'

'He's very silver!' Daniel seemed to have warmed to the synesthesia theme.

'By which do you mean very good looking?' Holly asked.

Carl was one of the best-looking men she knew.

'Oh, you think he's good looking, do you?' Daniel raised an eyebrow.

'Well, he is, by any standards,' she said. 'But he is my friend's husband so no need to raise your eyebrows.'

'You can still fancy him.' Daniel appeared to be teasing her in a way he had never done before.

Holly wondered if he was flirting. To date, he'd been affectionate and tactile but never flirtatious. She'd tried to imagine how she might appear through his eyes and could only think that she seemed old and staid, especially compared to his beautiful wife.

'The funny thing is, I actually don't. He is very nice, and what you might call devastatingly good looking, but he's very . . . ' Holly paused, trying to put her finger on what it was that stopped her from fancying Carl. 'Smooth. There's no edge to him, I suppose.'

She'd stopped short of saying he was safe, knowing how much she'd resented being described that way by Dimitri.

'Plus, of course,' she added, 'because he is my friend's husband, I know all about all his bad points and annoying habits.'

'God, do women always tell each other everything?' Daniel grimaced.

'Pretty much.' Holly lowered her voice. 'You see, I know Carl snores terribly and always hangs one leg out of the bed when he's asleep. Hannah says it trips her up every time she has to get up in the night.'

'That doesn't sound too off-putting,' Daniel said. 'I thought you meant things that were a little more intimate.'

'Oh, I know those too.' Holly smiled. 'But I couldn't tell you them. Plus all the usual moans about never doing the washing up, not knowing the children's names, barely tolerating the mother-in-law — though that's pretty standard stuff.'

'So do women tell each other this stuff to warn their friends off their husbands then?' Daniel asked. 'Is gossiping just a slightly more friendly way of saying, ''Hands off, he's mine!'?'

'I hadn't thought of it like that before.' She considered Daniel's remark. 'It's an interesting theory. You should be doing my job. It's the sort of thing we might discuss on *Antennae*.'

She could imagine this. They'd find a social anthropologist, who would tell them how cavewomen used to tell their friend that their husbands grunted like mammoths during sex and were equally hairy too. This, the required expert would explain, was not because they wanted to bond with their fellow gatherers, but rather to put them off trying to lure someone else's mammoth-hunter into their cave.

'So am I right?' Daniel looked at her quizzically. 'Is bitching about your partner behind their back a way of warning others off?'

'Possibly, but it might just be a way of letting off steam,' Holly said in response to his hypothesis. 'Men can be very difficult to live with.'

'So I am told,' he sighed, a slightly weary sound that suggested someone close to him had let it be known he was difficult to live with.

Holly couldn't imagine that he was. She found him considerate and quietly funny. She could now see why the beautiful Daisy had been attracted to him over all the other Alpha-males who had pursued her.

'I . . . ' Holly began to speak at the same time as Daniel also said, 'I . . . '

'You first,' she laughed.

'No, you go on,' he countered.

'I was going to say, I suppose no one is that easy to live with all of the time.' Especially not after sixteen years of marriage, Holly thought to herself. 'What were you going to say?'

'I was going to say that I'm glad you don't spend any time with Daisy,' Daniel said. 'I hate to think what she would tell you about me.'

Holly said nothing although she too was glad Daisy was not among her circle of friends. She didn't want to hear his wife's version of what Daniel was like at home because, at the moment, Holly's loyalties were with him.

'Tickets, please!' The guard was making his way down the carriage.

Holly took out her ticket and wondered, not for the first time, what Daisy and Mark told each other about her and Daniel when they were out running together.

30

'I'll see you there then, shall I?' Natalie unhooked her coat from the back of the door.

'Yes, I won't be long.' Holly glanced up briefly from her computer screen, but carried on typing an email. 'I said I'd let this guest know who else was appearing with him on the programme and give him an idea of the questions. You go ahead.'

'OK.' Natalie smiled. 'I told Guy we'd be there from six, and if he arrives and I'm not there yet, he may not stick around.'

'Of course,' Holly answered.

Natalie had told her earlier that Guy's parents were staying for the weekend and had offered to baby-sit, so that they could go out together.

Holly wasn't sure if they realised that going out together constituted Guy coming along to the pub with Natalie and her colleagues, who were celebrating a minor professional success.

Antennae had won a Sony award. Holly had overheard Dimitri telling his mother it was the radio equivalent of an Oscar, on a long-distance call to Athens. The award was for Best Radio Feature, for a piece they had done about kidney donors, broadcast during National Organ Donation Week.

James Darling had interviewed a mother who had donated a kidney to her daughter, then developed a serious infection in her remaining good organ and needed a donor herself. He'd also spoken to a newly married man who had previously had a kidney transplant where the donor had been his brother. This organ had just failed and his new wife wanted to donate hers.

Darling had been praised by the Sony judges for his sensitive and compassionate treatment of the guests while at the same time managing to ask probing and thoughtful questions. The piece had prompted a debate about the ethics of organ donation, which had been picked up by other media and had run for several days.

'We all deserve a celebration,' Katherine announced after she and James returned from the awards ceremony. 'I'll put some money behind the bar of The Adam and Eve next Friday evening. Partners are invited too.'

'Is your husband coming?' Rebecca asked when Holly joined her and Dimitri, who were waiting by the lift.

'No.' she shook her head. 'He'd have to come up from Brighton specially.'

Holly didn't tell them that she hadn't even asked Mark. She didn't think he'd have been interested if she had, and she would have resented his disinterest.

She'd told him that the drinks were taking place and that she'd be home late. He hadn't seemed bothered, only said something about how he planned to run in the evening anyway and that Chloe wanted to cook dinner. The implication seemed to be that Holly would not be missed.

'Your boyfriend?' she asked Rebecca as the lift arrived and they filed inside.

'He might,' Rebecca said as she caught sight of her reflection in the mirror of the lift and adjusted her hair slightly. 'He wasn't sure what time he would finish work.'

'Yours?' Holly directed this question to Dimitri.

'I don't have a boyfriend, Holly.' He winked at her.

'You know what I meant,' she said ruefully.

'My girlfriend's waiting in reception,' he told them.

Rebecca checked her appearance in the mirror again as the doors opened to reveal the reception area.

Holly was curious to see what the Greek god's girlfriend looked like. She imagined Rebecca was too. She pictured a female version of Dimitri; someone beautiful, with dark exotic good looks, but petite and slender in contrast to tall, powerful Dimitri.

The only person waiting in reception was the exact opposite, but she was standing up and walking towards him. The word Amazonian sprang to Holly's mind, as she watched her colleague kissing a tall pale woman with shoulder-length reddish-blond hair. There was a squareness to her jaw which was almost masculine, and, while she was attractive, she wasn't the beauty Holly had been expecting.

'This is Anna,' Dimitri introduced her. 'Anna, this is Holly.'

Holly shook her hand while Rebecca mumbled a, 'Hi, Anna.' Holly wondered if they had met before.

'Pleased to meet you, Holly,' Anna said, and Holly detected an accent which she could not immediately place. She thought it might be German.

The four of them began walking towards The Adam and Eve. The pavements were crowded. There was not room for them all to walk abreast of each other. Rebecca and Holly found themselves falling behind.

'Have you met Anna before?' Holly asked.

'A couple of times,' Rebecca murmured, non-committally.

'She's not what I imagined,' Holly told her. 'Where is she from?'

'Berlin,' Rebecca confirmed her intuition about the accent, then changed the subject. 'Did you speak to the man who's on Monday's programme?'

★ ★ ★

Natalie and James were squashed on a bench seat behind a table, at the head of which Katherine was sitting. There were three bottles of champagne on the table and an array of glasses. They looked up as the newcomers walked over to join them.

'Anna, this is Katherine the boss, James the talent, and Natalie,' Dimitri said, introducing his girlfriend.

'What does that make me then, Dimitri?' Natalie raised her eyebrows. 'We have the boss, the talent, and then just me.'

'Natalie is the office pin-up,' he said, and she

raised her eyebrows and smiled at Anna.

'Nice to meet you at long last,' Natalie said as Anna took the spare seat next to her. 'I don't know how you put up with him. Champagne?'

'Thank you,' Anna replied, nodding her head slightly.

'Pass the bottle, Darling.' Natalie nudged James's elbow.

'Oh, where are my manners?' he responded, picking up the bottle and pouring all round.

'Are you two married?' Anna asked.

'No,' Natalie laughed. 'I mean, we are married, but not to each other.'

Holly was vaguely aware of a presence behind her as Natalie said this and turned round to see Guy hovering beside the table, not quite sure how to announce his presence.

'Guy!' Natalie said. 'Great. You're here.'

'I'm here,' he confirmed.

'Shove up,' Natalie said to James, and he shuffled further along the bench, making room for Natalie's husband.

'She's married to me,' Guy said, sitting down and introducing himself to Anna. 'I'm Guy.'

'Anna,' she said, looking confused. 'I am with Dimitri.'

'Anna overheard your wife calling our illustrious presenter Darling.' Dimitri extended his hand across the table to Guy. 'I'm Dimitri. I think we met briefly in the office once before.'

'Yes, I remember,' Guy said.

'James's surname is Darling,' Dimitri explained to Anna.

'Oh.' She paused to consider this and then her

face lit up as she realised her mistake. 'I see!'

Holly briefly thought back to the evening when she and Daniel had met Anne-Marie. She had asked if they were married. What was it, she wondered now, that had given that impression?

Anna began laughing at her mistake and the rest of them joined in.

'Have I missed a good joke?'

They all turned to look at the indisputably beautiful woman who was pulling up a spare chair.

'Hello, Darling,' she said. 'I hope I'm not late.'

James' wife Mila was as unlike him as Anna was from Dimitri. She was tall and slim, with thick dark hair and sparkling green eyes. There was a grace to her movements that made you want to stop and simply watch her as she dragged a stool closer to the table and leaned across it to kiss her husband.

'I can't remember who's met Mila and who hasn't,' he said. 'You know Natalie, and Katherine. Have you met Holly and Rebecca . . . or Dimitri? We've only just met Anna. Anna, this is Mila and Guy. Mila, this is Guy.'

'Hello.' Mila smiled and gave a slight wave to where Anna and Guy were sitting. She was too far away from them to shake hands.

'Who is she?' Anna whispered to Guy.

'James' wife, I think,' he said to her. 'She was probably using his surname as an actual term of endearment!'

Anna smiled, as if glad of a fellow outsider to feel slightly conspiratorial with.

'Hello, Natalie.' Mila had extended her hand

across the table to her.

Natalie took it with what Holly thought was slight reluctance.

'Good you could come,' she said. 'Who's looking after the children?'

'They are with friends,' Mila said matter-of-factly. 'Who is looking after yours?'

'Guy's mother.' Natalie nodded towards her husband.

Holly wasn't sure if she was imagining a coldness in this exchange. If there was she put it down to the suspicion with which working and non-working mothers tended to treat each other.

She'd seen similar exchanges take place numerous times between women who worked full-time and those who had stopped altogether. Because, for the time being, they had no common ground, their conversations often seemed obliquely to challenge each other's life decisions.

Natalie and Mila's brief exchange ended when Katherine clapped her hands.

'Before we all get too drunk,' she joked, 'I'd just like to say a few words.'

Katherine did indeed keep her words to a minimum, reminding them all why they were celebrating, congratulating the team on a wonderful programme, among many other wonderful programmes, and giving Darling a special mention on account of the quality of his interviewing technique.

'Congratulations!' Katherine raised her glass and there was a graduated murmur in response.

292

'What was the programme about?' Anna asked.

Dimitri had obviously not filled her in on the details. So Natalie did the honours.

'It was one of those interviews which raised lots of questions. James handled it perfectly,' she concluded.

'Humph,' Guy grunted.

'What do you do, Anna?' Natalie asked, ignoring him.

'I'm a photographer.'

'Really? Guy used to be a photographer too. Didn't you?'

'I still am,' he said through gritted teeth.

'Oh, well, I didn't mean . . . ' Natalie trailed off.

Holly imagined Guy would have perceived the remark as a putdown. She knew he wasn't working at the moment. His plans to go back to doing some of the things he used to do, now that the twins had started school, didn't seem to be bearing any fruit.

Guy drained his glass and glowered at his wife who reached across the table for a bottle but found it empty.

'I'll get another,' she said, to no one in particular, and got up to go the bar.

'I'll help you,' Holly offered. 'I'm just going to go to the Ladies first.'

'I'll get a couple more bottles. There's still money behind the bar,' Natalie said as Holly rounded the corner to where the Ladies were.

When she came out a small group of men in suits were blocking her path back to the body of

293

the pub. She hovered, wondering if she could squeeze past without having to say a loud 'excuse me' and, as she waited, heard Natalie and Guy talking in agitated, hushed voices.

'Why do you always put me down like that in front of your colleagues?' he hissed.

'I don't know what you mean.' Natalie sounded placatory.

'Yes, you do. Saying I used to be a photographer,' Guy returned.

'I just meant you are looking after the children at the moment,' she told him.

'Our children.' Guy sounded cross.

'Yes, our children, obviously.' Natalie was beginning to sound pissed off.

'You go on about what a wonderful inter-viewer James fucking Darling is, and in the next breath you say I'm an old has-been.' Guy was clearly rattled.

'That's not what I said.' Natalie sounded as if she were talking to a small child. 'Just calm down, will you? This is my evening.'

'Fuck you, Natalie,' he said. 'I'm going home. Tell your precious colleagues there's a childcare crisis, which your neutered husband has to deal with.'

'Excuse me.' Holly tapped one of the men in suits on the elbow and they moved aside. She walked past and saw Natalie crossing the bar with two bottles as Guy stomped towards the door.

'Is everything OK?' Holly asked her before they reached the others.

'Don't ask.' Natalie pulled a face and glanced

over at Guy, now smiling at Mila who also appeared to be leaving the party.

'Mila's gone to have a cigarette,' James explained her absence when they rejoined the group.

'She doesn't look like a smoker,' Katherine said. 'Her skin is far too good.'

'She only smokes occasionally.' He smiled, as if accepting the compliment on his wife's behalf. 'She gets a bit stressed when she's with people she doesn't know that well.'

He glanced over to where she stood chatting to Guy.

'So does Guy,' said Natalie.

31

'Oh, congratulations,' Natalie said, as Holly came into the office on Monday morning.

She'd been about to remark on Natalie's new haircut and wondered what she was being congratulated for.

'What for?' Holly felt momentary panic that she might have been promoted or moved to another programme. She was not sure she could cope with the added stress that either involved.

'Your new husband,' Natalie said, indicating her computer screen.

Holly looked over Natalie's shoulder, and saw she was looking at her Facebook page. Natalie hit a few keys and Mark's profile appeared.

'Look at this.' Natalie pointed to a heart icon which flashed and announced, 'Just married!'

'What's all that about?' Holly wondered if Mark had had some virtual Facebook wedding without telling her. 'Why is it saying that?'

'Don't look so worried,' Natalie soothed. 'He must have just updated his profile over the weekend. I've seen this happen before. If you set up with only sketchy details then go back to change it, the site flags all the new stuff up.'

'I see.' Holly was not sure that she did.

'Mark must have added that he's married and has children,' Natalie told Holly. 'Then Facebook puts out a 'just married' alert!'

'Oh, you had me slightly worried for a bit.'

She knew, obviously, that Mark had not gone out and married anyone real over the weekend but she was relieved he hadn't had a virtual wedding either.

Both Mark and Jake had been locked on to their computers when she came home after her office pub outing. Jake had been non-committal when she'd asked what he was up to and Mark had said he was working on the logistics of Jimmy Finlay's run.

He'd run twelve miles himself on Saturday morning and disappeared to the office in the afternoon. On Sunday, Holly had suggested that if he was going to go into the office, which he no longer seemed to be giving up, then perhaps they could meet for a coffee in town.

'OK,' Mark had acquiesced. 'How about two-thirty? There's a new Spanish deli down the road. I'll need something to eat by then.'

Holly wasn't sure if he'd agreed to meet so he wouldn't have to eat alone or if he actually liked the idea of spending a bit of time with her away from home.

In the event, he was with her in body but not in spirit. He had his phone on the table between them and kept checking it for messages and looking as if he wanted to get going again.

Mark had ordered a Spanish omelette and Holly asked for a pot of tea and something which looked like a custard tart, which the waitress said was called a *nata*.

'So I'm going to have a cuppa and a natter then,' Holly had joked but Mark had looked at her blankly.

'I can't stay too long,' he replied. 'I want to finish planning the itinerary by Monday.'

'It's OK, I was making a joke,' Holly said, unable to keep the irritation from creeping into her voice.

'What?' he asked, but was looking at the waitress as if willing her to bring their food quickly.

'A pun,' Holly replied, but decided the joke wasn't worth making again. 'Oh, it doesn't matter.'

Mark wolfed his omelette down and left her to have her tea and *nata* on her own.

He'd obviously done some updating of his Facebook site while he was back in the office.

'Now you come to mention it,' Holly said to Natalie, 'I do remember him saying something about using Facebook more. It was something to do with this Jimmy Finlay thing he's doing, I think.'

'Well, there you go then,' said Natalie. 'You should have a look at some of the messages he's been getting. They're quite funny.'

'I think I'll just get a coffee.' Holly desperately needed one. 'Want one?'

'I'm all right,' Natalie replied. 'Darling's just gone to get me one. He should be back in a minute.'

'OK.' Holly took her coat off and hung it on the back of the door, feeling slightly irritated that whenever Darling was in, working on the programme, he seemed to prefer their office to the one he'd been allocated.

'I'll see you in a bit then.' She took her purse from her bag and headed towards the canteen.

'Here's the blushing bride!' James Darling had rolled Holly's chair over to Natalie's side of the office and was looking at Mark's Facebook site with her. 'Your husband has three hundred and fifty-two friends.'

'Thank goodness he doesn't invite them all round for dinner.' Holly chose to ignore his bride joke. 'By the way, Natalie, I like your hair.'

'Oh, God, it's hideous, I look like Richard the Second,' she said.

Her hair, which had been long-ish, was now cut in a short bob.

'I think it's nice,' Darling said, reaching across and playing with the newly cut ends. 'It suits you.'

'Nice if you like Plantagenet hair!' Natalie laughed.

'I do like Plantagenet hair,' Darling said, looking at her closely. 'I like it a lot.'

Holly felt as if she ought not to be here, as if she was intruding in some way, but it was partly her office after all. She cleared her throat and James looked away from Natalie's hair and back to the computer screen.

'Not many of your husband's friends seem to know you,' he commented, and began reading aloud from the screen.

'*Congratulations, Mark, anyone we know? . . . You're a dark horse, who's the lucky woman?* And look at this one. *Congrats, Mark. Was it a wedding or a civil partnership?*'

'Let me see.' Holly crossed to Natalie's side of

the office and James got up so she could sit where he had been.

'Some of these names are familiar.' Holly began scrolling down the messages and paused when she reached a comment from a sender she thought she knew.

'A lot of them are probably work contacts,' Natalie said.

'Noel. Mark used to do a lot of work with him in Hong Kong . . . and Ted.' Holly read out the postings from names she recognised, although they belonged to people she had never actually met.

'*Congratulations, Mark. Let us know the name of your new wife. Where are you living now?*'

'I can't believe he spent years going back and forth to Hong Kong, doing business with these guys, and never once mentioned he had a wife.' She looked at Natalie for reassurance.

'They're probably just treading carefully,' Natalie said. 'If Mark hasn't been in touch with them for a while, they might think you two got divorced or something.'

'Well, listen to this one.' Holly read out another. '*Good news, Mark. Presume you finally married Holly? Better late than never. Neil Somerset.* Neil Somerset was at our wedding!'

'Think of it as a compliment,' James told her, sitting on the edge of Natalie's desk.

'How so?' Holly looked up at him.

'Well, perhaps not a compliment exactly.' He paused to reconsider. 'But testament to the strength of your marriage. You've been married

300

so long that even people who came to your wedding find it hard to believe you still are.'

'That's an interesting way of putting it,' Natalie interjected. 'But it's true. You and Mark have been married longer than anyone else I know, which is quite an achievement in this age of divorce.'

'Mmm.' Holly was only giving Natalie a small portion of her attention.

Mark had a new Facebook friend. It was Anne-Marie, which was decidedly odd. He didn't even know her. She must have seen that he was friends with Holly and sent him a request, but Holly wondered why and why Mark had confirmed it.

Then she was distracted by a new posting from Daisy.

'*Better to wait and marry late than marry young and green.*'

'Is that a famous quote?' She pointed at the on-screen message and Natalie leaned in and read it.

'It might be.' She didn't sound convinced.

'What do you think she means?' Holly asked.

'Maybe something about knowing the person you are marrying?' Natalie suggested. 'Rather than marrying when you are young and not quite sure what you're letting yourself in for.'

'Best not to know,' Darling said. He was now reading a newspaper article but obviously still keeping abreast of their conversation. 'You'd never do it if you knew what you were letting yourself in for.'

'Oh, I don't know.' Natalie looked at him. 'I

301

think it becomes harder to accommodate another person as you get older.'

Holly wondered if she was talking about herself and Guy. She was curious as to whether they'd continued the argument she'd overheard in the pub back home — and whether they'd resolved it or not.

Holly got up, moved her chair back to her desk and switched on her computer.

Darling shifted his position on the edge of Natalie's desk a bit, moving slightly closer to her. Holly would have found this annoying but Natalie didn't seem to mind. They had certainly known each other long enough to accommodate each other at work.

'Coincidentally,' Darling said, shaking out the paper he was reading, 'Katherine gave me this when I passed her office this morning. Thought it would make a good discussion.'

'Let's have a look.' Natalie put out her hand to take the paper from him and began to read out the headline. '*Till the Main Meal Do Us Part — Is Marriage for Life or Just for Starters?*'

Natalie carried on reading to herself, then handed the paper over to Holly.

'What do you think?' she asked.

' "You may set out thinking marriage is for life, yet all too often it can be a brief affair, especially amongst twenty-somethings. Should starter marriages, which end after a few years, often without children, be seen as failed relationships or a trial run for a lasting, more fulfilling, long-term second marriage?" '

'Maybe,' Holly said out loud. 'Though it

smacks a bit of some charlatan having coined the term 'starter marriages'.'

'Yes, we'd have to get a charlatan to take part in the discussion,' Darling nodded, as if in agreement with her.

'And we'd need to find someone with a brief failed marriage,' Natalie mused, 'and then preferably a longer, more successful one.'

'It seems a bit like doing a *Hello!* though,' Holly said. 'Inviting people to talk about their long and happy marriages.'

'I've always been fascinated by childhood sweet-hearts,' said Darling. 'They seem to fall into a category of their own. Every now and then you read about people who have known each other since they were at school and then get married. I wonder if their marriages last as far as dessert?'

'*Ikabaebae*,' Holly said, finding something that Mark had told her had suddenly floated to the top of her mind.

'What?' said Darling and Natalie together.

'*Ikabaebae*,' Holly repeated. 'It means to be engaged from childhood in some Pacific island language.'

'Know anyone who falls into that category?' Natalie asked both Holly and James.

'William and Kate,' James suggested. 'Although I suppose they met at university. Still, good going.'

Holly kept quiet.

The only person she could think of who fell into that category was Daniel, and she wasn't about to volunteer this information to her colleagues.

32

Holly wanted someone to be nice to her and hoped she might find Daniel on the train.

She felt unnerved after Mark's reaction to the posting she'd made on his Facebook wall and his refusal to tell the virtual world who his actual wife was.

Congratulations, Mark, she'd written. *I think you might have forgotten to divorce me first . . . wife no. 1.*

Holly had intended this to be a joke but Mark had not found it funny. He'd phoned her at work, saying it made him look stupid.

'I updated my page because I'm expecting more people to look at it, thanks to Jimmy's run.' He sounded very pompous.

'Well, it leaves me out altogether,' she retorted. 'Half your Facebook friends don't even seem to realise that I exist.'

'Now you know what it feels like,' Mark had muttered, but refused to be drawn when Holly had asked what he meant by this.

Their marital tiff had been cut short when she had to go to the studio to record an interview. She'd thought about calling Mark back later, but decided to save whatever 'discussion' they might need to have until she got home. Too often, lately, she seemed to be having minor tiffs with him that ended unresolved and with accusations unspoken.

At the moment he was making Holly feel that

304

she was not a very nice person, that everything she said or did was somehow wrong, but she always felt reassured by Daniel. There was something in his manner and his attitude towards her that made her feel that what she was doing was right.

As Holly reached the middle of the train, she saw him sitting next to a window, facing backwards but with an empty seat next to him. She smiled to herself, pleased that she would be able to sit there.

Daniel looked up and saw her.

'Hello,' she said, approaching the space where he was sitting. 'Mind if I sit here?'

'Please do.' Daniel stressed the *do*. 'Which way do you want to face?'

Holly had registered, as she approached the seat, that there was someone already sitting opposite him, but not who it was. Now she turned and saw that it was Anne-Marie.

'Oh, hello,' she said, hoping she sounded convincingly pleased to see her.

Holly had been hoping to have some time with Daniel on her own, if she discounted the other people in the carriage, which she did. Anne-Marie made Holly feel edgy and unnerved, partly because of the way she seemed to keep appearing: on the train, in John Lewis, at the meeting, in Brighton at the weekend, and now on Mark's Facebook site too. It didn't seem like pure coincidence.

'Hello, Holly.' Anne-Marie said, not sounding too pleased to see her either. Her tone was positively dejected.

'How are you?' Holly forced herself to sound cheery and decided, against her inclination, to sit down next to Anne-Marie.

'Not great,' she replied, and Holly's heart sank.

She wished now she'd grabbed a seat at the back of the train. She didn't like herself for wishing this. She could only imagine what Anne-Marie must be going through and knew she ought to be sympathetic. For some reason she felt anything but.

'Bad day?' Holly said, imagining that for her some must be worse than others.

'It's her wedding anniversary today,' Daniel explained, filling Holly in on the detail Anne-Marie had already shared with him.

'Oh.' Holly cursed herself for her attitude to Anne-Marie. What, she wondered, had made her become so hard-hearted?

'I'm sorry,' she said. 'How long were you . . . would you have been married, I mean?'

'This would have been our third wedding anniversary,' Anne-Marie told her. 'We were married on the fifteenth of June three years ago.'

That wasn't long, Holly thought to herself, although she knew this wasn't relevant. She wondered which was worse: losing your husband in the early stages of a marriage, when you were still madly in love and had plans for a future, or when you'd been together for years?

'Did you not want to take the day off?' Holly couldn't quite think of what else to say.

'I thought about it, but I decided it was best to carry on,' Anne-Marie told her.

As she was speaking, it occurred to Holly that, if Anne-Marie would have been married for three years on 15 June that meant she herself had been married for seventeen years on 8 June. Both she and Mark had forgotten their anniversary.

'Oh, no!' she said. 'That means I forgot our wedding anniversary. It was last week.'

She realised, as soon as she said this, that it was not tactful.

'Sorry,' she said to Anne-Marie. 'I know that sounds terrible. Especially when . . . '

'How long have you been married, Holly?' Anne-Marie interrupted.

'Seventeen years,' Holly said, feeling as if she should also apologise for this to Anne-Marie. It seemed to her somehow indecent to have been married so long when Anne-Marie's marriage had been cut short.

'And you, Daniel?' Anne-Marie turned to him, a touch of the inquisitor about her.

'Five,' he said. 'We got married when I was twenty-three.'

Holly wondered if Anne-Marie had forgotten that she had asked them both how long they'd been married when they'd met in the pub. Holly remembered the conversation but it seemed to have slipped Anne-Marie's mind.

'That's young,' she commented.

'We were at school together,' Daniel, said, as if having known each other from a young age made twenty-three not so young to get married at all.

Holly thought about telling them about the discussion they were having on her programme but knew this would also mean saying that statistically his marriage only had a certain chance of lasting.

Instead she decided to keep quiet and send what she hoped would be a conciliatory text to Mark.

'*Happy Wedding Anniversary, Mark. Sorry I forgot . . . Long-standing wife xx*

'Seventeen years is quite an achievement,' Anne-Marie said.

'You're telling me,' Holly laughed, but sensed that Anne-Marie was not in the mood for joking. 'It seemed to come round very quickly, though. It doesn't feel like seventeen years, except when I stop to think how much has happened over that time. I guess, before we know it, we'll have been married another seventeen.'

'You're very lucky, Holly,' she said. 'Not everyone is as committed as your husband obviously is.'

Holly wasn't quite sure what she meant by this remark or why she'd singled Mark out as the committed half of the marriage when obviously it took two to stay together.

She was saved from having to reply by a text from Mark.

Happy Anniversary to you, long-standing, long-suffering wife. I am sorry about my own Alzheimer's. Must have forgotten with all the excitement of recent wedding! Sorry, Hol. Will make up xx

Holly smiled.

'Forgiven?' Daniel said, as if he knew the text had been from Mark.

'I think so,' she said, putting her phone away.

'Can you imagine having been married seventeen years?' Anne-Marie asked Daniel, looking at him directly. There was something challenging in the way she put it.

'I suppose so.' He began to take his laptop out of his bag. 'I've imagined certain things in the future. But you can never be quite sure what will happen, can you?'

His answer was oblique and Holly wondered how Anne-Marie might interpret it. Would she think he was alluding to the accident that had ended her own brief marriage? Holly wondered if he was referring to the children he seemed unable to conceive with Daisy, or to something else.

She looked at him and, as he opened his laptop, he glanced up and held her eye briefly. Holly wondered if Anne-Marie had noticed.

'Must finish a presentation.' He nodded at his flickering screen.

'And I have some papers to read.' Anne-Marie fished in her bag and the three of them fell into companionable silence, until the train neared Haywards Heath and Anne-Marie began preparing to get off.

'Have a good evening. I hope . . . ' Holly stopped mid-sentence, then continued, 'I mean, I hope it's not too hard, going home alone tonight.'

'I know what you mean,' Anne-Marie said flatly. 'I hope you have a good evening, too, if you ever get round to celebrating your wedding anniversary.'

'Bye then,' Daniel said, as she got off the train. And then, to Holly, 'Did she seem a bit off to you? Perhaps she was upset.'

'Yes,' Holly agreed. 'And that's understandable. I thought she was pissed off with me too, though. Did I interrupt something when I arrived?'

'Not really. We were just chatting,' Daniel told her. 'She'd told me it would have been her wedding anniversary so she was feeling a bit down.'

'This may sound daft, but I felt she was cross with me for forgetting my wedding anniversary,' Holly said. 'As if I ought to appreciate what I have more. But we've never really made a big thing out of anniversaries anyway.'

'Will you celebrate it, now that you've remembered?' Daniel asked.

'I don't know,' Holly said, wondering if going out to mark the occasion might be just what she and Mark needed, or whether it would be best to let it pass this year.

I'm not sure who I am missing most today, Geoff or the baby that we never had.

I had a conversation in my head with Holly this morning. I imagined that rather than ignoring my text at the weekend and meeting up with Daniel, she had replied and agreed to meet me.

'Call me whenever you need to talk,' I would have said to her when we left together, instead of my walking out of the cafe on my own and bumping into her, then waiting a while and seeing Daniel turn up.

'And you call me too, if you need, any time,' I put the words into her mouth. 'Really, any time at all.'

I would have called her this morning, before I left for work, because I knew today would be hard.

'Are you sure you're up to going to London?' Holly would have asked.

And I would have told her that life goes on.

People keep saying that to me, as if they don't know what else to say.

'Life goes on,' they say, and it does go on but it's not the same, is it?

I would have told her that it was our wedding anniversary today, or rather it would have been, and that we would have been married for three years. Then I would have told her about the

311

baby, who would be two and a half years old.

'So you were pregnant when you got married?' she'd have asked.

'Just a couple of months,' I'd explain. 'I didn't want to be too huge walking down the aisle. We were going to get married anyway. But the baby made us decide to do it sooner rather than later.'

This isn't entirely true.

We might never have got married if I hadn't got pregnant. Geoff made that very clear last year, on our wedding anniversary. It was a registry office affair, not the big white wedding I'd imagined when I was younger. But I no longer wanted that anyway, not with Mum and Dad both dead.

There weren't that many people I would have wanted to invite, so a small intimate affair seemed more appropriate. And that was easier to organise quickly too. There was no rush on Horsham registry office on a Wednesday afternoon or the restaurant where we all went for a meal afterwards. It was a quiet family affair, with Geoff's mum and dad and sisters.

But it was still the best day of my life, because suddenly things seemed to be moving forward for me. I was going to be with Geoff and we were going to have a baby.

He'd been stunned at first, when I told him I was pregnant, because I was on the pill. But I'd had an upset stomach the week before so it probably hadn't absorbed properly.

He was angry initially, that I hadn't told him this, but then he apologised because he knew that I was upset and said it would be wonderful

312

for us to have a baby, it was just the shock of finding out that made him react that way.

I hadn't expected him to ask me to marry him, but of course I accepted when he did. I couldn't believe my luck. I was so happy. Looking back on it, those few weeks leading up to the wedding were probably the happiest of my life.

'Are you sure you want to do it so soon?' Geoff's mum had asked. 'You might not be feeling so good, Anne-Marie. I was sick with Geoff for nearly four months.'

'I feel great,' I told her.

I did. I'd felt really tired and nauseous at first, although I wasn't ever sick, but once I was past six weeks I felt fine — full of energy, in fact, which I put down to thinking about the wedding and our future. I never imagined for a moment how soon it would all start to go wrong.

That's why I thought I'd find it hard today; not because this time last year it had all been champagne and roses, but because it had been awful.

Geoff hadn't planned to do anything to celebrate our anniversary last year and that upset me. He said because it was midweek he was too tired to go out, but I really wanted to do something and we ended up going to an Italian in town.

I wished I hadn't insisted, as Geoff obviously didn't want to be there. He hardly spoke all evening and kept checking his phone.

I asked him if he couldn't forget about work or whatever it was that was bothering him and enjoy the evening.

That was when he said it.

'Let's face it, Anne-Marie,' he said. 'We'd never have got married if it hadn't been for the baby.'

That made me think back to the awful moment when we went for the scan. It felt like a bad joke on the part of the ultrasound operator.

I remembered her putting the gel on my stomach and Geoff holding my hand and both of us looking expectantly at the monitor, waiting for a grainy image of the baby to appear.

'There's nothing there,' the operator said.

'What do you mean, nothing?' Geoff asked. I was too stunned to speak.

'I mean, there's no baby. I'm afraid your wife's not pregnant,' she said gently.

'But I am.' I half-sat up, half-turned to look at the monitor, to make sure she hadn't missed anything. 'I took four tests. I've got a slight bump. My breasts are bigger. You must have made a mistake.'

'I am sure you were pregnant, Anne-Marie,' she said to me. 'Sometimes people conceive but the baby doesn't develop very far and the body simply reabsorbs the foetus rather than miscarrying. It's called a phantom pregnancy. I'm very sorry.'

It wasn't just the baby I lost that day, I realise now, it was my hopes for the future. Geoff was angry that I hadn't known I wasn't pregnant any more. He behaved as if he thought I'd tricked him into getting married with some fantasy I'd made up. We started arguing. We'd probably have argued again today, on our wedding anniversary, if he'd been here. And I'd have wondered, for the umpteenth time, if I hadn't lost the baby, would everything have been different?

33

'I'm off,' Holly said to Dimitri, as she walked past his desk on her way out.

'Why is everyone sloping off early today?' He looked up from his computer.

'It's not early.' Holly resisted the temptation to check her watch. She knew it was only 5.30 and she could also see from where she was standing that Dimitri was on Facebook.

He might still be in the office but he wasn't actually doing any work.

He was probably waiting for Rebecca, who was still in the studio, recording an interview for later in the week, so that they could slope off wherever it was they seemed to slope off to after work.

'I guess not,' Dimitri conceded her right to leave the office. Then, qualifying his earlier statement, added, 'Natalie left just after lunch.'

'I think you must have had a late lunch,' Holly told him. 'She left just before five.' She did this regularly on a Wednesday, as it was Guy's day for going to the gym.

'You'll miss your train if you stand here arguing with me.' Dimitri leaned back in his chair and smiled at her.

'Actually, I don't have a train to catch just yet,' Holly laughed. 'I'm meeting my dad for dinner.'

Her phone beeped as she spoke and she took it out of her pocket and was surprised to find a

316

text message from her father.

Train just in. CU L8r.

When and where, Holly wondered, had her dad learned to send a text message and use text speak while he was at it? She no longer entirely recognised her parents.

'I thought your parents were in Thailand doing yoga?' Dimitri said, underlining what she was just thinking.

Holly had forgotten that she'd mentioned her mother was in Thailand, when they were talking about protests at Bangkok airport earlier in the day.

'My mum is there,' she explained. 'My dad is usually in Northampton, but he's booked himself a theatre break and is taking me out to dinner before he goes to see the Danish Ballet with an old friend.'

'Oh, right,' Dimitri replied. 'So your parents are divorced?'

'No, they just aren't joined at the hip.' Holly echoed what her mother had said when she had elaborated on her plans to travel alone for four months.

She didn't understand her parents' relationship quite well enough herself to explain it to anyone else. They appeared to get on well when they were together and yet they seemed to spend increasing amounts of time apart.

'I've spent the last thirty years with him,' her mother had said when Holly mentioned this to her. 'Don't you think I'm entitled to do my own thing?'

Holly hadn't wanted to argue with her, and

as her father seemed to be perfectly happy with the arrangement, she'd not questioned it further.

'Right, well, have a nice evening.' Dimitri tapped his keyboard and closed his computer down as Rebecca came into the office.

He looked at her and inclined his head slightly towards the door, as if to say, Shall we be off?

★　★　★

Her father was already sitting at a table in the Australian brasserie in Exmouth Market when Holly arrived. Natalie and Guy lived not far from here and Natalie had recommended the place when Holly had asked if she knew of somewhere she could meet her dad that was near Sadler's Wells.

'Are you meeting someone?' an Aussie waiter asked as soon as she set foot inside.

'My dad.' Holly nodded towards her father who was watching the world go by, but hadn't seen her. His mind appeared to be elsewhere.

'Ah, right, you'll be going with him to the Danish Ballet then?' the waiter asked. He'd obviously already had a chat with her dad.

'No.' Holly walked over to join him. 'Just having dinner with him first. Hello, Dad.'

'Holly!' Her father pushed his chair back and stood up to kiss her, then waited for her to sit down before he sat himself. 'How are you?'

'Fine.' She sat down and the waiter handed her a menu.

'Everybody here seems to be Australian,' said

her dad, as the waiter retreated to the bar. 'That young man has recently arrived from Sumatra. I have never before met anyone who has been to Sumatra. What would you like to eat?'

Holly picked up the menu. It was fairly typical of her father to fall into conversation with strangers. He generally found them easier to talk to than members of his own family. But she also wondered if he'd started quizzing the waiter because he was lonely. Her mother had been gone for nearly a month and his days were spent largely on his own.

'Have you heard from Mum this week?' Holly thought her father's mention of Sumatra provided a natural segue to the subject of someone who was in Thailand. They were both in the Indian Ocean and, Holly was pretty sure, on the same fault line.

'She sent an electronic message last Friday.' He had reluctantly started to use email, forced to by Susan's use of it, but emphasised his reluctance by refusing to call it by its abbreviated name.

'She was about to take a train up into the mountains, but I've not had time to go to the public library and see if she has sent any more letters this week.'

'And are you getting on OK at home?' Holly and her sister had both been copied on to the email that her mum had sent on Friday.

She knew about the trip to the mountains but had hoped her mother would have sent her father his own, more personal email. Unless there was one waiting for him on the computer terminal at the local library, it seemed she had not.

'Pretty well,' her dad answered. 'I've been reading a biography of Stanley Baldwin. It's very good. Have you read it?'

'No.' Holly smiled to herself, thinking that her dad seemed quite happy to fill her mother's absence with a weighty tome and the odd trip to London. 'So who are you going to the theatre with tonight?'

'Jean Hayward,' her father said, as the waiter came back to take their order. 'She doesn't get out much these days, without Hugh around.'

Jean and Hugh used to travel a lot themselves and Holly wondered if Jean would start travelling on her own again or if the fact that Hugh had died after having a stroke on their trip to Petra would put her off.

'How is she?' Holly asked.

If she'd asked this question to someone of her generation, Holly thought, they would probably have answered that Jean was generally OK but rather lonely, having lost her partner of forty-plus years and not having any children nearby to keep an eye on her.

'She's very well,' her father maintained.

He was now looking up at the waiter who was standing expectantly with pen poised over notepad.

'Shall we order?'

Patrick ordered pork belly and white bean stew, and Holly asked for the gilt-head sea bream.

'I wonder what it was feeling guilty about?' she

quipped as the waiter left, but her dad appeared not to have heard.

'What have you been up to?' he asked. Perhaps he thought she'd said something about feeling guilty herself for leaving work early or not going home.

Over dinner, Holly told him that she'd interviewed a man who had held up a bank with a Toilet Duck. Held under his jacket, the staff thought it was a gun. She talked about Jake settling into secondary school and Chloe becoming so independent that they hardly saw her any more.

'And Mark's got some work with a Scottish comedian.' Holly didn't imagine his name would mean anything to her dad. 'Jimmy Finlay.'

'Oh, I love him!' he said, surprising her. 'He's the one on that dot dot dot *I Nearly Died* programme, isn't he?'

'Yes, I didn't think that was the sort of thing you watched?' Holly replied.

'I've been watching a lot of rubbish since your mother has been away.' Holly noted that her dad hardly ever referred to Susan by name, always as her mother. 'But I like that programme. Good for Mark. What's he doing?'

Holly told him briefly about the run and what she knew of his involvement in it.

'He's organising the run itself, plotting the itinerary and organising hotels and a back-up team,' she repeated some of what Mark had told her. 'And then he's trying to arrange a big press launch in a few weeks and more press coverage throughout.'

'It sounds like a lot of work,' her father commented, and Holly nodded and decided not to say that, what with one thing and another, she'd hardly seen him since he landed the job. 'And is he still running himself?'

'Yes,' Holly said. 'When he's not working on Jimmy Finlay's run.'

If she had been having dinner with her mother, Susan might have asked if she'd managed to see Mark at all in between all this running and working. Her father did not.

'I'd better get the bill,' he said, when they'd finished eating. 'I said I would meet Jean outside Sadler's Wells at seven forty-five. Are you going to come and say hello?'

Holly wasn't sure if her father wanted her to come and greet an old family friend or if he was simply unsure how to get rid of her. She suspected the latter.

'I should probably start heading home actually, Dad,' she said apologetically. 'There's a train in forty minutes, which I could probably make if I rush.'

'Jolly good,' he said, signalling to the waiter.

He paid the bill in cash and asked for his coat.

'I might just go to the cloakroom before we leave,' Holly said. 'So I'll say goodbye now.'

'Yes.' Her father was putting his coat on. 'Well, goodbye. Nice to see you. I'm glad everything's OK.'

Holly wondered, as he said this, if meeting up had been his idea or whether her mother had urged him to see her.

'Yes,' said Holly, kissing her father on both

cheeks, although she suspected he would prefer just to shake hands. 'Say hello to Jean from me, and send Mum my love when you hear from her next.'

'Yes,' he said, holding his hand up in a royal wave as he walked towards the door.

Holly waved back and looked about her.

'Downstairs,' the waiter said, interpreting her scanning of the room correctly.

'Thanks,' Holly said, and went downstairs.

When she came up, she noticed a table tucked around the corner. It wasn't visible from the main part of the restaurant and even now she could only see it reflected in the mirror on the stairs. If that hadn't been there, she wouldn't have noticed the table at all, or the two people sitting at it, holding hands.

She stopped on the stairs, unsure what to do next. If she walked up quickly, could she go past and pretend she hadn't seen them? Too late. They'd seen her and had quickly unclasped their hands and sat back, too far back, in their chairs, creating a yawning space between them.

'Oh, hi.' Holly tried to sound casual, as if it was quite normal to bump into a friend's husband holding hands in a restaurant with the wife of the presenter of the programme she worked on.

'Hi, Holly.' Guy stood up and kissed her, as if he too thought their meeting like this was quite normal. 'What are you doing in this neck of the woods?'

'I've just had dinner with my dad.' She nodded in the direction where they had been seated and

Guy looked, obviously expecting to see him.

'He's gone to meet someone at the theatre now,' Holly explained. 'I was just on my way home.'

'You know Mila, don't you?' Guy motioned towards James Darling's wife, who was wiping the edges of her mouth with a napkin.

'We've met a couple of times.' Holly smiled, unsure whether to shake her hand or kiss her or just leave out any sort of greeting altogether.

'Hi.' Mila glanced briefly in her direction but didn't make eye contact.

'Well, I'd best get going.' Holly looked at her watch to underline this fact. 'I've got a train to catch.'

34

'Do you have a number for Guy?' Mark asked, as Holly buttered a slice of toast. She'd overslept, was running late and would have to eat it on her walk to the station.

'No, why?' Holly picked up the toast and took a bite.

She'd been through the list of contacts on her phone last night, wondering if at any point Natalie had given her Guy's mobile number. But Gina and Giles were the only Gs.

She hadn't known exactly what she would have done with the number had she found it. Texted him and asked what he was doing with James Darling's wife? Unlikely. Called him and asked if Natalie knew where he'd been? She knew Natalie thought he was at the gym. Holly had no idea what to do about having caught him having dinner with Mila.

She'd wondered whether to tell Mark that she'd seen them together, but decided not to. This was partly because he was uncommunicative when she got home and partly because she kept telling herself there must be an innocent explanation.

For the time being doing nothing seemed the best option.

'He's a photographer, isn't he?' Mark said, pouring himself some coffee. 'Jimmy wants an official photographer to document his run. He asked if I knew of any.'

'Would that mean going to Scotland for the duration?' Holly asked, glancing at the kitchen clock and noting that she should have left by now.

'I guess.' Mark sloshed some milk into his drink.

'He *is* a photographer,' Holly said. 'But he looks after the twins these days. I don't know if he'd be able to do it.'

Jake appeared in his school uniform and nodded before taking a box of cornflakes from the cupboard and pouring what looked like almost the entire contents into a bowl

'Surely that's up to him.' Mark looked at her accusingly, although Holly was not sure what she was being accused of. 'He can probably work something out.'

'I suppose so,' Holly said, although she knew it would be difficult. In the days when Mark's business had been booming and he was almost always busy, it had not always been easy to sort out their childcare.

'We'll work something out' had always been Mark's verbal solution to any problem. In reality this meant 'I'm too busy to look after the kids. See if you can find someone else'.

'I'll ask Natalie for his number.' Holly grabbed her keys off the work surface. 'Got to go now.'

'OK. See you later.' Mark was making himself more coffee and giving the task his full attention. Holly noted that he seemed to have stopped kissing her goodbye in the mornings.

''Bye, Jake,' she said, kissing the top of his head.

He grunted and took a mouthful of cereal. The food seemed to trigger part of his brain.

'How was Granddad?' he asked. 'Is he missing Grandma?'

'He was fine,' she told him.

She wasn't sure what the correct answer to the second part of his question was.

★　★　★

'How was your dad?' Natalie asked the same question when she got into the office.

'Fine,' Holly said again.

'Did you have a nice meal?' Natalie enquired, looking up from her computer screen.

Holly wondered if she was just being polite or if she might have found a receipt from the restaurant in Guy's pocket and was asking Holly this to find out if she'd seen him there.

'Very good, actually.' Holly sifted though a pile of papers on her desk to avoid making eye contact with Natalie as she said this. She decided to say nothing, and then wondered if Guy might have mentioned seeing her there.

'Thanks for the recommendation. Have you and Guy been there often?'

'Neither of us has ever been.' Natalie's answer put paid to the possibility that he might have come clean. 'But our next-door neighbours have been several times.'

'Oh.' Holly was unsure what else to say.

'They don't have kids.' Natalie seemed to think an explanation of her next-door neighbours' eating habits was in order. 'So they eat out quite a lot.'

'Well, it was good. You should go,' Holly said, wondering how Guy would manage to keep up the pretence of never having been if he went again with Natalie.

'By the way,' Holly added, 'Mark is looking for a photographer to do some work. He was wondering if Guy might be interested?'

'Well, I'd be interested in Guy doing some work,' Natalie replied enthusiastically.

'Don't you need him to look after the twins?' Holly repeated the reservation she'd voiced to Mark earlier that morning.

'They're at nursery during the day,' Natalie said, 'and he doesn't seem to do anything useful while they're there. It would be great if he had some work.'

'Right.' Holly didn't feel like explaining that the work might involve his going away. 'Can you let me know his email or mobile number?' She tried to sound casual, knowing that once she had them she would most likely contact Guy herself as well. 'So that Mark can talk to him about it.'

'Yes.' Natalie began writing Guy's details down on a Post-it note, then looked up.

'That's odd actually,' she said. 'He was asking what your mobile number was this morning. Are you two having some sort of secret affair or something?'

'Nat . . . ' Holly was saved from having to answer by James Darling sticking his head in at the door of their office. 'Are we in the studio this morning?'

'Yes,' said Natalie, looking up and smiling at him. 'I'll be down in ten minutes. Do you have the interview script?'

'Right here.' He waved it at her, noticing Holly sitting at her desk. 'Morning, Miss Golightly.'

'Morning, Darling.' Holly smiled. She wondered when it had dawned on him that her name was taken from *Breakfast At Tiffany's*.

'Shall I get you a coffee on the way down?' James was addressing Natalie again.

'Oh, thank you, Darling!' She smiled at him. 'I'll be down in a sec.'

Holly looked at Natalie as she finished what she was writing on the yellow square of paper.

'There you go.' She handed over the email address and mobile number to Holly. 'Mark's probably best emailing him first off. He never seems to answer his phone. Not to me anyway.'

She picked up a script from her desk and walked out of the door with Darling.

'I tried to call Guy several times when he was the at gym last night,' Holly overheard her saying to James. 'Kirsty was coughing terribly and I wanted to know if he'd given her any medicine already. But he never answered once.'

⋆　⋆　⋆

'You were lost in thought.'

Holly looked up and smiled as Daniel slid into the seat next to her.

She had been staring out of the window and, as he rightly pointed out, lost in thought. She hadn't noticed him approaching.

'Hello,' she greeted him.

'Or were you just considering whether to

329

change your broadband provider?' Daniel indicated the poster outside the window, which had Holly been taking in her surroundings she might have noticed.

'No, you were right the first time,' she told him. 'I find myself with a bit of a conundrum.'

'A conundrum?' he said, questioningly.

'I went out for dinner with my dad last night,' she began.

'That's nice,' Daniel commented. 'Where did you go?'

'Oh, an Australian place near Sadler's Wells. He was going to a show later.' Holly tried to skim through the details of their meeting.

'So what is the conundrum?' Daniel asked.

'Well, someone I work with . . . ' Holly decided not to divulge Natalie's name ' . . . she and another colleague get on very well. They've worked together for years and they are good friends.'

'And?' Daniel prompted.

'Well, a lot of people at work make comments about them behind their back.'

'What sort of comments?' Daniel seemed unsure where she was going with this.

'Oh, you know,' Holly said vaguely. 'That there might be something going on between them. That sort of thing.'

'And is there?' Daniel asked.

'I used not to think so,' Holly said, truthfully. 'I thought they were just very good friends. I don't really like the man, to be honest, and the woman's husband is lovely, so why she might like someone else is beyond me.'

'So you're not sure?' he asked.

'I'm pretty sure they're not,' Holly said. 'But then last night, when I was having dinner with Dad . . .'

'Did you see them having a candlestine dinner?' Daniel guessed. 'I mean . . . What's the word?'

'Clandestine!' Holly smiled. 'But I like candlestine. It's a good word for a clandestine candlelit dinner!'

'And did you catch them having one?' he persisted.

'Not them,' Holly told him. 'But their spouses. They were in a quiet corner and I didn't see them until I went to the Ladies. His wife was sitting with her husband. They looked very cosy.'

'Maybe there's an innocent explanation?' Daniel suggested.

'I hope so,' Holly said. 'But it puts me in a difficult position.'

She'd sent Guy an email earlier in the day, outlining briefly why Mark wanted to get in touch and giving him both Mark's and her mobile number. She hadn't referred to the night before but he had her email address and her mobile number now. The ball was in his court.

And he'd batted it back almost immediately with a text message.

Hi, Holly. Mark's job sounds interesting. Will email him next. Btw I know how it must have looked last night. But not what you think. Hope to see you soon — maybe we can have a quick coffee later in the week? Guy x

That was a textbook cop out, 'not what you

331

think', and Holly wasn't sure she believed him.

'As far as I know,' she said to Daniel now, 'they'd never met, until we all had a drink after work last week.'

'What if the boot was on the other foot?' Daniel looked at her closely as he asked this, making her feel slightly flustered. 'What if your colleague had seen us having a drink and talking? What do you think she would have thought?'

'I don't know.' Holly looked away as she spoke.

'She might have wondered what you were doing in a pub with me, and you'd have told her there was a perfectly innocent explanation.'

Daniel lowered his voice as he said this. The passengers seated opposite both had earphones plugged in but he didn't seem to want them to hear what he was saying.

'Yes,' Holly agreed, though she couldn't think what the innocent explanation for Guy and Mila being together and holding hands might be.

'Sometimes two people can look very cosy together,' Daniel said. 'In fact, they can be very comfortable together. But that doesn't necessarily mean there is 'anything going on'.'

He made quotation marks in the air as he said this.

'Does it?' He looked directly at her again.

35

'I like it here.' Holly looked around at the solid wooden shelves that lined the walls, all groaning under the weight of jars of olives and tapenade. 'When did it open? Didn't there used to be a charity shop here?'

'I think it used to be the Alzheimer's shop,' Mark said, pouring her a glass from a carafe of Rioja. 'But I can't remember.'

'I don't remember there being an Alzheimer's shop here,' Holly began, then realised that Mark was probably joking. In the spirit of their conciliatory wedding anniversary dinner, she laughed.

'Mind you, I haven't been to the North Laine in ages. I just rush past on my way to and from the station.'

'Perhaps work will pick up for me, if this thing with Jimmy Finlay goes well.' Mark lifted his menu. 'Then you won't have to rush past quite so much.'

'Oh, well, no . . . I just meant . . . ' Holly stuttered, thinking that even her throwaway comment could be construed by Mark as criticism for his not having enough work. 'I meant I hadn't noticed how many of the shops have changed. Anyway, this is nice.'

She smiled at her husband, who looked up from the menu and smiled in return, not just a reflex facial tic or a quick curving of the mouth but a slow, spreading, proper smile, as if he were taking Holly in properly, and thinking of all the reasons he had to smile at her.

She hadn't given him many of late; Holly admitted that much to herself. But she wasn't entirely to blame for what seemed like the increasing distance between them.

'Happy Wedding Anniversary, Holly.' Mark put the menu down and raised his glass. 'Here's to you.'

'Happy Wedding Anniversary to us!' she said, and tapped his glass with hers. She was already beginning to sense that the job for Jimmy Finlay was re-energising her husband and making him feel more positive about everything. 'How did you hear about this place?'

'Chloe told me about it actually,' he said. 'I was wondering whether we should go to Terre à Terre, after the conversation we had with your parents, but she said it's always busy and you can't book. She said she'd heard this place was good.'

'Since when did our daughter become so knowledgeable about restaurants?' Holly took a sip of her wine. 'She's not really a child any more, is she?'

'No,' Mark agreed. 'She's quite a woman about town these days. She certainly seems to know more about what's going on than I do!'

'I know.' Holly began studying the menu as she spoke. 'Do you think she's OK? She does seem to go out a lot these days and she gets very tired. I never went out when I was her age.'

'It's not as if she's doing anything her friends

aren't,' he said. 'And school's fine. She deserves to go out and have some fun too.'

'I suppose.' Holly was not entirely convinced, but Mark was right about Chloe doing well at school. They didn't really have any reason to stop her going out, just because things were different when they were young.

'What about her and Ruaridh?' Holly asked.

'What about them?' Mark was studying the menu.

Holly had been about to ask if he thought they were sleeping together and if this might account for Chloe's tiredness, but then she decided not to. She couldn't quite face the subject of sex, as she and Mark had not had any for several months. Perhaps tonight, she thought to herself, smiling up at Mark and muttering 'nothing' in relation to Chloe and Ruaridh.

'So what do you fancy?' He picked up the menu again. 'I like the look of the pork and artichoke hearts . . . and would it put you off if I had the rabbit?'

'No.' Holly was not going to get sentimental about rabbits. 'I quite fancy the squid. Do you think that's what they've got?'

Mark looked in the direction of the table Holly had just nodded towards. A young couple were forking up rings from a plate of deep purple ink.

Mark nodded. 'It certainly looks like squid. Do you remember that restaurant we went to in Andalucia, before we were married?'

'That's just what I was thinking!' Holly presumed they were thinking of the same restaurant. 'The one in Ronda? With the waiter . . . '

'And the squid!' Mark sat back, laughing at the memory, and Holly felt a huge surge of warmth for her husband and their shared life. She was glad they had come out and were forgetting the strains of the last year; remembering, instead, some of the highlights from their past.

'I don't suppose the same thing will happen here,' she said, looking at the waiter who was approaching to take their food order.

'I don't know.' Mark sat back and looked at her while she asked the waiter about the squid.

The Andalucian incident they'd both been reminded of had happened not long after Holly and Mark met. The company he worked for at the time was doing the marketing for a firm of olive-oil importers. They had sent him to Andalucia to see where their products originated. Mark had told Holly she could come with him.

'They will pay for everything,' he'd said, but she'd discovered a credit-card bill, when they returned, and found Mark had bought her flights and paid for most of the meals they'd had too. He'd never told her because he'd thought she'd insist on paying for herself or else might not come. She would have gone, no matter what.

'I think he's thinking about it,' Mark said, when the waiter had taken their order for a selection of tapas and left them to chat again.

'What?' Holly had lost the thread of their former conversation.

'Finding a flagon somewhere.' Mark raised his eyebrows, referring again to the incident in Andalucia.

They'd been out for dinner on their last evening to a fairly rustic, rough-hewn restaurant with pots, pans and plates all over the walls. The waiter there had been a very intense individual; dark and brooding, with a rasping voice when he told them exactly what they would be eating. He hadn't wanted to know what they might choose for themselves. For Mark it had been a very dark, purple, smoky octopus and for Holly roast suckling pig.

The waiter had been so sycophantic towards her it was comical and, at the end of the evening, had marched over and rasped that he wanted to pay homage to her beauty. He then reached for a flagon of wine, announced that his next gesture was for her, and poured it all over his face, so that it ran down his cheeks and chin and spilled on to his chest. It was the most extraordinary gesture, very erotic, and the sort of thing you would never encounter in England, but had seemed quite natural in Spain.

Mark, who was beginning to suffer from the hallucinogenic effects of the octopus ink, had sat back, not entirely sure if this was really happening.

'I doubt it,' Holly said, remembering that, when they'd returned to their hotel at the end of the evening, they'd abandoned the slightly polite, considerate sex which they'd been having with each other to date and replaced it with something much more wild, abandoned and passionate. She wondered if Mark remembered this too.

'I've become invisible with middle age,' she told him now.

'No, you haven't.' Mark studied her. 'You're still a very beautiful woman, Holly. People still look at you.'

'Not sexy young waiters.' She smiled, appreciating his compliment but never quite able to accept one with grace. 'I'm way too old for him.'

'No, you're not. As I said, you're a very beautiful woman. I'm sure a lot of people find you very attractive.' He took a sip of his wine.

'Thank you.' She tried to find the grace that had eluded her earlier, then decided to change the subject.

'So, how's this thing with Jimmy Finlay shaping up?' she asked. Mark had told her what he'd been planning but she hadn't asked him much about it for a while.

'Well, I think. It all seems to be going ahead,' Mark said as the waiter returned with the first of their dishes.

'How far have you got with the planning then?' Holly asked, eyeing up the artichoke hearts.

'The route is more or less planned,' Mark told her. But I still need to arrange press coverage and I'm trying to get a hotel chain to sponsor it which will help with the accommodation en route.'

'If he's doing it all for charity, who pays *you*?' she asked, hoping not to dampen Mark's enthusiasm by voicing the thing that had been nagging at her since he first got the job.

'Jimmy's paying me out of his own pocket.' Mark did not seem to mind the question. 'He really wants to do it, because of his dad, and he's single and has no family. He must earn quite a lot from . . . *I Nearly Died*. That's what he wants to do with it.'

'He sounds like a nice man,' she said.

She was pleased Mark had this job. It could be just what he needed to kick-start the business, although she was slightly worried about how they would manage the family between them if he became busy again.

'Will you have to go to Scotland when he's actually doing the run?' she asked, thinking that she would miss him if he did. She'd been taking his presence for granted recently, and finding it irritating at the same time. Now she found herself thinking it would be lonely coming home to a house without him in it, especially if he went for the duration.

'I might go up every now and then, but not all the time,' Mark reassured her. 'He needs a team to accompany him though; a backup vehicle and driver plus a photographer and a PA. Do you want some of this?'

He pushed a dish of fried chorizo towards Holly who spooned some of it on to her plate.

'I had a chat with Guy about the photography but he's not sure he can do it.'

'It would be difficult for him to get away.' Holly reiterated what she'd said before.

'I said I might have a coffee with him, next

time I'm in London,' Mark told her. 'Discuss it anyway.'

'Right.' Holly tried to sound disinterested. She'd arranged to have coffee with Guy herself the day after next.

She liked Guy but she wasn't looking forward to this meeting. She'd been going over and over in her mind what reason he could have to be eating out with Mila and couldn't think of one, except for the obvious. She didn't want to be asked to keep that a secret.

'I thought I might ask Daisy to do the PA-ing,' Mark said, as Holly took a mouthful and was momentarily unable to comment.

'Daisy? Daniel's Daisy?' she asked, forgetting immediately about Guy and Mila. 'But she's not a PA . . . and anyway, does she want to go away for that length of time?'

'I don't know.' Mark moved some of the dishes on the table to make way for a plate of rabbit which the waiter had brought.

'I won't know until I ask her. She worked as a PA before, in HR at BT.'

'That sounds like something to do with the menopause,' Holly remarked.

'Human Resources for BT. She said she hated the job because it was mostly sacking people, so she took voluntary redundancy herself,' Mark explained. 'She's bright and efficient, I'm sure she'd be great. Jimmy wants someone with him to deal with admin stuff, and it would be useful if that person were a personal trainer too. She could help with the running.'

'But it's a long time to be away from home.'

340

Holly knew the run would take at least six weeks.

She wondered if Mark knew that Daisy and Daniel were trying to have a child.

'Well, that's up to her, isn't it? I thought I'd ask her if she wants to work on the press launch, which will be in a few weeks,' he said, spearing a piece of rabbit as he did so. 'Then she can see if she wants to do the actual run. Do you think it will be a problem with Daniel?'

'I don't know,' Holly said quickly. 'Is the rabbit good?'

'Try some.' Mark pushed the plate towards her. 'How often do you see Daniel anyway?'

'Not that often.' Holly avoided looking directly at him and concentrated on getting the rabbit from the dish to her plate. 'I bump into him on the train every now and then. Just to say hello to.'

She wondered if Mark would accept what she said or if he guessed that it wasn't entirely true. She wasn't sure why but she didn't want him to know just how much time she spent talking to Daniel, any more than she wanted him to have another reason to spend more time with Daisy.

36

Holly felt the need to put some physical distance between herself and Guy and Natalie. She wanted to be out of London and on her way home but the departure boards weren't showing any trains to Brighton.

She'd met Guy for a coffee in a shop off Tottenham Court Road at midday. She'd told Natalie that she was going to look for some web-studio software that Jake wanted. He did want some web-design software, and it gave her just the excuse to head out of the office in that direction for half an hour.

She hadn't liked lying to Natalie but couldn't very well tell her she was meeting her husband.

Cuppa Coffee was an unusually homely affair for this part of town. Faux-suede sofas strewn with embroidered cushions were parked around coffee tables, creating the impression of a front room rather than a cafe. It seemed to be frequented entirely by mothers with young children and infants.

'Hello,' Holly said, spotting Guy sitting in an armchair in a corner. 'We should have a baby!'

She indicated the mothers and babies.

'It's too soon,' Guy said, grinning as he got up to kiss her.

Holly laughed, despite feeling that laughter wasn't entirely appropriate given their reason for meeting up.

'And I don't really want any more babies,' he added, catching the eye of the waitress who was approaching them. 'I don't think I could bear to go back to the early years again. What will you have, Holly?'

'A cup of tea, please,' she said to the waitress. 'English Breakfast.'

'I'll have an Americano, please,' Guy said, settling back into his chair as the waitress left with their order.

'So . . . ' Holly was not sure how to start this conversation. 'You spoke to Mark about this Jimmy Finlay run?'

'Yes, it was good of him to consider me,' Guy replied. 'And previously I'd have jumped at the chance, but it's difficult. I mentioned it to Nat and she said it was impossible. Her career seems to have to come first.'

'It's not the sort of job you can leave behind at the end of the day.' Holly detected the note of pique in his voice.

'Look, I know what you're probably thinking,' Guy said, coming to the point. 'I know things looked bad the other night.'

'I don't know what to think,' Holly told him. 'But you two certainly seemed very cosy.'

'It's the first time I've met Mila,' Guy said. 'Well, obviously, I met her at the do for the programme, but that's the first and only time I've met up with her alone.'

Holly said nothing.

'The thing is . . . ' Guy paused as the waitress came back and put their drinks on the table between them ' . . . I had a bit of a chat with her

343

then when I went to have a cigarette, about being at home with young children and how you don't have time to do anything for yourself.'

'It goes with the territory,' Holly pointed out.

'I know.' Guy took a sip of his coffee. 'Anyway we just got chatting about what we used to do, my photography and stuff. She's a sculptor but hardly gets time for it any more.'

'I know,' Holly said.

'Well, anyway, we exchanged numbers and I said we should meet and talk about ways of doing our own work.' He paused. 'But that's not really why I wanted to meet.'

'No?'

'I wanted to find out if she gets as rattled about the way Natalie is with James as I do.' A frown started to crease Guy's face. 'Because, from where I'm sitting, Holly, they are more than just colleagues. Natalie denies that there is anything going on but I don't know whether to believe her or not.'

'Why wouldn't you believe her?' Holly asked, thinking of the idle office speculation that there already was about James and Natalie and wondering if he had any firmer evidence.

'Because he just seems to take precedence in our lives,' Guy said. 'She's always on the phone to him, ostensibly talking about something for the programme, or going to functions with him, and just generally dropping his name into the conversation. It drives me mad.'

Holly shrugged. 'They do work together every day.'

'But you don't phone him every evening, do

344

you?' Guy challenged.

She shook her head.

'Anyway, I met up with Mila. I wanted to ask how she found things.'

'What did she say?' Holly was curious to hear how Mila viewed her husband's relationship with Natalie.

'She said, 'I don't consider Natalie to be a threat,'' Guy mimicked her accent. 'There was something condescending in the way she said it, as if Natalie wasn't worthy of fucking James Darling.'

'And is *she* a threat to Natalie?' Holly asked. She knew Guy knew she had seen them holding hands.

'Oh, God, no,' he laughed. 'I think she thinks I'm rather pathetic. What you saw . . . she was treating me like a child, Holly. She put her hand over mine and talked to me as if I was a four year old . . . '

''I do not think you need to worry, Guy.'' He did a good imitation of Mila's voice again. ''You should stop worrying about your wife and do something to feel better about yourself. Do something you enjoy.''

'That's probably good advice.' Holly decided to choose to believe what he had told her, for the moment at least. 'Natalie said you'd been going to the gym, is that something you enjoy?'

'Yes.' Guy looked away, a bit shiftily, Holly thought. 'I used to stay fit just lugging cameras around the world, but I need to do a bit more these days. What about Mark? He said he was going to run a marathon?'

'So he says.' Holly was wondering how much of anything anyone said was to be believed.

She'd found it hard not saying anything to Natalie about Guy when she got back to the office and was relieved when it was time to go home, although now the trains seemed to be conspiring against her getting there.

★　★　★

'What's going on?' Daniel stood next to her as she scanned the train departure boards at Victoria.

'I've no idea,' she answered, surprised at just how often they managed to bump into each other, given the number of possible trains they might both choose to catch. 'All the trains to Brighton are coming up as cancelled but there's no more information.'

'I'll ask someone.' Daniel began walking towards the guard who was manning the ticket barrier. He turned and smiled at Holly just before he got there and she felt a surge of intense feeling that she told herself was contentment.

'A body on the line at Hassocks.' Daniel grimaced as he returned with the news. 'No trains to Brighton until they've dealt with it.'

'What about Hove?' Holly bit back the temptation to say something about the selfishness of killing yourself on this stretch of track. Didn't whoever it was know that people who hadn't wanted to end their lives had only recently died on this line? She took a deep breath, trying to calm herself.

'No, same stretch of track.' Daniel began scanning the boards again. 'We could take that train to Lewes. Then get the coastway service back to Brighton. It will probably be quicker than waiting to see what happens.'

'Good idea.' Holly checked the platform number. 'I'd rather be on the move anyway.'

★　★　★

'I used to live in Lewes,' Daniel said as the train pulled out of the station.

'Did you?' Holly couldn't quite see him in Lewes.

She took her phone out. It had just bleeped in her bag and she checked her messages, half-expecting, half-hoping it was Mark, asking when she'd be home.

It was from Anne-Marie.

Hi, Holly. No trains going home. Just wondered if you were at station and fancied a drink while we wait?

Holly put the phone away, deciding not to show it to Daniel.

'We lived there briefly, when we first moved out of London,' he was saying. 'We rented a flat in Southover to see if we liked it, but Daisy preferred Brighton.'

'And do you?' Holly couldn't quite work out if it was Daisy who had driven the move to the sea.

'I liked Lewes but I'm happy in Brighton too.' Daniel didn't seem particularly bothered about where he lived.

'Mark's over the moon about this work he's

347

got with Jimmy Finlay.' Holly presumed Daniel knew about the run. 'And he's hoping Daisy will work on it with him.'

'She said he had asked if she wanted to help set up a press launch too.' Daniel didn't give away how he felt about this.

'I knew he was thinking of that, yes,' Holly said, wondering if Daniel knew that Mark also wanted her to accompany Jimmy Finlay on the run for six weeks. 'Do you mind?'

'No,' he replied. 'She'll probably enjoy working on something like that. She never really set out to do personal training and she gets a bit bored with it. It will be good for her to do something more challenging for a few weeks.'

'Yes.' Holly decided not to mention that Mark had Daisy in mind for a role which might last longer than that.

'Do you ever go to Lewes any more?' she asked as the train began nearing the town.

'Every now and then, for a wander and meal in The Snowdrop,' Daniel replied.

'The Snowdrop?' Holly sounded surprised.

'Yes. Have you been there?' Daniel asked.

'I don't think I've been for nearly twenty years.' She realised this made her sound very old.

'It's changed hands a few times,' Daniel said. 'And been done up. It's decked out like an old canal boat, and the food is great.'

'Then it has changed quite a bit.'

Holly remembered being sent there when she was a local radio reporter, to interview a retired policeman. He'd worked on a case involving the murder of two young children and been so affected he'd taken early retirement, spending his days in the pub which then, if not exactly spit and sawdust, most definitely didn't scream gastropub.

'I'll have to go some time,' she remarked.

'We could have a quick drink now,' Daniel suggested, looking at his watch, then at her. 'If you don't need to rush back.'

'Not really . . . ' Holly hesitated slightly.

She had told Mark she would try and get back by 7. He was going for a twelve-mile run and she'd promised to make dinner.

But the weather was warm and the idea of a drink with Daniel, in a pub by the river, was appealing. The trains to Brighton had all been cancelled. She had the perfect excuse for being late.

'That's a lovely idea.' She smiled at Daniel. 'I'll text Mark and let him know what's going on.'

★   ★   ★

'You're right.' Holly looked around her, taking in the decor. 'It is much nicer than when I last came!'

'What are you having?' The pub was busy but Daniel had homed in on a free barman, with a skill she rather admired.

'I'll have a white wine spritzer,' Holly said. 'Shall I go and get us somewhere to sit?'

'A white wine spritzer and a pint of Harvey's,' Daniel said to the barman. Then to Holly, 'Do you want to sit outside?'

'That would be good.' She went to find a table in the beer garden.

There were plenty free, despite the sunshine. She watched Daniel coming out, his pace slower than usual as he carried the drinks across the uneven terrain. It was funny, she thought to herself. Before the crash she would have recognised Daniel if she'd seen him somewhere out of context, but she wouldn't have thought he was attractive.

She wasn't even sure she would have thought this a few weeks ago either. But now, as he put their two glasses down on the table, she definitely did. She frowned slightly, wondering what had changed and why.

'Penny for your thoughts,' he said.

'I was wondering why the pub was called The Snowdrop?' Holly said, looking up and spotting the sign.

It gave her something to say even though she was thinking something quite different.

'Why do you think?' Daniel's tone was questioning, rather than dismissive, and he nodded towards the sign which had prompted her question in the first place.

'I'm not sure.' Holly looked at it, taking it in properly.

When she'd looked the first time, she'd seen a landscape scene and expected, if she looked more closely, it would be dotted with clusters of snowdrops.

It wasn't. There was a row of houses, tiny beneath the vast chalky cliff — not a snowdrop in sight.

'Do the river banks here have a lot of snowdrops?' she asked.

'Appalling guess!' Daniel laughed. 'I thought you would know, having been a local journalist.'

'Go on then, tell me!' Holly gave his hand a playful shove because he was teasing her. Daniel caught her eye as she did so. Again, he seemed to hold her look, and Holly felt slightly uncomfortable. 'Why is it called The Snowdrop then?'

'It's the site of the UK's biggest ever avalanche,' Daniel told her.

'Really?' Holly looked around them. The gentle undulating curves of the South Downs provided an impressive backdrop, but these were hills not mountains. Surely you needed those for an avalanche. 'But where did the snow come from?'

'From that cliff.' Daniel nodded up towards it. 'There'd been heavy snow and wind, and a huge drift built up over days at the top of it. When it eventually came down, it covered the row of workers' cottages here. About fifteen people were buried and quite a few died.'

'When was that?' Holly shivered involuntarily. The thought of people trapped under a vast quantity of snow made her feel suddenly cold.

'It was just after Christmas, sometime in the early nineteenth century.' Daniel noticed that she was shivering. 'Are you OK?'

'Yes, it's just . . . ' She paused and pulled her cardigan more tightly around her. 'I had a sudden feeling of déjà vu almost. It's the thought of all those people being trapped, in the cold and dark, waiting . . . not knowing if they would get out alive or not.'

'I didn't think.' Daniel reached out his hand across the table, took hers and held it.

He didn't say anything else. He didn't need to. Holly knew that he knew he had revived memories for her. She squeezed his hand, as he had squeezed hers when he'd stayed with her, waiting for the emergency services to arrive.

'I don't know how I'd have got through it without you,' she said.

'I just happened to be there.' He shrugged. 'Anyone else would have done the same.'

'I don't just mean then.' Holly held his gaze. 'I mean afterwards too. These last few months. I don't quite know how to say this but . . . '

'It's OK.' Daniel was stroking her hand as he continued to hold it. 'You don't have to say anything, Holly. I understand. I feel the same way too.'

37

Jake was sitting at the kitchen table with Mark's laptop. It was Sunday afternoon and he had opted to set himself up in the kitchen, largely because he was about to undertake a homework assignment and from the table there would be able to enlist help from both his parents.

'What's a palindrome?' he'd asked as he finished off his English homework.

'It's a word or phrase that reads the same forwards and backwards,' Holly told him.

'Like Anna?' Jake asked.

'Well, yes. A man, a plan, a canal, Panama is a good one.' She wondered if Jake had to come up with examples.

'What's Panama?' he asked.

'A very famous canal.' Holly felt sure he must know this. 'Don't they teach you anything in geography?'

'I've got geography homework too,' he told her. 'We don't learn where anywhere is, though.'

'Never odd or even, no lemon no melon.' It didn't surprise Holly that Mark had a whole lot of palindromes up his sleeve. 'God's dog.'

'Isn't that blasphemy?' Jake queried.

'Ma is a nun, as I am.' Mark ignored him and continued running off palindromes.

'A good one for Daisy,' Holly commented, wanting to remind him of the gaffe he'd made when he first met her.

He ignored her, turning his attention to Jake. 'What's your geography homework about then?'

'It's about natural disasters. I've got to think of three different types of natural disaster and then write about the causes and effects.'

'That sounds fairly straightforward.' Mark was reading the Sunday papers at the other of the table. 'You only have to pick up the paper to find something about a volcano or an earthquake.'

'Yeah, I might do the Icelandic volcano.' Jake leaned back in his seat and played with the mouse pad. ''Cos then I can write something about us getting stuck in Italy.'

'Oh, yes.' Holly recalled the extra week's holiday they'd had, courtesy of an Italian drinks company.

Mark had been working on a contract for Italian firewater and had had meetings and site visits in Tuscany. The brief was to see where the drink was sold in Italy and who drank it.

'It's a research trip,' he'd said when he told Holly about it.

'It's a pub crawl,' she had teased him. 'You get paid to do what most people have to spend their hard-earned cash doing. Groups of men, moving round bars, drinking. It's a pub crawl!'

'The thing about this particular pub crawl,' Mark had said, putting his arm around her waist and pulling her close to him, 'is that they want to know if I want to bring my family. And I have to be sure my wife won't be rude about my job if I do.'

'It's a very important research trip, obviously!'

she had replied, and kissed him.

The trip was supposed to last a week but the Icelandic volcano erupted and their flight home was cancelled. Usually, Mark would have been stressed about not being able to get home, but he had imbibed a lot of Italian *gioia vivere* and, when one of his clients invited them to stay at his home for another week, quickly accepted.

The research trip turned into an idyllic holiday, being wined and dined by the most hospitable Italians. They had played tennis with Jake, flirted with Holly, and allowed their teenage sons to flirt with the just-pubescent Chloe so much that she never wanted to come home. Mark had been in his element, happy to be working but proud to have his wife and family there.

'I want to find something a bit unusual too.' Jake brought Holly's thoughts back to the present. 'Some sort of natural disaster that no one knows much about.'

'Oh, I've got a good one.' Holly had a sudden burst of enthusiasm for Jake's project. 'Did you know that the biggest ever avalanche in the UK was in Lewes?'

'That can't be right.' Mark was quick to dismiss her input. 'There are no mountains in Lewes, and you need mountains for avalanches.'

'That's what I thought.' Holly tried to be patient. 'But it was caused when a huge snowdrift built up on the cliff and then it collapsed on to a row of cottages in South Street.'

'Was anyone killed?' There had to be deaths

for Jake to be interested.

'Yes, about fifteen people who lived in the cottages,' Holly told him. 'There's a pub there now, called The Snowdrop.'

'Oh, that's perfect!' Jake was pleased with this bit of information.

Mark was not.

'How do you know that?' He sounded cross and Holly was not sure if it was because he suspected her of having been to The Snowdrop, without telling him, or because she had an interesting bit of information to pass on which he hadn't known himself. He liked to think of interesting facts as his preserve.

'I don't know.' She decided to sound vague. 'Someone told me.'

'Who?' Mark was pressing her for more details.

'I can't remember who.' Holly continued with the deliberately vague tack. 'Or maybe I read it somewhere.'

'I never knew that.' Mark said this as if his not knowing might make the information wrong. He did have a capacity for soaking up and retaining information. Mention a small African country and he seemed to know its history and the make up of its government. He was a good person to have on a pub quiz team, the person you would want for your phone-a-friend . . . although if you phoned him and he didn't know the answer, he would probably find fault with the question.

'There's something about it here.' Jake had Googled the Lewes avalanche and was looking at a Wikipedia article. 'It must have been awful, being stuck in the snow like that.' He looked up at Holly questioningly, as if asking about her own experience.

Holly looked at Mark, who was reading the paper and not meeting her eyes. She smiled at Jake, attempting to reassure him. 'It's OK, Jakey. It was bad but I don't go there any more. I'm OK.'

'It's a grotty pub,' Mark said grumpily.

'Apparently it's changed hands a few times since we last went,' Holly said, and almost immediately wished she hadn't.

'And the same mysterious source who told you its history told you that too?'

Holly shrugged and wondered if perhaps he already knew that she'd been to the pub with Daniel on her way home. There was only one way he could. Daisy must have told him. But that seemed unlikely because Daisy could only have known if Daniel had told her.

★   ★   ★

'When did you tell Mark you'd be back?' Daniel had asked in the pub on Friday evening. 'Have you got time for another drink?'

'I didn't give him a time,' Holly said. She hadn't told Mark she was finding an alternative route. 'I just said there were no trains to Brighton and I'd be late back.'

'Daisy's not expecting me.' Daniel began to get up, as if to make for the bar. 'She's doing a training session this evening.'

'I'll get these.' Holly stood up herself and began picking up their empty glasses. 'Same again?'

Daniel nodded as she went back inside. She wondered as she stood at the bar whether he knew Daisy's training session was with Mark or if he minded the time they were spending together. There was no reason why he should. It was her job after all. But if Daisy was going to work on the Jimmy Finlay job, they would be spending even more time together.

Every now and then it crossed Holly's mind that Mark might be using his personal training sessions as an opportunity to try to make a move on Daisy. But even if he did, she was fairly confident he would not succeed. Daisy could do better, she thought, and as she did realised it was not a particularly pleasant thing to think about your own husband.

'Here you are.' She handed Daniel another pint and sat down. Now that they were here, away from their different worlds, she wanted to talk to him. 'Do you ever get flashbacks?'

'Sometimes.' Daniel did not seem surprised by her question, as if he had been waiting for her to ask it for some time.

'It was the dark that scared me more than anything,' Holly told him. 'It was so total. Every now and then something happens that brings it back to me.'

'I find it happens when I'm least expecting it,' Daniel confided. 'I'll be with a client in a meeting, having a perfectly normal conversation, and suddenly I can hear people screaming. I just have to keep talking and focus on the job and it usually recedes.'

'I find it comes back in quieter moments,' Holly told him. 'Mark thinks I should see a counsellor but most of the time I'm fine. I don't want to keep going over stuff, I'd rather just get on with life and try to forget it.'

'I'm the same.' Daniel sipped his pint and considered what she'd said. 'I mean, if someone like Anne-Marie can carry on and get the train regularly, what have I got to complain about? I wasn't hurt. I didn't lose anyone. We spent half an hour stuck on the train . . . that's all, really.'

'Anne-Marie does seem very angry,' Holly ventured.

'Well, she's got good reason to be.' Daniel was pushing some spilled beer around the tabletop. 'I'm sure she has bad days.'

'Do you have bad days?' Holly asked.

'Sometimes.' He looked up at her. 'But talking to you helps.'

'Perhaps we should talk more?' she suggested. In response Daniel put his hand over hers but said nothing.

A barmaid had come into the garden, looking for empties to clear away. She approached Holly and Daniel and peered briefly at the half-empty glasses between which they were holding hands.

Holly wondered what she made of them. Did they look like any couple having a drink on a Friday night or did they look different? Would the barmaid go inside and comment that they didn't look right together, but she wasn't quite sure why?

'The thing I find hardest,' Daniel said, after a few moments' silence, 'is connecting with everyone around me. I can go through the motions . . . I can have conversations . . . I can walk along the seafront with Daisy . . . but I feel slightly apart from them.'

'I know what you mean.' Holly felt like this, even with Chloe and Jake. 'I feel as if my friends and family don't understand me.' She paused and took a sip of her drink then corrected herself. 'Can't understand me.'

'The only person I think might understand me is you,' Daniel told her.

Then his phone had rung, and he'd picked up because it was Daisy, and although he turned away from her slightly as he reassured his wife that he would be back soon, Holly could still see enough of his face to notice it soften into the expression people use when they're talking to someone they are close to.

'I ought to be getting back,' she said, as soon as he had finished his call.

★ ★ ★

'OK, I'm going to do the avalanche, the tsunami and an earthquake.' Jake had decided the direction his geography project would take.

'We were in the tsunami.' Mark looked up from the travel section. 'Don't you remember?'

'No!' Now it was Jake's turn to express disbelief. 'I think I would have remembered.'

'Not exactly in it,' Holly said. 'Only the shallow end anyway.'

'It was still the tsunami though.' Mark addressed this to Jake. 'We were on holiday in the north of Thailand. It was our tenth wedding anniversary, wasn't it, Hol?'

'Yes.' She'd forgotten they'd decided to mark this milestone by all going to Thailand for a couple of weeks.

'And there was one day we were on the beach,' he continued, 'and it was suddenly covered in water.'

'It wasn't deep,' Holly joined in the recollections. 'Not more than an inch really, was it?'

'No,' Mark agreed. 'We thought it was quite fun at the time. We didn't know then what devastation it was wreaking elsewhere.'

'We were lucky then,' Jake said.

'And we've been in an earthquake too.' As she said this Holly suddenly realised her life seemed to be a series of minor involvements in major incidents.

'Oh, yes, on our honeymoon,' Mark told Jake. 'We were in Chile and there was an earthquake in another part of the country. We just felt a small tremor where we were. Do you remember, Hol?'

'I remember the earth moving!' Holly smiled, feeling some of the old warmth between them revived by this spontaneous bout of reminiscing.

'Oh, pl-ease.' Jake grimaced. 'I just want to hear about the earthquake.'

'Don't worry, Jakey,' Mark said, suddenly serious again. 'There's no earth moving around your mother any more.'

Holly shot him a furious look.

'I'm going to make a phone call,' she said, and left the room.

38

Holly slowed her pace, not sure if she wanted to talk to Anne-Marie. She was pretty sure that was the person Daniel was chatting to. Holly had a slightly awkward conversation with her earlier in the day and didn't want to repeat it.

'We're doing something in the programme next week about Survivor's Syndrome,' the producer who'd introduced herself as Melanie had said. Her voice was quiet and concerned, and Holly wondered if she'd adopted that tone, specially to talk to her.

'Right . . . ' Holly waited for her to say more.

'I hope you don't mind my call?' Melanie went on. 'But someone told me that you were on the train which crashed near East Croydon earlier this year, and I wondered if you thought it might be something you could talk about?'

'I'm not sure,' Holly said, but she was. 'To be honest, I don't think I'm a particularly good example. I wasn't hurt in the crash and I don't know anyone who was.'

'It doesn't have to be anyone who was hurt. Sufferers from Survivor's Syndrome often feel guilty about having escaped.'

Holly felt lucky to have escaped unharmed. She didn't want to be pigeonholed as a survivor.

'I don't want to do it,' she told Melanie firmly.

'I also wondered if you might know of anyone else?' Melanie asked tentatively.

'There is someone.' Holly had thought of Anne-Marie. 'But I'll have to speak to her first.'

★ ★ ★

Holly took out her season ticket and passed it though the barrier. She could see Anne-Marie saying goodbye to Daniel and heading for the exit alongside W H Smith. He went the opposite way into the mini M&S on the opposite side of the station.

Suddenly an instant meal seemed like a very good idea.

'Fancy meeting you here.' Holly surprised him as he plucked a steak-and-kidney pie from the chiller cabinet.

'Hello.' He stood up and grinned, brandishing the pie. 'One meal for one! What are you here for?'

'Another meal for one.' Holly started looking in the chiller cabinet herself.

'No one cooking for you?' Daniel glanced at her sideways.

'No.' She tried to concentrate on the food. 'Mark's out running tonight and both the children are out, too. What about you?'

'Daisy has a few training sessions this evening,' he said. 'I think one of them is with Mark actually.'

Holly nodded as if she knew this, although she didn't. Mark must be seeing an awful lot of her at the moment. She'd also begun working on the Jimmy Finlay project. He wouldn't actually start his run until much later in the year, he needed to get a lot fitter first, but Mark was talking of setting up a press conference in a couple of weeks. Daisy was helping with that.

'Do you fancy a quick drink before your date with the microwave?' Daniel asked, as they stood in the checkout queue.

'Yes,' Holly said, emphatically. 'Did I see you talking to Anne-Marie?' she asked, giving away the fact that she had spotted him before he hit M&S.

'Yes, I bumped into her when I got off the train.'

'Did she say anything about talking to me today?' Holly asked, as they walked the short distance from the station to The Battle of Trafalgar.

'No, why?' Daniel said quizzically as they went into the pub. 'What are you having?'

'I'll get them.' Holly took out her purse. 'It's my turn, I'm sure.'

'A pint of Sussex Best then, thank you,' he said. 'What did Anne-Marie want then?'

'Oh, well, I called her.' Holly ordered the drinks and they carried them into the beer garden at the back. 'It was a bit awkward, really.'

'Why?' Daniel took a sip of his pint and looked around. Holly wasn't sure if he was taking in their surroundings or looking to see if there was anyone he knew there.

'A producer from *Woman's Hour* called me. Someone at work must have given them my name.' Holly followed the direction of Daniel's gaze.

The garden was fairly empty. A couple of gay

men sat in the corner holding hands and an elderly woman sat by herself, pulling a bright orange cardigan tight around her, even though it was warm, as she nursed what was left of a pint.

'They are doing a programme about Survivor's Syndrome,' she told Daniel. 'They wanted to know if I would talk to them, but I said I didn't have much to say and suggested Anne-Marie.'

'What is Survivor's Syndrome?' he asked.

'A mental condition that occurs when a person thinks they've done wrong surviving a traumatic event.' Holly parroted what Melanie had told her.

'And do you think Anne-Marie has it?' He looked sceptical.

'I don't know,' Holly said. 'I was just trying to fob off the producer with someone else, really. I know that's a terrible thing to do. But I suppose I also thought Anne-Marie probably does have mixed emotions about the fact that she wasn't on the train and her husband was.'

'What did she say when you called her?' Daniel asked.

'She was angry.' Holly hadn't given much advance thought to how Anne-Marie might react. 'She was really cross. Said I didn't understand anything about her and I had no right to go talking to journalists about her behind her back. Although she took the producer's number.'

Daniel put his arm around her in a brief gesture of reassurance.

'It was probably just a spur-of-the-moment

365

reaction. She seemed happy enough when I spoke to her.'

'I hope so.' Holly smiled at him gratefully.

'I haven't been here for a while,' he said, looking round the beer garden again.

'Me neither.' Holly couldn't think when the last time was. 'Mark and I used to come here a lot when we first met. He had a flat near here.'

She thought back to the early days, when she had first met him and had gone to visit him in the flat he had moved into by himself, not long after meeting her.

'It will give us more space together,' he'd said, as if he needed to justify moving out of the shared flat above her colleague from work. 'I don't want Tim getting in the way every time you come round.'

'He doesn't,' she'd laughed, but was flattered that, so early in their relationship, he was wanting to spend more time alone with her. Not long after he'd taken on the new flat, he'd asked her to move in with him.

'Isn't it a bit too soon?' she'd asked, worried that he seemed to be rushing things and might have second thoughts. But Mark had looked her in the eye and said, 'Why? I know I want to be with you. Why wait?'

Holly felt sad now, thinking back to those early heady days. She'd known the intensity of her relationship with him would not last, that it would become more settled and predictable, but she'd never imagined that they would start becoming strangers to each other, living side by side but failing to connect.

'You don't come here any more then?' Daniel asked, as if he could sense what she was thinking. 'With Mark? Or does he come with friends?'

'No, I don't think so.' Holly had never really thought about this. Perhaps Mark did still come here sometimes.

'Once the children came along, we stopped going out as much,' she said. 'We haven't really started again.'

She looked up and smiled. A cheerful smile that she hoped would pull her out of her slightly melancholy mood.

'Make the most of the time you have before the children arrive,' she said.

'If that ever happens.' Daniel stared into his pint and Holly wished she hadn't said it.

'No news then?' she asked.

'No.' He looked up at her. 'The consultant said to give it more time, but to be honest . . . '

He paused and Holly didn't say anything, unsure if he wanted to continue this line of conversation.

'We haven't really been getting on that well recently,' he said, looking at Holly again and holding the look. 'It's a bit of an issue and Daisy won't talk about it.'

'That's probably natural.' Holly felt slightly flustered. 'A lot of couples say it puts enormous pressure on them, trying for a baby.'

She wondered if Daniel had the same misgivings she'd had about Daisy and Mark working together so closely.

'It's not just that . . . ' He looked away.

Holly felt her phone vibrating in her bag, which was on the floor against her leg. She ignored it. She couldn't very well answer it now.

'The thing is ... ' said Daniel, then he appeared to be searching for the right words to communicate whatever it was he had to say.

'What is it?' Holly asked, looking at him again, which was when Daniel leaned forward and kissed her.

★   ★   ★

It was something of a relief when his phone rang. The ringtone was loud, which made it hard to ignore.

There'd been an awkwardness to the finishing of their drinks, the polite enquiries about whether they wanted another, the starting to ask questions at the same time and the 'you first', before saying something other than what they had meant to say.

Holly was reminded of an Ingrid Bergman quote: 'A kiss is a lovely trick designed by nature to stop speech when words become superfluous.' And she was tempted to kiss Daniel again because it had been nice, kissing him, very nice, but somehow not quite right. Not as in morally 'we are both married to other people so we shouldn't be kissing', but not what she'd expected.

She wondered, if she kissed him a second time, if it would feel different, and where it might lead. They were awkward with each other now; the kiss had done away with the old easy familiarity.

Holly drained her drink and smiled to herself, wondering what Dimitri would think if he'd seen her kissing Daniel in the beer garden of The Battle of Trafalgar.

She could imagine him teasing her. 'Nice try, Holly, but it was still a pretty safe kiss.'

'What's funny?' Daniel asked.

'I was just thinking of something a colleague said.' She left it at that.

'Listen, Holly, I . . . ' Daniel paused as his phone began to ring. He took it out of his pocket and looked at the caller ID.

'It's Daisy,' he said, apologetically. 'I'd better get it.'

Holly nodded and watched him.

'Hello,' he said.

There was something beautiful about his face, she thought as she watched him now. Something she'd only come to appreciate having got to know him.

'Is everything OK?' Daniel was saying to his wife, and a look of anxiety crossed his face as he glanced up and caught Holly looking at him.

She looked away quickly, embarrassed.

'No, I'm just having a quick drink,' she heard him saying as she studied the grain of the wood on the table instead of his face. 'I thought you were out for the evening?'

Holly ran her finger around the contours of a large knot, concentrating on this so as to try not to listen to his conversation with his wife.

'Yes, she is with me,' she heard him say. 'We just bumped into each other, coming out of the station.'

Holly caught his eye and felt alarm. Did Daisy suspect there was something going on between her and Daniel? She felt panic beginning to mount at the prospect of a confrontation, even though, apart from their one brief kiss, there was nothing really to confront anyone about. Or was there? She was confused.

'I guess she must have it switched off,' Daniel was saying, but he was still looking at Holly, no longer tuning in to his conversation with his wife.

Holly reached for the phone that was in her bag, remembering someone had been trying to reach her just before she had begun kissing Daniel.

She checked the call log and found she had one missed call. But it was from a number she did not recognise.

'Do you want to speak to her?' Daniel's face had gone pale and Holly felt the colour beginning to drain from hers too. Why would Daisy want to speak to her? Had Mark said something to her while they were training this evening?

She took a deep breath and held on to the edge of the table now, wondering what she would say to Daisy, but Daniel was still talking to her.

'OK, yes. Of course,' he was saying.

Holly strained to hear what Daisy was saying at the other end of the line.

'I'll tell her,' he said. 'And get a taxi from the station.'

Daniel was obviously being summoned somewhere, quickly. Holly breathed a small sigh of relief that Daisy no longer wanted to talk to her. Perhaps she would later.

She raised her eyebrows questioningly, in a way she hoped would convey 'Is everything OK?' and elicit a reassuring 'Yes, everything's fine' nod. But Daniel's face remained impassive.

'OK, see you in a bit.' He started to wind up the phone conversation. 'Daisy,' he said, as if she'd been about to hang up and he wanted to keep her on the line a moment longer.

'Yes?' Holly heard her reply.

'I'll see you in a bit.' Daniel had already said this. He had obviously been about to say something else to her, but had thought better of it in front of Holly.

'Is everything OK?' she asked, now that he was slowly putting the phone back in his pocket.

'Holly,' Daniel began. 'Something's happened.'

39

'Are you a relative?' The receptionist at A & E had an air of suspicion about her, as if people who weren't relatives turned up all the time, trying to gain access to Accident and Emergency patients.

'Yes, I'm his wife,' Holly said, which had the effect of making the receptionist transfer her suspicions to Daniel.

'And you?' she asked.

'I'm a friend,' he told her coolly. 'And my wife brought him in.'

If Holly's emotions hadn't been in the heightened state they were, she might have noticed that the receptionist raised her eyebrows ever so slightly. Fortunately she didn't.

'He's been transferred to the Albion and Lewes ward,' the woman revealed, after typing Mark's name into her computer. 'Take the lift to the eighth floor and let the staff there know who you are.'

'Thank you.' Holly began looking around for the lifts.

'You can go up with her, if you want,' the receptionist told Daniel grudgingly.

'I've no intention of doing anything else,' he muttered, as they made their way through the walking wounded to the lifts.

Holly had once been very familiar with A & E and didn't need to look around to know that there would be a few drunks, passed out or brought in by the police, some anxious parents thinking their child may have meningitis, and a couple of older people, waiting patiently, not wanting to trouble the doctors, even though they may have broken a hip falling several hours ago.

A few years back she and Mark had been the anxious parents, sitting with Jake on various occasions: after he'd stepped on a rusty nail and got blood poisoning; jumped from the roof of the shed and broken several toes; and fallen off his skateboard and cracked a rib.

Holly remembered how the woman who'd been living next-door when he was born had told her she'd get used to coming into Casualty. The neighbour had three boys and was wondering whether to keep trying for a girl.

'Boys injure themselves all the time,' she'd said cheerily as Holly cradled her day-old son and thought to herself that she would do all she could to protect him.

The neighbour had been right, though. A few months down the line, Jake had stuffed a Lego figure so far up his nose it required a surgeon's skill to remove it. Since then A & E had become a regular haunt. Holly had expected to be back there at some point, and frequently envisaged a scenario where a car knocked down Jake while he was walking to school, his hearing impaired by an iPod and his sight blinkered by the cowl of his hoody.

She hadn't expected to be here because Mark had had a heart attack.

She could feel her own heart racing as they emerged from the lift and was surprised by how pleased she felt to see Daisy as they crossed the newly disinfected floor to the nurses' desk.

'Holly,' she said, touching her arm. 'He's going to be OK.'

Holly managed a half-smile as Daisy told the nurse that this was Mark's wife.

'Can I see him?' she asked.

'Of course.' The nurse at the desk had picked up more of a beside manner than her colleague downstairs. She stood up and nodded to a young uniformed man. 'Ashwin, this is Mrs Constantine.'

Mark was lying on a bed with an oxygen mask over his face and a drip in his arm. He was wearing a hospital gown.

'Hello,' she said gently, not sure how much of his surroundings he was taking in.

'Holly,' Mark said, lifting the mask from his face and speaking with some effort. His skin looked grey. 'You were right about the marathon being a ridiculous idea!'

'Oh, Mark.' Holly bent down to kiss him. 'What happened?'

Ashwin spoke for him.

'He's had a minor heart attack.' He confirmed what Daisy had already relayed via Daniel. 'We are going to operate to unblock one of his arteries. He's going to need a local anaesthetic and we're just waiting for the cardiologist.'

'Who's that?' Holly asked because she felt she needed to ask questions and wasn't sure what else to ask.

'Dr Parkinson,' the nurse told her. 'He's very experienced.'

'I hope he doesn't . . . ' Mark was lifting his oxygen mask again and trying to speak.

'Doesn't what?' Holly asked.

'Have Parkinson's!' Mark said, smiling despite the effort and letting the mask fall over his face again.

Holly smiled back, wondering whether hospital etiquette allowed emergency patients to joke about their condition.

'No, his hands are perfectly steady,' the nurse laughed. 'He's a bit of a comedian, your husband, isn't he? Apparently he made the paramedics laugh in the ambulance too. I keep telling him he should be trying to relax.'

'He can't help himself.' Holly sniffed, finding that she was now beginning to cry. She took Mark's hand and squeezed it.

'I was trying to make you laugh,' he said through the mask.

'You did,' she said, stroking his hand and feeling overawed that despite the fact he was lying on a hospital trolley, waiting to have a heart operation, he had not lost his sense of humour. She wondered now how she could ever have found his relentless jokiness irritating. He was naturally funny, and how much better a man who tried to use his humour to get through the difficult times than one who just allowed himself to become depressed.

'You do.' She emphasised the *do* and bent down to kiss him.

'Ready for Mr Constantine,' announced a man in scrubs. He had heavily tattooed arms, was chewing gum, and would have looked more at home backstage at a heavy metal convention than in a hospital corridor.

Oh, God, don't let him be the surgeon, Holly thought, slightly ashamed of her innate prejudice against multiple tattoos.

'The porter will take him up for his operation,' Ashwin put her mind at rest. 'You'll have to wait here.'

'Yes.' Holly had watched enough episodes of *Casualty* to know this much.

'I love you,' she whispered to Mark.

He didn't reply and she wasn't sure if he'd heard her. He looked scared now and so was Holly — scared that the future she'd always thought she would have with him might be in jeopardy.

★   ★   ★

Daniel and Daisy were sitting side by side on plastic chairs in the reception area. They looked up at Holly with a mixture of sympathy and query as she walked towards them.

'Has he gone in?' Daisy asked.

Holly nodded.

'So what do you do now?' Daniel enquired.

'They suggested I go home and get him some clothes and stuff.' Holly looked at them both, seeking their approval for this course of action.

It seemed to her somehow callous and uncaring to leave the building while Mark was being operated on, but she could see that it might be better to do something practical rather than pace around Reception, feeling slightly sick.

'I can take you.' Daisy seemed to decide for her.

'Thank you.' Holly accepted the offer and, for the first time since Daniel had taken Daisy's call in the pub, realised she had not let the children know anything was amiss.

She'd thought about calling them as she sat in the taxi on her way to the hospital with Daniel, but had decided to find out exactly what was happening with Mark first.

'I need to let the children know what's going on.' She looked from Daniel to Daisy, wondering what Daisy would think if she'd known that an hour or so ago Holly had been kissing her husband in a pub garden. She wished it had never happened.

'I called them after I called you. I hope you don't mind?' Daisy said. 'Mark said Jake had been going for a sleepover but it was cancelled so he'd be at home. And he said Chloe was out but she'd want to know too.'

'Thank you.' Holly was grateful to her again. She hadn't wanted to call them out of the blue and tell them the news. She didn't know exactly what Daisy had told them but, whatever it had been, it would make it easier for her to call them now.

'I told them Mark had been taken ill while running.' Daisy appeared to read her thoughts and filled her in. 'And that he was going to hospital to be checked over. I didn't want to tell them any more than that.'

'You seem to have done everything absolutely right,' Holly said, thinking that Daniel and Daisy were well suited to one other. They both seemed to know instinctively what to do in a crisis.

'Shall I take you home then?' Daisy asked. 'The car's on a double yellow line around the corner. At least, I hope it's still there.'

'Shall I wait here?' Daniel suddenly seemed set apart from the unfolding drama, unsure what to do.

'I've got a Smart car,' Daisy said, to explain why he would not be coming with them.

'I could wait until you get back.' Daniel sat down again, as if this was what he'd decided to do, and again Holly realised it was the right thing. She felt better leaving Mark knowing there was someone else in the building, someone who could contact her if necessary, someone who would be there, looking familiar, when she walked back in.

'Thank you,' she said to him.

'See you in a bit then.' He stood up a little awkwardly as if wondering whether he should make any sort of parting gesture, but Daisy was already guiding Holly towards the lift.

'Are you OK?' she asked as they got in.

'No,' Holly answered.

She was anything but all right. She felt sick, brought up short by the sight of Mark and the shock of what was happening to him. She felt guilty for being in the pub with Daniel when her husband was suddenly seized by overwhelming pain, and she felt powerless to do anything to help him.

'He'll be OK,' Daisy said, looking at Holly as if she knew exactly what she was thinking. 'I'm sure you'll both be OK, Holly.'

40

Jake closed the computer hurriedly when Holly walked into the sitting room. He seemed furtive and, even in her emotional state, she made a mental note that she and Mark really must check what he did on it. She suspected he might be looking at porn, but her suspicions were based only on the general impression that that was what all teenagers were doing these days.

'Oh, hi Mum.' Jake got up from the sofa and put the laptop back on the desk.

Then he walked over and hugged her, burying his head in her chest as he used to do every morning when he woke up, until about a year ago when a new set of hormones kicked in and told him that all physical contact with your mother should be avoided.

'Is Dad OK?' he said, raising his head and seeing Daisy hovering in the corridor behind Holly. The sight of her caused him to spring away from Holly as if he'd been caught in a clinch with someone who was not his mother.

'Not really, Jakey.' Holly wished Jake was still holding her but she knew the teenage psyche was like a yo-yo on high-grade elastic. 'Shall we sit down?' She motioned towards the sofa and Jake obediently ambled over and sat.

'Shall I make you a cup of tea?' Daisy was the one now hovering in the doorway.

'Oh, yes, please.' Holly realised this was just what she needed.

'Jake?' Daisy asked.

'OK.' He was graceless in accepting her offer.

'Do you want sugar?' This was addressed to Holly again, and although Holly didn't take sugar, she realised that she wanted it.

She nodded, and as she listened to the footsteps going down the corridor to the kitchen she wondered if Daisy was going to be looking for the kettle and the tea and the cups, and having difficulty finding them, or whether she was already completely au fait with the layout of their kitchen.

'Dad's not very well,' Holly said, sitting down next to Jake on the sofa. 'I don't want you to be too alarmed, because it sounds worse than it is, but he had a minor heart attack while he was running. He's going to be OK though.'

'Oh, right.' Jake's reply was characteristically nonchalant.

Holly had expected this news might provoke an atypical reaction.

'Our headmaster had a heart attack when he was running,' Jake said, as if hearing about middle-aged men having heart attacks was something he was very used to. 'He had three months off last year.'

'And is he OK now?' Holly wondered why Jake had never mentioned this at the time, and why the school had never told them. Perhaps they'd sent a note which had never made it out of the depths of Jake's bag or, if it had, only as far as Mark's hands, not hers.

'Yeah, he's fine,' Jake told her. 'He was a fat bastard before but he looks much better now. Some of the girls think he's really fit.'

'Do they?' Holly wondered if this was his way of trying to reassure her. She found the image of the girls that Jake knew lusting after the headmaster somewhat unsettling.

'They say he looks like Richard Gere, but he looks more like a grey-haired David Cameron to me. His skin's all shiny too.' Jake began laughing, nervously at first, and then when Holly laughed too, more whole heartedly.

Holly was reminded of a time when she'd been away for a few days when he was six years old. She'd gone with a group of other mothers for a long weekend in Lisbon. Mark said the kids had been fine while she was away, but when she came back Jake had sat on her lap and laughed so hard that he almost cried. Holly had thought then that he probably wanted to cry because he had missed her while she was away, but had turned the tears into laughter instead.

She thought the same was probably true now and put her arm around him, trying to reassure and comfort him, even though he wasn't showing visible signs of distress.

'Declan's dad had a heart attack too,' Jake said, when he'd stopped laughing.

For someone in his early teens, he certainly seemed to know a lot of people with heart problems. 'Or was it heart failure? He has to take pills every day now.'

'Dad's having an operation.' Holly admired his easy acceptance of the situation but suspected he was using it to cover more mixed emotions. 'He's in hospital now. One of the tubes that goes into his heart got blocked and they are going to do something to make it bigger so that doesn't happen again.'

'Angioplasty?' Jake asked, a question Holly had not thought to ask when the procedure was being explained to her at the hospital.

'Yes. Do you do this in biology or something?' She wondered at her son's apparent knowledge, which certainly seemed to be more extensive than hers.

'No, I read about it on the internet,' he told her. 'I was looking into . . . '

He stopped as if he was revealing too much, Holly was not sure why.

'Tea.' Daisy came in and put two steaming mugs on the table in front of them.

'How are you, Jake?' she asked. 'I liked your pictures of your shadow friends.'

'Thank you,' Holly said, referring to the tea and wondering what Daisy was talking about. Who were Jake's shadow friends?

'Thanks.' Jake looked momentarily animated. 'Mr Bannister says I should enter them for this competition.'

'You should,' Daisy agreed. 'They're really good.'

Mr Bannister was Jake's art teacher, this much Holly knew, but he hadn't shown her the pictures which Daisy seemed to know all about. Holly wondered how she knew, and how she'd been able to find the sugar, which was fairly well hidden as no one normally took it.

'I saw the pictures on Jake's Facebook site,' Daisy commented, as if realising that her knowledge of Holly's son's life needed some explanation. 'We're friends.'

'Ah.' Holly should have guessed.

'By the way, Gran says to let her know about Dad,' Jake said.

'Did she call?' Holly wondered if super-efficient Daisy had somehow also got word to her mother's yoga camp in Koh Samui that Mark had been taken to hospital. She was beginning to understand why Mark had put her forward for being Jimmy Finlay's PA.

'No, I was Facebooking her earlier,' Jake said. 'She's always online around five o'clock. It's when she catches up with everyone.'

Except me and my dad, Holly thought to herself.

She took a sip of her tea and for a moment almost forgot that this cuppa was only a brief interlude before she went back to the hospital where her husband was currently undergoing heart surgery.

She shivered at the thought and Jake put his arm around her, as if he knew what was going through her mind.

'He'll be OK, Mum,' he said. 'Are you?'

Holly smiled at him, thinking she was the one who should be reassuring him.

'I'm just going to pack a few things for Dad,' she told him. 'He might need to stay in overnight. Then we'll go back to the hospital. Do you know where Chloe is?'

'She's out somewhere.' Jake was typically

vague. 'But she called. She said she'd meet us there. Are we driving?'

'I'm not sure I'm up to driving,' Holly said. 'We could get a taxi.'

'We won't all fit in my car,' Daisy said. 'Shall I call a cab while you're packing, Holly?'

'I'll do it,' Jake said, and Holly suddenly thought how like Mark he was, better able to cope with a situation if he was actually doing something.

'I'll be off then,' Daisy said. 'If you're OK? Daniel said he'd make his own way home after you got back. Let me know how Mark is, won't you?'

'Of course,' Holly said, wondering how imperative it was that Daisy knew how the operation had gone. Did she want to know because she was a friend or was she more than that?

'Are you sure you'll be OK?' she asked.

'No,' Holly said, laughing in the way that people do when they are trying not to cry. 'But I'm going to try to be.'

She went upstairs and could hear Daisy saying goodbye to Jake and telling him to look after his mother. She opened the door of their bedroom and surveyed the unmade bed and dirty clothes strewn across the floor. Mark usually tidied up a bit before she got home.

He knew it annoyed her to find the bed still unmade and yesterday's clothes where they'd landed. This evening, though, in Mark's absence, Holly felt comforted by the mess. The discarded shirt in the doorway provided evidence of his existence in the way his mess had done when she first met him.

Back then, when they had shuffled between their respective flats, Holly had delighted in seeing Mark's stuff strewn around her bedroom when he was not there. It had been a reminder that she had a gorgeous new boyfriend, rather than evidence of a husband who never tidied up.

She picked his shirt up off the floor and held it to her face, breathing in the smell of Mark and washing powder. She put it on the bed, thinking she might use it as a comforter that evening, if he was kept in overnight. She hoped he would not stay in for longer than that. She wanted him home as soon as possible.

Holly pulled an overnight bag from the top of the wardrobe in their room and opened the drawer under their bed, where Mark kept his underwear and t-shirts. Today the drawer seemed to hold more than just clean clothes. Like the rest of the room it held reminders of Mark, and rather than just pulling a few clean t-shirts from near the front of the drawer, Holly found herself sitting down and staring at its contents.

Nearest to her was the bottle green t-shirt that he usually wore while out running. He must have been wearing a different one today. Holly began leafing through the folded tops, much as someone would flick through files in a filing cabinet, briefly conjuring up images of the last time she had seen her husband in a particular shirt. She wasn't being maudlin. She had just realised, sitting here now, with Mark in hospital, how little attention she had been paying him recently and how much she regretted that.

Holly reached to the back of the drawer and pulled out a pale blue garment she had not seen him wear for years. She hadn't even realised he still had it. It was a nondescript t-shirt but she remembered it because it had been the one he was wearing at the party where they'd first met. It probably didn't even fit him any more and she wondered why Mark had kept it. Was it for sentimental reasons?

She pulled it out of the drawer, to look at it, not to pack it, and as she shook it out a white envelope fell out and into her lap.

'Holly' was written on the front, in Mark's writing. She turned it over but the flap at the back was stuck down. She wasn't sure what to do. The letter was addressed to her, but hidden. She obviously wasn't meant to find it. She thought she should probably wrap it up in the t-shirt and put it back, pretend she'd never disturbed it.

But lately, she hadn't been doing many of the things she ought to do.

41

Dear Holly,

I don't know if I will ever give you this letter. I am writing it because, right now, I am not sure what else to do. There are so many things I want to say, that I feel I need to say to you, but it may be better if some of those things are left unsaid. Perhaps what I am feeling at the moment is just me, now, and in a few weeks or months it will have passed. By then, I may breathe a sigh of relief that I never actually aired what I am about to write.

Or perhaps I will still feel the same, and I will give you this letter, or sit down and tell you exactly how I am feeling. I don't know. All I know is that now I am not happy and I need to do something. I know that writing you a letter I may never give you is not very pro-active, but I hope it will at least make me feel better without damaging us more than we already seem to be.

A lot has happened to us over the past couple of years, Holly, and I feel as if we are gradually coming unstuck. People talk about the glue that holds a marriage together but to me that always suggests that the marriage was something a bit broken in the first place. Glue is usually used to fix things that someone has dropped on the floor (in our house anyway). I think of marriage more as two people being joined together like links in a chain, and I used to think that you and I were a very strong chain. I'm no longer so sure. I feel as if someone has prised open a link and, while we are still together, it may take only a small swerve or sudden jolt to force us apart.

You used to joke, when we first met, that I was always doing something. I think it used to annoy you that I could never just sit in the garden of that first flat that we rented together, but would always be cutting something back or putting something up. It's true I do like to do things, it makes me feel more in control in this out-of-control world, as if by cutting back a bit of honeysuckle I am maintaining control over my life.

I feel I am losing that control now. There have been too many things beyond it, conspiring to change my life, and it scares me to feel so powerless over my own destiny.

I thought that knowing me, as no one else docs, you would realise how vulnerable losing contracts at work and struggling to keep my business going would make me feel. I thought you would support me, as you always have done, and that I would be able to get though a difficult patch with you behind me. But you seemed to think the only thing to do was take everything on yourself, and you seemed to despise me for my failure at work.

Or perhaps despise is too strong? I know, Holly, that I am no longer the strong, capable, outgoing, funny man you first fell in love with — not to you anyway.

I know it's not supposed to be this way any more, but not being the main breadwinner makes me feel completely emasculated. When my company began to suffer and you went back to work full-time, I felt like a failure. I know that lots of women are the main breadwinners and there are plenty of men left holding the fort. You see, I can't quite bear to admit to being responsible for domestic affairs. I have to refer to our home as the fort! Anyway, who am I kidding? You'd done the bulk of the strenuous childcare by the time you went back to work. Jake and Chloe pretty much look after themselves. Being in when the internet shopping arrives and cooking dinner hardly compares to what you did for the kids when they were little.

I am full of admiration for you, Holly, but at the same time it scares me how competent you are. My role in the family seems to be becoming more and more redundant. To be honest, I started to feel quite depressed about this but I tried not to let it get me down. That's why I started running, not in some mid-life crisis quest to retain what's left of my youthful looks and body (I know when age is winning), but so that I was doing something. Oh, we're back to the need to do something again.

But I do enjoy running (well, not actually the running bit but the feeling slightly better for having done it bit) and it has led me via Daisy to Jimmy Finlay, and I feel positive about that. If we pull this off, it may be just the boost my company needs, but it will also take me away from home and I'm scared how that will affect us.

In the past I hated leaving you for weeks at a time, to sell whisky to the Japanese, because I missed you so much, but I never worried that the time spent apart would damage our relationship. Now I worry that if I go to Scotland for a week or so, I may return and find there is even more distance between us.

I know things were a bit difficult already, but the thought keeps occurring to me that the train was not the only thing that came uncoupled when it did. We started to unlink as well.

This is a terrible thing to say, and I wish more than anything that you'd caught a later train that day and not had to endure what you did, but a small selfish part of me hoped that the accident would bring us closer. I thought you'd be shaken and scared and that you would need me again, in a way you have not seemed to need me recently. But the opposite was true.

I still worry that you went back to work too soon and that you protest too much that you are fine. It's incredible the way you have carried on, as if nothing at all happened, but something did happen, Holly. It shook me. I wonder what it really did to you. I wish you'd tell me but you don't want to talk — not to me anyway.

I don't know why I am trying to stop myself from sounding petulant and jealous, as I will probably delete this letter once it is written, but I hate to admit that the thing I most resent about the train crash is that Daniel was there and not me. If you'd been sitting somewhere else or been on another train, you and he might never have been thrown together.

Of course, I am glad that there was someone there who was big enough to stay with you, while you waited for the fire brigade to cut you free. At first, I was also pleased that you could talk to him about what happened. But the more time you seem to spend together, the more jealous I am of him.

I can hear you now, saying, 'Don't be ridiculous. He's half my age,' although that would make you fifty-six. I know I'm bad at remembering birthdays and dates of birth but I'm pretty sure neither of us is quite there yet!

Anyway, if in this hypothetical conversation you mean I am ridiculous to suggest that there is anything sexual between the two of you, that is not what I am suggesting. In fact, I think I might find it easier to deal with if there were. I would be jealous and devastated, of course, but I think we could put an affair behind us. It's the sudden emotional closeness you have with Daniel that I can't stand, but can't really do anything about.

What sort of a man would I be if I stopped you talking to the man who was there for you when you most needed someone? But, as time goes on, I fear you are growing ever closer to Daniel, and that inevitably means further away from me.

We used to share all the details of our lives. You used to come home and, even when you were tired after two hours on the train and ten hours in the office, tell me something about the programme or something funny that had happened on your journey, enough to allow me to imagine you in that world. You tell me nothing these days and the lack of detail in our daily lives is leaving our marriage a shell.

I know that Daisy is worried about Daniel and their future together too. I like Daisy, she's a lovely woman, and I don't like seeing her unhappy, any more than I like seeing you becoming closer to someone else.

I bumped into someone I used to work with many years ago the other day, who told me he'd just split up with his wife. He said they'd been living separate lives for some time and only stayed together for the sake of the children. Now the kids had left home, he said, there was no reason to stay together any more.

You hear people say things like that a lot. But that was the first time hearing it ever made me wonder if that could be me. I felt as if someone had punched me in the stomach and I started to panic.

I had to dart into the nearest public toilet to splash water on my face. When I looked up in the mirror, I wondered if I was looking at a man who was biding his time with a wife who no longer loved him, waiting for the children to leave home before they went their separate ways.

I love you, Holly. I think you still love me

too, but you don't seem to respect me any more or need me. I'll always love you but I'm not sure if this is enough any more, for you — or for me.

Bloody hell! Writing this has worn me out! I feel I have run an emotional marathon. Perhaps this will help me get some of those pent-up feelings out of my system. I hope so.

Mark xxx

42

'Do you want to come too? Holly asked Jake who was pouring chocolate-flavoured cereal into a bowl, absent-mindedly, so that the small puffs of whatever it was before it got turned into sugar overflowed on to the table.

It was only just 7 in the morning, early for Jake to be up, let alone having breakfast, and even earlier for him to be already dressed in his school uniform. Chloe was still fast asleep but Jake had obviously found it as hard to stay in bed as Holly had.

She'd kept checking the clock at regular intervals. The last time she consciously remembered looking it was 4 a.m. and she was pretty sure she hadn't slept at all up to that point. Then it was 6.30 and she decided to get up and make a cup of tea.

When Jake appeared, looking to all intents and purposes (or 'all in tents with porpoises' as Mark usually said when using this particular phrase) as if he was planning on going to school at the crack of dawn, Holly asked if he wouldn't rather have the day off. She would be going to see Mark, when visiting hours began.

'No, I need to go to school today,' Jake said, grabbing handfuls of excess cereal and shoving them back in the box. 'They're doing trials for the rugby team. I won't get in if I'm not there.'

Holly hadn't even been aware that he wanted

to get into the rugby team, and wasn't sure she wanted him to. With Mark lying in hospital, it suddenly seemed a dangerous sport for her son to be playing. Given his track record of injuring himself at every possible opportunity, she didn't see how he would escape breaking his neck, if surrounded by a group of bulky teenagers. But she didn't say anything. She suspected the rugby trials were a cover for simply not wanting to go back to the hospital.

★   ★   ★

Jake had seemed distinctly uncomfortable there last night even though Mark had been surprisingly upbeat, when the two of them had gone to deliver his overnight things.

'Hello,' Holly had said tentatively when they found him lying in bed, surrounded by monitors and with tubes attached to various parts of him. A doctor was in attendance. 'How are you?'

'Fine.' Mark looked sideways at her and Jake, who shuffled awkwardly by the bed. He needed somewhere to sit, ideally with a computer in front of him, to feel comfortable. 'Am I in Devon?'

The doctor looked up abruptly, sensing something was amiss.

'No, you're in hospital in Brighton,' he said sternly, and then to Holly, 'I might have to ask you to leave for a moment, Mrs Constantine. Your husband seems a little disorientated.'

'It's a joke,' Holly told him.

'I feel like I've died and gone to Devon,' Mark

396

explained, and the doctor laughed.

'Oh, yes,' he said. 'Wasn't there an advertising campaign for Devon that used that slogan a few years ago?'

'That was one of mine,' Mark said.

Holly wondered if he had already told the doctor enough about his work for him to understand from this that Mark's company had once had a contract to rebrand Devon. His brief had been to make it appear as appealing as the Caribbean and his 'Feels like I've died and gone to Devon' slogan had been a success. Off the back of it, he'd secured a contract with the Czech Republic. But neither Paignton nor Prague needed his help any more.

'Really?' The doctor sounded suitably interested and looked at Mark's notes once more before introducing himself to Holly.

'Mrs Constantine,' he said, extending his hand to her. 'I'm Dr Grant. I'm looking after your husband while he is in coronary care.'

'How's he doing?' A man in a striped shirt appeared on the scene then. His sleeves were rolled up and he had a general air of authority about him.

Holly wondered if this was the cardiologist. She remembered doing a piece on the programme a couple of years back about hospital doctors being stopped from wearing white coats in order to prevent the spread of MRSA. Experts had recommended the change because they thought regular clothes were washed more often than white coats. They had also banned ties and said sleeves must be worn rolled up as well. The move seemed sensible to Holly but had prompted more letters to the *British Medical Journal* than almost any other issue. The doctors were up in arms about the changes, which they said were unnecessary. The proposers said they just didn't like being told what to do, or being made to look like everyone else on the ward.

But this man cut a swathe through the place as he walked into it. There was no mistaking that he was in charge.

'Are you his wife?' he asked Holly now.

'This is Dr Parkinson,' Dr Grant introduced the newcomer. 'He operated on your husband.'

'Thank you.' Holly took the hand he had proffered and found herself noting how steady it was.

She could think of nothing to say or ask him, even though there should have been a million things about the operation, Mark's condition and his future prognosis. Instead, she found herself asking a question which sounded ridiculous to her as she asked it.

'Why is it that surgeons never call themselves doctors?' she heard herself saying, wondering as she said it why, if he'd operated on Mark, he was a doctor and not a surgeon.

'Your husband just asked me the very same question.' Dr Parkinson didn't seem to think it was out of place. 'It's because until the mid-nineteenth century surgeons didn't have to have any medical training. They just served an apprenticeship with another surgeon. Of course, that's all changed, but the title remains the same.'

'I see,' Holly said.

'Your husband's operation was straightforward enough to be done by a cardiologist,' Dr Parkinson added, answering her unasked question.

Holly looked at Mark and smiled, feeling a certain relief that, despite the letter she'd just found, they still seemed to be on a shared wavelength when it came to talking to doctors.

She felt sick every time she thought of that letter.

'So how did the operation go?' she continued, suddenly finding there were a lot of questions she wanted answers to. 'How long will it take him to recover? When will he be able to come home?'

'It was a success,' the doctor said, raising his hand like a traffic policeman to stem the flow of questions. 'But we'll be keeping him in overnight for observation.'

He paused and looked up as the door opened. A quizzical, slightly bemused expression crossed his face but he smiled as if he was pleased to see whoever it was who had come into the room.

'Did one of you order a takeaway?' he asked.

Holly turned and took in Chloe wearing some sort of uniform that was not her school one and carrying several bags, which did indeed look like takeaway food.

'Chloe?' She knew her eldest daughter would infer that she wanted to know what the uniform was and why the food, from the upward inflexion given to her name alone.

'I was at work and I didn't pick up your

message till I had my break.' Her daughter shrugged. 'The manager said I should bring some food. He said hospital food is crap. Is Dad OK?'

Chloe looked apologetically at Dr Parkinson as she said this.

'He's going to be fine,' he reassured her, smiling as he spoke. 'And your manager is right. The food is crap, and your dad needs to eat something. Where do you work?'

'Yes,' Holly pitched in. 'Where *do* you work, Chloe?'

'Terre à Terre,' she mumbled, putting the food down.

'I didn't know you had a job after school. Is that where you've been all the time?'

Chloe nodded.

'Did you know about this, Mark?' Holly could hear that her tone was slightly accusing, as if he had been keeping secrets from her.

The surgeon noticed too.

'Now is probably not the time,' he warned gently, as Mark shook his head.

'Yes, of course.' Holly was duly chastised.

★   ★   ★

'Do you want some toast?' she asked Jake now as she watched him slurp up the last of his cereal.

She hoped he did. Making it would give her something to do.

'Yeah, OK.' His answer implied he knew he was doing her a favour by having it.

'So when are the rugby trials?' she asked.

'Lunchtime,' he said non-committally.

'And will you be back after school?' It was always like trying to get blood out of a stone, trying to extract words from Jake in the mornings, but Holly pressed on.

'Yeah.' He pushed his empty bowl to one side. 'When will Dad be back?'

'Hopefully I'll bring him home this morning,' Holly said, jumping slightly as the toaster popped and her mobile phone beeped at the same time.

'I'll come straight back then,' he said.

Holly took the toast out and buttered it. There was something reassuring about the action of doing this. Normally Jake would get his own toast, or if she was making some anyway, she'd stick it on a plate and leave it to him to spread, but it felt surprisingly soothing.

'How much butter are you going to put on that toast?' Jake stopped her in her reverie. 'You're doing it the way Gran does.'

'Sorry.' Holly stopped buttering and passed the toast to Jake, thinking about her mother as she put the plate on the table.

Susan did have a lot of butter on her toast. She claimed it was having grown up with rationing that made her lather it on. When butter was still rationed, she told them she used to eat most of her toast unbuttered and save her entire ration for one corner, savouring the taste of the butter melting right into the bread. Now that she could have as much as she wanted, she tried to create the same effect with the whole piece of toast.

Her cholesterol levels ought to be sky high,

Holly thought, yet she seemed incredibly fit and healthy for her age.

Holly wished her mother were here now. She wanted someone else to be the responsible adult; to make breakfast and go through the motions of normality so that she could stop trying to keep everything and everyone together.

Holly shook her head to stop herself feeling maudlin and checked her phone while Jake appeared to be concentrating on the shape left after he took each mouthful of toast.

There were three messages.

The first was from Anne-Marie.

Sorry I was short with you on the phone the other day, it said. *Would like to talk to you. Could you call me? AM x*

The next was from Daniel and the other was from a number that was not in her phonebook. She opened that next.

Hi, Holly, it read. *Hope you managed to get some sleep last night. Let us know how Mark is. Daisy x*

She wondered if they had both texted at the same time and were aware that the other was doing so as they did. Daniel's read: *Are you OK? Hardly slept wondering how you were. Let me know. D xx*

'I'm going to go in early.' Jake scraped his chair back, making her shiver with the noise of metal on the stone floor.

'Are you sure you don't want to take the day off and come to hospital to get Dad?' Holly asked him again.

'I'll see him after school,' Jake said, putting his

plate and bowl in the dishwasher, which Holly suspected was a gesture of appeasement for preferring lessons in one institution to waiting around in another.

Holly wasn't surprised he would prefer to go to school rather than come to see Mark in hospital. She wanted him to come with her because she felt uncomfortable about seeing her husband alone. She'd only read it once, but she had all but memorised the contents of Mark's letter to her and kept going over it in her mind.

She wanted Jake to go with her for moral support. But she could understand why he wanted to carry on as if everything was normal, the way she'd been trying to carry on for the past few months, apparently without success.

43

'Would you like a cup of tea? Or something to eat?' Holly felt as if she was talking to a new acquaintance she had just brought back to her house for the first time, not her husband of seventeen years.

Mark, for all his chirpiness in the hospital, was still weak from the operation. When she'd arrived to take him home, he'd been chatting to a doctor about his work and Jimmy Finlay's run around Scotland.

'He wants to raise awareness of heart disease,' Mark was telling the surgeon. 'It would have been better for me if he'd done it last year, then I might not be lying here now.'

'Ironic,' said the doctor, scrutinising the clipboard at the end of Mark's bed as Holly came into the room.

'And I always thought that was getting your newly ironed shirt crumpled when you tried to fold the ironing board,' Mark said.

'What?' the doctor said, as the joke, which Holly had heard several times before, slowly dawned on him. 'Oh, I see. That's very good.'

Holly had been surprised by how normal Mark seemed, but now as he got out of the car he had the gait of a much older man, and seemed to struggle as he walked up the steps to their front door, refusing her arm when it was offered, saying he needed to do it on his own.

'A cup of tea and maybe a piece of toast, please,' Mark said, sitting down on the sofa in the living room, looking unsure what he should do next. No wonder he felt like a stranger to her, Holly thought, looking at him. He must feel like a stranger to himself too.

He was not someone you would expect to have had a heart attack. He was fit and healthy and increasingly active. He must have felt completely floored by yet another unexpected turn of events.

'I'll take your bag upstairs and then go and make some,' Holly said tentatively.

She was scared of leaving him. He had seemed fine in the hospital and the doctor had signed him off to go home, but she felt as she had when she first brought Chloe home as a baby, frightened that something might happen to her precious charge now there were no doctors or nurses on call.

She didn't feel entirely confident that she would do the right thing if Mark had chest pains or collapsed again. And, realising now how he had been feeling about their relationship, she didn't quite know how she should behave around him.

Mark nodded, as if to dismiss her, and she went to the kitchen, rubbing her eyes as she walked down the hallway from the living room.

*   *   *

Holly had felt the empty space in their bed where Mark should have been acutely during the night, and had held one of his shirts close to her

405

chest as she'd begun to wonder if emptiness might become a regular feature in their bedroom.

Suddenly just getting on with things and keeping going no longer seemed enough. She'd realised she needed to do more to get her life back on track, but she wasn't sure what.

There didn't appear to be any simple solutions. Holly had held Mark's discarded shirt to her face, breathing in the scent of him, and begun to cry. She'd wished she could get up and climb into bed with Jake, but suspected the teenager he was turning into would be horrified by the idea.

She missed now the disturbed nights when she would wake to see him standing by the bedroom door, looking at her and Mark in bed to see if they were awake or else waiting until his mere presence caused them to wake, before reporting that he'd had a bad dream or wet the bed or couldn't sleep because his room was too dark. Then she would either tell him to come and sleep with them and curl around him until he decided they were 'too squashy' and went back to his own bed, or get up and change his sheets then climb into bed with him until he went back to sleep or decided she alone was 'too squashy' and dismissed her back to her own bed.

Chloe had gained her night-time independence much earlier than Jake, sleeping with the lights off from a very early age, getting up to take herself to the toilet in the night almost as soon as she could walk, and barely ever seeking reassurance from her parents. Holly remembered one occasion when, aged six, she'd gone to bed complaining of feeling sick and Holly had told her to get some sleep but to come and find her if she felt ill in the night. When Holly woke in the morning she presumed Chloe's sickness had gone and she'd slept right through, but Chloe informed them she'd thrown up twice during the night. She'd taken the waste bin from the bathroom, in case she didn't make it to the toilet, and gone back to bed without disturbing anyone.

Holly wondered if this independence was a residual character trait or one foisted upon her because she was the oldest and had had to look after herself more when the needier, more demanding Jake arrived on the scene.

Because she'd always seemed independent, it shouldn't really have come as a surprise to Holly that Chloe had decided to go out and get herself a job.

'How long have you been working at Terre à Terre?' she'd said when they got home from the hospital.

'A few weeks,' Chloe had replied. 'I'm only a kitchen assistant. It's just stock checking and sorting salad leaves, and sometimes I get to help the *pâtissier*. But the people are nice.'

'Why didn't you tell us?' Holly wasn't cross but she was put out that their daughter felt she'd had to keep her job from them.

'I was trying to help,' Chloe told her. 'I know things have been difficult, with Dad's business not doing well and you having to work such long hours. I didn't want to keep asking for money, and one of Ruaridh's older brothers works as a waiter in Terre à Terre and he said they were looking for kitchen assistants. So I applied.'

'Oh, Chloe.' Holly exhaled. 'It's good that you've got a job. But you don't have to worry about money. Things aren't that bad. Is this because of the school trip?'

'Sort of,' she said.

'What do you mean?'

'I'm not really that bothered about the school trip. It just made me realise,' Chloe's voice became quieter and Holly had to strain to hear her, 'it's difficult for you at the moment. Dad not having much work seems to make things strained. I wanted to do something to try and make things better.'

She was like her father, Holly thought proudly, realising she had stopped thinking of Mark with any pride recently.

'Do things seem that bad?' She'd asked her daughter gently.

'Kind of,' Chloe muttered, looking away from her. 'You and Dad haven't been the same.'

Holly tried to formulate a reply that would reassure her but Chloe spoke first.

'Megan's parents are getting separated,' she said, staring hard at the floor, avoiding all eye contact.

'That's very sad for them all,' Holly said. 'But it might not be permanent. Sometimes couples go through a patch where they are not as close as they once were, but they can get over it.'

She hoped this would give Chloe the reassurance she appeared to need but was not going to ask for, and hoped this would be true for herself and Mark.

'Will Dad be OK?' Chloe asked.

'Yes,' Holly had said. 'And we'll be OK too.'

She'd replayed the conversation in her head several times during the night, as she lay in her bed alone, unable to sleep.

★ ★ ★

'Are you OK?' Holly said now to Mark as she passed the sitting room after taking his bag upstairs.

She popped her head in at the door and saw he was on his BlackBerry.

'I just need to let someone know something,' he said, looking up. 'There are a few things I should be doing today . . . '

'You don't need to do anything today,' Holly reprimanded him. 'You are to take it easy. You heard what the doctor said.'

'I know.' Mark gave a guilty shrug and looked down at his phone again. 'Sent now! Where's that tea and toast you promised me?'

'I'm just going to make it,' she said. 'But I have to keep making sure you are behaving yourself!'

'Sorry, miss.' Mark put his phone on the table next to the sofa. 'But the press conference is in a couple of weeks. There are people I need to let know what's happened.'

'I could do it for you,' she volunteered.

'It's done now,' he said, getting up. 'I'm just going to the loo before my tea and toast.'

'Can you manage?' Holly wondered if he would be OK with the stairs.

'It's my heart, not my bladder, that's been giving me trouble,' Mark said, walking slowly towards the door.

'I'll take that as a no then,' Holly said to herself as she went into the kitchen, listening to him taking the stairs slowly, one at a time, and shuffling across the landing to the bathroom.

She put the kettle on and took a jar of coffee out of the cupboard. She wasn't usually a coffee drinker but felt she needed something slightly stronger than tea to keep her going. It was too early for a drink. The doctor had said that Mark wasn't allowed coffee. He'd also told Holly he must take it easy for a few weeks.

'And leave it a couple of weeks before having sex,' the surgeon had added. 'It puts an enormous strain on the heart. You were lucky your husband collapsed while running. You'd be surprised how many men of his age come in having had a heart attack in flagrante.'

Holly laughed, because she thought he was trying to amuse her. But his comments only served to remind her that she and Mark had not had sex for months. As she was laughing, an image of Daisy crossed her mind. It was not one she wanted to see but one which began to make her wonder if Mark had actually been running when he'd had the heart attack.

He was taking his time in the bathroom and Holly checked her phone for messages before taking the tea and toast into the sitting room.

Another from Anne-Marie.

Worried by your silence, please call. AM x

Holly knew she ought to call her but couldn't face it so she put her phone down, picked up the tray and carried Mark's food and drink to the living room. She put it on the table just as his phone began vibrating to alert him to an incoming message.

Holly could see that the sender was Daisy. The temptation to read it was great but she knew she couldn't do so without Mark knowing. She could, she realised, read the message he had sent before he went upstairs though.

Back home feeling as if the last few days were all a dream. Have you spoken to Daniel yet? You have to tell him. Speak soon. M xx

44

'When did you get back?' Holly looked across the kitchen table at her mother.

Susan looked different but Holly could not quite pinpoint how. It wasn't just the tan and the slightly longer hair, which she'd pinned up with a souvenir mother-of-pearl clasp. She looked freer, Holly thought, somehow less encumbered. Although, now that she thought about it, her mother had not been looking particularly burdened in the first place.

Holly regarded Susan as having led a fairly easy life. She'd worked for a few years, as a secretary, until she met Patrick and they'd been married the same year.

'We couldn't wait,' had been her breezy explanation of the speed at which they'd tied the knot. Holly didn't like to ask what it was they couldn't wait for. They met in the sixties so she didn't imagine they were waiting for sex, but didn't like to give this too much thought. She had wondered vaguely if her mother had been pregnant and examined the few black-and-white wedding photos carefully for any signs of a tell-tale bump, but there was nothing and her sister Fay had not been born until two years later. Of course, it was possible her mother had lost a baby.

As soon as she became pregnant with Fay, she gave up work. 'People did in those days,' she'd told Holly, and she'd only started working again, part-time as a PA in a local restaurant, when Holly had started secondary school.

'For pin money,' Patrick had said dismissively, as if he wasn't entirely happy with his wife dirtying her hands in the world of work. But Holly had remembered her mother seeming happy at the time, making friends with the other restaurant staff, buying herself new clothes with her 'pin money' and generally coming alive.

She'd lost her job when the restaurant went into liquidation. Susan had said this was not because it was losing money but because the owner had been sleeping with the pastry chef. He'd wanted to get divorced but did not want his wife to get her hands on his hard-earned profits. Holly couldn't remember the ins and outs of it. She did remember that her mother had been at a bit of a loss when the restaurant closed down but had told her there was no point in looking for another job. She was too old and Patrick would be retiring in a few years' time so they'd want to be doing things together.

Holly's father had duly retired but they'd actually seemed to spend more time apart then, if anything, he on the golf course, she at a succession of Adult Education classes: flirting with Spanish and Per the Brazilian teacher, book-keeping because she thought she might want to do a bit of work one day, and latterly yoga and Thailand.

Had something happened in Thailand, Holly wondered, to make her mother look different? Perhaps she had had an affair with a Thai yoga teacher. Again, she didn't want to dwell on this. The idea of your mother having sex with a young Thai man, who could hook his left foot behind his ear, was not something she wanted to think about, any more than she wanted to think of her parents having sex before or after their marriage.

'I flew back in on Monday,' Susan said, rousing Holly from her contemplation of her parents' sex life. 'I've been a bit jet-lagged for the past couple of days, but I seem to be back on track again now.'

'You look well.' Holly began pouring tea for them both. 'But you came home earlier than planned?'

'Thailand was wonderful,' her mother answered the question that hung in the air even though Holly had not actually asked it. 'But I'd had enough of travelling. I'm too old to be on the move all the time. And when I heard about Mark, I wanted to come back and see you.'

'You didn't need to come home on my account,' Holly said, pushing a cup of tea across the table and taking the lid off the biscuit tin. 'Biscuit?'

'I know.' Susan poured milk into the cup. 'But I wanted to see you anyway. I felt a long way away in Thailand. They say modern communication makes everything closer, but it doesn't really. If anything had happened, I would still be on the other side of the world. I know you were there for Mark, but what if anything had happened to your father?'

'Dad's OK, isn't he?' Holly thought back to what Fay had said, about their mother being worried about him dying before her.

'Yes, he's fine.' Her mother stirred her tea. She looked as if she was thinking about something else.

'I think he missed you while you were away.' Holly appreciated her having come home. She felt better for simply knowing that she was in the country. Even though she was forty-four, and often found her mother difficult, she liked her to be there.

Feeling well disposed towards her now, Holly wondered if Susan might tell her a little more about her reasons for having gone in the first place.

'Dad phoned more often than he usually does while you were away, and wanted to meet up with me and Fay more too.' Holly paused then decided to say out loud the thing that had been worrying her slightly about her father. 'Jean Hayward seemed to be keeping him company quite a lot.'

Her mother looked up sharply. Holly expected her to say 'nonsense' the way she usually did if she disagreed with anything that was said.

'Well, that had started before I went,' Susan surprised her by saying. 'That's partly why I did.'

Holly said nothing; she wasn't used to this sort of discussion with her mother. She rarely talked to either of her parents openly.

They just about did tea and sympathy but definitely not cappuccinos and counselling.

Holly had thought the amount of time her father seemed to be spending with Jean was a bit odd but put it down to loneliness on both their parts. Jean had recently lost her husband and Susan had gone off to Thailand. They were simply keeping each other company, she reasoned to herself. Although, if she allowed herself to think about it, there were other women who, at times, her father had seemed suddenly to be spending a lot of time with.

As if she could tell what Holly was thinking, her mother carried on talking.

'Your father likes a project,' she said. 'And he was at a bit of a loose end when he retired. When Jean's husband died, I think it made him feel useful, being able to help her out a bit. And to be honest, it got him out from under my feet. I'd been used to having the place to myself.'

She paused and took another sip of her tea.

'Well, you probably don't want to listen to me going on.'

Holly filled up her mother's cup, saying nothing, and Susan carried on.

'Like I said,' her mother looked up, but not at Holly, 'he started going over to Jean's house quite a lot before I went away. I knew people were talking, but I don't think there's anything going on between them.'

'And it doesn't bother you?' Holly asked, cautiously. 'Dad spending so much time with her?'

'Yes.' This time her mother looked directly at her. 'It does bother me, but what can I do? He's being good to a mutual and old friend of ours. I don't think they're having an affair or anything.'

Holly looked down. The idea of her father having an affair embarrassed her even at her age.

'But they're close?' she ventured.

'Yes,' Susan said quietly. 'It happens some-times. I'm sure it will pass. I've been there myself.'

'Mum?' Holly waited for her to go on.

'Do you remember there was an awful car crash when you'd just started secondary school?'

Holly nodded. It was one of the few things she did remember about starting secondary school. She could recall quite clearly, even now, her father taking a phone call one evening, then saying he needed to speak to Susan. They'd gone into another room and closed the door. When they came out they'd said nothing but their mood had changed completely.

The next day her mother had told Holly and Fay that there'd been a car crash and Pat, a woman who lived a few streets from them, had been killed along with her two sons. Her husband, David, never really got over it. Holly knew the family slightly, but Susan knew Pat and David from the Parish Council.

'We all tried to do what we could for David afterwards,' Holly's mother said now. 'I used to take him meals, and after a while he started asking me to stay and eat them with him. He was lonely. He wanted company.'

Holly had begun dunking a digestive into her cup of tea but forgotten to take it out again. She cursed inwardly when the soggy biscuit broke off from the dry half and sank to the bottom of her cup. But she carried on listening to her mother.

'I thought I was being a good neighbour,' her mother told her. 'But it all got a bit out of hand.

David said he'd fallen in love with me. I'm sure he hadn't really, he was confused and grieving, but it made things difficult.'

'So what happened?' Holly realised how little she really knew about her parents.

'I stopped going round to him after I came home one day and found your father breaking up the garden table.' She said this as if it explained everything. But Holly needed more.

'I don't understand?'

'Patrick knew what was happening. He was worried he might lose me, but said he'd not wanted to say anything in case it made things worse. He broke up the table because he was so angry and frustrated, he needed to take it out on something.'

'That doesn't sound like Dad.' Holly thought of the mild-mannered man she knew, who rarely raised his voice or lost his temper and never resorted to physical violence.

'It wasn't,' Susan said. 'But he said he couldn't think of anything else to do. I had no idea how he was feeling. To be honest, I wasn't really thinking about him at all, Holly. I was concerned for David and didn't stop to think how that might be affecting your dad.'

Holly began scooping the soggy biscuit from her cup of tea and tried to take this all in.

'But if that was how Dad felt then, Mum,' she said, 'doesn't he realise how you must feel about him spending time with Jean?'

'Probably,' Susan said quietly. 'But I didn't want to stop him being a friend to her. Anyway, I know where his priorities lie. As soon as he heard about Mark, he called the retreat where I was and we had a long talk. He was worried about you both. It's you and Fay and me he really cares about. I know that, even if at times it might seem otherwise.'

'I had no idea, Mum.' Holly looked at her mother and saw her in a slightly different light.

'Anyway . . . ' Susan signalled a change in the direction of the conversation. 'I didn't come here to talk about me. I came to see how you are, and Mark of course?'

'He's pretty well, considering.' Holly wondered if what her mother had just told her would ever be mentioned again.

As she'd sat listening to her reveal details of her marriage, which were news to Holly, she'd wondered if Susan was telling her because she could see her former situation mirrored in her daughter's. Did she know that Holly had allowed herself to drift closer to a man who was not her husband, and taken her eye off her own family in the process?

'Mark's a bit more tired than usual and he's been told to take it easy. But he's anxious to get back to work. He should be down in a minute,' she said.

Mark was upstairs 'resting', though she suspected he was probably checking emails and giving her space to talk to her mother. He'd taken a call on his mobile earlier from Daisy and gone upstairs to speak to her. When he came down again, he said they'd been talking about the press launch.

'We need to get interest going before he

actually starts the run,' Mark had said, and Holly had nodded.

She'd wondered why calls from Daisy had to be taken in a separate room and if they'd yet discussed whatever it was that Mark had asked her if she'd told Daniel, in the text he'd sent her on first coming out of hospital. Holly had read a few more of his texts in the past week, too. Some of them appeared to be genuinely work-related. Others were more ambiguous and raised questions to which Holly could only think of answers she didn't want to contemplate.

How did Daniel take the news? one had read. Mark must have deleted the texts leading up to this as it didn't make sense in isolation. *Are you OK?*

She'd not found a reply from Daisy. Although she had a text of her own from Daniel later that day.

When are you back at work, Holly? How are things at home? Not so good here. Would be good to see you but realise you are needed there. D x

'I can see why you want to fix it up soon for Jimmy,' Holly had said about the press conference to Mark. 'But it might be too soon for you, don't you think?'

She was worried that, although he seemed fine, he was not taking things easy enough.

'If I was on my own, yes,' Mark agreed. 'But with Daisy helping me, it should be fine. It'll be in Edinburgh and I'll probably have to stay up there for a night or so . . . '

'Good. I'm looking forward to seeing him,'

Susan was saying with a smile. 'I missed you all while I was away.'

Holly forced herself to smile back. She'd been making the comparison between herself and Mark and her parents, and it suddenly struck her that perhaps instead of taking himself off out of the country, so he could turn a blind eye to herself and Daniel, Mark might have taken himself off to be with Daisy.

'I nearly forgot,' her mother said, fumbling in her bag, 'I brought you something.'

It was a hand-sized carved wooden elephant, intricate in all its detail, right down to the wrinkles and sagging folds of skin on its legs.

'It's an elephant,' Susan said, unnecessarily. 'I got one for your father too. I thought it might give you and Mark something to talk about.'

'Sometimes people find it helps to talk about these things,' Caroline, the radio reporter, said to me. 'Or others might find that hearing what you have to say might help them.'

I'd been going to say no, to insist that I wouldn't do the interview and tell her that Holly should never have given my number to her in the first place.

'It wouldn't be live,' she said. 'We'd pre-record the interview beforehand.'

'OK,' I said, suddenly realising that what she said might be true. 'When would you like me to come in?'

It occurred to me that if perhaps it could help others, and if I couldn't talk to Holly about it first, perhaps the only thing to do was to go ahead and do the interview.

I haven't seen Holly for over a week, or Daniel either, and she hasn't returned my texts. I sent one a week ago, to apologise for being angry with her on the phone, but she never replied.

So I sent another. Not immediately, I didn't want to appear to be hassling her, but a couple of days later, saying I hadn't heard from her for a while and that I hoped she was OK. She didn't reply to that one either.

Then I let her know I was going to do the interview. I thought she might be pleased that I'd agreed, and that, as I would be going to her office, we might meet for lunch or something. Again no reply, which worried me.

'Radio silence,' as Geoff used to say.

I never really stopped to think exactly what radio silence meant, so I asked Caroline as we walked to the studio to do the interview.

'It's when a station stops transmitting,' she said, opening a huge baize-covered door. 'We're in here.'

The room was empty but for a table with several microphones arranged around it and a few chairs. On the other side of a large glass window was a much busier room, full of stuff and several people.

Caroline sat on one of the chairs and pressed a button, which allowed her to talk them.

'This is Anne-Marie,' she said, nodding towards me. They all smiled. 'We're just going to have a bit of chat before we start recording.'

They smiled some more and began shuffling papers, as if they were minding their own business, although I knew they'd be listening to every word I said.

I felt slightly intimidated by this but I'd rehearsed in my head what I was going to say and, like a politician, planned to stick to the script, no matter what Caroline asked me.

'I asked you about radio silence earlier,' I said, when she asked how I was managing now, without Geoff. 'Well, it's like that, really. I still keep expecting Geoff to be there, to be home when I get there, or on the other end of the phone if I call him, or to get a text or email in reply to one I've sent. But all I get is radio silence.'

'That's wonderful, Anne-Marie, thank you,' Caroline said, then told the gathering behind the glass to stop recording.

'Thank you so much for coming in,' she said as we walked to the lift which would take us back to Reception. 'It was a really moving interview.'

Another woman appeared, just as the lift doors were opening, and got in with us.

'I was wondering,' I said to Caroline, 'could I pop in and say hello to Holly, as I'm here?'

'Holly?' Caroline queried. She didn't seem to know who I was talking about.

'Holly's a friend who works here,' I explained. 'She commutes as well. It was her who gave you my number. Holly Holt.'

'Oh, I work with Holly,' the other occupant of the lift piped up. 'But she's not in. She's been away all week.'

'Oh,' I said. 'Is she on holiday?'

That might have explained her not returning my texts.

'Not exactly.' The woman looked slightly flustered now, as if she might be about to give something away. 'It's more of a personal matter.'

'Oh, yes.' I tried to give the impression that I knew all about it. 'Do you know when she'll be back?'

'I'm not sure,' she replied. Then the lift stopped at the ground floor and Caroline gestured for me to get out, putting a stop to any further questioning of this woman who worked with Holly.

45

'Well, it's lucky you're back, Holly, as we seem to be rather depleted this morning.' Katherine looked around the table in the meeting room.

This, Holly thought to herself, was her editor's way of not saying, 'Hello, Holly. Nice to have you back. How is your husband? I do hope he's all right now. You must have had a terrible shock. Are you sure you were quite ready to come back to work?'

It was unlikely Katherine would ever say that but Holly would have appreciated her at least acknowledging the reason for her absence over the past week, rather than just treating it as an annoyance. It was like the way she had behaved after the train crash, although Holly had been glad that she'd ignored that.

'Right . . . ' Katherine took a pen out of her bag. 'Before we talk about this week's programme, I do have something I need to tell you all.'

'Are we not waiting for the others?' Holly asked.

There were only five of them around the table: Katherine, herself, Dimitri, Rebecca and a man called Andy, who Katherine had told her, as they walked into the meeting room, would be 'helping out'.

The meeting was when they tried to set the agenda for that week's programme, and unless he had a more pressing news assignment, it was almost always attended by James Darling, and, of course, Natalie.

Holly caught Dimitri and Rebecca exchanging a look. They seemed to exchange a lot of looks these days, so she did not regard it as particularly significant.

'Natalie and James are not with us for the moment,' Katherine said. 'For personal reasons.'

Holly looked at her boss who smiled a closed smile, giving nothing away.

Rebecca raised her eyebrows and mouthed something, which Holly presumed to be 'Later'. Now, the look which she had just given Dimitri seemed to take on more significance.

'It's unlikely James will be back,' Katherine said, surveying the assembled company to see what reaction her statement produced.

Holly was surprised but tried hard not to give Katherine the satisfaction of showing it.

'And I hope Natalie will be back soon,' she continued. 'In the meantime, Dimitri will continue acting up as senior producer.'

Holly noted the word 'continue' and presumed this arrangement must have begun last week, when she was at home looking after Mark.

He always joked about the BBC term 'acting up', used to describe someone temporarily doing a more senior job. He imagined all the researchers, temporarily working as producers, and the producers working as senior producers, running around like over-excited children, shouting and doing everything they could to get themselves noticed. This was not, Holly told him, an inaccurate description.

'And Andy is an extra pair of hands,' Dimitri piped up, keen to show his acting seniority. 'He's worked with Dylan a lot in the past.'

'Dylan?' Holly had only been off for a week, admittedly a week during which she hadn't bothered to check her emails, but nevertheless, she hadn't expected to come back to work and find so much had changed.

'Dylan Williams,' Katherine said, adopting the tone a mother might use to calm a child who was acting up. 'He stepped in at the last minute to present the programme in James' absence. He will be presenting for the next few weeks as well.'

Holly knew Dylan Williams. He had gone to work as a reporter at Radio Sussex not long after she'd left and, by all accounts, was very driven. He'd begun acting up almost immediately and was news editor within a few months of joining the station.

Holly only felt she'd been working in London a few months before Dylan Williams followed her up there to work as a reporter on the *Today* programme. In less than the time it took her to get a cup of coffee in the morning, he'd become the presenter of the lunchtime news. So it wasn't exactly a surprise that if anyone was going to fill James Darling's size 12 shoes, it was Dylan Williams.

'I produce Dylan on the one o'clock.' Andy spoke for the first time in the meeting. 'I know how he works.'

Holly looked at him more closely and decided,

for no particular reason, that she didn't like Andy and wasn't looking forward to working with him.

'Anyway,' Katherine held up her pen, commanding an end to banal chitter chatter, 'as I said earlier, before we start to discuss this week's programme, I do have something I need to tell you all.'

They looked dutifully in her direction, silenced by the brandished pen which, Holly noticed, had been filched from a Hilton Hotel.

'The listening figures for the programme are in and I am afraid they are not good.' Katherine paused, allowing her words to sink in.

The listening figures for programmes were the stuff of numerous management meetings. The producers were never over-concerned with them. They just carried on making programmes and didn't worry too much if anyone was listening to them or not. But analysing and discussing listening figures was the stuff which justified huge management salaries.

'As you all know, *Antennae* is a relatively new programme,' she continued. 'And we had hoped it would attract a new audience, but over the past year the figures actually seem to have diminished.'

'Whereas audience figures for the same slot on other stations have increased.' Andy spoke again. He seemed to be enjoying their pain, not that Holly was feeling particularly pained. She was listening but wishing that Katherine would hurry up with her precious announcement and get the meeting over with, so that she could call Natalie and find out the cause of her mysterious absence.

'*Antennae* was a bold experiment,' Katherine said.

'Boldly going . . . ' Dimitri was acting up again, but Katherine silenced him with an angry look.

'But the audience seemed to find it too serendipitous.' This was a word she often ascribed to the programme. Holly preferred to describe it as a mish-mash of items, but she could see that serendipitous was more elegant.

'There's no easy way to say this . . . ' Katherine paused again, underlining just how hard it was for her even to reach the end of a sentence. Holly suspected she was loving every second of the delay. 'The department has decided to replace the programme from the end of the month.'

'What's it going to be replaced with?' Holly asked, paraphrasing the question she wanted to ask which was, What's going to happen to all of us then?

'An obituary programme,' Katherine told them, and answered the question in Holly's mind with her next sentence. 'It's the idea of a producer in the Arts Unit who will be making it with a fairly small team.'

'Well, that's apt,' Dimitri commented on the irony of the situation. 'I suppose we will all be asked to contribute to its first episode?'

'I don't see why . . . ' Katherine said slowly as it dawned on her Dimitri was definitely acting up in a childish way rather than a senior producer-ish way. 'Oh, I see. Very funny. But perhaps not very appropriate, Dimitri.'

'Who's going to present?' he asked, rubbing his wrist as he spoke, as if he had actually been slapped rather than just verbally admonished.

'Gus O'Hagan,' Katherine told them.

Gus O'Hagan was the elderly editor of *Down But Not Out* — a periodical aimed at the over-fifties. It ran far more obituaries than any other publication and Holly imagined most of them were about people Gus had personally known. She supposed he was a good choice to present. Management, she thought to herself, had obviously done an about turn on attracting younger listeners and decided to try and pander more to their existing ones.

'Can't see him lasting long,' Dimitri said, and then, as if he had only meant to think this and realised he had said it out loud, 'Oops, sorry!'

'Anyway,' Katherine continued, 'I know this has come as a shock to all of you and I will talk to you individually about your futures. In the meantime, I don't want the two final episodes of *Antennae* to suffer in any way. So, does anyone have any ideas for this week's programme?'

'Before we try and think of some,' Dimitri spoke again, 'I have some news of my own. I was hoping Darling and Natalie would be here too, but as you're not sure when they're coming back, I might as well tell the rest of you.'

46

Holly felt as if she was deserting the sinking ship by sneaking out at lunchtime, but Andy seemed keen to show everyone that he was more than capable of producing the entire programme on his own. He'd come up with a hundred and one suggestions in the meeting, compared to the combined one that the rest of the usual team had managed.

Holly suspected Andy might well be lining himself up to work on the new obituaries programme. It was fortuitous for him that *Antennae's* deputy editor and presenter were both absent, giving him an opportunity to jump at.

As it was her first day back, after a week's compassionate leave, Holly had thought she needed at least to look as if she was pulling her weight. She'd envisaged a sandwich at her desk, rather than swanning off out to lunch, but felt as if she hadn't really had any time to herself in the past week. She wanted to get out and think her own thoughts without family or colleagues in the background.

Now she thought she'd buy a sandwich and walk up to Regent's Park.

Holly had called Natalie, as soon as she'd left the meeting, to ask if everything was OK.

'Not really. Not at all,' her friend had said. 'Have you got time for a drink after work, Holly?

I could do with a talk.'

'I'm sorry.' She had felt bad about not making the time for her friend, but she'd promised to get home early. She felt she needed to be around in the evening, to monitor Mark both in terms of his health and his attitude to her.

'Later in the week?' Natalie had asked. 'I need to get out of the house.'

Holly sensed that something was up. And she knew she could do with talking to a friend too. The events of the past week were preoccupying most of her thoughts and she felt she needed to get some of them out in the open. Airing them seemed like one way of making things clearer for herself.

Holly wondered if Natalie already knew that their programme was being axed. She definitely sounded preoccupied. As she put the phone down, she realised her friend hadn't even asked how she and Mark were. There must be something wrong.

She had called Mark after speaking to Natalie, to ask how he was and tell him about the programme being axed, but he'd sounded distracted so she'd decided to save the news until later.

'I think we're going to have the press conference next week,' he'd said to her on the phone. 'That's right, isn't it?'

She couldn't tell, down the line, if he was asking the question of himself or whether Daisy was with him and he was asking her.

Holly knew she had to sit down with Mark and talk to him, soon. Until she did, she felt everything about their life seemed unreal. They appeared to be operating in different spheres at the moment and she knew that something needed at least to get them overlapping again. But Mark was busy with the press launch for Jimmy Finlay and Holly was wary of upsetting him, lest it put undue strain on his heart. He already seemed to be putting enough pressure on himself with the organisation of the run.

The Ladies' toilets on the fifth floor of Broadcasting House were usually empty. Just off the stairwell, they were tucked away behind the new library, which was almost entirely staffed by men. Holly usually used them on her way out, knowing there was unlikely to be a queue.

Today, a woman wearing a familiar-looking tunic was bending over the washbasin, splashing her face with water. She didn't look up as the door closed behind Holly, but turned the tap off and picked up a paper towel and began drying her face.

'Rebecca?' Holly knew it was her but there was something about her being here and the way she was dabbing her face with the towel that seemed not quite right.

'Oh, Holly, hi.' Rebecca stopped patting her face with the towel and blew her nose on it.

'Are you OK?' Holly didn't think she looked it.

'Yes.' Rebecca sniffed decisively. 'I'm fine.'

'Are you sure?' Holly thought she looked as if she'd been crying and might be about to cry again. She suspected she'd come down to the fifth floor to cry in privacy, not expecting anyone she knew to use these backwater toilets or Holly to be on her way out.

'I think so.' Rebecca sounded less certain this time. 'It just came as a bit of a shock, that's all.'

'You'll be OK,' Holly reassured her. 'They'll move you on to another programme, somewhere in the department. It can only be a better one. You won't be out of a job.'

Holly had worked for the BBC long enough to know that these sudden changes in programming were unsettling, but that everyone who wanted one usually ended up finding a new home somewhere.

'Oh, I know. It's not that.' Rebecca unzipped a make-up bag that was on the ledge by the sink, and took out a tube of foundation, She began dotting some around her slightly reddened eyes.

'I don't want to pry,' Holly said, and went into the nearby toilet cubicle, giving Rebecca the opportunity to confide what was bothering her, if she wanted, or to put her make-up on and run if she didn't.

'I've obviously completely misunderstood the situation,' Holly heard Rebecca say as she closed the door.

'I'm not with you?' Holly raised her voice to be heard though the door and tried to wee as quickly as she could.

'May I ask you a question, Holly?' Rebecca called.

Holly felt the slight dread she always felt when anyone asked that.

'You can ask, but I might not answer,' she said,

coming out of the cubicle and starting to wash her hands.

'Did you ever think there might be anything between Dimitri and me?' Rebecca looked at Holly's reflection in the mirror, rather than directly at her.

'Why? Was there? Is there?' Holly answered Rebecca's reflection with more questions. It was odd, she thought, addressing each other indirectly in this way. It gave the impression that what was said between them now could be forgotten about later.

'I thought you were good friends,' she said slowly, realising that she was probably getting herself into a conversation that was not going to be quick.

The news that Dimitri had brought to the more than usually eventful morning meeting was that he was getting married.

They'd all been suitably congratulatory. Even Andy who'd only just met him had stood up and shaken his hand a bit too vigorously. Dimitri had made a face at Holly over his shoulder and shaken his arm gingerly when Andy wasn't looking.

Rebecca, now that Holly thought back to the scene, had been slightly more reticent in coming forward and congratulating her friend. Holly had presumed this was because he'd probably already told her his news and she was just going through the motions along with everyone else.

'We are,' Rebecca said, looking at Holly directly this time. 'Very good friends. Dimitri is

435

really good company and I can talk to him about everything.'

'Yes?' Holly looked back at her and waited.

'He talked to me about things too.' Rebecca looked down again, as if concerned she might be breaking a confidence. 'About Anna and their life together. He said she was thinking about moving back to Germany and he wasn't sure what to do about it. I thought . . . '

Holly took a paper towel and began slowly drying her hands.

'I thought he was going to split up with her,' Rebecca concluded.

'Is that what you wanted?' Holly asked.

'I thought that's what he wanted too.' Rebecca paused and looked at herself in the mirror again. 'There'd been a bit of . . . well, you know, a couple of things had happened . . . '

Rebecca wiped something Holly couldn't see from her face and then took a deep breath as if she was either going to let it all out or change the subject.

Holly was slightly relieved that it was the latter. She didn't want to know if Rebecca and Dimitri had been sleeping together. If true, it was the sort of thing that was best kept between them.

'Anyway, it doesn't matter now. He's getting married and we'll be working on different programmes,' Rebecca said. 'Life goes on.'

She zipped up her make-up bag. Holly thought this was the best way for the conversation to end. She didn't want Rebecca to tell her too much about her feelings for Dimitri

436

and whatever it was they had shared together. She suspected her colleague might regret it in a few days, when she was less raw from the shock of hearing that he was going to marry someone else.

But Holly didn't want to appear insensitive either. She took a step closer to Rebecca and gave her a big hug.

'Sometimes,' Holly said, speaking aloud some of the thoughts which had been circulating in her head for some time, 'it's almost impossible to tell what another person is thinking, and all too easy to misinterpret the way they feel about you.'

'Thanks, Holly,' Rebecca said quietly, then picked up her bag and went towards the door. 'I'll see you later.'

'And sometimes,' Holly said to herself in the mirror, 'you're not even sure yourself how you feel about someone.'

47

'Sorry I'm late.' Holly didn't think she was but Natalie appeared to have been here for some time, judging by the near-empty glass in front of her. She was sitting alone, in the corner of the pub, with a gin and tonic, most of which had already been drunk.

'You weren't really.' She didn't seem to mind that she'd been kept waiting. 'I was early. I had to get out of the house.'

'Are you OK?' Holly knew the answer was going to be negative. Natalie didn't look it. She looked awful; pale, tired and thin. She had all the signs of someone who'd been going through something and Holly knew she was about to find out what.

'No, I'm bloody awful.' Natalie drained what was left of her drink.

Holly wondered how long she'd been sitting there and how many she'd had already. This wasn't like Natalie at all. Even when they went for drinks after work, she usually held back, citing early mornings or key interviews to be recorded the next day as her reason for staying relatively sober.

'Shall I get you another drink?' Holly asked, wondering if this was wise but knowing she was gong to need one herself.

'A large gin and tonic,' Natalie pushed her empty glass across the table to Holly and shrugged, as if acknowledging she was drinking too much but wasn't sure what else to do.

Holly went to the bar and texted Mark while she was waiting.

Natalie not good. Might be a bit later than I thought. Hope you OK xxx

She had asked him if it was all right for her to go for a drink after work with her friend this evening. She'd told him that Natalie had been away from work for a few days and had called, asking to meet.

'I guess you two need to discuss your futures,' Mark had said. He seemed to think the programme being axed was a good thing.

'Perhaps you can work part-time again?' he'd suggested, and Holly had bitten back the urge to say that his doing one job for Jimmy Finlay did not mean they didn't need her to contribute any more.

Under normal circumstances, she would have gone ahead and made an arrangement with Natalie without consulting her husband. But at the moment, she felt she had to ask Mark's permission. This was because she knew he was supposed to be taking it easy and she ought to get home in time to cook dinner, although Chloe had done a lot of the cooking in the past week and was also doing a rather better job of looking after Mark than Holly was.

She still hadn't talked to him properly. She'd been putting it off, using the doctor's admonition that he needed to avoid stressful situations as her excuse for doing so.

For the first time in her life Holly was unsure

439

of Mark's feelings towards her and scared of what he might say if she asked him. She'd never felt like this before. He had always been such a constant man. Even when they'd had major arguments about things, which now seemed silly, she'd never for a moment doubted his feelings for her.

'Sure,' Mark had said, when she'd asked. 'No problem.'

Holly had wondered if this response was because he genuinely didn't mind her being back late from work or because it gave him more time with Daisy. She knew they were meeting up today, not because he'd told her but because she'd looked through his emails and found several from Daisy. They were all warm and jokey in tone, ostensibly to do with Jimmy Finlay's run and organising the press conference, but Holly couldn't help wondering if there was more to *See you tomorrow x* than the fact that Daisy would be seeing Mark tomorrow!

Holly hadn't seen Daniel since that day at the hospital. She wondered if he was having the same misgivings as she was.

Allowing Natalie to unburden herself wasn't going to help her own state of mind. But what choice did Holly have? Natalie was her friend and something was obviously very wrong. That much she could tell just by looking.

'A small white wine and a gin and tonic, please,' Holly said to the barman, who looked suspiciously in Natalie's direction. Holly avoided eye contact as he got the drinks ready. She feared that if she made it, he might say something about the length of time Natalie had already spent in her corner and the amount of gin she's already downed. It wasn't for him to pass judgment.

Instead she read Mark's reply when her phone beeped a message alert.

OK. Send her my love. All fine here. Later x

Mark's texts seemed to lack their customary warmth these days, but perhaps Holly was just trying to read too much into them. That was the trouble with texting. It was far too easy to misinterpret a smiley face or a kiss or the lack of either. She wanted his text to reassure her that he didn't mind her staying up in London later than usual, but that he'd look forward to seeing her when she got home. What she read in those few brief words was that she wasn't really needed at home; they could all manage quite well without her.

At least there is a kiss, she thought to herself, although she knew that Mark invariably ended all his texts with a kiss and, on the occasions she's snooped, had seen he sent more than one to Daisy.

She gave the barman the best part of a tenner for the drinks and took them over to the corner.

'Here you are,' she said, putting Natalie's down on a beer mat, which appropriately (or perhaps inappropriately) was advertising a certain brand of gin.

'Thanks.' She took a sip. 'And thanks for coming too. I know you've not been having an easy time. How is Mark?'

'He seems OK,' Holly said. 'Quite normal, considering. Thanks for the flowers, by the way.'

Natalie had sent him some flowers when he came out of hospital. *That confirms my suspicion that exercise is bad for you. Look after yourself. Nat x* the card had read. Mark had laughed when he read it, and been genuinely cheered by the flowers.

'Oh, that's all right.' Natalie put her drink down on the table, picked up the beer mat and began fiddling with it.

'What's up?' Holly asked. Then, thinking that it was often easier to talk about something difficult if you began by talking about something else, added, 'The office is like the *Marie-Celeste*. Darling's not been in all week either.'

'Really?' Natalie seemed genuinely surprised. Holly had thought she probably already knew. They were usually in more or less daily contact. 'I suppose the rumour mill has gone into overdrive then?'

'You know what people are like.' Holly wished now she hadn't brought up the subject of Darling. It was true that there was much speculation about why Natalie and James were both off at the same time.

Rather than the absences being regarded as coincidence, they seemed to confirm people's suspicions that the two of them were having an affair. Holly herself thought that James, being the slippery character he was, had probably got wind of the fact the programme was going to be axed and jumped ship straight away. He wouldn't want to tarnish his career by having to present a programme that everyone now knew was to be taken off air in a couple of weeks.

'Does everyone think he and I are having an affair?' Natalie looked directly at Holly, her look implying she wanted an honest answer.

'Well, I don't. I know you are close and people do gossip about you, but I never believed it. Why would you, when you've got Guy and the twins?'

Holly didn't air her private thoughts about James Darling. But she wondered why a liaison with someone arrogant, short and with the perfect face for radio was worth having, when, for Natalie, it would mean risking losing a tall, good-looking, charming husband.

Moreover Holly knew what it was like to have young children and a job. It didn't leave much time for hair-washing, let alone anything else.

'Guy thinks that I am,' Natalie said. 'Or at least he did. He thought . . . he thinks . . . '

She stopped talking and Holly thought she was going to cry, but she took a deep breath and carried on.

'He thinks it's been going on for years, since before I met him.'

She took another swig of her drink and began talking again before Holly had quite taken in what she was saying.

'And he thinks that because he believes I've been having an affair with Darling all along, that vindicates him for going on dates with a string of women he's been meeting on the internet.'

'What?' Holly couldn't quite believe what Natalie was telling her.

She knew about his meeting with Mila, obviously, and she'd decided to believe the

443

explanation he'd given her when they'd met for coffee, but now she wondered if she'd chosen to believe him because his explanation was credible or simply because she wanted it to be true. If there were other women, Guy hadn't exactly told her the whole truth.

'I opened a credit-card bill,' Natalie said. 'I didn't mean to. It was in a pile with a load of bills. I wonder if Guy actually wanted me to find it. He left it there with the gas and the electricity and all the other stuff he says he never has time to deal with, despite being at home all day.'

'I can't believe he meant you to find it,' Holly began. 'And anyway, perhaps there was a reason for whatever you found on the bills.'

'Don't defend him,' Natalie said abruptly. 'There were payments for restaurants, and sometimes hotels, and a website which I looked up. Every Wednesday, when I thought he was going to the gym, he was having a quick drink with some woman he'd met on an internet site for bored married people, and if he liked them they'd go off to a hotel and have sex.'

'Are you sure?' Holly felt sick just listening to her.

'Yes, I'm sure.' Natalie started to cry now. 'I asked him outright and he admitted it. He didn't even seem sorry. He said I was as much to blame as he was.'

'How did he work that one out?' Holly felt the familiar feeling of anger she'd experienced on previous occasions when friends had told her they'd found a partner had cheated on them.

'He said it was common knowledge that I was

having an affair with James Darling.' Natalie was getting angry now. 'He went and slept with other women because of a fucking rumour, Holly! Can you believe it?'

'No.' She took her friend's hand and held it, at a loss for words and unsure what to believe.

'And do you know what makes it worse?'

Holly shook her head. She couldn't think of anything much worse than discovering your husband had been having brief affairs with virtual strangers.

'He said it didn't really make any difference if I wasn't actually having sex with James or not. He said he was cuckolded by my relationship with him anyway.' Natalie took another sip of her drink. 'He said my loyalties were with James and he couldn't take it any more. I suppose he thought screwing other women would help mend his precious hurt ego.'

'Natalie . . . ' Holly could think of no good way to phrase this so she just asked it. 'Is there anything between you and Darling?'

'No,' she said emphatically. 'We are good friends, you know that. We go back a long way and I really respect him. He's great at his job . . . unlike Guy, who is turning out to be a complete waster.'

'Sorry,' Holly apologised for asking. 'I never really thought there was anything more than that.'

But I can see that Guy might have, she thought to herself. And look what's happened. She could hear Mark's voice in her head now, saying what he'd said in the letter she'd read about her closeness to Daniel, leaving their marriage a shell.

'What will you do now?' she asked Natalie, wondering if the answer would help her too decide what she should do herself.

48

Mark was lying on the sofa chatting to someone on the phone and laughing when Holly got home. He appeared to be enjoying the conversation so much that he didn't hear her opening the door or come into the sitting room.

'Oh, that's great,' he was saying. 'You're brilliant! That's perfect.'

Holly stood by the door, feeling as if she was eavesdropping on something but not sure what.

'And how are you feeling?' Mark's tone became more serious suddenly and he sat up slightly, hunching over the phone, apparently unaware still that Holly was watching him. 'Are you OK? Are things really bad?'

Holly froze, almost sure now that he was talking to Daisy and wondering why things might be bad. She suspected it had to do with Daniel; he'd insinuated as much to her by text.

Holly had no idea what it was all about but felt uneasy about the cosy concerned way Mark was talking to Daisy now.

Ironically, her freezing seemed to alert him to her presence and he sat up suddenly, looking round at Holly angrily, as if she had been spying.

'Got to go now,' he said into the phone. 'I'll speak to you in the morning.'

'You frightened the life out of me,' he said. 'How long have you been standing there?'

'I've only just come in.' She was defensive in

reaction to his slightly accusatory tone. 'Who were you talking to?'

'Daisy,' he said. 'She's found the perfect venue for the press conference. It's a café in Princes Street Gardens. So Jimmy can talk and then do a bit of running round the park for a photo call.'

'Next week?' Holly asked. 'Will you be strong enough to go?'

'Yes,' Mark dismissed her concern. 'I've got a check up with the doctor later this week, but I feel fine. It's only for a night.'

'Are you sure?' Holly felt apprehensive about the prospect of him spending a night away from home, especially if he was going to have company. 'Where will you stay?'

'We're staying at the Scotsman.' Mark replied. 'And I'll be fine. Don't worry. It's just a meeting to give Daisy a chance to spend a bit of time with Jimmy. If she's going to be his PA and trainer when he does the run, they'll need to get on reasonably well. I am sure they will. Daisy's very easy to be with, but it'll give them a chance to get to know each other.'

'Right,' said Holly, wondering if it was Jimmy who wanted the chance to get to know Daisy or Mark himself.

'How was Natalie?' he asked, getting up. 'Do you want a cup of tea or something?'

'Yes, please.' She followed him into the kitchen. 'Natalie wasn't good actually. The planets must be out of sync at the moment, everyone seems to be having some sort of crisis.'

Mark had his back turned to her as he filled the kettle up. He said nothing.

'Mark,' she ventured, 'can we talk?'

She hoped he would realise that she meant a proper sit-down serious talk.

'Yep.' His reply sounded casual. 'I'll just make the tea.'

'Where are the kids?' Holly asked, wondering if they would be uninterrupted.

'Chloe has gone to the cinema with Ruaridh,' Mark said. 'His dad is going to bring her home later. And Jake is in his room.'

'Has he gone to bed?' Holly asked. It was nearly ten and she would have preferred Chloe to be home by now. She had school tomorrow. But at the same time Holly was glad she was out enjoying herself instead of working.

'No, I think he's on the computer.'

'I'll go and say hello while you make the tea,' Holly said, putting her bag on the chair and walking upstairs.

When she came back down again Mark had made a pot of tea and was sitting at the kitchen table, as if he had heeded her request and was ready and waiting.

'So what's up with Natalie?' he asked, which seemed as good a way into the conversation as any.

'Guy's been screwing around,' Holly said. She didn't really like the word 'screwing' but it was the only way she could think of to describe what he had been up to. She'd thought about it on the train on the way home and wondered if it would have been better or worse if he had been having an affair.

The fallout would have been different, and

perhaps harder to deal with if he'd formed an attachment to someone else. If, that is, he was telling the truth to Natalie, and had told Holly the truth about his meeting with Mila as well.

'In what way?' Mark poured her a cup of tea but had none himself.

Holly knew he was being careful, watching his caffeine intake — she just hoped he wasn't indulging in anything else that might stimulate his heart.

'The usual way. The seeing other women way.' She looked at Mark to see if he reacted at all to this, whether he would give away something that would make her suspect Guy wasn't the only one. His face remained impassive so she continued.

'He'd started going to the gym . . . except he wasn't going there at all, he was meeting up with women he'd contacted on the internet. Sometimes he'd just meet them for a drink, and sometimes if he liked them they'd go to a hotel. Natalie found his credit-card statements and it all came out.'

'Bloody hell!' Mark looked genuinely shocked. 'Poor Natalie. How long had this been going on?'

'Not long, which I suppose is something,' Holly said. 'But long enough to have a devastating effect on her. She's in bits. She's been off work for the past week or so. I can't see her coming back any time soon, not the state she was in.'

'I'm sure it helped, being able to talk to you.'

Mark smiled at Holly and put his hand briefly over hers.

It was a small gesture but something he hadn't done spontaneously for so long that she found herself immediately questioning its significance.

'The thing is, there's something else.' She looked up at him as Mark took his hand away again. 'I'm not sure how good a friend I'm being because I know something else that Natalie doesn't, and I don't know whether to tell her or not.'

'What's that?' Mark was leaning back in his chair now, looking at her curiously.

'When I went for dinner with my dad that night, Guy was in the restaurant with James Darling's wife,'

'What — the presenter?'

'Yes.' Holly couldn't remember how much she had told Mark about the gossip that surrounded Natalie and Darling or if he'd even taken it in. 'Natalie and James are very good friends, but people at work insinuate that they are more than that.'

'And are they?' Mark wasn't usually interested in office gossip but he looked interested now.

'Natalie says not,' Holly told him. 'And I believe her. For one thing, Darling is a creep, although she seems to like him. But that was one of the reasons Guy cited for seeing these other women. He told Natalie he felt cuckolded by their friendship, even if it was innocent.'

'I can understand that,' Mark said, looking at Holly and holding her gaze for a moment as if to impart extra significance to what he'd just said.

'What do you think he was doing with James Darling's wife?'

'They'd met before at some drinks after work,' Holly said, remembering she'd not invited him to come. 'Guy was very jumpy when I saw them and asked to meet me a couple of days later. I haven't told Natalie any of this.'

'And what did he tell you then?' Mark asked.

'He said they'd just met to talk.' Holly wondered if her husband was bothered that she hadn't shared any of this with him at the time. 'He told me Mila was quite dismissive, condescending even towards him, treating the very suggestion that her husband might want anything to do with someone like Natalie as ridiculous.'

'I'd have thought it would be the other way round,' Mark commented. 'Surely she's more of a catch than James Darling.'

'You'd think so, wouldn't you? But his wife is this incredibly beautiful sculptress. I was amazed myself when I met her. Darling obviously has some very well-hidden qualities which make him attractive to some women.'

'Or perhaps the circumstances in which they met had some bearing.' Mark was looking hard at her again.

Holly could feel the conversation heading towards the topic she'd wanted to raise with him, but now she felt anxious and unsure.

'Anyway . . . ' She carried on talking about Natalie and James to put off the moment when they might start talking about her and Daniel. And Mark and Daisy. 'Later I wondered if Guy

452

had really met her because he was hoping that Mila . . . '

' . . . might be tempted back to one of his hotels?' Mark said what she had been about to say. 'Redress the balance by sleeping with the wife of the person he thought was taking all his wife's time and attention?'

'I suppose so.' Holly swallowed hard, wondering if Mark was saying what she thought he might be saying to her. 'But from what Guy told me, she seemed to treat him as if he was rather pathetic.'

She was going to say 'which he is', but decided not to until she'd heard Mark's response.

'He wouldn't be the first man to try it on with an attractive woman, and I'm sure he won't be the last.' Mark was looking at her again. 'I'm not making excuses for Guy, but sometimes if you're not feeling great about your own relationship and find yourself in the company of another woman who seems to like you, you think it's worth a try. Men do anyway. Sometimes, I suppose, the women respond, but I'm sure most of the time they treat the very suggestion as ridiculous.'

'Do you think I should tell Natalie?' Holly asked, while mentally mulling over what Mark had just said and wondering if he was talking about Guy and Mila, or himself and Daisy, or if he had somehow got wind of the fact that she had kissed Daniel? 'I'm sure it's bound to come out and then she'll be angry with me for keeping it from her.'

'If I were you,' Mark said, looking straight into

her eyes and holding her gaze as he spoke, 'I would keep quiet. If what you say is right and nothing happened between Guy and Mila, talking about it might make everyone say things that would be best left unsaid. Don't you think?'

'Maybe. If they are things that don't really matter in the long run.' Holly looked back at him, wondering what the subtext of his remarks was.

'Did you say anything to Natalie at all?' he asked, shifting in his seat and looking away as if it had been decided that they wouldn't talk about themselves, not now.

'I asked if she knew that James Darling had been off work,' Holly told him, feeling relieved that the conversation appeared to have been averted for the time being at least. 'The rumour mill at work had noted they were both off at the same time.'

'And did she know?' Mark asked.

'Yes, she did. That's the thing about Natalie and James. They seem to know more about each other than anyone else does, and Natalie seems to know more about what he's up to than her own husband.'

'So where is he?'

'He'd gone to cover a story about gay rights in Belgrade. That's where Mila, his wife, is from. Apparently he'd got wind that the correspondent there might be moving to Kiev and thought he'd make his face known.'

Mark picked up the elephant Holly's mother had brought them from Thailand and began fiddling with it absent-mindedly.

'It's very realistic, isn't it?' he said.

'Yes, very.'

'The elephant in the room. I wonder if that's why your mother gave it to us.'

'What?' Holly asked.

Then it dawned on her what he meant, and what her mother had meant when she gave it to her.

'I'm starving. Is there anything to eat?' Jake wandered into the kitchen and asked, oblivious to the fact that his parents were deep in conversation.

'There's some leftover stew in the fridge,' Mark said, getting up as if the conversation were over. 'You can heat it up if you want, Jake. I'm off to bed. I'm absolutely exhausted.'

'I'll be up in a minute,' Holly said, needing a pause to go back over the conversation and try to work out what exactly had been said about their situation.

Jake had gone for buttering half a loaf of bread over heating up leftover stew, and taken it in front of the TV to eat.

'You ought to go to bed soon,' Holly said to him, and he nodded before disappearing, giving her a moment to text Daniel.

49

'I'm sorry if it makes things difficult for you.' Anne-Marie was looking nervously around the café, afraid to meet Holly's eye.

'It doesn't,' Holly tried to reassure her. She looked like a frightened rabbit and Holly half-expected her to jump up at any minute and make a bolt for the door. 'Do you want some tea? Or coffee? And maybe some cake?'

Holly thought that her mother would be proud of her, sitting here pretending everything was perfectly normal in a peculiarly British way, talking about tea and cake.

She'd called Anne-Marie on her mobile as soon as the producer from *Woman's Hour* had left earlier that morning. Holly had thought when she looked up and saw the familiar face appear in her office that perhaps *Woman's Hour* was her fate once *Antennae* came off air. It wasn't Melanie who had called her before to ask about Survivor's Syndrome, but a more senior producer, Helen Clark, who had come to see her.

Holly had worked on *Woman's Hour* before she'd had Chloe. She had loved it, but as the programme was on air daily there was never any down time and she wasn't sure she could cope with that right now.

She hadn't for a moment imagined the conversation Helen was about to have with her would give her another major headache, at a time when her head already felt as if it would explode with the number of worries, secrets and problems she was carrying around in it.

'May I have a word?' Helen had asked, before sitting in the seat usually occupied by Natalie.

'Did anything ever come of the woman from the train? The one I put Melanie in touch with?' Holly asked, wondering if Anne-Marie had agreed to talk to them despite her concerns.

'That's what I wanted to talk to you about. I just wondered how well you know her?'

'Not that well.' Holly began to feel guilty as she nearly always did when the subject of Anne-Marie came up. She still couldn't quite put her finger on what it was about Anne-Marie that made her feel uneasy.

She seemed a perfectly nice woman and Holly wished she could feel a bit more warm and friendly towards her, but she always made her feel slightly uncomfortable. Daniel didn't seem to feel the same, or if he did he'd never said anything. She felt herself flinching slightly at the way things had been left with Daniel too.

She hadn't seen him to talk to for a few weeks. He'd texted her a couple of times, asking how Mark was and suggesting 'catching up for a quick chat'. She knew she needed to talk to him but was not sure what she wanted to say, so she avoided it. There were too many other people needing to talk to her right now. One of them was sitting in her office.

'I met her at a meeting after the train crash,' Holly told Helen. 'And we went for a drink a few weeks after. I bump into her on the train from time to time.'

'So you're not exactly friends?' she asked.

'To be honest, I feel bad about her,' Holly confessed. 'She sort of latched on to me and another man I know who commutes.'

'Did you know her by sight before you met?'

'No.' Holly remembered thinking it odd that she'd never seen Anne-Marie on the train before, but then she'd explained that she was an infrequent commuter. 'I don't think I'd seen her before. She doesn't go on the train that often. Maybe that's why she talks to us. She doesn't understand the etiquette.'

'What etiquette?' Helen looked confused.

'Oh, you know,' Holly said, although she clearly didn't. 'The 'you don't speak to people you see on the train every day or you might just end up talking to them every day for the rest of your life' rule!'

'But Anne-Marie did?'

'Yes,' Holly answered. 'She seemed keen to meet up. I didn't really want to but then I felt a bit mean. She's lost her husband and she seems to be coping really well. I felt as if I ought at least to talk to her. You know how it is?'

'The thing is,' Helen said, 'she really does need to talk to someone and I was hoping you might be able to have a chat with her first off.'

★ ★ ★

'Do you take sugar?' Holly asked Anne-Marie, pouring from the pot of tea for two they'd asked for and eyeing up the cake she'd ordered. Anne-Marie had said she was not hungry.

'No,' Anne-Marie said, taking the cup and holding it close to her, like a comforter. 'So what happens now?' she asked.

'Nothing happens. I just wanted to see if you were OK,' Holly said, trying to reassure her again. Holly had always thought she was in her early thirties. She looked about thirteen now, like a schoolgirl who had been caught stealing from her parents and knew there would be trouble, even if the offence didn't carry a custodial sentence.

'The interview you did won't go out, and the bit that went out in the trailer was only a few seconds. I don't suppose anyone noticed.'

'Except him,' said Anne-Marie, looking up and meeting her eye for the first time.

'Except him,' Holly agreed, thinking that things could have gone a whole lot worse for Anne-Marie if he hadn't.

She didn't fully understand why but she did feel sorry for Anne-Marie now, who was looking as if her world was about to crumble.

'I didn't mean for this to happen,' she said quietly.

'I'm sure you didn't.' Holly put her hand across the table and took Anne-Marie's and held it. She felt quite comfortable with her now that she knew her misgivings had not been entirely unfounded.

She could empathise with her too. Both she and Anne-Marie had been through something that day and allowed themselves to be swept up in the ripple of repercussions without ever stopping to think how it would all turn out. Now they were both trying to sort out the resulting mess.

⋆ ⋆ ⋆

'Caroline Mills arranged to interview her,' the *Woman's Hour* producer had told Holly back in her office. 'She can be very persuasive.'

'Really?' Holly had heard Caroline Mills on air but didn't know her personally. She knew Anne-Marie had been reluctant to be interviewed. Perhaps that persuasiveness explained why she'd agreed.

'I heard her on the phone, setting it up,' Helen went on. 'I could tell whoever was at the other end of the line was hesitant, to say the least, but Caroline always brings people round.'

'Always?' Holly asked.

'Well, almost always,' Helen told her. 'She told Anne-Marie it would be more of a chat really. Said they'd talk about everything first and then, only if she was happy, they'd record a bit of what she had to say. She told Anne-Marie her contribution was only going to be a small part of a bigger piece about the subject. You know how it works.'

'Yes.' Holly had spent long enough working in radio to know that the desperation of a producer with empty air space to fill often outweighed the reluctance of a potential interviewee to talk about something deeply personal.

'Well, anyway,' Helen told her, 'Anne Marie agreed to meet her and they recorded the interview.'

She paused and looked around the office, as if to make sure no one else was listening. The door was shut.

'Between you and me,' Helen adopted a confidential tone, 'Caroline does tend to put words into people's mouths a bit. I edited an interview she'd done once and there was a lot of 'why don't you just tell me' . . . Then she'd tell them more or less exactly what to say.'

'So what did Anne-Marie say?' Holly was getting a little wary of the slightly conspiratorial nature of this meeting.

'She said more or less what we thought she would say,' Helen continued. 'She said she hadn't been on the train that day but that she'd lost her husband in the crash. She didn't go into detail about what actually happened to him and, for once, Caroline was sensitive enough not to probe.'

Holly kept quiet, waiting for Helen to reveal whatever it was she thought she needed to tell Holly, the reason she thought Holly needed to speak to Anne-Marie.

'It was a good interview. There were a few clips that worked well with the rest of the piece,' Helen told her. 'Anne-Marie seemed to have had an almost text-book experience.'

'So what was the problem?' Holly asked, urging her to get to the point.

'We used a clip of her in a trailer for the programme. It went out at the weekend,' Helen told her. 'By Monday morning, there were several messages on the answerphone in our office. They were from her husband.'

It wasn't how I first imagined meeting up with Holly for coffee would be. I thought once we'd met and exchanged numbers she'd contact me, or reply to one of my texts and we'd meet for lunch one day and talk openly about our different experiences of events that day. I thought out of our shared experiences a friendship would grow.

Instead we seemed to get off on a series of misunderstandings, and by the time I realised this, I didn't know how to put things right. If Holly had ever replied and agreed to meet me, I could have tried. But she never did. Now I know she had good reason, but at the time I thought she was just ignoring me and that made me determined to press on.

So I never envisaged sitting nervously, waiting for her to arrive, dreading what she was going to say to me, and hating myself for having misled her.

I could tell when she called that she knew. Her voice sounded different, not cross but perplexed and a bit disappointed.

'Hi, Holly,' I said, when I heard it was her on the other end of the line. 'I haven't seen you for a while.'

'No,' she replied, sounding strained. 'I've been away.'

But I already knew that.

Then she said, 'I think we ought to meet, don't you?'

And I knew then that she would want an explanation; that I owed her one.

I thought she would be angry, but she wasn't.

She looked tired, when she arrived, and I wondered where she'd been.

She didn't look as if she'd had a holiday. She wasn't tanned or relaxed, rather stressed and exhausted looking, and I wanted to reach out and take her hand and ask if she was OK. I wanted to be a friend to her, which is all that I'd ever wanted really, but now everything was a mess.

I'd misled her and I feared she'd not forgive me, but she was surprisingly kind and understanding, even before I'd explained everything.

Holly said she'd listened to the interview. Caroline had played it to her in her office and she thought I came across well, especially the part about my mother and the store stampede.

'That must have been very traumatic,' she said to me. 'Did you have nightmares afterwards?'

'I don't remember,' I said, honestly. I don't remember the immediate aftermath; I only really started thinking about it in hindsight when Mum got ill.

'It must have been hard, your mother being in hospital and having to go and live with friends,' Holly continued, and she talked as if she could understand that. 'Did you realise it was bothering her, even before it became obvious?'

'Perhaps.' I thought about this. My mother

and I had always been close, and afterwards she did seem a little distant, but if I ever thought about it I'd supposed it was because I was growing up, getting older and more private, wanting my own space.

It wasn't until she went into hospital that I realised how much I missed that closeness.

'Geoff always said I was too clingy,' I said, knowing we needed to broach the subject sooner or later. 'He said I used to suffocate him because I was too needy, and I think now maybe that's why.'

'That's a very harsh thing to say,' Holly said gently, as if she understood. 'I mean for Geoff to say — that you suffocated him.'

'I don't think he thought that at first,' I said, because I know he didn't. I am sure we were happy when we started out.

'Things are different when you start a relationship,' Holly said. 'People want to be . . .'

She paused and looked down at the table, trying to think of the right way to put whatever it was she meant to say.

'There's a fine line between suffocation and being completely wrapped up in another person,' she continued. 'When you first meet someone, you want to be wrapped up in them and vice versa. You want to be needed by the other person because you want to be with them. You want them to be unable to live without you really, don't you? So that they want to commit to you?'

'I'd never thought of it like that,' I said, stirring my tea and thinking that Holly was just like I thought she would be: kind and understanding.

'But then, when you've been with someone a long time, sometimes one of you starts reasserting their independence, and if the other's not ready for that . . . ' Holly was staring at the table again and she never finished her sentence.

'Geoff once said that I didn't really love him,' I told her, looking around the coffee shop to see if anyone could hear us.

It felt strange to be telling all this to a virtual stranger in a public place, but I also felt relieved at the same time.

'He said I wanted someone to love so I put all my energy into loving the first person who happened to come along, without really considering if I did love him or not.' I paused and Holly looked at me. 'But I did love him, Holly. I really did. And I thought he loved me too.'

'I'm sure he did,' she said, and then she put her hand across the table and over mine, saying, 'Tell me what happened, Anne-Marie. I want to know.'

That's when I started crying, because I'd wanted to talk to someone for so long but I'd been holding it all in. Now that Holly was sitting there, asking me to tell her, the emotions I'd been keeping in check started to flood out.

I knew that people were looking at us but I didn't care, and Holly didn't seem to mind either.

'I'm sorry, Holly,' I said when I'd finished. 'I didn't mean for it to turn out like this.'

'There's no need to apologise,' she said, and I

realised her hand was still over mine, she hadn't taken it away all the time I'd been talking, telling her about everything: about Mum and Dad and living with Lisa, about meeting Geoff and the baby, and then Julia.

All the time she was stroking my hand gently with hers, smiling like the friend I had hoped she might become.

'I've wanted to talk to you ever since I saw you on the news,' I sobbed.

She stopped stroking my hand then and took hers away, ostensibly to have a drink of water but she didn't put it back.

'You were being carried out of the tunnel on a stretcher,' I told her. 'I was watching the news because I didn't know what else to do after I heard, and I saw you and I wanted to talk to you.'

'Why?' Holly asked, taking small sips from her glass.

'I can't really explain,' I said, but I tried. 'There was just something about the look on your face that made me think you might understand. I thought I could talk to you. I thought you might be able to help me.'

I hadn't meant to say this. I hadn't meant to say that I needed help. I knew I was finding it difficult, obviously, but I thought I could get through it one way or another.

'I think you probably need to talk to someone else, Anne-Marie,' Holly said, looking at me. 'I'd like to be able to help you, really I would, but there are things I need to sort out in my own life first.'

50

'Holly, it's really good to see you!' Daniel stood up and gave her a hug, which she felt lasted slightly too long.

He seemed reluctant to release her from his embrace and allow her to sit down and Holly wasn't sure if the hug was one of sympathy, because her husband had had a heart attack, or given because the last time she had seen him they had kissed.

Are you around at all? she had texted him earlier in the week. *There's something I need to tell you.*

Working from home this week. Are you in London every day? I really want to see you, D x

Wednesday? she had suggested.

Antennae was still on air until the end of the month but the production team were unenthusiastic and no one seemed to mind about their presence in the office any more.

Wednesday was the day before Mark and Daisy were due to fly to Edinburgh for the press conference. They'd be spending the night there.

Holly didn't recognise Daniel at first when she looked around Brown's, not only because he was in t-shirt and jeans, but also because he looked older, more tired and resigned.

'Holly,' he'd called out as she walked right past the table he was sitting at. She'd focused and seen him, looking what she could only describe as crushed.

'How are you?' she asked, thinking that if he said fine, he would be lying.

'Fine,' he said.

Holly laughed, feeling some of the awkwardness she had felt disappear.

'What's funny?' Daniel asked.

'You don't look fine,' she told him.

'Is that funny?' He raised his eyebrows questioningly and a hint of the expression of permanent half-amusement that she usually associated with him returned to his face.

'No,' Holly agreed. 'I think that's why someone came up with the expression 'you've got to laugh' — for precisely those moments when laughter is entirely inappropriate. To explain away its inappropriateness.'

'So you don't actually find the fact that I am not fine funny?' He was smiling now.

'You said you were fine,' she reminded him.

'Well, I'm not.' Daniel was serious again. 'Do you want something to eat or drink?'

Holly noticed that he already had a beer and a plate of steak and fries, which was hardly touched.

'I'll have a cup of tea.' She wondered how long he had already been there. 'And I might nick a few of your chips, if you're not eating them?'

'No, I'm not hungry,' he said, pushing his plate slightly towards her.

'So what's made you lose your appetite?' she asked, taking a chip and dipping it in a swirl of mayonnaise.

'I'll tell you in a bit.' Daniel signalled to the waitress who was clearing a nearby table. 'You said there was something you needed to tell me, when you texted?'

'Well, yes, something's happened,' Holly told him as the waitress approached. 'Could I get a pot of tea and a glass of water, please? Do you want anything else, Daniel?'

When he said he didn't, the waitress left.

'Is Mark OK?' Daniel asked. 'Daisy seems completely wrapped up in this press conference, but I thought Mark was supposed to take things easy?'

'He's been busy too but he seems to be OK,' Holly answered, wondering if Daniel knew something she didn't.

'I met Anne-Marie earlier in the week.' This was the reason Holly had needed to talk to him. 'She wasn't in a good way.'

Holly stopped talking when the waitress came back and put a large pot of tea and a glass of water on the table.

'Thank you,' she said, as she unloaded a cup and a jug of milk.

'Did you just bump into her on the train, or arrange to meet?' Daniel asked.

'We arranged to meet.' Holly poured some milk into the bottom of her cup. 'Do you remember I told you I'd put someone from *Woman's Hour* in touch with her?'

'Yes.' He nodded. 'You said you thought she was angry at the time.'

'I did,' Holly told him. 'But apparently she agreed to do the interview anyway. I didn't know about it. I was off work for a week, after Mark . . . '

Daniel reached out and put his hand on hers as her voice trailed off. She pulled it back and put it on her lap, finding this physical contact slightly oppressive, in the same way she had found the hug he'd given her earlier slightly claustrophobic.

'When I got back to work, the producer came and told me she'd done the interview. She said it was good and they'd used a small part of it to trail the programme over the weekend.'

'Trail?' Daniel asked.

'To advertise the programme before it goes out,' Holly told him. 'If you'd tuned in to Radio Four over the weekend, you might have heard Anne-Marie talking about losing her husband the day the train crashed.'

'So did it stir things up for her?' he asked. 'You said you thought she was coping too well, didn't you?'

'I did.' Holly nodded. 'I didn't know why, but I always thought there was something not quite right about Anne-Marie. And, it turns out, I was right.'

'What was it then?' Daniel was looking at her expectantly.

'It seems her husband didn't die in the crash that day at all,' she told him. 'He was on the train but got out and walked out through the tunnel, alive and unharmed.'

'So why did she say that he died?' Daniel's expression was incredulous. 'I don't understand.'

'The funny thing is, she never actually did say

that he died,' Holly tried to explain. 'That was one of the things that struck me as odd about Anne-Marie, the way she said things. Even when she recorded this interview for *Woman's Hour*, she never actually said that he'd died. She said that she'd lost him.'

'Same difference surely?' Daniel asked.

'Not to her.' Holly tried to explain some of what Anne-Marie had told her when they'd met. 'She knew he was on that train, and she heard on the news in the morning that it had crashed and there were likely to be casualties.'

Holly screwed up her face as she said the word. She didn't like this euphemism for deaths but she couldn't quite bring herself to say the word either.

'Anne-Marie told me she tried to contact him but the mobile phone lines were down. She was at home, waiting for news.' Holly paused then.

When Anne-Marie had described the waiting to her, it had forced her to consider what it must have been like for Mark, waiting to find out if his wife was all right.

Anne-Marie had told her the waiting was agonising. That she'd jumped every time someone walked past the house, and sat by the phone willing it to ring with positive news. Mark had been at home, alone when he was waiting for news, but Anne-Marie had had company.

Holly concentrated on these facts as Anne-Marie spoke to her, and tried not to think where she had been while Anne-Marie was sitting at home.

'She told me her best friend came round, after

she'd heard the news on the radio, and sat with her. She was thankful for the company. She said having someone else to wait with her broke the silence of the phone not ringing.'

'Go on,' Daniel urged her.

Holly thought back to the afternoon she'd spent with Anne-Marie.

★   ★   ★

'It was eerie,' Anne-Marie had told her. 'Usually I get lots of calls from people selling life insurance, or debt management services, or trying to make me switch electricity providers. But in that hour no one at all called until . . . '

She'd paused and looked up at Holly, her eyes filling with tears as she did so. Then she'd drunk a whole glass of water and afterwards carried on.

'Julia seemed more agitated than I was.' Anne-Marie described how her best friend kept getting up and sitting down again, and had eventually gone into the garden to have a cigarette. 'She'd given up a few years ago but she still had the occasional one.'

'When she was in the garden her phone started ringing inside her bag,' Anne-Marie told Holly. 'I took it out. I took it out and then I noticed that the number calling was Geoff's.'

'Did you answer?' Holly asked her.

'No,' she said. 'I froze. I thought that someone else must have his phone and be calling from it. I thought maybe they were going through the contacts, trying to find out who his wife was. It didn't occur to me at the time that of course I am one of the first names on the list.'

'So who was it, calling Julia?' Holly asked her.

'It was Geoff. He left a message and I listened to it while Julia was still smoking at the bottom of the garden. He was calling to tell her he was OK. He said he wanted to let her know that he was all right. Then he said he had to go because he ought to call me.'

★　★　★

'But I still don't understand?' Daniel said, looking to Holly for further explanation.

'They'd been having an affair.' Holly hadn't needed Anne-Marie to spell it out for her. 'Geoff had been seeing her best friend for months, apparently. That's why she'd come round — not to look after Anne-Marie, but because she too was desperate to find out if Geoff was alive.'

Daniel took a sip of his drink but said nothing as he took this all in.

'If he hadn't been on that train, the affair might have gone on much longer without Anne-Marie knowing,' Holly said. 'He told her that evening he'd been planning to leave her but hadn't worked out how to tell her. Then he packed his bags and left.'

'So that's why she said she lost her husband that day?' Daniel was beginning to understand.

'Yes.' Holly nodded. 'She lost her best friend as well. The ultimate betrayal.'

'How was she when you saw her?' Daniel asked, picking up a paper napkin and absent-mindedly shredding it as he talked.

'Not good, obviously. She was mortified that she'd misled us. She said she never meant to. It was just that we assumed that he'd died, and she said she found it easier to let us believe that than to tell us what had really happened.'

'But why did she go to the meeting? I still don't really understand,' Daniel said. 'And why did she agree to do the radio interview?'

'She said she went to the meeting because her husband had ceased all contact with her. She wanted to get some sense of what had happened and who else had been on the train,' Holly told him. 'She told me that, even after what he'd done to her, she hoped they might have a future and thought his decision to leave her might have been affected by his having been in the crash.'

'And the radio?' Daniel asked.

'She didn't want to do it at first,' Holly told him. 'But the reporter who called her was very persuasive. And she hadn't been able to speak to Geoff since. When she said she'd lost him, she really had. He hadn't returned her calls. He'd refused to meet or talk to her. She told me she thought that if she did the interview, it would force his hand.'

'It worked then, didn't it?' Daniel commented.

'It makes sense now,' Holly said. 'All the things she said, the way she was with us and even the fact that she said she had lost him. He may not have died that day but what she went through was like a bereavement. I can't imagine how she must have been feeling.'

'I can imagine, Holly,' Daniel said, looking straight at her. 'I know how she must have felt.

That's why I'm not at work. That's why I needed to talk to you. I know what it feels like to find out that your partner doesn't want to be with you any more.'

51

'Do you know where Dad is?' Holly had knocked and put her head tentatively round the door of Jake's room.

He didn't like her walking in unannounced any more. Gone were the days when she could stand by the door and watch him, so completely absorbed in a Lego construction that he didn't even notice she was there, and then, when he did, beam at her presence and show her the beginnings of a complex battleship, or whatever it was he was making.

'Don't know.' Jake had been sitting at his desk, doing something on a laptop. He closed it hurriedly as soon as he saw his mother. 'He said he might be late back, though.'

'Did he say how late?' Holly asked, wondering why he had closed the computer so fast

'He's all right,' Mark would say, when she told him she didn't like the amount of time Jake spent on it. 'That's what boys do.'

'But what if he's doing stuff he shouldn't?' she would press him.

'My parents used to worry about me listening to punk music.' Mark often used this line of reasoning. 'Thought it would turn me into a juvenile delinquent, but I turned out all right.'

As if to prove his point, Jake got up and came over to where Holly was standing near the radiator. He sat down on the edge of his bed opposite her and smiled.

'Dad said he might be late because he needed to make sure he had everything ready before he goes to Edinburgh tomorrow.' Jake appeared to be in chatty mode.

Tomorrow was the official press launch for the Jimmy Finlay run. Mark had been working hard on it ever since he'd come out of hospital. Too hard, Holly thought, since he was supposed to be taking things easy. He was flying up to Edinburgh first thing in the morning, with Daisy. They needed to be at the airport early. Holly had presumed he'd get home at a reasonable hour before that and not burn the candle at both ends.

'Where've you been anyway? I thought you were working from home today.'

'Well, I didn't really feel like working, so I bunked off and went for a wander round town.' Holly didn't like lying to Jake. She found it much more difficult than lying to Mark, but she wasn't sure he'd understand her reasons for seeing Daniel today and she didn't want him to ask about their meeting now.

'Do you know what you'll be doing yet, when *Antennae* goes off air?' Jake asked.

'Not yet.' Holly wondered if he was worried that she might be out of a job. 'I'm sure they have something in mind but have chosen not to share it with me yet.'

'Are you all right, Mum?' Jake eased himself back on his bed and lay down so that he was looking at the ceiling as he asked her this.

'Yes, I'm fine, darling.' She tried to sound reassuring, though she was anything but fine.

'But why?' Holly had asked Daniel, when he'd told her Daisy wanted to leave him. 'When did this happen? Where will she go? What will you do?'

The world suddenly seemed to be falling apart. Everywhere she turned couples were coming unstuck. Holly didn't want them to come unstuck, not just because she cared about the people involved but because it meant it could happen to her too.

'The day Mark went into hospital.' Daniel chose to answer the when part of her question first. 'When we got home, Daisy said she needed to talk.'

'Yes,' Holly said, feeling suddenly nauseous. She remembered reading the text Mark had sent Daisy, when he came out of hospital the following day. *Have you told Daniel?* it had read, and Holly had told herself it was probably work-related and tried, unsuccessfully, to dismiss any thought of what else it might be about from her head.

She took a deep breath, trying to calm herself in anticipation of Daniel now telling her something she didn't want to hear.

'She'd been a bit off earlier in the week,' he said. 'I thought there was something wrong but I wasn't sure what and I didn't ask her. I thought it would probably pass.'

'But it didn't?' Holly asked, not wanting to ask what it was that had been wrong.

'No.' Daniel had taken a deep breath himself

and then explained, 'Daisy had had a miscarriage the week before. I didn't even know she was pregnant. She hadn't told me.'

'How pregnant was she?' Holly asked, wondering why Daisy would keep news like that from her husband.

'Only a couple of weeks. She'd only been sure she was pregnant for a few days before she miscarried.'

'And she didn't tell you?' Holly was thinking to herself that a few days was an eternity in which not to tell your husband you were pregnant, especially when you had been trying for a while.

'No.' He looked incredibly sad. 'Not until it was over.'

'But why?' Holly asked. She could only think of one reason why you wouldn't tell your husband that you were having a baby — and that was if it was someone else's.

'She said that when she found out she was pregnant she realised it was not what she wanted.' Daniel looked at Holly then as if perhaps she could explain this to him.

'You don't always feel as you think you should feel.' She thought back to when she'd discovered she was expecting Chloe. She'd thought in advance that she would be delighted, but found she felt strangely detached from the whole process yet terrified at the same time.

'I was really scared when I was pregnant with Chloe. I didn't feel blooming and expectant. I was scared of what it would be like having a baby . . . of what I would be like as a mother. I

479

didn't think I'd be able to do it. But it worked out all right in the end.'

'We'll never find out now.' Daniel stared at the table.

'At least it means you know she can get pregnant,' Holly tried to comfort him. 'People often miscarry their first child. It's quite common. So if it's happened once, it can happen again.'

'It won't happen again though, Holly.' He looked up at her and his expression was one of abject resignation. 'Because Daisy doesn't want to get pregnant again, not soon and not with me anyway.'

'She can't be sure of that,' Holly tried to reassure him, and herself in the process. She couldn't get the thought out of her head that Daisy hadn't wanted the baby because it wasn't Daniel's. And if it wasn't Daniel's, whose was it? She tried to recall the exact wording of some of the texts to and from Mark that she had read. Did he know about this? She thought that he must.

'She's just been pregnant for the first time and then lost the baby,' Holly continued. 'Her hormones will be all over the place, and her emotions too. Wait a while, I'm sure she will see things differently, Daniel.'

'She was adamant,' he insisted. 'And to be honest, Holly, I'm beginning to wonder if she ever really wanted to try for a baby. I really wanted one and I thought she did too. But I'm beginning to think I misinterpreted things.'

Holly said nothing, waiting for him to explain further.

'I was the one who suggested we start trying. Daisy said she wasn't sure if it was the right time.'

'There never seems to be a right time,' Holly said.

'I should have listened to her then,' Daniel said. 'I shouldn't have let things go this far . . .'

'What things?' Holly asked.

'When Daisy got pregnant, she told me it made her realise that this wasn't what she wanted.' Daniel paused.

'A baby?' Holly asked.

'And the rest,' he said slowly. 'She said she didn't tell me she was pregnant because it had made her realise that she didn't want the life she has now. She said she didn't want to be married and living off my earnings, and she didn't want to be stuck at home with a child. She said doing this work for Mark had made her realise what she'd been missing out on, and she didn't feel ready to start settling down.'

'I can understand why she felt like that.' Holly hoped this would reassure Daniel. 'It can seem as if life, as you know it, is over when you're expecting a child, and no amount of people telling you it's only just beginning will make you believe that's true. It's a major change. It makes you run scared.'

'But Daisy said she was already running scared.' Daniel slumped back in his chair. 'She said she felt we'd married too young, and that I'm making her lead a life she doesn't want to lead. She really wants this job with Jimmy Finlay. I think she was relieved she lost the baby, Holly,

481

because it means she can go off and do whatever it is she wants to do.'

'Perhaps it will work out for the best.' Holly wondered how much of this Mark knew and why he hadn't mentioned anything to her. 'Perhaps she can do the job for a while, and in a year or so she may feel ready to try for another baby.'

'I've been though all of this with her,' Daniel sighed. 'We've been going round and round in circles, talking about what we both want — and it's not the same thing.'

'I'm sorry.' Holly didn't know what else to say.

'The thing is,' Daniel carried on talking, 'I could never quite believe it when Daisy agreed to marry me. I never thought someone like her would want to settle down with someone like me. It seemed too good to be true. And now it turns out I was right all along.'

★   ★   ★

'That sounds like Dad.' Jake sat up on his bed, listening to the sound of a key being turned in the door.

'Mark?' Holly called out, without moving.

'Hello,' his familiar voice came up the stairs. 'Where are you?'

'In Jake's room,' she called back, hearing the exchange as if she were not taking part in it. 'I'll be down in a moment.'

It all sounded completely normal, this exchange between husband and wife, but Holly was no longer sure if everything was normal or if this was just an illusion.

52

'How was your day?' Holly studied Mark's face closely for signs that anything might be amiss.

'Good.' He sounded upbeat but turned away to hang his coat on the hook in the hall so she could only see his profile. 'Everything seems to be ready for tomorrow. I'm really excited about it.'

'What time are you leaving?' Holly asked, wondering when she would find time to sit him down and talk.

'The flight's not till nine but we need to be there by seven-thirty.' Holly noted how casually Mark managed to make the 'we' that meant himself and Daisy sound. 'I'll book a cab for six-thirty and pick up Daisy on the way.'

'Right.' Holly wasn't sure what else to say, but the silence was filled by Chloe opening the front door.

'Hello!' She sounded cheery too.

Holly wondered if her family were really all in buoyant mood or whether they just appeared more up in contrast to the way she felt.

'Hello, darling,' she said to Chloe. 'What have you been doing since school finished?'

'I've been at Ruaridh's house.' She smiled at her mother. 'And I stopped at the Open Market on the way back. I thought I'd cook dinner tonight, as Dad's going away tomorrow morning.'

'That's very kind,' Holly said. 'Are you sure

you have time? You don't have any homework or anything to do?'

'I did it at Ruaridh's house,' Chloe answered, heading for the kitchen with a plastic bag that appeared to be bursting with vegetables.

Holly had nothing in mind for dinner, so was glad not to have to dream up something from whatever she could find. Nevertheless she felt a bit redundant. They didn't really seem to need her here, any of them.

As she thought this, Holly realised this was exactly what Mark must have been thinking for the past year.

'Can you come up to my room?' Jake stood at the top of the stairs, making this unusual request. His room was usually the last place he wanted either of his parents.

'Me or Dad?' she asked.

'Well, Dad, but both of you,' Jake answered.

'Yes, both of you,' Chloe said, as if she already knew what this was about.

'OK.' Holly started going up the stairs and could feel Mark following her.

'I need to pack for tomorrow,' he said, apparently unperturbed by the novelty of Jake inviting them both into his room.

'Do you want to sit on my bed?' he asked, sitting on the swivel chair by his desk.

Holly felt unnerved by the way he was behaving. He was obviously about to tell them something and she had no idea what. But she wasn't sure if she could take any more surprises.

★   ★   ★

'I'm really sorry,' Holly said to Daniel as they walked down an alleyway connecting the street the brasserie was in to the one that ran parallel.

'What for?' The alley was too narrow for them to walk abreast of each other. Daniel had been ahead of her but stopped now and turned to face her.

'I feel partly responsible,' Holly said. 'Because of Mark putting her up for the job with Jimmy Finlay.'

'It was Daisy who put Mark in touch with him,' Daniel reminded her.

'Oh, yes.' Holly had forgotten this. 'Still, I feel bad. Is there . . . ?'

She wanted to start walking again. She felt she could ask the question she wanted to ask more easily if they were in motion, but Daniel was blocking the way.

'Is there someone else?' Holly looked down at the pavement as she asked it.

'She says not.' He seemed momentarily rooted to the spot.

'And you don't think there is?' Holly could not get out of her head the thought that there might be, and that it might be Mark.

'I don't think there is anyone else,' Daniel said slowly, looking straight at her. 'Not for Daisy anyway.'

'What do you mean?' Holly wondered if Daisy had told him something about Mark and someone else. Was Daniel going to be the bearer of bad tidings?

He didn't answer.

Instead, he took a step closer to Holly, took

hold of her and began kissing her, more passionately than the last time, more urgently too, and pushing her so that her back was against the wall of the alley and his hand was on her breast but moving down towards the top of her skirt.

Holly tried to wriggle away and say 'no', but he was kissing her too hard for her to speak, forcing her mouth open with his tongue and pushing his hand between her legs.

Holly was trying to force him away but it appeared to be having little effect. Daniel was much stronger than he looked. He was pressing himself against her now and Holly could feel herself becoming aroused although she knew this was definitely not what she wanted. She squirmed again, putting her free hand up and pulling sharply on Daniel's hair.

He stopped kissing her and moved his face away far enough for her to speak.

'What's wrong?' he asked.

'This is wrong,' Holly said. 'This isn't going to help.'

'I thought it was what you wanted, Holly.' Daniel moved back slightly but he was still too close for her to move.

'It's not.' She tried to edge sideways and put some space between them. 'It's not what I want at all.'

'I'm sorry.' He stepped back abruptly, as if suddenly realising what he'd been doing, then turned away and began walking fast down the alley.

'Wait!' Holly called after him. 'Daniel, wait.'

But he carried on walking, too fast for her to catch up without running, and she didn't want to run after him. As he turned out of the alleyway he turned back briefly and said to her, as she gained ground, 'What do you want, Holly?'

His voice was raised but she didn't think it was in anger, just so she could hear across the distance.

She stopped as she neared the end of the alley and said quietly, so that he wouldn't hear, but out loud, as if saying it might make it happen: 'I want things back the way they were.'

★ ★ ★

Mark sat next to her on the bed, but not right next to her. There was a time when he would automatically have sat close, with his arm around her, or they would both have squeezed into bed with Jake, giving him a cuddle before he went to sleep. Now Mark's preferred position was about a foot away. Whatever news it was Jake was about to deliver, it wasn't going to be received together. Holly and Mark were going to react separately to it from different ends of his bed.

'What is it you wanted to tell us, Jake?' Holly looked across the room to where he was sitting at his desk, now fiddling with the laptop. She dreaded hearing what he might be going to say. Was he in trouble at school? Worried about things at home? Was he going to tell them he thought he was gay, or was there something on the computer he was going to show them?

The latter seemed the most likely as he was saying 'hang on a sec' and tapping away at the keyboard.

'Take a look at this,' he said, nervously, as if they might be angry with what they saw.

'What is it, Jake?' Holly asked, feeling she needed to prepare herself for whatever it was he was going to show them.

'Have a look, Mum.' Jake was smiling now. He still looked apprehensive but not scared of what their reaction might be.

Mark got up first and peered over his shoulder.

'Oh my god!' he said, sounding surprised. 'That's amazing, Jakey. Incredible, in fact. When did you do that?'

'Have a look, Dad,' Jake encouraged him. 'Enter the site.'

'I don't know what to say.' Mark was tooling around with the mouse. Holly wondered what site Jake had discovered that could be so incredible it merited inviting both his parents up to his room to have a look at it.

'Look at this, Holly.' Mark swung his head in her direction. She got up and looked over Jake's other shoulder.

'Oh, Jake,' she said, putting her arms around him. 'Did you do that?'

53

Holly saw Daniel immediately, through the window of the carriage, even though she was trying to walk past without looking and without being seen. She didn't know what she would say to him when she next saw him. He hadn't called or texted her after leaving her in the alleyway, and she hadn't contacted him. So it was still there, hanging in the air, whatever it was that had happened.

She got on the train further down, feeling slightly nervous not just about her life but about the journey. Why now? she asked herself. You've done it scores of times, since the crash. But she still felt a slight feeling of dread. A week ago, Daniel's presence on the train would have made her feel safe. Now it had the opposite effect. She realised she'd been stupid, thinking he could carry on looking after her the way he had done in the immediate aftermath of the crash. He wasn't the person she needed, it was Mark.

Holly checked her watch. It was just before 8. Mark would be at the airport now, with Daisy. Holly wondered what they would be doing. Would they be having a coffee and something to eat somewhere? Or filling time separately in the airport shops? Or would they be waiting at the departure gates together? Holly had a sudden vivid mental picture of the latter. Mark and

Daisy were holding hands in the transit lounge, knowing that there, airside, they were unlikely to be seen by anyone they knew.

Holly shook her head to try and remove the image from her mind, but she also cursed herself for not having found the right time to sit down and have a proper talk with her husband during the past couple of weeks. It should have been easy but initially she'd shied away from any confrontation, knowing that Mark was supposed to be taking things easy. Then, when they both went back to work, they never seemed to be in the same space at the same time, or if they were the children were always there too. And when they did find themselves together, Holly became suddenly unsure what it was she needed to talk to him about.

Last night she'd been clear what she needed to say to Mark and that she needed to say it before he went away to Edinburgh with Daisy, but then the evening took a new direction and she couldn't bring herself to spoil the mood.

She thought back now, as the train began inching out of the station, to the look on Mark's face when Jake had opened the laptop. He had been amazed and delighted and incredibly proud. And so was she.

All those hours Jake had spent on the computer, when she'd thought he'd been chatting to friends on Facebook or suspected he might be looking at porn, he'd been developing a new website for Mark.

'It's incredible, Jake, really incredible,' his father told him. 'I should have done something myself really, but I never got round to it.'

'I reckoned a lot of Jimmy Finlay fans will want to follow the run, so you needed something on your site before it started.' Jake sounded like a professional who'd been consulted about this, rather than a thirteen year old, who'd done it all off his own bat.

'If you click on the map, you'll be able to see where Jimmy is.' He carried on showing them round the site. 'And get daily updates, which you or Daisy can add in. I did talk to Daisy about it a bit.'

He said this a little sheepishly, as if he had somehow been going behind their backs, but Mark didn't seem to notice.

'Well, I don't know what to say, Jakey.' Mark sounded almost tearful.

'It's really good, isn't it?' Chloe had come upstairs and the smell of something delicious, cooking downstairs, followed her.

'Did you know about this?' Holly asked her.

'Well, yes,' Chloe admitted. 'I've seen it. He's really clever, isn't he? By the way, dinner's ready.'

'You're both incredible,' Holly had said, amazed that they had each found a way of helping out the family.

Holly had been wrong to worry about what they were both up to when they were out or in their rooms. They'd simply being trying to help in whatever way they could. She'd thought they were off elsewhere, Chloe in body and Jake in spirit, when in fact they'd both been focused on their family.

She was the one who'd been elsewhere and

she wanted to be back now, but wasn't quite sure how to get there.

'The kids are amazing, aren't they?' Mark said when they went to bed that night.

The evening had become celebratory. Chloe had produced a wonderful dinner and Mark had opened a bottle of sparkling wine and toasted both children. Then Chloe had wished him luck with Jimmy Finlay's press conference. It felt as if everyone was moving forward, excited about the future for the first time in a long while. Only Holly felt scared about what the next few weeks might bring.

Mark cuddled up to her after he got into bed, and when he put his arm around her and began stroking her back in circular motions, she wondered if they might end up having sex. His caress wasn't exactly foreplay but it was more physical contact than they'd had in months.

She found his face in the dark and kissed him, but Mark sat up suddenly.

'Damn, I forgot!' He broke whatever mood there had been. 'I need to text Daisy the time the cab is coming.'

He got out of bed and reached for his dressing gown, which hung on the back of the bedroom door.

'Sorry,' he said, cheerily. 'I won't be long.'

He wasn't. But long enough for Holly to wonder why her kissing him had reminded him he needed to text Daisy. And long enough for him to want to go straight to sleep when he came back.

'Better get some rest,' he said, climbing into

492

bed. It sounded like a warning to Holly not to get any ideas about coming on to him now.

'Yes.' She felt like someone watching a film of her own life.

The actress in it was waiting for direction. Should she accuse her husband of something she had no real grounds to accuse him of, or keep quiet and let him go off to Edinburgh with a woman she knew no longer wanted to be with her own husband?

The imaginary director asked her to keep quiet for the moment, but to lean over and kiss Mark.

'I love you, Mark,' she said quietly.

'You too,' he said, rearranging his pillows and turning his back on her.

★ ★ ★

Holly took out her book and began reading but she wasn't taking anything in. The train was moving incredibly slowly and seemed to take forever to get to Preston Park, which was only two minutes away.

She decided to text Mark, feeling that if he was going to be away for a few days, she had to maintain contact.

My train is crawling. Hope you are on your way and that today goes really well. Am sure it will be a great success. Love you. Holly x

She sent the message just before the train entered a short tunnel on the outskirts of Brighton. When it came out again her phone showed she had a reply.

Flight delayed too! Waiting for gate to come up. Will speak to you later. Mark xx

Holly felt like a teenager, trying to analyse the true meaning of the few liquid-crystal words. He hadn't said he loved her, but he had put two kisses. Was the omission because he didn't think it needed to be said? Was it implied with the kisses, or were they simply habit?

The train picked up a little speed before slowing again as it entered the tunnel which ran under the Downs. It crept along slowly until the carriage was in the dark void and then stopped.

People began sighing and looking at their watches and phones, as if the very act of staring at their timepieces would make the train go again.

It didn't. An hour and a few gratuitous announcements by the guard later, they were still sitting there, unsure what was causing the delay or when they would get going again. Then the lights went out and they were plunged into darkness, alleviated only by the LED displays from mobile phones and laptop screens.

Holly experienced a huge wave of nausea and found she was having trouble drawing the deep breath she needed to take to quell it. She could hear herself taking short, sharp, rasping breaths. She sounded as if she was having an asthma attack but knew she was having a panic attack.

'Are you OK?' the woman sitting next to her asked.

Holly shook her head, although she knew the woman wouldn't be able to see the movement in the dark.

Holly could feel herself getting hotter and thought she might be about to faint.

'I have to get out,' she said, so quietly she wasn't sure if anyone could hear her, but her travelling companion did.

Holly felt her hand being taken.

'It's OK,' the woman tried to reassure her. 'We'll get going again soon. You just have to try and relax for a few minutes.'

'What's wrong with her?' another male voice asked.

Holly was aware of a male outline but could only think that she had to get out of the carriage. She couldn't just sit here waiting in the dark. It might happen again. She might not be so lucky this time. She couldn't just sit here waiting.

'No, I have to get out,' she said, struggling to her feet.

'You can't get out, love. We're in the middle of the tunnel,' the male voice said. 'Sit down.'

'Yes, sit next to me.' The woman's voice was more soothing, as if she was used to dealing with this sort of thing. She was still holding her hand and pulled Holly gently back into her seat.

'Take a deep breath,' she said as the train spluttered back to life, the lights came on and it moved through the tunnel and out again.

Several people were looking at her curiously now as the train gathered speed.

'Are you OK?' the woman sitting next to her said again. Holly saw that she was young, smart in a suit, and very pretty.

'I think so.' Holly smiled, trying to deflect the

unwanted attention. 'I think I'll just splash my face with water.'

She picked up her bag and began walking out of the carriage. She wondered if the woman would follow her, but found she was on her own, stumbling slightly in the corridor as the train gathered speed before slowing again to stop at Haywards Heath.

The platform there was crowded with the backlog of commuters that had built up while they sat in the tunnel. Holly knew that they would all try to cram into the carriage and it would become unbearably crowded.

She stood by the doors, waiting for them to open, anticipating the crush as people pushed by to make sure they were not left behind.

There was only a couple of seconds' delay between the train stopping and the doors opening but it felt like an eternity. She fought against the flow of passengers, making her way to a bench, where she sat down and wondered what she was going to do next.

*I feel better today than I have done for weeks
. . . years if I am honest. In fact, I almost feel
ready to stop writing things down and put these
pages up in the attic, with the diary I stopped
writing after Mum came out of hospital.*

*The last few months have felt strange but I
think things are starting to get better. At least,
I'm beginning to see how things are and how
they were more clearly.*

*Geoff knocked on the door a few nights ago,
the same day I'd met Holly and told her what
really happened. It was early evening but I
wasn't expecting anyone. I never am. I thought it
would be someone trying to sell something. So I
opened the door reluctantly, and there was
Geoff.*

'Can I come in, A–M?' he asked.

*He looked tired, older too, a lot greyer than he
was the last time I saw him, and thinner. He
didn't look happy. I'd tried not to picture him
because I didn't want to think of him somewhere
else, with someone else, enjoying his life without
me. But when I failed to shut out the images of
what his life might be like now, he was happy,
fatter, wearing new clothes, a new man. He
wasn't the one standing on the doorstop now,
the old Geoff but looking beaten.*

*'Of course,' I said, because even just seeing
him there, without knowing what he was going*

497

to say to me or how we would go from here, made me feel hopeful.

'How are you?' he said, stepping inside and then waiting for me to tell him where to go.

'Fine,' I said, although I knew he knew that wasn't true. We were being very polite with each other. 'Shall we go into the sitting room? How's Julia?'

I asked this, as he sat down, casually, as if it was of no importance to me.

'I haven't seen her since,' Geoff surprised me by saying.

I sat down too.

'But I thought you'd been with her?' I said. 'I thought that's where you went.'

'I've been at my mum's,' he told me. 'Trying to sort my head out.'

'And have you?' I asked him.

'Not completely.' He looked at me and smiled then. 'It's very muddled up, my head. It's not easy to sort.'

'Mine's a complete and utter mess,' I said, and saying it made me start laughing.

Then the laughter turned to tears, and before I knew it I was sitting there bawling and Geoff had come over and put his arms round me. 'I'm sorry. I'm so so sorry. I never meant for any of this to happen,' he said.

'It did happen though, didn't it?' I answered. Then, taking a deep breath, ready to talk, 'Why did you let it happen, Geoff?'

'I don't know,' he replied, sitting up. 'I just felt I needed an escape. I know that sounds pathetic and I'm not blaming you because I know that none of this is your fault. I know that I've behaved really badly but I felt there seemed to be so much that had gone wrong in your life and you wanted me to make it all better. But I couldn't, could I? I couldn't turn the clock back. I couldn't make any of the things that had happened to you and around you go away. I felt you wanted too much from me, so I started backing off.'

'And then there was Julia?' I said this as a question.

'Julia was just there,' he said. 'She was around and she was willing and so I started sleeping with her as an escape. But it wasn't an escape, I realised that when the train got hit.'

'What happened to you then?' I asked because I still didn't know.

'I was fine,' Geoff said. 'I was in the carriage in the tunnel, but I got up and walked out. I can't have been in there more than five or ten minutes but it was like a huge wake-up call. I realised I could have died, but I didn't, and I realised that I had to sort my life out. I had to stop seeing Julia and I had to work out what I wanted with you.'

I didn't know what to say, so I said nothing and Geoff continued.

'And it also made me understand, just a little bit, some of what you must have gone through in your life,' he continued. 'I know you'd told me all this stuff, but it always felt as if you weren't really involved because you were one step removed. Then when I walked off that train, scot-free, I felt as if I had been involved in something major, something awful, but didn't feel I had the right to say that, not really.'

I nodded.

'Can we try again, A-M?' he asked. 'Because I do love you. I just don't think I can be everything that you want me to be.'

'No,' I said, agreeing with a negative that I realised might confuse him. 'I mean, no, you can't be everything to me, I'm beginning to realise that now. I need to talk to someone, someone qualified, and then maybe we can talk too, about us?'

I had the first session with a counsellor yesterday. She's quite old, much older than Helen was, and I told her about the sessions I had with her and why I stopped going. Then we talked about everything: the department store, Mum, Lisa, Geoff, the baby, the crash and Julia. And I told her about Holly and Daniel, and the whole mess of misunderstandings that I seem to have created throughout my life.

By the end of the session I was beginning to feel that I was actually starting to sort things out properly for the first time. I felt better for that.

But Holly, when I saw her this morning, looked a whole lot worse.

She was getting off the train as I got on but she didn't see me. I tried to smile and ask why she was getting off at Haywards Heath but she just pushed past me, as if she couldn't wait to get off the train. She looked drained, like she did when we met the other day and she told me she had stuff to sort out. But she looked worse today, paler and more tired.

I knew the train had been delayed because of a power failure and the way Holly looked, it was as if it had all come back to her, as if she couldn't face being on the train any more. I thought about turning round and going after her, missing my train so I could talk to her but I wasn't sure I would be of any help. Instead, I got on the train and walked up it, looking for Daniel.

He was there, and he looked tired and down as well. I didn't ask why. I told him about Holly and he said he didn't know what to do. So I told him what to do.

'Do you know how to get hold of her husband?' I asked, and he nodded.

54

Holly wasn't sure how long she'd been sitting on the bench but she knew it was long enough for the early crowds of commuters to have thinned. The platform was no longer crowded, people were no longer cramming themselves into trains like sardines, and the early morning chill had given way to warm sunshine.

Holly stared ahead of her, only dimly aware of her surroundings. She could hear her phone ringing from inside her bag and knew she ought to answer it but didn't want to. She needed to focus on what she was going to do now and she didn't seem able to, so she carried on looking into the middle distance, letting the world go on around her, as if she had no place in it.

Then something caught her attention. She didn't look but she sensed someone bounding up the steps to the platform and striding purposefully towards her. The energy of whoever it was roused her from her torpor and she turned her head and saw a tall dark-haired man approaching her. There was something about him which made her realise that everything was going to be all right. The way he was walking towards her with such clear intent made her think that whoever this was would know what she should do. Only when he sat down next to her on the bench did she realise it was Mark.

'Holly.' He put his arms around her and she

found the feel and smell of him made her start sobbing uncontrollably.

Mark tightened his grip on her, saying nothing but holding her so close that Holly felt as if she was absorbing some of his strength and calm. Gradually her sobs subsided and Mark began stroking her hair and talking to her.

'It's OK,' he said. 'Everything will be OK, Holly, I promise.'

'What are you doing here?' She looked up at him, remembering that he had been on his way to Edinburgh. 'How did you know I was here?'

'Daniel saw you get off the train. He called Daisy,' Mark told her, taking her hand and stroking it gently while he talked. 'I was still in transit. I got a cab from the airport.'

'But you need to go to Scotland,' she said. 'It's the start of the run. Jimmy Finlay needs you to be there.'

'Daisy's on her way,' Mark told her. 'She can deal with everything. I need to be with you.'

'But it's your big day. You've been working up to this,' Holly protested, but Mark raised his fingers to her lips to silence her.

'I want to be with you, Holly.' He took his fingers away and kissed her gently, clasping her hand in his as he did so.

Holly felt so relieved at the familiarity of Mark's touch that she began to cry again, but this time the tears were quieter and gentler.

'I'm so sorry,' she said quietly.

'You've got nothing to be sorry for,' he said. 'I'm the one who should be sorry.'

'What for?' Holly asked, and hoped against

503

hope that he wasn't going to tell her anything she didn't want to hear.

'For not realising how you really were,' Mark said, squeezing her hand. 'I thought you were OK, Holly. I thought you didn't need me. You've always been so strong, I thought you were coping with the crash and going back to work full-time. I should have seen this coming.'

'How could you?' She squeezed his hand this time, trying to reassure him. 'How could you have known that anything was wrong when I didn't realise it myself?'

55

'Do you remember when we went to that gig at Wembley and missed the last train home?' Mark asked.

They had been sitting on the bench together talking for almost an hour now.

'I'd forgotten but I remember it now.' Mark had his arm around her and Holly was resting her head against his chest. She didn't want to move. It felt right now, being here with Mark, sitting like this, talking. She wanted to stay like this for as long as possible.

'We ended up going to Gatwick and sitting on a bench there for half the night,' he reminisced. 'Until the mail train to Brighton arrived. I remember thinking then, when we sat on that bench talking, that I wanted to be with you for the rest of my life.'

'What made you decide then?' Holly asked, thinking that she had thought this about him on the very first night they'd met.

'It was cold and rainy and we had a three-hour wait ahead of us,' he continued. 'I remember thinking that if I'd been with anyone else, I'd have been really pissed off. But I'd have happily sat there for ever, as long as I was with you.'

'There was another thing about that evening.' Holly smiled at her husband. 'We didn't go to the gig together. We met there, do you remember?'

'Vaguely.' He raised his eyebrows.

'You'd been to meet a client in London or something, and we'd arranged to meet outside the tube station at Wembley.' Holly could recall the evening clearly now. 'When we made that arrangement, I thought I'd be the only person there and you'd come out of the tube and look around and see me, but when I arrived there were so many people, all milling around, that I thought we'd never find each other.'

'That was before mobile phones, I suppose, wasn't it?' he queried.

'Yes. There was no way I could contact you if we didn't bump into each other.' Holly remembered the waiting and thinking she'd never find him, not in that crowd.

'Then I saw someone pushing their way through a huge mass of people and making their way towards me.'

'Me?' Mark obviously didn't remember this part of the night the way that Holly did.

'Yes, it was you,' she told him. 'And I asked you how you'd managed to see me, through all those people. Do you remember what you said?'

'That I was 'looking for you in the world'.' Mark smiled, clearly remembering the moment too. 'It was a D. H. Lawrence quote and I'm sure I patronised you with my sketchy knowledge of his late poetry!'

'You told me it was from one of his poems, yes.' Holly smiled. 'And I remember thinking then how perfectly that summed up what a long-term relationship is about, having someone who looks for you in the world.'

Mark said nothing but looked directly at Holly now, holding her eyes and excluding the rest of the world.

'I could hear you saying that again when you walked towards me along the platform earlier,' she told him. 'I didn't even know it was you until you sat down. You didn't stop to look around. It was as if you knew exactly where I was.'

'Maybe after so long together, Holly,' he said slowly, 'I don't have to look for you in the world any more. I know where to find you.'

'Except I haven't been in the right place for a while.' She looked down, unable to meet his gaze any longer.

'And maybe I wasn't looking hard enough.' Mark tilted her chin up with his hand so that she was forced to look at him again. 'But I have always been looking for you in the world, Holly. You and Chloe and Jake. No one else.'

'I know,' she said, believing him and thinking now that all her fears about Daisy were unfounded. 'Sometimes other people look out for you because they happen to be there, but they're not really looking for you.'

Holly could see clearly now, as if the past few months were in the distant past, that Daniel was someone who just happened to be there and get caught up in her life at a certain time. But Mark, she realised, was the one who was there and always would be.

'Do you mean Daniel?' he said, gently. He appeared to be asking, not accusing her of anything.

'Yes.' Holly looked down at her lap, feeling

embarrassed now at how she'd let Daniel take precedence in her thoughts. 'I know it sounds ridiculous, Mark, but he somehow made me feel safe. I felt that if he was around, everything would be OK. Does that sound ridiculous?'

'No, not entirely,' Mark said, taking her hand. 'He was there for you then, wasn't he? He could understand something that I couldn't.'

'I'm sure you could have, if I'd let you,' Holly said softly. 'I know I blocked you out. It was my way of dealing with things.'

'It doesn't matter now.' He squeezed her hand. 'I was preoccupied with work and then the running. I was trying to prove something to you, but I should have been more supportive. It was the least I could have done.'

'It's hard to be supportive if the person you are trying to support won't let you.' Holly looked at him and was struck by how handsome he was, how kind and strong his face was, and how much she loved him.

How could she have lost sight of this, she wondered, and how much damage had she done in the process?

'I have to ask you this, Mark,' she said, looking directly at him. 'I don't want you to be angry, but I have to ask you.'

'You want to know if there is anything going on between me and Daisy?' Mark seemed to know her better than she knew herself.

She nodded.

'There isn't,' he answered his own question. 'Although . . .'

'What?' Holly began to feel cold again,

wondering what 'although' preceded.

'I did try to kiss her once.' Mark shrugged and smiled as he said this.

It wasn't a smile of self-satisfaction, more one of mild embarrassment.

'She pushed me away with a firm 'I don't think so', as if the very idea were ridiculous. Which it was.'

'It's not that ridiculous.' Holly laughed, now feeling slightly offended that Daisy had thought kissing Mark was out of the question. 'I would have wanted to kiss you, if I'd been her.'

'Thank you.' He smiled. 'But I can see myself though her eyes. Some overweight, middle-aged man who kept going on about his wife not respecting him any more.'

'That's not true,' Holly cut in.

Mark carried on talking. 'I kissed her because she was young and pretty but, to be honest, I was relieved she didn't respond. It wasn't what I wanted. I was just feeling lonely and Daisy seemed to need looking after. She's not very happy, Holly. I have talked to her about you, while we were running, and she's told me stuff about her and Daniel too.'

'I saw him yesterday,' Holly confessed now. 'He told me she'd had a miscarriage and that she didn't want to be with him any more. Did you know?'

'Yes.' Mark nodded. 'She'd told me about the miscarriage. I should have told you, but I promised her I wouldn't. From what she said, I think she feels too young to settle down and have a baby.'

'Daniel's devastated,' Holly said. She decided not to tell him the rest, not yet anyway.

'I think Daniel and I are probably the same, and Guy too.' Mark considered what he was saying before carrying on. 'We all have some Darwinian desire to be the great male protector, but we're all with strong independent women and don't seem to be very good at dealing with that.'

Holly wondered if she should tell him that Daniel had kissed her, but Mark prevented her from doing so by leaning forward and kissing her himself. She felt herself becoming lost in the moment, forgetting everyone else and everything that had happened, wanting nothing more than to stay here for as long as possible.

It was the arrival of a train travelling south towards Brighton which signalled the end of their kiss.

'We should probably think about going home now,' Mark said gently.

'I'm not sure I want to get on another train.' Holly didn't move. 'I don't think I can face it. Not just now, Mark, not yet.'

'I know,' he said, getting to his feet and putting his hand out to her. 'We'll get a taxi or . . . '

He stopped talking and looked down at her feet. Holly was wearing sandals. Her feet had been cold when she'd set off in the morning but she'd known the temperature would rise by midday and she'd have been hot in London.

'Or?' she asked Mark.

'Can you walk in those shoes?'

'Yes.' Holly was not sure what he had in mind.

'We'll walk home then,' Mark said decisively as he stood up and put his hand out to her.

'Are you sure?' It was a long way home and she had no idea how long it would take them. 'It's quite a distance, and you are supposed to be taking it easy still.'

'I feel fine,' he said. 'Let's go.'

He was his old self again, the decisive man of action who could sweep people along with his good-humoured conviction. Or perhaps, Holly thought to herself, he had never been anything other than his old self. It was she who had changed and stopped seeing him properly

'We don't need to rush. We'll stop for lunch somewhere on the way back,' he said, as they walked towards the station exit. 'It doesn't really matter how long it takes, as long as we're together.'

Holly wasn't sure if he was talking about the walk home or more than that. She put her arm around his waist and felt the familiar fit of him as they walked out of the station.

'OK?' Mark asked, folding his arm around her shoulder.

A tannoy announcement made it difficult for her to answer.

'Please stand clear of the train about to arrive on platform four,' a voice coming from a speaker directly above boomed out. 'This is the southbound train from London Victoria. The front eight carriages will be going to Lewes and Eastbourne. The rear four coaches are for Hove

511

and Littlehampton. Please stand clear of the platform while the train is divided.'

Holly didn't answer Mark, just tightened her arm around his waist as they set off towards Brighton.

Acknowledgements

Thanks to all who were positive and encouraging about my first book. You stopped me getting so anxious and paranoid that I could not finish this one!

To my writers group and other writers for keeping me going and being generous and supportive, when I am sure you were inclined to be otherwise.

Thanks also to all my friends who have continued to talk to me, even though they know that by doing so they risk their best anecdotes being fictionalised. You know who you are. So do my family.

To Ruth and Nigel, for their medical advice, Barney and Al for theirs on marketing, and Caroline and Amanda for the lowdown on restaurants.

Thank you also to Peter Straus and Jenny Hewson at RCW and everyone at Headline, most especially my editor, Imogen Taylor, for nagging me, in the nicest possible way, until I got there.

And to Mick, who came up with the title, and looks for *me* in the world.

Other titles published by
The House of Ulverscroft:

WHAT YOU DON'T KNOW

Lizzie Enfield

With a lovely husband, two gorgeous children, and a job in the real world, some would think that Helen Collins has it all. So when plain, bald Graham Parks walks into her office, ready to be cross-questioned about his book, Helen isn't expecting to fall for him. He's the exact opposite of her good-looking husband Alex, who woos women daily in his role as a TV character. But after fifteen years together, Helen wonders what it would be like to sleep with someone else. What begins as harmless flirtation quickly develops into something far more threatening, pulling Helen to the edge of something that may just turn her world upside down. It's exciting, alluring, all-consuming. But is it worth the risk?

THE BOOK OF SUMMERS

Emylia Hall

Beth Lowe is given a package. It contains a letter informing her that her long-estranged mother has died . . . and something she's never seen before — her mother's scrapbook. The Book of Summers, stuffed with photographs and mementos, records the seven glorious childhood summers Beth spent in rural Hungary. Then, she trod the tightrope between separated parents and two very different countries; her bewitching but imperfect Hungarian mother and her gentle English father; the dazzling house of a Hungarian artist and an empty-feeling cottage in deepest Devon. It was a time which brutally ended the year Beth turned sixteen. Beth never again allowed herself to think about those childhood days. But The Book of Summers will bring the past tumbling back; as vivid, painful and vital as ever.

ALYS, ALWAYS

Harriet Lane

Frances is a thirty-something sub-editor, an invisible production drone on the books pages of the *Questioner*. Her routine and colourless existence is disrupted one winter evening when she happens upon the aftermath of a car crash and hears the last words of the driver, Alys Kyte. When Alys's family makes contact in an attempt to find closure, Frances is given a tantalising glimpse of a very different world: one of privilege and possibility. The relationships she builds with the Kytes will have an impact on her own life, both professionally and personally, as Frances dares to wonder whether she might now become a player in her own right . . .

THE MAN WHO FORGOT HIS WIFE

John O'Farrell

Lots of husbands forget things: they forget that their wife had an important meeting that morning; they forget to pick up the dry cleaning; some of them even forget their wedding anniversary. But Vaughan has forgotten he even has a wife. Her name, her face, their history together, everything she has ever told him, everything he has said to her — it has all gone, mysteriously wiped in one catastrophic moment of memory loss. And now he has rediscovered her — only to find out that they are getting divorced. Now Vaughan will try anything to turn the back the clock and have one last chance to reclaim his life.

THE EXPATS

Chris Pavone

When her husband accepts a job in Luxembourg, Kate Moore thinks she is leaving behind her covert life, working for the CIA, for good. She throws herself into her new life as an expatriate in the genteel European city, home-making and meeting new friends. But when Kate and her husband, Dexter, are befriended by another American couple, Julia and Bill, Kate can't help but sense that they may not be who they say they are. Charming and sociable, they are also vague about their past in ways that make Kate suspicious . . .

THE LIGHT BETWEEN OCEANS

M. L. Stedman

Tom Sherbourne, released from the horrors of the First World War, is now a lighthouse keeper, cocooned on a remote island off Western Australia with his young, bold and loving wife. Izzy is content in everything but her failure to have a child. Years later, after two miscarriages and a stillbirth, a boat washes ashore carrying a dead man — and a crying baby . . . now the path of the couple's lives hits an unthinkable crossroads. Safe from the real world, Tom and Izzy break the rules and follow their hearts. It is a decision with devastating consequences . . .

THE WORLD'S GREATEST
AIRCRAFT

Christopher Chant

CRESCENT

Photographic Acknowledgements

Brian Trodd Publishing House Limited: 6,
8, 9, 12, 15, 19, 20, 23, 25, 28, 30, 33, 34,
36, 40, 44, 47, 48, 52, 53, 54, 55, 56, 57,
58, 59, 61, 63, 64, 67, 68, 69, 72, 73, 75,
76, 78, 86, 89, 90, 93, 94, 96 97, 98, 99,
100, 102, 103, 104, 105, 107, 109, 112,
114, 115, 117, 121, 122, 123, 126, 128,
129, 131, 133, 135, 137, 139, 140, 142,
143, 145, 151, 152, 153, 159, 161, 162,
163, 164, 166, 169, 173, 174, 178, 179,
180, 182, 187, 188, 189, 190, 194, 195,
196, 197, 198, 198, 200, 201, 202, 204,
206, 212, 213, 214, 215, 216, 218, 219,
225, 226, 234, 244, 245, 247, 248, 249;
Aermacchi: 157; Air Transport World:
211; Airbus Industries: 227, 230, 232;
Beech Aircraft Corporation: 236, 239,
242; Boeing: 144, 228; British Airways:
222; British Aerospace: 110, 111, 156,
233; Nikk Burridge: 27, 39, 41, 42, 81,
82, 130, 147, 148, 149, 150, 208, 217,
221, 229, 232, 235, 238, 240, 241, 243,
246, 251, 252, 253; Hugh W. Cowin: 18,
45, 62; Czechoslovak Embassy (London):
154; Dassault: 66, 155; De Havilland
Canada: 209; Department of Defense
(U.S.): 60, 65, 71, 74, 83, 85, 106, 108,
113, 116, 124, 136, 138, 170, 171, 175,
176, 177; Dornier: 46, 101; Embraer: 205,
210; General Dynamics: 80; McDonnell
Douglas Corporation: 79, 172, 220;
National Air and Space Museum: 4, 5, 7,
10, 11, 13, 14, 16, 17, 22, 24, 26, 29, 38,
51, 87, 88, 91, 95, 118, 119, 125, 132,
160, 165, 167, 168, 183, 185, 186, 190,
191, 192, 193, 237, 250; National
Archives (U.S.): 35, 127, 146; Northrop:
141; Northwest: 223; Plane's of Fame: 37;
Rockwell: 120; Saab: 77; Shorts: 207;
Sirpa-Air: 84; VFW-Fokker: 184, 224,
203; Brian Walters: 158.
TRH Pictures: 21, 49, 70, 92, 134, 181;
Grumman/TRH Pictures: 43; Richard
Winslade/TRH Pictures: 50.

This 1991 edition published by Crescent
Books.
Distributed by Outlet Book Company,
Inc.
a Random House Company
225 Park Avenue South
New York, New York 10003

Copyright © 1991 Brian Trodd Publishing
House Limited

ISBN 0-517-03766-1

8 7 6 5 4 3 2 1

Printed in Italy

Editor: Loulou Brown

Aircraft specifications: Hugh Cowin

Colour illustrations: Maltings Partnership.
John Batchelor

Line drawings: Annabel Trodd, David
Dedman, Elaine Knight, Andrew Wright.

CONTENTS

MILITARY AIRCRAFT

RESEARCH AIRCRAFT

CIVIL AIRCRAFT

BRISTOL F.2 FIGHTER Series (United Kingdom)

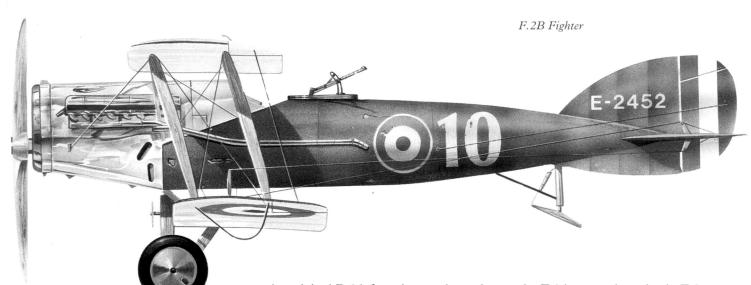

F.2B Fighter

The F.2 Fighter was the best two-seat combat aircraft of World War I, even though it was designed in 1916 as a reconnaissance type. The design was an equal-span biplane of fabric-covered wooden construction, and in its original R.2A form it was planned round an 89-kW (120-hp) Beardmore engine. The availability of the 112-kW (150-hp) Hispano-Suiza engine resulted in the concept's revision as the slightly smaller R.2B sesquiplane, and further revision was then made so that the R.2B could also be fitted with the 142-kW (190-hp) Rolls-Royce Falcon engine. In August 1916, two prototypes and 50 production aircraft were ordered. Before the first prototypes flew in September 1916 the type had been reclassified as the F.2A fighter. All 50 aircraft were delivered together with the Falcon engine, and the F.2A entered service in February 1917.

The type's combat debut was disastrous, four out of six aircraft being lost to an equal number of Albatros D III fighters. But as soon as pilots learned to fly their F.2As as if they were single-seaters, with additional firepower provided by the gunner, the type became highly successful. The rest of the Fighter's 5,308-aircraft production run was of the F.2B variant with successively more powerful engines and modifications to improve fields of vision and combat-worthiness. Other designations were F.2C for a number of experimental re-enginings, F.2B Mk II for 435 new and reconditioned and tropicalized machines for army co-operation duties in the Middle East and India, Fighter Mk III for 80 strengthened aircraft delivered in 1926 and 1927, and Fighter Mk IV for Mk III conversions with strengthened structure and landing gear as well as a balanced rudder and automatic leading-edges slots. The RAF retired its last Fighters in 1932.

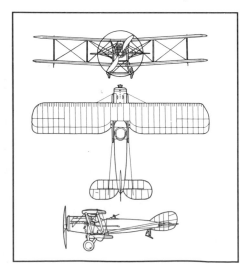

Bristol F.2B Fighter

BRISTOL F.2B
Role: Fighter
Crew/Accommodation: Two
Power Plant: One 275-hp Rolls-Royce Falcon III water-cooled inline
Dimensions: Span 11.96 m (39.25 ft); length 7.87 m (25.83 ft); wing area 37.6 m² (405 sq ft)
Weights: Empty 875 kg (1,930 lb); MTOW 1,270 kg (2,800 lb)
Performance: Maximum speed 201 km/h (125 mph) at sea level; operational ceiling 6,096 m (20,000 ft); endurance 3 hours
Load: Two or three .303 inch machine guns plus up to 54.4 kg (120 lb) of bombs

Bristol Fighter Mk III.

NIEUPORT 11 BEBE and 17 (France)

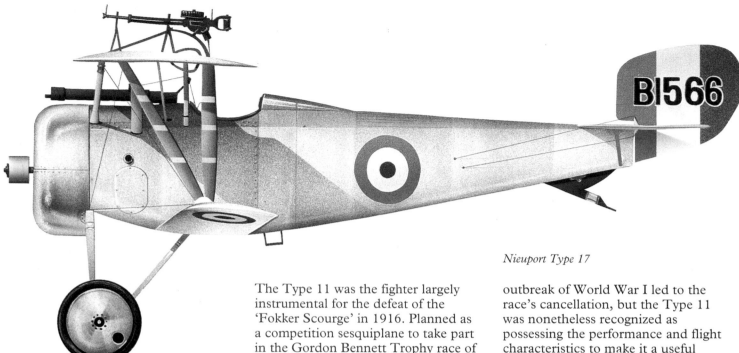

Nieuport Type 17

The Type 11 was the fighter largely instrumental for the defeat of the 'Fokker Scourge' in 1916. Planned as a competition sesquiplane to take part in the Gordon Bennett Trophy race of 1914, the first Type 11 was designed and built in a mere four months. The outbreak of World War I led to the race's cancellation, but the Type 11 was nonetheless recognized as possessing the performance and flight characteristics to make it a useful military aircraft. Early Type 11 aircraft were powered by the 60-kW (80-hp) Le Rhône rotary engine, and were used by the French and British as scouts from 1915. The aircraft's apparent daintiness led to the nickname Bébé (Baby). The Type 11 was then turned into a fighter by the addition of a machine-gun on the upper-wing centre section to fire over the propeller's swept disc.

Many more aircraft were built under licence in Italy by Macchi with the designation Nieuport 1100. The Type 16 was a version with the 82-kW (110-hp) Le Rhône rotary for better performance. The Type 17 was a further expansion of the same design concept with a strengthened airframe but the same 82-kW (110-hp) Le Rhône. The new model retained its predecessors' excellent agility but offered superior performance, including a sparkling rate of climb. The fighter's 7.7-mm (0.303-in) Lewis gun was located on a sliding mount that allowed the pilot to pull the weapon's rear down, allowing oblique upward fire and also making for easier reloading.

The slightly later Type 17bis introduced the 97-kW (130-hp) Clerget rotary and a synchronized machine-gun on the upper fuselage. Still later models were the Type 21 with the 60-kW (80 hp), later the 82-kW (110 hp), Le Rhône and larger ailerons, and the slightly heavier Type 23 with 60- or 89-kW (120 hp) Le Rhône engines.

Nieuport 11.

NIEUPORT TYPE 11
Role: Fighter
Crew/Accommodation: One
Power Plant: One 80 hp Gnome or Le Rhône 9C air-cooled rotary
Dimensions: Span 7.55 m (24.77 ft); length 5.8 m (19.03 ft); wing area 13 m² (140 sq ft)
Weights: Empty 344 kg (759 lb); MTOW 550 kg (1,213 lb)
Performance: Maximum speed 156 km/h (97 mph) at sea level; operational ceiling 4,600 m (15,090 ft); range 330 km (205 miles) with full bombload
Load: One .303 inch machine gun

Nieuport Type 11 Bébé

5

ROYAL AIRCRAFT FACTORY S.E.5 (United Kingdom)

S.E.5a

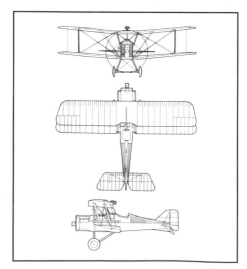

Royal Aircraft Factory S.E.5

The best aircraft to be designed by the Royal Aircraft Factory, and also the mount of several celebrated British aces of World War I, the S.E.5 was designed by H.P. Folland. Given the minimal levels of training received by pilots before their posting to the front, Folland decided to make his new aircraft easy to fly; thus a static inline engine was preferred to a rotary engine with all its torque problems, and a fair measure of inherent stability was built into the design. At the same time, Folland opted for an extremely strong airframe that was also easy to manufacture. Construction was entirely orthodox for the period, with fabric covering over a wooden primary structure. The result was a fighter that was an exceptionally good gun platform but, without sacrifice of structural strength, possessed good performance and adequate agility. The armament was an unusual variant on the standard pair of 7.7-mm (0.303-in) machine guns; one was synchronized a Vickers gun located in the forward fuselage and firing through the disc swept by the propeller, while the other was a Lewis located on a rail over the centre section and firing over the propeller. The Lewis gun could be pulled back and down along a quadrant rear extension of its rear so that the pilot could change ammunition drums. The S.E.5 was powered by a 112-kW (150-hp) Hispano-Suiza 8 inline and began to enter service in April 1917.

From the summer of the same year it was complemented and then supplanted by the S.E.5a version with a 149-kW (200-hp) engine. There were at first a number of teething problems with the engine and the Constantinesco synchronizer gear, but once these had been overcome the S.E.5a matured as a quite superlative fighter that could also double in the ground-attack role with light bombs carried under the wings. Total production was 5,205 aircraft.

ROYAL AIRCRAFT FACTORY S.E.5a
Role: Fighter
Crew/Accommodation: One
Power Plant: One 200 hp Wolseley W.4A Viper water-cooled inline
Dimensions: Span 8.12 m (26.63 ft); length 6.38 m (20.92 ft); wing area 22.84 m² (245.8 sq ft)
Weights: Empty 635 kg (1,399 lb); MTOW 880 kg (1,940 lb)
Performance: Maximum speed 222 km/h (138 mph) at sea level; operational ceiling 5,182 m (17,000 ft); endurance 2.5 hours
Load: Two .303 inch machine guns, plus up to 45 kg (100 lb) of bombs

The Royal Aircraft Factory S.E.5a was an outstanding fighter

SOPWITH CAMEL (United Kingdom)

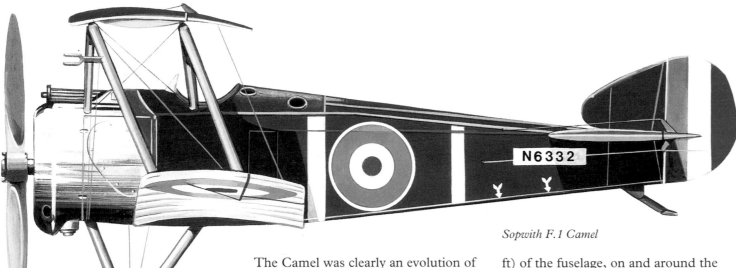

Sopwith F.1 Camel

The Camel was clearly an evolution of the Pup's design concept and was in fact designed to supplant this type, but had all its major masses (engine, fuel/lubricant, guns/ammunition and pilot) located in the forward 2.1 m (7 ft) of the fuselage, on and around the centre of gravity to offer the least inertial resistance to agility. The type was therefore supremely manoeuvrable; the torque of the powerful rotary meant that a three-quarter turn to the right could be achieved as swiftly as a quarter turn to the left, but this also meant that the type could easily stall and enter a tight spin if it was not flown with adequate care.

In configuration Camel was a typical single-bay braced biplane with fixed tailwheel landing gear, and was built of wood with fabric covering except over the forward fuselage, which had light alloy skinning. The type was more formally known to its naval sponsors as the Sopwith Biplane F.1, the nickname deriving from the humped fuselage over the breeches of the two synchronized 7.7-mm (0.303-in) Vickers machine guns that comprised the armament. Production of 5,490 aircraft made this the most important British fighter of late 1917 and 1918. The type was powered in its production forms by a number of Bentley, Clerget, Gnome and Le Rhône rotary engines in the power class between 75 and 112 kW (100 and 150 hp), though some experimental variants had engines of up to 134-kW (180-hp) rating. Some F.1s were operated from ships, but a specialized derivative for this role was the 2F.1 with folding wings. Other variants were the F.1/1 with tapered wing panels, and the TF.1 trench fighter (ground-attack) model with a pair of 7.7-mm Lewis guns arranged to fire obliquely downward and forward through the cockpit floor, but neither of these entered production.

The Sopwith F.1 Camel.

SOPWITH F.1 CAMEL
Role: Fighter
Crew/Accommodation: One
Power Plant: One 130 hp Clerget 9B air-cooled rotary
Dimensions: Span 8.53 m (28 ft); length 5.71 m (18.75 ft); wing area 21.5 m² (231 sq ft)
Weights: Empty 436 kg (962 lb); MTOW 672 kg (1,482 lb)
Performance: Maximum speed 168 km/h (104.5 mph) at 3,048 (10,000 ft); operational ceiling 5,486 m (18,000 ft); endurance 2.5 hours
Load: Two .303 inch machine guns

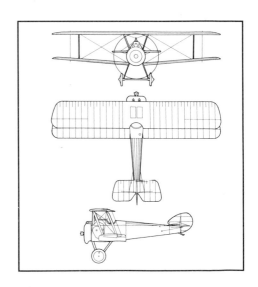

Sopwith F.1 Camel

7

ALBATROS D III and D V (Germany)

D Va

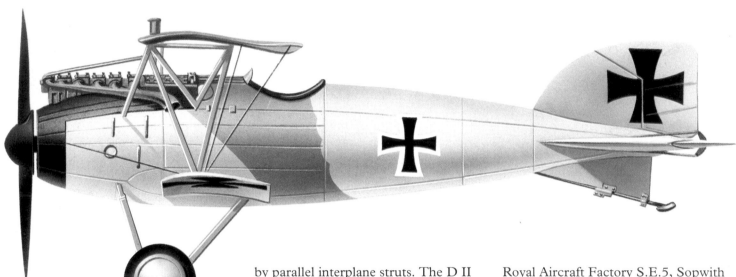

The first Albatros fighter was the excellent D I with virtually identical but staggered upper and lower wings connected toward their outboard ends by parallel interplane struts. The D II was basically similar, apart from the lowering of the upper wing to provide the pilot with improved forward and upward fields of vision. In an effort to improve manoeuvrability, designer Robert Thelen then moved to the D III with a revised and unstaggered wing cellule in which an increased-span upper wing was connected to the smaller and narrower-chord lower wing by V-section interplane struts.

The D III entered service in spring 1917 and proved most successful until the Allies introduced types such as the Royal Aircraft Factory S.E.5, Sopwith Camel and Spad S.13 in the late summer of the same year. During the course of the fighter's production, engine power was raised from 127- to 130-kW (170- to 175-hp) by increasing the compression ratio, and the radiator was shifted from the upper-wing centre section into the starboard upper wing so that the pilot would not be scalded if the radiator was punctured.

Albatros introduced the D V in May 1917 with features such as a still further lowered upper wing, a modified rudder, a revised aileron control system, and a larger spinner providing nose entry for a deeper elliptical rather than flat-sided plywood fuselage to reduce drag and so boost performance. Greater emphasis was then placed on this model and its D Va derivative with the upper wing and aileron control system of the D III. In fact the D V and D Va were outclassed by Allied fighters, and their lower wings were structurally deficient in the dive.

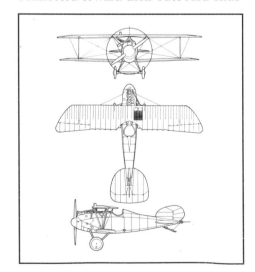

Albatros D Va

ALBATROS D III
Role: Fighter
Crew/Accommodation: One
Power Plant: One 175 hp Mercedes D.IIIa water-cooled inline
Dimensions: Span 9.05 m (29.76 ft); length 7.33 m (24 ft); wing area 20.5 m² (220.7 sq ft)
Weights: Empty 680 kg (1,499 lb); MTOW 886 kg (1,953 lb)
Performance: Maximum speed 175 km/h (109 mph) at 1,000 m (3,280 ft); operational ceiling 5,500 m (18,045 ft); endurance 2 hours
Load: Two 7.92 mm machine guns

Albatros D Va.

FOKKER Dr I (Germany)

Dr I

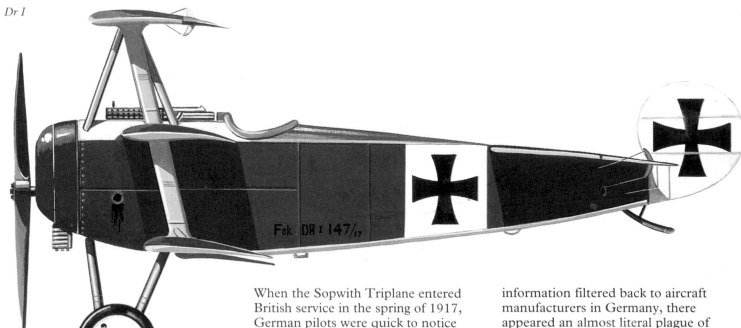

When the Sopwith Triplane entered British service in the spring of 1917, German pilots were quick to notice and appreciate this novel type's high climb rate and excellent manoeuvrability. When this information filtered back to aircraft manufacturers in Germany, there appeared an almost literal plague of triplane fighter prototypes. One of these manufacturers was Fokker, whose V 3 prototype was designed by Reinhold Platz, who had become Fokker's chief designer after the death of Martin Kreutzer in a flying accident during June 1916.

Platz decided on a rotary-engined fighter of light weight for maximum agility rather than high performance, and to the typical Fokker fuselage and tail unit (welded steel tube structures covered in fabric) added triplane wings. These were of thick section and wooden construction, with plywood covering as far aft as the spar, and were cantilever units that did not require bracing wires or interplane struts. In flight the wings vibrated, however, and Platz added plank-type interplane struts on the V 4 second prototype that also incorporated a number of aerodynamic refinements. The type was put into production during the summer of 1917 as the F I, though this designation was soon altered to Dr I. The new triplane soon built up a phenomenal reputation, though this was the result not of the type's real capabilities, which were modest in the extreme, but of the fact that it was flown by a number of aces who had the skills to exploit the Dr I's superb agility in the defensive air combat waged by Germany over the Western Front. The type was grounded late in 1917 because of structural failures in the wing cellule, but with this defect remedied, the type was swiftly restored to service. Production ended in May 1918 after the delivery of about 300 aircraft.

Fokker Dr I

FOKKER Dr I
Role: Fighter
Crew/Accommodation: One
Power Plant: One 110 hp Oberursel U.R. II air-cooled rotary
Dimensions: Span 7.17 m (23.52 ft); length 5.77 m (18.93 ft); wing area 16 m² (172.2 sq ft)
Weights: Empty 405 kg (893 lb); MTOW 585 kg (1,289 lb)
Performance: Maximum speed 185 km/h (115 mph) at sea level; operational ceiling 5,975 m (19,603 ft); range 210 km (130 miles)
Load: Two 7.92 mm machine guns

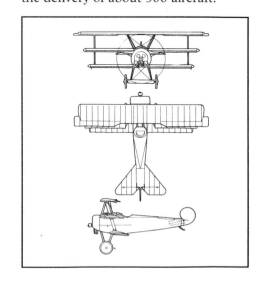

Fokker Dr I

SPAD S.7 AND S.13 (France)

SPAD S.13

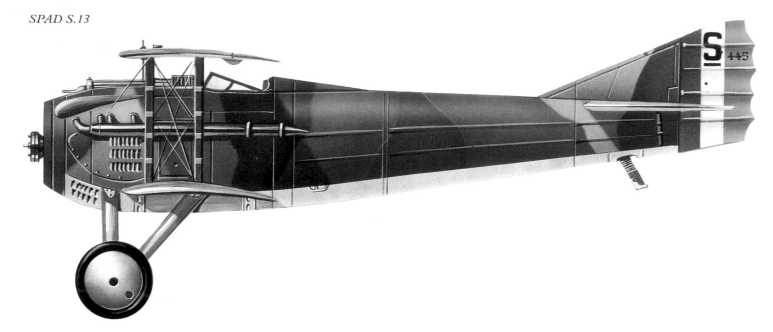

These two closely related aircraft were France's best fighters of World War I, combining high performance and structural strength without too great a sacrifice of agility. The result was an excellent gun platform comparable with the S.E.5a in British service. After experience with the A1 to A5 aircraft, designer Louis Béchereau turned to the conventional tractor biplane layout for the S.5 that first flew in the closing stages of 1915 and became in effect the prototype for the S.7, which was the first genuinely successful warplane developed by the Société Pour l'Avions et ses Dérives which is what the original but bankrupt Société Pour les Appareils Deperdussin became after its purchase by Louis Blériot.

The first S.7 flew early in 1916 with a 112-kW (150-hp) Hispano-Suiza 8Aa inline and a single synchronized 7.7-mm (0.303-in) Vickers machine-gun, and was a sturdy two-bay biplane with unstaggered wings, fixed tailskid landing gear, and a wooden structure covered with fabric except over the forward fuselage, which was skinned in light alloy. Delivery of the essentially similar first production series of about 500 aircraft began in September 1916, being followed by some 6,000 examples of an improved model with the 134-kW (180-hp) HS 8Ac engine and wings of slightly increased span. In 1917 the company flew two development aircraft, and the S.12 with the 149-kW (200-hp) HS 8Bc paved the way for a production series of some 300 aircraft including some with the 164-kW (220-hp) HS 8Bec engine between the cylinder banks of which nestled a 37-mm *moteur canon.* Further development produced the S.13 that first flew in April 1917 for service from May of the same year. This has two guns rather than one, more power, slightly greater span and a number of aerodynamic refinements. Production of this superb fighter totalled 8,472 aircraft.

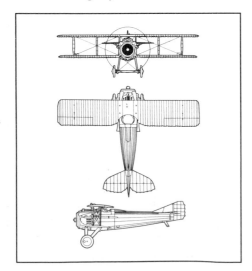

SPAD S.7

SPAD S.13
Role: Fighter
Crew/Accommodation: One
Power Plant: One 220 hp Hispano-Suiza 8BEC water-cooled inline
Dimensions: Span 8 m (26.3 ft); length 6.2 m (20.33 ft); wing area 21.1 m² (227.1 sq ft)
Weights: Empty 565 kg (1,245 lb); MTOW 820 kg (1,807 lb)
Performance: Maximum speed 222 km/h (138 mph) at sea level; operational ceiling 5,400 m (17,717 ft); range 402 km (250 miles)
Load: Two .303 inch machine guns

SPAD S.13

FOKKER D VII (Germany)

Fokker D VII

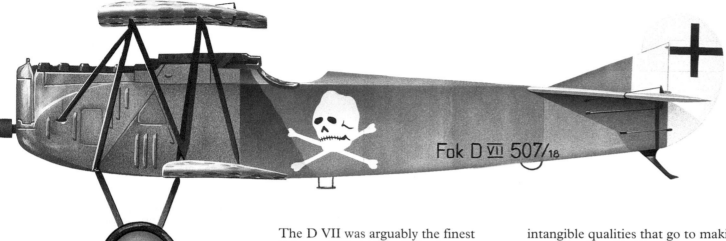

The D VII was arguably the finest fighter of World War I, for it was a package that featured great structrual strength, considerable agility, good firepower and a combination of those intangible qualities that go to making a 'pilot's aircraft'. The type was developed for Germany's first single-seat fighter competition, and the VII prototype made its initial flight just before this during January 1918. This machine had many similarities to the Dr I triplane in its fuselage, tail unit and landing gear. Reinhold Platz, designer of the D VII, intended his new fighter to offer considerably higher performance than that of the Dr I, and for this reason a more powerful inline engine, the 119-kW (160-hp) Mercedes D.III, was installed. This dictated the use of larger biplane wings. Despite the N-type interplane struts, these were cantilever units of Platz's favourite thick aerofoil section and wooden construction with plywood-covered leading edges.

As a result of its success in the competition, the type was ordered into immediate production as the D VII. Within three months, the type was in operational service, and some 700 had been delivered by the time of the Armistice. The type proved a great success in the type of defensive air fighting forced on the Germans at this stage of World War I.

It was particularly impressive in the high-altitude role as it possessed a good ceiling and also the ability to 'hang on its propeller' and fire upward at higher aircraft. Later examples were powered by the 138-kW (185-hp) BMW III inline for still better performance at altitude, and a number of experimental variants were built. Fokker returned to his native Netherlands at the end of the war, in the process smuggling back components for a number of D VIIs as a prelude to resumed construction.

The Fokker D VII was perhaps the best fighter of World War I

FOKKER D VII
Role: Fighter
Crew/Accommodation: One
Power Plant: One 160 hp Mercedes D.III water-cooled inline
Dimensions: Span 8.9 m (29.2 ft); length 6.95 m (22.8 ft); wing area 20.25 m² (218 sq ft)
Weights: Empty 700 kg (1,543 lb); MTOW 878 kg (1,936 lb)
Performance: Maximum speed 188 km/h (117 mph) at 1,000 m (3,281 ft); operational ceiling 6,100 m (20,013 ft); range 215 km (134 miles)
Load: Two 7.9 mm machine guns

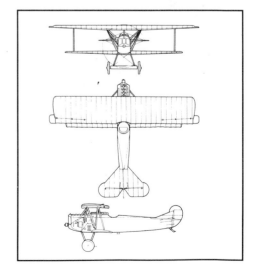

Fokker D VII

11

ARMSTRONG WHITWORTH SISKIN (United Kingdom)

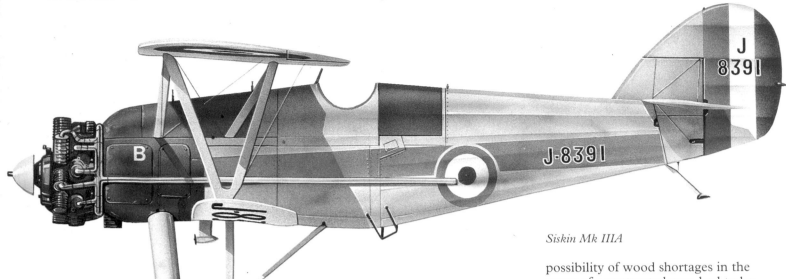

Siskin Mk IIIA

The Siskin was the mainstay of the Royal Air Force's fighter arm in the mid-1920s, and originated from the Siddeley Deasy S.R.2 of 1919. This was designed to use the 224-kW (300-hp) Royal Aircraft Factory 8 radial engine, a promising type whose final development was later passed to Siddeley Deasy but then put to one side so that the company could concentrate its efforts on the Puma.

The type first flew with the 239-kW (320-hp) A.B.C. Dragonfly radial and then as the Armstrong Siddeley Siskin with the definitive 242-kW (325-hp) Armstrong Siddeley Jaguar radial in 1921. The Siskin offered promising capabilities but, because the Air Ministry now demanded a primary structure of metal to avoid the possibility of wood shortages in the event of a protracted war, had to be recast as the Siskin Mk III of 1923 with a fabric-covered structure of aluminium alloy.

The 64 examples of the Siskin Mk III began to enter service in May 1924 with the 242-kW (325-hp) Jaguar III. These were later supplemented by 348 examples of the Siskin Mk IIIA, together with the supercharged Jaguar IV and 53 examples of the Siskin Mk IIIDC dual-control trainer variant. The Siskin Mk IIIB, Mk IV and Mk V were experimental and racing machines. In October 1924, Romania placed an order for the Siskin, however unfortunately the balance of the 65-aircraft contract was cancelled after the fatal crash of one of the first seven aircraft to be delivered. In British service, the Siskin was replaced by the Bristol Bulldog from October 1932, but in Canadian service the type was not replaced by the Hawker Hurricane until as late as 1939.

ARMSTRONG WHITWORTH SISKIN Mk IIIA
Role: Fighter
Crew/Accommodation: One
Power Plant: One 400 hp Armstrong Siddeley Jaguar IVS
Dimensions: Span 10.11 m (33.16 ft); length 7.72 m (25.33 ft); wing area 27.22 m² (293 sq ft)
Weights: Empty 997 kg (2,198 lb); MTOW, 1,260 kg (2,777 lb)
Performance: Maximum speed 227 km/h (141 mph) at sea level; operational ceiling 6,401 m (21,600 ft); endurance 2.75 hours
Load: Two .303 inch machine guns

Armstrong Whitworth Siskin Mk IIIA

Armstrong Whitworth Siskin is here represented by a Siskin Mk IIIAMk IIIA.

CURTISS P-1 and F6C HAWK Series (United States)

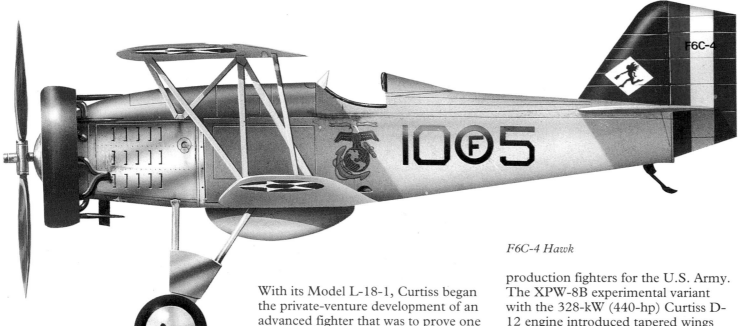

F6C-4 Hawk

With its Model L-18-1, Curtiss began the private-venture development of an advanced fighter that was to prove one of the decisive designs of the 1920s. The type first flew late in 1922, but was followed by only 25 PW-8 production fighters for the U.S. Army. The XPW-8B experimental variant with the 328-kW (440-hp) Curtiss D-12 engine introduced tapered wings and other alterations, resulting in an order for 10 examples of the P-1 production variant. This was then produced in a bewildering number of developed variants, of which the most significant were the 25 P-1As with detail improvements, the 25 P-1Bs with the 324-kW (435-hp) Curtiss V-1150-3 engine and larger-diameter wheels, and the 33 P-ICs with the V-1150-5 wheel brakes and provision for alternative ski landing gear. The type was also developed as the AT-4 advanced trainer. The type was based on the P-1A but engined with the 134-kW (180-hp) Wright-Hispano E, and of the 40 aircraft ordered, 35 became P-1Ds when re-engined with the V-1150, and the other five became AT-5s with the 164-kW (220-hp) Wright Whirlwind J-5 radial; they were later converted to P-1Es with the V-1150 engine. Some 31 AT-5As with a longer fuselage were ordered, but soon became P-1F fighters with the V-1150 engine.

The army's P-1 series was also attractive to the U.S. Navy, which ordered the type with the designation F6C. The F6C-1 was intended for land-based use by the U.S. Marine Corps and was all but identical with the P-1, but only five were delivered as such, while the four others were delivered as F6C-2s with carrier landing equipment including an arrester hook. The F6C-3 was a modified F6C-2, and these 35 aircraft were followed by 31 of the F6C-4 that introduced the 313-kW (420-hp) Pratt & Whitney R-1340 Wasp radial in place of the original D-12 inline.

Curtis Hawk F6C-3.

CURTISS F6C-3
Role: Naval carrierborne fighter
Crew/Accommodation: One
Power Plant: One 400 hp Curtiss D.12 Conqueror water-cooled inline
Dimensions: Span 9.63 m (31.6 ft); length 6.96 m (22.83 ft); wing area 23.41 m² (252 sq ft)
Weights: Empty 980 kg (2,161 lb); MTOW 1,519 kg (3,349 lb)
Performance: Maximum speed 248 km/h (154 mph) at sea level; operational ceiling 6,187 m (20,300 ft); range 565 km (351 miles)
Load: Two .303 inch machine guns

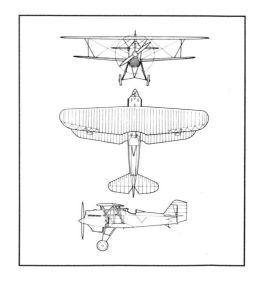

Curtiss F6C Hawk

13

BOEING PW-9 and FB (United States)

Boeing PW-9D

by 25 PW-9As with the D-12C and duplicated flying and landing wires, 40 PW-9Cs with the D-12D and revised fittings for the flying and landing wires, and 16 PW-9Ds with a balanced rudder that was retrofitted to earlier aircraft. A total of 14 FB-1s was ordered for the U.S. Marines, this model being virtually identical to the PW-9. Only 10 were delivered as such, the last four being used for experimental purposes with different engines (the Packard 1A-1500 inline in the first three and the Wright P-1 then Pratt & Whitney Wasp radial in the last) and designations in the sequence from FB-2 to FB-6 except FB-5. This was reserved for 27 aircraft with the Packard 2A-1500 engine, revised landing gear and in addition to this increased wing stagger.

After learning the craft from the manufacture of other company's designs, most notably the Thomas-Morse MB-3A, Boeing entered the fighter market with the Model 15 that first flew in June 1923 as an unequal-span biplane with a massive 324-kW (435-hp) Curtiss D-12 inline engine. The fixed landing gear was of the through-axle type, and while the flying surfaces were of wooden construction the fuselage was of welded steel tube; most of the airframe was covered in fabric. Performance was impressive, and after the type had been evaluated by the U.S. Army as the XPW-9, two more XPW-9s were ordered.

The second of these aircraft had divided landing gear, and it was this type that was ordered into production for the U.S. Army as the PW-9 series and the U.S. Marine Corps as the FB series. The 30 PW-9s were followed

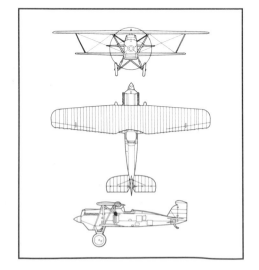

Boeing PW-9D

BOEING PW-9
Role: Fighter
Crew/Accommodation: One
Power Plant: One 435 hp Curtiss D-12 water-cooled inline
Dimensions: Span 9.75 m (32 ft); length 7.14 m (23.42 ft); wing area 24.15 m² (260 sq ft)
Weights: Empty 878 kg (1,936 lb); MTOW 1,415 kg (3,120 lb)
Performance: Maximum speed 256 km/h (159.1 mph) at sea level; operational ceiling 5,768 m (18,925 ft); range 628 km (390 miles)
Load: One .5 inch and one .303 inch machine guns

Boeing PW-9D.

BRISTOL BULLDOG (United Kingdom)

Bulldog Mk IVA

By the mid-1920s, the performance of light day bombers such as the Fairey Fox was outstripping the defensive capabilities of fighters such as the Armstrong Whitworth Siskin, and in an effort to provide the British fighter arm with a considerably improved fighter, the Air Ministry in 1926 issued a fairly taxing specification for a high-performance day/night fighter armed with two fixed machine guns and powered by an air-cooled radial engine. Several companies tendered designs, and the Type 105 proposal from Bristol narrowly beat the Hawfinch from Hawker. The Type 105 was a conventional biplane of its period, with a fabric-covered metal structure, unequal-span wings and fixed landing gear of the spreader-bar type. The Bulldog Mk I prototype first flew in May 1927, and was later fitted with larger wings for attempts on the world altitude and time-to-height records. A second prototype introduced the lengthened fuselage of the Bulldog Mk II production model, which was powered by the 328-kW (440-hp) Bristol Jupiter VII radial, and had a number of modern features such as an oxygen system and short-wave radio.

The Bulldog Mk II entered service in June 1929, and the Bulldog became the U.K.'s most important fighter of the late 1920s and early 1930s. Total production was 312, including 92 basic Bulldog Mk IIs, 268 Bulldog Mk IIAs of the major production type with a strengthened structure and the 365-kW (490-hp) Jupiter VIIF engine, four Bulldog MK IIIs for Denmark with the Jupiter VIFH, two interim Bulldog MK IIIAs with the 418-kW (560-hp) Bristol Mercury IVS.2, 18 Bulldog Mk IVAs for Finland with strengthened ailerons and the 477-kW (640-hp) Mercury VIS.2, and 59 Bulldog TM trainers with a second cockpit in a rear fuselage section that could be replaced by that of the standard fighters in times of crisis.

Bristol Bulldog Mk IIA.

BRISTOL BULLDOG Mk IVA
Role: Fighter
Crew/Accommodation: One
Power Plant: One 640 hp Bristol Mercury VIS2 air-cooled radial
Dimensions: Span 10.26 m (33.66 ft); length 7.72 m (25.33 ft); wing area 27.31 m² (294 sq ft)
Weights: Empty 1,220 kg (2,690 lb); MTOW 1,820 kg (4,010 lb)
Performance: Maximum speed 360 km/h (224 mph) at sea level; operational ceiling 10,180 m (33,400 ft); endurance 2.25 hours
Load: Two .303 inch machine guns, plus up to 36 kg (80 lb) of bombs

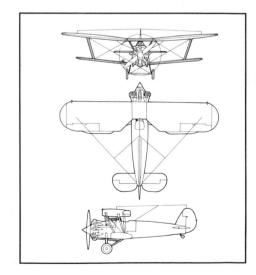

Bristol Bulldog Mk IIA

15

BOEING F4B and P-12 (United States)

F4B-4

The U.S. Army ordered the type as the P-12, the first 10 aircraft being generally similar to the Model 89; later aircraft were 90 P-12Bs with revised ailerons and elevators, 95 P-12Cs similar to the F4B-2, 36 improved P-12Ds, 110 P-12Es with a semi-monocoque fuselage, and 25 P-12Fs with the Pratt & Whitney SR-1340 engine for improved altitude performance. There were also several experimental and even civil models, and also a number of export variants in a total production run of 586 aircraft. The aircraft began to enter American service in 1929, and were the mainstay of the U.S. Army's and U.S. Navy's fighter arms into the mid-1930s, and at that time they were replaced by more modern aircraft. Many aircraft were then used as trainers, mainly by the U.S. Navy, right up to the eve of the entry of the U.S.A. into World War II.

In an effort to produce replacements for the PW-9 and F2B/F3B series, Boeing developed its Models 83 and 89; the former had through-axle landing gear and an arrester hook, while the latter had divided main landing gear units and an attachment under the fuselage for a bomb. Both types were evaluated in 1928, and a hybrid variant with divided main units and an arrester hook was orderd for the U.S. Navy as the F4B-1 with tailskid landing gear. These 27 aircraft were followed by 46 F4B-2s with a drag-reducing cowling ring and through-axle landing gear with a tailwheel, 21 F4B-3s with a semi-monocoque fuselage and 92 F4B-4s with a larger fin and, to be found in the last 45 aircraft, a liferaft in the pilot's headrest.

BOEING F4B-4
Role: Naval carrierborne fighter bomber
Crew/Accommodation: One
Power Plant: One 500 hp Pratt & Whitney R-1340-D Wasp air-cooled radial
Dimensions: Span 9.14 m (30 ft); length 7.75 m (25.42 ft); wing area 21.18 m² (228 sq ft)
Weights: Empty 1,049 kg (2,312 lb); MTOW 1,596 kg (3,519 lb)
Performance: Maximum speed 301 km/h (187 mph) at sea level; operational ceiling 8,382 m (27,500 ft); range 941 km (585 miles)
Load: One .5 inch and one .303 inch machine guns, plus one 227 kg (500 lb) bomb

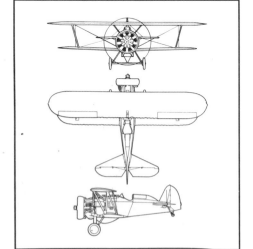

Boeing P-12E

Boeing F4B-3.

CURTISS P-6 HAWK and F11C Series (United States)

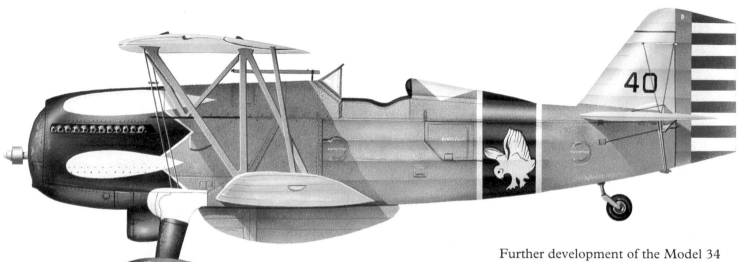

kW (700-hp) V-1570C Conqueror. This was the finest of the army's Hawk fighters, and was the Curtiss Model 35.

There were many experimental variants including the radial-engined P-3 and P-21, and the turbocharged P-5 and P-23.

The type also secured comparatively large export orders under the generic designation Hawk. The Hawk I was sold to the Netherlands East Indies (eight aircraft), Cuba (three) and Japan (one), while the same basic type with a Wright Cyclone radial was sold with the name Hawk II to Bolivia (nine), Chile (four plus licensed production), China (50), Colombia (26 float-equipped aircraft), Cuba (four), Germany (two), Norway (one), Siam (12) and Turkey (19).

In addition, the U.S. Navy ordered a version of the Hawk II with the 522-kW (700-hp) Wright R-1820-78 Cyclone radial and the designations F11C-2 (28 aircraft), and with manually operated landing gear that retracted into a bulged lower fuselage, another type, the BF2C-1 (27 aircraft).

Further development of the Model 34 (P-1 and F6C series) led to the P-6 series with the Curtiss V-1570 Conqueror engine. The development was pioneered in two P-1 conversions, namely the XP-6 with tapered wings and the XP-6A with the uptapered wings of the PW-8 and low-drag wing surfaced radiators. Both these aircraft were successful racers in 1927, and paved the way for the production series later on.

The main variants were the original P-6 of which nine were delivered with refined fuselage lines, the nine P-6As with Prestone-cooled engines, and the P-6E of which 46 were delivered in the winter of 1931-32 with the 522-

Curtiss P-6E Hawk.

CURTISS P-6E
Role: Fighter
Crew/Accommodation: One
Power Plant: One 700 hp Curtiss V-1570C Conqueror water-cooled inline
Dimensions: Span 9.6 m (31.5 ft); length 6.88 m (22.58 ft); wing area 23.4 m² (252 sq ft)
Weights: Empty 1,231 kg (2,715 lb); MTOW 1,558 kg (3,436 lb)
Performance: Maximum speed 311 km/h (193 mph) at sea level; operational ceiling 7,285 m (23,900 ft); range 393 km (244 miles)
Load: Two .303 inch machine guns

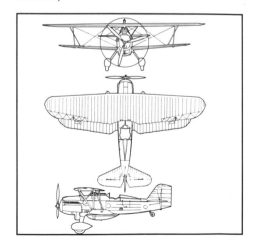

Curtiss P-6E

HAWKER FURY I and II BIPLANES (United Kingdom)

placed in production for service from May 1931. The fighter was of metal construction covered with panels of light alloy and with fabric, and the powerplant was a single 391-kW (525-hp) Rolls-Royce Kestrel IIS engine driving a large two-blade propeller. Production of the Fury (later the Fury I) for the RAF totalled 118, though another 42 were built for export with a number of other engine types. Hawker developed the basic concept further in the Intermediate Fury and High-Speed Fury prototypes that led to the definitive Fury II with the 477-kW (640-hp) Kestrel VI and spatted wheels. This entered service in 1937, and the 98 aircraft were used as interim fighters pending large-scale deliveries of the Hawker Hurricane monoplane fighter. The Fury II was exported to Yugoslavia, which took 10 aircraft. The Nimrod was a naval equivalent; 100 were produced for British and Danish service.

This single-seat fighter resulted from a 1927 requirement that led to the construction of prototype first flew with the 336-kW (450-hp) Bristol Jupiter radial specified by the Air

Ministry. The aircraft failed to win a production contract, but its experience with this prototype stood the company in good stead. After its Hart high-speed day bomber had entered service as a pioneer of a new breed of high-performance warplanes, Hawker developed as a private venture fighter prototype. Sydney Camm decided not to follow current Air Ministry preference for radial engines, but instead opted for the Rolls-Royce

F.XIX inline engine in an elegantly streamlined nose entry. The whole prototype was of very clean lines, and after purchase by the Air Ministry was renamed Fury.

Trials confirmed the type's capabilities as the first British fighter capable of exceeding 200 mph (322 km/h) in level flight, and the type was

HAWKER FURY Mk II
Role: Interceptor
Crew/Accommodation: One
Power Plant: One 525 hp Rolls-Royce Kestrel IIS water-cooled inline
Dimensions: Span 9.15 m (30 ft); length 8.13 m (26.67 ft); wing area 23.4 m² (251.8 sq ft)
Weights: Empty 1,190 kg (2,623 lb); MTOW 1,583 kg (3,490 lb)
Performance: Maximum speed 309 km/h (192 mph) at 1,525 m (5,000 ft); operational ceiling 8,534 m (28,000 ft); range 491 km (305 miles)
Load: Two .303 inch machine guns

Hawker Fury Mk I

The Fury series was always notable for the elegance of its lines.

BOEING P-26 'PEASHOOTER' (United States)

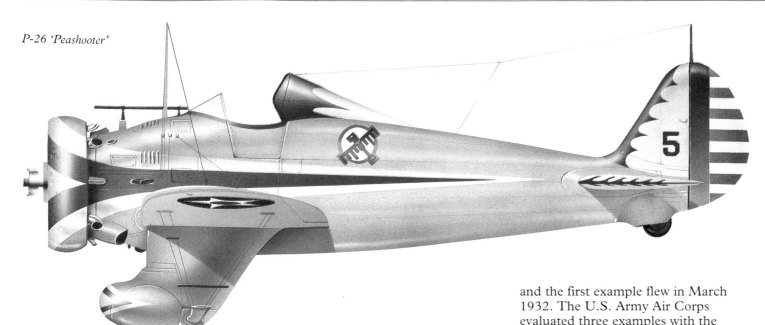

P-26 'Peashooter'

production version with a revised structure, flotation equipment, and radio. The P-26As were often known as 'Peashooters', and were delivered between January 1934 and June 1934.

Later aircraft had a taller headrest for improved pilot protection in the event of a roll-over landing accident, and were produced with the trailing-edge split flaps that had been developed to reduce landing speed; in-service aircraft were retrofitted with the flaps. Other variants were two P-26Bs with the fuel-injected R-1340-33 radial, and 23 P-26Cs with modified fuel systems.

Some 11 aircraft were also exported to China, and surplus American aircraft were later delivered to Guatemala and Panama. Ex-American aircraft operated by the Philippine Air Corps saw short but disastrous service in World War II.

and the first example flew in March 1932. The U.S. Army Air Corps evaluated three examples with the designation XP-936, and then ordered 111 examples of the Model 266

The Model 266 was a step, but only an interim step, towards the 'modern' monoplane fighter of all-metal construction that appeared in definitive form during the mid-1930s.

The Model 266 was indeed a monoplane fighter, but the wing was not a cantilever structure and had, therefore, to be braced by flying and landing wires. This bracing was in itself an obsolescent feature, and so too were the open cockpit and fixed landing gear, though the latter's main units were well faired. Boeing began work on its Model 248 private-venture prototype during September 1931,

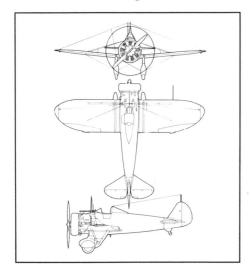

Boeing P-26A

BOEING P-26C
Role: Fighter
Crew/Accommodation: One
Power Plant: One 600 hp Pratt & Whitney R-1340-33 Wasp air-cooled radial
Dimensions: Span 8.52 m (27.96 ft); length 7.24 m (23.75 ft); wing area 13.89 m² (149 sq ft)
Weights: Empty 1,058 kg (2,333 lb); MTOW 1,395 kg (3,075 lb)
Performance: Maximum speed 378 km/h (235 mph) at sea level; operational ceiling 8,230 m (27,000 ft); range 1,022 km (635 miles)
Load: Two .5 inch machine guns, plus 90.8 kg (200 lb) of bombs

Boeing P-26A.

19

FIAT CR.32 and CR.42 FALCO (Italy)

CR.32

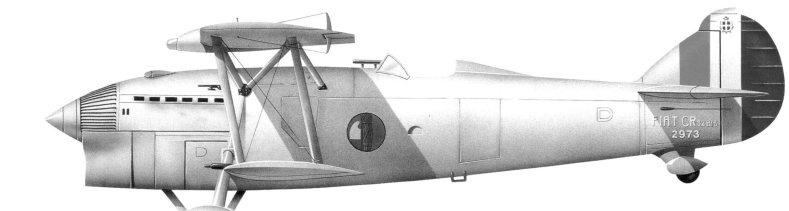

The CR.32 was Italy's finest fighter of the late 1930s, and marks one of the high points in biplane fighter design. The type was planned as successor to the CR.30 with smaller dimensions and reduced weight so that the type would have a comparably high level of agility but better overall performance on the same power. The prototype first flew in April 1933 with the 447-kW (600-hp) Fiat A.30 RAbis inline engine, and the successful evaluation of this machine led to production of slightly more than 1,300 aircraft in four series. These were about 350 CR.32 fighters with two 7.7-mm (0.303-in) machine guns, 283 CR.32bis close-support fighters with two 12.7-mm (0.5-in) and two 7.7-mm guns as well as provision for two 50-kg (110-lb) bombs, 150 CR.32ter fighters with two 12.7-mm (0.5-in) guns and improved equipment, and 337 CR.32quater fighters with radio and reduced weight. Another 100 or more of this last type were built in Spain as Hispano HA-132-L 'Chirri' fighters.

The Spanish Civil War led to the CR.42 Falco (Falcon) that first flew in prototype form during May 1938. This could be regarded as an aerodynamically refined version of the CR.32 with cantilever main landing gear units and more power in the form of a 626-kW (840-hp) Fiat A.74 R1C radial. More than 1,780 aircraft in five series were produced. The original CR.42 was armed with one 12.7-mm and one 7.7-mm machine guns. The CR.42AS was a close-support fighter with two 12.7-mm guns and two 10-kg (220-lb) bombs. The CR.42bis fighter was produced for Sweden with two 12.7-mm guns. The CR.42CN night fighter had two searchlights in underwing fairings. And the CR.42ter was a version of the CR.42bis with two 7.7-mm guns in underwing fairings.

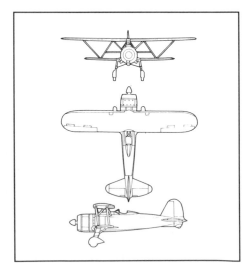

The Fiat CR.42bis Falco

FIAT CR.32bis
Role: Fighter
Crew/Accommodation: One
Power Plant: One 600 hp Fiat A30 RAbis water-cooled inline
Dimensions: Span 9.5 m (31.17 ft); length 7.47 m (24.51 ft); wing area 22.1 m² (237.9 sq ft)
Weights: Empty 1,455 kg (3,210 lb); MTOW 1,975 kg (4,350 lb)
Performance: Maximum speed 360 km/h (224 mph) at 3,000 m (9,840 ft); operational ceiling 7,700 m (25,256 ft); range 750 km (446 miles)
Load: Two 12.7 mm and two 7.7 mm machine guns, plus provision to carry up to 100 kg (220 lb) of bombs

The Fiat CR.42 bis Falco.

POLIKARPOV I-16 (U.S.S.R.)

I-16 Type 24

The I-16 was the first low-wing monoplane fighter to enter full service with retractable landing gear. The aircraft had a cantilever wing of metal construction married to a monocoque fuselage of wooden construction and, in addition to the manually retracted main landing gear unit, the type had long-span split ailerons that doubled as flaps. The type first flew in 1933 as the TsKB-12 with the 358-kW (480-hp) M-22 radial. The TsKB-12bis flew two months later with an imported 529-kW (710-hp) Wright

SR-1820-F3 Cyclone radial and offered better performance. The handling qualities of both variants were tricky, because the short and very portly fuselage reduced longitudinal stability to virtually nothing, but its speed and rate of climb ensured that the machine was ordered into production, initially as an evaluation batch of 10 I-16 Type 1 fighters with the M-22.

Total production was 7,005 in variants with progressively more power and armament: the I-16 Type 4

used the imported Cyclone engine, the I-16 Type 5 had the 522-kW (700-hp) M-25 licensed version of the Cyclone and improved armour protection, the I-16 Type 6 was the first major production model and had the 544-kW (730-hp) M-25A, the I-16 Type 10 had the 559-kW (750-hp) M-25V and four rather than two 7.62-mm (0.3-in) machine-guns, the I-16 Type 17 was strengthened and had 20-mm cannon in place of the two wing machine guns plus provision for six 82-mm (3.2-in) rockets carried under the wings, the I-16 Type 18

had the 686-kW (920-hp) M-62 radial and four machine guns, the I-16 Type 24 had the 746-kW (1,000-hp) M-62 or 820-kW (1,100-hp) M-63 radial, strengthened wings and four machine guns, and the I-16 Types 28 and 30 that were reinstated in production during the dismal days of 1941 and 1942 had the M-63 radial. There were also SPB dive-bomber and I-16UTI dual-control trainer variants.

The I-16 was the world's first 'modern' monoplane fighter.

POLIKARPOV I-16 TYPE 24
Role: Fighter
Crew/Accommodation: One
Power Plant: One 1,000 hp Shvetsov M-62 air-cooled radial
Dimensions: Span 9 m (29.53 ft); length 6.13 m (20.11 ft); wing area 14.54 m² (156.5 sq ft)
Weights: Empty 1,475 kg (3,313 lb); MTOW 2,050 kg (4,519 lb)
Performance: Maximum speed 525 km/h (326 mph) at sea level; operational ceiling 9,000 m (29,528 ft); range 700 km (435 miles)
Load: Two 20 mm cannon and two 7.62 mm machine guns, plus six rocket projectiles

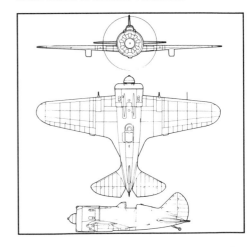

Polikarpov I-16 Type 24

21

CURTISS P-36 and HAWK 75 (United States)

P-36C

In 1934 Curtiss decided on the private-venture design of a modern fighter that might interest the U.S. Army Air Corps as a successor to the Boeing P-26 and would also have considerable export attractions.

The Model 75 prototype first flew in May 1935 as a low-wing monoplane of all-metal construction with an enclosed cockpit, retractable landing gear and a 671-kW (900-hp)

Wright XR-1670-5 radial. The type was evaluated by the USAAC as the Model 75B with the 634-kW (750-hp) Wright R-1820 radial, but was initially beaten for a production order by the Seversky prototype that became the P-35.

The Curtiss machine was reworked into the Model 75E with the 783-kW (1,050-hp) Pratt & Whitney R-1830-13 derated to 708 kW (950 hp) and then re-evaluated as the Y1P-36. This was clearly a superior fighter, and in July 1937 the type was ordered into production as the P-36A with the fully rated version of the R-1830-13 driving a constant-speed propeller. Some 210

of the type were ordered, but only 31 were completed to P-36C standard with the 895-kW (1,200-hp) R-1830-17 engine and the two fuselage-mounted guns (one of 12.7-mm/0.5-in and the other of 7.62-mm/0.3-in calibre) complemented by two wing-mounted 7.62-mm guns.

The type was exported in fairly large numbers as the H75A, principally to France and the United Kingdom, but in smaller numbers to other countries. British aircraft were

named Mohawk and comprised four main variants. Some 30 repossessed Norwegian aircraft were taken in charge by the Americans with the designation P-36G. In addition to this, Curtiss developed a less advanced version as the Hawk 75, in the main similar to the pre-production Y1P-36 but with a lower-powered 652-kW (875-hp) Wright GR-1820 radial and fixed landing gear.

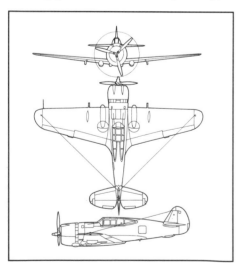

Curtiss P-36C

CURTISS P-36C (RAF MOHAWK)
Role: Fighter
Crew/Accommodation: One
Power Plant: One 1,200 hp Pratt & Whitney R-1830-17 Twin Wasp air-cooled radial
Dimensions: Span 11.35 m (37.33 ft); length 8.72 m (28.6 ft); wing area 21.92 m² (236 sq ft)
Weights: Empty 2,095 kg (4,619 lb); MTOW 2,790 kg (6,150 lb)
Performance: Maximum speed 501 km/h (311 mph) at 3,048 m (10,000 ft); operational ceiing 10,272 m (33,700 ft); range 1,320 km (820 miles) at 322 km/h (200 mph) cruise
Load: Four .303 inch machine guns

Curtiss P-36C.

DEWOITINE D.500 and D.510 Series (France)

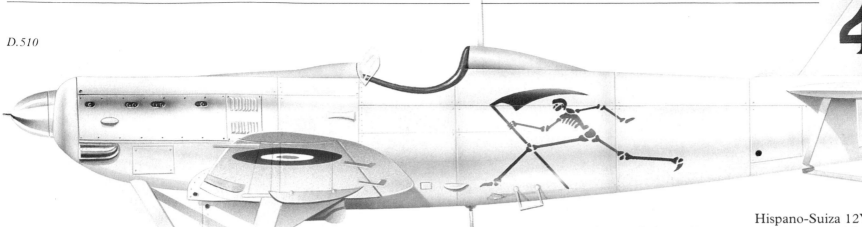

D.510

The ungainly but impressive D.500 spanned the technological gap between the fabric-covered biplanes of the 1920s and the all-metal monoplane fighters of the mid-1930s. Designed as a successor to the Nieuport 62 and 622, the D.500 was of all-metal construction with a low-set cantilever wing, but these modern features were compromised by obsolescent items such as an open cockpit and fixed tailwheel landing gear the main legs of which carried large fairings. The D.500.01 prototype first flew in June 1932 with the 492-kW (660-hp) Hispano-Suiza 12Xbrs inline engine, and the type was ordered into production. The initial D.500 was produced to the extent of 101 aircraft, later aircraft with 7.5-mm (0.295-in) Darne machine guns in place of the original 7.7-mm (0.303-in) Vickers guns. There followed 157 D.501s with the 515-kW (690-hp) Hispano-Suiza 12Xcrs engine and a hub-mounted 20-mm cannon in addition to the two machine guns.

Projected variants were the D.502 catapult-launched floatplane fighter, the D.504 parachute trials aircraft, and the D.505 to D.509 with different engines. The main variant in service at the beginning of World War II was the D.510 based on the D.501 but powered by the 641-kW (860-hp) Hispano-Suiza 12Ycrs inline in a longer nose and featuring a number of refinements such as modified landing gear, greater fuel capacity and, in late aircraft, 7.5-mm MAC 1934 machine guns in place of the Darne weapons. Production of the D.510 totalled 120 aircraft in all.

An interesting experimental derivative was the D.511 of 1934: this had a smaller wing, cantilever main landing gear units, and the HS 12Ycrs engine. The type was never flown, as it was modified as the D.503 with the HS 12Xcrs and proving inferior to the D.501 aircraft.

Dewoitine D.500

DEWOITINE D.510
Role: Fighter
Crew/Accommodation: One
Power Plant: One 860 hp Hispano-Suiza 12Y crs water-cooled inline
Dimensions: Span 12.09 m (39.67 ft); length 7.94 m (26.05 ft); wing area 16.5 m² (177.6 sq ft)
Weights: Empty 1,427 kg (3,145 lb); MTOW 1,915 kg (4,222 lb)
Performance: Maximum speed 402 km/h (250 mph) at 4,850 m (15,912 ft); operational ceiling 8,350 m (27,395 ft); range 985 km (612 miles)
Load: One 20 mm cannon and two 7.5 mm machine guns

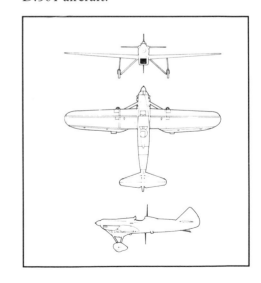

DeWoitine D.500

HAWKER HURRICANE (United Kingdom)

Hurricane Mk I

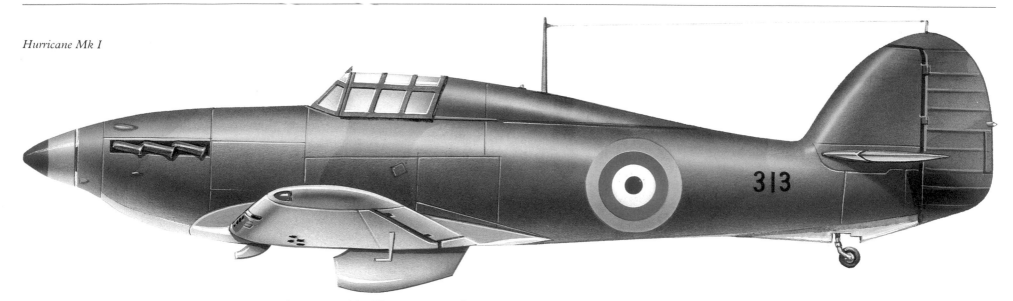

The Hurricane was the first British example of the 'modern' monoplane fighter, even though it lacked the stressed-skin construction of later machines such as the Supermarine Spitfire. The initial design was created as a private venture, and offered such advantages over current biplane fighters that a 1934 specification was written round it. The prototype first flew in November 1935 and revealed itself as a mix of advanced features (retractable landing gear, flaps and an enclosed cockpit) and an obsolescent structure of light alloy tube covered in fabric. This last did facilitate construction and repair, but limited the Hurricane's longer-term development potential despite an overall production total of 14,232 aircraft.

The Hurricane Mk I entered service in December 1937 with an armament of eight 7.7-mm (0.303-in) machine guns and the 768-kW (1,030-hp) Rolls-Royce Merlin II inline driving a two-blade propeller, and in the Battle of Britain was the RAF's most important and successful fighter with the 767-kW (1,029-hp) Merlin III driving a three-blade propeller. British production of 3,164 Mk Is was complemented by 140 Canadian-built Hurricane Mk Xs and a few Belgian- and Yugoslav-produced machines. Adoption of the 954-kW (1,280-hp) Merlin XX resulted in the Hurricane Mk II, of which 6,656 were produced in the U.K. in variants such as the Mk IIA with eight 7.7-mm machine-guns, the Mk IIB with 12 such guns and provision for underwing bombs, the Mk IIC based on the Mk IIB but with four 20-mm cannon, and the Mk IID with two 40-mm cannon in the anti-tank role; Canadian production amounted to 937 similar Hurricane Mks X, XI and XII aircraft. The final version was the Hurricane Mk IV, of which 2,575 were built with the 1208-kW (1,620-hp) Merlin 24 or 27 and a universal wing allowing the use of any of the standard armament combinations. About 825 aircraft were converted into Sea Hurricane Mks I and II.

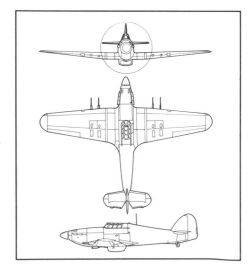

Hawker Hurricane Mk IIB

HAWKER HURRICANE Mk II B
Role: Fighter bomber
Crew/Accommodation: One
Power Plant: One 1,280 hp Rolls-Royce Merlin XX water-cooled inline
Dimensions: Span 12.19 m (40 ft); length 9.75 m (32 ft); wing area 23.9 m² (257.5 sq ft)
Weights: Empty 2,495 kg (5,500 lb); MTOW 3,311 kg (7,300 lb)
Performance: Maximum speed 722 km/h (342 mph) at 6,706 m (22,000 ft); operational ceiling 10,973 m (36,000 ft); range 772.5 km (480 miles) on internal fuel only
Load: Twelve .303 inch machine guns, plus up to 454 kg (1,000 lb) bombload

The Hawker Hurricane was the RAF's first 'modern' monoplane fighter.

MESSERSCHMITT Bf 109 (Germany)

Bf 109F-2

The Bf 109 was Germany's most important fighter of World War II in numerical terms, and bore the brunt of the air war until supplemented by the Focke-Wulf Fw 190 from 1941. The type went through a large number of production variants, and in common with other German aircraft was developed within these basic variants into a number of subvariants with factory- or field-installed modification packages.

The Bf 109 was designed from 1934 to provide the German Air Force with its first 'modern' fighter of all-metal stressed-skin construction with a low-set cantilever wing, retractable landing gear and enclosed cockpit. The first prototype flew in May 1935 with a 518-kW (695-hp) Rolls-Royce Kestrel inline, but the second had the 455-kW (610-hp) Junkers Jumo 210A for which the aircraft had been designed. The overall production figure has not survived, but it is thought that at least 30,500 aircraft were produced, excluding foreign production. The limited-number Bf 109A, B and C variants can be regarded mostly as pre-production

and development models with differing Jumo 210s and armament fits. The Daimler-Benz DB 600A inline was introduced on the Bf 109D, paving the way for the first large-scale production variant, the Bf 109E produced in variants up to the E-9 with the 820-kW (1,100-hp) DB 601A. The Bf 109F introduced a more refined fuselage with reduced armament, and in addition was powered by the DB 601E or N in variants up to the F-6.

The most important production model was the Bf 109G with the DB 605 inline and provision for cockpit pressurization in variants up to the G-16. Later in the war there appeared comparatively small numbers of the Bf 109H high-altitude fighter with increased span in variants up to the H-1, and the Bf 109K improved version of the Bf 109G with the DB 605 inline in variants up to the K-14.

MESSERSCHMITT Bf 109G-6
Role: Fighter
Crew/Accommodation: One
Power Plant: One 1,475 hp Daimler-Benz DB605A water-cooled in line
Dimensions: Span 9.92 m (32.55 ft); length 9.02 m (29.59 ft); wing area 16.5 m² (172.75 sq ft)
Weights: Empty 2,700 kg (5,953 lb); MTOW 3,150 kg (6,945 lb)
Performance: Maximum speed 623 km/h (387 mph) at 7,000 m (22,967 ft); operational ceiling 11,750 m (38,551 ft); range 725 km (450 miles)
Load: One 30 mm cannon, two 20 mm cannon and two 13 mm machine guns, plus a 500 kg (1,102 lb) bomb

Bf 109F.

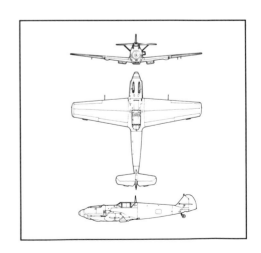

Messerschmitt Bf 109E-3

NAKAJIMA Ki-27 'NATE' (Japan)

Ki-27 'Nate'

The Ki-27 was the Imperial Japanese Army Air Force's equivalent to the Navy's Mitsubishi A5M, and though it was an interim 'modern' fighter with fixed landing gear (selected because of its light weight) it had more advanced features such as flaps and an enclosed cockpit. The type was evolved from the company's private-venture Type PE design, and the first of two prototypes flew in October 1936 with the 485-kW (650-hp) Nakajima Ha-1a radial. Flight trials with the prototypes confirmed the Ki-27's superiority to competing fighters, and 10 examples of the type with a modified clear-vision canopy were ordered for evaluation. These aircraft proved highly effective, and the first full-production type was ordered with the company designation Ki-27a and the service designation Army Type 97 Fighter Model A.

The production programme lasted from 1937 to 1942 and totalled 3,384 aircraft in the original Ki-27a and modestly improved Ki-27b variants. The Ki-27a had an uprated Ha-1b (Army Type 97) engine and a metal-faired canopy, while the Ki-27b reverted to the clear-vision canopy and featured light ground-attack capability in the form of the four 25-kg (55-lb) bombs that could be carried under the wings. A number of the fighters were converted as two-seat armed trainers, and two experimental lightweight fighters were produced with the designation Ki-27 KAI. The Ki-27 was used operationally up to 1942, when its light structure and poor armament forced its relegation to second-line duties. The type was initially known to the Allies in the China-Burma-India theatre as the 'Abdul', but 'Nate' later became the standard reporting name.

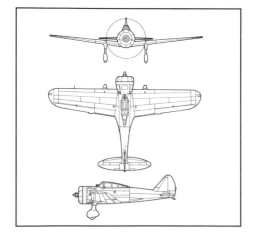

Nakajima Ki-27b 'Nate'

NAKAJIMA Ki-27 'NATE'
Role: Fighter
Crew/Accommodation: One
Power Plant: One 710 hp Nakajima Ha-1b air-cooled radial
Dimensions: Span 11.3 m (37.07 ft) length 7.53 m (24.7 ft); wing area 18.6 m² (199.7 sq ft)
Weights: Empty 1,110 kg (2,447 lb); MTOW 1,650 kg (3,638 lb)
Performance: Maximum speed 460 km/h (286 mph) at 3,500 m (11,480 ft); operational ceiling 8,600 m (28,215 ft); range 1,710 m (1,060 miles)
Load: Two 7.7 mm machine guns, plus up to 100 kg (220 lb) of bombs

The Nakajima Ki-27.

SUPERMARINE SPITFIRE and SEAFIRE (United Kingdom)

Spitfire Mk IX

The Spitfire was the most important British fighter of World War II and remained in production right through the conflict for a total of 20,334 aircraft bolstered by 2,556 new-build Seafire naval fighters. The prototype first flew in March 1936 with a 738-kW (900-hp) Rolls-Royce Merlin C engine, and was soon ordered into production as the Spitfire Mk I with the 768-kW (1,030-hp) Merlin II and eight 7.7-mm (0.303-in) machine guns or, in the Mk IB variant, four machine guns and two 20-mm cannon; the suffix A indicated eight 7.7-mm machine-guns, B four such machine-guns and two 20-mm cannon, C four cannon, and E two

cannon and two 12.7-mm (0.5-in) machine-guns.

Major fighter variants with the Merlin engine were the initial Mk I, the Mk II with the 876-kW (1,175-hp) Merlin XII, the Mks VA, VB and VC in F medium- and LF low-altitiude forms with the 1974-kW (1,440-hp) Merlin 45 or 1096-kW (1,470-hp) Merlin 50, the HF.Mk VI high-altitude interceptor with the 1055-kW (1,415-hp) Merlin 47 and a pressurized cockpit, the HF.Mk VII with the two-stage Merlin 61, 64 or 71, the LF, F and HF.Mk VIII with the two-stage Merlin 61, 63, 66 or 70 but an unpressurized cockpit, the LF, F and HF.Mk IX using the Mk V

airframe with the two-stage Merlin 61, 63 or 70, the LF and F.Mk XVI using the Mk IX airframe with a cutdown rear fuselage, bubble canopy and Packard-built Merlin 226.

The Spitfire was also developed in its basic fighter form with the larger and more powerful Rolls-Royce Griffon inline, and the major variants of this sequence were the LF.Mk XI with the 1294-kW (1,735-hp) Griffon II or IV, the LF and F.Mk XIV with the 1529-kW (2,050-hp) Griffon 65 or 66 and often with a bubble canopy, the F.Mk XVIII with the two-stage Griffon and a bubble canopy, the F.Mk 21 with the Griffon 61 or 64, the

F.Mk 22 with the 1771-kW (2,373-hp) Griffon 85 driving a contra-rotating propeller unit, and the improved F.Mk 24.

The Spitfire was also used as a unarmed reconnaissance type, the major Merlin-engined types being the Mks IV, X, XI and XIII, and the Griffon-engined type being the Mk XIX. The Seafire was the naval counterpart to the Spitfire, the main Merlin engined versions being the Mks IB, IIC and III, and the Griffon-engined versions being the Mks XV, XVII, 45, 46 and 47.

Supermarine Spitfire F.Mk XIV

SUPERMARINE SPITFIRE F.Mk XIV E
Role: Fighter
Crew/Accommodation: One
Power Plant: One 2,050 hp Rolls-Royce Griffon 65 water-cooled inline
Dimensions: Span 11.23 m (36.83 ft); length 9.96 m (32.66 ft); wing area 22.48 m² (242 sq ft)
Weights: Empty 2,994 kg (6,600 lb); MTOW 3,856 kg (8,500 lb)
Performance: Maximum speed 721 km/h (448 mph) at 7,925 m (26,000 ft); operational ceiling 13,106 m (43,000 ft); range 740 km (460 miles) on internal fuel only
Load: Two 20 mm cannon and two .303 machine guns, plus up to 454 kg (1,000 lb) of bombs

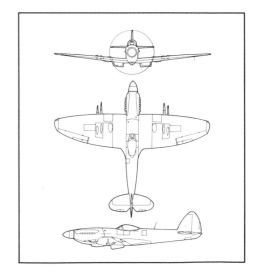

Supermarine Spitfire F.Mk 24

BELL P-39 AIRACOBRA (United States)

P-39 Airacobra Mk I

The P-39 Airacobra was an attempt to create a fighter that possessed greater manoeuvrability and more powerful nose-mounted armament than contemporary fighters. The engine was located behind the cockpit on the aircraft's centre of gravity. It drove the propeller by means of an extension shaft, and the nose volume was left free for the forward unit of the retractable tricycle landing gear and also for heavy fixed armament including one 37-mm cannon firing through the propeller shaft. The XP-39 prototype flew in April 1938, and was followed by 13 YP-39 pre-production aircraft including one YP-39A with an unturbocharged Allison V-1710 engine. This last became the prototype for the production version, which was ordered in August 1939 as the P-45. These aircraft were in fact delivered as 20 P-39Cs and 60 P-39Ds with heavier armament and self-sealing tanks. Large-scale production followed. Total P-39 production was 9,590, even though the Airacobra was never more than adequate as a fighter and found its real mileu in the low-level attack role.

The main models were the 229 P-39Fs modelled on the P-39D but with an Aeroproducts propeller, the 210 P-39Ks with the V-1710-63 engine and a Curtiss propeller, 240 P-39Ms with the V-1710-83 engine and a larger propeller, 2,095 P-39Ns with the V-1710-85 engine but less fuel and armour, and 4,905 P-39Qs with two underwing gun gondolas. Large numbers were supplied to the U.S.S.R. in World War II.

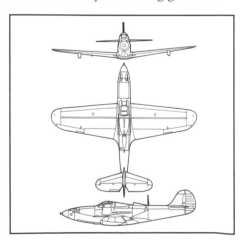

BELL P-39D AIRACOBRA
Role: Fighter
Crew/Accommodation: One
Power Plant: One, 1,150 hp Allison V-1710-35 water-cooled inline
Dimensions: Span 10.36 m (34 ft); length 9.19 m (30.16 ft); wing area 19.79 m² (213 sq ft)
Weights: Empty 2,478 kg (5,462 lb); MTOW 3,720 kg (8,200 lb)
Performance: Maximum speed 592 km/h (368 mph) at 4,206 m (13,800 ft); operational ceiling 9,784 m (32,100 ft); range 1,287 km (800 miles) with 227 kg (500 lb) of bombs
Load: One 37mm cannon, plus two .5 inch and four .303 inch machine guns, along with 227 kg (500 lb) of bombs

P-39N of the Italian Air Force

BLOCH M.B. 151 and M.B. 152 (France)

M.B. 152 C1

The M.B. 151 was one of France's first 'modern' monoplane fighters, and resulted from the unsuccessful M.B. 150 prototype produced to meet a 1934 requirement. The M.B.150 could not at first be persuaded to fly, but after it had been fitted with a larger wing, revised landing gear and a 701-kW (940-hp) Gnome-Rhône 14N radial, the type first flew in October 1937. In 1938 further improvement in flight performance was achieved with a slightly larger wing and the Gnome-Rhône 14N-7 engine, and a pre-production batch of 25 M.B. 151 fighters was ordered with slightly reduced wing span and the 695-kW (920-hp) Gnome-Rhône 14N-11 radial. The first of these flew in August 1938, and there followed 115 production aircraft with the identically rated Gnome-Rhône 14N-35 radial.

The type was deemed to lack the performance required of a first-line fighter, and was generally used as a fighter trainer. An improved version was developed as the M.B. 152 with the more powerful 768-kW (1,030-hp) Gnome-Rhône 14N-25 or 790-kW (1,060-hp) Gnome-Rhône 14N-49. Production was slow, and only a few M.B. 152s were combat–ready in time for the German invasion of May 1940; more than 30 aircraft had been delivered by January 1940, but most lacked the right propeller. The airworthy examples served with success during the German invasion of mid-1940, and then remained operational with the Vichy French air force. Some aircraft were used by the Luftwaffe as trainers, and 20 were passed to Romania.

The Bloch M.B. 151.

BLOCH M.B. 152
Role: Fighter
Crew/Accommodation: One
Power Plant: One 1,000 hp Gnome-Rhône 14N-25 air-cooled radial
Dimensions: Span 10.54 m (34.58 ft); length 9.1 m (29.86 ft); wing area 17.32 m² (186.4 sq ft)
Weights: Empty 2,158 kg (4,758 lb); MTOW 2,800 kg (6,173 lb)
Performance: Maximum speed 509 km/h (316 mph) at 4,500 m (14,765 ft); operational ceiling 10,000 m (32,808 ft); range 540 km (335 miles)
Load: Two 20 mm cannon and two 7.5 mm machine guns

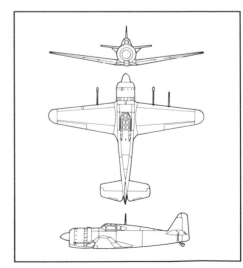

Bloch M.B. 155

BOULTON PAUL DEFIANT (United Kingdom)

Defiant Mk II

In the mid-1930s there was considerable enthusiasm among Royal Air Force planners for the two-seat fighter in which all the armament would be concentrated in a power-operated turret. Such a fighter, its protagonists claimed, would be able to penetrate into enemy bomber streams and wreak havoc. A first expression of this concept was found in the Hawker

Demon, of which 59 were manufactured in 1934 by Boulton Paul with a Frazer-Nash turret. The company was therefore well placed to respond to a 1935 requirement for a more advanced two-seat turret fighter. The P.82 design was for a trim fighter of the 'modern' monoplane type, little larger than current single-seaters and fitted with a four-gun turret immediately aft of the cockpit. The first of two Defiant prototypes flew in

August 1937 with a 768-kW (1,030-hp) Rolls-Royce Merlin I inline engine, and the Defiant Mk I fighter began to enter service in December 1939.

After early encounters with German warplanes, in which the Defiant scored some success because of the novelty of its layout, operations soon revealed the inadequacy of a type in which the turret's weight and drag imposed severe performance and handling limitations and also left the pilot without fixed forward-firing

armament. It was decided to convert existing fighters to Defiant NF.Mk IA night fighter standard with primative AI.Mk IV or VI radar. Mk I production totalled 723, and another 210 night fighters were built as Defiant NF.Mk IIs with the more powerful Merlin XX engine and larger vertical tail surfaces. Many were later converted to Defiant TT.Mk I target-tugs and another 140 were built as such; similarly converted Mk Is became Defiant TT.Mk IIIs. Total production was 1,075.

Boulton Paul Defiant Mk I

BOULTON PAUL DEFIANT Mk II
Role: Night fighter
Crew/Accommodation: Two
Power Plant: One 1,280 hp Rolls-Royce Merlin XX water-cooled inline
Dimensions: Span 11.99 m (39.33 ft); length 10.77 m (35.33 ft); wing area 23.23 m² (250 sq ft)
Weights: Empty 2,850 kg (6,282 lb); MTOW 3,773 kg (8,318 lb)
Performance: Maximum speed 507 km/h (315 mph) at 5,029 m (16,500 ft); operational ceiling 9,251 m (30,350 ft); range 748 km (465 miles)
Load: Four .303 inch machine guns in power-operated turret.
Note: The Defiant Mk III was retrofitted to embody AIMk4 radar.

Boulton Paul Defiant Mk I

GRUMMAN F4F WILDCAT (United States)

F4F-4 Wildcat

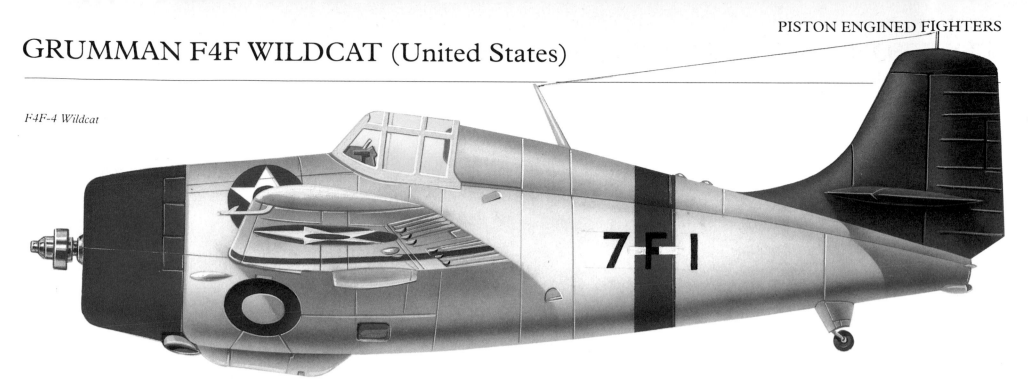

The F4F designation was first used for the G-16 biplane ordered as the XF4F-1 in competition to the Brewster monoplane prototype that was accepted for service as the F2A Buffalo carrierborne fighter. Grumman did not build the biplane prototype, but instead reworked the design as the G-18 monoplane. Re-evaluation of Grumman's proposal led the U.S. Navy to call for an XF4F-2 monoplane prototype, and this first flew in September 1937 with a 783-kW (1,050-hp) Pratt & Whitney R-

1830-66 Twin Wasp radial. This initial model was judged slightly inferior to the Buffalo, but was revised as the G-36 with a redesigned tail, a larger wing and the XR-1830-76 engine.

This XF4F-3 first flew in March 1939, and its performance and handling were so improved that the type was ordered as the F4F-3, the British taking a similar version as the Martlet Mk I; the armament was four 12.7-mm (0.5 in) machine guns and production totalled 369 excluding 95

F4F-3As with the R-1830-90 engine. The F4F/Martlet was the first Allied carrierborne fighter able to meet land-based opponents on anything like equal terms, and proved invaluable during the early war years up to 1943 in variants such as the 1,169 examples of the F4F-4 (Martlet Mks II, III and IV) with wing folding, armour, self-sealing tanks and six rather than four machine guns, and the 21 examples of the F4F-7 unarmed long-range reconnaissance version. The Eastern Aircraft Division of General Motors built 1,060 of the FM-1 (Martlet Mk V) equivalent to the F4F-4 with the R-

1830-86 engine, four wing guns, and provision for underwing stores, and 4,127 of the FM-2 (Martlet Mk V) based on Grumman's XF4F-8 prototype with the 1007-kW (1,350-hp) Wright R-1820-56 Cyclone, taller vertical tail surfaces and, on the last 826 aircraft, provision for six 127-mm (5-in) rockets under the wings.

Grumman F4F-4 Wildcat.

GRUMMAN F4F-4 WILDCAT
Role: Naval carrierborne fighter
Crew/Accommodation: One
Power Plant: One 1,200 hp Pratt & Whitney R-1830-86 Twin Wasp air-cooled radial
Dimensions: Span 11.58 m (38 ft); length 8.76 m (28.75 ft); wing area 24.16 m² (260 sq ft)
Weights: Empty 2,624 kg (5,785 lb); MTOW 3,607 kg (7,952 lb)
Performance: Maximum speed 512 km/h (318 mph) at 5,913 m (19,400 ft); operational ceiling 10,638 m (34,900 ft); range 1,239 km (770 miles) on internal fuel only
Load: Six .5 inch machine guns

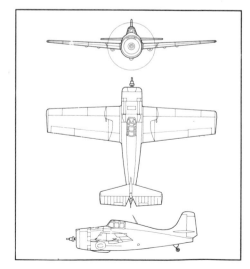

Grumman F4F-4 Wildcat

CURTISS P-40 WARHAWK Family (United States)

P-40 B Warhawk

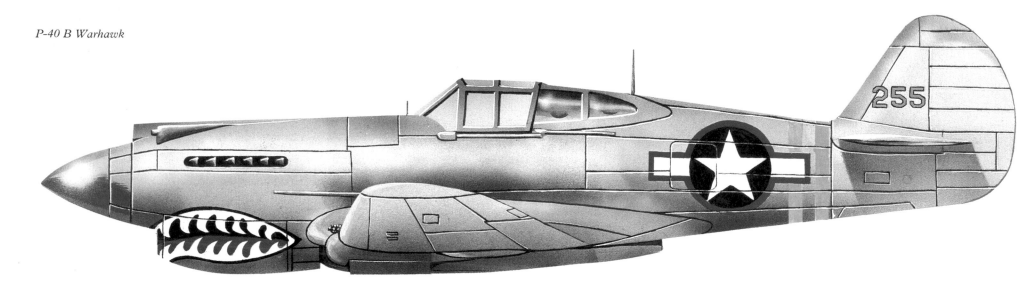

The P-40 series was in no way an exceptional warplane, but nonetheless proved itself a more than adequate fighter-bomber. It was exceeded in numbers by only two other American fighters, the Republic P-47 Thunderbolt and North American P-51 Mustang. The basis for the P-40 series was the Model 75I, a Model 75/

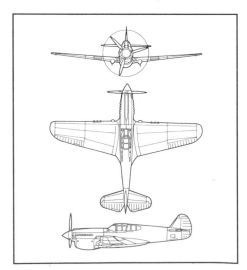

Curtiss P-40E Warhawk

XP-37A airframe modified to take the 858-kW (1,150-hp) Allison V-1710-11 inline engine. This became the first U.S. fighter to exceed 300 mph (483 km/h) in level flight, and the type was ordered by the U.S. Army Air Corps in modified form with the designation P-40 and the less powerful V-1710-33; export versions were the Hawk 81-A1 for France and Tomahawk Mk I for the UK.

Improved models were the P-40B (Tomahawk Mk IIA) with self-sealing

---

CURTISS P-40F WARHAWK
Role: Fighter
Crew/Accommodation: One
Power Plant: One 1,300 hp Packard-built Rolls-Royce V-1650-1 Merlin water-colled inline
Dimensions: Span 11.38 m (37.33 ft); length 10.16 m (33.33 ft); wing area 21.93 m² (236 sq ft)
Weights: Empty 2,989 kg (6,590 lb); MTOW 4,241 kg (9,350 lb)
Performance: Maximum speed 586 km/h (364 mph) at 6,096 m (20,000 ft); operational ceiling 10,485 m (34,400 ft); range 603 km (375 miles)
Load: Six .5 inch machine guns, plus up to 227 kg (500 lb) of bombs

tanks, armour and better armament, the P-40C (Tomahawk Mk IIB) with improved self-sealing tanks and two more wing guns, the P-40D (Kittyhawk Mk I) with the 858-kW (1,150-hp) V-1710-39 with better supercharging to maintain performance to a higher altitude, and the P-40E with four wing guns plus the similar Kittyhawk Mk IA with six wing guns. The P-40 series had all along been limited by the indifferent supercharging of the V-1710, and this situation was remedied in the P-40F and generally similar P-40L

(Kittyhawk Mk II) by the adoption of the 969-kW (1,300-hp) Packard V-1650-1 (licence-built Rolls-Royce Merlin). The type's forte was still the fighter-bomber role at low altitude, and further developments included the P-40K (Kittyhawk Mk III) version of the P-40E with the V-1710-33 engine, the P-40M with the V-1710-71 engine, and the definitive P-40N (Kittyhawk Mk IV) with the V-1710-81/99/115 engine and measures to reduce weight significantly as a means of improving performance.

Curtiss P-40 Warhawk

DEWOITINE D.520 (France)

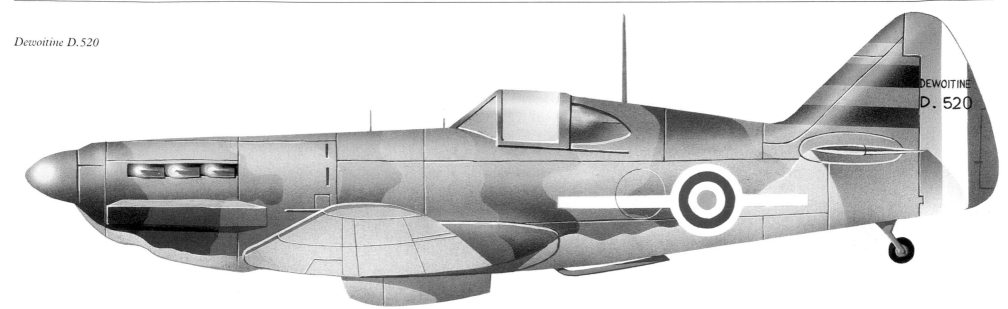

Dewoitine D.520

Dewoitine's first 'modern' low-wing monoplane fighter was the D.513 that first flew in January 1936 with a 641-kW (860-hp) Hispano-Suiza 12Ycrs inline. The type introduced advanced features such as an enclosed cockpit and retractable landing gear, but its low performance and severe instability problems proved very disappointing. The type was extensively revised but still had problems, so it was abandoned.

The company used the lessons learned from the D.513 fiasco in the creation of the D.520 which proved a far more satisfactory type and was ordered in substantial numbers. One of the most advanced fighters to serve with the French Air Force in the disastrous early campaign of 1940, the D.520 was a modern fighter of considerably trimmer and more pleasing lines than the D.513. It embodied an enclosed cockpit, trailing-edge flaps, retractable tailwheel landing gear and a variable-pitch propeller for the engine located in a much cleaner nose installation.

The D520.01 prototype first flew in October 1938 with the 664-kW (890-hp) Hispano-Suiza 12Y-21 inline, though the two following prototypes had wing, vertical tail and cockpit canopy modifications as well as the 746-kW (1,000-hp) HS 12Y-51 and 619-kW (830-hp) HS 12Y-31 engines respectively. Substantial orders were placed for the D.520 with the 686-kW (920-hp) HS 12Y-45 or -49, but only 403 aircraft had been delivered before the fall of France in June 1940. The in-service fighters did well in combat with German aircraft, and 478 aircraft were built for the Vichy French Air Force. Surviving aircraft remained up to the early 1950s. There were several experimental variants including the very promising D.524 with the 895-kW (1,200-hp) HS 12Y-89.

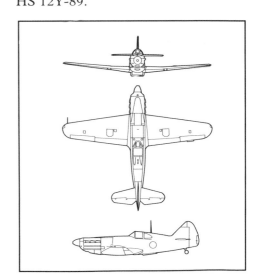

Dewoitine D.520

Dewoitine D.520.

DEWOITINE D.520
Role: Fighter
Crew/Accommodation: One
Power Plant: One 920 hp Hispano-Suiza 12Y45 water-cooled inline
Dimensions: Span 10.2 m (33 ft); length 8.76 m (28 ft); wing area 15.95 m² (171.7 sq ft)
Weights: Empty 2,092 kg (4,612 lb); MTOW 2,783 kg (6,134 lb)
Performance: Maximum speed 535 km/h (332 mph) at 6,000 m (19,685 ft); operational ceiling 11,000 m (36,090 ft); range 900 km (553 miles)
Load: One 20 mm cannon and four 7.5 mm machine guns

BRISTOL BEAUFIGHTER (United Kingdom)

Beaufighter Mk I

The Beaufighter was born of the Royal Air Force's shortage of heavy fighters (especially heavily armed night fighters and long-range escort fighters) as perceived at the time of the 'Munich crisis' late in 1938. The Type 156 was planned round the wings, tail unit and landing gear of the Type 152 Beaufort torpedo bomber married to a new fuselage and two Hercules radials.

The first of four prototypes flew in July 1939, and production was authorized with 1119-kW (1,500-hp) Hercules XI engines. Development of the Beaufighter at this time divided into two role-orientated streams. First of these was the night fighter as exemplified by the 553 Beaufighter Mk IFs with Hercules XIs, nose radar and an armament of four 20-mm nose cannon and six 7.7-mm (0.303-in) wing machine-guns. This model entered service in July 1940, and further evolution led to the 597 Beaufighter Mk IIFs with 954-kW (1,280-hp) Rolls-Royce Merlin XX inlines, and finally the 879 Beaufighter Mk VIFs with 1245-kW (1,675-hp) Hercules VIs or XVIs and improved radar in a 'thimble' nose.

With its high performance and capacious fuselage, which made the installation of radar a comparatively simple matter, the Beaufighter night fighter provided the RAF with its first truly effective method of combating nocturnal German bombers. More significant in the longer term, however, was the anti-ship version first developed as the 397 Beaufighter Mk ICs and then evolved via the 693 torpedo-carrying Beaufighter Mk VICs and 60 Beaufighter Mk VI (ITF)s with eight 27-kg (60-lb) rockets in place of the wing guns, to the 2,205 Beaufighter TF.Mk Xs with search radar and an armament of one torpedo plus light bombs or eight rockets. The 163 Beaufighter TF.Mk XIs were similar, while the 364 Beaufighter TF.Mk 21s were the Australian-built equivalents of the TF.Mk X.

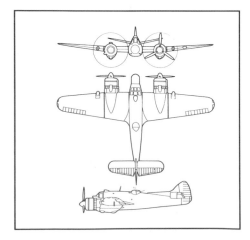

Bristol Beaufighter TF.Mk X

BRISTOL BEAUFIGHTER Mk IF
Role: Night fighter
Crew/Accommodation: Two
Power Plant: Two 1,400 hp Bristol Hercules XI air-cooled radials
Dimensions: Span 17.63 m (57.83 ft); length 12.60 m (41.33 ft); wing area 46.7 m² (503 sq ft)
Weights: Empty 6,382 kg (14,069 lb); MTOW 9,525 kg (21,000 lb)
Performance: Maximum speed 520 km/h (323 mph) at 4,572 m (15,000 ft); operational ceiling 8,839 m (29,000 ft); range 2,413 km (1,500 miles) internal fuel only
Load: Four 20 mm cannon and six .303 machine guns (interception guided by AI Mk IV radar)

TF.Mk X.

FOCKE-WULF FW 190 and Ta 152 (Germany)

Focke-Wulf FW 190A

The FW 190 was Germany's best fighter of World War II, and resulted from the belief of designer Kurt Tank that careful streamlining could produce a radial-engined fighter with performance equal to that of an inline-engined type without the extra complexity and weight of the latter's water-cooling system. The first of three prototypes flew in June 1939, and an extensive test programme was required to develop the air cooling system and evaluate short- and long-span wings, the latter's additional 1.0 m (3 ft 3.7 in) of span and greater area reducing performance but boosting both agility and climb rate. This wing was selected for the FW 190A

production type in a programme that saw the building of about 19,500 FW 190s. The FW 190A was powered by the BMW 801 radial, and was developed in variants up to the Fw 190A-8 with a host of subvariants optimized for the clear- or all-weather interception, ground-attack, torpedo attack and tactical reconnaissance roles, together with an immensely diverse armament.

The FW 190B series was used to develop high-altitude capability with longer-span wings and a pressurized cockpit, and then pioneered the 1304-kW (1,750-hp) Daimler-Benz DB 603 inline engine. The FW 190C was another high-altitude development

model with the DB 603 engine and a turbocharger. The next operational model was the Fw 190D, which was developed in role-optimized variants between FW 190D-9 and FW 190D-13 with the 1324-kW (1,776-hp) Junkers Jumo 213 inline and an annular radiator in a lengthened fuselage. The FW 190E was a proposed reconnaissance fighter, and the FW 190F series, which preceded the FW 190D model, was a specialized ground-attack type based

on the radial-engined FW 190A-4. Finally in the main sequence came the FW 190G series of radial-engined fighter-bombers evolved from the FW 190A-5. An ultra-high-altitude derivative with longer-span wings was developed as the Jumo 213-engined Ta 152, but the only operational variant was the Ta 152H.

FOCKE-WULF FW 190 A-8
Role: Fighter
Crew/Accommodation: One
Power Plant: 1,600 hp BMW 801C-1 air-cooled radial
Dimensions: Span 10.5 m (34.45 ft); length 8.84 m (29 ft); wing area 18.3 m² (196.98 sq ft)
Weights: Empty 3,170 kg (7,000 lb); MTOW 4,900 kg (10,805 lb)
Performance: Maximum speed 654 km/h (408 mph) at 6,000 m (19,686 ft); operational ceiling 11,400 m (37,403 ft); range 805 km (500 miles)
Load: For 20 mm cannon and two 13 mm machine guns, plus up to 1,000 kg (2,205 lb) of bombs

Focke-Wulf FW 190

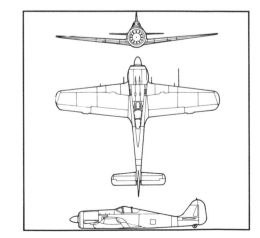

Focke-Wulf FW 190A

LOCKHEED P-38 LIGHTNING (United States)

P-38J Lightning

The Lightning was one was the more important fighters of World War II and, though it was not as nimble as a machine as single-engined types, found its métier in the long-range role with heavy armament and high performance. The machine resulted from a 1937 specification issued by the U.S. Army Air Corps for a high-performance fighter providing such speed, climb rate and range that a single-engined aircraft was virtually out of the question. Having opted for the twin-engined configuration, the design team then chose an unconventional layout with a central nacelle and twin booms extending as rearward extensions of the engine nacelle to accommodate the turbochargers and support the wide-span tailplane and oval vertical surfaces.

The XP-38 prototype flew in January 1939 with 716-kW (960-hp) Allison V-1710-11/15 engines driving opposite-rotating propellers. Development was protracted, and the first of 30 P-38s, with V-1710-27/29 engines, did not enter service until late 1941. Production totalled 10,037 in variants that included 36 P-36Ds with a revised tail unit and self-sealing fuel tanks, 210 P-38Es with the nose armament revised from one 37-mm cannon and four 12.7-mm (0.5-in) machine guns to one 20-mm cannon and four machine guns, 527 P-38Fs for tropical service with V-1710 49/53 engines, 1,082 F-38Gs with V-1710-55/55 engines and provision for 907-kg (2,000-lb) of underwing stores, 601 P-38Gs with 1062-kW (1,425-hp) V-1710-89/91s and greater underwing stores load, 2,970 P-38Js with an improved engine installation and greater fuel capacity, 3,810 P-38Ls with 1193-kW (1,600-hp) V-1710-111/113s, provision for underwing rockets and, in some aircraft, a revised nose accommodating radar or a bomb-aimer for use as a bomber leader, the P-38M conversions of P-38L as two-seat night fighters, and the F-4 and F-5 conversions.

LOCKHEED P-38L LIGHTNING

Role: Long-range fighter bomber
Crew/Accommodation: One
Power Plant: Two 1,475 hp Allison V-1710-111 water-cooled inlines
Dimensions: Span 15.85 m (52 ft); length 11.53 m (37.83 ft); wing area 30.47 m² (327 sq ft)
Weights: Empty 5,806 kg (12,800 lb); MTOW 9,798 kg (21,600 lb)
Performance: Maximum speed 666 km/h (414 mph) at 7,620 m (25,000 ft); operational ceiling 13,410 m (44,000 ft); range 725 km (450 miles) with 1,451 kg (3,200 lb) of bombs
Load: One 20 mm cannon and four .5 inch machine guns, plus up to 1,451 kg (3,200 lb) of bombs

Lockheed P-38J Lightning

Lockheed P-38L Lightning

MITSUBISHI A6M REISEN 'ZEKE' (Japan)

A6M5 Reisen 'Zeke'

The A6M Reisen (Zero Fighter) will rightly remain Japan's best known aircraft of World War II, and was in its early days, without doubt, the finest carrierborne fighter anywhere in the world. The A6M was the first naval fighter able to deal on equal terms with the best of land-based fighters, and was notable for its heavy firepower combined with good performance, great range and considerable agility. This combination could only be achieved with a lightweight and virtually unprotected airframe. Thus from 1943 the Zero

could not be developed effectively to maintain it as a competitive fighter.

The A6M was planned to an Imperial Japanese Navy Air Force requirement for a successor to the Mitsubishi A5M, a low-wing fighter with an open cockpit and fixed landing gear. The first of two A6M1 prototypes flew in April 1939 with a 582-kW (780-hp) Mitsubishi Mk2 Zuisei radial. The new fighter was a cantilever low-wing monoplane with retractable tailwheel landing gear, an enclosed cockpit and powerful armament. Performance and agility

were generally excellent, but the type was somewhat slower than anticipated. The sole A6M2 prototype therefore introduced the 690-kW (925-hp) Nakajima NK1C Sakae radial, and this was retained for the first series-built A6M2 aircraft that entered service with the designation Navy Type 0 Carrier Fighter Model 11. Production of the series amounted to 11,283 aircraft to the end of World War II, and major variants after the A6M2 were the A6M3 with the 843-kW (1,130-hp) Sakae 21 and clipped wingtips, the A6M5 with improved

armament and armour in three subvariants, the A6M6 with the Sakae 31, and the A6M7 dive-bomber and fighter. There were also a number of experimental and development models as well as the A6M2-N floatplane fighter built by Nakajima. The principal Allied reporting name for the type was 'Zeke'.

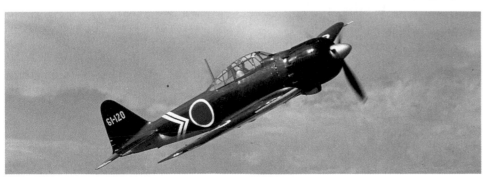

A Mitsubishi A6M5 Reisen

MITSUBISHI A6M5 'ZEKE'
Role: Naval carrierborne fighter
Crew/Accommodation: One
Power Plant: One 1,130 hp Nakajima Sakae 21 air-cooled radial
Dimensions: Span 11 m (36.09 ft); length 9.09 m (29.82 ft); wing area 21.3 m² (229.3 sq ft)
Weights: Empty 1,894 kg (4,176 lb) MTOW 2,952 kg (6,508 lb)
Performance: Maximum speed 565 km/h (351 mph) at 6,000 m (19,685 ft); operational ceiling 11,740 m (38,517 ft); range 1,570 km (976 miles)
Load: Two 20 mm cannon and two 7.7 mm machine guns

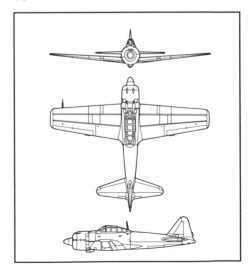

Mitsubishi A6M3 32 Reisen

37

MIKOYAN-GUREVICH MiG-1 and MiG-3 (U.S.S.R.)

MiG-3

To design the new interceptor fighter requested by the Soviet Air Force in 1938, Artem Mikoyan and Mikhail Gurevich started a collaboration that led eventually to a succession of world-famous fighters. The two men's first effort was not so successful. As the starting point for the new interceptor, the MiG team produced I-65 and I-61 design concepts, the latter in variants with the Mikulin AM-35A and AM-37 inlines. The I-61 was deemed superior and ordered in the form of three I-200 prototypes.

The first of these flew in April 1940, and on the power of the AM-35A the type proved to have the excellent speed of 630 km/h (391 mph), making it the world's fastest interceptor of the period. The type was ordered into production as the MiG-1 with an open cockpit or a side-hinged canopy, and an armament of one 12.7-mm (0.5-in) and two 7.62-mm (0.3-in) machine guns. But range and longitudinal stability were both minimal, and structural integrity was inadequate after battle damage had been suffered, so only 100 were delivered before the MiG-1 was superseded by the strengthened and aerodynamically refined MiG-3. This had a rearward-sliding canopy, increased dihedral on the outer wing panels, greater fuel capacity, better armour protection and provision for weightier armament in the form of 200-kg (440-lb) of bombs or six 82-mm (3.2-in) rockets carried under the wings. Some 3,322 such aircraft were built, but these saw only limited use; the MiG-3 performed well at altitudes over 5000 m (16,405 ft), but most air combats with the generally better flown German fighters of the period took place at the low and medium altitudes below this height.

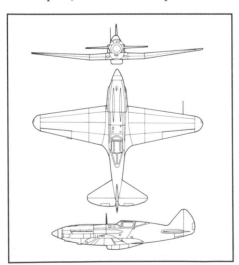

Mikoyan-Gurevich MiG-3

MIKOYAN-GUREVICH MiG-3
Role: Fighter
Crew/Accommodation: One
Power Plant: One 1,350 hp Mikulin AM-35A water-cooled inline
Dimensions: Span 10.3 m (33.79 ft); length 8.15 m (26.74 ft); wing area 17.44 m² (187.7 sq ft)
Weights: Empty 2,595 kg (5,720 lb); MTOW 3,285 kg (7,242 lb)
Performance: Maximum speed 640 km/h (398 mph) at 7,000 m (22,965 ft); operational ceiling 12,000 m (39,370 ft) range 820 km/h (510 miles) with full warload
Load: Three 12.7 mm machine guns, plus up to 200 kg (441 lb) of bombs or rockets

Mikoyan-Gurevich MiG-3

NORTH AMERICAN P-51 MUSTANG (United States)

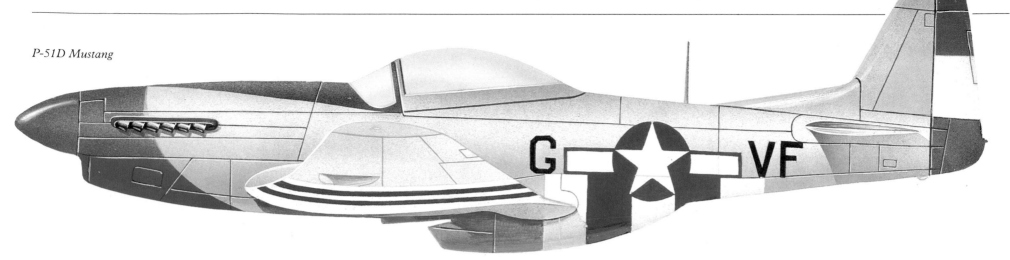

P-51D Mustang

The Mustang was perhaps the greatest fighter of World War II in terms of all-round performance and capability, and resulted from a British requirement of April 1940 that stipulated a first flight within 120 days of contract signature. The NA-73X flew in October of the same year with an 820-kW (1,100-hp) Allison V-1710-F3R inline. Mustang production totalled 15,469, and the first variant was the Mustang Mk I reconnaissance fighter with an armament of four 12.7-mm (0.5-in) machine-guns; two of these 620 aircraft were evaluated by the U.S. Army Air Corps with the designation XP-51. The next variants were the 93 Mustang Mk IAs and 57 cquivalent P-51s with four 20-mm cannon, and the 50 longer-range Mustang Mk IIs and 250 equivalent P-51As with more power and four machine-guns. U.S. Army offshoots were the F-6 and F-6A reconnaissance aircraft and the A-36A Apache dive-bomber and ground-attack aircraft.

Tactical capability was hampered by the V-1710 engine, so the basic airframe was revised to take the Rolls-Royce Merlin built under licence in the United States by Packard as the V-1650. Production versions were the 910 Mustang Mk IIIs with four machine-guns and the equivalent P-51B and P-51C, respectively 1,988 and 1,750 aircraft with original and bubble canopies; there were also F-6C reconnaissance aircraft. The classic and most extensively built variant was the P-51D (7l,966, of which 875 became British Mustang Mk IVs) with a cutdown rear fuselage, a bubble canopy, six machine-guns, greater power and more fuel; the F-6D was the reconnaissance version. The P-51D had the range to escort U.S. bombers on deep raids, and was the decisive fighter of the second half of World War II.

Later variants expanded on the theme of the P-51D: the 555 P-51Hs were of a lightened version, the 1,337 P-51Ks were of a similarly lightened variant with an Aeroproducts propeller, and the F-6K was the reconnaissance conversion of the P-51K. The type was also built under licence in Australia with designations running from Mustang Mk 20 to Mustang Mk 24.

North American P-51D Mustang

NORTH AMERICAN P-51D MUSTANG
Role: Day fighter
Crew/Accommodation: One
Power Plant: One 1,450 hp Packard/Rolls Royce Merlin V-1650-7 water-cooled inline
Dimensions: Span 11.28 m (37 ft); length 9.83 m (32.25 ft); wing area 21.83 m² (235 sq ft)
Weights: Empty 3,466 kg (7,635 lb); MTOW 5,493 kg (12,100 lb)
Performance: Maximum speed 703 km/h (437 mph) at 7,625 m (25,000 ft); operational ceiling 12,192 m (40,000 ft); range 2,655 km (1,650 miles) with maximum fuel
Load: Six .5 inch machine guns, plus up to 907 kg (2,000 lb) of externally carried bombs or fuel tanks

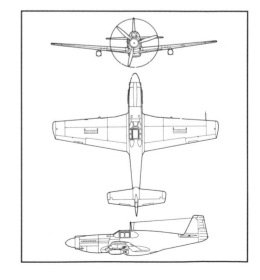

North American A-36A Apache

VOUGHT F4U CORSAIR (United States)

A-7P Corsair II

One of several fighters with a realistic claim to having been the best fighter of World War II, the Corsair was certainly the war's best fighter-bomber and a truly distinguished type in this exacting role with cannon, bombs and rockets. The type originated as the V.166A design in response to a U.S. Navy requirement of 1938 for a high-performance carrierborne fighter. The

design team produced the smallest possible airframe round the most powerful engine available, the 1491-kW (2,000-hp) Pratt & Whitney XR-2800 Double Wasp radial. This engine required a large-diameter propeller, and to provide this with adequate ground clearance without recourse to stalky main landing gear legs, the design team opted for inverted gull wings that allowed short main gear legs and also helped to keep the type's height as low as possible with the wings folded.

The V.166B prototype first flew in May 1940 as the XF4U-1, and after a troubled development in which the U.S. Navy refused to allow carrierborne operations until after the British had achieved these on their smaller carriers, the type entered service as the F4U-1. Total production was 12,571 up to the early 1950s, and the main variants were the baseline F4U-1 (758 aircraft), the F4U-1A (2,066) with a frameless canopy, the F4U-1C (200) with four 20-mm cannon in place of the wing

machine-guns, the F4U-1D (1,375) fighter-bomber, the F4U-1P photo-reconnaissance conversion of the F4U-1, the FG-1 built by Goodyear in three subvariants (1,704 FG-1s, 2,302 FG-1Ds and FG-1E night fighters in the FG-1 total), the F3A built by Brewster in two subvariants (735 F3A-1s and F3A-1Ds), the F4U-4 (2,351) with the 1827-kW (2,450-hp) R-2800-18W(C), a few of the F25 Goodyear version of the F4U-4, and several F4U-5, F4U-7 and AU-1 post-war models.

Vought F4U-1D Corsair

VOUGHT F4U-1D CORSAIR
Role: Naval carrierborne fighter bomber
Crew/Accommodation: One
Power Plant: One 2,000 hp Pratt & Whitney R-2800-8 Double Wasp air-cooled radial
Dimensions: Span 12.50 m (41 ft); length 10.16 m (33.33 ft); wing area 29.17 m² (314 sq ft)
Weights: Empty 4,074 kg (8,982 lb); MTOW 6,350 kg (14,000 lb)
Performance: Maximum speed 578 km/h (359 mph) at sea level; operating ceiling 11,247 m (36,900 ft); range 1,633 km (1,015 miles)
Load: Six .5 inch machine guns plus up to 907 kg (2,000 lb) of bombs

A Vought AU-1 Corsair with the markings of the US Marine Corps

FAIREY FIREFLY (United Kingdom)

Firefly AS.Mk 6

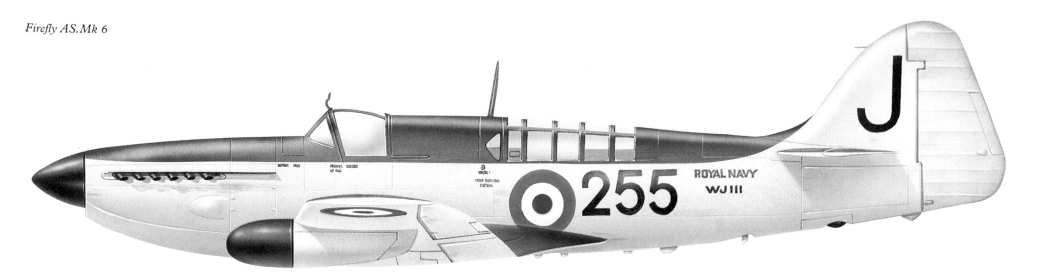

Designed to a requirement for a carrierborne two-seat reconnaissance fighter and first flown in December 1941 as the first of four prototypes powered by the 1290-kW (1,730-hp) Rolls-Royce Griffon IIB inline engine, the Firefly was one of the Royal Navy's most successful warplanes of the 1940s. The type had an all-metal construction, low-set cantilever wings, retractable tailwheel landing gear, and naval features like folding wings and an arrester hook.

The Firefly Mk I initial production series featured wings spanning 13.55 m (44 ft 6 in) and the 1484-kW (1,990-hp) Rolls-Royce Griffon XII with a chin radiator, and was produced in F.Mk I fighter, FR.Mk I fighter reconnaissance, NF.Mk I night-fighter and T.Mk I trainer versions to the extent of 937 aircraft. The 37 Firefly NF.Mk II night fighters had a longer nose and different radar, but were soon converted to Mk I standard.

Post-war conversions of the Mk I were the Firefly T.Mk 1 pilot trainer, T.Mk 2 operational trainer, and T.Mk 3 anti-submarine warfare trainer. The Firefly Mk IV switched to the 1566-kW (2,100-hp) Griffon 61 with root radiators in wings spanning 12.55 m (41 ft 2 in), and was produced in F.Mk IV and FR.Mk 4 versions. The Firefly Mk 5 introduced power-folding wings, and was produced in FR.Mk 5, NF.Mk 5, T.Mk 5 and anti-submarine AS.Mk 5 versions. The AS.Mk 6 was identical to the AS.Mk 5 other than in its use of British rather than American sonobuoys. The last production model, which raised the overall construction total to 1,623 aircraft, was the Firefly AS.Mk 7, which had the original long-span wing and a 1678-kW (2,250-hp) Griffon 59 with a chin radiator. Surplus Fireflies were also converted as remotely controlled target drones for the British surface-to-air missile programme.

The Fairey Firefly FR.Mk 5 was a two-seat reconnaissance fighter

FAIREY FIREFLY FR. Mk 5
Role: Fighter reconnaissance
Crew/Accommodation: Two
Power Plant: One 2,250 hp Rolls-Royce Griffon 74 water-cooled inline
Dimensions: Span 12.55 m (41.17 ft); length 11.56 m (37.91 ft); wing area 30.65 m² (330 sq ft)
Weights: Empty 4,389 kg (9,674 lb); MTOW 6,114 kg (13,479 lb)
Performance: Maximum speed 618 km/h (386 mph) at 4,270 m (14,000 ft); operational ceiling 8,660m (28,400 ft); range 2,090 km (1,300 miles) with long-range tankage
Load: Four 20 mm cannon, plus up to 454 kg (1,000 lb) of externally underslung bombs

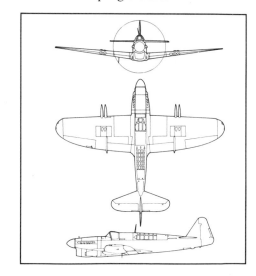

Fairey Firefly F.Mk I

41

REPUBLIC P-47 THUNDERBOLT (United States)

P-47D Thunderbolt

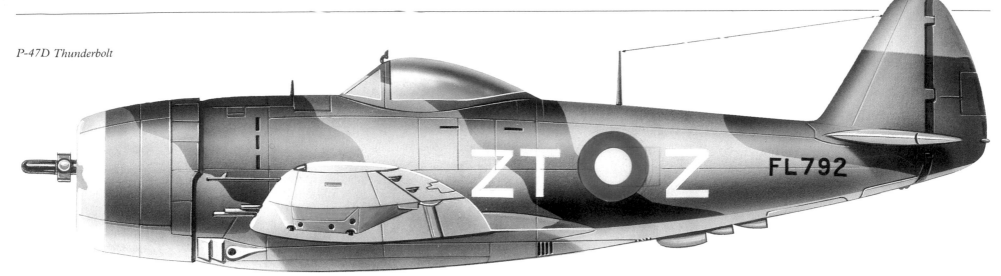

The Thunderbolt was one of a trio of superb American fighters to see extensive service in World War II. The massive fuselage of this heavyweight fighter was dictated by the use of a large turbocharger, which was located in the rear fuselage for balance reasons and therefore had to be connected to the engine by extensive lengths of wide-diameter ducting. The type was clearly related

to Republic's early portly-fuselage fighters, the P-35 and P-43 Lancer, but was marked by very high performance, high firepower and great structural strength.

The XP-47B prototype flew in May 1941 with the 1380-kW (1,850-hp) XR-2800 radial, later revised to develop 1491 kW (2,000 hp). This formed the basis of the 171 P-47B production aircraft with the R-2800-21 radial, and the 602 P-47Cs with a longer forward fuselage for the same engine or, in later examples, the 1715-kW (2,300-hp) R-2800-59 radial; the type also featured provision for a drop

tank or bombs. The P-47D was the main production model, 12,602 being built with the 1715-kW (2,300 hp) R-2800-21W or 1890-kW (2,535-hp) R-2800-59W water-injected radials, as well as a greater load of external stores that could include 1134-kg (2,500-lb) of bombs or ten 127-mm (5-in) rockets in the fighter-bomber role that became an increasingly important part of the Thunderbolt's repertoire. Early aircraft had the original 'razorback' canopy/rear fuselage, but later machines introduced a 360° vision

bubble canopy and a cutdown rear fuselage. P-47G was the designation given to 354 Wright-built P-47Ds. and the only other production models were the 130 P-47M 'sprinters' with the 2088-kW (2,800-hp) R-2800-57(C) radial and the 1,816 P-47N long-range aircraft with a strengthened and longer wing plus the 2088-kW (2,800-hp) R-2800-77 radial. The Thunderbolt was never an effective close-in fighter, but excelled in the high-speed dive-and-zoom attacks useful in long-range escort.

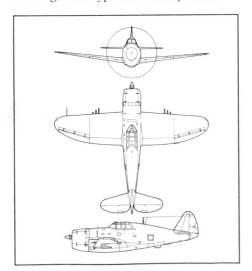

Republic P-47C Thunderbolt

REPUBLIC P-47C THUNDERBOLT
Role: Fighter
Crew/Accommodation: One
Power Plant: One 2,000 hp Pratt & Whitney R-2800-21 Double Wasp air-cooled radial
Dimensions: Span 12.42 m (40.75 ft); length 10.99 m (36,08 ft); wing area 27.87 m² (300 sq ft)
Weights: Empty 4,491 kg (9,900 lb); MTOW 6,770 kg (14,925 lb)
Performance: Maximum speed 697 km/h (433 mph) at 9,144 m (30,000 ft); operational ceiling 12,802 m (42,000 ft); range 722 km (480 miles) with a 227 kg (500 lb) bomb
Load: Eight .5 inch machine guns, plus up to 227 kg (500 lb) of bombs

The Republic P-47D Thunderbolt

GRUMMAN F6F HELLCAT (United States)

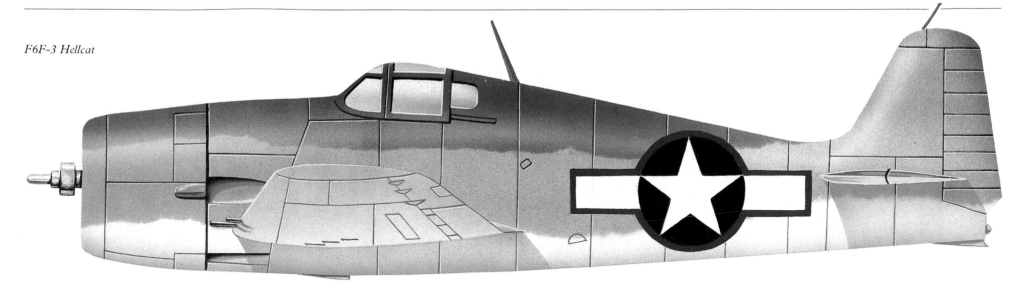

F6F-3 Hellcat

The Hellcat was the logical successor to the Wildcat with more size and power in a generally similar airframe with a low- rather than mid-set wing. A number of operational improvements suggested by Wildcat experience were incorporated in the basic design, and after evaluating this, the U.S. Navy contracted in June 1941 for a total of four XF6F prototypes. These were built with different Wright and Pratt & Whitney engine installations (normally aspirated and turbocharged R-2600 Cyclone and R-2800 Double Wasp units respectively). In June 1942, the

XF6F-1 became the first of these to fly, and the type selected for production was the XF6F-3 powered by the 1491-kW (2,000-hp) R-2800-10 Double Wasp with a two-stage turbocharger. This model entered production as the F6F-3 and reached squadrons in January 1944; the Fleet Air Arm designated the type Gannet Mk I, but later changed the name to Hellcat Mk I. Production lasted to mid-1944, and amounted to 4,423 aircraft including 18 F6F-3E and 205 F6F-3N night fighters with different radar equipments in pods under their starboard wings.

That the Hellcat was in all significant respects 'right' is attested by the relatively few variants emanating from a large production run that saw the delivery of 12,275 aircraft in all. From early 1944, production switched to the F6F-5 (Hellcat Mk II) with aerodynamic refinements including a revised cowling, new ailerons, a strengthened tail unit, and the R-2800-10W radial the suffix of which indicated the water injection system that produced a 10 per cent power boost for take-off and combat. These 6,436 aircraft also

featured provision for underwing bombs or rockets. There were also 1,189 examples of the F6F-5N (Hellcat NF.Mk II) night fighter, and some F6F-5 and F6F-5N fighters were also converted as F6F-5P photo-reconnaissance aircraft. Hellcat pilots claimed 4,947 aircraft shot down in combat, more than 75 per cent of all 'kills' attributed to U.S. Navy pilots in World War II.

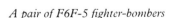

A pair of F6F-5 fighter-bombers

GRUMMAN F6F-5 HELLCAT
Role: Naval carrierborne fighter
Crew/Accommodation: One
Power Plant: One 2,000 hp Pratt & Whitney R-2800-10W Double Wasp air-cooled radial
Dimensions: Span 13.06 m (42.83 ft); length 10.31 m (33.83 ft); wing area 31.03 m² (334 sq ft)
Weights: Empty 4,100 kg (9,060 lb); MTOW 5,714 kg (12,598 lb)
Performance: Maximum speed 612 km/h (380 mph) at 7,132 m (23,400 ft); operational ceiling 11,369 m (37,300 ft); range 1,521 km (945 miles)
Load: Two 20 mm cannon and four .5 inch machine guns, plus up to 975 kg (2,150 lb) of weapons, including one torpedo

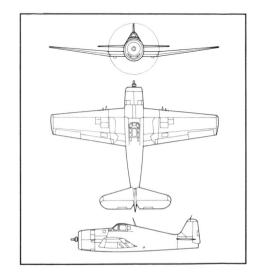

Grumman F6F-3 Hellcat

43

MACCHI MC.200 to MC.205 Series (Italy)

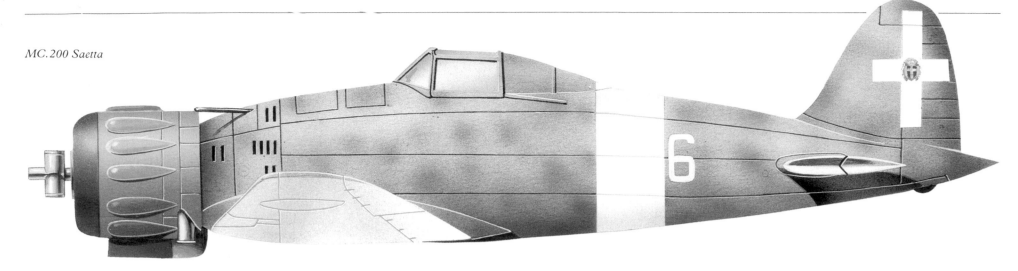

MC.200 Saetta

In 1936 the Italian Air Force belatedly realized that the day of the biplane fighter was effectively over, and requested the development of a 'modern' monoplane fighter with stressed-skin metal construction, a low-set cantilever monoplane wing, an enclosed cockpit and retractable landing gear. Macchi's response was the MC.200 Saetta (lightning) that first flew in December 1937 with the

649-kW (870-hp) Fiat A.74 RC 38 radial engine. The type was declared superior to its competitors during 1938 and ordered into production to a total of 1,153 aircraft in variants that 'progressed' from an enclosed to an open and eventually a semi-enclosed cockpit.

The MC.200 was a beautiful aircraft to fly, but clearly lacked the performance to deal with the higher-performance British fighters. There was no Italian inline engine that could offer the required performance, so the MC.202 Folgore (Thunderbolt) that flew in August 1940 with an enclosed

cockpit used an imported Daimler-Benz DB 601A engine. About 1,500 production aircraft followed, initially with imported engines but later with licence-built Alfa-Romeo RA.100 RC 41-I Monsone engines rated at 876-kW (1,175-hp). The MC.205V Veltro (Greyhound) was a development of the MC.202 with the 1100-kW (1,475-hp) DB 605A engine and considerably heavier armament. The

MC.205 was first flown in April 1942 but production had then to await availability of the licensed DB 605A, the RA.1050 RC 58 Tifone, so deliveries started only in mid-1943. Production amounted to 252, and most of these aircraft served with the fascist republic established in northern Italy after the effective division of Italy by the September 1943 armistice with the Allies.

MACCHI MC.205V VELTRO Series II
Role: Fighter
Crew/Accommodation: One
Power Plant: One 1,475 hp Fiat-built Daimler-Benz DB605A water-cooled inline
Dimensions: Span 10.58 m (34.71 ft); length 8.85 m (29.04 ft); wing area 16.8 m² (180.8 sq ft)
Weights: Empty 2,581 kg (5,690 lb); MTOW 3,224 kg (7,108 lb)
Performance: Maximum speed 642 km/h (399 mph) at 7,200 m (2,620 ft); operational ceiling 11,000 m (36,090 ft); range 950 km (590 miles)
Load: Two 200 mm cannon, plus up to 320 kg (706 lb) of bombs

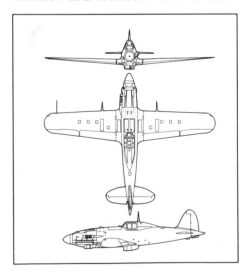

Macchi Mc.205V Veltro

The Macchi MC.205V Veltro

YAKOVLEV Yak-9 (U.S.S.R.)

Yak-9D

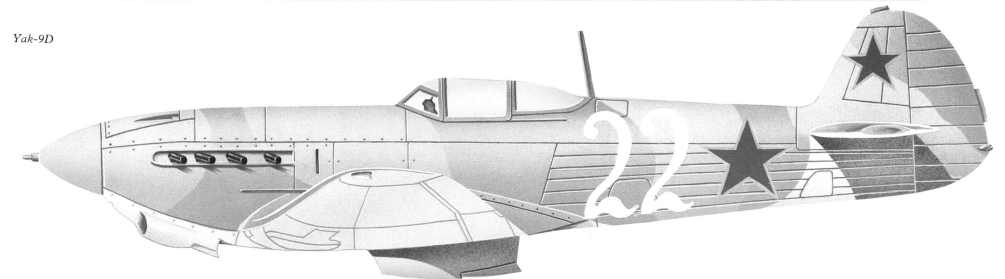

The Yak-9 was one of the finest fighters of World War II, and was the most prolific culmination of the evolutionary design philosophy that started with the Yak-1. The Yak-9 entered combat during the Battle of Stalingrad late in 1942, and was a development of the Yak-7DI that was notable for its mixed wood and metal primary structure.

Production lasted to 1946 and totalled 16,769 aircraft in several important and some lesser variants. These included the original Yak-9 with the 969-kW (1,300-hp) Klimov VK-105PF-1 or 1014-kW (1,360-hp) VK-105PF-3 inline engine plus an armament of one 20-mm cannon and one or two 12.7-mm (0.5-in) machine guns, the Yak-9M with revised armament, the Yak-9D long-range escort fighter with the VK-105PF-3 engine and greater fuel capacity, the Yak-9T anti-tank variant with one 37- or 45-mm cannon and provision for anti-tank bomblets under the wings, the Yak-9K heavy anti-tank fighter with a 45-mm cannon in the nose, the Yak-9B high-speed light bomber with provision for four 100-kg (220-lb) bombs carried internally as part of a 600-kg (1,323-lb) total internal and external warload, the Yak-9MPVO night fighter carrying searchlights for the illumination of its quarry, the Yak-9DD very long-range escort fighter based on the Yak-9D but fitted for drop tanks, the Yak-9U conversion trainer in three subvariants, the YAK-9P post-war interceptor with the 1230-kW (1,650-hp) Klimov VK-107A inline and two fuselage-mounted 20-mm cannon, and the Yak-9R reconnaissance aircraft.

Yakovlev Yak-9DD long-range fighters

YAKOVLEV Yak-9D
Role: Fighter
Crew/Accommodation: One
Power Plant: One 1,360 hp Klimov VK-105PF-3
Dimensions: Span 9.74 m (32.03 ft); length 8.55 m (28.05 ft); wing area 17.1 m² (184.05 sq ft)
Weights: Empty 2,770 kg (6,107 lb); MTOW 3,080 kg (6,790 lb)
Performance: Maximum speed 602 km/h (374 mph) at 2,000 m (6,560 ft); operational ceiling 10,600 m (34,775 ft); range 1,410 km (876 miles)
Load: One 20 mm cannon + one 12.7 mm machine gun

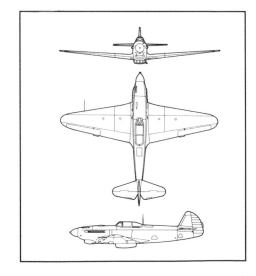

Yakovlev Yak-9D

DORNIER Do 335 PFEIL (Germany)

Do 335A Pfeil

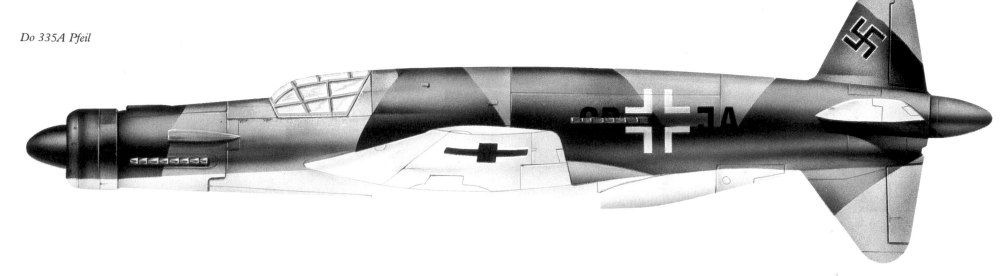

The unusual configuration of the Do 335 Pfeil (Arrow) was designed to allow the installation of two powerful engines in a minimum-drag layout that would also present no single-engined asymmetric thrust problems. Dr Claudius Dornier patented the concept in 1937, and the configuration was successfully evaluated in the Göppingen Gö 9 research aircraft during 1939. Dornier then developed the basic concept as a high-performance fighter, but the Do P.231 type was adopted by the Reichsluftfahrtministerium (German Air Ministry) as a high-speed bomber. Initial work had reached an advanced stage when the complete project was cancelled. There then emerged a German need for a high-performance interceptor, and the wheel turned full circle as Dornier was instructed to revive its design in this role.

The resulting aircraft was of all-metal construction, and in layout was a low-wing monoplane with sturdy retractable tricycle landing gear, cruciform tail surfaces, and two 1342-kW (1,800-hp) Daimler-Benz DB 603 inline engines each driving a three-blade propeller. One engine was mounted in the conventional nose position, and the other in the rear fuselage powering a propeller aft of the tail unit by means of an extension shaft. The first of 14 prototypes flew in September 1943. Considerable development flying was undertaken by these one- and two-seater models, and 10 Do 335A-O pre-production fighter-bombers were evaluated from the late summer of 1944. The first production model was the Do 335A-1, of which 11 were completed. None of these entered full-scale service, though some were allocated to a service test unit in the spring of 1945. The only other aircraft completed were two examples of the Do 335A-12 two-seat trainer. There were also many projected variants.

DORNIER Do 335A-O PFEIL
Role: Long range day fighter
Crew/Accommodation: One
Power Plant: Two 2,250 hp Daimler-Benz DB 603E/MW50 liquid-cooled inlines
Dimensions: Span 13.80 m (45.28 ft); length 13.85 m (45.44 ft); wing area 38.50 m² (414.41 sq ft)
Weights: Empty 7,400 kg (16,315 lb); MTOW 9,600 kg (21,160 lb)
Performance: Maximum speed 768 km/h (477 mph) at 6,890 m (21,000 ft); operational ceiling 11,400 m (37,400 ft); radius 1,397 km (868 miles) at military power
Load: One 30 mm and two 15 mm cannons, plus a 500 kg (1,103 lb) bomb

Dornier Do 335A-O Pfeil

Dornier Do 335 Pfeil

HAWKER TEMPEST (United Kingdom)

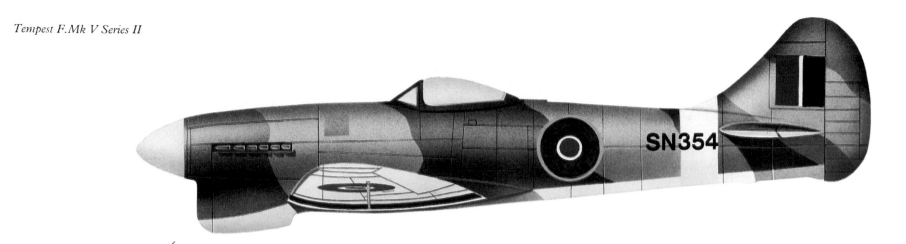

Tempest F.Mk V Series II

The failure of the Hawker Typhoon in its designed interceptor role left the British short of an advanced interceptor; in 1941 it was suggested the Typhoon be revised with a thinner, elliptical wing with low-drag radiators in the leading edges to replace the Typhoon's chin radiator. In November 1941 two prototypes were ordered with the Napier Sabre inline. Early in 1942, the type was renamed Tempest. The two original prototypes became the Tempest F.Mks I and V with the Sabre IV and II respectively, and another four prototypes were ordered as two Tempest F.Mk IIs with the 1879-kW (2,520-hp) Bristol Centaurus radial and two Tempest F.Mk IIIs with the Rolls-Royce Griffon IIB inline, the latter becoming Tempest F.Mk IVs when fitted with the Griffon 61.

Initial orders were placed for 400 Tempest F.Mk Is, and the first such fighter flew in February 1943. The engine suffered development problems, however, and the variant was abandoned. The first Tempest to fly had been the Tempest F.Mk V in September 1942, and an eventual 800 were built as 100 Tempest F.Mk V Series I and 700 Series II aircraft with long- and short-barrel cannon respectively, some later being converted as Tempest TT.Mk 5 target tugs. The Tempest Mk II materialized with the Centaurus V radial, and production for post-war service amounted to 136 F.Mk II fighters and 338 FB.Mk II fighter-bombers. The only other production model was the Tempest F.Mk VI, of which 142 were produced for tropical service with the 1745-kW (2,340-hp) Sabre V. Some of these were later adapted as Tempest TT.Mk 6s.

HAWKER TEMPEST Mk V
Role: Stike fighter
Crew/Accommodation: One
Power Plant: One 2,180 hp Napier Sabre IIA water-cooled inline
Dimensions: Span 12.49 m (41 ft); length 10.26 m (33.67 ft); wing area 28.05 m² (302 sq ft)
Weights: Empty 4,196 kg (9,250 lb); MTOW 6,187 kg (13,640 lb)
Performance: Maximum speed 700 km/h (435 mph) at 5,180 m (17,000 ft); operational ceiling 11,125 m (36,500 ft); range 1,191 km (740 miles) on internal fuel only
Load: Four 20 mm cannon, plus up to 907 kg (2,000 lb) of bombs or rockets

Tempest F.Mk V

Hawker Tempest F.Mk II

47

KAWANISHI N1K 'REX' and 'GEORGE' (Japan)

N1K2-1 'George'

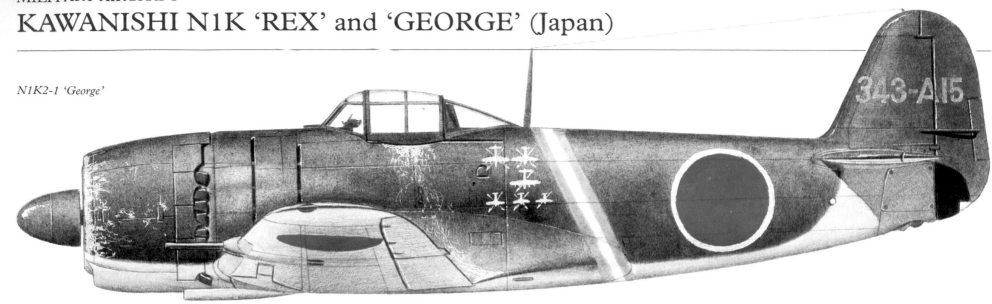

Designed from 1940 as a fighter able to protect and support amphibious landings, the N1K was schemed as a substantial seaplane with single main/ two stabilizing floats and a powerful engine driving contra-rotating propellers that would mitigate torque problems during take-off and landing. The first prototype flew in May 1942 with the 1089-kW (1,460-hp) Mitsubishi MK4D Kasei radial, but

problems with the contra-rotating propeller unit led to the use of a conventional propeller unit. The type began to enter service in 1943 as the N1K1 Kyofu (Mighty Wind), but the type's *raison d'être* had disappeared by this stage of the war and production was terminated with the 97th machine. The Allied reporting name for the N1K1 was 'Rex'.

The N1K2 with a more powerful engine remained only a project, but in 1942 the company began development of a landplane version as the N1K1-J Shiden (Violet Lightning) with

retractable tailwheel landing gear and the 1357-kW (1,820-hp) Nakajima NK9H Homare 11 radial. This suffered a number of teething problems, and its need for a large-diameter propeller dictated the design of telescoping main landing gear legs. The new type flew in prototype form during December 1942, but development difficulties delayed the type's service debut to early 1944. N1K1-J production totalled 1,007 in three subvariants known to the Allies

as the 'George'. Yet this had been planned as an interim version pending deliveries of the N1K2-J version with a low- rather than mid-set wing, a longer fuselage, a revised tail unit, and less complicated main landing gear units. Only 423 of this version were produced. The N1K3-J, N1K4-J and N1K5-J prototypes had a longer forward fuselage, the 1491-kW (2,000-hp) Homare 23 engine and the 1641-kW (2,200-hp) Mitsubishi MK9A radial engine respectively.

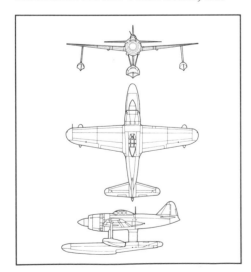

Kawanishi N1K1 'Rex'

KAWANISHI N1K1 'REX'
Role: Fighter floatplane
Crew/Accommodation: One
Power Plant: One 1,460 hp Mitsubishi Kasei 14 air-cooled radial
Dimensions: Span 12 m (39.37 ft); length 10.59 m (34.74 ft); wing area 23.5 m² (252.9 sq ft)
Weights: Empty 2,700 kg (5,952 lb); MTOW 3,712 kg (8,184 lb)
Performance: Maximum speed 482 km/h (300 mph) at 5,700 m (18,701 ft); operational ceiling 10,560 m (34,646 ft); range 1,690 km (1,050 miles) with full bombload
Load: Two 20 mm cannon, two 7.7 mm machine guns, plus up to 60 kg (132 lb) of bombs

The Kawanishi N1K2-J Shiden KAI.

de HAVILLAND D.H.103 HORNET (United Kingdom)

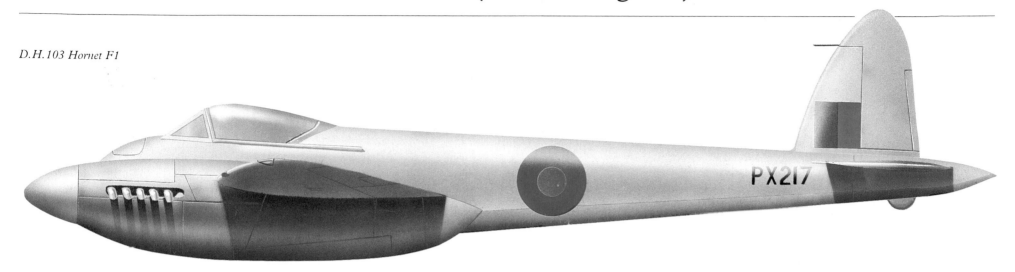

D.H.103 Hornet F1

The D.H.103 was designed to provide the British forces fighting the Japanese with a long-range fighter with the advantages of a twin-engined layout. The type was based on the aerodynamics of the Mosquito multi-role warplane, and so impressive were the estimated performance figures that a specification was written round the type in 1943. The D.H.103 retained the Mosquito's plywood/balsa/plywood structure for its single-seat fuselage, but featured new wood and metal wings. Work began in June 1943, and the first prototype flew in July 1944 with two Merlin 130/131 inline engines. Performance and handling were excellent, and initial deliveries were made in April 1945. This first model was the Hornet F.Mk 1, of which 60 were built, but it was too late for service in World War II.

The major variant of this land-based series was the Hornet F.Mk 3 with a dorsal fillet (retrofitted to earlier aircraft), greater internal fuel capacity, and provision for underwing loads of weapons or drop tanks. The last of 120 aircraft were delivered to Hornet FR.Mk 4 reconnaissance fighter standard with the rear fuselage fuel tank deleted to provide accommodation for a single camera. The basic design also appealed to the Fleet Air Arm, which ordered the navalized Sea Hornet series. Deliveries included 78 Sea Hornet F.Mk 20 fighters based on the F.Mk 3 and first flown in August 1946 for a final delivery in June 1951, 79 Sea Hornet NF.Mk 21 two-seat night fighters based on the F.Mk 20 but with radar in a revised nose, and 43 Sea Hornet PR.Mk 23 photo-reconnaissance aircraft based on the F.Mk 20 but with one night or two day cameras. The last Sea Hornets were retired in 1955.

Hornet F.Mk 3 of No.64 Squadron.

de HAVILLAND D.H.103 HORNET F.Mk 1
Role: Long range fighter
Crew/Accommodation: One
Power Plant: Two 2,070 hp Rolls-Royce Merlin 130/131 liquid-cooled inlines
Dimensions: Span 13.72 m (45.00 ft); length 11.18 m (36.66 ft); wing area 33.54 m² (361 sq ft)
Weights: Empty 5,671 kg (12,502) lb; MTOW 8,029 kg (17,700 lb)
Performance: Maximum speed 760 km/h (472 mph) at 6,706 m (22,000 ft); operational ceiling 11,430 m (37,500 ft); range 4,023 km (2,500 miles)
Load: Four 20 mm cannons

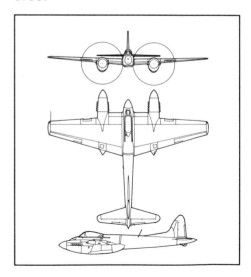

de Havilland Hornet F.Mk 3

HAWKER SEA FURY (United Kingdom)

Sea Fury FB.Mk 11

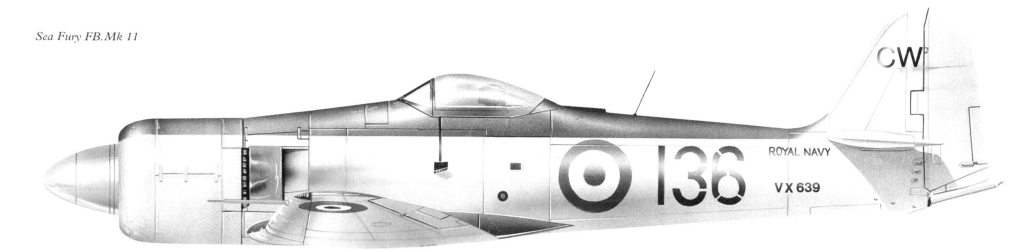

The origins of Hawker's second Fury fighter lay in a 1942 requirement for a smaller and lighter version of the Tempest, and was developed in parallel land-based and naval forms to 1943 specifications. Hawker was responsible for the overall design, with Boulton Paul allocated the task of converting the type for naval use. By December 1943, six prototypes had been ordered, one with the Bristol Centaurus XII radial, two with the Centaurus XXI radial, two with the Rolls-Royce Griffon inline, and one as a test airframe. The first to fly was a Centaurus XII-powered machine that took to the air in September 1944, followed in November by a Griffon-powered machine that was later re-engined with the Napier Sabre inline. Orders were placed for 200 land-based Fury and 100 carrierborne Sea Fury fighters, but the Fury order was cancelled at the end of World War II. The first Sea Fury flew in February 1945 with the Centaurus XII, and development continued after the war to produce the first fully navalized machine with folding wings and the Centaurus XV. This flew in October 1945, and paved the way for the Sea Fury F.Mk X, of which 50 were built.

The first type to enter widespread service was the Sea Fury FB.Mk 11 of which 615 were built including 31 and 35 for the Royal Australian and Royal Canadian Navies respectively. The Fleet Air Arm also took 60 Sea Fury T.Mk 20 trainers, of which 10 were later converted as target tugs for West Germany. Additional operators of new-build aircraft were the Netherlands with 22 Sea Fury F.Mk 50s and FB.Mk 50s, and Pakistan with 93 Sea Fury FB.Mk 60s and five T.Mk 61s. Other buyers were Burma (21 ex-British aircraft), Cuba (17 aircraft) and Iraq (60 aircraft).

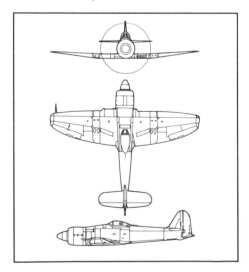

Hawker Sea Fury FB.Mk 11

HAWKER SEA FURY FB.Mk 11
Role: Carrierborne fighter bomber
Crew/Accommodation: One
Power Plant: One 2,480 hp Bristol Centaurus 18 air-cooled radial
Dimensions: Span 11.70 m (38.40 ft); length 10.57 m (34.67 ft); wing area 26.01 m² (280.00 sq ft)
Weights: Empty 4,191 kg (9,240 lb); MTOW 5,670 kg (12,500 lb)
Performance: Maximum speed 740 km/h (460 mph) at 5,486 m (18,000 ft); operational ceiling 10,912 m (35,800 ft); radius 1,127 km (700 miles) without external fuel tanks
Load: Four 20 mm cannons, plus up to 907 kg (2,000 lb) of bombs or twelve 3 inch rocket projectiles

The Hawker Sea Fury FB.Mk 11.

KAWASAKI Ki-61 HIEN and Ki-100 'TONY' (Japan)

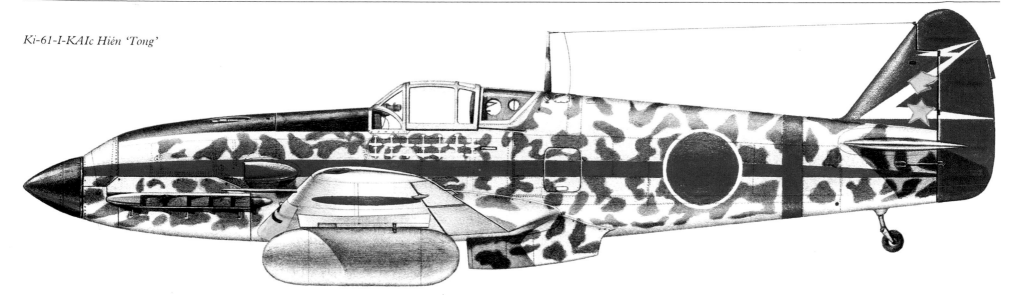

Ki-61-I-KAIc Hién 'Tong'

The Ki-61 Hien (Swallow) was the only inline-engined Japanese fighter to see substantial use in World War II, and was developed in parallel with the unsuccessful Ki-60 though using the same Kawasaki Ha-40 engine, a licence-built version of the Daimler-Benz DB 601A. The first Ki-61 prototype flew in December 1941. The Ki-61-I entered combat in April 1943 and soon acquired the Allied reporting name 'Tony'. By the time production ended in January 1945, 2,666 aircraft had been built in variants such as the Ki-61-I with two

7.7-mm (0.303-in) fuselage and two 12.7-mm (0.5-in) wing machine guns, the Ki-61-Ia with two 20-mm wing cannon, the Ki-61-Ib with 12.7-mm (0.5-in) fuselage machine guns, the Ki-61-Ic with a rationalized structure, and the Ki-61-Id with 30-mm wing cannon.

The Ki-61-II had a larger wing and the more powerful Ha-140 engine, but was so delayed in development that only 99 had been produced before United States Air Force bombing destroyed engine production capacity. Variants were the Ki-61-II KAI with

the Ki-61-I's wing, the Ki-61-IIa with the Ki-61-Ic's armament, and the Ki-61-IIb with four 20-mm wing cannon. With the Ha-140 engine unavailable for a comparatively large number of completed Ki-61-II airframes, the Japanese army ordered the type adapted to take the Mitsubishi Ha-112-II radial engine, the 1119-kW (1,500-hp) rating of which was identical to that of the Ha-140. The resulting Ki-100 first flew in 1945 and proved an outstanding interceptor, perhaps Japan's best fighter of World War II, also known to the Allies as 'Tony'. The army ordered completion

of the 272 Ki-61-II airframes as Ki-100-Ia fighters, while new production amounted to 99 Ki-100-Ib aircraft with the cut-down rear fuselage and bubble canopy developed for the proposed Ki-61-III fighter. The designation Ki-100-II was used for three prototypes with the Mitsubishi Ha-112-IIru turbocharged radial for improved high-altitude performance.

This is a Ki-61-I.

KAWASAKI KI-100-II 'TONY'
Role: Fighter
Crew/Accommodation: One
Power Plant: One 1,500 hp Mitsubishi Ha-112-II air-cooled radial
Dimensions: Span 12 m (39.37 ft); length 8.82 m (28.94 ft); wing area 20 m² (215.3 sq ft)
Weights: Empty 2,522 kg (5,567 lb); MTOW 3,495 kg (7,705 lb)
Performance: Maximum speed 590 km/h (367 mph) at 10,000 m (32,808 ft); operational ceiling 11,500 m (37,500 ft); range 1,800 km (1,118 miles)
Load: Two 20 mm cannon and two 12.7 mm machine guns

Kawasaki Ki-61 KAIc

MESSERSCHMITT Me 262 SCHWALBE (Germany)

Me 262A-1a Schwalbe

The Me 262 Schwalbe (Swallow) could have been the world's first operational jet fighter, but was enormously delayed by manoeuvrings within the German political and aircraft establishments; with its clean lines, tricycle landing gear, slightly swept wings and axial-flow turbojets it was certainly the most advanced fighter to see service in World War II.

Design work was launched in 1938 to meet a specification that called for a fighter powered by two of the new turbojet engines then under development by BMW, and eventually an order was placed for three prototypes powered by the 600-kg (1,323-lb) thrust BMW P-3302 engines. Work on the airframe proceeded more rapidly than development of the engine, so the Me 262 V1 first flew in April 1941 with a single nose-mounted Junkers Jumo 210G piston engine and retractable tailwheel landing gear, a type replaced by tricycle landing gear in later prototypes and all production aircraft.

The piston engine was later supplemented by two BMW 003 turbojets, but these proved so unreliable that they were replaced by 840-kg (1,852-lb) thrust Junkers 004As in a programme that required some redesign as the Junkers engines were larger and heavier than the BMW units. The five prototypes were followed by 23 pre-production Me 262A-0s before the Me 262A-1 entered service as the first production variant: the -1a had four 30-mm cannon and the -1b added 24 air-to-air unguided rockets. Total production was about 1,100 aircraft; later variants were the Me 262A-2 fighter-bomber, the Me 262A-5 reconnaissance fighter, the Me 262B-1a two-seat conversion trainer and the Me 262B-2 night fighter. By 1945, many variants were being considered or developed.

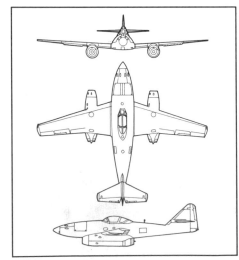

MA52 to come

MESSERSCHMITT Me 262A-1a SCHWALBE
Role: Fighter
Crew/Accommodation: One
Power Plant: Two 990 kgp (1,984 lb s.t.) Junkers Jumo-004B turbojets
Dimensions: Span 12.5 m (41.01 ft); length 10.605 m (34.79 ft); wing area 21.68 m² (233.3 sq ft)
Weights: Empty 4,000 kg (8,820 lb); MTOW 6,775 kg (14,938 lb)
Performance: Maximum speed 868 km/h (536 mph) at 7,000 m (22,800 ft) operational ceiling 11,000 m (36,080 ft); range 845 km (524 miles) at 6,000 mm (19,685 ft) cruise altitude
Load: Four 30 mm cannon

Me 262-1A fighters

de HAVILLAND D.H.100, 113 and 115 VAMPIRES (United Kingdom)

D.H. 115 Vampire T.Mk 11

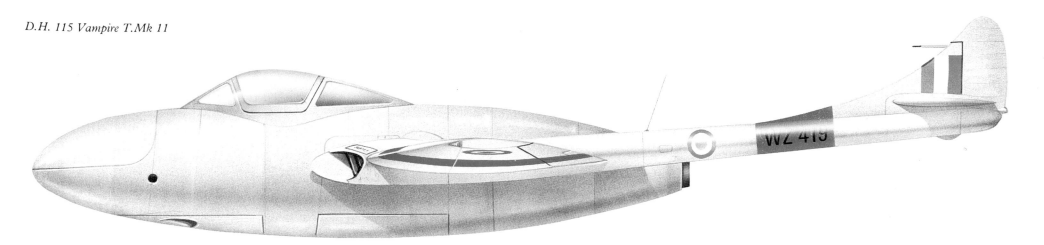

The Vampire, the second turbojet-powered British fighter, was too late for service in World War II. The type, known originally as the Spider Crab, was planned round a portly central nacelle and twin booms to allow the use of a short and therefore less inefficient jetpipe for the de Havilland Goblin engine, which was of the centrifugal-flow type and therefore of greater diameter than axial-flow types.

The first prototype flew in September 1943, a mere 16 months after the start of detail design.

The Vampire F.Mk 1 entered service in 1946 with the 1225-kg (2,700-lb) thrust de Havilland Goblin I turbojet, and was followed by the Vampire F.Mk 3 with provision for underwing stores and modifications to improve longitudinal stability. Next came the Vampire FB.Mk 5 fighter-bomber with a wing of reduced span but greater strength for the carriage of underwing stores, and finally in the single-seat stream the Vampire FB.Mk 9 for tropical service with a cockpit air conditioner. British variants on the Vampire FB.Mk 5 theme were the Sea Vampire FB.Mks 20 and 21 for carrierborne use, while export variants included the generally similar Vampire FB.Mk 6 for Switzerland and a number of Vampire FB.Mk 50 variants with Goblin and Rolls-Royce Nene engines, the latter featuring in the licence-built French version, the Sud-Est S.E.535 Mistral. A side-by-side two-seater for night fighting was also produced as the Vampire NF.Mk 10 (exported as the Vampire NF.Mk 54 to France), and a similar accommodation layout was retained in the Vampire T.Mk 11 and Sea Vampire T.Mk 22 trainers. Australia produced the trainer in Vampire T.Mks 33, 34 and 35 variants, and de Havilland exported the type as the Vampire T.Mk 5.

de Havilland Vampire

de HAVILLAND D.H.100 VAMPIRE FB Mk 5
Role: Strike fighter
Crew/Accommodation: One
Power Plant: One 1,420 kgp (3,100 lb s.t.) de Havilland Goblin 2 turbojet
Dimensions: Span 11.6 m (38 ft); length 9.37 m (30.75 ft); wing area 28.7 m² (266 sq ft)
Weights: Empty 3,310 kg (7,253 lb); MTOW 5,600 kg (12,290 lb)
Performance: Maximum speed 861 km/h (535 mph) at 5,791 m (19,000 ft); operational ceiling 12,192 m (40,000 ft); range 1,883 km (1,170 miles) with maximum fuel
Load: Four 20 mm cannon, plus up to 904 kg (2,000 lb) of ordnance

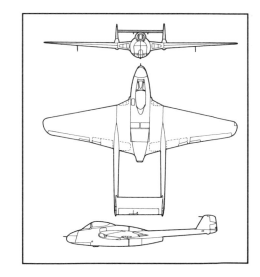

de Havilland Vampire FB.Mk 5

53

GLOSTER METEOR (United Kingdom)

Meteor N F.Mk 11

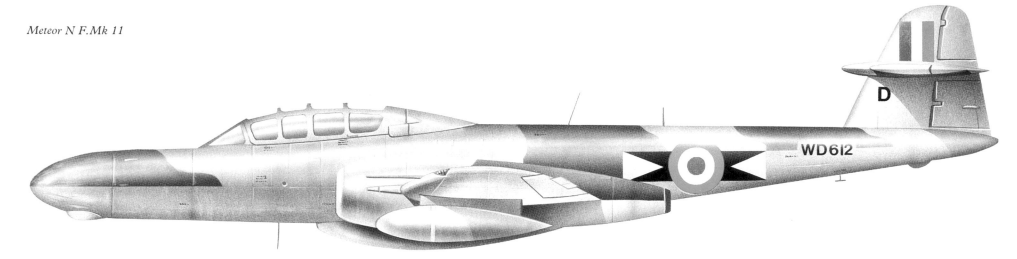

The Meteor was the only Allied jet fighter to see combat in World War II, and just pipped the Germans' Me 262 to the title of becoming the world's first operational jet aircraft. Given its experience with the E.28/39, the research type that had been the first British jet aircraft, Gloster was the logical choice to develop a jet fighter especially as this would leave 'fighter companies' such as Hawker and

Supermarine free to concentrate on their definitive piston-engined fighters. The G.41 design took shape comparatively quickly. The first of eight prototypes started taxiing trials in July 1942 with 454-kg (1,000-lb) thrust Rover W.2B engines, but it was March 1943 before the fifth machine became the first Meteor to fly, in this instance with 680-kg (1,500-lb) thrust de Havilland H.1 engines.

Trials with a number of engine types and variants slowed development of a production variant, but the 20 Meteor F.Mk Is finally entered service in July 1944 with 771-kg (1,700-lb) thrust Rolls-Royce

W.2B/23C Welland I turbojets. The Meteor remained in RAF service until the late 1950s with the Derwent turbojet that was introduced on the second production variant, the Meteor F.Mk III, of which 280 were built, in most cases with the 907-kg (2,000-lb) thrust Rolls-Royce W.2B/37 Derwent I.

The type underwent considerable development in the post-war period when 3,237 were built. The main streams were the Meteor F.Mks 4 and

8 single-seat fighters of which 657 and 1,183 were built with Derwent I and 1633-kg (3,600-lb) thrust Derwent 8s respectively, the Meteor FR.Mk 9 reconnaissance fighter of which 126 were built, the Meteor NF.Mks 11 to 14 radar-equipped night fighters, the Meteor PR.Mk 10 photo-reconnaissance type of which 58 were built, and the Meteor T.Mk 7 two-seat trainer of which 712 were built. Surplus aircraft were often converted into target tugs or target drones.

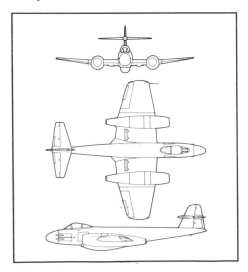

Gloster Meteor F.Mk 8

GLOSTER METEOR F. Mk 8
Role: Fighter
Crew/Accommodation: One
Power Plant: Two 1,723 kgp (3,800 lb s.t.) Rolls-Royce Derwent 9 turbojets
Dimensions: Span 11,33 m (37.16 ft); length 13.59 m (44.58 ft); wing area 32.5 m² (350 sq ft)
Weights: Empty 4,846 kg (10,684 lb); MTOW 7,121 kg (15,700 lb)
Performance: Maximum speed 962 km/h (598 mph) at 3,048 m (10,000 ft); operational ceiling 13,106 m (43,000 ft); endurance 1.2 hours with ventral and wing fuel tanks
Load: Four 20 mm cannon

This is a Gloster Meteor F.Mk 8 fighter

LOCKHEED F-80 SHOOTING STAR and T-33 (United States)

F-80C Shooting Star

The Shooting Star was the best Allied jet fighter to emerge from World War II, though the type was in fact just too late for combat use in that conflict. The design was launched in June 1943 on the basis of a British turbojet, the 1834-kg (2,460-1b) thrust de Havilland (Halford) H. 1B, and the first XP-80 prototype with this engine flew in January 1944 as a sleek, low-wing monoplane with tricycle landing gear and a 360° vision canopy. The two XP-80As switched to the 1746-kg (3,850-lb) thrust General Electric I-40 (later J33) engine, and this powered all subsequent models. The P-80A version began to enter service in January 1945, and just 45 had been delivered before the end of World War II. Production plans for 5,000 aircraft were then savagely cut, but the development of later versions with markedly improved capabilities meant that as many as 5,691 of the series were finally built.

The baseline fighter was redesignated in the F- (fighter) series after World War II, and variants were the 917 F-80As with the J33-GE-11 engine, the 240 improved F-80Bs with an ejector seat and provision for RATO, and the 749 F-80Cs with 2087- or 2449-kg (4,600- or 5,400-lb) thrust J33-GE-23 or -35 engines and provision for underwing rockets in the ground-attack role. The versatility of the design also resulted in 222 F-14 and later RF-80 photo-reconnaissance aircraft, 5,871 TF-80 (later T-33A) air force and TO-1/2 (later TV-1/2) navy flying trainers that were in numerical terms the most important types by far, 150 T2V SeaStar advanced naval flying trainers with the 2767-kg (6,100-lb) thrust J33-A-24 and a boundary-layer control system, many AT-33A weapons trainers for the export and defence aid programmes, and many other variants.

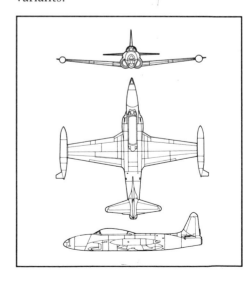

The P-80B version of the Lockheed Shooting Star

LOCKHEED F-80B SHOOTING STAR
Role: Day fighter
Crew/Accommodation: One
Power Plant: One 2,041 kgp (4,500 lb s.t.) Allison J33-A-21 turbojet
Dimensions: Span 11.81 m (38.75 ft); length 10.49 m (34.42 ft); wing area 22.07 m² (237.6 sq ft)
Weights: Empty 3,709 kg (8,176 lb); MTOW 7,257 kg (16,000 lb)
Performance: Maximum speed 929 km/h (577 mph) at 1,830 m (6,000 ft); operational ceiling 13,870 m (45,500 ft); range 1,270 km (790 miles) without drop tanks
Load: Six .5 inch machine guns

T-33A Shooting Star

55

REPUBLIC F-84 Family (United States)

F-84F Thunderflash

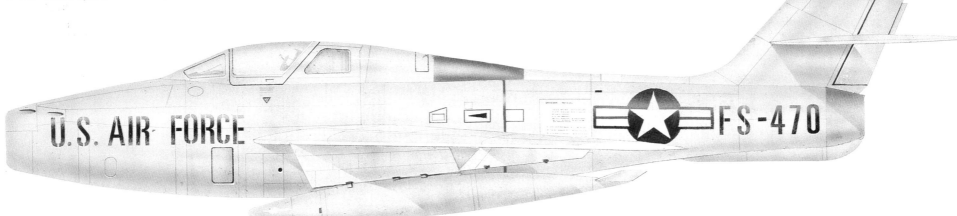

The Thunderjet was Republic's first jet-powered fighter, a straight-winged successor to the P-47 Thunderbolt that first flew in February 1946 as the first of three XP-84 prototypes with the 1701-kg (3,750-lb) thrust General Electric J35-GE-7 turbojet. The 25 YP-84A service trial aircraft switched to the 1814-kg (4,000-lb) thrust Allison J35-A-15, the type chosen for the 226 P-84B initial production aircraft. The 191 P-84C (later F-84C) aircraft had the similarly rated J35-A-13C but a revised electrical system, while the 154 F-84Ds had the 2268-kg (5,000-lb) thrust J35-A-17D engine, revised landing gear and thicker-skinned wings.

Korean War experience resulted in the F-84E, of which 843 were built with a lengthened fuselage, enlarged cockpit and improved systems. The F-84G was similar but powered by the 2540-kg (5,600-lb) thrust J35-A-29, and the 3,025 of this variant were able to deliver nuclear weapons in the tactical strike role. The basic design was then revised as the Thunderstreak to incorporate swept flying surfaces and the more powerful Wright J65 turbojet for significantly higher performance. Some 2,713 such F-84Fs were built, the first 375 with the J65-W-1 and the others with the more powerful 3275-kg (7,220-lb) thrust J65-W-3.

The final development of this tactically important warplane series was the RF-84F Thunderflash reconnaissance variant with the 3538-kg (7,800-lb) thrust J65-W-7 aspirated via root inlets, a modification that left the nose clear for the camera installation.

There were a number of experimental and development variants, the most interesting of these being the GRF-84F (later RF-84K) designed to be carried by the Convair B-36 strategic bomber for aerial launch and recovery.

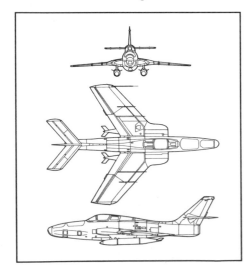

Republic RF-84F Thunderflash

REPUBLIC F-84B THUNDERJET
Role: Fighter bomber
Crew/Accommodation: One
Power Plant: One 1,814 kgp (4,000 lb s.t.) Allison J35-A-15 turbojet
Dimensions: Span 11.1 m (36.42 ft); length 11.41 m (37.42 ft); wing area 24.15 m² (260 sq ft)
Weights: Empty 4,326 kg (9,538 lb); MTOW 8,931 kg (19,689 lb)
Performance: Maximum speed 945 km/h (587 mph) at 1,219 m (4,000 ft); operational ceiling 12,421 m (40,750 ft); range 2,063 km (1,282 miles)
Load: Six .5 inch machine guns and thirty-two 5 inch rocket projectiles

Republic RF-84F Thunderflash reconnaissance aircraft

MIKOYAN-GUREVICH MiG-15 'FAGOT' Family (U.S.S.R.)

Mig-17 'Fresco'

The MiG-15 was the North American F-86 Sabre's main opponent in the Korean War, and was the production version of the I-310 prototype that first flew in late 1947. The MiG-15 was the U.S.S.R.'s first swept-wing fighter to enter large-scale production. The type was powered by the Soviet version of the Rolls-Royce Nene turbojet, which was initially known as the Klimov RD-45 but then in further developed form as the VK-1.

The MiG-15 proved itself a competent fighter, but the type's only major variant, the improved MiG-15bis, could outclimb and out-turn the Sabre in most flight regimes. Many thousands of the series were produced, most of them as standard day fighters, but small numbers as MiG-15P all-weather fighters and MiG-15SB fighter-bombers. The type was given the NATO reporting name 'Fagot', and there was also an important MiG-15UTI tandem-seat advanced and conversion trainer known as the 'Midget'. Licensed production was undertaken in Czechoslovakia and Poland of the S.102 and LIM variants. The MiG-17 'Fresco' was the production version of the I-330 prototype developed to eliminate the MiG-15's tendency to snap-roll into an uncontrollable spin during a high-speed turn. A new wing of 45° rather than 35° sweep was introduced, together with a longer fuselage, a revised tail unit and more power. Several thousand aircraft were delivered from 1952 in variants such as the MiG-17 day fighter, MiG-15F improved day fighter with the VK-1F afterburning engine, MiG-17PF limited all-weather fighter, and MiG-17PFU missile-armed fighter. The type was also built in China, Czechoslovakia, and Poland with the designations J-5 (or export F-5), S.104 and LIM-5/6 respectively.

MiG-15UTI 'Midget' was a two-seat trainer

MIKOYAN-GUREVICH MiG-17PF 'FRESCO-D'

Role: Fighter
Crew/Accommodation: One
Power Plant: One 3,380 kgp (7,452 lb s.t.) Klimov VK/1FA turbojet with reheat
Dimensions: Span 9.63 m (31.59 ft); length 11.26 m (36.94 ft); wing area 22.6 m² (243.26 sq ft)
Weights: Empty 4,182 kg (9,220 lb); MTOW 6,330 kg (13,955 lb)
Performance: Maximum speed 1,074 km/h (667 mph) at 4,000 m (13,123 ft); operational ceiling 15,850 m (52,001 ft); range 360 km (224 miles) with full warload
Load: Three 23 mm cannon, plus up to 500 kg (1,102 lb) of bombs or unguided rockets

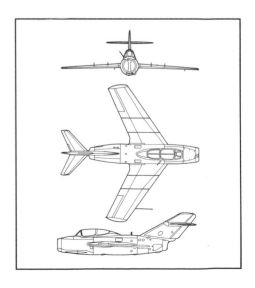

MiG-15UTI 'Midget'

57

NORTH AMERICAN F-86 SABRE (United States)

F-86F Sabre

The Sabre was the most important American air combat fighter in the Korean War. In 1944 the U.S. Army Air Forces contracted for three XP-86 prototypes for a day fighter that could also double in the escort and ground-attack roles. When the fruits of German aerodynamic research became available to the Americans after World War II, the type was reworked to incorporate swept flying surfaces, and the first such prototype flew in October 1947 with a 1701-kg (3,750-lb) thrust General Electric TG-180 (later J35-GE-3) axial-flow turbojet. The type was then re-engined with the General Electric J47 turbojet to become the YP-86A, leading to the P-86A (later F-86A) production model with the 2200-kg (4,850-lb) thrust J47-GE-1 engine.

These 554 aircraft with four J47 marks up to a thrust of 2359-kg (5,200-lb) were followed in chronological order by the 456 F-86Es with a slab tailplane and the 3877-kg (5,200-lb) thrust J47-GE-27, the 2,540 F-86Fs with the 2708-kg (5,970-lb) thrust J47-GE-27 and, in later aircraft, the '6-3' wing with extended leading edges, the 2,504 F-86D redesigned night and all-weather fighters with the 2517-kg (5,550-lb) thrust J47-GE-33, the 473 F-86H fighter-bombers with the 4037-kg (8,900-lb) thrust J73-GE-3, greater span and a deeper fuselage, the 341 examples of the F-86K simplified version of the F-86D with the 2461-kg (5,425-lb) J47-GE-17B, and the 981 examples of the F-86L rebuilt version of the F-86D with a larger wing and updated electronics. The Sabre was also built in Australia as the CAC Sabre in Mk 30, 31 and 32 versions with two 30-mm cannon and the Rolls-Royce Avon turbojet, and in Canada as the Canadair Sabre in Mk 2, 4 and 6 versions with the Orenda turbojet.

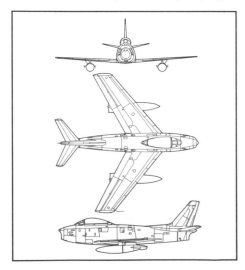

North American F-86E Sabre

NORTH AMERICAN F-86F SABRE
Role: Day fighter
Crew/Accommodation: One
Power Plant: One 2,708 kgp (5,970 lb s.t.) General Electric J47-GE-27 turbojet
Dimensions: Span 11.3 m (37.08 ft); length 11.43 m (37.5 ft); wing area 26.76 m² (288 sq ft)
Weights: Empty 4,967 kg (10,950 lb); MTOW 7,711 kg (17,000 lb)
Performance: Maximum speed 1,110 km/h (690 mph) at sea level; operational ceiling 15,240 m (50,000 ft); range 1,263 km (785 miles) without external fuel
Load: Six .5 inch machine guns, plus up to 907 kg (2,000 lb) of bombs or fuel carried externally

Examples of the F-86F variant of the F-86 Sabre

HAWKER HUNTER (United Kingdom)

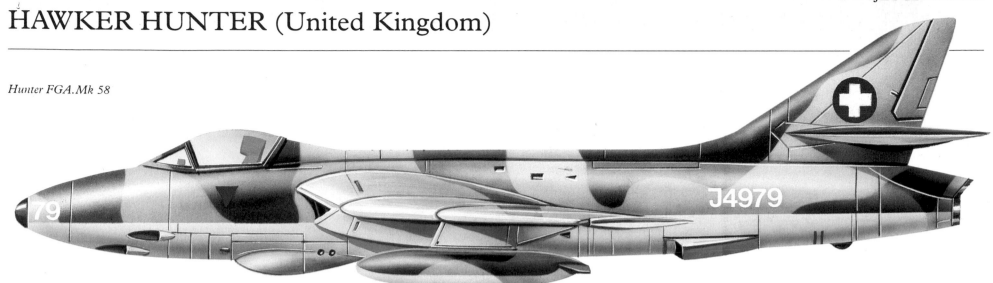

Hunter FGA.Mk 58

The Hunter was the most successful of British post-World War II fighters, with a total of 1,972 built including 445 manufactured under licence in Belgium and the Netherlands, and the type still serves in modest numbers as a first-line type with smaller air forces. This superb fighter resulted from a British need to replace the obsolescent Gloster Meteor with a more advanced type offering transonic performance, and the P.1067 prototype first flew in

July 1951, and was followed just one month later by the first Hunter F.Mk 1 pre-production aircraft.

The first production article flew in May 1953, and the Hunter F.Mk 1 entered squadron service in July 1954. These aircraft were powered by the Rolls-Royce Avon turbojet, but the Hunter F.Mk 2 used the Armstrong Siddeley Sapphire Mk 101 turbojet. Further evolution led to the similar Hunter F.Mks 4 and 5 with more fuel

and underwing armament capability, the former with the Avon Mk 115/121 and the latter with the Sapphire Mk 101. The Hunter F.Mk 6 introduced the Avon Mk 200 series turbojet in its Mk 203/207 forms, greater fuel capacity, along with the underwing armament of the F.Mk 4. The F.Mk 6 was later developed as the Hunter FGA.Mk 9 definitive ground-attack fighter with the dogtoothed leading edges and Avon Mk 207 engine.

There were also tactical reconnaissance variants based on the FGA.Mk 9 and produced in Hunter FR.Mk 10 and PR.Mk 11 forms for

the RAF and Fleet Air Arm respectively. Another variant was the side-by-side two-seat trainer, pioneered in the P.1101 prototype that first flew in mid-1955. This was produced in Hunter T.Mks 7 and 8 forms for the RAF and Fleet Air Arm respectively. Export derivatives of the single- and two-seat varieties were numbered in the Hunter Mks 50, 60, 70 and 80 series.

A Hawker Hunter F.Mk 1 used as an instructional airframe

HAWKER HUNTER F.Mk 6
Role: Day fighter
Crew/Accommodation: One
Power Plant: One 4,605 kgp (10,150 lb s.t.) Rolls-Royce Avon Mk 207 turbojet
Dimensions: Span 10.25 m (33.33 ft); length 13.97 m (45.83 ft); wing area 32.42 m² (349 sq ft)
Weights: Empty 6,505 kg (14,22 lb); MTOW 8,051 kg (17,750 lb)
Performance: Maximum speed 1,002 km/h (623 mph) at 10,975 m (36,000 ft); operational ceiling 14,630 m (48,000 ft); range 789 km (490 miles) on internal fuel only
Load: Four 30 mm cannon

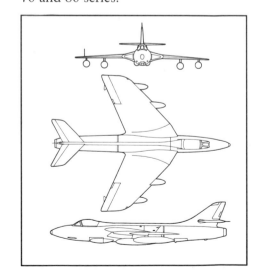

Hawker Hunter FGA.Mk 9

CONVAIR F-102 DELTA DAGGER and F-106 DELTA DART (United States)

F-106A Delta Dart

These two delta-winged fighters were designed specifically for air defence of the continental United States and were among the first aircraft in the world designed as part of a complete weapon system integrating airframe, sensors, and weapons. The YF-102 was developed on the basis of data derived from the experimental programme undertaken with the XF-92A, which itself was derived from American assessment of German research into delta-winged aircraft during World War II. The Model 8 was planned to provide the U.S. Air Force with an 'Ultimate Interceptor' for the defence of North American airspace, and was intended to possess Mach 2+ performance and carry the very advanced MX-1179 Electronic Control System. The resulting Model 8-80 was ordered as a single YF-102 prototype and first flew in October 1952 with a 4400-kg (9,700-lb) thrust Pratt & Whitney J57-P-11 turbojet. This prototype was soon lost in an accident but had already displayed disappointing performance.

The airframe of the succeeding YF-102A was redesigned with Whitcomb area ruling to reduce drag, and this improved performance to a degree that made feasible the introduction of F-102A single-seat fighter and TF-102A two-seat trainer variants. The MX-1179 ECS had proved too difficult for the technology of the time, so the less advanced MG-3 fire-control system was adopted for these models, of which 875 and 111 respectively were built.

Greater effort went into the development of the true Mach 2 version, which was developed as the F-102B but then ordered as the F-106 before the first of two YF-106A prototypes flew in December 1956. The F-106A single-seat fighter and F-102B two-seat trainer versions were produced to the extent of 277 and 63 aircraft respectively, and these served into the later 1980s.

Convair F-106A Delta Dart

CONVAIR-F-106A DELTA DART
Role: All-weather interceptor
Crew/Accommodation: One
Power Plant: One 11,115 kgp (24,500 lb s.t.) Pratt & Whitney J75-P-17 turbojet with reheat
Dimensions: Span 11.67 m (38.29 ft); length 21.56 m (70.73 ft); wing area 64.83 m² (697.8 sq ft)
Weights: Empty 10,904 kg (24,038 lb); MTOW 17,779 kg (39,195 lb)
Performance: Maximum speed 2,135 km/h (1,152 knots) at 10,668 m (35,000 ft); operational ceiling 16,063 m (52,700 ft); radius 789 km (490 miles) on internal fuel only
Load: One 20 mm multi-barrel cannon, plus one long-range and four medium-range air-to-air missiles

A Convair F-106A Delta Dart

DASSAULT MYSTERE and SUPER MYSTERE (France)

Mystère IVA

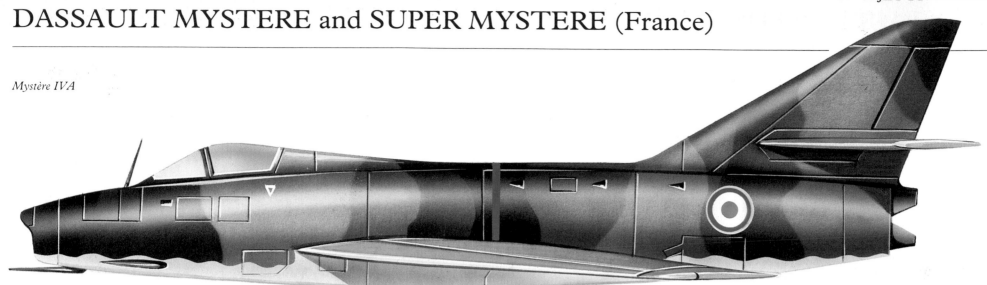

At the end of World War II, Marcel Bloch was released from a German concentration camp, promptly changed his named to Dassault and started to rebuild his original aircraft company as Avions Marcel Dassault, the premier French manufacturer of warplanes. After gaining experience in the design and construction of jet-powered fighters with the straight-winged M.D. 450 Ouragan fighter-bomber, Dassault turned his attention to a swept-wing design, the Mystère (Mystery). This first flew in the form of the M.D. 452 Mystère I prototype form during February 1951, and was followed by eight more prototypes each with the Rolls-Royce Tay turbojet: two more Mystère Is, two Mystère IIAs and four Mystère IIBs. Then came 11 pre-production Mystère IICs with the 3000-kg (6,614-lb) thrust SNECMA Atar 101 turbojet, and these paved the way for the Mystère IV production prototype that first flew in September 1952 with the Tay turbojet but thinner and more highly swept wings, a longer oval-section fuselage, and modified tail surfaces. There followed nine Mystère IVA pre-production aircraft and finally more than 480 production fighters, of which the first 50 retained the Tay but the others used the 3500-kg (7,716-lb) thrust Hispano-Suiza Verdun 350 turbojet.

Further development led to the Mystère IVB prototype with a Rolls-Royce Avon turbojet, a thinner and more highly swept wing, and a revised fuselage of lower drag. The resulting Super Mystère B1 production prototype flew in March 1955 with an afterburning turbojet as the first genuinely supersonic aircraft of European design, and was followed by 185 examples of the Super Mystère B2 production model with the 4460-kg (9,833-lb) thrust Atar 101G-2/3 afterburning turbojet. Some aircraft were supplied to Israel, which modified a number with the 4218-kg (9,300-lb) thrust Pratt & Whitney J52-P-8A non-afterburning turbjojet.

Dassault Mystère IVA fighters of the French Air Force's EC 8 wing

DASSAULT MYSTERE IVA
Role: Strike fighter
Crew/Accommodation: One
Power Plant: One 3,500 kgp (7,716 lb s.t.) Hispano-Suiza Verdun 350 turbojet
Dimensions: Span 11.13 m (36.5 ft); length 12.83 m (42.1 ft); wing area 32 m² (344.5 sq ft)
Weights: Empty 5,875 kg (12,950 lb); MTOW 9,096 kg (20,050 lb)
Performance: Maximum speed 1,120 km/h (604 knots) at sea level; operational ceiling 13,716 m (45,000 ft); range 460 km (248 naut. miles)
Load: Two 30 mm DEFA cannon, plus to up 907 kg (2,000 lb) of externally carried bombs

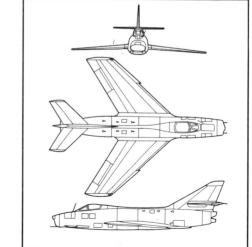

Dassault Super Mystère BZ

SUD-OUEST S.O.4050 VAUTOUR (France)

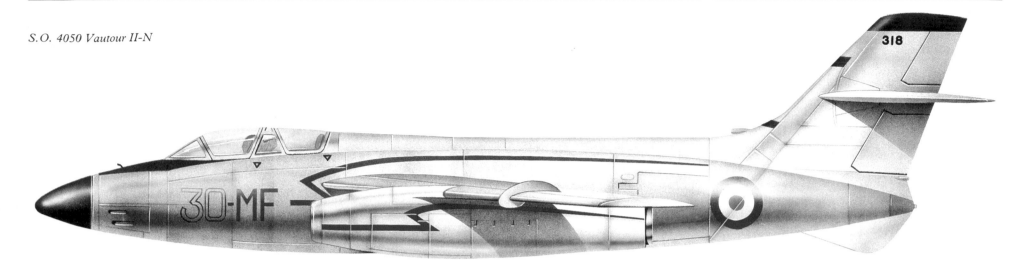

S.O. 4050 Vautour II-N

In the late 1940s, Sud-Ouest produced two half-scale research aircraft as the S.O.M.1 air-launched research glider and its powered version, the S.O.M.2 with a Rolls-Royce Derwent turbojet. The company then evolved the S.O.4000 full-scale prototype with two Rolls-Royce Nene turbojets (licence-built by Hispano-Suiza) in the rear fuselage and the unusual landing gear of a single nosewheel and four main wheels, the latter arranged in tandem pairs.

The S.O.4000 first flew in March 1951, and paved the way for the S.O.4050 Vautour (Vulture) prototype with swept flying surfaces and a landing gear arrangement comprising two-twin wheel main units in tandem under the fuselage and single-wheel outriggers under the nacelles of the wing-mounted engines. The first of three prototypes was a two-seat night fighter and flew in October 1952 with 2400-kg (5,291-lb) thrust SNECMA Atar 101B turbojets; the second machine was a single-seat ground-attack type with 2820-kg (6,217-lb) thrust Atar 101Ds; and the third machine was a two-seat bomber with Armstrong Siddeley Sapphire turbojets. There followed six pre-production aircraft before it was decided to procure all three variants with a powerplant standardized as two 3500-kg (7,716-lb) thrust Atar 101Es. Even so, production totalled just 140 aircraft. These comprised 30 single-seat Vautour II-A ground-attack aircraft, 40 two-seat Vautour II-B bombers, and 70 two-seat Vautour II-N night fighters, with equipment and armament optimized for the three types' specific role. The first of these three types flew in April 1956, July 1957 and October 1956 respectively. Some 18 aircraft were later supplied to Israel, and after retrofit with slab tailplanes, the Vautour II-N became the Vautour II-1N.

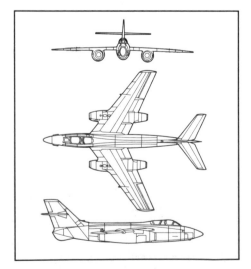

Sud-Ouest S.O. 4050 Vautour II

SUD S.O. 4050 VAUTOUR II-N
Role: All-weather/night fighter
Crew/Accommodation: Two
Power Plant: Two 3,300 kgp (7,275 lb s.t.) SNECMA Atar 101E-3 turbojets
Dimensions: Span 15.1 m (49.54 ft); length 16.5 m (54.13 ft); wing area 45.3 m² (487.6 sq ft)
Weights: Empty 9,880 kg (21,782 lb); MTOW 17,000 kg (37,479 lb)
Performance: Maximum speed 958 km/h (595 mph) at 12,200 m (40,026 ft); operational ceiling 14,000 m (45, 932 ft); range 2,750 km (1,709 miles) with maximum fuel
Load: Four 20 mm cannon

Sud-Ouest S.O.4050 Vautour

LOCKHEED F-104 STARFIGHTER (United States)

F-104S Super Starfighter

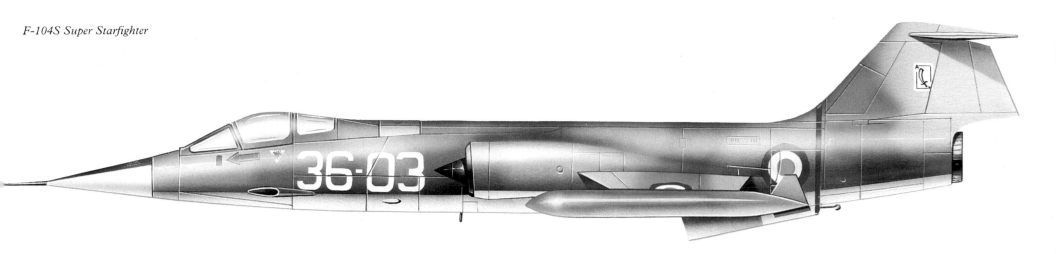

The Starfighter resulted from the U.S. Air Force's experiences in the Korean War, where the need for a fast-climbing interceptor became clear. The type was planned by 'Kelly' Johnson with the smallest airframe that would accommodate the most powerful available axial-flow turbojet. This resulted in a fighter possessing a long and basically cylindrical fuselage with unswept and diminutive wings, plus a large T-tail assembly.

The first of two XF-104 prototypes first flew in March 1954 with an interim engine, the 4627-kg (10,200-lb) thrust Wright XJ65-W-6, and four years of troubled development followed with 17 YF-104As before the F-104A entered service with a longer fuselage accommodating the 6713-kg (14,800-lb) thrust J79-GE-3 engine, and an armament of one 20-mm multi-barrel cannon and two AIM-9 Sidewinder air-to-air missiles. The USAF eventually ordered only 296 examples of the Starfighter in variants that included 153 F-104A interceptors, 26 F-104B tandem-seat trainers, 77 F-104C tactical strike fighters with provision for a 907-kg (2,000-lb) external load, and 21 F-104D tandem-seat trainers. The commercial success of the type was then ensured by the adoption of the much-improved F-104G all-weather multi-role type by a NATO consortium. This model had a strengthened airframe, a larger vertical tail, greater power, and more advanced electronics, and itself spawned the F-104J interceptor that was built in Japan. This mutli-national programme resulted in the largely licensed production of another 1,986 aircraft up to 1983. The F-104G itself produced TF-104 trainer and RF-104 reconnaissance variants, and Italy developed the special F-104S variant as a dedicated interceptor with better radar and medium-range Sparrow and Aspide air-to-air missiles.

Lockheed F-104G Starfighters of European air forces

LOCKHEED F-104A STARFIGHTER
Role: Interceptor
Crew/Accommodation: One
Power Plant: One 6,713 kgp (14,800 lb s.t.) General Electric J79-GE-3B turbojet with reheat
Dimensions: Span 6.63 m (21.75 ft); length 16.66 m (54.66 ft); wing area 18.2 m² (196.1 sq ft)
Weights: Empty 6,071 kg (13,384 lb); MTOW 11,271 kg (25,840 lb)
Performance: Maximum speed 1,669 km/h (1,037 mph) at 15,240 m (50,000 ft) operational ceiling 19,750 m (64,795 ft); range 1,175 km (730 miles) with full warload
Load: One 20 mm multi-barrel cannon and two short-range air-to-air missiles

Lockheed F-104G Starfighter

SAAB 35 DRAKEN (Sweden)

F35 Draken

An even more remarkable achievement than the Saab 32, the Saab 35 Draken (Dragon) was designed as an interceptor of transonic bombers. This role demanded supersonic speed, a very high rate of climb, better than average range and endurance, and a sizeable weapon load. The tactical philosophy of the Swedish Air Force also dictated that the new type should have STOL capability so that it could operate from lengths of straight road during dispersed operations. The fighter was therefore designed on the basis of a slender circular-section fuselage and a double-delta wing in a combination that provided large lifting area and fuel capacity at minimum profile drag. To achieve much the same performance as the slightly later English Electric Lightning powered by two Rolls-Royce Avon afterburning turbojets, the design team opted for such a single example of the same engine built under licence in Sweden as the Flygmotor RM6. The layout was evaluated successfully in the Saab 210 research aircraft that was in essence a scaled-down Saab 35 and first flew in February 1952 with the 476-kg (1,050-lb) thrust Armstrong Siddeley Adder turbojet.

The first prototype of the Saab 35 flew in October 1955, and the J 35A initial production variant began to enter service in 1958. Production totalled 525 in variants such as the J 35A fighter with the 7000-kg (14,432-lb) thrust RM6B, the J 35B improved fighter with collision-course radar and a data-link system, the Sk 35C tandem-seat operational trainer, the J 35D fighter with the 7830-kg (17,262-lb) thrust RM6C and more advanced electronics, the S 35E tactical reconnaissance aircraft and the J 35F with more advanced radar and Hughes Falcon air-to-air missiles. The type was also exported as the Saab 35X, and surviving J 35Fs have been upgraded to J 35J standard for service into the 1990s.

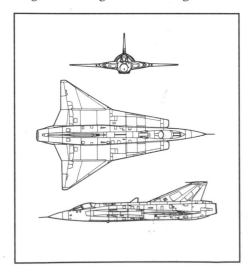

Saab 35 Draken

SAAB 35/J 35 DRAKEN
Role: Interceptor/strike/reconnaissance
Crew/Accommodation: One
Power Plant: One 7,830 kgp (17,262 lb s.t.) Flygmotor-built Rolls-Royce Avon RM6C turbojet with reheat
Dimensions: Span 9.4 m (30.83 ft); length 15.4 m (50.33 ft); wing area 50 m² (538 sq ft)
Weights: Empty (not available); MTOW 16,000 kg (35,274 lb)
Performance: Maximum/Cruise speed 2,150 km/h (1,160 mph) Mach 2.023 at 11,000 m (36,090 ft); operational ceiling 18,300 m (60,039 ft); range 1,149 km (620 naut. miles) with 2,000 lb warload
Load: Two 30 mm cannon, plus up to 4,082 kg (9,000 lb) of bombs

The J 35F was the definitive interceptor of the Saab Draken family

VOUGHT F-8 CRUSADER (United States)

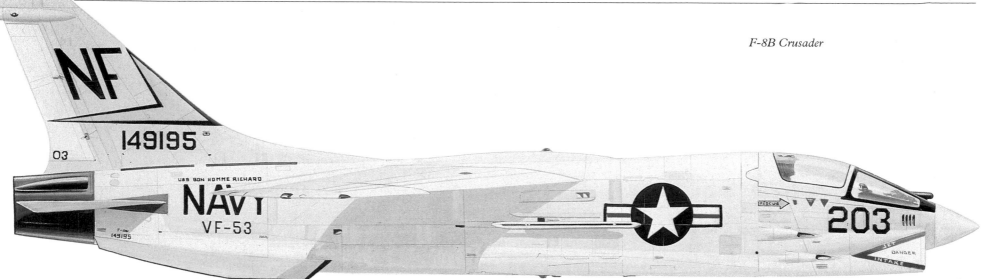

F-8B Crusader

A slightly later contemporary of the North American F-100 Super Sabre that used practically the same powerplant, the Crusader carrierborne fighter was an altogether more capable machine despite the additional fixed weight of its naval equipment. The design's most interesting feature was a variable-incidence wing that allowed the fuselage to be kept level during take-off and landing, thereby improving the pilot's fields of vision. The type resulted from a 1952 U.S. Navy requirement for an air-superiority fighter with truly supersonic performance, and from eight submissions the Vought design was selected in May 1953 for hardware development in the form of two XF8U-1 prototypes.

The first of these flew in March 1955 with the 6713-kg (14,800-lb) thrust Pratt & Whitney J57-P-11 turbojet. Deliveries to operational squadrons began in March 1957 of the F8U-1 with the 7348-kg (16,200-lb) thrust J57-P-4A, four 20-mm cannon, rockets in an underfuselage pack and, as a retrofit, Sidewinder air-to-air missiles. Production totalled 318, and from 1962 these aircraft were redesignated F-8A. There followed 30 examples of the F8U-1E (F-8B) with limited all-weather capability, 187 examples of the F8U-2 (F-8C) with the 7666-kg (16,900-lb) thrust J57-P-16, 152 examples of the F8U-2N (F-8D) with the 8,165-kg (18,000-lb) thrust J57-P-20, extra fuel and four Sidewinder missiles, and 286 examples of the F8U-2NE (F-8E) with the 8165-kg (18,000-lb) thrust J57-P-20A, advanced radar and provision for 1814 kg (4,000 lb) of external stores on four underwing hardpoints. The F-8H to L were rebuilds of older aircraft to an improved standard with a strengthened airframe and blown flaps, and a reconnaissance variant was the F8U-1P (RF-8A) without any weapons and a camera bay in the forward fuselage; 73 were later rebuilt to RF-8G standard with the J57-P-20A.

VOUGHT F-8E CRUSADER
Role: Naval carrierborne fighter
Crew/Accommodation: One
Power Plant: One 8,165 kgp (18,000 lb s.t.) Pratt & Whitney J57-P-20 turbojet with reheat
Dimensions: Span 10.9 m (35.7 ft); length 16.5 m (54.2 ft); wing area 34.8 m² (375 sq ft)
Weights: Empty 8,960 kg (19,750 lb); MTOW 15,420 kg (34,000 lb)
Performance: Maximum speed 1,802 km/h (973 knots) Mach 1.7 at 12,192 m (40,000 ft); operational ceiling 17,374 m (57,000 ft); radius 966 km (521 naut. miles)
Load: Four 30 mm cannon, plus up to 2,268 kg (5,000 lb) of externally carried weapons, which can include four short-range air-to-air missiles

The French Navy's version of the Vought Crusader is the F-8E(FN)

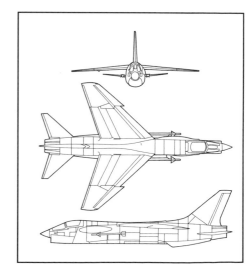

Vought F8U-2 Crusader

DASSAULT MIRAGE III Family (France)

IAI Kfir C-7

The Mirage was designed to meet a 1954 French requirement for a small all-weather supersonic interceptor, and emerged as the delta-winged M.D.550 Mirage prototype for a first flight in June 1955 with two 980-kg (2,160-lb) thrust Armstrong Siddeley Viper turbojets. The type was too small for any realistic military use, and a slightly larger Mirage II was planned; this was not built, both these

initial concepts being abandoned in favour of the still larger Mirage III that first flew in November 1956 with an Atar 101G-1 afterburning turbojet. Further development led to the Mirage IIIA pre-production type with an Atar 9B of 6000-kg (13,228-lb) afterburning thrust boosting speed from Mach 1.65 to 2.2 at altitude.

The type went into widespread production for the French forces and for export, and as such was a considerable commercial success for

Dassault, especially after Israeli success with the type in the 1967 'Six-Day War'. The basic variants are the Mirage IIIB two-seat trainer, the Mirage IIIC single-seat interceptor, the Mirage IIIE single-seat strike fighter and the Mirage IIIR reconnaissance aircraft. The Mirage 5 was produced as a clear-weather type, though the miniaturization of electronics in the 1970s and 1980s have allowed the installation or retrofit of avionics that make most Mirage 5 and up-engined Mirage 50 models

superior to the baseline Mirage III models. Israel produced a Mirage 5 variant as the IAI Kfir with a General Electric J79 afterburning turbojet and advanced electronics, and this has spawned the very impressive Kfir-C2 variant with canard foreplanes for much improved field and combat performance. Many surviving Mirage III aircraft have been modernized to similar aerodynamic and electronic standard, and have also featured improved nav/attack systems and modern weapons.

Dassault-Breguet Mirage 5

DASSUALT MIRAGE IIIE
Role: Strike fighter
Crew/Accommodation: One
Power Plant: One 6,200 kgp (13,670 lb s.t.) SNECMA Atar 9C turbojet, plus provision for one 1,500 kgp (3,307 lb s.t.) SEPR 844 rocket engine
Dimensions: Span 8.22 m (27 ft); length 15.03 m (49.26 ft); wing area 34.85 m² (375 sq ft)
Weights: Empty 7,050 kg (15,540 lb); MTOW 13,000 kg (29,760 lb)
Performance: Maximum speed 2,350 km/h (1,268 knots) Mach 2.21 at 12,000 m (39,375 ft); operational ceiling 17,000 m (55,775 ft); radius 1,200 km (648 naut. miles)
Load: Two 30 mm DEFA cannon, plus up to 1,362 kg (3,000 lb) of externally carried ordnance

A Dassault-Breguet Mirage IIING

FIAT G91 (Italy)

G91Y

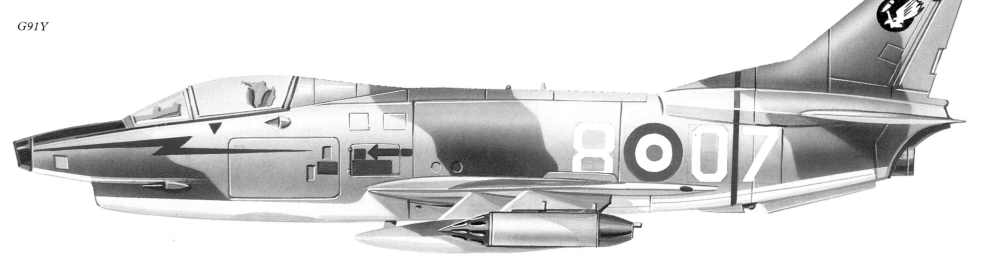

First flown in August 1956, the G91 was the winning design in a large-scale competition resulting from a 1954 NATO requirement for a light attack fighter. This was to be a technically simple and affordable type, offering good operational capabilities in combination with good short-field performance. Although the G91 met all the requirements, in the event it was produced only in modest numbers for the Italian and West German Air Forces, with second-hand aircraft

being passed to Portugal later in the type's career.

The initial version was the G91R with a 2268-kg (5,000-lb) thrust Fiat-built Bristol Siddeley (later Rolls-Royce) Orpheus Mk 803 non-afterburning turbojet, and this was produced in a number of variants with different armament and, in the type's secondary role, reconnaissance equipment. The G91R/1 had a fixed armament of four 12.7-mm (0.5-in) machine guns, the G91R/1A was

similar but had the R/3's navigation package, the G91R/1B had a strengthened structure, the G91R/3 was the West German model with upgraded electronics and a fixed armament of two 30-mm cannon, and the G91R/4 was a G/3 version with the armament of the G/1; there was also a G91T operational trainer version produced in T/1 Italian and T/2 West German forms. The basic design was later reworked as the G91Y with a twin-engined powerplant in the form of two 1850-kg (4,080-lb)

thrust General Electric J85-GE-13 turbojets. This first flew in December 1966, and production of 77 aircraft was undertaken as the type offered not only the additional reliability of a twin-engined powerplant, but the operational advantage of better payload/range performance derived from the availability of 63 per cent more thrust for only an 18 per cent increase in empty weight.

Aeritalia (Fiat) G91 warplanes of the Italian air force

FIAT G91R
Role: Strike fighter/reconnaissance
Crew/Accommodation: One
Power Plant: One 2,268 kgp (5,000 b.s.t.) Bristol Siddeley Orpheus 803 turbojet
Dimensions: Span 8.56 m (28.08 ft); length 10.3 m (33.79 ft); wing area 16.4 m² (176.7 sq ft)
Weights: Empy 3,100 kg (6,835 lb); MTOW 8,700 kg (19,180 lb)
Performance: Maximum speed 1,075 km/h (580 knots) Mach 0.877 m at sea level; operational ceiling 13,100 m (42,979 ft); radius 315 m (170 naut. miles) with full warload
Load: Four 12.7 mm machine guns, plus up to 907 kg (2,000 lb) of externally-carried weapons-fuel

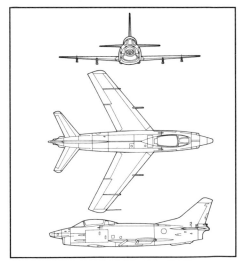

Fiat (Aeritalia) G91R/1A

MIKOYAN-GUREVICH MiG-21 'FISHBED' (U.S.S.R.)

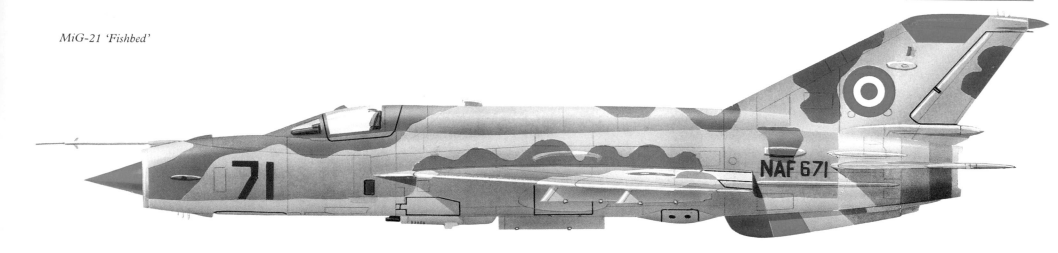

MiG-21 'Fishbed'

The MiG-21 'Fishbed' was designed after the U.S.S.R. had digested the implications of the Korean War to provide a short-range interceptor. The type was analogous to the Lockheed F-104 Starfighter in rationale, but was a radically different aircraft based on a tailed delta configuration, small overall size, and light weight to ensure adequate performance on just one relatively low-powered afterburning turbojet, the Tumansky R-11 that was only slightly larger and heavier than the RD-9 used in the preceding MiG-19's twin-engined powerplant.

Differently configured Ye-2A and Ye-5 prototypes were flown in 1956, the latter paving the way for the definitive Ye-6 prototype that flew in 1957. More than 11,000 examples of the MiG-21 were produced in variants such as the MiG-21 clear-weather interceptor, MiG-21PF limited all-weather fighter with search and track radar, MiG-21PFS fighter with blown flaps and provision for RATO units,

MiG-21FL export version of the MiG-21PFs but without blown flaps or RATO provision, MiG-21PFM improved version of the MiG-21PFS, MiG-21PFMA second-generation dual-role fighter with a larger dorsal hump and four rather than two underwing hardpoints, MiG-21M export version of the MiG-21PFMA, MiG-21R tactical reconnaissance version, MiG-21MF with the more powerful but lighter R-13-30 engine,

MiG-21RF reconnaissance version of the MiG-21MF, MiG-21SMT aerodynamically refined version of the MiG-21MF with increased fuel and ECM capability, MiG-21bis third-generation multi-role fighter, and MiG-21Mbis definitive third-generation fighter with a re-engineered airframe, updated electronics and R-25 engine. There have also been three MiG-21U 'Mongol' conversion trainer variants.

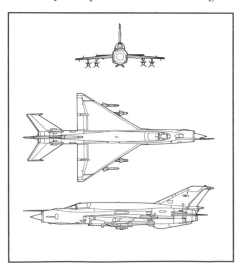

MiG-21 'Fishbed-K'

MIKOYAN-GUREVICH MiG-21SMT 'FISHBED-K'

Role: Strike fighter
Crew/Accommodation: One
Power Plant: One 6,600 kgp (14,550 lb s.t) Tumansky R-13 turbojet with reheat
Dimensions: Span 7.15 m (23.46 ft); length 13.46 m (44.16 ft); wing area 23 m² (247.57 sq ft)
Weights: Empty 5,450 kg (12,015 lb); MTOW 7,750 kg (17,085 lb)
Performance: Maximum speed 2,230 km/h (1,386 mph) Mach 2.1 at 12,000 m (39,370 ft); operational ceiling 18,000 m (59,055 ft); radius 500 km (311 miles) with full warload
Load: Two 23 mm cannon, plus up to 1,000 kg (2,205 lb) of air-to-air missiles or bombs depending upon mission

The Mikoyan-Gurevich MiG-21

ENGLISH ELECTRIC LIGHTNING (United Kingdom)

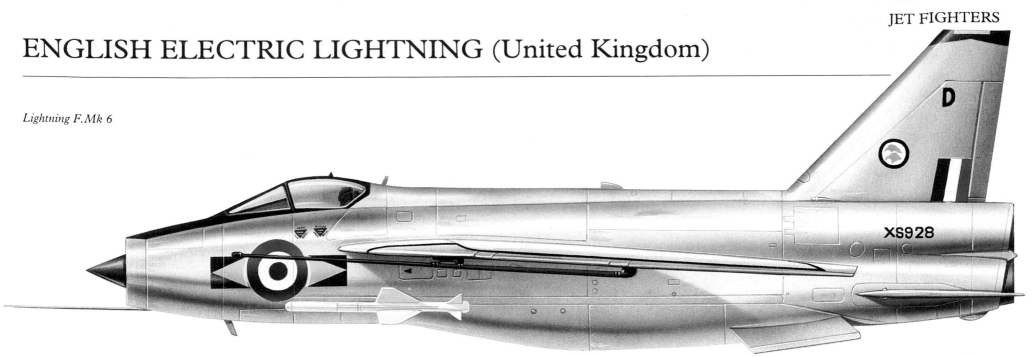

Lightning F.Mk 6

The Lightning was the United Kingdom's first supersonic fighter. The type offered superlative speed and climb performance, but was always limited by poor range and indifferent armament. The origins of the type lay in the P.1A, which resulted from a 1947 requirement for a supersonic research aircraft. The first of three prototypes flew in August 1954 and later revealed supersonic performance on two Bristol Siddeley non-afterburning turbojets. It was seen that the type had the makings of an interceptor, and the type was revised as the P.1B that first flew in April 1957 with two superimposed Rolls-Royce Avon turbojets. After a lengthy development with 20 pre-production aircraft, the type began to enter service in 1960 as the Lightning F.Mk 1 with two 30-mm cannon and two Firestreak air-to-air missiles.

Later variants were the Lightning F.Mk 1A with inflight-refuelling capability, the Lightning F.Mk 2 with improved electronics and fully variable afterburners, the Lightning F.Mk 3 with 7420-kg (16,360-lb) thrust Avon Mk 300 series engines, provision for overwing drop tanks, a square-topped vertical tail, improved radar, no guns, and a pair of Red Top air-to-air missiles that offered all-aspect engagement capability in place of the earlier marks' pursuit-course Firestreak missiles.

The final variant was the Lightning F.Mk 6 (originally lightning F.Mk 3A) with a revised wing with cambered and kinked leading edges, and a ventral tank that virtually doubled fuel capacity while also accommodating a pair of 30-mm cannon. There were also two side-by-side trainer models, the Lightning T.Mks 4 and 5; these were based on the F.Mk 1A and F.Mk 3 respectively, and retained full combat capability. For export there was the Lighting Mk 50 series of fighters and trainers.

An English Electric Lightning F.Mk 53

ENGLISH ELECTRIC/BAC LIGHTNING F.Mk 6
Role: Interceptor fighter
Crew/Accommodation: One
Power Plant: Two 7,420 kgp (16,360 lb s.t.) Rolls-Royce Avon 300 turbojets with reheat
Dimensions: Span 10.61 m (34.9 ft); length 16.84 m (55.25 ft); wing area 44.08 m² (474.5 sq ft)
Weights: Empty 11,340 kg (25,000 lb); MTOW 18,144 kg (40,000 lb)
Performance: Maximum speed 2,230 km/h (1,203 knots) Mach 2.1 at 10,975 m (36,000 ft); operational ceiling 17,375 m (57,000 ft); radius 972 km (604 miles)
Load: Two Red Top missiles, plus two 30 mm Aden cannon

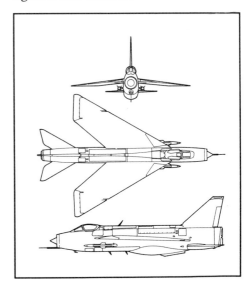

Lightning F.Mk 6

AVRO CANADA CF-105 ARROW (Canada)

CF-105 Arrow Mk I

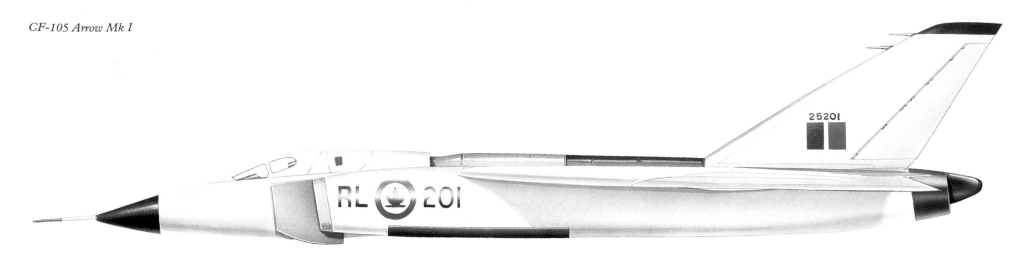

The CF-105 was an ambitious attempt to create a successor to the same company's CF-100 with considerably better performance and its radar, fire-control system, and missile armament integrated into a weapon system. Intended as an interceptor with long range and highly supersonic performance, the CF-105 entered the design phase of its life in 1953, the year that the CF-100

entered service. By 1954 the five CF-105 Mk I prototypes were being built, and the type had received the name Arrow in recognition of the design's sharp needle nose and high-set delta-wing. The two crew members (pilot and systems operator) were seated in tandem on ejector seats in a pressurized cockpit, and beside this were the inlets for the two large afterburning turbojet engines, which were located in the rear fuselage and aspirated through rectangular-section trunks channelling air from the

advanced inlets. In the prototypes the engines were a pair of Pratt & Whitney J75 turbojets, but for the Arrow Mk II production fighter it was planned to use an engine type developed in Canada by Avro's Orenda engine division, namely the PS-13 Iroquois turbojet with a planned thrust of 12,700-kg (28,000-lb) in afterburning mode.

The first Arrow Mk I flew in March 1958, and all five prototypes were

firmly involved in the development programme when the Arrow was cancelled in February 1959. Despite its considerable promise, the type had fallen foul of political pressures. Like the U.K., the Canadian government had in 1957 concluded that manned warplanes had been made redundant by the advent of effective missiles. The five Arrow Mk Is were scrapped, together with one complete and four incomplete Arrow Mk IIs.

Avro Canada CF-105 Arrow

AVRO CANADA CF-105 ARROW Mk I
Role: All-weather, long range interceptor
Crew/Accommodation: Two
Power Plant: Two 10,699 kgp (23,500 lb s.t.) Pratt & Whitney J75-P-3 turbojets with reheat
Dimensions: Span 15.24 m (50 ft); length 23.71 m (77.82 ft); wing area 113.8 m² (1,225 sq ft)
Weights: Empty 22,211 kg (48,923 lb); MTOW 31,144 kg (68,600 lb)
Performance: Maximum speed 1,297 km/h (700 knots) Mach 1.05 at sea level; operational ceiling 15,240 m (50,000 ft); radius 663 km (358 naut. miles with 5 mins at M1.5)
Load: Six Douglas AIR-2 Genie air-to-air missiles carried internally

The Avro Canada CF-105 Arrow

McDONNELL DOUGLAS F-4 PHANTOM II (United States)

IAI F-4 Phantom 2000

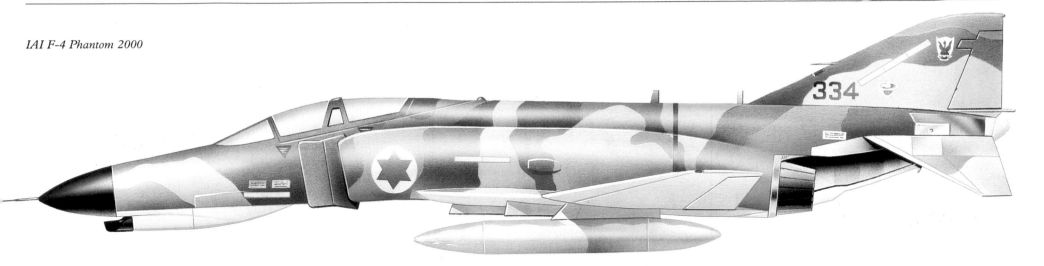

In October 1979, the 5,057th Phantom II was completed, ending the West's largest warplane production programme since World War II. The programme was devoted to an exceptional type that must be numbered in the five most important warplanes of all time. It was planned initially as an all-weather attack aircraft, but then adapted during design into an all-weather fleet-defence and tactical fighter. The first of two XF4H-1 prototypes flew in May 1958 with early examples of the equally classic J79 afterburning turbojet. The 45 F4H-1Fs (later F-4As) were really pre-production types with 7326-kg (16,150-lb) thrust J79-GE-2/2A engines.

True operational capability came with 649 F4H-1 (later F-4B) with 7711-kg (17,000-lb) thrust J79-GE-8 engines, 46 RF-4B reconnaissance aircraft for the U.S. Marine Corps, 635 F-4C (originally F-110A) attack fighters for the U.S. Air Force with 7711-kg (17,000-lb) thrust J79-GE-15 engines, 499 RF-4C USAF tactical reconnaissance aircraft, 773 F-4Ds based on the F-4C but with electronics tailored to USAF rather than U.S. Navy requirements, 1,405 F-4Es for the USAF with 8119-kg (17,900-lb) thrust J79-GE-17 engines, improved radar, leading-edge slats and an internal 20-mm rotary-barrel cannon, 175 F-4F air-superiority fighters for West Germany, 512 F-4Js for the U.S. Navy with 8119-kg (17,900-lb) thrust J79-GE-10 engines, a revised wing and modified tail, 52 F-4Ks based on the F-4J for the Royal Navy with Rolls-Royce Spey turbofans, and 118 F-4Ms based on the F-4K for the Royal Air Force.

There have been several other versions produced by converting older airframes with more advanced electronics as well as other features, such as the similar F-4N and F-4S developments of the F-4B and F-4J for the U.S. Navy, the F-4G for the USAF's 'Wild Weasel' radar-suppression role, and the Super Phantom (or Phantom 2000) rebuild of the F-4E by Israel Aircraft Industries.

The RF-4C is a version of the McDonnell Douglas Phantom II land-based fighter series

McDONNELL DOUGLAS F-4E PHANTOM II
Role: All-weather strike fighter
Crew/Accommodation: Two
Power Plant: Two 8,119 kgp (17,900 lb s.t.) General Electric J79-GE-17 turbojets with reheat
Dimensions: Span 11.71 m (38.42 ft); length 19.2 m (63 ft); wing area 49.2 m² (530 sq ft)
Weights: Empty 13,397 kg (29,535 lb); MTOW 27,965 kg (61,651 lb)
Performance: Maximum speed 2,390 km/h (1,290 knots) Mach 2.2 at 12,190 m (40,000 ft); operational ceiling 18,975 m (62,250 ft); radius 960 km (518 naut. miles) typical combat mission
Load: One 20 mm multi-barrel cannon and four medium-range air-to-air missiles, plus up to 7,257 kg (16,000 lb) of externally carried weapons or fuel

F-4E Phantom II

71

NORTHROP F-5 Family (United States)

F-5E Tiger II

The F-5 Freedom Fighter was developed from Northrop's private-venture N-156 design as a modestly supersonic fighter and attack aircraft with the light weight, compact dimensions and simple avionics that would suit it to operation by American allies requiring an essentially defensive type of low purchase and operating costs combined with relatively simple maintenance requirements. The concept's first concrete expression was the N-156T supersonic trainer that first flew in April 1959 as the YT-38 with two 953-kg (2,600-lb) thrust General Electric J85-GE-1 non-afterburning turbojets, though the third to sixth prototypes had the 1633-kg (3,600-lb) afterburning thrust J85-GE-5 engines that paved the way for the 1746-kg (3,850-lb) thrust J85-GE-5As used in the T-38A Talon version, of which 1,139 were built for the U.S. Air Force.

The N-156F fighter was developed in F-5A single-seat and F-5B two-seat variants, and first flew in July 1959 with 1850-kg (4,850-lb) thrust J85-GE-13 turbojets. Production of the F-5A and F-5B totalled 818 and 290 respectively for various countries in differently designated versions that included the Canadair-built CF-5 for Canada and NF-5 for the Netherlands, and the CASA-built SF-5 for Spain. There was also an RF-5A reconnaissance model with four cameras in a modified nose. The mantle of the Freedom Fighter was then assumed by the more capable Tiger II variant produced in F-5E single-seat and F-5F two-seat forms with an integrated fire-control system as well as 2268-kg (5,000-lb) thrust J85-GE-21 engines and aerodynamic refinements for much improved payload and performance.

The type first flew in March 1969, and deliveries began in 1973. Large-scale production followed before the line was closed in the mid-1980s, and this sequence also included a small number of RF-5E Tigereye reconnaissance aircraft.

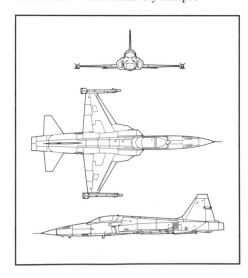

Northrop F-5E Tiger II

NORTHROP F-5E TIGER II
Role: Strike fighter
Crew/Accommodation: One
Power Plant: Two 2,268 kgp (5,000 lb s.t.) General Electric J85-GE-21 turbojets with reheat
Dimensions: Span 8.13 m (26.66 ft); length 14.68 m (48.16 ft); wing area 17.3 m² (186.2 sq ft)
Weights: Empty 4,392 kg (9,683 lb); MTOW 11,195 kg (24,680 lb)
Performance: Maximum speed 1,730 km/h (934 knots) Mach 1.63 at 11,000 m (36.090 ft); operational ceiling 15,790 m (51,800 ft); radius 222 km (138 miles) with full warload
Load: Two 20 mm cannon, plus up to 3,175 kg (7,000 lb) of ordnance, including two short-range air-to-air missiles

The Northrop E-5F Tiger II is the two-seat version of the F-5E single-seater

MIKOYAN-GUREVICH MiG-25 'FOXBAT' Series (U.S.S.R.)

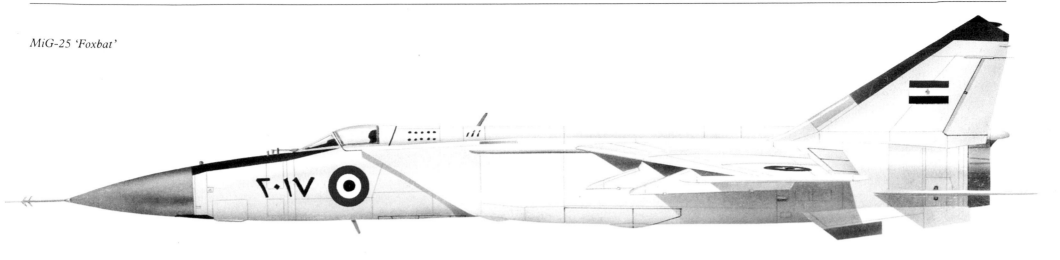

MiG-25 'Foxbat'

The MiG-25 was designed to provide the Soviets with an interceptor capable of dealing with the United States' North American B-70 Valkyrie Mach 3 high-altitude strategic bomber. When the B-70 was cancelled, the Soviets continued to develop this very high-performance interceptor which first flew as the Ye-266 in 1964. The type is built largely of stainless steel with titanium leading edges to deal with friction-generated heat at Mach 3, but at such a speed is virtually incapable of manoeuvre.

The type entered service in 1970 with valve-technology radar that lacked the sophistication of current Western equipments but offered very high power, and thus the ability to 'burn through' the defences provided by the enemy's electronic counter-measures. Current variants are the 'Foxbat-A' interceptor with four air-to-air missiles, the 'Foxbat-B' operational-level reconnaissance aircraft, the 'Foxbat-C' two-seat conversion trainer, and the 'Foxbat-D' improved reconnaissance aircraft.

The MiG-25 is obsolete as an interceptor, but surplus airframes have been utilized for more effective warplanes produced as two converted types; the 'Foxbat-E' is the 'Foxbat-A' interceptor converted to deal with low-level intruders such as penetration bombers and cruise missiles, and the 'Foxbat-F' is another such conversion, in this instance for air-defence suppression role with a specialized radar-warning suite and AS-11 'Kilter' anti-radar missiles. The MiG-31 'Foxhound' entered service in the mid-1980s and is a development of the MiG-25 with greater power and the combination of pulse-Doppler look-down/shoot-down radar and more modern missiles to destroy low-level attackers. The type's maximum speed is a 'mere' Mach 2.4.

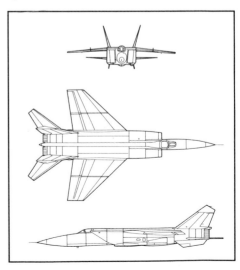

MiG-25 'Foxbat-A'

Mikoyan-Gurevich Mig-25 'Foxbat-A'

MIKOYAN-GUREVICH MiG-25 'FOXBAT-A'
Role: High speed high altitude interceptor
Crew/Accommodation: One
Power Plant: Two 12,250 kgp (27,010 lb s.t.) Tumansky R-31 turbojets with reheat
Dimensions: Span 13.95 m (45.75 ft); length 23.82 m (78.15 ft); wing area 56.83 m² (611.7 sq ft)
Weights: Empty 20,000 kg (44,100 lb); MTOW 37,425 kg (82,500 lb)
Performance: Maximum speed 3,006 km/h (1,622 knots) at 10,975 m (36,000 ft); operational ceiling 24,385 m (80,000 ft); range 1,450 km (782 naut. miles)
Load: Four medium-range and two short-range air-to-air missiles

REPUBLIC F-105 THUNDERCHIEF (United States)

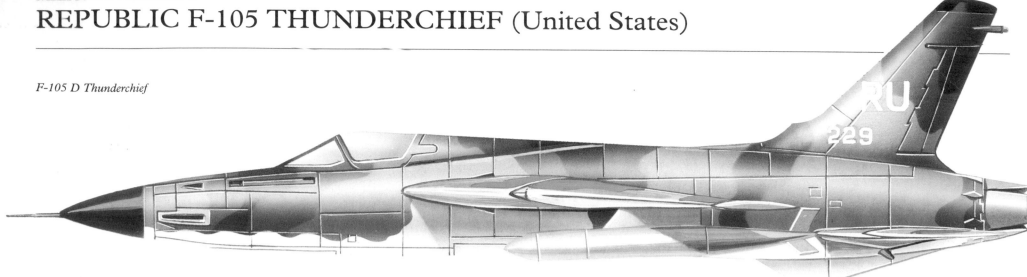

F-105 D Thunderchief

The Thunderchief was the final major type to come from the Republic company before its merger into the Fairchild organization, and accorded well with its manufacturer's reputation for massive tactical warplanes. The type was schemed as a successor to the F-84F Thunderstreak and was therefore a strike fighter, but one that offered the advantages of an internal weapons bay able to accommodate 3629-kg (8,000-lb) of stores and fully supersonic performance. This last was provided by the use of a powerful afterburning turbojet in an advanced airframe incorporating the lessons of the area-rule principle.

Two YF-105A prototypes were ordered, and the first of these flew in October 1956 with the 6804-kg (15,000-lb) thrust Pratt & Whitney J57-P-25 turbojet and an 'unwaisted' fuselage. No production followed, for the availability of the new J75 engine and the area-rule theory resulted first in another four prototypes designated YF-105B and powered by 7471-kg (16,470-lb) thrust J75-P-3. Production thus began with 71 F-105B aircraft modelled on the YF-105B and its area-ruled 'waisted' fuselage and forward-swept inlets in the wing roots for the 7802-kg (17,200-lb) thrust J75-P-5 engine. The major variant was the F-105D, of which 610 were built with all-weather avionics, an improved nav/attack system, the 7802-kg (17,200-lb) J75-P-19W turbojet and provision for up to 6350-kg (14,000-lb) of ordnance carried on four underwing hardpoints as well as in the internal load.

The final version was the F-105F tandem two-seat conversion trainer, and of 86 aircraft 60 were later converted to EF-105F (and then F-105G) 'Wild Weasel' defence-suppression aircraft. These were fitted with special radar-detection equipment and anti-radar missiles, and played an important part in American air operations over North Vietnam.

Republic F-105G Thunderchief

REPUBLIC F-105D THUNDERCHIEF
Role: Fighter
Crew/Accommodation: One
Power Plant: One 11,113 kgp (24,500 lb s.t.) Pratt & Whitney J75-P-15W turbojet with reheat
Dimensions: Span 10.65 m (34.94 ft); length 19.58 m (64.25 ft); wing area 35.76 m² (385 sq ft)
Weights: Empty 12,474 kg (27,500 lb); MTOW 23,834 kg (52,546 lb)
Performance: Maximum speed 2,369 km/h (1,279 knots) Mach 2.23 at 11,000 m (36,090 ft); operational ceiling 12,802 m (42,000 ft); radius 1,152 km (662 naut. miles)
Load: One 20 mm multi-barrel cannon, plus up to 6,350 kg (14,000 lb) of weapons/fuel

Republic F-105D single-seaters and, in the foreground, an F-105F two-seater

DASSAULT-BREGUET MIRAGE F1 (France)

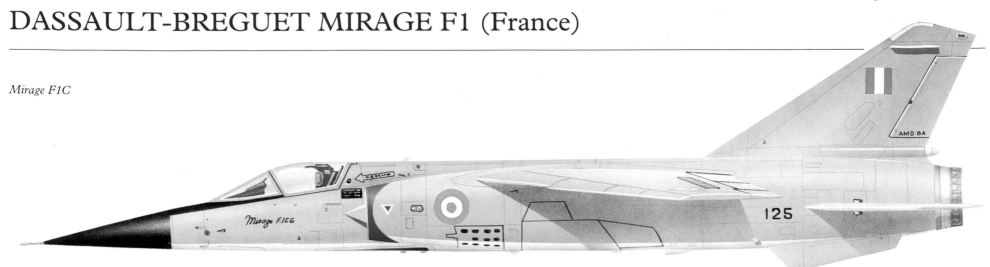

Mirage F1C

The Mirage F1 was developed by Dassault-Breguet as a successor to the Mirage III/5 family, but is a markedly different aircraft with 'conventional' flying surfaces. The French Air Force originally wanted a two-seat warplane, and such a type was evolved by the company as the Mirage F2 to government contract and powered by a SNECMA/Pratt & Whitney TF306 turbofan. At the same time the company worked as a private venture on the Mirage F1, a smaller and lighter single-seater sized to the SNECMA Atar turbojet.

The Mirage F2 flew in June 1966, but cost too much for a profitable production contract. The Mirage F1 first flew in December 1966 with the Atar 9K-31 turbojet. After the Mirage F2 programme was cancelled the French government ordered three pre-production examples of the Mirage F1. These displayed excellent performance and overall capabilities as multi-role warplanes, their primary advantages over the Mirage III/5 family being larger warload, easy handling at low altitude, good rate of climb, and 40 per cent greater fuel capacity (through the use of integral rather than bladder tanks) all combined with semi-STOL field performance thanks to the use of droopable leading edges and large trailing-edge flaps on the sharply swept wing, which is mounted in the shoulder position.

The Mirage F1 was ordered into production with the Atar 9K-50 afterburning turbojet. Like the preceding Mirage III/5 series, the Mirage F1 has been a considerable if not outstanding commercial success. The main variants have been the Mirage F1A clear-weather ground-attack fighter, the Mirage F1B two-seat trainer, the Mirage F1C (and Mirage F1C-200 long-range) multi-role fighter, the Mirage F1E strike fighter, and the Mirage F1CR-200 long-range reconnaissance aircraft. Some French aircraft are also being adapted as Mirage F1CT tactical fighters.

Dassault-Breguet Mirage F1C

DASSAULT-BREGUET MIRAGE F1C
Role: Strike fighter
Crew/Accommodation: One
Power Plant: One 7,200 kgp (15,873 lb s.t.) SNECMA Atar 9K-50 turbojet with reheat
Dimensions: Span 8.4 m (27.55 ft); length 15 m (49.24 ft); wing area 25 m² (270 sq ft)
Weights: Empty 7,400 kg (16,315 lb); MTOW 14,900 kg (32,850 lb)
Performance: Maximum speed 2,335 km/h (1,260 knots) Mach 2.2 at 12,000 m (39,370 ft); operational ceiling 20,000 m (65,600 ft); range 3,300 km (1,781 miles)
Load: Two 30 mm DEFA cannon, plus up to 4,000 kg (8,818 lb) of externally carried weapons

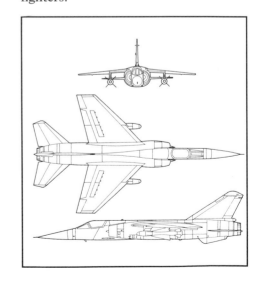

Dassault-Breguet Mirage F1C

MIKOYAN-GUREVICH MiG-23 AND MiG-27 'FLOGGER' Series (U.S.S.R.)

MiG-27 'Flogger'

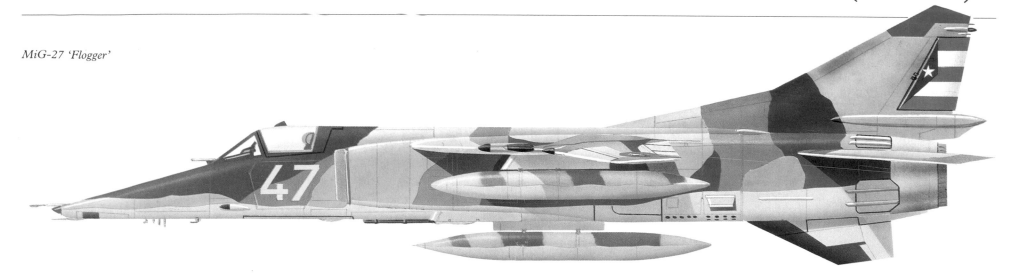

In 1966, the MiG bureau flew its Ye-231 prototype for evaluation against the Ye-230 tailed-delta prototype powered by a single Lyul'ka AL-7F-1 turbojet propulsion engine and given V/STOL capability by the incorporation of a battery of Koliesov lift jets in the centre of the fuselage. The Ye-231 proved superior, and in 1968 a derivative, the MiG-23 with the new Tumansky R-27 R-29 series of turbojets was produced.

The Ye-231 and MiG-23 marked a new development in design by introducing variable-geometry wings to reconcile the apparently incompatible features of good field and cruise performance with high dash speed in a type with STOL capability. The MiG-23 was developed as an air-combat fighter with useful secondary attack capability, and entered service in 1970 with interim radar and the R-27 engine.

The full-capability 'High Lark' radar and the R-29 engine were introduced in 1975, and since that time the type has been extensively developed in terms of its electronics and overall capabilities, the latest variant being that known in the West only by its NATO reporting designation 'Flogger-K'. The MiG-27 is the dedicated attack derivative of the MiG-23 with a revised forward fuselage offering heavy armour protection and fitted with terrain-avoidance rather than search radar. The MiG-27 also has a less advanced powerplant with fixed inlets and a simple nozzle for its reduced-performance role at low altitude; special target-acquisition and weapon-guidance equipment are installed, as are a multi-barrel cannon and additional hardpoints for the larger offensive load. Two variants are the 'Flogger-D' and 'Flogger-J', while export aircraft are the MiG-23 'Flogger-F' and 'Flogger-H' combining the airframe of the MiG-23 with the armoured nose of the MiG-27.

MiG-23 'Flogger-B'

MIKOYAN-GUREVICH MiG-27 'FLOGGER-J'
Role: Strike fighter with variable/geometry wing
Crew/Accommodation: One
Power Plant: One 11,500 kgp (25,350 lb s.t.) Tumansky R-29-300 turbofan with reheat
Dimensions: Span 14.25 m (46,75 ft) swept 8.17 m (26.8 ft); length 16.5 m (54.13 ft); wing area 27.26 m² (293,42 sq ft)
Weights: Empty 10,818 kg (23,849 lb); MTOW 18,000 kg (39,683 lb)
Performance: Maximum speed 1,102 km/h (594 knots) Mach 0.95 at 305 m (1,001 ft); operational ceiling 13,000+ m (46,650+ ft); radius 390 km (210 naut. miles) with full weapons load
Load: One 23 mm cannon, plus up to 3,000 kg (6,614 lb) of weapons

This 'Flogger-D' aeroplane has terrain-avoidance radar

SAAB 37 VIGGEN (Sweden)

JA 37 Viggen

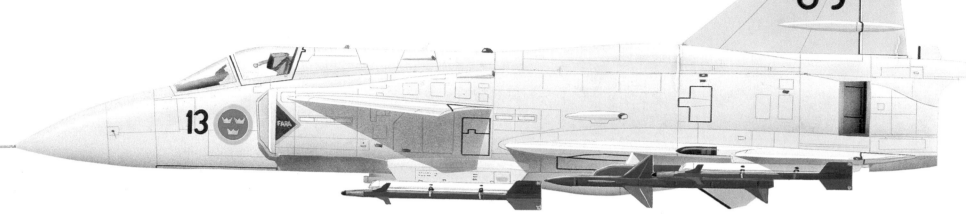

With the Saab 37 Viggen (Thunderbolt), first flown in February 1967, Sweden produced a true multi-role fighter with a thrust-reversible afterburning turbofan and a canard layout for true STOL capability using short lengths of road. The type was schemed on the integrated weapon system concept pioneered in the United States, and was based on a Swedish licence-built version of the Pratt & Whitney JT8D turbofan, basically a civil engine offering great reliability and fuel economy, but fitted in this application with Swedish-designed afterburning and thrust-reversing units. The combination of the flapped canard configuration and sturdy landing gear allows the type to be flown straight onto the runway (or length of road) after a no-flare approach, and a combination of aerodynamic braking, thrust reversing and wheel braking by units with anti-skid systems keeps the landing run exceptionally short. The advanced electronics include pulse-Doppler radar, a head-up display and other items linked by a digital fire-control system to maximize the type's offensive and defensive capabilities with effective weapons and electronic countermeasures.

Production totalled 329, and the variants have been the AJ 37 attack aircraft with the 11,790-kg (25,992-lb) thrust RM8A, the SF 37 overland reconnaissance aircraft with a modified nose accommodating seven cameras and an infra-red sensor, the SH 37 overwater reconnaissance aircraft with search radar, and the Sk 35 tandem two-seat operational trainer with a taller vertical tail. A 'Viggen Mk 2' development is the JA 37 interceptor with the 12,750-kg (28,109-lb) thrust RM8B turbofan, a number of airframe modifications, an underfuselage pack housing the extremely potent Oerlikon-Bührle KCA 30-mm cannon, together with a revised electronic suite with much improved radar.

The SH 37 is the overwater reconnaissance variant of the Saab Viggen family

SAAB JA 37 VIGGEN
Role: Interceptor
Crew/Accommodation: One
Power Plant: One 12,750 kgp (28,109 lb s.t.) Volvo Flyg motor RM8B turbofan with reheat
Dimensions: Span 10.6 m (34.78 ft); length 16.4 m (53.81 ft); wing area 52.2 m² (561.9 sq ft)
Weights: Empty 12,200 kg (26,455 lb); MTOW 22,500 kg (49,604 lb)
Performance: Maximum speed 2,231 km/h (1,204 knots) Mach 2.10 at 11,000 m (36,090 ft); operational ceiling 18,300 m (60,039 ft); radius 483 km (260 naut. miles) with 1,360 kg warload
Load: One 30 mm cannon, plus up to 6,000 kg (13,277 lb) of externally-carried weapons/fuel, including two medium range and four short-range air-to-air missiles

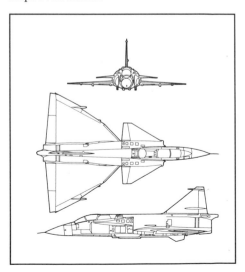

Saab AJ 37 Viggen

GRUMMAN F-14 TOMCAT (United States)

F-14 Tomcat

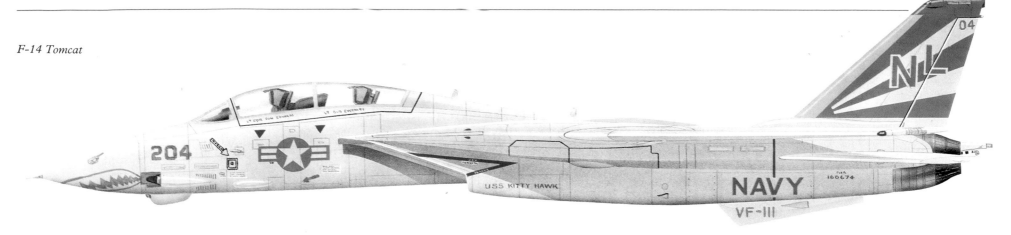

After the cancellation of the F-111B, developed primarily by Grumman as the fleet defence fighter equivalent of the General Dynamics F-111A land-based interdictor, the U.S. Navy issued a requirement for a new fighter. Submissions were received from five companies, but Grumman had a head-start with its G-303 design that made valuable use of the company's experience of variable-geometry wings, and also incorporated the F-111B's TF30 engines, AIM-54

Phoenix long-range air-to-air missiles, and AWG-9 radar fire-control system. In January 1969, the G-303 was selected for development as the F-14, and the first of 12 YF-14A pre-production aircraft flew in December 1970. The Tomcat was aerodynamically more tractable because of its 'glove vanes', small surfaces extending from the leading-edge roots of the main wings' fixed structure as the outer surfaces swept aft, which regulated movement in the centre of pressure to reduce pitch alterations.

The F-14A initial model entered service in October 1972 and immediately proved itself a classic fighter of its type in terms of performance, manoeuvrability, and weapon system capability. Some aircraft have been adapted for the reconnaissance role as the F-14A/TARPS with a ventral equipment pod. The only limitation to the F-14's total success has been the powerplant of two 9480-kg (20,900-lb) thrust Pratt & Whitney TF30-P-412A turbofans,

which were not designed for fighter use and therefore lack the flexibility required for this role. In the F-14A Plus variant introduced in the later 1980s, the TF30 has been replaced by the altogether more capable General Electric F110-GE-400 delivering a thrust of 10,478 kg (23,100 lb), which will also be used in the F-14D(R) rebuilt version of the F-14A together with a mass of electronic improvements in the offensive and defensive suites.

GRUMMAN F-14A TOMCAT
Role: Naval carrierborne fighter
Crew/Accommodation: Two
Power Plant: Two, 9,480 kgp (20,900 lb s.t.) Pratt & Whitney TF30-P-312A turbofans
Dimensions: Span unswept 19.6 m (64.1 ft) swept 11.7 m (38.2 ft); length 19.1 m (62.7 ft); wing area 52.5 m² (565 sq ft)
Weights: Empty 18,036 kg (39,762 lb); MTOW 31,945 kg (70,426 lb)
Performance: Maximum speed 2,498 km/h (1,348 knots), Mach 2.35 at 11.276 m (37,000 ft); operational ceiling 18,288+ m (60,000 ft); radius of action unrefuelled 1,232 km (665 miles)
Load: Up to 2,913 kg (6,423 lb) of externally mounted missiles, typically 6 AIM-554 Phoenix and 2 AIM-9 Sidewinders, plus an internal 6-barrel 20 mm General Electric M61 Vulcan cannon

Grumman F-14A Tomcat

A Grumman F-14A Tomcat in the markings of US Naval Aviation

McDONNELL DOUGLAS F-15 EAGLE (United States)

F-15C Eagle

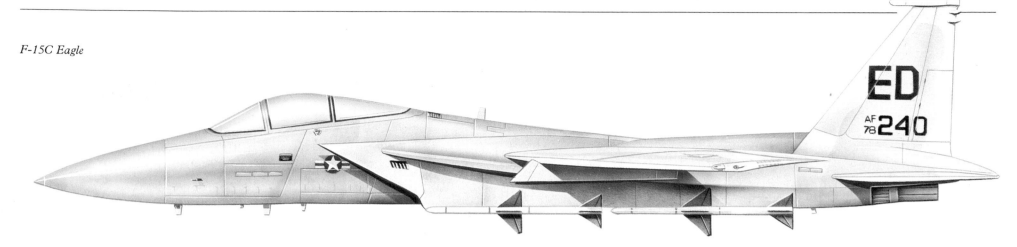

The F-15 was planned as the U.S. Air Force's successor to the F-4 in the air-superiority role. After three years of design studies the type was selected for hardware development in December 1969. The first of two YF-15A prototypes emerged for its first flight in July 1972 as a massive aircraft with two 10,809-kg (23,830-lb) thrust Pratt & Whitney F100-P-100 turbofans, sophisticated aerodynamics, advanced electronics including the APG-63 multi-role radar and a pilot's head-up display, and the world's first production cockpit of the HOTAS (Hands-On-Throttle-And-Stick) type.

The Eagle entered service in November 1974, and has since proved itself a first-class and versatile warplane. Its powerful engines allow the type to carry a large weight of widely assorted weapons in the primary air-to-air and secondary air-to-ground roles, and also generate a thrust-weight ratio in the order of unity for an exceptionally high rate of climb and very good manoeuvrability.

The initial F-15A single-seat model was complemented by the F-15B (originally TF-15A) two-seat combat-capable version.

In 1979 production switched to the F-15C and F-15D respectively. These are powered by 10,637-kg (23,450-lb) thrust F100-P-220 engines, and have more advanced systems, including the improved APG-70 radar from 1985 production onward, as well as provision for external carriage of the so-called FAST (Fuel And Sensor Tactical) packs that provide considerably more fuel and weapons

at a negligible increase in drag and weight. The F-15C and D are built under licence in Japan as the F-15J and F-15DJ. In 1989 the USAF received its first example of the F-15E two-seat interdiction aircraft derived from the F-15D, and developments currently in hand centre on a long-range strike version able to operate from short lengths of damaged runway with the aid of 2D vectoring nozzles and canard foreplanes controlled by an advanced fly-by-wire system.

A McDonnell Douglas F-15E Eagle of the 4th Tactical Fighter Wing

---

McDONNELL DOUGLAS F-15E EAGLE
Role: All-weather strike fighter
Crew/Accommodation: Two
Power Plant: Two 10,637 kgp (23,450 lb s.t.) Pratt & Whitney F100-PW-220 turbofans with reheat
Dimensions: Span 13.05 m (42 ft); length 19.43 m (63.75 ft); wing area 56.5 m² (608 sq ft)
Weights: Empty 14,379 kg (31,700 lb); MTOW 36,741 kg (81,000 lb)
Performance: Maximum speed 2,698 km/h (1,456 knots) Mach 2.54 at 12.192 m (40,000 ft); operational ceiling 18,300 m (60,000 ft); radius 1,420 km (670 naut. miles) with 3,175 kg (7,000 lb) of weapons
Load: Up to 10,659 (23,500 lb) of weaponry, including one 20 mm multi-barrel cannon mounted internally

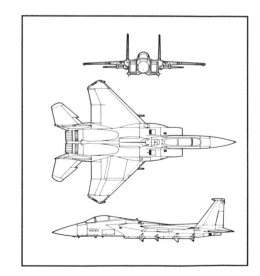

McDonnell Douglas F-15C Eagle

GENERAL DYNAMICS F-16 FIGHTING FALCON (United States)

F-16A Fighting Falcon

During the Vietnam War the United States Air Force discovered that its fighters were in general handicapped by their very large size, weight and Mach 2 performance, all of which were factors which were liabilities that seriously eroded reliability and combat agility in the type of turning dogfight that became increasingly common at low and medium altitudes. To help to find a solution to this problem, in

1971 the U.S. Air Force instituted a Light-Weight fighter competition, and General Dynamics produced its Model 401 design.

The first of two YF-16 prototypes flew in January 1974, and 12 months later the type was declared winner of the LWF competition. The basic type was adopted as the U.S. Air Force's Air-Combat Fighter, and in June 1975 it was announced that the same type had been adopted by a four-nation European consortium. The first production models were the single-

seat F-16A and two-seat F-16B, which entered service in August 1978 and received the name Fighting Falcon in 1980. The type has gone on to become numerically the most important fighter in the inventory of the Western world. The type is based on blended contours and relaxed stability controlled by a fly-by-wire system the sidestick joystick of which is operated by a semi-reclining pilot. Powered by the 10,814-kg (23,840-lb) afterburning thrust Pratt & Whitney F100-P-200 turbofan, the first two variants matured as exceptional multi-role fighters which were able to carry and deliver with great accuracy a large load of widely assorted weapons.

Many structural and electronic improvements, including a more capable radar, have created the latest F-16C single-seat and F-16D two-seat variants, which can use the F100 or General Electric F110 turbofan in their most recent and powerful forms. There have been a number of experimental variants, and future developments are centred on the A-16 close support and RF-16 reconnaissance models for the U.S.

Air Force, and the FSX next-generation derivative to be produced in Japan.

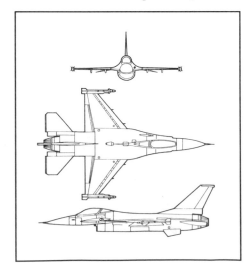

F-16C Fighting Falcon

GENERAL DYNAMICS F-16A FIGHTING FALCON
Role: Day strike fighter
Crew/Accommodation: One
Power Plant: One 10,814 kgp (23,840 lb s.t.) Pratt & Whitney F100-P-200 turbofan
Dimensions: Span 10.01 m (32.83 ft); length 14.52 m (47.64 ft); wing area 17.87 m² (300 sq ft)
Weights: Empty 6,613 kg (14,567 lb); MTOW 17,010 kg (37,500 lb)
Performance: Maximum speed 2,146 km/h (1,158 knots) Mach 2.02 at 12,190 m (40,000 ft); operational ceiling 15,850 m (52,000 ft); range 580 km (313 naut. miles) with 3,000 lb bombload
Load: One 20 mm cannon, plus up to 6,894 kg (15,200 lb) of bombs

The General Dynamics F-16C Fighting Falcon

MIKOYAN-GUREVICH MiG-29 'FULCRUM' (U.S.S.R.)

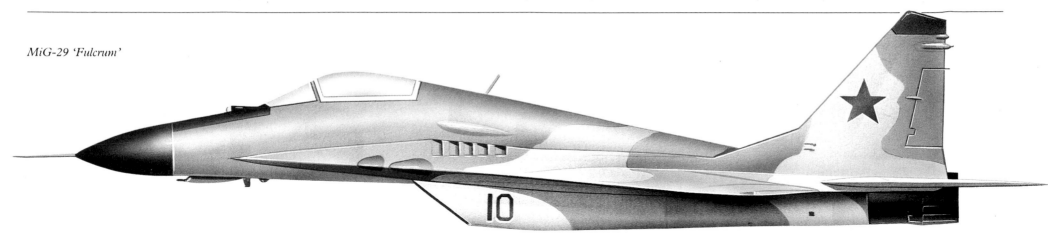

MiG-29 'Fulcrum'

Entering service in 1985, the MiG-29 is also known by the NATO reporting name 'Fulcrum' and is a dual-role fighter optimized for the air combat role with a secondary attack capability. Despite its use of a conventional control system in an airframe of basically conventional configuration, the type possesses great agility. Moreover, a genuine look-down/shoot-down capability is offered by the combination of a 40-km (25-mile) range radar and the new AA-10 snap-

down air-to-air missile. The 'Fulcrum-A' has undergone a number of changes since it was first seen, the consensus being that these indicate a number of fixes to bring the design up to its present standard.

The first variant was probably a pre-production model and carried small ventral fins reminiscent of those carried by the Sukhoi Su-27 'Flanker'. The next model was first revealed at Kuopio Risalla in Finland during July 1986, and was probably the first

service variant. The third variant has wider-chord rudders. The MiG-29UB 'Fulcrum-B' is the two-seat combat-capable conversion and continuation trainer derivative of the 'Fulcrum-A' with a ranging radar in place of the pulse-Doppler unit of the 'Fulcrum-A'. The next variant is known only by its NATO reporting name of 'Fulcrum-C' and is distinguishable by its larger dorsal fairing for more fuel, or, more probably, upgraded electronics. Since 1989, the U.S.S.R. has been testing a navalized 'Fulcrum' as a possible part of the complement

for the U.S.S.R.'s new conventional aircraft-carriers. The naval version has folding wings, an arrester hook, provision for a 'buddy' refuelling pack and a steerable infra-red sensor forward of the cockpit. From May 1990, the U.S.S.R. has been trialling an improved version of the MiG-29 which has fly-by-wire controls in place of the original mechanical type.

A Mikoyan-Gurevich MiG-29 'Fulcrum-A'

MIKOYAN-GUREVICH MiG-29 'FULCRUM-A'
Role: Fighter
Crew/Accommodation: One
Power Plant: Two 8,300 kgp (18,300 lb s.t.) Tumansky R-33D turbofans with reheat
Dimensions: Span 11.36 m (37.27 ft); length 17.32 m (56.83 ft); wing area 35.2 m² (378.9 sq ft)
Weights: Empty 8,175 kg (18,025 lb); MTOW 18,000 kg (39,700 lb)
Performance: Maximum speed 2,440 km/h (1,320 knots) Mach 2.3 at 11,000 m (36,090 ft); operational ceiling 17,000 m (56,000 ft); range 2,100 km (1,130 naut. miles)
Load: One 30 mm cannon, plus two medium-range and four short-range air-to-air missiles

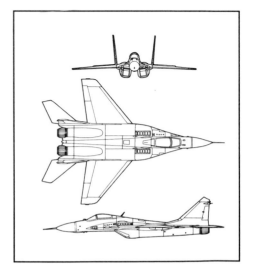

MiG-29 'Fulcrum-A'

81

SUKHOI Su-27 'FLANKER' (U.S.S.R.)

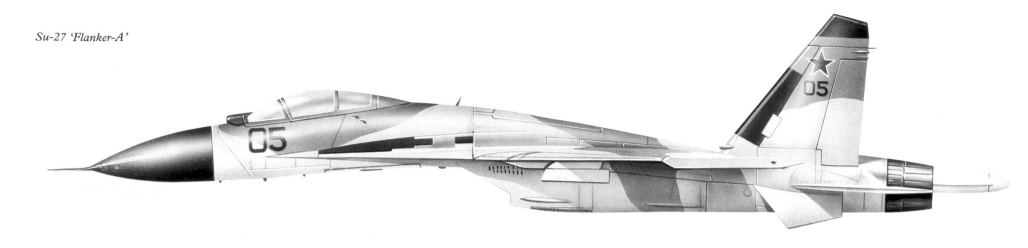

Su-27 'Flanker-A'

Developed during the 1970s as a direct counterpart to the U.S. Air Force's McDonnell Douglas F-15 Eagle air-superiority fighter, the Su-27 is a high-performance type with a fly-by-wire control system, and is almost certainly the U.S.S.R.'s first genuine look-down/shoot-down fighter with its pulse-Doppler radar and ten air-to-air missiles. The type entered service in 1985 in the initial form known to

NATO as the 'Flanker-A', though it is now thought that this was the pre-production type with the vertical tail surfaces located centrally above the engine installations, rounded wingtips lacking the missile launch rails of the 'Flanker-B'. and 12,500-kg (27,557-lb) thrust R-31F engines.

The full-production version is the 'Flanker-B' with squared-off wingtips carrying missile launch rails, plus a number of refinements such as leading-edge flaps and vertical tail surfaces located farther outboard. This type entered service early in 1986, and

the fly-by-wire control system automatically limits manoeuvres to a maximum 30° angle of attack and the load factor to 9 *g*, and the leading- and trailing-edge flaps are scheduled automatically to maximize lift and minimize drag during combat manoeuvres.

The 'Flanker-B2' is the navalized version of the 'Flanker-B' under test from 1989 as a possible component of the air group for the U.S.S.R.'s new conventional aircraft carriers. The version has folding wings, an arrester

hook, strengthened landing gear as well as provision for a 'buddy' refuelling pack.

The 'Flanker-C' is a tandem two-seat variant first revealed in 1989 with a normal take-off weight of 22,500-kg (49,603-lb). This model has improved radar in a slightly longer nose, and is probably an interdictor rather than a trainer, with the rear-seat officer tasked with management of the electronic and weapon systems, which are in all probability more advanced than those of the 'Flanker-B'.

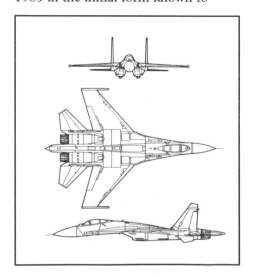

Sukhoi Su-27 'Flanker-B'

SUKHOI Su-27 'FLANKER A'
Role: Interceptor
Crew/Accommodation: One
Power Plant: Two 13,608 kgp (30,000 lb s.t.) Tumansky R-32 turbofans with reheat
Dimensions: Span 14.5 m (47.57 ft); length 21 m (68.9 ft); wing area 71 m² (764.2 sq ft)
Weights: Empty 15,400 kg (33,951 lb); MTOW 28,400 kg (62,611 lb)
Performance: Maximum speed 2,125+ km/h (1,147+ knots) Mach 2.0+ at 11,000 m (36,090 ft); operational ceiling 16,400+ m (53,806+ ft); range 1,500 km (809 naut. miles) with full missile warload
Load: One 30 mm multi-barrel cannon, plus six long-range and four short-range air-to-air missiles

A Sukhoi Su-27 'Flanker-B'

BRITISH AEROSPACE SEA HARRIER (United Kingdom)

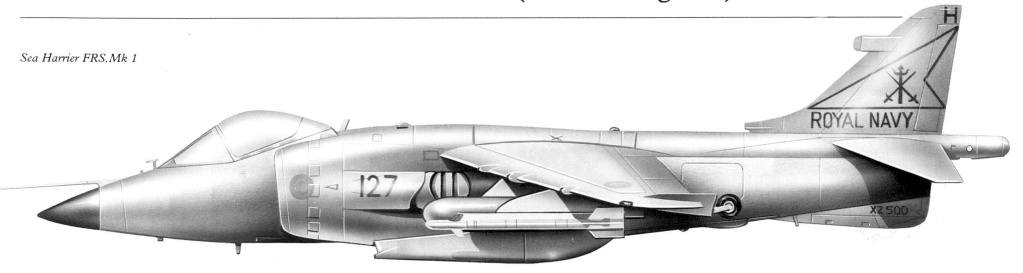

Sea Harrier FRS.Mk 1

Despite the fact that land-based Harriers had performed large numbers of VTOL and STOVL demonstrations on all manner of surface warships, it was many years before the Royal Navy took the decision to procure a navalized version of the Harrier for what were then called 'through-deck cruisers' to conceal their real light aircraft carrier nature from political opposition. The decision was taken in 1975, after the failure of an Anglo-American project to achieve sufficient common ground, and was designed to provide the three 'Invincible' class carriers with a multi-role warplane. As a result, the basic Harrier GR.Mk 3 was adapted with a raised cockpit offering much improved all-round fields of vision, updated and more comprehensive avionics, more advanced electronics including Ferranti Blue Fox multi-role radar, and weapons that include air-to-air missiles. The first Sea Harrier FRS.Mk 1 fighter, reconnaissance, and strike aircraft were hurriedly pushed into service during 1982 in time for the Falklands war with Argentina, and proved a decisive weapon in the British victory. A similar model is operated by the Indian Navy, whose Sea Harrier FRS. Mk 51s have provision for Matra Magic rather than AIM-9 Sidewinder air-to-air missiles.

The latest British standard is the Sea Harrier FRS.Mk 2 able to engage multiple targets at long range thanks to the provision of Ferranti Blue Vixen radar and AIM-120A AMRAAM missiles. This mid-life updated version also has improved defensive electronics, a HOTAS (Hands-On-Throttle-And-Stick) cockpit, modern 25-mm cannon in place of the elderly 30-mm weapons of the FRS.Mk 1, a digital databus for the better integration of the electronics with modern weapons, and two additional underwing hardpoints.

A British Aerospace Sea Harrier FRS.Mk 1 of 800 Squadron, Fleet Air Arm

BRITISH AEROSPACE SEA HARRIER FRS.Mk 1
Role: Strike fighter/reconnaissance
Crew/Accommodation: One
Power Plant: One 9,752 kgp (21,500 lb s.t.) Rolls-Royce Pegasus 104 vectored thrust turbofan
Dimensions: Span 7.7 m (25.25 ft); length 14.52 m (47.58 ft); wing area 18.68 m² (201.1 ft)
Weights: Empty 6.374 kg (14,052 lb); MTOW 11,880 kg (26,200 lb) with take-off roll
Performance: Maximum speed 1,185 km/h (640 knots) at sea level; operational ceiling 15,240+ m (50,000+ ft); radius 520 km (280 naut. miles) with two anti-ship missiles
Load: Two 30 mm cannon, plus up to 3,630 kg (8,000 lb) of externally carried ordnance

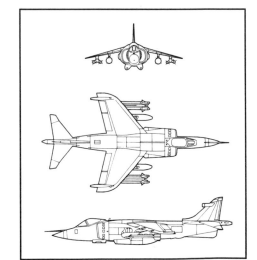

Sea Harrier FRS.Mk 1

DASSAULT-BREGUET MIRAGE 2000 (France)

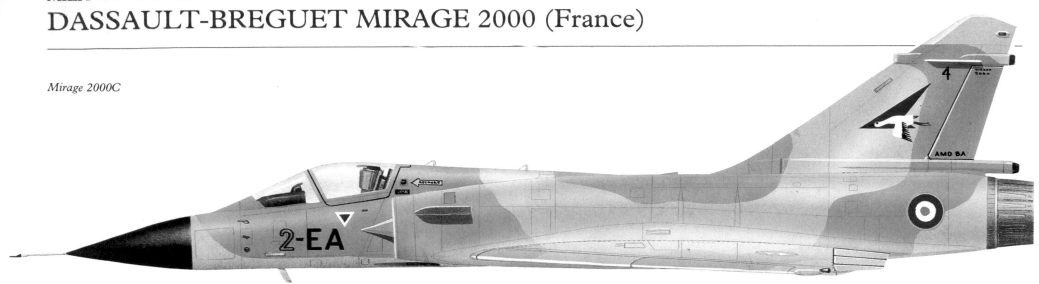

Mirage 2000C

With the Mirage 2000 the manufacturer reverted to the delta-wing planform, but, in this instance, of the relaxed-stability type with an electronic 'fly-by-wire' control system to avoid many of the low-level handling and tactical limitations suffered by the aerodynamically similar Mirage III/5 family. In the early and mid-1970s, Dassault was working on a prototype to meet the

French Air Force's ACF (Avion de Combat Futur) requirement, but this was cancelled in 1975 when the service decided that a warplane powered by two SNECMA M53-3 turbofans was too large. In December 1975, therefore, the French government authorized the design and development of a smaller single-engined machine. This emerged as the Mirage 2000 with the 9000-kg (19,840-lb) thrust SNECMA M53-5 turbofan in the smallest and lightest possible airframe for a high power/weight ratio.

The first of five prototypes flew during March 1978 and the prototypes soon demonstrated the Mirage 2000's complete superiority to the Mirage III in all flight regimes. The type remains in production, and the primary variants are the Mirage 2000B two-seat trainer with a lengthened fuselage, the Mirage 2000C single-seat interceptor and multi-role fighter (now with the 9700-kg/21,384-lb thrust M53-P2 turbofan and RDI pulse Doppler radar in place of the original RDM multi-mode radar), the Mirage 2000N two-seat

nuclear strike fighter based on the airframe of the Mirage 2000B and optimized for the low-level penetration role with the ASMP stand-off missile, the Mirage 2000N-1 two-seat conventional attack fighter based on the Mirage 2000N, the Mirage 2000R single-seat reconnaissance fighter, the Mirage 2000-3 multi-role export derivative of the Mirage 2000N-1 with RDY multi-function radar and the ability to carry a large range of advanced weapons, and the Mirage 2000-5 air-defence counterpart of the Mirage 2000-3.

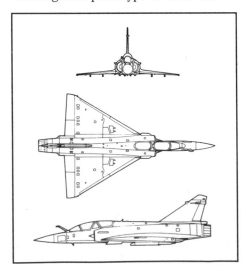

Mirage 2000-5

DASSAULT-BREGUET MIRAGE 2000C
Role: Air superiority fighter
Crew/Accommodation: One
Power Plant: One 9,700 kgp (21,385 lb s.t.) SNECMA M53-P2 turbofan with reheat
Dimensions: Span 9.13 m (29.95 ft); length 15 m (49.2 ft); wing area 41 m² (441.3 sq ft)
Weights: Empty 7,500 kg (16,534 lb); MTOW 17,000 kg (37,480 lb)
Performance: Maximum speed 2,335 km/h (1,260 knots) Mach 2.2 at 11,000 m (36,000 ft); operational ceiling 18,000 m (60,000 ft); range 1,600+km (850+ naut. miles) with external fuel
Load: Two 30 mm DEFA cannon, two Matra 550 Magic and two Matra Super 530 missiles

A Dassault-Breguet Mirage 2000C

McDONNELL DOUGLAS F/A-18 HORNET (United States)

F/A-18A Hornet

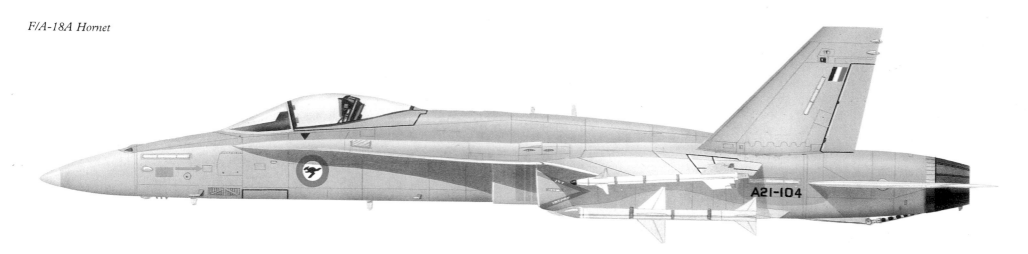

Serving with the U.S. Navy and Marine Corps as replacement for the F-4 and A-7 in the fighter and attack roles respectively, the dual-capability F/A-18 is one of the West's most important carrierborne warplanes, and has also secured useful export orders for land-based use. The type was derived from the Northrop YF-17 (losing contender to the YF-16 in the USAF's Light-Weight Fighter competition) in order to meet the requirements of the Navy Air Combat Fighter requirement.

In the development programme undertaken by Northrop and McDonnell Douglas, the YF-17 was enlarged, aerodynamically refined, re-engined and fitted with advanced mission electronics to emerge as the first of 11 YF-18A pre-production aircraft that flew from November 1979. Initial plans to procure separate F-18 and A-18 fighter and attack variants had been abandoned when it was realized that different software in the mission computers would allow a single type to be optimized in each role. McDonnell Douglas assumed production leadership, and the F/A-18As entered service late in 1983 as the F/A-18A single-seater and its combat-capable two-seat partner, the F/A-18B, originally designated the TF/A-18A.

The F/A-18A has been replaced in production by the F/A-18C with a number of electronic and system improvements and can carry more advanced weapons. The F/A-18B has been complemented by the next two-seat variant: the F/A-18D. This is a combat type optimized for the night attack role, and this night attack capability is common to all F/A-18C and D aircraft delivered since October 1989. Another variant, due to enter service in the early 1990s, is the RF-18D tactical reconnaissance platform to replace the RF-4B.

A McDonnell Douglas F/A-18A Hornet

McDONNELL DOUGLAS F/A-18A HORNET
Role: Naval carrierborne strike fighter
Crew/Accommodation: One
Power Plant: Two 7,257 kgp (16,000 lb s.t.) General Electric F404-GE-400 turbofans with reheat
Dimensions: Span 11.4 m (36.5 ft); length 17.1 m (56 ft); wing area 37.16 m² (400 sq ft)
Weights: Empty 12,700 kg (28,000 lb); MTOW 25,401 kg (56,000 lb)
Performance: Maximum speed 1,457 km/h (786 knots) Mach 1.18 at sea level; operational ceiling 15,240 m (50,000 ft); radius 740 km (399 naut. miles) with missiles and internal fuel only
Load: One 20 mm multi-barrel cannon, two medium-range and two short-range air-to-air missiles, plus externally carried weapons that in total exceed 7,711 kg (17,000 lb)

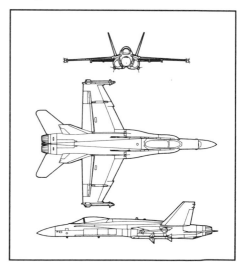

McDonnell Douglas F/A-18A Hornet

85

BREGUET Bre. 14 (France)

Bre.14B2

mounted Renault in line engine proved both powerful and reliable.

An initial 150 aircraft were ordered in the A.2 two-seat artillery observation category during April 1917, and by the end of that year orders had been placed for 2,650 aircraft to be produced by Breguet and five licensees in two-seat A.2 artillery and B.2 bomber variants, the latter with wings of increased span and flaps on the trailing edges of the lower wing. Other World War I variants were the Bre. 14B.1 single-seat bomber and Bre. 14S ambulance. Production up to the end of World War I totalled 5,300 aircraft with a variety of engine types, and more than 2,500 additional aircraft were built before production ended in 1928. Many of the post-war aircraft were of the Bre. 14 TOE type for use in France's colonial possessions. The Bre. 14 was finally phased out of French service only in 1932. Substantial exports were also made.

The Breguet Bre. 14 was France's single most important and successful warplane of World War I, and perhaps the best known French combat plane until the advent of the Dassault Mirage III series. The type began to take shape on the drawing boards of the company's designers during the summer of 1916, and the first AV Type XIV flew in November 1916 with the AV (Avant, or forward) signifying that the plane was of the tractor type. Though not notable for its aesthetic qualities, the machine that soon became the Type 14 and later the Bre. 14 was immensely sturdy as a result of its steel, duralumin and wooden construction covered in fabric and light alloy panels and supported on strong landing gear of the spreader type. The pilot and gunner were located close together in the optimum tactical location, and the front

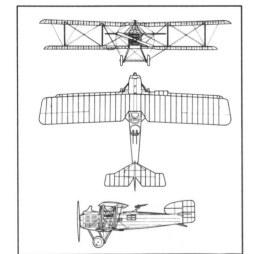

Breguet Bre.14

BREGUET Bre.14B2
Role: Fast day bomber/reconnaissance
Crew/Accommodation: Two
Power Plant: One 300 hp Renault 12 Fcy water-cooled inline
Dimensions: Span 14.91 m (48.92 ft); length 8.87 m (29.10 ft); wing area 51.1 m² (550 sq ft)
Weights: Empty 1,035 kg (2,282 lb); MTOW 1,580 kg (3,483 lb)
Performance: Maximum speed 195 km/h (121 mph) at sea level; operational ceiling 4,265 m (13,993 ft); range 485 km (301 miles) with full warload
Load: Two/three .303 inch machine guns, plus up to 260 kg (573 lb) of externally-carried bombs

A Breguet Bre.14 in Portuguese service

AIRCO D.H.9 (United Kingdom)

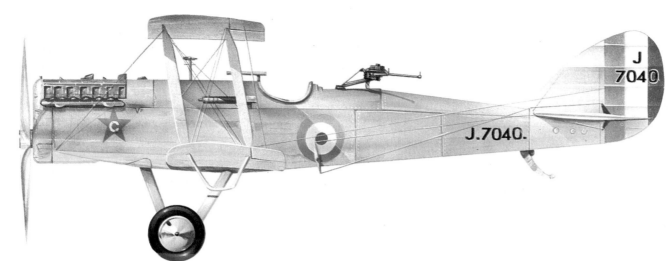

D.H.9A

The D.H.9 was planned as a longer-range successor to the D.H.4. To speed production, the D.H.4's flying surfaces and landing gear were combined with a new fuselage that located the pilot and gunner close together and provided better streamlining for the engine, in this instance a 171.5-kW (230-hp) Galloway-built BHP engine. The type first flew in July 1917, and proved so successful that outstanding D.H.4 contracts were converted to the D.H.9, which therefore entered large-

scale production with the 224-kW (300-hp) lightweight version of the BHP developed by Siddeley-Deasy and known as the Puma. The engine was unreliable and generally derated to 171.5 kW (230 hp), which gave the D.H.9 performance inferior to that of the D.H.4. As a result, the D.H.9 suffered quite heavy losses when it entered service during April 1918 over the Western Front, though it fared better in poorer defended areas, such as Macedonia and Palestine. Some 3,200 D.H.9s were built by Airco and 12 subcontractors.

Given the fact that the D.H.9's failing was its engine, it was hoped that use of the excellent 280-kW (375-hp) Rolls-Royce Eagle VIII would remedy the situation, but demands on this motor were so great that an American engine, the 298-kW (400-hp) Packard Liberty 12, was used instead to create the D.H.9A, which was perhaps the best strategic bomber of World War I. British production of 885 aircraft was complemented by 1,415 American-built Engineering Division USD-9 aircraft.

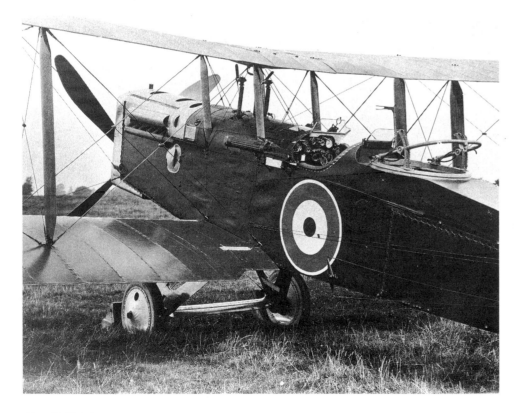

Airco D.H.9A

AIRCO D.H.9
Role: Light day bomber
Crew/Accommodation: Two
Power Plant: One 230 hp Siddeley-Deasy B.H.P. water-cooled inline
Dimensions: Span 12.92 m (42.4 ft); length 9.28 m (30.46 ft); wing area 40.32 m² (430 sq ft)
Weights: Empty 1,012 kg (2,230 lb); MTOW 1,508 kg (3,325 lb)
Performance: Maximum speed 177 km/h (110 mph) at 3,048 m (10,000 ft); operational ceiling 4.724 m (15,500 ft); endurance 4.5 hours
Load: Two .303 inch machine guns, plus up to 412 kg (908 lb) bombload

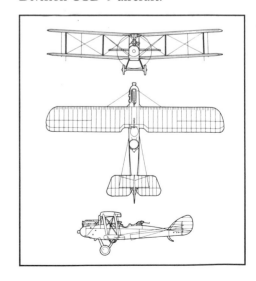

Airco (de Havilland) D.H.9

BREGUET Bre. 19 (France)

Bre. 19TR

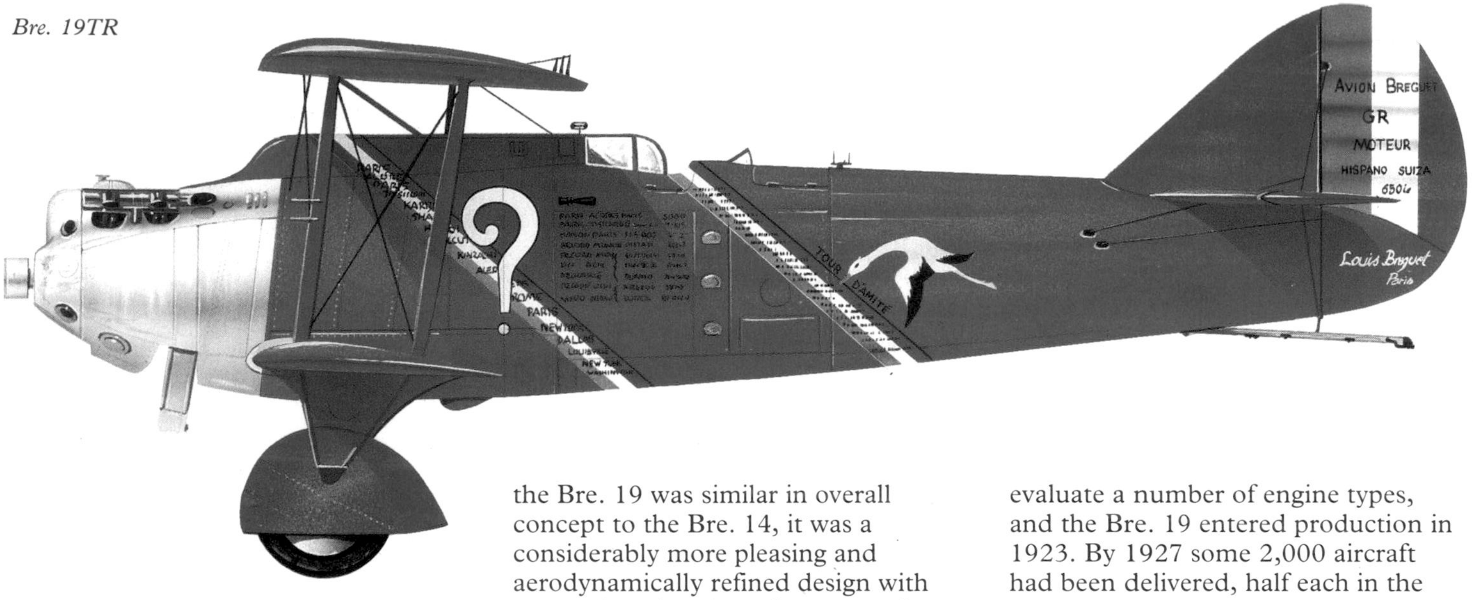

First flown in March 1922 with a 336-kW (450-hp) Renault 12Kb inline engine, the Bre. 19 was planned as successor to the Bre. 14 but was produced in parallel with its predecessor for service with units based in metropolitan France. Though the Bre. 19 was similar in overall concept to the Bre. 14, it was a considerably more pleasing and aerodynamically refined design with unequal- rather than almost-equal span wings with single outward sloping I-type interplane struts, a circular-section rather than slab-sided fuselage, and a much cleaner landing gear arrangement with a spreader-type main unit. The structure was primarily of duralumin with fabric covering, though the forward fuselage as far aft as the gunner's cockpit was covered with duralumin sheet.

The prototype was followed by 11 development aircraft that were used to evaluate a number of engine types, and the Bre. 19 entered production in 1923. By 1927 some 2,000 aircraft had been delivered, half each in the B.2 bomber and A.2 spotter/reconnaissance roles. Most aircraft in French service were powered by the Renault 12K or Lorraine-Dietrich 12D/E engines, and with each type gave invaluable service mainly at home but also in France's colonial wars of the 1920s in Morocco and Syria. The Bre. 19 soldiered on into obsolescence, and late in its career equipped four night fighter squadrons before being relegated to the reserve and training roles during 1934. The type also secured considerable export success (direct sales and licensed production) mainly of the Bre. 19GR long-range variant. The Bre. 19 was also developed in Bidon (petrol can) and Super Bidon variants for a number of classic record-breaking distance flights.

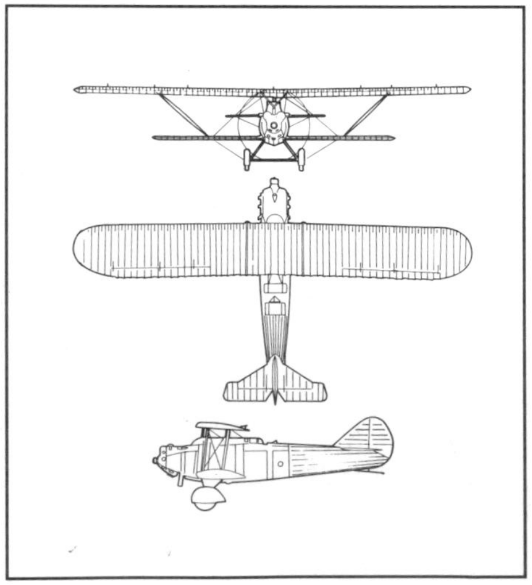

Caption?

BREGUET Bre. 19 B2
Role: Light day bomber
Crew/Accommodation: Two
Power Plant: One 550 hp Renault 12Kc water-cooled inline
Dimensions: Span 14.8 m (48.5 ft); length 8.89 m (29.16 ft); wing area 50 m^2 (538.4 sq ft)
Weights: Empty 1,485 kg (3,273 lb); MTOW 2,301 kg (5,093 lb)
Performance: Maximum speed 240 km/h (149 mph) at sea level; operational ceiling 7,800 m (25,590 ft); range 800 km (497 miles) with full warload
Load: Three/four .303 inch machine guns, plus up to 700 kg (1,543 lb) of bombs

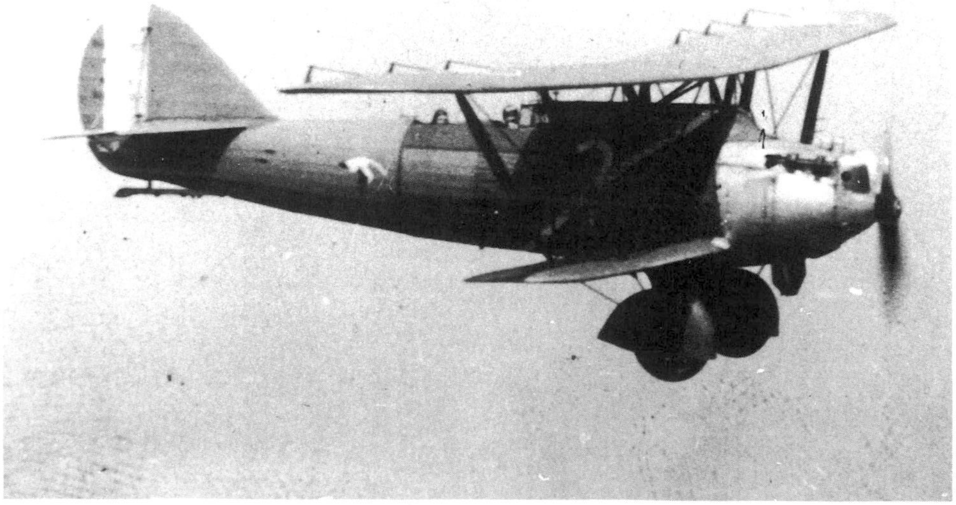

The Breguet 19

JUNKERS Ju 87 (Germany)

Ju 87B-1

A pair of Ju 87B aircraft

The Ju 87 was planned as a dedicated dive-bomber, a type known to the Germans as the *Sturzkampfflugzeug* or Stuka, and proved a decisive weapon in the opening campaigns of World War II. The type delivered its weapons with great accuracy, and came to be feared so highly that the appearance of its inverted gull wings and the sound of the 'Jericho trumpet' sirens on its landing gear legs often caused panic.

The first of four prototypes flew late in 1935 as the Ju 87 V1 with the 477-kW (640-hp) Rolls-Royce Kestrel V inline engine and endplate vertical surfaces. The next two prototypes had single vertical tail surfaces and were powered by the 455-kW (610-hp) Junkers Jumo 210Aa inline, while the last prototype introduced a larger

vertical tail. The type entered service in the spring of 1937 as the Ju 87A with the 477-kW (640-hp) Jumo 210C, and production of this variant totalled 210 aircraft.

Later variants included the Ju 87B with the 895-kW (1,200-hp) Jumo 211D, a larger canopy, and the wheel fairings replaced by spats, the Ju 87D dive-bomber and ground-attack type with the 1051-kW (1,410-hp) Jumo 211J, in a revised cowling, a redesigned canopy, a still larger vertical tail, simplified landing gear, and upgraded offensive and defensive features, the Ju 87G anti-tank model with two 37-mm underwing cannon, the Ju 87H conversion of the Ju 87D as a dual-control trainer, and the Ju 87R version of the Ju 87B in the long-range anti-ship role. From 1941 the Ju 87's limitations in the face of effective anti-aircraft and fighter defences were fully evident, but Germany lacked a replacement and the type had to remain in service as increasingly specialized ground-attack and anti-tank aircraft. Production of the series totalled 5,709 aircraft.

JUNKERS Ju 87B
Role: Dive bomber
Crew/Accommodation: Two
Power Plant: One 1,200 hp Junkers Jumo 211 Da water-cooled inline
Dimensions: Span 13.8 m (45.3 ft); length 11 m (36.83 ft); wing are a 31.9 m² (343.3 sq ft)
Weights: Empty 2,750 kg (6,063 lb); MTOW 4,250 kg (9,321 lb)
Performance: Maximum speed 380 km/h (237 mph) at 4,000 m (13,124 ft); operational ceiling 8,100 m (26,575 ft); range 600 km (372 miles) with full warload
Load: Three 7.9 mm machine guns, plus 1,000 kg (2,205 lb) bombload

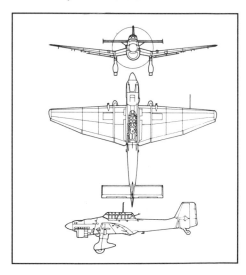

Junkers Ju 87B-2

BRISTOL BLENHEIM (United Kingdom)

Blenheim Mk IF

In 1934 Lord Rothermere commissioned Bristol to produce a fast and capacious light personal transport. This appeared as the Type 142 that first flew in April 1935 with two 485-kW (650-hp) Bristol Mercury VIS radials. The aircraft caused a great stir as it was 48 km/h (30 mph) faster than the U.K.'s latest fighter, and it was presented to the nation by the air-minded Rothermere after the Air Ministry asked for permission to evaluate the machine as a light bomber. As a result, Bristol developed the Type 142M bomber prototype that first flew in June 1936. The type offered higher performance than current light bombers, and was ordered in large numbers for service from 1937 onwards.

BRISTOL BLENHEIM Mk I
Role: Medium bomber
Crew/Accommodation: Three
Power Plant: Two 840 hp Bristol Mercury VIII air-cooled radials
Dimensions: Span 17.17 m (56.33 ft); length 12.11 m (39.75 ft); wing area 43.57 m² (469 sq ft)
Weights: Empty 3,674 kg (8,100 lb); MTOW 5,670 kg (12,500 lb)
Performance: Maximum speed 459 km/h (285 mph) at 4,572 m (15,000 ft); operational ceiling 8,315 m (27,280 ft); range 1,810 km (1,125 miles) with full bombload
Load: Two .303 inch machine guns, plus up to 454 kg (1,000 lb) of bombs

The main variants were the original Blenheim Mk I of which 1,365 were built in the U.K. and 61 under licence (45 in Finland and 16 in Yugoslavia) with 626-kW (840-hp) Mercury VIII radials, the Blenheim Mk IF interim night fighter of which about 200 were produced as conversions with radar and a ventral pack of four machine guns, the generally improved Blenheim Mk IV of which 3,297 were built in the U.K. and another 10 under licence in Finland with 686-kW (920-hp) Mercury XV engines, more fuel and a lengthened nose, the Blenheim Mk IVF extemporized night fighter, the Blenheim Mk IVF fighter conversion, and the Blenheim Mk V of which 945 were built with 708-kW (950-hp) Mercury 25 or 30 engines and a solid nose housing four machine-guns in Mk VA bomber, Mk VB close support, Mk VC operational trainer and Mk VD tropicalized bomber subvariants. The Blenheim Mk IV was built in Canada as the Bolingbroke coastal reconnaissance and light bomber aircraft, of which 676 were built as Mk Is with Mercury VIIIs, Mk IVs with Mercury XVs and MK IV Ws with Pratt & Whitney R-1830 Wasp radials.

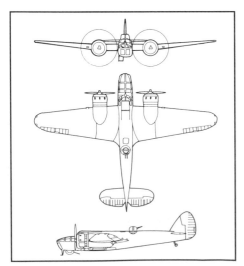

Bristol Blenheim Mk IV

Bristol Blenheim Mk IV

JUNKERS Ju 88 Family (Germany)

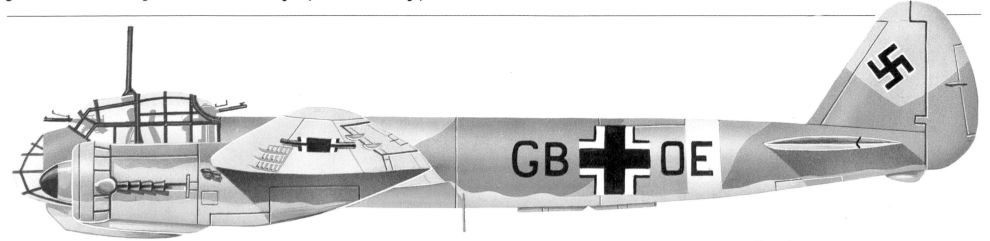

Ju 88A-4

The Ju 88 can be considered Germany's equivalent to the British Mosquito and with that type was certainly the most versatile warplane of World War II. Production of the Ju 88 family totalled about 15,000 aircraft. The type was schemed as a high-speed bomber and first flew in December 1936 with 746-kW (1,000- hp) Daimler-Benz DB 600A inlines, subsequently changed to Junkers Jumo 211s of the same rating, a low/mid-set wing and, in the standard German fashion, the crew grouped closely together in an extensively glazed nose section that proved comparatively vulnerable despite steadily heavier defensive armament. With the Jumo 211, the Ju 88A entered widespread service, being built in variants up to the Ju 88A-17. Six manufacturers produced about 7,000 of this series alone.

The next operational bomber was the Ju 88S in three subvariants with the 1268-kW (1,700-hp) BMW 801G radial, smoother nose contours, and reduced bomb load to improve performance; companion reconnaissance models were the two variants of the Ju 88T and the three variants of the longer-range Ju 88H. Production of the Ju 88H/S/T series totalled some 550 aircraft. From the Ju 88A was developed the Ju 88C heavy fighter; this had BMW 801A radials and a 'solid' nose for the heavy gun armament, together with radar in a few night fighter variants. The definitive night fighter series with steadily improving radar and effective armament was the Ju 88G, together with the improved Ju 88R version of the Ju 88C. Other series were the Ju 88D long-range reconnaissance and Ju 88P anti-tank aircraft. Development of the same concept yielded the high-performance Ju 188 and high-altitude Ju 388 series.

Junkers Ju 88A-4 bombers

JUNKERS Ju 88A-4
Role: Light fast bomber
Crew/Accommodation: Four
Power Plant: Two 1,340 hp Junkers Jumo 211J-1 water-cooled inlines
Dimensions: Span 20 m (65.63 ft); length 14.4 m (47.23 ft); wing area 54.5 m² (586.6 sq ft)
Weights: Empty 9,860 kg (21,737 lb); MTOW 14,000 kg (30,870 lb)
Performance: Maximum speed 470 km/h (292 mph) at 5,300 m (17,390 ft); operational ceiling 8,200 m (26,900 ft); range, 1,790 km (1,112 miles) with full bombload
Load: Two 13 mm and three 7.9 mm machine guns, plus up to 2,000 kg (4,409 lb) bombload

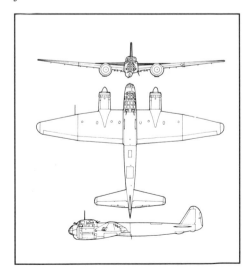

Junkers Ju 88A-4

AICHI D3A 'VAL' (Japan)

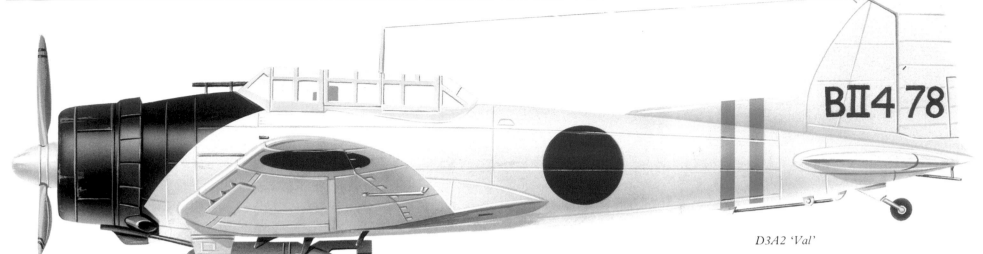

D3A2 'Val'

Designed as successor to the same company's D1A and first flown in 1938 with the 544-kW (730-hp) Kinsei 3 radial engine, the D3A was

Japan's most important naval dive-bomber at the beginning of World War II, and played a major part in the Pearl Harbor attack. Known to the Allies as the 'Val', the D3A played a decisive part in Japan's expansionist campaign in South-East Asia and the South-West Pacific, but was eclipsed by American carrierborne fighters from mid-1942 onward.

The type's elliptical flying surfaces were aerodynamically elegant, and the combination of a lightweight structure and fixed but spatted landing gear provided good performance. Production aircraft were based on the second prototype, but with slightly reduced span and also a long dorsal fin to improve directional stability. Total construction was 1,495 aircraft, and the main variants were the D3A1 and D3A2, which totalled 476 and 1,007 respectively.

The D3A1 entered service in 1940 with the 746-kW (1,000-hp) Kinsei 43

that was altered later in the production run to the 1,070-hp (798-kW) Kinsei 44 radial. The D3A2 was fitted with a propeller spinner and a modified rear cockpit canopy, and was powered by the 969-kW (1,300-hp) Kinsei 54 that could draw on greater fuel capacity for better performance and range. The D3A2-K was a trainer conversion of the earlier models. From late 1942 the type was relegated to the land-based attack role, and then to second-line tasks such as training before final use as kamikaze attack aircraft.

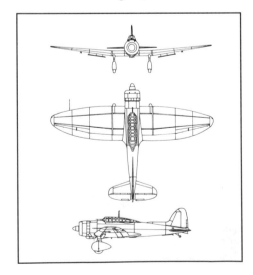

Aichi D3A2 'Val'

AICHI D3A2 'VAL'
Role: Naval carrierborne dive bomber
Crew/Accommodation: Two
Power Plant: One 1,300 hp Mitsubishi Kinsei 54 air-cooled radial
Dimensions: Span 14.37 m (47.1 ft); length 10.23 m (33.6 ft); wing area 23.6 m² (254 sq ft)
Weights: Empty 2,618 kg (5,722 lb); MTOW 4,122 kg (9,087 lb)
Performance: Maximum speed 430 km/h (232 knots) at 9,225 m (20,340 ft); operational ceiling 10,888 m (35,720 ft); range 1,561 km (842 naut. miles) maximum
Load: Three 7.7 mm machine guns, plus up to 370 kg (816 lb) of bombs

The Aichi D3A2

DOUGLAS DB-7/A-20 HAVOC Series (United States)

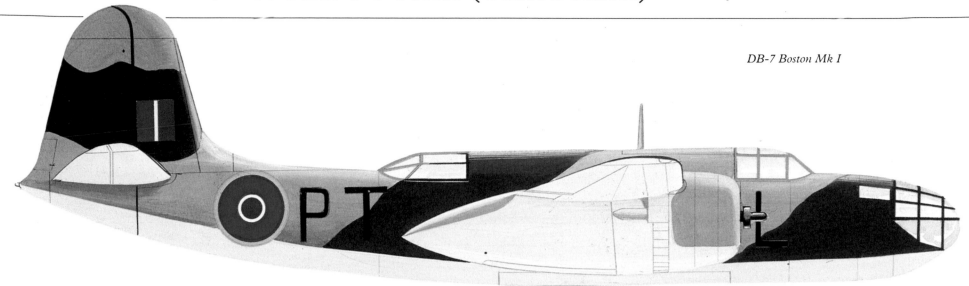

DB-7 Boston Mk I

The Model 7 was a basic twin-engined light bomber design that was evolved as a private venture and then went through a number of important forms during the course of an extensive production programme that saw the delivery of 7,478 aircraft in World War II up to September 1944. The type originated as a possible replacement for the U.S. Army's current generation of single-engined attack aircraft, and first flew as the Model 7B in October 1938 with 820-kW (1,100-hp) Pratt & Whitney R-1830 radials in place of the 336-kW (450-hp) engines of the originally proposed Model 7A. Initial orders came from France for a Douglas Bomber 7 (DB-7) variant with 895-kW (1,200-hp) R-1830-S3C4-G engines and a deeper fuselage, followed by the improved DB-7A with 1119-kW (1,500-hp) Wright R-2600-A5B engines.

Most of these aircraft were delivered to the U.K. after the fall of France, and were placed in service with the name Boston Mks I and II, though several were converted to Havoc radar-equipped night-fighters. A redesigned DB-7B bomber variant with larger vertical tail surfaces and British equipment became the Boston Mk III, and the same basic type was ordered by the U.S. Army as the A-20 Havoc. The latter were used mainly as reconnaissance aircraft, though a batch was converted to P-70 night fighter configuration. Thereafter the U.S. Army accepted large numbers of the A-20A and subsequent variants up to the A-20K with more power, heavier armament, and improved equipment. Many of these passed to the RAF and other British Commonwealth Air Forces in variants up to the Boston Mk V. The steady increases in engine power maintained the performance of these types despite their greater weights and warloads. In addition to the Western Allies, the U.S.S.R. operated comparatively large numbers of the series received under Lend-Lease and often fitted with locally modified armament.

A A-20G of the US Army Air Force

DOUGLAS A-20B HAVOC
Role: Light day bomber
Crew/Accommodation: Three
Power Plant: Two 1,600 hp Wright R-2600-11 Double Cyclone air-cooled radials
Dimensions: Span 18.69 m (61.33 ft); length 14.48 m (47.5 ft); wing area 43.1 m² (464 sq ft)
Weights: Empty 6,727 kg (14,830 lb); MTOW 10,796 kg (23,800 lb)
Performance: Maximum speed 563 km/h (350 mph) at 3,658 (12,000 ft); operational ceiling 8,717 m (28,600 ft); range 1,328 km (825 miles) with 454 kg (1,000 lb) of bombs
Load: Three .5 inch and one or three .303 inch machine guns, plus to 1,089 kg (2,400 lb) of bombs

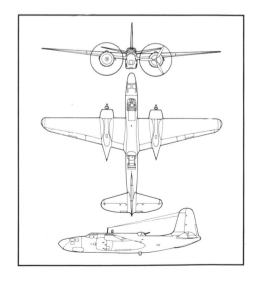

Douglas A-20J Havoc

DOUGLAS SBD DAUNTLESS (United States)

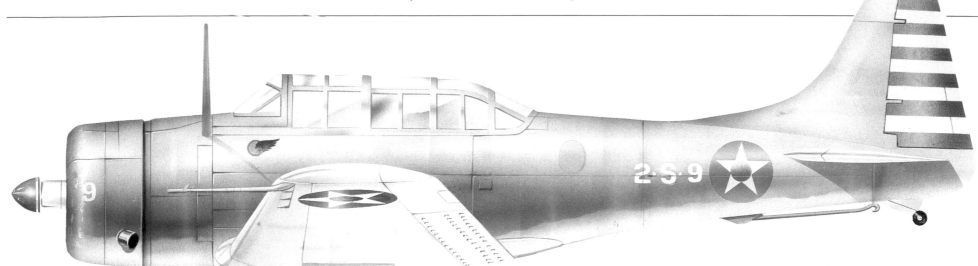

SBD-3 Dauntless

The SBD Dauntless was the most successful dive-bomber produced by the Americans during World War II, and assumed historical importance as one of the weapons that checked the tide of Japanese expansion in the Battles of the Coral Sea and Midway during 1942. The type began life as a development of the 1938 Northrop

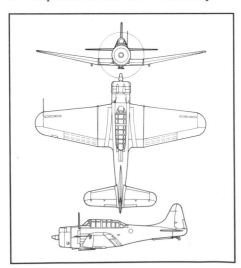

SBD-5 Dauntless

BT-1 after Northrop's acquisition by Douglas. The Douglas development was first flown in July 1938 as the XBT-2 low-wing, monoplane with the 746-kW (1,000-hp) Wright R-1820-32 Cyclone radial engine, perforated split trailing-edge flaps that also served as airbrakes, and the main bomb carried under the fuselage on a crutch that swung it clear of the propeller before it was released in a steep dive.

DOUGLAS SBD-5 DAUNTLESS
Role: Naval carrierborne dive bomber
Crew/Accommodation: Two
Power Plant: One 1,200 hp Wright R-1820-60 Cyclone air-cooled radial
Dimensions: Span 12.66 m (41.54 ft); length 10.09 m (33.1 ft); wing area 30.19 m² (325 sq ft)
Weights: Empty 2,905 kg (6,404 lb); MTOW 4,853 kg (10,700 lb)
Performance: Maximum speed 410 km/h (255 mph) at 4,265 m (14,000 ft); operational ceiling 7,780 m (25,530 ft); range 1,795 km (1,115 miles) with 726 kg (1,600 lb) bombload
Load: Two .5 inch and two .303 inch machine guns, plus up to 1,021 kg (2,250 lb) of bombs

The type began to enter U.S. Navy carrierborne and U.S. Marine Corps land-based service as the SBD-1, of which 57 were built with one trainable and two fixed 7.62-mm (0.3-in) machine guns. The 87 SBD-2s had greater fuel capacity and revised offensive armament. Next came the 584 SBD-3s which introduced the R-1820-52 engine, a bulletproof windscreen, armour protection, self-sealing fuel tanks of greater capacity, and the definitive machine gun armament of two 12.7-mm (0.5-in) fixed guns and two 7.62-mm (0.3-in) trainable guns. The 780 SBD-4s had a revised electrical system. The 3,025

SBD-5s had the 895-kW (1,200-hp) R-1820-60 engine and greater ammunition capacity. The 451 examples of the final SBD-6 had the yet more powerful R-1820-66 engine and increased fuel capacity.

Subvariants of this series were the SBD-1P, SBD-2P and SBD-3P photo-reconnaissance aircraft. The U.S. Army ordered an A-24 version of the SBD-3, further contracts specifying A-24A (SBD-4) and A-24B (SBD-5) aircraft, but these were not successful. The Fleet Air Arm received nine SBD-5s that were designated Dauntless DB.Mk I but not used operationally.

Douglas SBD Dauntless

PETLYAKOV Pe-2 (U.S.S.R.)

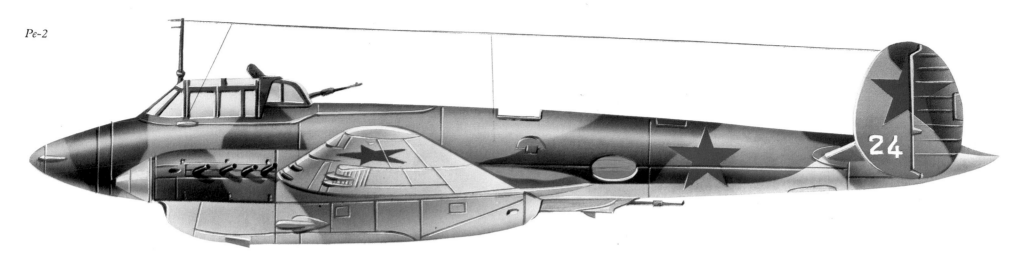

Pe-2

The Pe-2 was one of the U.S.S.R.'s most important tactical aircraft of World War II, and resulted from the VI-100 high-altitude fighter prototype with the 783-kW (1,050-hp) Klimov M-105 inlines. The planned role was then changed to dive-bombing, resulting in the PB-100 design for a dive-bomber with a crew of three rather than two, dive-brakes and other modifications including provision of a bomb aimer's position and elimination

of the pressure cabin. The type was of all-metal construction and a thoroughly modern concept with a cantilever low-set wing, endplate vertical tail surfaces, a circular-section fuselage, and retractable tailwheel landing gear. The aircraft entered service in November 1940 as the Pe-2 with two 902-kW (1,210-hp) VK-105RF engines, and when production ended early in 1945 some 11,427 aircraft of the series had been built.

The versatility of the type is attested by the development and production of variants intended for the bombing, reconnaissance, bomber destroyer, night fighter and conversion trainer roles. In addition to the baseline Pe-2, the main variants were the Pe-2R photo-reconnaissance type with cameras and greater fuel capacity, the Pe-2UT dual-control trainer with a revised cockpit enclosure over tandem seats, and the Pe-3 multi-role fighter, of which some 500 were built as 200 Pe-3 bomber destroyers and 300 Pe-3bis night fighters; the Pe-3 had the fixed nose

armament of two 20-mm cannon, two 12.7-mm (0.5-in) and two 7.62-mm (0.3-in) machine guns plus one 12.7-mm gun in the dorsal turret, while the Pe-3bis entered production with a nose armament of one 20-mm cannon, one 12.7-mm machine gun and three 7.62-mm machine guns but ended with two 20-mm cannon, two 12.7-mm guns and two 7.62-mm guns.

Petlyakov Pe-2

PETLYAKOV Pe-2
Role: Dive bomber
Crew/Accommodation: Three/four
Power Plant: Two 1,100 hp Klimov M-105R water-cooled inlines
Dimensions: Span 17.16 m (56.23 ft); length 12.66 m (41,54 ft); wing area 40.5 m² (435.9 sq ft)
Weights: Empty 5,876 kg (12,954 lb); MTOW 8,496 kg (18,730 lb)
Performance: Maximum speed 540 km/h (336 mph) at 5,000 m (16,404 ft); operational ceiling 8,800 m (28,871 ft); range 1,500 km (932 miles)
Load: One 12.7 mm and two 7.62 mm machine guns, plus up to 1,200 kg (2,646 lb) of bombs

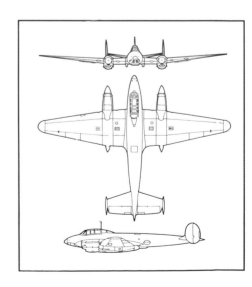

Petlyakov Pe-2

CURTISS SB2C HELLDIVER (United States)

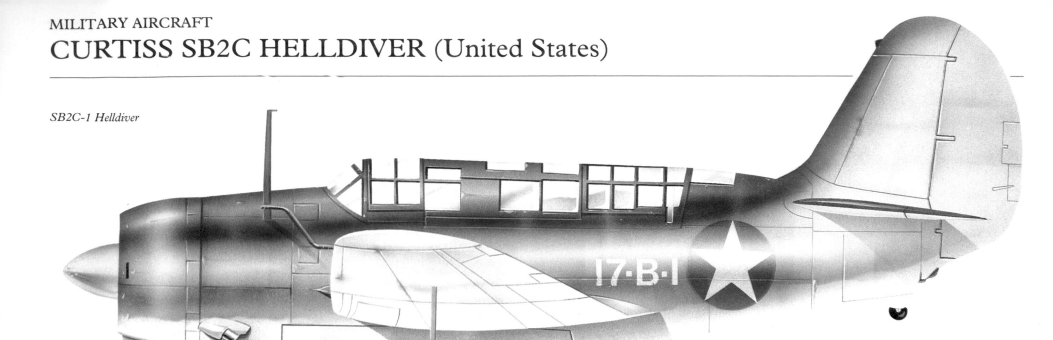

SB2C-1 Helldiver

The SB2C was the third Curtiss design to bear the name Helldiver, the first two having been the F8C/O2C biplanes of the early 1930s and SBC biplane of the late 1930s. The Model 84 (or SB2C) monoplane was designed in competition to the Brewster XSB2A Buccaneer as successor to the Model 77 (or SBC) biplane in the carrierborne scout

bomber/dive bomber role. The type was designed as a substantial all-metal monoplane of the low-wing variety with retractable tailwheel landing gear (complete with arrester hook), a substantial tail unit, and a deep oval-section fuselage characterized by extensive glazing over the rear compartment. The X2B2C-1 prototype flew in December 1940 but was lost in an accident only a short time later. The U.S. Navy had considerable faith in the type,

however, and large-scale production had already been authorized to launch a programme that saw the eventual delivery of 7,200 aircraft. But because of the need to co-develop an A-25A version for the U.S. Army, the first SB2C-1 production aeroplane with the 1268-kW (1,700-hp) Wright R-2600-8 Cyclone 14 radial did not emerge until June 1942. The A-25A in fact entered only the most limited of army service, and the majority of the army's aircraft were reassigned to the U.S. Marine Corps in the land-based

role with the designation SB2C-1A.

Other variants were the SB2C-1C with the four wing-mounted 12.7-mm (0.5-in) machine guns replaced by two 20-mm cannon, the SB2C-3 with the 1417-kW (1,900-hp) R-2600-20 engine, the SB2C-4 with underwing bomb/rocket racks, the radar-fitted SB2C-4E, and the SB2C-5 with greater fuel capacity. Similar versions were built by Fairchild and Canadian Car & Foundry with the basic designation SBF and SBW respectively.

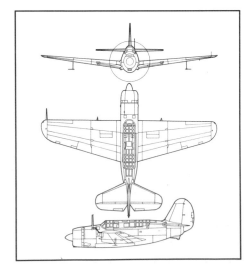

SB2C-1C Helldiver

CURTISS SB2C-5 HELLDIVER
Role: Naval carrierborne bomber/
  reconnaissance
Crew/Accommodation: Two
Power Plant: One 1,900 hp Wright R-2600-20
  Double Cyclone air-cooled radial
Dimensions: Span 15.15 m (49.75 ft); length
  11.17 m (36.66 ft); wing area 39.2 m² (422
  sq ft)
Weights: Empty 4,799 kg (10,580 lb); MTOW
  7,388 kg (16,287 lb)
Performance: Maximum speed 418 km/h (260
  mph) at 4,907 m (16,100 ft); operational
  ceiling 8,047 m (26,400 ft); range 1,875 m
  (1,165 miles) with 454 kg (1,000 lb)
  bombload
Load: Two 20 mm cannon and two .303 inch
  machine guns, plus up to 907 kg (2,000 lb)
  of bombs

Curtiss SB2C Helldiver

de HAVILLAND D.H.98 MOSQUITO (United Kingdom)

Mosquito B.Mk VI

Perhaps the most versatile warplane of World War II and certainly one of the classic warplanes of all time, the 7,785 Mosquitoes began from a private venture based on the company's composite plywood/balsa construction principal. It was planned as a high-performance but unarmed light bomber. The Mk I prototype flew in November 1940. Photographic reconnaissance, fighter, trainer and bomber variants followed.

The PR versions were the Mosquito PR.Mk IV with four cameras, PR.Mk VIII with two-stage Merlins, PR.Mk IX with greater fuel capacity, PR.Mk XVI with cockpit pressurization, PR.Mk 32 based on the NF.Mk XV, PR.Mk 34 with extra fuel in a bomb bay 'bulge', PR.Mk 40 Australian development of the FB.Mk 40, and PR.Mk 41 version of the PR.Mk 40 with two-stage engines.

The fighters were the Mosquito NF.Mk II night fighter, FB.Mk VI fighter-bomber with bombs and underwing rockets, NF.Mk XII and XIII with improved radar, NF. Mk XV conversion of the B. Mk IV for high-altitude interception, NF.Mk XVII conversion of the NF.Mk II with U.S. radar, FB.Mk XVIII anti-ship conversion or the FB.Mk VI with a 57-mm gun and rockets, NF.Mk XIX with British or U.S. radar, FB.Mk 21 Canadian-built FB.Mk VI, FB.Mk 26 version of the FB.Mk 21 with Packard-built Merlin engines, NF.Mk 30 high-altitude model with two-stage Merlins, TR.Mk 33 naval torpedo fighter, NF.Mk 36 higher-altitude equivalent to the NF.Mk 30, TR.Mk 37 version of the TR.Mk 33 with British radar, and FB.Mk 40 Australian-built equivalent of the FB.Mk VI.

The trainer versions were the Mosquito T.Mk III, T.Mk 22 Canadian-built equivalent to the T.Mk III, T.Mk 27 version of the T.Mk 22 with Packard-built engines, T.Mk 29 conversion of the FB.Mk 26, and T.Mk 43 Australian-built equivalent to the T.Mk III.

The bomber versions were the basic Mosquito B.Mk IV, B.Mk VII Canadian-built type with underwing hardpoints, B.Mk IX high-altitude type with a single 1814-kg (4,000-lb) bomb, B.Mk XVI development of the B.Mk IX with pressurized cockpit, B.Mk 20 B.Mk 25 version of the B.Mk 20 and B.Mk 35 long-range high-altitude model.

This is a de Havilland Mosquito T.Mk III trainer of the Royal Air Force

---

de HAVILLAND D.H.98 MOSQUITO NF. Mk 36

Role: Night/all-weather fighter
Crew/Accommodation: Two
Power Plant: Two 1,690 hp Rolls-Royce Merlin 113 water-cooled inlines
Dimensions: Span 16.51 m (54.17 ft); length 12.34 m (40.5 ft); wing area 42.18 m² (454 sq ft)
Weights: Empty 7,257 kg (16,000 lb); MTOW 9,707 kg (21,400 lb)
Performance: Maximum speed 650 km/h (404 mph) at 8,717 m (28,600 ft); operational ceiling 10,972 m (36,000 ft); range 2,704 km (1,680 miles)
Load: Four 20 mm cannon (interception guided by AI Mk 10 radar)

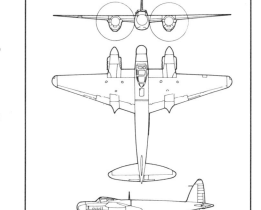

Mosquito NF.Mk 36

ILYUSHIN Il-2 (U.S.S.R.)

Il-2M3

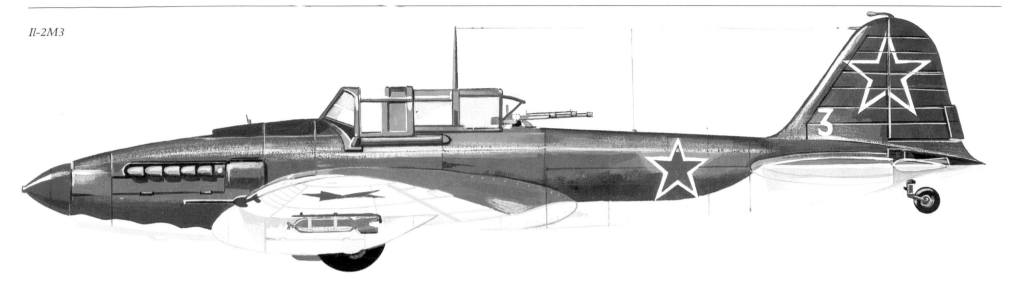

The Il-2 was probably the finest ground-attack aircraft of World War II and was built to the extent of some 36,165 aircraft. The type began life as the TsKB-55 (alternatively BSh-2 or DBSh) two-seat prototype that first flew in December 1939 with the 1007-kW (1,350-hp) Mikulin AM-35 inline engine. Flight tests indicated that the type was too heavy because of its massive armour 'bath' structural core,

so the basic design was developed into the single-seat TsKB-57 that flew in October 1940 with a 1268-kW (1,700-hp) Mikulin AM-38 inline. This entered production as the single-seat BSh-2, a designation that was altered to Il-2 during April 1941, and by August production had risen to some 300 aircraft per month.

Early operations confirmed the design bureau's initial objections to the removal of the TsKB-55's rear gunner, for the Il-2 was found to be especially vulnerable to rear attack. The Il-2 was therefore refined as the

Il-2M with the cockpit extended aft for a rear gunner equipped with a 12.7-mm (0.5-in) machine gun but separated from the pilot by a fuel tank. The original two wing-mounted 20-mm cannon were replaced by 23-mm weapons offering greater armour-penetration capability, and provision was made for the eight 82-mm (3.2-in) rockets to be replaced by four 132-mm (5.2-in) weapons. Later the type was also produced in the aerodynamically improved Il-2 Type 3 version with a 1320-kW (1,770-hp) engine, a refined canopy and faster-

acting doors for the bomb cells in the wings that carried 200 2.5-kg (5.51-lb) anti-tank bomblets. There was also an Il-2 Type 3M variant with further aerodynamic refinement, and a fixed forward-firing armament of two 37-mm cannon complemented by up to 32 82-mm (1 in) rockets on a two-stage zero-length installation. Other Il-2 versions were the Il-2T torpedo bomber with one 533-mm (21-in) torpedo under the fuselage and the I1-2U tandem-seat trainer. Production ended in late 1944 to allow for the much improved Il-10.

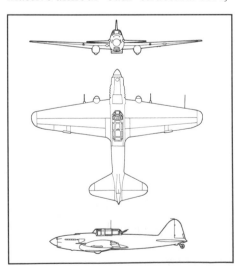

ILYUSIHN Il-2M
Role: Strike/close air support
Crew/Accommodation: Two
Power Plant: One 1,700 hp AM-38F water-cooled inline
Dimensions: Span 14.6 m (47.9 ft); length 11.6 m (38.06 ft); wing area 38.5 m² (414.41 sq ft)
Weights: Empty 4,525 kg (9,976 lb); MTOW 6,360 kg (14,021 lb)
Performance: Maximum speed 404 km/h (251 mph) at 1,500 m (4,921 ft); operational ceiling 6,000 m (19,685 ft); range 765 km (475 miles) with full warload
Load: Two 23 mm cannon and two 7.62 mm machine guns, plus up to 600 kg (1,321 lb) of bombs or anti-armour rockets

Ilyushin Il-2 Type 3M

GRUMMAN TBF AVENGER (United States)

TBF-1 Avenger

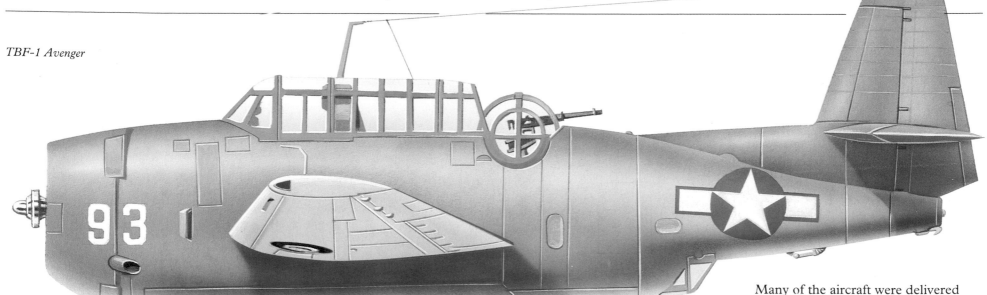

Despite a disastrous combat debut in which five out of six aircraft were lost, the TBF Avenger was a decisive warplane of World War II, and may rightly be regarded as the Allies' premier carrierborne torpedo bomber. The TBF resulted from a 1940 requirement for a successor to the Douglas TBD Devastator. Orders were placed for two Vought XTBU-1 prototype in addition to the two XTBF-1s, and the Grumman type first flew in August 1941 on the power of the 1268-kW (1,700-hp) Wright R-

2600-8 Cyclone radial. The type was of typical Grumman design and construction, and despite the fact that it was the company's first essay in the field of carrierborne torpedo bombers, the Avenger proved itself a thoroughbred and immensely strong.

The type was ordered into production as the TBF-1 or, with two additional heavy machine-guns in the wings plus provision for drop tanks, TBF-1C; production totalled 2,291 aircraft. The Royal Navy also received the type as the Tarpon Mk I, later

changed to Avenger Mk I. The Eastern Aircraft Division of General Motors was also brought into the programme to produce similar models as 550 TBM-1s and 2,336 TBM-1Cs (Avenger Mk IIs), and the only major development was the TBM-3. Eastern produced 4,657 of this model, which had been pioneered as the XTBF-3 with the 1417-kW (1,900-hp) R-2600-219 engine and strengthened wings for the carriage of drop tanks or rockets.

Many of the aircraft were delivered without the initial model's heavy power-operated dorsal turret.

Late in World War II and after the war, the series was diversified into a host of other roles, each indicated by a special suffix, such as photo-reconnaissance, early warning, electronic warfare, anti-submarine search/attack, transport, and target towing. Total production was 9,839 aircraft.

GRUMMAN TBF-1 AVENGER
Role: Naval carrierborne strike
Crew/Accommodation: Three
Power Plant: One 1,700 hp Wright R-2600-8 Double Cyclone air-cooled radial
Dimensions: Span 16.51 m (54.16 ft); length 12.23 m (40.125 ft); wing area 45.52 m² (490 sq ft)
Weights: Empty 4,572 kg (10,080 lb); MTOW 7,214 kg (15,905 lb)
Performance: Maximum speed 436 km/h (271 mph) at 3,658 m (12,000 ft); operational ceiling 6,828 m (22,400 ft); range 1,955 km (1,215 miles) with torpedo
Load: One .5 inch and two .303 inch machine guns, plus up to 726 kg (1,600 lb) of internally-stowed torpedo or bombs

A version of the Grumman TBF Avenger, the TBM, built by General Motors

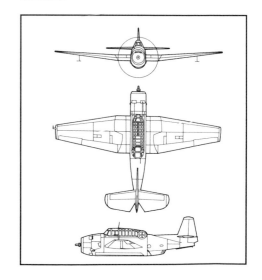

Grumman TBF-1 Avenger

DOUGLAS A-1 SKYRAIDER (United States)

A-1B Skyraider

The massive single-seat Skyraider was designed as a carrierborne dive- and torpedo-bomber, and the first of 25 XBT2D-1 Destroyer II prototype and service test aircraft flew in March 1945. The capabilities of the new aircraft were so impressive that large-scale production was ordered and it proved an invaluable U.S. tool in the Korean and Vietnam Wars.

The type went through a number of major marks, the most significant being the 242 AD-1s with the 1864-kW (2,500-hp) R-3350-24W radial and an armament of two 20-mm cannon plus 3629 kg (8,000 lb) of disposable stores, the 156 improved AD-2s with greater fuel capacity and other modifications, the 125 AD-3s with a redesigned canopy and longer-stroke landing gear as well as other improvements, the 372 AD-4s with the 2014-kW (2,700-hp) R-3350-26WA and an autopilot, the 165 nuclear-capable AD-4Bs with four 20-mm cannon, the 212 AD-5 anti-submarine search and attack aircraft with a widened fuselage for a side-by-side crew of two, the 713 examples of the AD-6 improved version of the AD-4B with equipment for highly accurate low-level bombing, and the 72 examples of the AD-7 version of the AD-6 with the R-3350-26WB engine and strengthened structure.

From 1962 all surviving aircraft were redesignated in the A-1 sequence. The Skyraider's large fuselage and greater load-carrying capability also commended the type for adaptation to other roles, and these roles were generally indicated by a letter suffix to the final number of the designation; E indicated anti-submarine search with radar under the port wing, N three-seat night attack, Q two-seat electronic counter-measures, S anti-submarine attack in concert with an E type, and W three/four-seat airborne early warning with radar in an underfuselage radome. Total production was 3,180 aircraft up to 1957, and from 1962 the series was redesignated in the A-1 series.

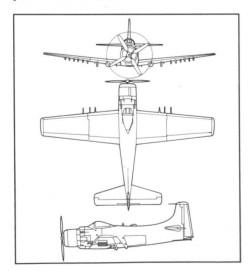

Douglas A-1J Skyraider

DOUGLAS AD-1 SKYRAIDER
Role: Naval carrierborne strike
Crew/Accommodation: One
Power Plant: One 2,500 hp Wright R-3350-24W air-cooled radial
Dimensions: Span 15.24 m (50.02 ft); length 12 m (39.35 ft); wing area 37.19 m² (400.3 sq ft)
Weights: Empty 4,749 kg (10,470 lb); MTOW 8,178 kg (18,030 lb)
Performance: Maximum speed 517 km/h (321 mph) at 5,580 m (18,300 ft); operational ceiling 7,925 m (26,000 ft); range 2,500 km (1,554 miles)
Load: Two 20 mm cannon, plus up to 2,722 kg (6,000 lb) of weapons

A Douglas A-1H Skyraider with the markings of the South Vietnamese Air Force

DORNIER Do 17 Family (Germany)

Do 217K

The origins of this important German bomber lie with a 1933 Deutsche Lufthansa requirement for a six-passenger mailplane, though this requirement was also responsible for the narrow 'pencil' fuselage that was one of the main hindrances to the type's later development as a warplane. The Do 17 first flew in the autumn of 1934, and its performance suggested a military development with the single vertical tail surface replaced by endplate surfaces to increase the dorsal gunner's field of fire. Six military prototypes were followed by two pre-production types, the Do 17E-1 bomber with a shortened but glazed nose and 500-kg (1,102-lb) bomb load, and the Do 17F-1 photographic reconnaissance type, both powered by 559-kW (750-hp) BMW VI inlines.

There followed a number of experimental and limited-production variants before the advent of the Do 17Z definitive bomber built in several subvariants with the 746-kW (1,000-hp) BMW-Bramo 323 Fafnir radials in 1939 and 1940. Do 17 production was perhaps 1,200 aircraft, and from this basic type was developed the Do 215, of which 112 were produced with Daimler-Benz DB 601A inline engines. The two main models were the Do 215B-4 reconnaissance type and the Do 215B-5 night fighter. The Do 217 that first flew in September 1938 was essentially a Do 17 with 802-kW (1,075-hp) DB 601A engines, a larger fuselage, and a revised empennage.

Production was 1,750 aircraft in three basic series: the Do 217E heavy bomber and anti-ship type with stepped forward fuselage and 1178-kW (1,580-hp) BMW 801 radial engines, the Do 217K and Do 217M heavy night bomber and missile-armed anti-ship types with unstepped forward fuselage plus 1268-kW (1,700-hp) BMW 801 radials and 1305-kW (1,750-hp) DB 603A inline engines, and the Do 217N night fighter and intruder types with radar, specialist weapon fit, and 1379-kW (1,850-hp) DB 603A inline engines.

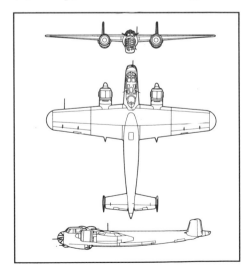

Dornier Do 217E-2

The Do 217P, the final development of the Dornier Do 217 series

DORNIER Do 17Z-2
Role: Medium bomber
Crew/Accommodation: Five
Power Plant: Two 1,000 hp BMW Bramo 323P Fafnir air-cooled radials
Dimensions: Span 18 m (59.06 ft); length 15.8 m (51.84 ft); wing area 55 m² (592 sq ft)
Weights: Empty 5,210 kg (11,488 lb); MTOW 8,590 kg (18,940 lb)
Performance: Maximum speed 410 km/h (255 mph) at 4,000 m (13,124 ft); operational ceiling 8,200 m (26,904 ft); radius 330 km (205 miles) with full bombload
Load: Eight 7.9 mm machine guns, plus up to 1,000 kg (2,205 lb) of bombs

ENGLISH ELECTRIC CANBERRA AND MARTIN B-57 (United Kingdom)

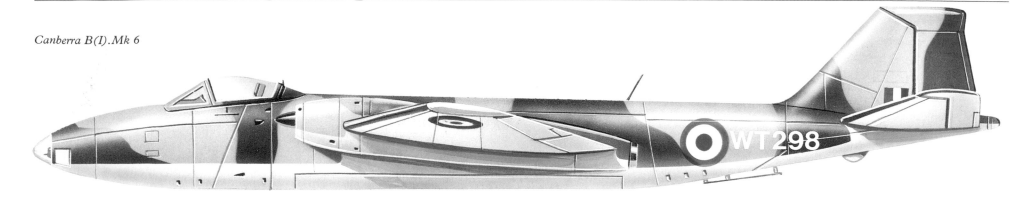

Canberra B(I).Mk 6

The Canberra was planned as a nuclear-capable medium bomber with turbojet engines, and as a high-altitude type it was designed round a large wing and a crew of two using a radar bombing system. The Canberra in fact matured as a medium/high-altitude type with optical bomb aiming by a third crew member, and first flew in May 1949. Its great development potential ensured that the type enjoyed a long first-line career as well as diversification into other roles. The main bomber stream began with the Canberra B.Mk 2

powered by 2948-kg (6,500-lb) Avon RA.3 Mk 101 turbojets, and then advanced to the B.Mk 6 with greater fuel capacity and 3357-kg (7,400-lb) thrust Avon Mk 109s, the B.Mk 15 conversion of the B.Mk 6 with underwing hardpoints, the B.Mk 16 improved B.Mk 15, and the B.Mk 20 Australian-built B.Mk 6; there were also many export versions. The intruder/interdictor series began with the Canberra B(I).Mk 6 version of the B.Mk 6 with underwing bombs and a ventral cannon pack, and continued with the B(I).Mk 8 multi-role version; there were also several export versions. The reconnaissance models began with the Canberra PR.Mk 3 based on the B.Mk 2, and then moved through variants including the PR.Mk 7

equivalent of the B.Mk 6, and the PR.Mk 9 high-altitude model with increased span, extended centre-section chord, and 4990-kg (11,000-lb) thrust Avon Mk 206s; there were also a few export models. Other streams included trainer, target tug and remotely controlled target drone models, and apart from first-line PR aircraft, the machines that still survive are used mainly for electronic roles. The importance of the Canberra is also attested by the fact that it became the first non-U.S. type to be manufactured under licence in the United States after World War II. This variant was the Martin B-57, the first version of which was the B-57A with Wright J65-W-1 (licence-built Armstrong Siddeley Sapphire) turbojets.

The main production model was

the B-57B, an extensively adapted night intruder with two seats in tandem and a fixed armament of four 20-mm cannon plus eight 12.7-mm (0.5-in) machine-guns as well as the standard bomb bay and underwing loads. Other variants were the B-57C dual-control version of the B-57B, and the B-57E target-tug version of the B-57B. The aircraft were also extensively converted as RB-57 photo-reconnaissance and EB-57 electronic warfare platforms, the most radical such version being the General Dynamics-produced RB-57F with span increased to 37.19 m (122 ft 0 in) for ultra-high flight with two 8165-kg (18,000-lb) thrust Pratt & Whitney TF33-P-11 turbofans and, in underwing nacelles, two 1497-kg (3,300-lb) thrust Pratt & Whitney J60-P-9 turbojets.

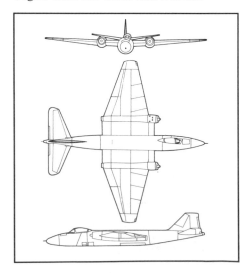

Canberra PR.Mk 9

ENGLISH ELECTRIC CANBERRA B.Mk 2
Role: Bomber reconnaissance
Crew/Accommodation: Two
Power Plant: Two 2,948 kgp (6,500 lb s.t.) Rolls-Royce Avon RA.3 Mk 101 turbojets
Dimensions: Span 19.49 m (63.96 ft); length 19.96 m (65.5 ft); wing area 89.2 m² (960 sq ft)
Weights: Empty 10,070 kg (22,200 lb); MTOW 20,865 kg (46,000 lb)
Performance: Maximum speed 917 km/h (570 mph) at 12,192 m (40,000 ft); operational ceiling 14,630 m (48,000 ft); range 4,281 km (2,660 miles)
Load: Up to 2,722 kg (6,000 lb) of ordnance all carried internally

This Argentine bomber is a English Electric Canberra B.Mk 62

DOUGLAS A-4 SKYHAWK (United States)

A-4S Super Skyhawk

Another great warplane from the Douglas stable, the Skyhawk, was designed as a private-venture successor to the AD Skyraider. At this time the U.S. Navy envisaged a turboprop-powered machine in the role, but Douglas produced its design to offer all the specified payload/range capability in an airframe that offered higher-than-specified performance and about half the planned maximum take-off weight. The concept was sufficiently attractive for the service to order two XA4D-1 prototypes, and the first of these flew in June 1954 as a low-wing delta monoplane with

integral fuel tankage and the 3266-kg (7,200-lb) Wright J65-W-2 version of a British turbojet, the Armstrong Siddeley Sapphire. Production deliveries began in October 1956 and continued to February 1979 for a total of 2,960 aircraft.

The first version was the A4D-1 (A-4A from 1962), of which just 19 were delivered with the 3493-kg (7,700-lb) thrust Wright J65-W-4 and an armament of two 20-mm cannon and 2268 kg (5,000 lb) of disposable

stores. The main successor variants were the 542 A4D-2s (A-4Bs) with more power and inflight-refuelling capability, the 638 A4D-2Ns (A-4Cs) with terrain-following radar and more power, the 494 A4D-5s (A-4Es) with the 3856-kg (8,500-lb) thrust Pratt & Whitney J52-P-6 turbojet and two additional hardpoints for a 3719-kg (8,200-lb) disposable load, the 146 A-4Fs with a dorsal hump for more advanced electronics, the 90 examples of the A-4H based on the A-4E for

Israel with 30-mm cannon and upgraded electronics, the 162 A-4Ms with an enlarged dorsal hump and more power, and the 117 examples of the A-4N development of the A-4M for Israel. There have been a number of TA-4 trainer models, and other suffixes have been used to indicate aircraft built or rebuilt for export. There is currently a considerable boom in upgraded aircraft, often with a General Electric F404 turbofan.

A McDonnell Douglas A-4M Skyhawk II of the VMA-324 squadron

DOUGLAS A4D-5/A-4E SKYHAWK
Role: Naval carrierborne strike
Crew/Accommodation: One
Power Plant: One 3,856 kg (8,500 lb s.t.) Pratt & Whitney J52-P-6A turbojet
Dimensions: Span 8.38 m (27.5 ft); length 12.23 m (40.125 ft); wing area 24.16 m² (260 sq ft)
Weights: Empty 4,469 kg (9,853 lb); MTOW 11,113 kg (24,500 lb)
Performance: Maximum speed 1,083 km/h (584 knots) at sea level; operational ceiling 11,460 m (37,600 ft); range 1,865 km (1,006 naut. miles) with 1,451 kg (3,200 lb) bombload
Load: Two 20 mm cannon, plus up to 3.719 kg (8,200 lb) of weapons

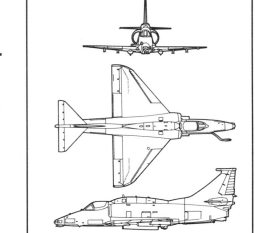

Douglas A-4N Skyhawk II

103

SUKHOI Su-7 'FITTER' Family (U.S.S.R.)

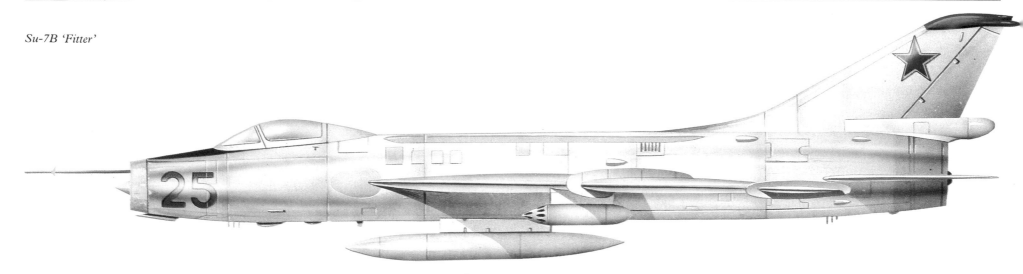
Su-7B 'Fitter'

Though now obsolete and disappearing from first-line service, in its time the Su-7 had a superb reputation as a ground-attack fighter able to absorb virtually any amount of combat damage yet still deliver its ordnance with great accuracy. On the other side of the coin, however, the type has an engine so prodigiously thirsty that at least two hardpoints have to be used for drop tanks rather than ordnance.

Various S-1 and S-2 prototypes flew in the mid-1950s, the latter introducing a slab tailplane, and during 1958 the Su-7 was ordered with the 9000-kg (19,841-lb) thrust Lyul'ka AL-7F turbojet as the service version of the S-22 pre-production derivative of the S-2 with an area-ruled fuselage. The type was developed in steadily improved Su-7 variants, known to NATO by the reporting name 'Fitter-A', with greater power, soft-field capability and six rather than four hardpoints. This effective yet short-ranged type was then transformed into the far more potent Su-17 with variable-geometry outer wing panels. The Su-7IG prototype of 1966 confirmed that field performance and range were markedly improved. With the 10,000-kg (22,046-lb) AL7F-1 turbojet in early aircraft and the 11,200-kg (24,691-lb) thrust AL-21F-3 in later aircraft, the variable-geometry type has been extensively built since then for Soviet, Warsaw Pact and allied use. The main Soviet and Warsaw Pact models are the Su-17 variants known to NATO as the 'Fitter-C', 'Fitter-D' with a drooped nose, 'Fitter-H' with two extra hardpoints, and 'Fitter-K' with improved electronic countermeasures. The main export variant is the Su-20 with inferior electronics to the Soviet 'Fitter-C', while the Su-22 is a Third-World export model with the 11,500-kg (25,353-lb) Tumansky R-29BS-300 turbojet and inferior electronics.

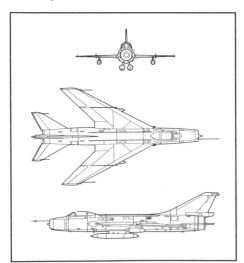
Sukhoi Su-7B 'Fitter-A'

SUKHOI Su-7BMK 'FITTER A'
Role: Strike-fighter
Crew/Accommodation: One
Power Plant: One 9,600 kgp (21,164 lb s.t.) Lyulka AL-7F-1 turbojet with reheat
Dimensions: Span 8.77 m (28.77 ft); length 16.8 m (55.12 ft); wing area 34.5 m² (371.4 sq ft)
Weights: Empty 8,616 kg (18,995 lb); MTOW 13,500 kg (29,762 lb)
Performance: Maximum speed 1,160 km/h (720 mph) Mach 0.95 at 305 m (1,000 ft); operational ceiling 13,000+ m (42,650 ft); radius 460 km (285 miles) with 1,500 kg (3,307 lb) warload
Load: Two 3 mm cannon, plus up to 2,500 kg (5,512 lb) of weapons/fuel carried externally

Sukhoi Su-7 'Fitter'

BLACKBURN BUCCANEER (United Kingdom)

Buccaneer S.Mk 2B

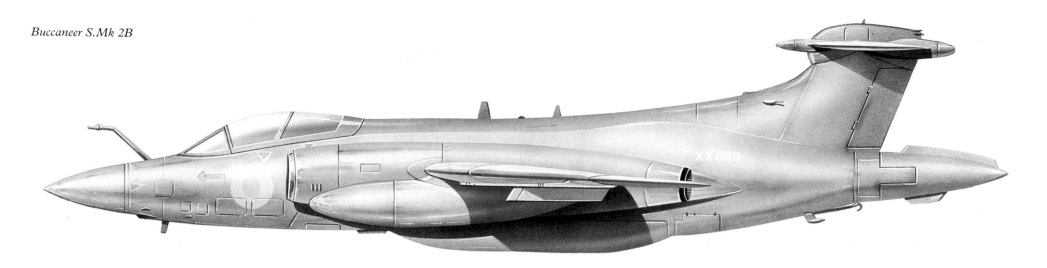

This superb aircraft was planned as the B-103 to meet the NA.39 requirement for a carrierborne low-level transonic strike warplane, and was designed with a boundary layer control system for the wings and tailplane, an area-ruled fuselage, a sizeable weapon bay with a rotary door carrying the main weapons, and a vertically split tail cone that could be opened into large-area air brakes. The prototype was the first of 20 pre-production aircraft, and first flew in April 1958 with two 3175-kg (7,000-lb) thrust de Havilland Gyron Junior DGJ.1 turbojets.

Forty Buccaneer S.Mk 1s were ordered with the 3221-kg (7,100-lb) thrust Gyron Junior 101, and these began to enter service in July 1962. To overcome the S.Mk 1's lack of power, the 84 Buccaneer S.Mk 2s were powered by the 5105-kg (11,200-lb) thrust Rolls-Royce Spey Mk 101 turbofan, and with this engine displayed an all-round improvement in performance. The Royal Navy received its first aircraft in October 1965. The type had greater range than the S.Mk 1, but was also equipped for inflight refuelling. The similar Buccaneer S.Mk 50 was procured by South Africa, this model also having a 3629-kg (8,000-lb) thrust Bristol Siddeley Stentor rocket motor for improved 'hot and high' take-off.

With the demise of the Navy's large carriers, some 70 S.Mk 2s were reallocated to the RAF from 1969 Buccaneer S.Mk 2As. Updated aircraft with provision for the Martel ASM are designated Buccaneer S.Mk 2B, and another 43 new aircraft were ordered to this standard. The aircraft have been upgraded for service into the mid-1990s.

A British Aerospace Buccaneer S.Mk 2B

BLACKBURN BUCCANEER S.Mk 2
Role: Low-level strike
Crew/Accommodation: Two
Power Plant: Two 5,035 kgp (11,100 lb s.t.) Rolls-Royce Spey Mk 101 turbofans
Dimensions: Span 13.41 m (44 ft); length 19.33 m (63.42 ft); wing area 47.82 m² (514.7 sq ft)
Weights: Empty 13,517 kg (29,800 lb); MTOW 28,123 kg (62,000 lb)
Performance: Maximum speed 1,040 km/h (561 knots) Mach 0.85 at 76 m (250 ft); operational ceiling 12,192 m (40,000+ ft); radius 1,738 km (938 naut. miles) with full warload
Load: Up to 3,175 kg (7,000 lb) of ordnance, including up to 1,815 kg (4,000 lb) internally, the remainder, typically Martel or Sea Eagle anti-ship missiles, being carried externally under the wings

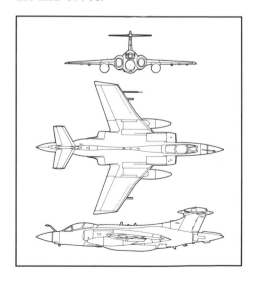

Buccaneer S.Mk 2B

GRUMMAN A-6 INTRUDER (United States)

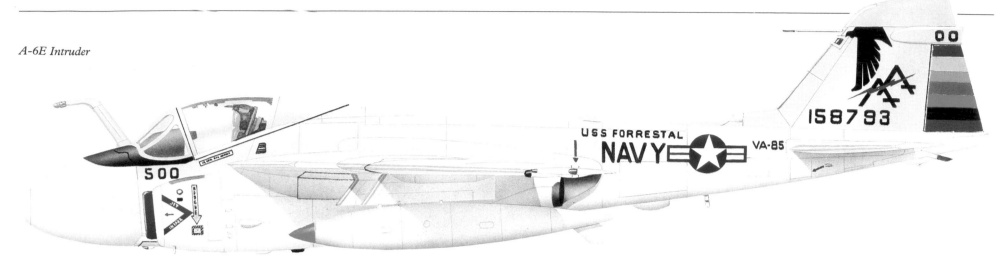

A-6E Intruder

After the Korean War, the U.S. Navy wanted a jet-powered attacker able to undertake the pinpoint delivery of large warloads over long ranges and under all weather conditions. The resulting specification attracted 11 design submissions from eight companies, and at the very end of 1957 the G-128 design was selected for development as the A2F. Eight YA2F-1 development aircraft were ordered, and the first of these flew in April 1960 with two 3856-kg (8,500-lb) thrust Pratt & Whitney J52-P-6 turbojets. In 1962 the type was designated A-6, and in February 1963 the first of 484 A-6A production aircraft were delivered with 4218-kg (9,300-lb) thrust J52-P-8A/B engines, a larger rudder, and the world's first digital nav/attack system. The Intruder had high maintenance requirements, but proved itself a superb attack platform during the Vietnam War.

The next three models were conversions, and comprised 19 A-6B day interdictors with simplified avionics and capability for the AGM-78 Standard anti-radar missile, 12 A-6C night attack aircraft with forward-looking infra-red and low-light-level TV sensors in an underfuselage turret, and 58 KA-6D 'buddy' refuelling tankers with a hose-and-drogue unit in the rear fuselage. This paved the way for the definitive A-6E attack model with J52-P-8B or -408 engines and an improved nav/attack system based on solid-state electronics for greater reliability and reduced servicing requirements. Some 192 A-6As were converted to this standard, with additional new-build aircraft coming from a programme that is only now coming to an end. In-service aircraft have been upgraded to A-6E/TRAM standard with the Target Recognition and Attack Multisensor package in a small undernose turret. Some of these aircraft are to be further upgraded with composite wings, modernized engines, and enhanced electronics.

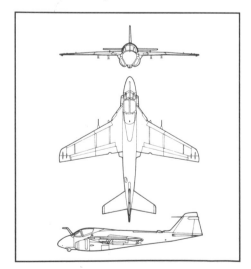

Grumman A-6E/TRAM Intruder

GRUMMAN A-6E INTRUDER
Role: Naval carrierborne all-weather heavy strike (bomber)
Crew/Accommodation: Two
Power Plant: Two 4,218 kgp (9,300 lb s.t.) Pratt & Whitney J52-P-8B turbojets
Dimensions: Span 16.15 m (53 ft); length 16.7 m (54.75 ft); wing area 49.15 m² (529 sq ft)
Weights: Empty 12,000 kg (26,456 lb); MTOW 27,395 kg (60,395 lb)
Performance: Maximum speed 1,038 km/h (560 knots) Mach 0.85 at sea level; operational ceiling 12,954 m (42,500 ft); radius 595 km (316 naut. miles) with 6,350 kg (14,000 lb) bombload
Load: Up to 8,165 kg (18,000 lb) of weapons — all externally carried

A Grumman A-6A Intruder

BRITISH AIRCRAFT CORPORATION TSR-2 (United Kingdom)

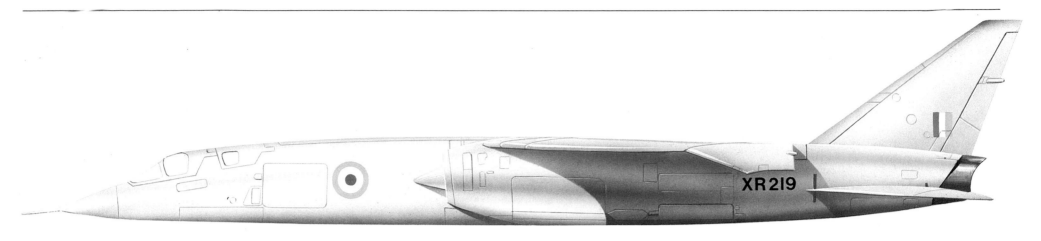

This is one of history's great 'aircraft that might have been'. The type resulted from attempts, started as early as the 1950s, to produce a successor to the English Electric Canberra. There were considerable difficulties in defining the type of aircraft required, and in envisaging the technology required. Eventually it was announced in 1959 that the concept offered by the partnership of English Electric and Vickers-Armstrong was to be developed as the TSR-2 weapons system providing the capability for

supersonic penetration of enemy airspace at very low level for the accurate delivery of conventioned and/or nuclear weapons. In configuration the TSR-2 was a high-wing monoplane with tandem seating for the crew of two, highly swept wings with downturned tips and wide-span blown trailing-edge flaps to provide STOL peformance, and a swept tail unit the surfaces of which provided control in all three planes. The onboard electronic suite includied an air-data system, inertial navigation

system, forward-looking radar, and side-looking radar the data of which were integrated via an advanced computer to provide terrain-following capability and, on the pilot's head-up display and navigator's head-down displays, navigation cues and information relevant to weapon arming and release.

The result was an advanced but potentially formidable warplane that first flew in September 1964. As was only to be expected in so complex a machine, there were a number of

problems. These were in the process of being solved when rising costs and political antipathy persuaded the Labour government to cancel the project in April 1965. Only the first of four completed aircraft had flown, and any resumption of production was made impossible by the destruction of all jigs and tooling.

British Aircraft Corporation TSR-2

BRITISH AIRCRAFT CORPORATION TSR-2
Role: Long range, low-level strike and reconnaissance
Crew/Accommodation: Two
Power Plant: Two 13,800 kgp (30,600 lb s.t) Bristol-Siddeley Olympus B.01.22R turbojets with reheat
Dimensions: Span 11.32 m (37.14 ft) length 27.14 m (89.04 ft); wing area 65.30 m^2 (702.90 sq ft)
Weights: Empty 24,834 kg (54,750 lb) MTOW 46,357 kg (102,200 lb)
Performance: Maximum speed 1,344+ km/h (725+ knots) Mach 1.1+ at sea level; operational ceiling 17,374+ m (57,000+ ft); radius 1,853 km (1,000 naut. miles)
Load: Up to 4,536 kg (10,000 lb) of weaponry/fuel

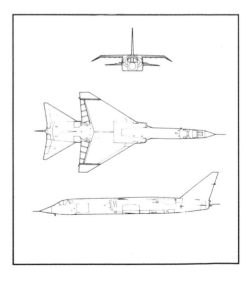

British Aircraft Corporation TSR-2

GENERAL DYNAMICS F-111 (United States)

EF-111A Raven

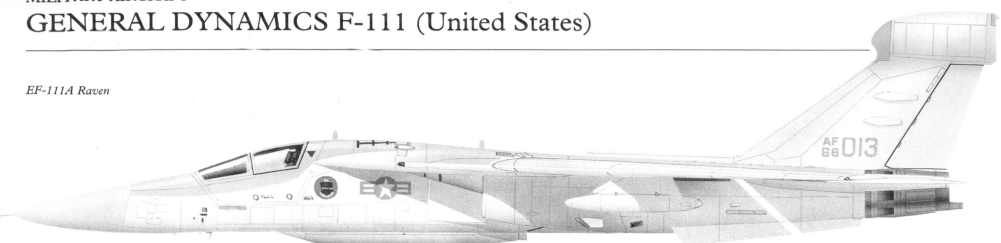

The F-111 was the world's first operational 'swing-wing' aircraft, and remains in valuable service as the U.S. Air Force's most potent all-weather long-range interdiction platform. The type originated from a 1960 requirement for a strike platform with the variable-geometry wings the positions of which at minimum sweep would provide semi-STOL field performance at very high weights, at intermediate sweep long cruising range at high subsonic speed, and at maximum sweep very high dash performance. So versatile a tactical warplane suggested to the Department of Defense's civilian leadership the economic advantages of cheaper development and production costs if this land-based type could also be used as the basis for a new fleet defence fighter. Despite technical objections, the Tactical Fighter Experimental requirement was drawn up and orders placed for 23 pre-production aircraft (18 F-111As and five naval F-111Bs). The first of these flew in December 1964, but weight and performance problems led to the July 1968 cancellation of the F-111B. The F-111A also had problems before and after its October 1967 service debut, but despite an indifferent powerplant it has matured as an exceptional type.

The most important tactical models have been 158 F-111As with 8391-kg (18,500-lb) thrust TF30-P-3 engines, 24 F-111Cs for Australia with the FB-111A's longer-span wings, 96 F-111Ds with 8890-kg (19,600-lb) thrust TF30-P-9s, 94 F-111Es based on the F-111As with improved inlets, and 106 F-111Fs with 11,385-kg (25,100-lb) thrust TF30-P-100s and improved electronics; 42 of the F-111As have been modified into EF-111A Raven electronic warfare platforms. There is also a strategic model in the form of 76 FB-111As with wings of 2.13 m (7 ft 0 in) greater span, eight rather than six hardpoints, 9185-kg (20,150-lb) thrust TF30-P-7 engines, and revised electronics; most of these are to be converted as F-111G tactical aircraft for use in the European theatre.

GENERAL DYNAMICS F-111F
Role: Long-range low-level variable-geometry strike
Crew/Accommodation: Two
Power Plant: Two 11,385 kgp (25,100 lb s.t.) Pratt & Whitney TF30-P-100 turbofans with reheat
Dimensions: Span 19.2 m (63.0 ft), swept 9.74 m (31.95 ft); length 23.02 m (75.52 ft); wing area 48.77 m² (525 sq ft)
Weights: Empty 23,525 kg (47,500 lb); MTOW 45,360 kg (100,000 lb)
Performance: Maximum speed 1,471 km/h (794 knots) Mach 1.2 at sea level; operational ceiling 17,650 m (57,900 ft); range 1,480 km (799 naut. miles)
Load: One 22 mm multi-barrel cannon, plus up to 11,340 kg (25,000 lb) of ordnance/fuel

General Dynamics F-111

A General Dynamics F-111 in flight with its wings extended

VOUGHT A-7 CORSAIR II (United States)

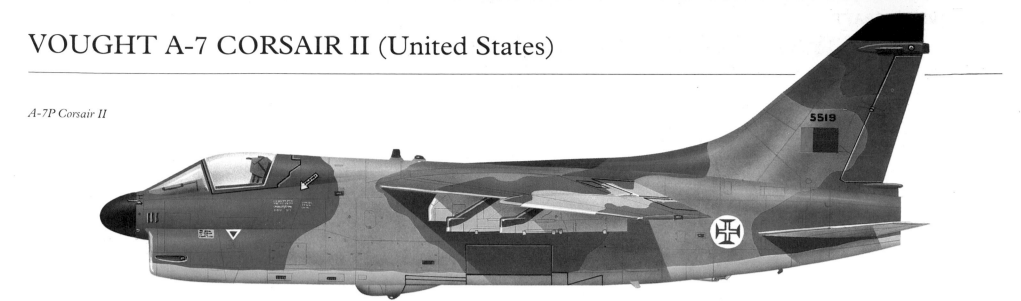

A-7P Corsair II

The A-7 was developed with great speed on the aerodynamic basis of the F-8 Crusader to provide the U.S. Navy with a medium-weight replacement for the light-weight Douglas A-4 Skyhawk in the carrierborne attack role, and in March 1964 the navy ordered three YA-7A prototypes. The first of these flew in September 1965 with the 5148-kg (11,350-lb) thrust Pratt & Whitney TF30-P-6 non-afterburning turbofan, and the flight test programme moved ahead with great speed. This allowed the Corsair II to enter service during February 1967 in the form of the A-7A with the same engine as the YA-7A. Production totalled 199 aircraft of this initial model, and was followed by 196 examples of the A-7B with the 5534-kg (12,200-lb) thrust TF30-P-8 that was later upgraded to -408

standard, and by 67 examples of the A-7C with the 6078-kg (13,400-lb) thrust TF309-P-408 and the armament/avionics suite of the later A-7E variant.

In December 1965 the U.S. Air Force decided to adopt a version with a different engine, the Rolls-Royce Spey turbofan in its licence-built form as the Allison TF41. The USAF series was now named Corsair II, and the first model was the A-7D, of which 459 were built with the 6577-kg (14,500-lb) thrust TF41-A-1, a 20-mm six-barrel rotary cannon in place of the Corsair II's two 20-mm single-barrel cannon, a much improved nav/attack package and, as a retrofit,

manoeuvring flaps and the 'Pave Penny' laser tracker. This model was mirrored by the Navy's A-7E, of which 551 were built with the 6804-kg (15,000-lb) thrust TF41-A-2 and, as a retrofit, a forward-looking infra-red sensor. There have been some two-seat versions and limited exports, but nothing came of the A-7 Plus radical development that was evaluated as the YA-7F with advanced electronics and the combination of more power and a revised airframe for supersonic performance.

A Vought A-7E Corsair II

VOUGHT A-7E CORSAIR II
Role: Naval carrierborne strike
Crew/Accommodation: One
Power Plant: One 6,804 kgp (15,000 lb s.t.) Allison/Rolls-Royce TF41-A-1 turbofan
Dimensions: Span 11.8 m (38.75 ft); length 14.06 m (46.13 ft); wing area 34.83 m² (375 sq ft)
Weights: Empty 8,592 kg (18,942 lb); MTOW 19,051 kg (42,000 lb)
Performance: Maximum speed 1,060 km/h (572 knots) at sea level; operational ceiling 13,106 m (43,000 ft); range 908 km (489 naut. miles) with 2,722 kg (6,000 lb) bombload
Load: One 6-barrel 20 mm cannon, plus up to 6,804 kg (15,000 lb) of weapons

Vought A-7E Corsair II

BRITISH AEROSPACE HARRIER (United Kingdom)

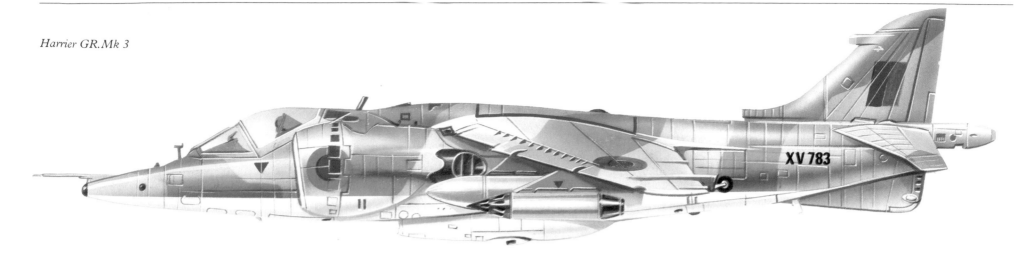

Harrier GR.Mk 3

The Harrier was the world's first operational VTOL combat aircraft, and at its core is the remarkable Rolls-Royce (Bristol Siddeley) Pegasus vectored-thrust turbofan. The type was pioneered in the form of six P. 1127 prototypes. The first of these made its initial hovering flights, in tethered mode, during October 1960, and the first transition flights between direct-thrust hovering and wingborne forward flight followed during September 1961. Such was the potential of this experimental type that nine Kestrel F(GA).Mk 1 evaluation aircraft were built for a combined British, U.S. and West German trials squadron.

The Harrier is the true operational version, and the main types have been the Harrier GR.Mk 1 with the 8618-kg (19,000-lb) thrust Pegasus Mk 101, the GR.Mk 1A with the 9072-kg (20,000-lb) thrust Pegasus Mk 102, and the GR.Mk 3 with the 9752-kg (21,500-lb) thrust Pegasus Mk 103 and revised nose accommodating a laser ranger and marked-target seeker. Combat-capable two-seat trainer equivalents are the Harrier T.Mk 2, T.Mk 2A and T.Mk 4. The U.S. Marine Corps used the Harrier as the AV-8A single-seater (of which many were upgraded to AV-8C standard) and TAV-8A two-seater and examples were exported to Spain with the local name Matador. A much improved variant has been developed by McDonnell Douglas and BAe as the Harrier II with the 11,340-kg (25,000-lb) F402-RR-408 (Pegasus 11-61) turbofan, a larger wing of composite construction, and a number of advanced features in its aerodynamics and electronics. This serves with the U.S. Marine Corps as the AV-8B and with the RAF as the Harrier GR.Mk 5 or, with night-vision capability, the Harrier GR.Mk 7. The companies are also working on a radar-fitted Harrier II Plus model.

British Aerospace Harrier GR.Mk 3

BRITISH AEROSPACE HARRIER GR Mk 3
Role: Strike fighter
Crew/Accommodation: One
Power Plant: One 9,760 kgp (21,500 lb s.t.) Rolls-Royce Pegasus 103 vectored thrust turbofan
Dimensions: Span 7.70 m (25.25 ft); length 13.91 m (45 ft); wing area 18.68 m² (201.10 sq ft)
Weights: Empty 5,624 kg (12,400 lb); MTOW 8,165 kg (18,000 lb in vertical take-off mode
Performance: Maximum speed 1,160 km/h (626 knots) Mach 0.95 at 305 m (1,000 ft); operational ceiling 15,240+ m (50,000+ ft); radius 644 km (400 miles) with external fuel tanks
Load: Two 30 mm externally mounted cannons, plus up to 2,268 kg (5,000 lb) of ordnance/fuel

A McDonnell Douglas/BAe Harrier GR.Mk 7

SEPECAT JAGUAR (France/United Kingdom)

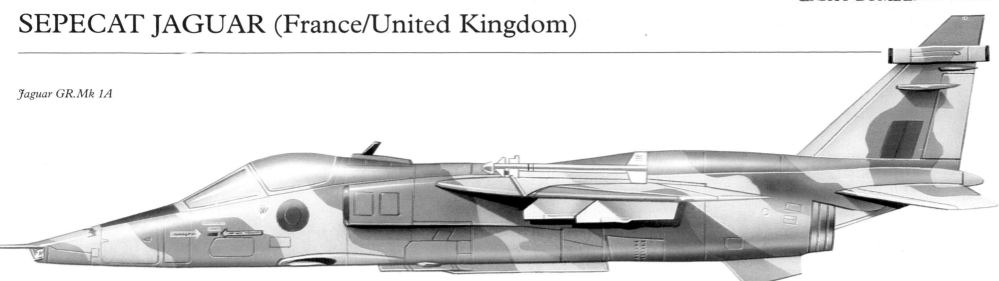

Jaguar GR.Mk 1A

In the early 1960s, the British and French Air Forces each evinced an interest in a dual-role supersonic warplane able to operate as a tandem-seat operational trainer and single-seat attack aircraft. The similarity of the two requirements suggested a collaborative design, development, and production programme, and in May 1965 the British and French governments signed an agreement for such a programme. Several British and French designs were studied before the Breguet Br.121 concept was selected as the basis for the new

warplane the development of which was undertaken by the Société Européenne de Production de l'Avion Ecole de Combat et d'Appui Tactique (SEPECAT) formed by the British Aircraft Corporation and Breguet. An equivalent engine grouping combined the talents of Rolls-Royce and Turboméca for the selected Adour afterburning turbofan.

The Jaguar first flew in September 1968 as a conventional monoplane with swept flying surfaces and retractable tricycle landing gear, a shoulder-set wing being selected as

this provided good ground clearance for the wide assortment of disposable stores carried on four underwing hardpoints in addition to a centreline hardpoint under the fuselage.

Such were the capabilities of the type that the major production variants were the Jaguar A and S attack aircraft (160 and 165 aircraft respectively for the French and British Air Forces, of which the latter has considerably upgraded its aircraft with greater power and a more advanced

nav/attack system) plus only a few Jaguar E and Jaguar B trainers (40 and 38 aircraft respectively for the French and British Air Forces). There has also been the Jaguar International for the export market, absorbing just over another 150 aircraft with overwing hardpoints, uprated engines and, in Indian aircraft, an improved nav/attack system including radar in some aircraft.

A SEPECAT Jaguar GR.Mk 1 of the RAF's No. 6 Squadron

SEPECAT JAGUAR INTERNATIONAL
Role: Low-level strike fighter
Crew/Accommodation: One
Power Plant: Two 3,811 kgp (8,400 lb s.t.) Rolls-Royce/Turbomeca Adour Mk 811 turbofans with reheat
Dimensions: Span 8.69 m (28.5 ft); length 16.8 m (55.1 ft); wing area 24.18 m² (280.3 sq ft)
Weights: Empty 7,000 kg (15,432 lb); MTOW 15,422 kg (34,000 lb)
Performance: Maximum speed 1,350 km/h (729 knots) Mach 1.1 at sea level; operational ceiling (not available); radius 852 km (460 naut. miles) with 3,629 kg (8,000 lb) warload
Load: Two 30 mm cannon, plus up to 4,762 kg (10,500 lb) of weapons, including bombs, rockets or air-to-surface missiles, plus two short-range air-to-air missiles

SEPECAT Jaguar GR.Mk 1A

YAKOVLEV Yak-38 'FORGER' (U.S.S.R.)

Yak-38 'Forger'

Developed from the Yak-36 VTOL prototype and initially thought to be designated Yak-36MP, the Yak-38 is a carrierborne tactical warplane with STOVL capability, known in the West by the NATO reporting name 'Forger'. Up to 1984, Western analysts thought the 'Forger' capable only of VTOL performance, but the relevation of its STOVL capability meant an upward reassessment of

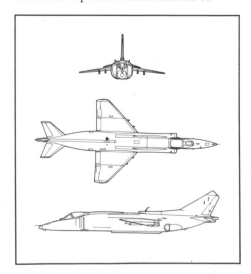

Yak-38 'Forger-A'

the warload that could be carried by the YAK-38.

The type first flew in the early 1970s with the thrust-vectoring turbojet in the rear fuselage complemented by two 3750-kg (7,870-lb) thrust Koliesov ZM straight-lift turbojets in the forward fuselage, and entered service in 1976. The 'Forger-A' is a single-seat type designed principally to provide Soviet naval forces with experience in the operation of such aircraft. The type is therefore limited in terms of

YAKOVLEV Yak-38 'FORGER-A'
Role: Vertical take-off and landing naval strike fighter
Crew/Accommodation: One
Power Plant: One 8,200 kgp (18,078 lb s.t.) Lyul'ka vectored thrust turbofan and two 4,100 kgp (9,039 lb s.t.) Koliesov lift turbojets
Dimensions: Span 7.5 m (24.6 ft); length 16 m (52.5 ft); wing area 15.5 m² (167 sq ft)
Weights: Empty 5,500 kg (12,125 lb); MTOW 9,980 kg (22,002 lb)
Performance: Maximum speed 1,164 km/h (628 knots) Mach 0.95 at sea level; operational ceiling 11,887 m (39,000 ft); radius 371 km (200 naut. miles)
Load: Up to 1,000 kg (2,205 lb) of externally carried weapons, including two medium-range air-to-air missiles

performance, warload and electronics, but still provides Soviet helicopter carriers and aircraft carriers with useful interception and attack capabilities in areas too distant for the involvement of land-based air defences. Until the first months of 1990 it was thought that the vectoring engine was an 8160-kg (17,989-lb) thrust Lyul'ka AL-21F, but this is now known to be a 6800-kg (14,991-lb) thrust Tumansky R-27V-300 unit. The Yak-38UV is known to NATO as the 'Forger-B' and is the tandem two-seat conversion trainer variant, and

has its fuselage lengthened to 17.68 m (58 ft 0 in) to accommodate the pupil's cockpit. It is thought that the Soviets are developing a Yak-41 successor to the Yak-38 with search radar in a revised nose, twin vertical tail surfaces and, possibly, vectored thrust of the four-poster type to remove the need for the two direct-lift engines which are so much dead weight except for take-off and landing. The resulting aircraft has been under evaluation from 1989, and probably possesses supersonic performance.

Yak-38 'Forger-As'

FAIRCHILD REPUBLIC A-10 THUNDERBOLT II (United States)

A-10A Thunderbolt II

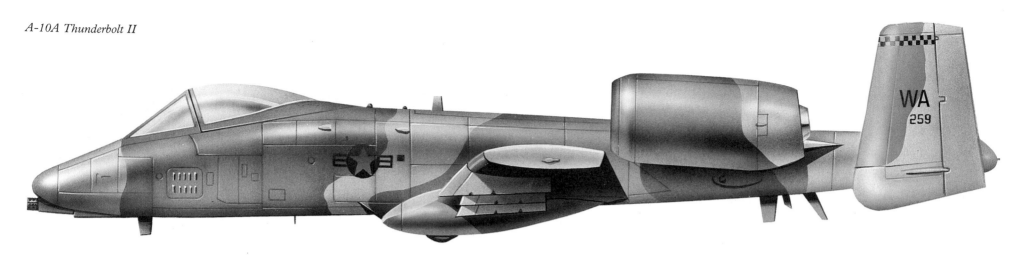

First flown in May 1972 as the YA-10A after Republic Aviation had become a division of Fairchild, the Thunderbolt II was developed to meet the U.S. Air Force's Attack Experimental requirement of 1967. The two YA-10A prototypes were competitively evaluated against the two YA-9As produced by Northrop, and the Fairchild Republic design was declared winner of the competition in January 1973. The requirement called for a specialist close-support and anti-tank aircraft offering high rates of survival from ground fire.

The particular nature of its role dictated the Thunderbolt II's peculiar configuration with two turbofan engines located high on the fuselage sides between the wings and tailplane, and straight flying surfaces that restrict outright performance but enhance take-off performance and agility at very low level. To reduce the effect of anti-aircraft fire, all major systems are duplicated, extensive armour is carried, and vulnerable systems such as the engines are both duplicated and shielded as much as possible from ground detection and thus from ground fire. The first of more than 700 production aircraft were delivered in 1975, and though the type remains in valuable service, it is to be replaced by an A-16 dedicated attack version of the General Dynamics F-16 Fighting Falcon fighter. The core of the A-10A is the massive GAU-8/A seven-barrel cannon that occupies most of the forward fuselage and carries 1,174 rounds of anti-tank ammunition delivering a pyrophoric penetrator of depleted uranium. A large load of other weapons, both 'smart' and 'dumb', can be carried on no fewer than 11 hardpoints.

A Fairchild Republic A-10A Thunderbolt II

FAIRCHILD REPUBLIC A-10 THUNDERBOLT II
Role: Anti-armour close air support
Crew/Accommodation: One
Power Plant: Two 4,112 kgp (9,065 lb s.t.) Genreal Electric TF34-GE-100 turbofans
Dimensions: Span 17.53 m (57.5 ft); length 16.25 m (53.33 ft); wing area 47.01 m² (506 sq ft)
Weights: Empty 9,006 kg (19,856 lb); MTOW 22,221 kg (46,786 lb)
Performance: Maximum speed 697 km/h (433 mph) at sea level; operational ceiling 10,575 m (34,700 ft); radius 974 km (605 miles) with 4,327 kg (9,540 lb) bombload
Load: One 30 mm multi-barrel cannon, plus up to 7,250 kg (16,000 lb) of externally-carried weapons

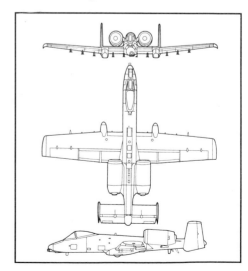

DASSAULT-BREGUET ETENDARD Family (France)

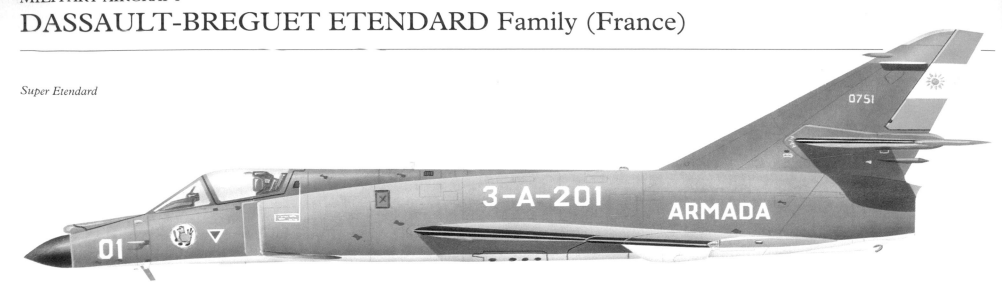

Super Etendard

By the middle of the 1950s the growing complexity of modern warplanes was beginning to dictate types of such size, weight, cost and lengthy gestation that considerable thought was given to lightweight attack fighters that could be developed comparatively quickly and cheaply for use on small airfields or even semi-prepared airstrips that would remove the need to build the large and costly air bases that were becoming

increasingly vulnerable. NATO formulated the requirement, and one of several contenders was the Etendard (Standard). Three prototypes were built, one of them with company funding, and the first of these flew in July 1956 as the Etendard II with two 1100-kg (2,425-lb) thrust Turboméca Gabizo turbojets; the second prototype had the 2200-kg (4,850-lb) thrust Bristol Siddeley Orpheus BOr.3 turbojet. The competition was won by the Fiat G91, but the company's own Etendard IV prototype, the Etendard IVM, larger

than its half-brothers and designed to accommodate more powerful engines, first flew in July 1956 and soon attracted naval interest as a carrierborne attack fighter.

One prototype and six pre-production aircraft validated revisions such as folding wingtips, naval equipment, a larger rudder, beefed-up landing gear, and the 4400-kg (9,700-lb) thrust SNECMA Atar 8B turbojet. Production totalled 90 aircraft including 21 of the Etendard IVP

reconnaissance/tanker variant. From 1970 Dassault revised the basic type as the Super Etendard, and the first of two prototype conversions flew in October 1974. This model has aerodynamic and structural revisions for supersonic performance, and a modern nav/attack system including Agave multi-role radar for targeting of the AM.39 Exocet anti-ship missile. Some 50 aircraft have been upgraded electronically as launchers for the ASMP nuclear-tipped missile.

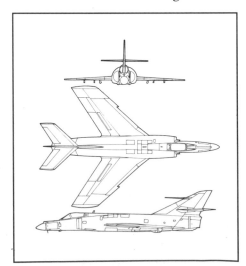

Dassault-Breguet Super Etendard

DASSAULT-BREGUET SUPER ETENDARD
Role: Carrierborne strike fighter
Crew/Accommodation: One
Power Plant: One 5,000 kgp (11,023 lb s.t.) SNECMA Atar 8K50 turbojet with reheat
Dimensions: Span 9.60 m (31.50 ft); length 14.31 m (46.90 ft); wing area 28.40 m² (307.00 sq ft)
Weights: Empty 6,250 kg (13,780 lb); MTOW 11,500 kg (25,350 lb)
Performance: Maximum speed 1,164 km/h (628 knots) Mach 0.95 at sea level; operational ceiling 12,497 m (41,000 ft); radius 649 km (350 naut. miles) with one Exocet
Load: Two 30 mm cannons, plus up to 2,087 kg (4,600 lb) of externally carried weapons/missiles/fuel

Dassault-Breguet Super Etendard strike fighter

PANAVIA TORNADO (Italy/United Kingdom/ West Germany)

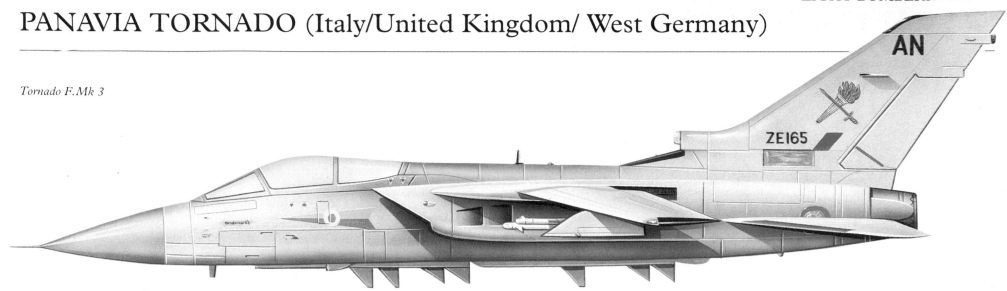

Tornado F.Mk 3

Currently one of the NATO alliance's premier front-line aircraft types, the Tornado was planned from the late 1960s as a multi-role combat aircraft able to operate from and into short or damaged runways for long-range interdiction missions at high speed and very low level. The keys to the mission are a variable-geometry design with wings able to sweep through 430° and carrying an extensive array of high-lift devices on their leading and

trailing edges, compact turbofan engines fitted with thrust reversers, and an advanced sensor and electronic suite. This suite is based on a capable nav/attack system that includes attack and terrain-following radars, an inertial navigation system, and a triplex fly-by-wire control system.

The first of nine Tornado prototypes flew in August 1974, and after a protracted development the first of 1,000 Tornados for the

domestic markets of Italy, the United Kingdom and West Germany and for the export market began to enter service in 1980. The three main variants are the Tornado IDS baseline interdiction and strike warplane, the Tornado ADV air-defence fighter with different radar and weapons (including four semi-recessed Sky Flash air-to-air missiles) in a longer fuselage, and the Tornado ECR electronic combat and reconnaissance type. The British version of the IDS is the Tornado GR.Mk 1 and its

Tornado GR.Mk 1A reconnaissance derivative, and the ADV is the Tornado F.Mks 1, 2 and 3 with steadily improved engines as well as enhanced control and manoeuvring systems. From the mid-1990s the type is to be updated with digital rather than the original analog electronics, and these will make the Tornado better suited to both the carriage and delivery of the most advanced 'smart' weapons.

Panavia Tornado IDSs of the German navy's Marinefliegergeschwader 1

PANAVIA TORNADO GR. Mk 1
Role: All-weather, low-level strike reconnaissance
Crew/Accommodation: Two
Power Plant: Two 7,257 kgp (16,000 lb s.t.) Turbo-Union RB199 Mk 101 turbofans with reheat
Dimensions: Span 13.9 m (45.6 ft); swept 8.6 m (28.2 ft); length 16.7 m (54.8 ft); wing area 30 m² (322.9 sq ft)
Weights: Empty 10,433 kg (23,000 lb); MTOW 26,490 kg (58,400 lb)
Performance: Maximum speed 1,483 km/h (800 knots) Mach 1.2 at 152 m (500 ft); operational ceiling 15,240+ m (50,000+ ft); range 1,062 km (573 naut. miles) unrefuelled with 1,657 kg (3,652 lb) warload
Load: Two 27 mm cannon, plus up to 7,257 kg (16,000 lb) of externally carried weaponry or fuel

Panavia Tornado F.Mk 3

LOCKHEED F-117

F-117A

Very little of a definite nature is known of this important machine, the world's first 'stealth' aircraft to reach operational status after development from 1978 via the XST (Experimental Stealth Technology) aircraft, of which six were built in the 1970s. The first F-117A flew in June 1981 and the type entered service in October 1983, but until November 1988 the U.S. Air Force denied the type's very existence. The aircraft was planned after a number of Israeli setbacks with U.S. aircraft pitted against Soviet surface-to-air weapon systems in the 1973

'Yom Kippur' War. But though it was first imagined that development was undertaken on the conceptual basis of the Lockheed A-12/SR-71 series with highly curvaceous surfaces and a large proportion of radar-absorbent materials to create an aircraft designated F-19A, the release of a poor photograph in 1988 revealed that the real F-117A is a highly angular type of flying-wing basic design (based on relaxed stability and a quadruplex fly-by-wire control system) with a butterfly tail and elements of lifting-body vehicle design, the whole concept being schemed not so much to trap or absorb incoming electro-magnetic radiation as to reflect such radiation away from the emitter.

The F-117A is intended to penetrate enemy airspace in a mission

to detect and then destroy high-value SAM systems and their associated radar systems, relying on low visual, electromagnetic and IR signatures (the last aided by the use between the wings and tail of exhaust-spreading slot nozzles that also mix cold air and hot gas) to achieve undetected penetration of hostile airspace. The

weapon bay appears to measure some 4.72 m (15 ft 6 in) in length and 1.75 m (5 ft 9 in) in width, and the payload is one or two precision-guided munitions. Production totalled 59 aircraft up to July 1990 (out of a planned 100) and was then terminated. Up to mid-1989 three had been lost in accidents.

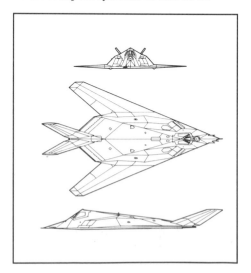

LOCKHEED F-117A
Role: Low-observability strike
Crew/Accommodation: One
Power Plant: Two 4,899 kgp (10,800 lb s.t.) General Electric F404-GE-F1D2 non-reheated turbofans
Dimensions: Span 13.20 m (43.33 ft) length 20.08 m (65.92 ft); wing area 88.68 m² (954.54 sq ft)
Weights: MTOW 23,814 kg (52,500 lb)
Performance: Maximum speed 1,234+ km/h (666+ knots) Mach 1.0+ at sea level
Load: Reportedly in the 2,270 kg (5,000 lb) range, based on the need to carry all weapons internally

SAVOIA-MARCHETTI SM. 79 SPARVIERO (Italy)

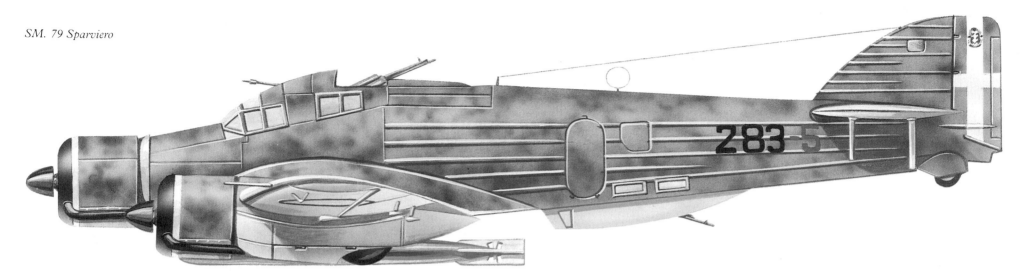

SM. 79 Sparviero

The SM. 79 Sparviero (Sparrowhawk) was Italy's most important bomber of World War II and, in its specialist anti-ship version, the best torpedo bomber of the war. The type was evolved from the company's earlier tri-motor types, and first flew in late 1934 as the SM. 79P prototype of a planned eight-passenger civil transport, and in this form was powered by three 455-kW (610-hp) Piaggio Stella radials. The type was a cantilever low-wing monoplane of mixed construction with retractable tailwheel landing gear, and its considerable capabilities soon

prompted the adoption of a more warlike role with a revised cockpit, a vental gondola, provision for offensive and defensive armament, and 582-kW (780-hp) Alfa Romeo 125 RC 35/126 RC 34 radial engines.

Production of the series totalled about 1,370 for Italy and for export, and the initial variant was the SM. 79-I bomber with 582-kW (780-hp) Alfa-Romeo 126 RC 34 radials and no windows in the fuselage sides. This type was successfully evaluated in the Spanish Civil War in both the level bomber and the torpedo bomber roles,

and proved so admirable in the latter that a specialized variant was then ordered as the SM. 79-II torpedo bomber with 746-kW (1,000-hp) Piaggio P.XI RC 40 or 768-kW (1,030-hp) Fiat A.80 RC 41 radials and provision for two 450-mm (17.7-in) torpedoes. The SM. 79-III was an improved version of the SM. 79-II without the ventral gondola and with heavier defensive armament. Production of the SM. 79-I, II and III totalled 1,230. Other variants were the SM. 79B twin-engined export version

of the SM. 79-I with a variety of radials, the SM.79C (and SM. 79T long-range) prestige conversion of the SM. 79-I without dorsal and ventral protusions, the SM. 79JR model for Romania with two Junkers Jumo 211Da inline engines, the SM.79K version of the SM. 79-I for Yugoslavia, and the SM. 83 civil transport version.

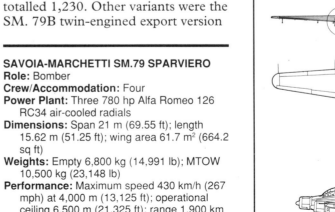

SM. 79-II Sparviero

Savoia-Marchetti SM. 79C

SAVOIA-MARCHETTI SM.79 SPARVIERO
Role: Bomber
Crew/Accommodation: Four
Power Plant: Three 780 hp Alfa Romeo 126 RC34 air-cooled radials
Dimensions: Span 21 m (69.55 ft); length 15.62 m (51.25 ft); wing area 61.7 m² (664.2 sq ft)
Weights: Empty 6,800 kg (14,991 lb); MTOW 10,500 kg (23,148 lb)
Performance: Maximum speed 430 km/h (267 mph) at 4,000 m (13,125 ft); operational ceiling 6,500 m (21,325 ft); range 1,900 km (1,180 miles) with full bombload
Load: Three 12.7 mm and two 7.7 mm machine guns, plus up to 1,250 kg (2,756 lb) of bombs or one torpedo

HEINKEL He 111 (Germany)

He 111H-5

The He 111 was Germany's most important bomber of World War II, and was built to the extent of 7,300 or more aircraft. The type was designed supposedly as an airliner, and in its first form it was basically an enlarged He 70 with two 492-kW (660-hp) BMW VI 6,0Z inline engines mounted on the wings. The first prototype flew in February 1935, and considerable development was necessary in another prototype, 10 pre-production aircraft and finally another prototype before the He 111B began to enter military service with 746-kW (1,000-hp) Daimler-Benz DB 600 inlines, which were also used for the six He 111C 10-passenger airliners. The DB 600 was in short supply, so the He 111E used the 746-kW (1,000-hp) Junkers Jumo 211A and was developed in five subvariants to a total of about 190 aircraft.

The 70 He 111Fs combined the wing of the He 111G with Jumo 211A-3 engines, and at the same time the eight He 111Gs introduced a wing of straight rather than curved taper and was built in variants with BMW 132 radial or DB 600 inline engines. The He 111H was based on the He 111P and became the most extensively built model, some 6,150 aircraft being produced in many important subvariants, both built and converted, up to the He 111H-23 with increasingly powerful engines (including the Jumo 211 and 213), heavier armament and sophisticated equipment. The He 111J was a torpedo bomber, and about 90 were delivered. Despite its late designation, the He 111P was introduced in 1939 and pioneered the asymmetric and extensively glazed forward fuselage in place of the original stepped design, and about 40 aircraft were built in subvariants up to the He 111P-6.

The oddest variant was the He 111Z heavy glider tug, which was two He 111H-6 bombers joined by a revised wing section incorporating a fifth Jumo 211F engine.

Heinkel He 111D-1

HEINKEL HE 111H-16
Role: Bomber
Crew/Accommodation: Five
Power Plant: Two 1,350 hp Junkers Jumo 211F-2 water-cooled inlines
Dimensions: Span 22.6 m (74.15 ft); length 16.4 m (53.81 ft); wing area 86.5 m² (931 sq ft)
Weights: Empty 8,680 kg (19,136 lb); MTOW 14,000 kg (30,865 lb)
Performance: Maximum speed 435 km/h (270 mph) at 6,000 m (19,685 ft); operational ceiling 6,700 m (21,982 ft); range 1,950 km (1,212 miles) with maximum bombload
Load: Two 20 mm cannon and five 13 mm machine guns, plus up to 3,600 kg (7,937 lb) of bombs

Heinkel He 111H bombers

VICKERS WELLINGTON (United Kingdom)

Wellington B.Mk III

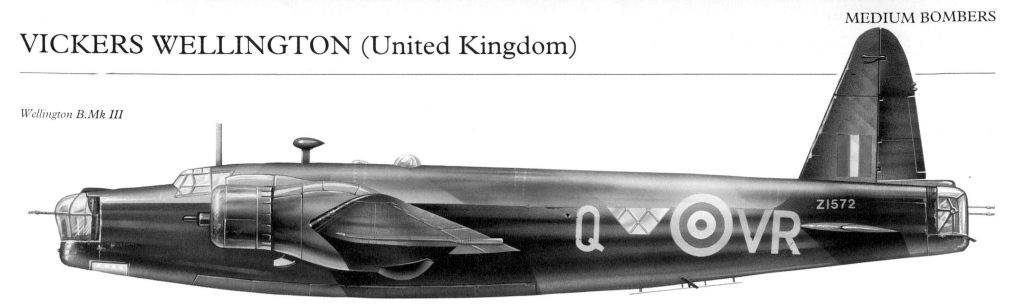

The Wellington was the most important British medium bomber of World War II, and indeed during the early stages of the war was perhaps the only truly effective night bomber after the type was switched to this role in the aftermath of some disastrously heavy losses in early daylight raids. The type used the kind of geodetic construction pioneered in the Type 246 Wellesley, and was thus immensely strong if somewhat ungainly in appearance. This latter factor was reduced in later models by the adoption of power-operated turrets that blended into the fuselage contours more satisfactorily than the original manual units.

Designed to meet a 1932 requirement, the prototype first flew in June 1936 with 682-kW (915-hp) Bristol Pegasus X radials. When production ceased in October 1945, no fewer than 11,461 Wellingtons had been produced in versions with the 746-kW (1,000-hp) Pegasus XVIII radial (the Wellington B.Mks I, IA and IC with steadily improved defensive capability, and the Wellington GR.Mk VIII with searchlight and provision for anti-submarine weapons), the 1119-kW (1,500-hp) Bristol Hercules radial (the Wellington B.Mk III with the Hercules XI and B.Mk X with the Hercules VI or XVI, and the Wellington GR.Mks XI, XII, XIII and XIV with the Hercules VI or XVI and steadily improved anti-submarine equipment), the 783-kW (1,050-hp) Pratt & Whitney Twin Wasp radial (the Wellington B.Mk IV) and the 854-kW (1,145-hp) Rolls-Royce Merlin X inline (the Wellington B.Mks II and VI). Wellingtons were extensively converted later in the type's career into alternative roles such as freighting and training. Several aircraft were also used as engine test-beds, and the basic concept was developed considerably further in the Type 294 Warwick that was designed as a heavy bomber but actually matured as a maritime reconnaissance aircraft.

Vickers Wellington Mk III

VICKERS WELLINGTON B.Mk IC
Role: Heavy bomber
Crew/Accommodation: Five/six
Power Plant: Two 1,050 hp Bristol Pegasus XVIII air-cooled radials
Dimensions: Span 26.27 m (86.18 ft); length 19.69 m (64.6 ft); wing area 78 m² (848 sq ft)
Weights: Empty 8,709 kg (19,200 lb); MTOW 12,927 kg (28,500 lb)
Performance: Maximum speed 378 km/h (235 mph) at 1,440 m (4,724 ft); operational ceiling 5,486 m (18,000 ft); range 2,575 km (1,600 miles) with 925 kg (2,040 lb) bombload
Load: Six .303 inch machine guns, plus up to 2,041 kg (4,500 lb) internally stowed bombload

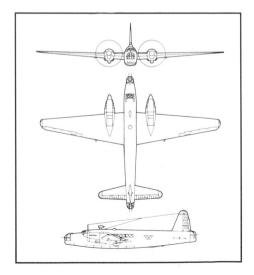

Vickers Wellington Mk II

119

NORTH AMERICAN B-25 MITCHELL (United States)

B-25J Mitchell

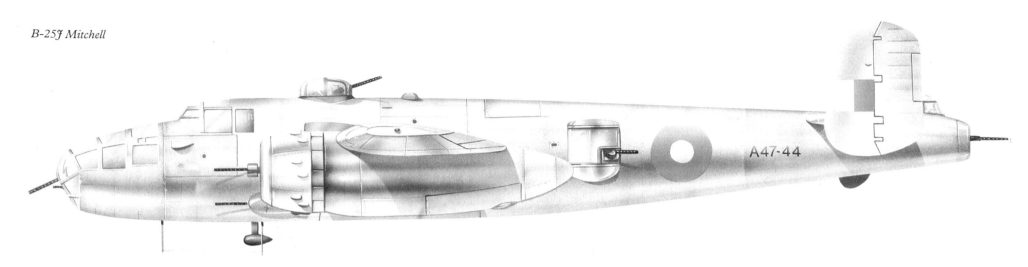

Immortalized as the mount of Doolittle's Tokyo Raiders when flown off the deck of USS *Hornet* in April 1942, the NA-40 was designed to meet a U.S. Army requirement for a twin-engined attack bomber, and emerged for its first flight in January 1939 as a shoulder-wing monoplane with tricycle landing gear and 820-kW (1,100-hp) Pratt & Whitney R-1830-S6C3-G radials that were soon replaced by 969-kW (1,300-hp) Wright GR-2600-A71 radials. The R-2600 was retained throughout the rest of the type's 9,816-aircraft production run. Further development produced the NA-62 design with the wing lowered to the mid-position, the fuselage widened for side-by-side pilot seating, the crew increased from three to five, greater offensive and defensive armament, and 1268-kW (1,700-hp) R-2600-9 engines. In this form the type entered production as the B-25, and the first of 24 such aircraft flew in August 1940.

Development models produced in small numbers were the B-25A (40 with armour and self-sealing fuel tanks) and B-25B (119 with power-operated dorsal and ventral turrets but with the tail gun position removed). The major production models began with the B-25C; 1,625 of this improved version were built with an autopilot, provision for an underfuselage torpedo, underwing racks for eight 113-kg (250-lb) bombs and, in some aircraft, four 12.7-mm (0.5-in) machine guns on the fuselage sides to fire directly forward. The 2,290 B-25Ds were similar but from a different production line. A few experimental versions intervened, and the next series-built models were the B-25G (405 with a 75-mm/2.95-in nose gun) and similar B-25H (1,000 with the 75-mm gun and between 14 and 18 12.7-mm machine-guns).

The final production version was the B-25J (4,390 with R-2600-92 radials and 12 12.7-mm machine-guns). Other variants included in the total were the F-10 reconnaissance, the AT-25 and TB-25 trainers, together with the PBJ versions, the last provided for the U.S. Navy.

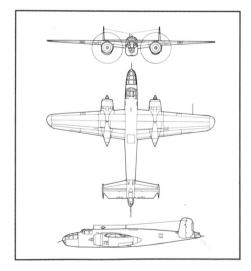

North American B-25A Mitchell

NORTH AMERICAN B-25C MITCHELL
Role: Medium bomber
Crew/Accommodation: Five/six
Power Plant: Two 1,700 hp Wright R-2600-19 Cyclone air-cooled radials
Dimensions: Span 20.6 m (67.58 ft); length 16.13 m (52.92 ft); wing area 56.67 m² (610 sq ft)
Weights: Empty 9,208 kg (20,300 lb); MTOW 15,422 kg (34,000 lb)
Performance: Maximum speed 457 km/h (284 mph) at 4,572 mph (15,000 ft) operational ceiling 6,041 m (21,200 ft); range 2,414 m (1,500 miles) with full bombload
Load: Four .5 inch machine guns, plus up to 1,361 kg (3,000 lb) of bombs

North American B-25J Mitchell

MARTIN B-26 MARAUDER (United States)

B-26F Marauder

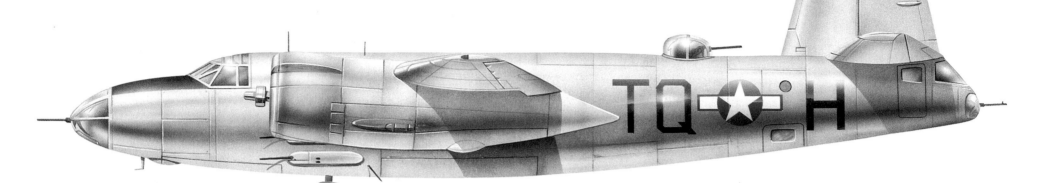

The Marauder was designed to meet a particularly difficult specification issued in 1939 by the U.S. Army Air Corps for a high-performance medium bomber, and was ordered 'off the drawing board' straight into production without any prototype or even pre-production aircraft. The first B-26 flew in November 1940 with two 1380-kW (1,850-hp) Pratt & Whitney R-2800-5 radials as a highly streamlined mid-wing monoplane with

tricycle landing gear. The type was able to deliver the required performance, but because of the high wing loading low-speed handling was poor, resulting in a spate of accidents.

Total production was 4,708 aircraft, and in addition to the 201 B-26s the main variants were the B-26A (139 aircraft) with 1380-kW (1,850-hp) R-2800-9 or -39 engines, greater fuel capacity and provision for an underfuselage torpedo, the B-26C

(1,883) with 1491-kW (2,000-hp) R-2800-41 engines and, from the 642nd aircraft, a wing increased in span by 1.83 m (6 ft 0 in) as a means of reducing wing loading, though this was negated by inevitably increased weight, the B-26C (1,210) generally similar to the B-26B but from a different production line, the B-26F (300) which introduced a higher wing incidence angle to improve field performance, and the B-26G (893) generally similar to the B-26F. There were two target tug-gunnery trainer variants produced by converting

bombers as 208 AT-23As (later TB-26Bs) and 375 AT-23Bs (later TB-26Cs); 225 of the latter were transferred to the U.S. Navy as JM-1s. There was also the new-build TB-26G crew trainer, and 47 of these 57 aircraft were transferred to the U.S. Navy as JM-2s. Comparatively large numbers of several models were used by the British and, to a lesser extent, the French and South Africans.

This Martin B-26B Marauder shows evidence of protracted services

---

MARTIN B-26B MARAUDER
Role: Medium bomber
Crew/Accommodation: Seven
Power Plant: Two 2,000 hp Pratt & Whitney R-2800-41 Double Wasp air-cooled radials
Dimensions: Span 21.64 m (71 ft); length 17.75 m (58.25 ft); wing area 61.13 m² (658 sq ft)
Weights: Empty 10,660 kg (23,500 lb); MTOW 17,328 kg (38,200 lb)
Performance: Maximum speed 454 km/h (282 mph) at 4,572 m (15,000 ft); operational ceiling 4,572+ m (15,000+ ft); range 1,086 km (675 miles) with maximum bombload
Load: Twelve .5 inch machine guns, plus up to 1,815 kg (4,000 lb) of internally carried bombs, or one externally carried torpedo

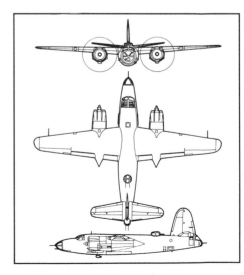

Martin B-26G Marauder

MITSUBISHI Ki-67 HIRYU 'PEGGY' (Japan)

Ki-67-I Type 4 'Peggy'

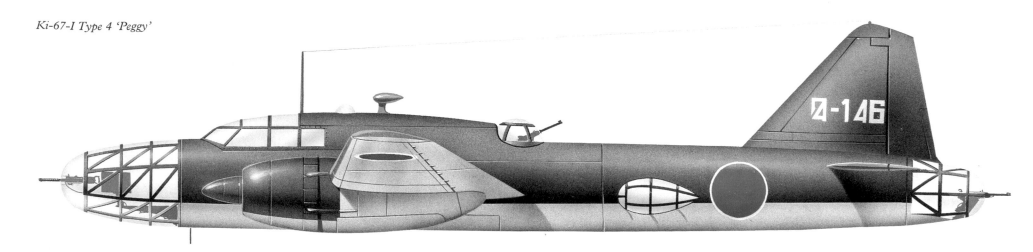

In February 1941, Mitsubishi received instructions from the Imperial Japanese Army Air Force to design a tactical heavy bomber, and the company responded with a type that secured good performance and agility through the typically Japanese defects of minimal protection (armour and self-sealing fuel tanks) combined with a lightweight structure that was little suited to sustain battle damage.

The first of 19 Ki-67 prototypes and pre-production aircraft flew in December 1942 with two 1417-kW (1,900-hp) Mitsubishi Ha-104 radials. Production was delayed as the Japanese army considered a whole range of derivatives based on this high-performance basic aircraft, but in December 1943, the army belatedly decided to concentrate on just a single heavy bomber type capable of the level and torpedo bombing roles. The type entered production with the company designation Ki-67-I and entered

service as the Army Type 4 Heavy Bomber Model 1 Hiryu (Flying Dragon). Only 679 of these effective aircraft were built, all but the first 159 having provision for an underfuselage rack carrying one torpedo to give the type an anti-ship capability. Many were converted as three-seat Ki-67-I KAI *kamikaze* aircraft with the defensive gun turrets removed and provision made for two 800-kg (1,764-lb) bombs or 2900 kg (6,393 lb) of explosives. Further production

was to have been of the Ki-67-II version with two 1789-kW (2,400-hp) Mitsubishi Ha-214 radials, however, the only other production was in fact of the Ki-109 heavy fighter variant. This type was armed with a 75-mm (2.95-in) nose gun in the bomber destroyer role, and production totalled just 22 aircraft before the end of World War II. The Ki-67 was known to the Allies as the 'Peggy', however the Ki-109 received no reporting name.

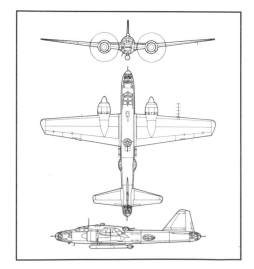

Mitsubishi Ki-67-I Hiryu

MITSUBISHI Ki-67-I OTSU HIRYU 'PEGGY'
Role: Bomber
Crew/Accommodation: Eight
Power Plant: Two 1,900 hp Mitsubishi Ha-104 air-cooled radials
Dimensions: Span 22.5 m (73.82 ft); length 18.7 m (61.35 ft) wing area 65.85 m² (708.8 sq ft)
Weights: Empty 8,649 kg (19,068 lb); MTOW 13,765 kg (30,347 lb)
Performance: Maximum speed 537 km/h (334 mph) at 6,090 m (19,980 ft); operational ceiling 9,470 m (31,070 ft) range 2,800 km (1,740 miles) with 500 kg (1,102 lb) bombload
Load: One 20 mm cannon and four 12.7 mm machine guns, plus up to 1,080 kg (2,359 lb) of ordnance, including one heavyweight torpedo

Mitsubishi Ki-67-iB

TUPOLEV Tu-16 'BADGER' (U.S.S.R.)

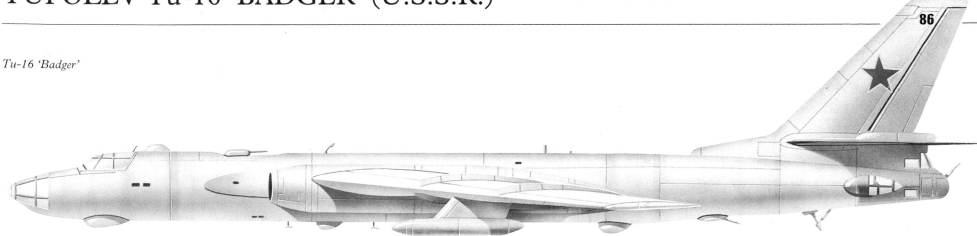

Tu-16 'Badger'

A great technical achievement in the fields of aerodynamics and structures by the Tupolev design bureau, the Tu-16 twin-jet strategic bomber entered service in 1953 after the Tu-88 prototype had flown in the winter of 1952 and confirmed the success of this swept-wing strategic medium bomber design with its mid-wing configuration with two powerful turbojets buried in the roots. About 2,000 aircraft were produced, and though the baseline 'Badger-A' bomber with free-fall weapons is still in limited service, other variants are now important.

The 'Badger-B' was originally developed as a launcher for anti-ship missiles, but is now used as a free-fall bomber. The 'Badger-C' is an anti-ship type carrying either one AS-2 'Kipper' under the fuselage or two AS-6 'Kingfish' missiles under the wings. The 'Badger-D' is an electronic and/or maritime reconnaissance platform. The 'Badger-E' is a free-fall bomber with strategic photo-reconnaissance capability aircraft. The 'Badger-F' is a variant of the 'Badger-E' but with electronic support measures equipment carried in two underwing pods. The 'Badger-G' is an improved anti-ship missile carrier and can carry two AS-5 'Kelt' or, in its 'Badger-G (Modified)' form, AS-6 'Kingfish' missiles under its wings. The 'Badger-H, J, K and L' are all electronic counter-measures aircraft optimized for the escort and/or stand-off, locator jamming, revised locator jamming and electronic intelligence/jamming roles respectively. Many of the older aircraft have been converted into either of two types of inflight-refuelling tanker. The same basic type is produced in China as the Xian H-6 bomber and anti-ship missile carrier.

The Tupolev Tu-16

TUPOLEV Tu-16 'BADGER G'

Role: Missile-carrying bomber, reconnaissance, electronic warfare

Crew/Accommodation: Six to nine dependent upon mission

Power Plant: Two 8,750 kgp (19,290 lb s.t.) Mikulin AM-3M turbojets

Dimensions: Span 32.93 m (108 ft); length 34.8 m (114.2 ft); wing area 164.65 m² (1,772 sq ft)

Weights: Empty 40,000 kg (88,185 lb); MTOW 77,000 kg (169,756 lb)

Performance: Maximum speed 941 km/h (508 knots) at 11,000 m (36,090 ft); operational ceiling 12,200 m (40,026 ft); radius 2,895 km (1,562 naut. miles) unrefuelled with full warload

Load: Three 23 mm cannon, plus up to 9,000 kg (19,842 lb) of bombs

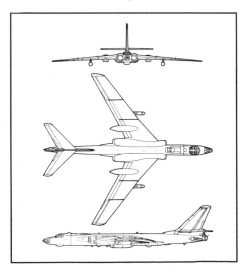

Tupolev Tu-16 'Badger-A'

NORTH AMERICAN A-5 VIGILANTE (United States)

RA-5C Vigilante

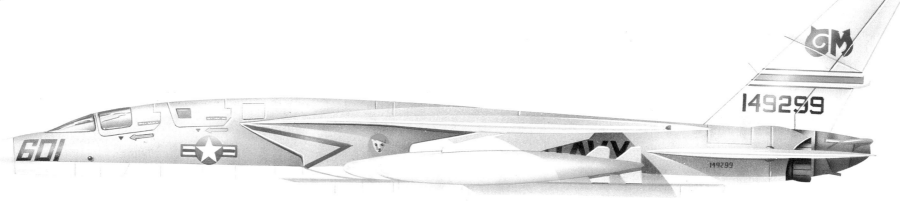

The Vigilante was designed as a Mach 2 all-weather strike aircraft to provide the U.S. Navy with a carrierborne type able to deliver strategic nuclear weapons, and the design known as the North American General Purpose Attack Weapon was ordered in the form of two YA3J-1 prototypes. The first of these flew in August 1958 with two 7326-kg (16,150-lb) thrust General Electric J79-GE-2

RA-5C Vigilante

afterburning turbojets aspirated via the first variable-geometry inlets fitted on any operational warplane. The overall design was of great sophistication, and included wing spoilers for roll control in conjunction with differentially operating slab tailplane halves that worked in concert for pitch control. Considerable problems were caused by the design's weapon bay, which was a longitudinal tunnel that contained fuel cells as well as the nuclear weapon in a package that was ejected to the rear as the Vigilante flew

---

NORTH AMERICAN A-5A VIGILANTE
Role: Naval carrierborne nuclear bomber
Crew/Accommodation: Two
Power Plant: Two 7,324 kgp (16,150 lb s.t.) General Electric J79-GE-2/4/8 turbojets with reheat
Dimensions: Span 16.15 m (53 ft); length 23.11 m (75.83 ft); wing area 71.45 m² (769 sq ft)
Weights: Empty 17,009 kg (37,498 lb); MTOW 36.287 kg (80,000 lb)
Performance: Maximum speed 2,229 km/h (1,203 knots) Mach 2.1 at 12.192 m (40,000 ft); operational ceiling 14,326 m (47,000 ft); range 3,862 km (2,084 naut. miles) with nuclear weapons
Load: One multi-megaton warhead class nuclear weapon

over the target.

The A3J-1 began to enter service in June 1961 with the 7711-kg (17,000-lb) thrust J79-GE-8, and just over a year later the type was redesignated A-5A. These 57 aircraft were followed by the A-5B long-range version with additional fuel in a large dorsal hump, wider-span flaps, blown leading-edge flaps, and four underwing hardpoints. Only six of this variant were built as a change in the U.S. Navy's strategic

nuclear role led to the Vigilante's adaptation for the reconnaissance role with additional tankage and cameras in the weapon bay and side-looking airborne radar in a ventral canoe fairing. Production of this RA-5C model totalled 55 with 8101-kg (17,860-lb) thrust J79-GE-10 engines and revised inlets, in addition, extra capability was provided by 59 conversions (53 A-5As and the six A-5Bs).

The North American RA-5C Vigilante

DASSAULT-BREGUET MIRAGE IV (France)

Mirage IVA

Requiring a supersonic delivery platform for the atomic bomb that was then the French nuclear deterrent weapon, the French Air Force in 1954 issued a requirement for a bomber offering long range as well as high speed. Dassault headed a consortium that looked first at a development of the Sud-Ouest S.O. 4050 Vautour but from 1956 turned its attentions to the potential of an earlier aborted Dassault twin-engined night fighter

design. This resulted in the design of the Mirage IV of what was in essence a scaled-up Mirage III with two engines and provision for a 60-kiloton AN22 free-fall bomb semi-recessed under the fuselage.

The prototype first flew in June 1959 on the power of two 6000-kg (13,228-lb) thrust SNECMA Atar 9 turbojets, and soon demonstrated its ability to maintain Mach 2 speed at high altitude. There followed three

pre-production aircraft with slightly larger overall dimensions and two 6400-kg (14,110-lb) thrust Atar 9C turbojets. The first of these flew in October 1961, and was more representative of the Mirage IVA production model with a circular radome under the fuselage for the antenna of the bombing radar. The last of these three aircraft was fully representative in its Atar 9K engines, inflight refuelling probe and definitive nav/attack system. Mirage IVA production totalled 62 aircraft. Twelve aircraft were later coverted as Mirage IVR strategic reconnaissance

platforms with the CT52 mission package in the erstwhile bomb station, and from the mid-1980s another 18 aircraft were converted as Mirage IVP missile carriers. These have a new nav/attack system and upgraded electronic defences, and are designed for low-level penetration of enemy airspace as the launchers for the ASMP nuclear-tipped stand-off missile.

The fourth Dassault Mirage IVA prototype

DASSAULT MIRAGE IVA
Role: Supersonic strategic bomber
Crew/Accommodation: Two
Power Plant: Two 7,000 kgp (15,432 lb s.t.) SNECMA Atar 09K turbojets with reheat
Dimensions: Span 11.85 m (38.88 ft); length 23.50 m (77.08 ft); wing area 78.00 m² (839.58 sq ft)
Weights: Empty 14,500 kg (31,965 lb); MTOW 31,600 kg (69,665 lb)
Performance: Maximum speed 2,124 km/h (1,146 knots) Mach 2.2 at 11,000 m (36,088 ft); operational ceiling 20,000 m (65,616 ft); radius 1,600+ km (994+ miles) unrefuelled
Load: One megaton range nuclear bomb carried semi-recessed beneath fuselage

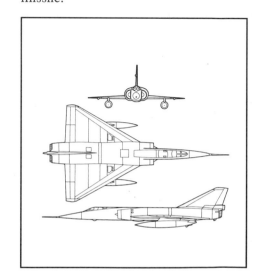

Dassault Mirage IVA

TUPOLEV Tu-26 'BACKFIRE' (U.S.S.R.)

Tu-26 'Backfire'

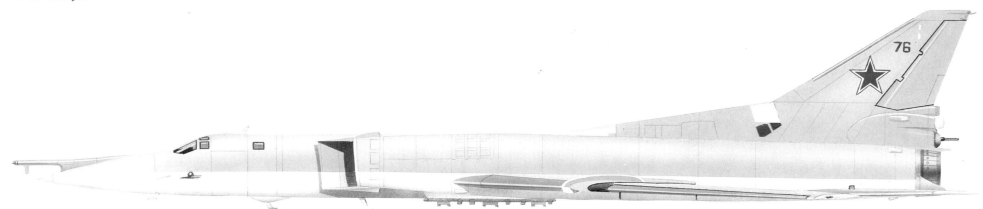

The bomber known to NATO as the 'Backfire' may be regarded as the successor to the Tu-16 'Badger' via the interim Tu-22 'Blinder'. In comparison with the Tu-16 the type offers supersonic performance, and in comparison to the Tu-22 it was designed to provide significantly longer range through the adoption of variable-geometry outer wing panels and a different powerplant with two afterburning turbofans located in long fuselage trunks rather than two afterburning turbojets located in nacelles on the upper sides of the rear fuselage.

The new bomber first flew during 1969 in the form of the Tu-136 prototype, and a pre-production series entered service in 1973 in the form of aircraft designated 'Backfire-A' by NATO and Tu-22M by the Soviets. As the Soviet designation indicates, these machines were probably Tu-22 conversions and retained the Tu-22's type of landing gear with main units that retracted rearward into large fairings projecting aft of the wing trailing edges. The Tu-22M was still deficient in range, probably as a result of the drag associated with the landing gear pods, so the definitive Tu-26 'Backfire-B' was a redesigned type that retained only the vertical tail, fuselage shell and inner wing structure of the Tu-22M in combination with new outer wings and inward-retracting main landing gear units; all 'Backfire-B' bombers were in fact built as such.

The 'Backfire-C' was introduced in 1983 and has more advanced ramp inlets. These permit higher dash performance, and also suggest that a new type of engine has been installed. The 'Backfire-C' also possesses revised defensive armament, with one rather than two 23-mm twin-barrel cannon in a tail barbette of improved aerodynamic form.

Tupolev Tu-26 'Backfire-C'

TUPOLEV Tu-26 'BACKFIRE'
Role: Bomber/reconnaissance with variable-geometry wing
Crew/Accommodation: Four/five
Power Plant: Two 21,000 kgp (46,297 lb s.t.) Kuznetsov NK-144 turbojets with reheat
Dimensions: Span 34.4 m (112.9 ft); swept 26.2 m (86 ft); length 40.2 m (131.9 ft); wing area 170 m² (1,830 sq ft)
Weights: Empty 47,000 kg (103,617 lb); MTOW 122,500 kg (270,066 lb)
Performance: Maximum speed 2,126 km/h (1,147 knots) Mach 2 at 11,000 m (36,090 ft); operational ceiling 17,983+ m (59,000+ ft); radius 8,700 km (4,695 naut. miles) with one air-to-air refuelling
Load: Two 23 mm cannon, plus up to 8,000 kg (17,637 lb) of weapons, including one long-range anti-ship missile

A Tupolev Tu-26 'Backfire-B'.

BOEING B-17 FLYING FORTRESS (United States)

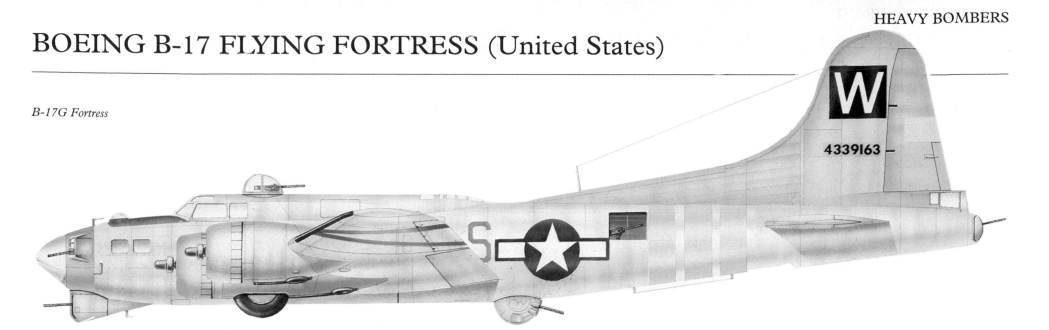

B-17G Fortress

The Flying Fortress was one of the United States' most important warplanes of World War II, and resulted from a 1934 requirement for a multi-engined bomber with the ability to carry a 907-kg (2,000-lb) bomb load over minimum and maximum ranges of 1640 and 3540 km (1,020 and 2,200 miles) at speeds between 322 and 402 km/h (200 and 250 mph). Boeing began work on its Model 299 design in June 1934, and the prototype flew in July 1935 with four 599-kW (750-hp) Pratt & Whitney R-1680-E Radials.

Although it crashed during a take-off in October 1935 as a result of locked controls, the prototype had demonstrated sufficiently impressive performance for the U.S. Army Air Corps to order 14 YB-17 (later Y1B-17) pre-production aircraft including the static test airframe brought up to flight standard. Twelve of these aircraft were powered by 694-kW (930-hp) Wright GR-1820-39 radials, while the thirteenth was completed as the Y1B-17A with 746-kW (1,000-hp) GR-1820-51 radials, each fitted with a turbocharger for improved high-altitude performance. The early production models were development variants and included 39 B-17Bs, 38 B-17Cs with 895-kW (1,200-hp) R-1820-65 engines, and 42 B-17Ds with self-sealing tanks and better armour. The tail was redesigned with a large dorsal fillet, which led to the first of the definitive Fortresses, the B-17E and B-17F, of which 512 and 3,405 were built, the latter with improved defensive armament.

The ultimate bomber variant was the B-17G with a chin turret and improved turbochargers for better ceiling, and this accounted for 8,680 of the 12,731 Flying Fortresses built. The type was discarded almost immediately after World War II, only a few special-purpose variants remaining in service. In addition, there were a number of experimental and navy models.

The definitive B-17G version of the Boeing B-17 Flying Fortress

BOEING B-17G FORTRESS
Role: Long-range day bomber
Crew/Accommodation: Ten
Power Plant: Four 1,200 hp Wright R-1820-97 Cyclone air-cooled radials
Dimensions: Span 31.62 m (103.75 ft); length 22.66 m (74.33 ft); wing area 131.92² (1,420 sq ft)
Weights: Empty 16,391 kg (36,135 lb); MTOW 29,484 kg (65,000 lb)
Performance: Maximum speed 462 km/h (287 mph) at 7,620 m (25,000 ft); operational ceiling 10,851 m (35,600 ft); range 5,472 km (3,400 miles)
Load: Twelve .5 inch machine guns, plus up to 2,722 kg (6,000 lb) of bombs

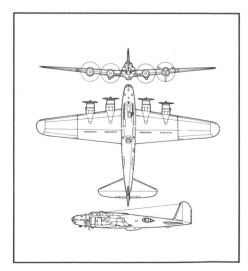

Boeing B17-C Flying Fortress

CONSOLIDATED B-24 LIBERATOR (United States)

B-24H Liberator

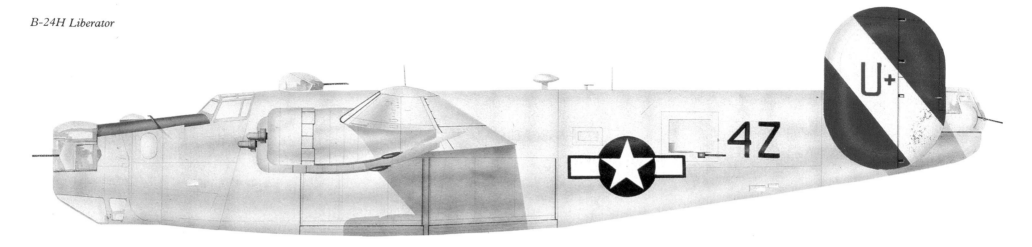

The Liberator was a remarkably versatile aircraft, and was built in greater numbers than any other U.S. warplane of World War II. The Model 32 was designed to a U.S. Army Air Corps request of January 1939 for a successor to machines such as the Boeing XB-15 and Douglas XB-19, neither of which entered production, and offering higher performance than the Boeing B-17.

The design was based on the exceptional wing of the Model 31 flying boat, the high aspect ratio of which offered low drag and thus the possibility of high speed and great range. The XB-24 prototype flew in December 1939 with 895-kW (1,200-hp) R-1830-33 radial engines, and the seven YB-24 pre-production machines were followed by nine B-24As with two 7.62-mm (0.3-in) tail guns and six 12.7-mm (0.5-in) guns in nose, ventral, dorsal and waist positions, and nine B-24Cs with turbocharged R-1830-41 engines and eight 12.7-

mm guns in single-gun nose, ventral, and twin waist positions, and twin-gun dorsal and tail turrets. These paved the way for the first major model, the B-24D based on the B-24C but with R-1830-43 engines, self-sealing tanks and, in later aircraft, a ventral ball turret together with two 12.7-mm guns.

These 2,381 aircraft were followed by 801 B-24Es with modified propellers. Then came 430 B-24Gs with R-1830-43 engines and a power-operated nose turret carrying twin 12.7-mm guns, and 3,100 improved B-24Hs with a longer nose. The most important variant was the slightly

modified B-24J, of which 6,678 were built with R-1830-65 engines, an autopilot and an improved bombsight. The 1,667 B-24Ls were similar to the B-24Js but had hand-operated tail guns, as did the 2,593 B-24Ms in a lighter mounting. There were also a number of experimental bomber variants, while other roles included transport (LB-30, air force C-87 and navy RY variants), fuel tanking (C-109), photographic reconnaissance (F-7), patrol bombing (PB4Y-1 and specially developed PB4Y-2 with a single vertical tail surface) and maritime reconnaissance (British Liberator GR models).

Consolidated B-24D Liberator

CONSOLIDATED B-24J LIBERATOR
Role: Long-range day bomber
Crew/Accommodation: Ten
Power Plant: Four 1,200 hp Pratt & Whitney R.1830-65 Twin Wasp air-cooled radials
Dimensions: Span 33.53 m (110 ft); length 20.47 m (67.16 ft); wing area 97.36 m² (1,048 sq ft)
Weights: Empty 16,556 kg (36,500 lb); MTOW 29,484 kg (65,000 lb)
Performance: Maximum speed 467 km/h (290 mph) at 7,620 m (25,000 ft); operational ceiling 8,534 m (28,000 ft); range 3,379 km (2,100 miles) with full bombload
Load: Ten .5 inch machine guns, plus up to 3,992 kg (8,800 lb) of internally carried bombs

A Consolidated B-24D Liberator in USAAF markings

HANDLEY PAGE HALIFAX (United Kingdom)

Halifax B.Mk II

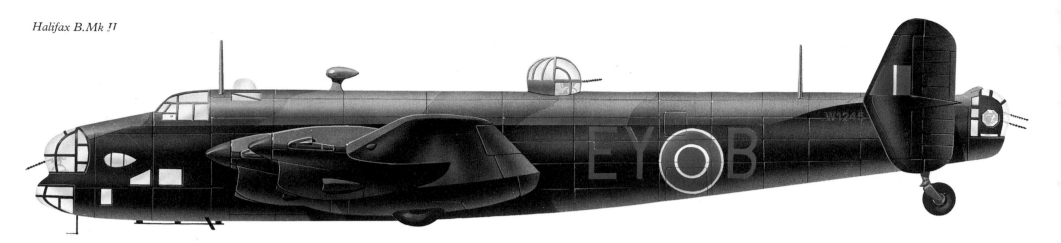

The Halifax was one of the RAF's trio of four-engined night bombers in World War II, and while not as important in this role as the Lancaster, it was more important in secondary roles such as maritime reconnaissance transport, and airborne forces' support. The type originated from a 1936 requirement for a medium/heavy bomber powered by two Rolls-Royce Vulture inline engines, and the resulting H.P.56 design was ordered

in prototype form. The company had doubts about the Vulture, and began to plan an alternative H.P.57 with four Rolls-Royce Merlin inlines. In September 1937, two H.P.57 prototypes were ordered. The first flew in October 1939.

The type entered service as the Halifax B.Mk I with 954-kW (1,280-hp) Merlin Xs, and these 84 aircraft were produced in three series as the initial Series I, the higher-weight

Series II, and the increased-tankage Series III. Later bombers were the 1,977 Halifax B.Mk IIs with Merlin XXs or 22s and a two-gun dorsal turret, the 2,091 Halifax B.Mk IIIs with 1204-kW (1,615-hp) Bristol Hercules VI or XVI radials, the 904 Halifax B.Mk Vs based on the Mk II with revised landing gear, the 467 Halifax B.Mk VIs based on the Mk III but with 1249-kW (1,675-hp) Hercules 100s, and the 35 Halifax B.Mk VIIs that reverted to Hercules XVIs; there were also bomber subvariants with important

modifications. The other variants retained the same mark number as the relevant bomber variant, and in the transport type these were the C.Mks II, VI and VII, in the maritime role GR.Mks II, V and VI, and in the airborne support role the A.Mks II, V and VII. Post-war development produced the C.Mk 8 and A.Mk 9 as well as the Halton civil transport, and total production was 6,178 aircraft.

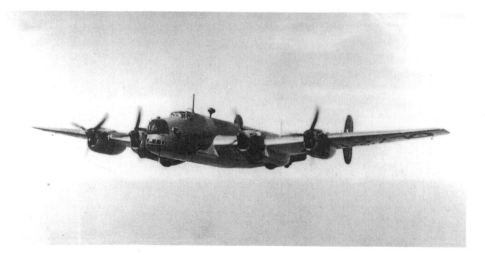

Handley Page Halifax Mk I

HANDLEY PAGE HALIFAX B.Mk III
Role: Heavy night bomber
Crew/Accommodation: Seven
Power Plant: Four 1,615 hp Bristol Hercules XVI air-cooled radials
Dimensions: Span 30.12 m (98.83 ft); length 21.82 m (71.58 ft); wing area 116.3 m² (1,250 sq ft)
Weights: Empty 17,346 kg (38,240 lb); MTOW 29,484 kg (65,000 lb)
Performance: Maximum speed 454 km/h (282 mph) at 4,115 m (13,500 ft); operational ceiling 7,315 m (24,000 ft); range 2,030 km (1,260 miles) with full warload
Load: Nine .303 inch machine guns, plus up to 5,897 kg (13,000 lb) of internally-stowed bombload

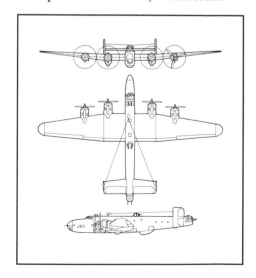

Handley Page Halifax B.Mk III

AVRO LANCASTER (United Kingdom)

Lancaster B.Mk III

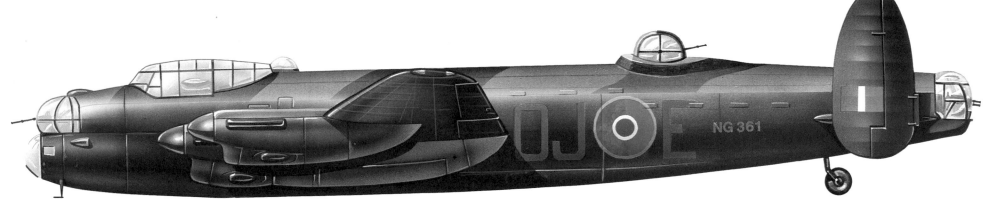

Certainly the best night bomber of World War II, the Lancaster was conceived as a four-engined development of the twin-engined Type 679 Manchester, which failed because of the unreliability of its Rolls-Royce Vulture engines. The first Lancaster flew in January 1941 with 854-kW (1,145-hp) Rolls-Royce Merlin Xs and the same triple vertical tail surfaces as the Manchester,

though these were later replaced by the larger endplate surfaces that became a Lancaster hallmark. The type was ordered into large-scale production as the Lancaster Mk I (later B.Mk I), of which 3,435 were produced. Defensive armament was eight 7.7-mm (0.303-in) machine-guns in three powered turrets: twin-gun nose and dorsal units, and a four-gun tail unit.

The first aircraft had 954-kW (1,280-hp) Merlin XXs or XXIIs, but later machines used the 1208-kW (1,620-hp) Merlin XXIVs. A feared shortage of Merlin inline engines led

to the development of the Lancaster Mk II with 1294-kW (1,735-hp) Bristol Hercules VI or XVI radial engines, but only 301 of this model were built as performance was degraded and Merlins were in abundant supply. The Lancaster Mk I was soon supplemented by the Lancaster B.Mk III and Canadian-built Lancaster B.Mk X, both powered by Packard-built Merlins.

Production of the Mk III and Mk X totalled 3,039 and 430 respectively. The final production version was the Lancaster B.Mk VIII with an American dorsal turret containing two 12.7-mm (0.5-in) heavy machine guns, and deliveries totalled 180 bringing overall Lancaster production to 7,377. After the war Lancasters were modified to perform a number of other roles.

AVRO LANCASTER Mk I
Role: Heavy night bomber
Crew/Accommodation: Seven
Power Plant: Four 1,640 hp Rolls-Royce Merlin 24 water-cooled inlines
Dimensions: Span 31.09 m (102 ft); length 21.18 m (69.5 ft); wing area 120.49 m² (1,297 sq ft)
Weights: Empty 16,780 kg (37,000 lb); MTOW 29,408 kg (65,000 lb)
Performance: Maximum speed 394 km/h (245 mph) at sea level; operational ceiling 6,706 m (22,000 ft); range 3,589 km (2,230 miles) with 3,182 kg (7,000 lb) bombload
Load: Eight .303 inch machine guns, plus up to 8,165 kg (18,000 lb) of bombs

Avro Lancaster Mk I

This is the RAF's preserved Avro Lancaster B.Mk I

BOEING B-29 and B-50 SUPERFORTRESS (United States)

B-29A Superfortress

The B-29 was the world's first genuinely effective long-range strategic bomber, and was designed from January 1940 as the Model 345 to meet the U.S. Army Air Corps' extremely ambitious plan for a 'hemisphere defense' bomber. The type was an extremely advanced design with pressurized accommodation, remotely controlled defensive armament, a formidable offensive load, and very high performance including great ceiling and range. The first of three XB-29 prototypes flew in September 1942 with four Wright R-3550 twin-row radials; each fitted with two turbochargers. By this time, Boeing already had contracts for more than 1,500 production bombers. The XB-29s were followed by 14 YB-29 pre-production aircraft, of which the first flew in June 1943.

A prodigious effort was made to bring the Superfortress into full service, and a wide-ranging programme of subcontracting delivered components to four assembly plants. The type entered full service in time to make a major contribution to the war against Japan in World War II, which it ended with the A-bombings of Hiroshima and Nagasaki in August 1945.

Some 2,848 B-29s were complemented by 1,122 B-29As with slightly greater span and revised defensive armament, and by 311 B-29Bs with no defensive armament but a radar-directed tail barbette. The type was also developed for reconnaissance and experimental roles, and was then revised with a sturdier structure and Pratt & Whitney R-4360 engines as the B-29D, which entered production as the B-50A. This was followed by its own series of bomber, reconnaissance and tanker aircraft.

B-29 Superfortress heavy bomber

BOEING B-29A SUPERFORTRESS
Role: Long-range, high altitude day bomber
Crew/Accommodation: Ten
Power Plant: Four 2,200 hp Wright R-3350-23 Cyclone Eighteen air-cooled radials
Dimensions: Span 43.05 m (141.25 ft); length 30.18 m (99 ft); wing area 161.56 m² (1,739 sq ft)
Weights: Empty 32,369 kg (71,360 lb); MTOW 62,823 kg (138,500 lb)
Performance: Maximum speed 576 km/h (358 mph) at 7,620 m (25,000 ft); operational ceiling 9,708 m (31,850 ft); range 6,598 km (4,100 miles) with 7,258 kg (16,000 lb) bombload
Load: One 20 mm cannon and twelve .5 inch machine guns, plus up to 9,072 kg (20,000 lb) of bombs

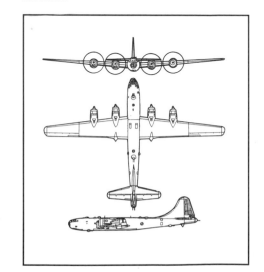

Boeing B-29 Superfortress

CONSOLIDATED B-36 'PEACEMAKER' (United States)

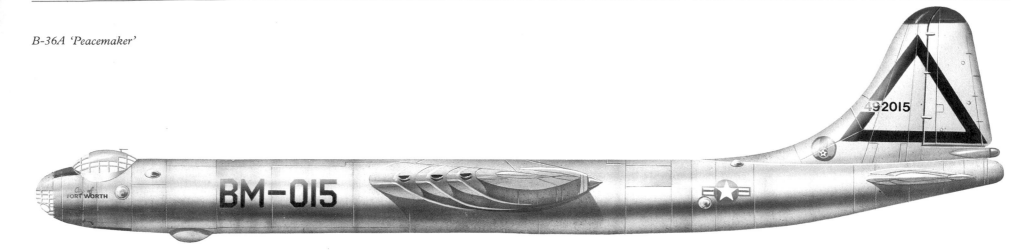

B-36A 'Peacemaker'

Designed as the Model 36 while the company was still Consolidated but built after it had become Convair, this extraordinary machine was the world's first genuinely intercontinental strategic bomber. The type resulted from an April 1941 requirement of the U.S. Army Air Corps for a machine able to carry a maximum bomb load of 32,659 kg (72,000 lb) but more realistically to deliver 4536 kg (10,000

lb) of bombs on European targets from bases in the United States. From four competing designs, the Model 36 was selected by the U.S. Army Air Forces for construction as the XB-36 prototype. This first flew in August 1946 and featured a pressurized fuselage and pusher propellers on the six 2237-kW (3,000-hp) R-4360-25 radial engines buried in the trailing edges of wings sufficiently deep to afford inflight access to the engines. The service trials model was the YB-

36 with a raised cockpit roof, and this was subsequently modified as the YB-36A with four- rather than single-wheel main landing gear units. These were features of the first production model, the B-36A unarmed crew trainer of which 22 were built without armament. The 104 B-36Bs introduced 2610-kW (3,500-hp) R-4360-41 engines and a defensive armament of 16 20-mm cannon in nose, tail and six fuselage barbettes. Some 64 were later revised as B-36D strategic reconnaissance aircraft with greater weights and performance through the addition of four 2359-kg (5,200-lb) thrust General Electric J47-

GE-19 turbojets in podded pairs under the outer wing, and in this role they complemented 22 aircraft which were built as such.

Later bombers with greater power and improved electronics were the 34 B-36Fs with 2833-kW (3,800-hp) R-04360-53s and J47-GE-19s, 83 B-36Hs with an improved flight deck, and 33 B-36Js with strengthened landing gear. There were also RB-36D, E, F and H reconnaissance versions, and even the GRB-36F with an embarked fighter for protection over the target area. Plans for jet- and even nuclear-powered versions resulted in no production variants.

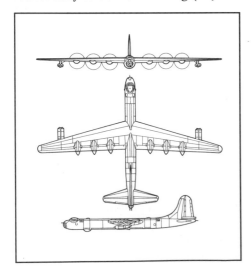

Convair B-36H

CONSOLIDATED/CONVAIR B-36D
Role: Long-range heavy bomber
Crew/Accommodation: Fifteen, including four relief crew members
Power Plant: Six 3,500 hp Pratt & Whitney R-4360-41 air-cooled radials, plus four 2,359 kgp (5,200 lb s.t.) General Electric J47-GE-19 turbojets
Dimensions: Span 70.1 m (230 ft); length 49.4 m (162.08 ft); wing area 443 m² (4,772 sq ft)
Weights: Empty 72,051 kg (158,843 lb); MTOW 162,161 kg (357,500 lb)
Performance: Maximum speed 706 km/h (439 mph) at 9,790 m (32,120 ft); operational ceiling 13,777 m (45,200 ft); range 12,070 km (7,500 miles) with 4,535 kg (10,000 lb bombload)
Load: Twelve 20 mm cannon, plus up to 39,009 kg (86,000 lb) of bombs

A Convair B-36B in its original form

BOEING B-47 STRATOJET (United States)

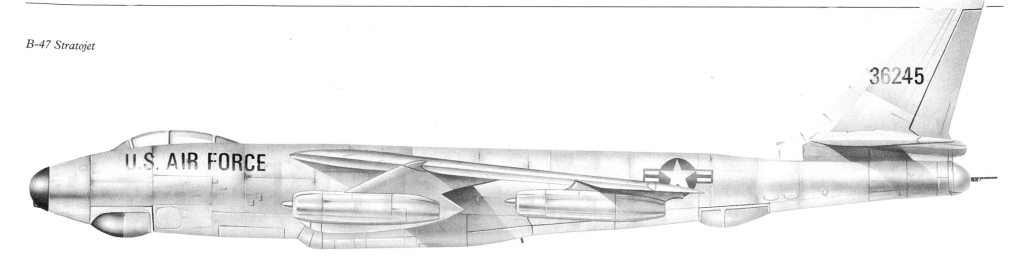

B-47 Stratojet

The B-47 was a great achievement, and as a swept-wing strategic bomber in the medium-range bracket it formed the main strength of the U.S. Strategic Air Command in the early 1950s. The U.S. Army Air Forces first considered a jet-powered bomber as early as 1944; at that time four companies were involved in producing preliminary designs for such a type. The Model 424 failed to attract real interest, but the later Model 432 was thought more acceptable and initial contracts were let. The company then recast the design as the Model 448 with the swept flying surfaces that captured German research data had shown to be desirable, but the USAAF was unimpressed. The design was finalized as the Model 450 with the six engines relocated from the fuselage to two twin-unit and two single-unit underwing nacelles.

In the spring of 1946, the USAAF ordered two Model 450 prototypes with the designation XB-47 and the first of these flew in December 1947. The type was notable for many of its features including the 'bicycle' type landing gear the twin main units of which retracted into the fuselage. The 10 B-47As were essentially development aircraft, and the first true service variant was the 399 B-47Bs, followed by 1,591 B-47Es with a host of operational improvements including greater power, inflight refuelling capability, and ejector seats. The B-47B and B-47E were both strengthened structurally later in their lives, leading to the designations B-47B-II and B-47E-II. There were also RB-47 reconnaissance together with several special-purpose and experimental variants.

Boeing B-47E bomber

BOEING B-47E STRATOJET
Role: Heavy bomber
Crew/Accommodation: Three
Power Plant: Six 3,266 kgp (7,200 lb s.t.) General Electric J47-GE-25 turbojets, plus a 16,329 kgp (36,000 lb s.t.) rocket pack for Jet Assisted Take-Off (JATO)
Dimensions: Span 35.36 m (116 ft); length 32.92 m (108 ft); wing area 132.67 m² (1,428 sq ft)
Weights: Empty 36.631 kg (80,756 lb); MTOW 93,759 kg (206,700 lb) with JATO rocket assistance
Performance: Maximum speed 975 km/h (606 mph) at 4,968 m (16,300 ft); operational ceiling 12,344 m (40,500 ft); range 6,228 km (3,870 miles) with 4,536 kg (10,000 lb) bombload
Load: Two rear-firing 20 mm cannon, plus up to 9,979 kg (22,000 lb) of bombs

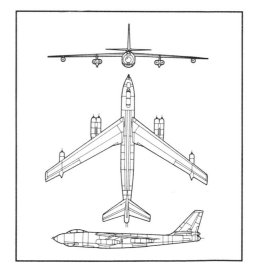

Boeing B-47E Stratojet

133

VICKERS VALIANT (United Kingdom)

Valiant B(K).Mk 1

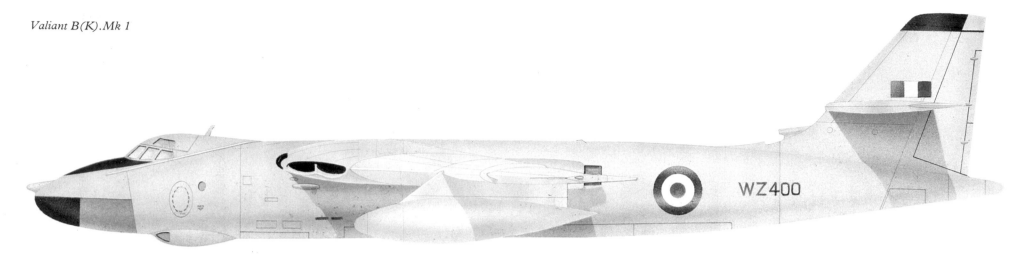

The Valiant was the first of the U.K.'s trio of strategic V-bombers to enter service and, though not as advanced or capable as the later Avro Vulcan and Handley Page Victor, it was nonetheless a worthy warplane. The Type 667 was originated in response to a 1948 requirement for a high-altitude bomber to carry the British free-fall nuclear bomb that would be dropped with the aid of a radar bombing system. The type was based on modestly swept flying surfaces that included a shoulder-set cantilever wing with compound-sweep leading edges, a circular-section fuselage accommodating the five-man crew in its pressurized forward section, retractable tricycle landing gear, and, in addition, four turbojets buried in the wing roots.

The prototype first flew in May 1951 with 2948-kg (6,500-lb) Rolls-Royce Avon RA.3 turbojets, improved to 3402-kg (7,500-lb) thrust Avon RA.7s in the second prototype that took over the flight test programme after the first had been destroyed by fire. The first five of 36 Valiant B.Mk 1 bombers served as pre-production aircraft, and this type began to enter squadron service in 1955. The type was used operationally as a conventional bomber in the Suez campaign of 1956, and was also used to drop the first British atomic and hydrogen bombs in October 1956 and May 1957 respectively. Production for the RAF totalled 104 aircraft in the form of 36 Valiant B.Mk 1 bombers, 11 Valiant B(PR).Mk. 1 strategic reconnaissace aircraft, 13 Valiant B(PR).Mk 1 multi-role aircraft usable in the bomber, reconnaissance and inflight refuelling tanker tasks, and 44 Valiant B(K).Mk 1 bomber and tanker aircraft. The Valiant B.Mk 2 did not pass the prototype stage, and all surviving aircraft were retired in 1965 as a result of fatigue problems.

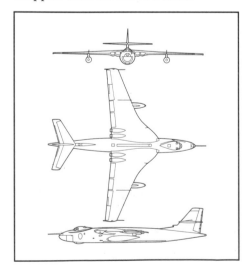

Vickers Valiant B(K).Mk 1

VICKERS VALIANT B.Mk 1
Role: Strategic bomber
Crew/Accommodation: Five
Power Plant: Four 4,536 kgp (10,000 lb s.t.) Rolls-Royce Avon 28 turbojets
Dimensions: Span 34.85 m (114.33 ft); length 32.99 m (108.25 ft); wing area 219.4 m² (2,362 sq ft)
Weights: Empty 34,419 kg (75,881 lb); MTOW 63,503 kg (140,000 lb)
Performance: Maximum speed 912 km/h (492 knots) at 9,144 m (30,000 ft); operational ceiling 16,459 m (54,000 ft); range 7,242 km (3,908 naut. miles) with maximum fuel
Load: No defensive armament, but internal stowage for up to 9,525 kg (21,000 lb) of bombs

Vickers Valiant B.Mk 1 bomber

AVRO VULCAN (United Kingdom)

Vulcan B.Mk 2

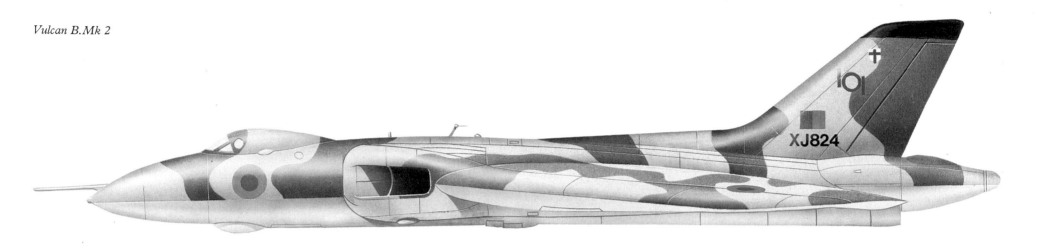

The Type 698 was a massive delta-winged bomber, and by any standards was an extraordinary aerodynamic feat that, with the Handley Page Victor and Vickers Valiant, was one of the U.K.'s trio of nuclear 'V-bombers' in the 1950s and 1960s. The type was planned as a high-altitude bomber able to deliver the British free-fall nuclear bomb over long ranges. A radical aerodynamic approach was selected, and various features were proved in five Type 707 one-third scale research aircraft. The first of two Type 698 prototypes flew in August 1952 with four 2948-kg (6,500-lb) thrust Rolls-Royce Avon RA.3 turbojets, later replaced by 3629-kg (8,000-lb) thrust Armstrong Siddeley Sapphire turbojets. The initial production model, the Vulcan B.Mk 1, had Olympus turbojet in variants increased in thrust from 4990 to 6123-kg (11,000 to 13,500-lb).

In 1961 existing aircraft were modified to Vulcan B.Mk 1A standard with a bulged tail containing electronic counter-measures gear. The definitive model was the Vulcan B.Mk 2 with provision for the Avro Blue Steel stand-off nuclear missile, a turbofan powerplant offering considerably greater fuel economy as well as more power, and a much-modified wing characterized by a cranked leading edge and offering greater area as well as elevons in place of the Mk 1's separated elevators and ailerons. The type was later modified as the Vulcan B.Mk 2A for the low-level role with conventional bombs and ECM equipment, and the Vulcan SR.Mk 2 was a strategic reconnaissance derivative.

An Avro Vulcan B.Mk 2

AVRO VULCAN B.Mk 2
Role: Long-range bomber
Crew/Accommodation: Five
Power Plant: Four 9,072 kgp (20,000 lb s.t.) Bristol Siddeley Olympus 301 turbojets
Dimensions: Span 33.83 m (111 ft); length 30.45 m (99.92 ft); wing area 368.29 m² (3,964 sq ft)
Weights: Empty 48,081 kg (106,000 lb); MTOW 98,800 kg (200,180 lb)
Performance: Maximum speed 1,041 km/h (562 knots) Mach 0.98 at 12,192 m (40,000 ft); operational ceiling 19,912 m (65,000 ft); radius 3,701 km (2,300 miles) at altitude with missile
Load: Up to 9,525 kg (21,000 lb) of bombs, or one Blue Steel Mk 1 stand-off missile

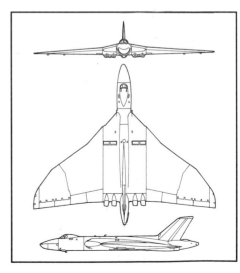

Avro Vulcan B.Mk 2A

135

BOEING B-52 STRATOFORTRESS (United States)

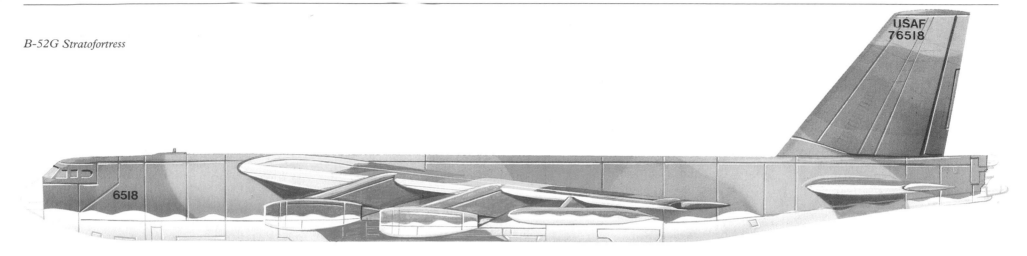

B-52G Stratofortress

In numerical terms, the B-52 is still the most important bomber in the U.S. Strategic Air Command inventory. It offers an excellent combination of great range and very large payload, though the type's radar signature is large and its operational capabilities ensured only by constantly updated offensive and defensive electronic systems.

The Stratofortress was first planned as a turboprop-powered successor to the B-50, but was then recast as a turbojet-powered type using eight 3402-kg (7,500-lb) thrust Pratt & Whitney J57s podded in four pairs under the swept wings. The B-52 employs the same type of 'bicycle' landing gear as the B-47, and after design as the Model 464 the XB-52 prototype first flew in April 1952 with a high-set cockpit that seated the two pilots in tandem. The current cockpit was adopted in the B-52A, of which three were built as development aircraft. The 50 B-52Bs introduced the standard nav/attack system, and the 35 B-52Cs had improved equipment and performance. These were in reality development models, and the first true service version was the B-52D, of which 170 were built with revised tail armament. This model was followed by 100 B-52Es with improved navigation and weapon systems, 89 B-52Fs with greater power, 193 B-52Gs with a shorter fin, remotely controlled tail armament, integral fuel tankage and underwing pylons for two AGM-28 Hound Dog stand-off nuclear missiles, and 102 B-52Hs with Pratt & Whitney TF33 turbofans, a rotary-barrel cannon as tail armament, and structural strengthening for the low-altitude role.

The only types currently in service are the B-52G and H, and most of these are now configured for a combination of AGM-69 SRAM supersonic defence-suppression missiles and AGM-86B subsonic cruise missiles.

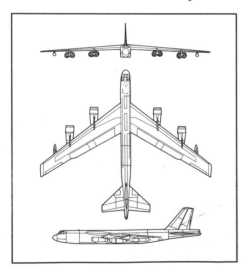

BOEING B-52H STRATOFORTRESS
Role: Long-range bomber
Crew/Accommodation: Six
Power Plant: Eight 7,718 kgp (17,000 lb s.t.) Pratt & Whitney TF33-P-3 turbofans
Dimensions: Span 56.42 m (185 ft); length 48.03 m (157.6 ft); wing area 371.6 m²
Weights: Empty 78,355 kg (172,740 lb); MTOW 221,350 kg (488,000 lb)
Performance: Maximum speed 1,013 km/h (630 mph) at 7,254 m (23,800 ft); operational ceiling 14,540 m (47,700 ft); radius 7,000 km (4,350 miles) with maximum bombload
Load: Up to 16,330 kg (36,000 lb) of bombs or missiles

A Boeing B-52G Stratofortress

HANDLEY PAGE VICTOR (United Kingdom)

Victor SR.Mk 2

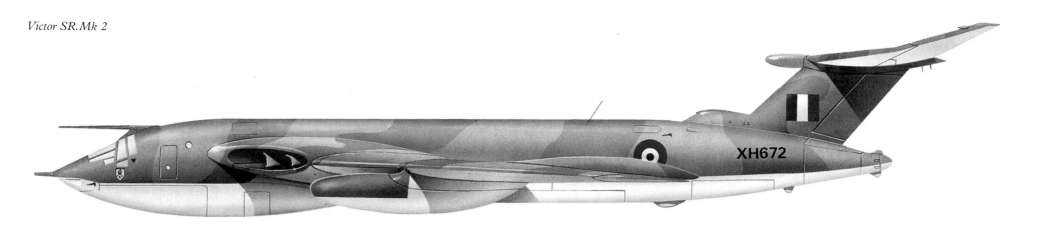

The last of the United Kingdom's trio of nuclear 'V-bombers' to enter service, it is now the only one still in service, albeit as a tanker. The type was planned against the requirements of a 1946 specification for a bomber able to carry a free-fall nuclear bomb over long range at a speed and altitude too high for interception by the fighters of the day. The H.P.80 was based on what was in effect a pod-and-boom fuselage that supported crescent-shaped flying surfaces. For its time it was a very advanced type. The

first of two prototypes flew in December 1952.

After considerable development, the type entered squadron service in November 1957 with 5012-kg (11,050-lb) thrust Armstrong Siddeley Sapphire ASSa.7 Mk 202 turbojets. Production totalled just 50 aircraft that were formally designated Victor B.Mk 1H with better equipment and electronic counter-measures than the basic Victor B.Mk 1 that had originally been planned; soon after delivery, 24 aircraft were modified to

Victor B.Mk 1A standard with improved defensive electronics. Though planned with Sapphire ASSa.9 engines in a wing increased in span to 34.05 m (115 ft 0 in), the radically improved Victor B.Mk 2 was delivered with Rolls-Royce Conway turbofans, initially 7824-kg (17,250-lb) thrust RCo.11 Mk 200s, but then in definitive form 9344-kg (20,600-lb) thrust Conway Mk 201s. Production totalled 34 aircraft, and of these 21 were modified to Victor B.Mk 2R standard with provision for the Avro Blue Steel stand-off nuclear missile that allowed the Victor to avoid flight

over heavily defended targets. Soon after this, the Victor was retasked to the low-level role as Soviet defensive capability was thought to have made high-altitude overflights little more than suicidal. Later conversions were the nine Victor B(SR).Mk 2 maritime reconnaissance and the tanker models that included 11 Victor K.Mk 1s, six Victor B.Mk 1A(K2P)s, 14 Victor K.Mk 1As and 24 Victor K.Mk 2s.

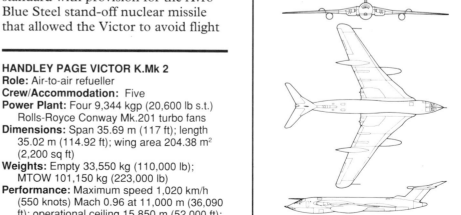

Handley Page Victor B.Mk 2

HANDLEY PAGE VICTOR K.Mk 2
Role: Air-to-air refueller
Crew/Accommodation: Five
Power Plant: Four 9,344 kgp (20,600 lb s.t.) Rolls-Royce Conway Mk.201 turbo fans
Dimensions: Span 35.69 m (117 ft); length 35.02 m (114.92 ft); wing area 204.38 m² (2,200 sq ft)
Weights: Empty 33,550 kg (110,000 lb); MTOW 101,150 kg (223,000 lb)
Performance: Maximum speed 1,020 km/h (550 knots) Mach 0.96 at 11,000 m (36,090 ft); operational ceiling 15,850 m (52,000 ft); range 7,403 km (3,995 naut. miles) unrefuelled
Load: Up to 15,876 kg (35,000 lb)

A Handley Page Victor B.Mk 2

TUPOLEV Tu-95 'BEAR' (U.S.S.R.)

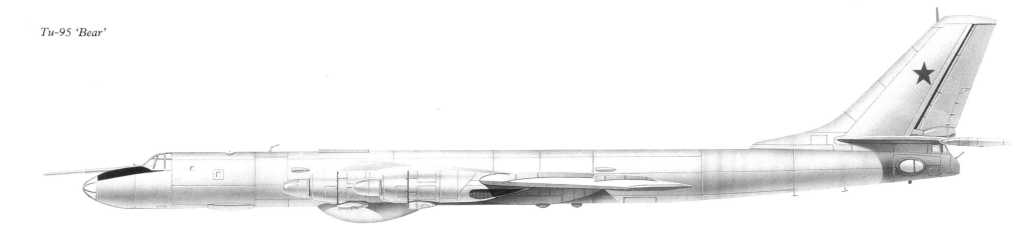

Tu-95 'Bear'

The Tu-95 prototype first flew during the summer of 1954 and the type entered service in 1955, originally with the service designation Tu-20 that has now been dropped in favour of Tu-95. The 'Bear-A' was the original bomber version and is still in limited service. First seen in 1961, the 'Bear-B' carries the AS-3 'Kangaroo' missile semi-recessed under the fuselage, while retrofits later added inflight refuelling

and, in some aircraft, strategic reconnaissance capabilities. Introduced in about 1963, the 'Bear-C' is a dedicated maritime reconnaissance and Elint (electronic intelligence gathering) derivative of the 'Bear-B' but retains missile capability. The 'Bear-D' was introduced in about 1966 as a multi-sensor maritime reconnaissance and missile-support version produced by converting 'Bear-As'. Introduced in the later 1960s, the 'Bear-E' is a multi-sensor maritime reconnaissance aircraft produced by converting 'Bear-

As' with inflight refuelling capability plus more fuel and a conformal pallet for six or seven cameras and other sensors. The designation 'Bear-G' applies to 'Bear-Bs' and 'Bear-Cs' reworked as Elint aircraft and launch platforms for two AS-4 'Kitchen' missiles carried under the wings, and 'Bear-J' to older aircraft which were reworked as submarine communication relay aircraft.

The Tu-142 designation is believed to apply to new-build aircraft produced from the late 1960s with a number of design, engineering, and

equipment improvements allowing take-off at a higher maximum weight. This 'Bear-F' was designed for the long-range anti-submarine role and entered service in 1972; there are now four subvariants. The 'Bear-H' is a new-build variant based on the 'Bear-F' but with a shorter fuselage for use as a launch platform for the AS-15 'Kent' cruise missile. (Six are carried internally in the weapon bay with an additional four or eight as twins or quadruplets respectively placed on two pylons under the wing roots).

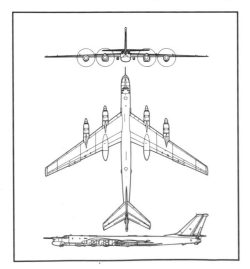

Tupolev Tu-142 'Bear-H'

TUPOLEV Tu-142 'BEAR F'
Role: Long range bomber and maritime reconnaissance
Crew/Accommodation: Eleven to 13 (mission dependent)
Power Plant: Four 17,795 shp Kuznetsov NK-12MV turboprops
Dimensions: Span 51.10 m (167.66 ft); length 49.50 m (162.42 ft); wing area 292.60 m² (3,150.00 sq ft)
Weight: MTOW 188,000 kg (414,470 lb)
Performance: Maximum speed 897 km/h (484 knots) Mach 0.82 at 9,000 m (29,528 ft); operational ceiling 13,500 m (44,290 ft); radius 8,285 km (4,475 naut. miles) unrefuelled
Load: Two 23 mm cannons and up to 30,000 kg (66,189 lb) of weaponry

A variant of the Tupolev Tu-95 family, a 'Bear-D'

GENERAL DYNAMICS B-58 HUSTLER (United States)

B-58A Hustler

The B-58 Hustler resulted from a 1949 U.S. Air Force requirement for a supersonic medium strategic bomber and was a stupendous technical achievement. In 1952 the Convair Model 4 was selected for development as an initial 18 aircraft. Convair's own experience in delta-winged aircraft, themselves based on German data captured at the end of World War II, was used in the far-sighted concept. The smallest possible airframe required advances in aerodynamics,

structures, and materials, and was designed on Whitcomb area ruling principles with a long but slender fuselage that carried only a tall vertical tail and a small delta wing. This latter supported the nacelles for the four afterburning turbojets. The airframe was too small to accommodate sufficient fuel for both the outbound and return legs of the Hustler's mission, so the tricycle landing gear had very tall legs that raised the fuselage high enough off the ground to

accommodate a large underfuselage pod 18.90 m (62 ft 0 in) long. This pod contained the Hustler's nuclear bombload and also the fuel for the outward leg, and was dropped over the target. The crew of three was seated in tandem escape capsules.

In July 1954 the order was reduced to two XB-58 prototypes, 11 YB-58A pre-production aircraft, and 31 pods. The first XB-58 flew in November 1956, and proved tricky to fly. Extensive development was undertaken with the aid of another 17

YB-58As ordered in February 1958 together with 35 pods; the last 17 YB-58As were later converted to RB-58A standard with ventral reconnaissance pods. The type became operational in 1960, but as the high-altitude bomber was clearly obsolescent, full production amounted to only 86 B-58As plus 10 upgraded YB-58As. Training was carried out in eight TB-58A conversions of YB-58As.

The Convair B-58A Hustler

CONVAIR B-58A HUSTLER
Role: Supersonic bomber
Crew/Accommodation: Three
Power Plant: Four 7,076 kgp (15,600 lb s.t.) General Electric J79-GE-3B turbojets with reheat
Dimensions: Span 17.32 m (56.83 ft); length 29.49 m (96.75 ft); wing area 143.26 m² (1,542 sq ft)
Weights: Empty 25,202 kg (55,560 lb); MTOW 73,936 kg (163,000 lb)
Performance: Maximum speed 2,126 km/h (1,147 knots) Mach 2.1 at 12,192 m (40,000 ft); operational ceiling 19,202 m (63,000 ft); range 8,247 km (4,450 naut. miles) unrefuelled
Load: One 20 mm multi-barrel cannon, plus up to 8,820 kg (19,450 lb) of stores and fuel carrier in mission pod

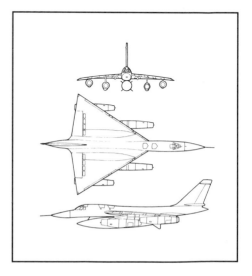

Convair B-58A Hustler

ROCKWELL B-1 (United States)

B-1A

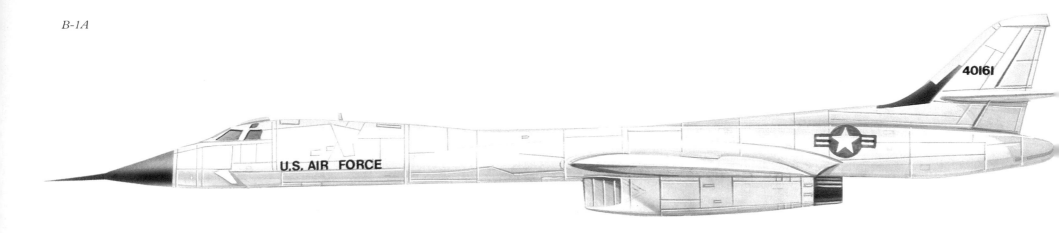

Entering service from 1986 to replace the Boeing B-52 in the penetration bomber role, the B-1B resulted from a protracted development history from the time the U.S. Air Force issued its 1969 requirement for a high-level bomber with dash capability of Mach 2.2+ for delivery of free-fall and stand-off weapons. The Rockwell submission was accepted as the B-1 in 1970, and the full-scale development

of the initial production version was soon under way, this B-1A being a complex variable-geometry type with General Electric F101 turbofans and variable inlets.

The prototype first flew in December 1974 and the flight test programme moved ahead without undue delay. In June 1977 the obsolescence of the high-level role was recognized in President Carter's

decision to scrap the programme in favour of cruise missiles, but the administration of President Reagan decided in October 1981 to procure 100 B-1B bombers in the revised low-level penetration role with fixed inlets and modified nacelles (reducing maximum speed to Mach 1.25) and a strengthened airframe and landing gear for operation at higher weights. Other changes were concerned with reduction of the type's already low radar signature: S-shaped ducts with streamwise baffles shielded the face of the engine compressors, and radar absorbent materials were used in sensitive areas to reduce reflectivity.

The second and fourth B-1As were used from March 1983 to flight-test features of the B-1B, which first flew in September 1984 with the advanced offensive and defensive electronic systems. From the ninth aircraft the type was built with revised weapons bays, the forward bay having a movable bulkhead allowing the carriage of 12 AGM-86B ALCMs internally, as well as additional fuel tanks and SRAMs. When the Northrop B-2 enters service in the 1990s as the USAF's penetration 'stealth' bomber, the B-1B will be relegated increasingly to the stand-off and conventional bombing roles.

Rockwell B-1B

ROCKWELL B-1B
Role: Long-range low-level variable-geometry stand-off bomber
Crew/Accommodation: Four
Power Plant: Four 13,608 kg (30,750 lb s.t.) General Electric F101-GE-102 turbofans with reheat
Dimensions: Span 41.66 m (136.68 ft); swept 23.83 m (78.23 ft); length 44.43 m (145.76 ft); wing area 181.2 m² (1,950 sq ft)
Weights: Empty 87,090 kg (192,000 lb); MTOW 213,367 kg (477,000 lb)
Performance: Maximum speed 978 km/h (529 knots) Mach 0.8 at 61 m (200 ft); operational ceiling 15,240+ m (50,000+ ft); range 10,378 m (5,600 naut. miles) with 34,020 kg (75,000 lb) internal warload
Load: Up to 56,699 kg (125,000 lb) of weapons, including up to 24 short-range attack missiles carried on rotary launcher within the aircraft's three internal weapon bays

Rockwell B-1B Lancer

NORTHROP B-2 (United States)

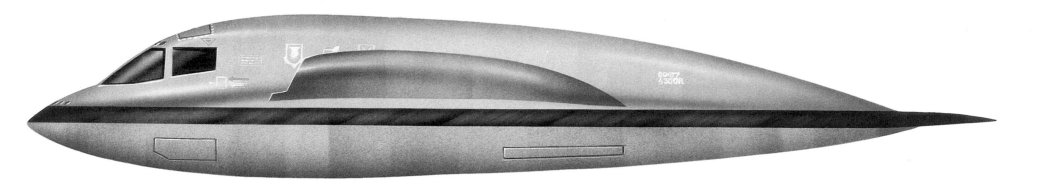

Developed at enormous cost during the late 1970s and 1980s, and first revealed in November 1988 for an initial flight in July 1989, the B-2 was designed as successor to the Rockwell B-1B in the penetration bomber role. Unlike the low-altitude B-1B, however, the B-2 is designed for penetration of enemy airspace at medium and high altitudes, relying on its stealth design and composite structure to evade detection by enemy air defence systems until it has closed to within a few miles of its target, where attack accuracy is enhanced by use of the APQ-181 main radar, which has features in common with the APG-70 used in the McDonnell Douglas F-15C/D/E Eagle.

The B-2 is a design of the relaxed-stability type, and is a flying wing with 40° swept leading edges and W-shaped trailing edges featuring simple flight-control surfaces (elevons for pitch and roll control, and 'differential drag' surfaces for yaw control) operated by a fly-by-wire control system. The design emphasis was placed on completely smooth surfaces with blended flightdeck and nacelle bulges. Radar reflectivity is very low because of the use of radiation-absorbent materials and a carefully optimized shape (including shielded upper-surface inlets), and the head-on radar cross-section is only about one-tenth of that of the B-1B. Additionally, the careful mixing of hot exhaust gases with cold freestream air before release through the type's 2D nozzles reduces thermal and acoustic signatures to a very significant degree in this firmly subsonic design. Production of 132 B-2s was originally planned, but this total may now be trimmed to just 75 aircraft used in primary bomber (with 2,000 of the USAF's 4,850 nuclear weapons) and secondary maritime surveillance and attack roles.

B-2A is a costly but potentially decisive warplane

NORTHROP B-2
Role: Long-range, low-detectability bomber
Crew/Accommodation: Two/three
Power Plant: Four 8,620 kgp (19,000 lb s.t.) General Electric F118-GE-100 turbofans
Dimensions: Span 52.43 m (172 ft); length 21.03 m (69 ft)
Weights: MTOW 136,080 kg (300,000 lb)
Performance: Maximum speed 1,012 km/h (546 knots) at 15,240 m (50,000 ft); range 11,110+ km (6,000+ naut. miles) unrefuelled
Load: Up to sixteen SRAM II, AGM-129 or B83 nuclear bombs stowed internally and carried on rotary dispensers within three weapons bays.
Note: data on empty weight and operational ceiling remain classified

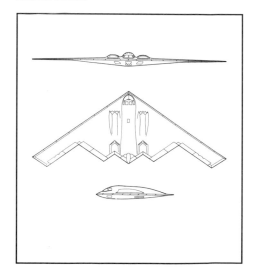

GRUMMAN E-2 HAWKEYE (United States)

E-2C Hawkeye

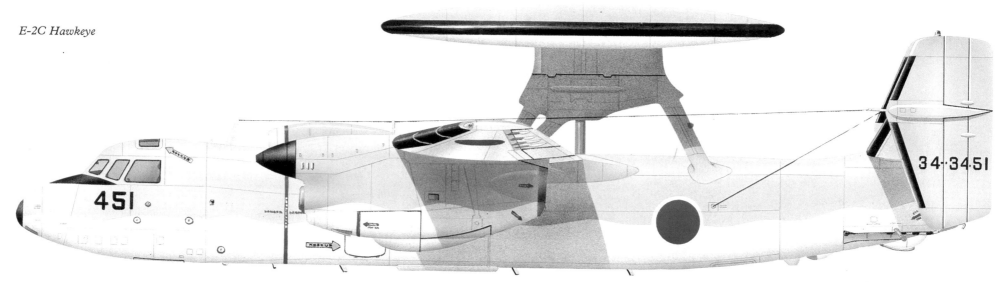

Grumman developed its G-89 concept as the world's first pupose-designed airborne early warning platform to meet a U.S. Navy requirement for the aerial component of the Naval Tactical Data System, and the Grumman design was selected in March 1957 for hardware development as the W2F-1. The first aerodynamic prototype flew in October 1960, while the second machine, which flew in April 1961, introduced the APS-96 surveillance radar (with its antenna in a large-diameter rotodome) and the advanced data-processing system that allowed the three-man tactical crew to watch and control all air activity within a large radius. The first aircraft were delivered with the designation W2F-1, but these 62 aircraft entered service from January 1964 as E-2As. This model was limited to overwater operations, but from 1969 most aircraft were modified to the E-2B standard adding overland capability. This resulted from the combination of APS-120 radar and a digital central computer; other improvements were inflight refuelling capability and larger vertical tail surfaces.

In January 1971 Grumman flew the prototype of the E-2C that entered service in November 1973 with the more capable APS-125 radar able to detect air targets out to a range of 370 km (230 miles) even in ground clutter and also able to track more than 250 air and surface targets simultaneously, allowing the tactical crew to control 30 or more interceptions at the same time. Later aircraft have the APS-138 radar for the tracking of 600 targets to a range of 483 km (300 miles) and enhanced electronic support measures capability. From 1988 the APS-139 radar added the capability to track even stationary targets, and further improvement will accrue from the APS-145 radar able to work over normal rather than featureless terrain. There is also a C-2 Greyhound carrier onboard delivery variant with provision for 39 passengers.

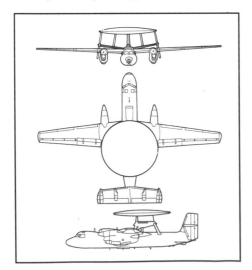

Grumman E-2C Hawkeye

GRUMMAN E-2C HAWKEYE
Role: Naval carrierborne airborne early warning and control
Crew/Accommodation: Five
Power Plant: Two 4,910 hp General Electric T56A-425 turboprops
Dimensions: Span 24.6 m (80.6 ft); length 17.5 m (57.6 ft); wing area 65.03 m² (700 sq ft)
Weights: Empty 17,212 kg (37,945 lb); MTOW 23,503 kg (51,817 lb)
Performance: Maximum speed 602 km/h (325 knots) at 4,877 m (16,000 ft); operational ceiling 9,388 m (30,800 ft); endurance 6.1 hours
Load: None, other than special-to-task onboard equipment

A Grumman E-2B Hawkeye of US Naval Aviation

GRUMMAN EA-6 PROWLER (United States)

EA-6B Prowler

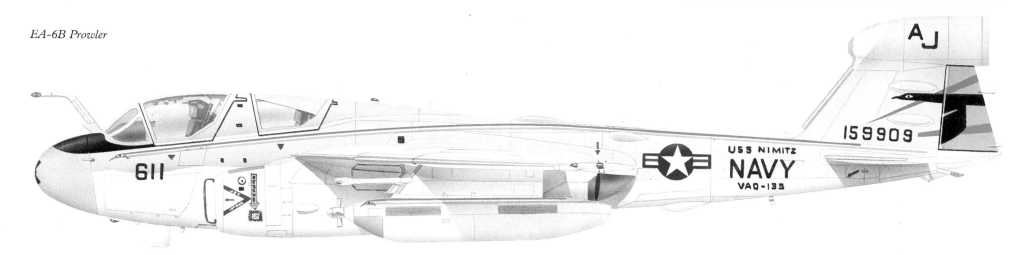

From early in the programme to develop the A2F, the U.S. Navy realized the importance of producing a support version fitted with the specialized electronic systems that could aid the pure warplane version's passage through enemy airspace. The result was the development of the EA-6A (initially the A2F-1Q) as an electronic support variant that also retained partial attack capability. The first example of this variant flew in 1963 as a conversion from YA-6A (initially YA2F-1) standard, and was

followed by another two YA-6A and four A-6A conversions, and by 21 new-build aircraft. The variant is distinguishable by its revised vertical tail surfaces, which are surmounted by the large fairing that accommodates the receiver antennae for the electronic warfare system, which had internal and external jammers.

The U.S. Navy called for a dedicated electronic warfare variant that appeared as the EA-6B Prowler with its fuselage lengthened by 1.37 m (4 ft 6 in) to allow the insertion of a

stretched cockpit accommodating, in addition to the standard two crew, two specialist operators for the ALQ-99 system to detect, localize and analyse enemy radar emissions before finding the right jamming set-on frequency for any of the five windmill-powered jammer pods carried under the fuselage and wings. The EA-6B has undergone enormous electronic development in the form of steadily more comprehensive and wide-ranging standards known as the

Expanded Capability, Improved Capability, Improved Capability 2, Defensive Electronic Counter-Measures, and Advanced Capability. Together with aerodynamic and powerplant enhancements, this process is being continued to ensure that the Prowler remains capable of handling all electronic threats until well into the next century.

A Grumman EA-6B Prowler

GRUMMAN EA-6B PROWLER
Role: Naval carrierborne, all-weather electronic warfare
Crew/Accommodation: Four
Power Plant: Two 5,080 kgp (11,200 lb s.t.) Pratt & Whitney J52-P-40B turbojets
Dimensions: Span 16.16 m (53 ft); length 18.1 m (59.25 ft); wing area 49.15 m² (529 sq ft)
Weights: Empty 14,589 kg (32.162 lb); MTOW 27,493 kg (60,610 lb)
Performance: Maximum speed 1,002 km/h (541 knots) Mach 0.82 at sea level; operational ceiling 11,582 m (38,000 ft); radius 639 km (345 naut. miles) with full 5-jammer warload
Load: Up to in excess of 11,340 kg (25,000 lb) of electronic broad-band jammers and other specialized electronic warfare systems

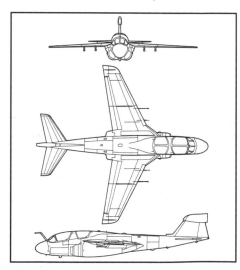

Grumman EA-6B Prowler

BOEING E-3 SENTRY (United States)

E-3A Sentry

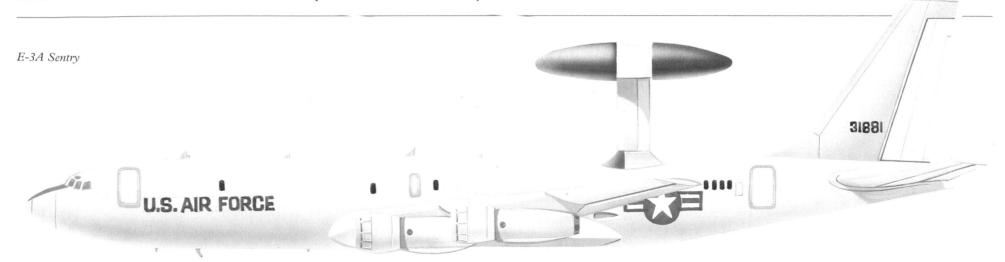

One of the most expensive but important current military aircraft, the Sentry is a highly capable Airborne Warning And Control System type designed for three-dimensional surveillance of a massive volume of air and the direction of aerial operations within that volume as a force multiplier. The type is based on the Model 707-300B airliner, and two EC-137D prototypes were used to evaluate the Westinghouse APY-1 and Hughes APY-2 radars. The former was chosen for the 34 E-3A production aircraft, which were delivered between 1977 and 1984. The first 24 aircraft were Core E-3As with only an overland capability, CC-1 computer, nine situation display consoles and two auxiliary display units, while the last 10 were standard E-3As with additional overwater sensor capability, a faster CC-2 computer, secure voice communications, and Joint Tactical Information Distribution System.

The Standard E-3A type (though with improved APY-1 radar and provision for self-defence AAMs) was ordered for the multi-national NATO early warning force, and these 18 aircraft were delivered between January 1982 and April 1985. Another five have been delivered to Saudi Arabia as E-3A/Saudi aircraft with slightly less capable electronics and four 9979-kg (22,000-lb) thrust CFM56-A2-2 turbofans. The Core E-3As (and two EC-137Ds) have been raised to E-3B standard with the CC-2 computer, 14 display consoles, JTIDS, improved ECM capability, and limited overwater sensor capability, while the Standard E-3As have been raised to E-3C standard with five extra situation display consoles and the 'Have Quick-A' communications system. The type also has the capability to carry small underwing pylons, which could carry AIM-9 Sidewinder AAMs for a modest self-defence facility. Comparable aircraft for the British and French Air Forces are seven E-3Ds (that is, Sentry AEW.Mk 1s) and four E-3Fs with CEM56 engines.

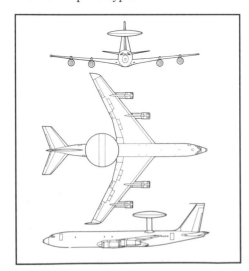

Grumman E-3 Sentry

BOEING E-3D SENTRY
Role: Airborne early warning and command
Crew/Accommodation: Four, plus 13 AWACS specialists
Power Plant: Four 10,886 kgp (24,000 lb s.t.) General Electric/SNECMA CFM-56-2 turbofans
Dimensions: Span 44.43 m (145.75 ft); length 46.62 m (152 ft); wing area 284.40 m² (3,050 sq ft)
Weights: Empty 77,238 kg (170,277 lb); MTOW 151,995 kg (335,000 lb)
Performance: Maximum speed 805 km/h (434 knots) at 8,839 m (29,000 ft); operational ceiling 11,430 m (37,500 ft); range 9,250 km (5,000 naut. miles)
Load: Nil

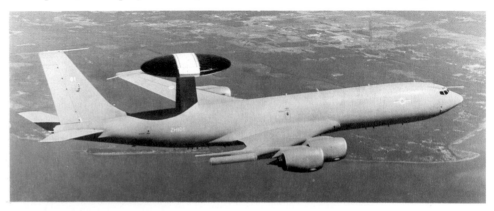

A Boeing E-3D Sentry in RAF markings as a Sentry AEW.Mk 1

AVRO 504 (United Kingdom)

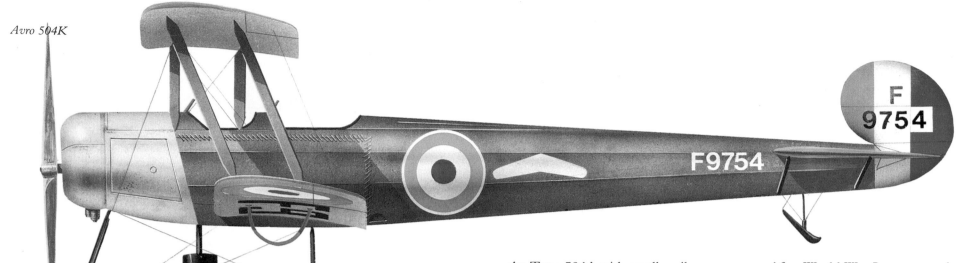

Avro 504K

One of the most remarkable aircraft of all time, the Type 504 was developed from the Type 500 basic trainer, and first flew in July 1913 with a 60-kW (80-hp) Gnome rotary that in fact yielded only about 46-kW (62-hp). In the summer of 1913 the British army

and navy ordered the Type 504 as a general-purpose aeroplane. After a limited amount of front-line service, which included the successful bombing of the Zeppelin sheds at Friedrichshafen in November 1914, the Type 504 was relegated to second-line duties. Here it found its métier as a trainer.

The main variants were Type 504,

the Type 504A with smaller ailerons, the Type 504B with a larger fin, the Type 504C anti-Zeppelin single-seater, and the Type 504D, all powered by the 60-kW (80-hp) Gnome Monosoupape rotary engine. Trainer and civil variants were the Type 504E with less wing stagger, the classic Type 504J of 1916 with the same 75-kW (100-hp) Gnome Monosoupape as the Type 504E, the Type 504K standard trainer with a universal engine mounting able to accommodate a variety of inline, radial and rotary engines, the Type 504L floatplane and the Type 504M cabin transport.

After World War I, many surplus Type 504 models were converted to improved Type 504N standard with a number of structural revisions, revised landing gear that eliminated the central skid of earlier models, and a 134-kW (180-hp) Armstrong Siddeley Lynx IV radial engine. Well over 8,000 Type 504s were built in World War I, and post-war conversions were supplemented by 598 Type 504Ns built between 1925 and 1932.

Avro Type 504K

AVRO 504K
Role: Reconnaissance/trainer
Crew/Accommodation: Two
Power Plant: One 130 hp Clerget air-cooled rotary
Dimensions: Span 10.97 m (36 ft); length 7.75 m (25.42 ft); wing area 30.66 m² (330 sq ft)
Weights: Empty 558 kg (1,231 lb); MTOW 830 kg (1,829 lb)
Performance: Maximum speed 153 km/h (95 mph) at sea level; operational ceiling 5,486 m (18,000 ft); endurance 3 hours
Load: A number of 504s were converted into home defence single-seat fighters with one .303 inch machine gun, plus stowage for hand-released small bombs

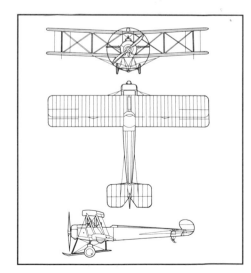

Avro Type 504K

CURTISS JN 'JENNY' (United States)

4002

LOVE FIELD
SC4002
15

JN-4 appeared later in the production run.

The JN-4A had a larger tailplane and engine downthrust; the slightly earlier JN-4B introduced the larger tailplane and used the OX-2 engine; the JN-4C was an experimental model of which just two were produced, the JN-4 Can (generally known as the Canuck) was a development by the Curtiss company's Canadian associate and was a very successful evolution of the JN-3; the JN-4D combined features of the JN-4A and the JN-4 Can to become the nearest there was to a standard variant; the JN-4H was the JH-4D re-engined with the 112-kW (150-hp) Wright-built Hispano-Suiza inline. JHN-4H variants were the JN-4HT, JN-4HB and JN-4HG dual-control trainer, bombing and gunnery trainers. A variant of the JN family produced in smaller but still useful numbers was the JN-6, which evolved via the JN-5 with a stronger aileron structure and was developed in several subvariants.

JN-4H 'Jenny'

Generally known as the 'Jenny', this celebrated trainer resulted from the Model J. This had a 67-kW (90-hp) Curtiss O inline engine and unequal-span biplane wings with upper-wing ailerons operated by the obsolete Deperdussin-type control system. The contemporary Model N had the 75-kW (100-hp) Curtiss OXX inline and interplane ailerons. Features of both types were included in the JN-2 that appeared in 1915 with equal-span biplane wings each carrying an aileron, and powered by a 67-kW (90-hp) Curtiss OX engine. The succeeding JN-3 was essentially an interim type and had unequal-span wings with ailerons only on the upper surfaces, but these control surfaces were operated by a wheel on the joystick rather than a shoulder-yoke. In July 1916 there appeared the definitive JN-4, and this was built in large numbers for useful service well into the 1920s. As first delivered, the JN-4 had unequal-span wings of the two-bay type, and spreader-bar landing gear, so the definitive form of the

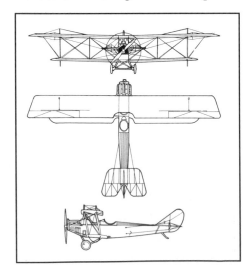

CURTISS JN-4D
Role: Primary trainer
Crew/Accommodation: Two
Power Plant: One 90 hp Curtiss OX-5 water-cooled inline
Dimensions: Span 13.29 m (43.6 ft); length 8.33 m (27.33 ft); wing area 32.7 m² (352 sq ft)
Weights: Empty 630.5 kg (1,390 lb); MTOW 871 kg (1,920 lb)
Performance: Cruise speed 97 km/h (60 mph) at sea level; operational ceiling 1,981 m (6,500 ft); range 402 km (250 miles)
Load: None

Curtiss JN-4N

2453

This 'Jenny' is a Curtiss JN-4D

de HAVILLAND D.H.82 TIGER MOTH (United Kingdom)

D.H.82 Tiger Moth

The success of its various lightplane designs convinced de Havilland that there was a large market for flying trainers, especially for military use, and from the D.H.60M version of its

The de Havilland D.H.82A Tiger Moth was a first-class elementary trainer

Moth biplane with a metal rather than wooden structure the company evolved the D.H.60T Moth Trainer as a two-seat basic trainer with a strengthened airframe and the 89-kW (120-hp) de Havilland Gipsy II engine. From this latter the company derived the D.H.82 Tiger Moth for the specifically military market with a sturdier airframe for operation at higher weights with equipment such as a camera gun or practice bombs.

Eight pre-production aircraft were built with the same D.H.60T designation as the Moth Trainer, and these also retained the straight lower wing and dihedralled upper wing of

the Moth Trainer; stagger was increased as the upper-wing centre section was moved forward to ease movement into and out of the front cockpit. The aircraft were powered by the 89-kW (120-hp) Gipsy III engine in a cowling, the sloping upper line of which improved the pilot's field of vision, and the lower wing was given dihedral for improved ground clearance. The definitive form was reached in the D.H.82 prototype that first flew in October 1931 with increased lower-wing dihedral and sweepback. Large-scale production followed, and of the 8,280 aircraft all but a few were of the Tiger Moth Mk II (D.H.82A) variant in which the ridged stringer/fabric rear decking of the Tiger Moth Mk I was replaced by a smooth plywood decking. The D.H.82B was the Queen Bee remotely controlled target drone, and the D.H.82C was a winterized variant built by de Havilland Canada. Surplus military aircraft found a ready civilian market, and the well loved Tiger Moth is even today flying in fairly large numbers.

de HAVILLAND D.H.82A TIGER MOTH
Role: Trainer/tourer
Crew/Accommodation: Two
Power Plant: One 130 hp de Havilland Gipsy Major I air-cooled inline
Dimensions: Span 8.94 m (29.3 ft); length 7.3 m (23.95 ft); wing area 22.2 m² (239 sq ft)
Weights: Empty 506 kg (1,115 lb); MTOW 828 kg (1,825 lb)
Performance: Maximum speed 167 km/h (104 mph) at sea level; operational ceiling 4,267 m (14,000 ft); range 483 km (300 miles)
Load: 81.6 kg (180 lb)

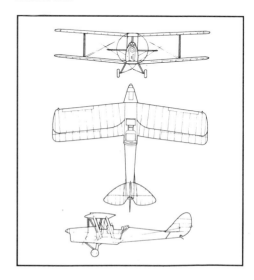

D.H.82 Tiger Moth

BOEING/STEARMAN MODEL 75/PT-13 and PT-17 (United States)

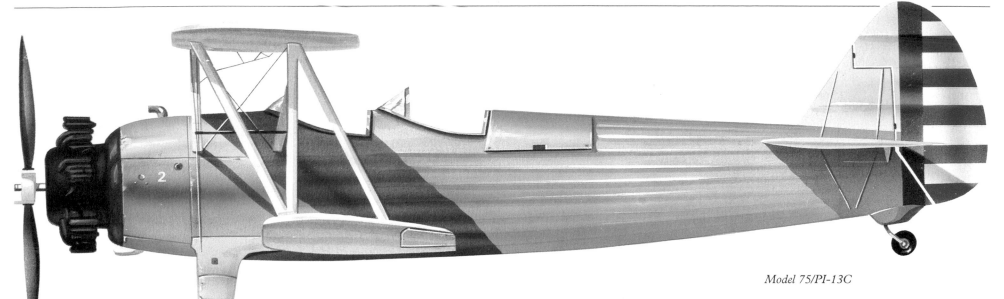

Model 75/PI-13C

In 1939 Boeing bought Stearman Aircraft, and as a result acquired the excellent Model 75 developed by Stearman from the X-70 first flown in December 1933. The U.S. Navy had taken 61 of the Model 73 production type with the designation NS-1, and development had then led to the Model 75 accepted by the U.S. Army as the PT-13 with the 160-kW (215-hp) Lycoming R-680-5 radial.

These 26 aircraft were just the beginning of a major development and production programme. Further evolution led to 92 PT-13As with the 164-kW (220-hp) R-680-7 engine and improved instrumentation, 255 PT-

13Bs with the R-680-11 engine, and six PT-13Cs with night-flying instrumentation. A change was then made to the 164-kW Continental R-670-5 radial for the PT-17, of which 3,510 were built in 1940. Specialist versions were the 18 blind-flying PT-17As and three pest-control PT-17Bs. The navy also operated the Model 75 as the N2S, and this series included 250 N2S-1s with the R-670-14 engine, 125 N2S-2s with the R-680-8 engine, 1,875 N2S-3s with the R-670-

4, and 1,051 N2S-4s with the R-670-5 engine. Then came a common army/navy model produced as 318 PT-13Ds and 1,450 N2S-5s with the R-680-17 engine. Variants with Jacobs R-755-7 radials were designated PT-18 and, in the blind-flying role, PT-18A.

Some 300 aircraft supplied to Canada were designated PT-27 by the U.S.A. but were called Kaydet in the receiving country. This name is usually given to all Model 75 variants.

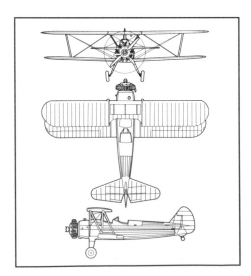

Boeing Stearman PT-13D

BOEING/STEARMAN PT-17A
Role: Basic trainer
Crew/Accommodation: Two
Power Plant: One 220 hp Continental R-670-5 air-cooled radial
Dimensions: Span 9.8 m (32.16 ft); length 7.32 m (24.02 ft); wing area 27.63 m² (297.4 sq ft)
Weights: Empty 878 kg (1,936 lb); MTOW 1,232 kg (2,717 lb)
Performance: Maximum speed 200 km/h (124 mph) at sea level; operational ceiling 3,414 m (11,200 ft); range 813 km (505 miles)
Load: None

A Boeing (Stearman) Kaydet

NORTH AMERICAN T-6/SNJ TEXAN AND FOREBEARS (United States)

T-6G Texan

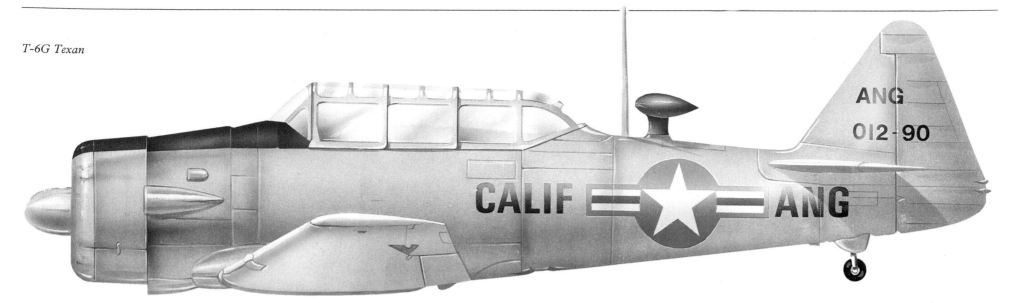

This series comprised the Western Alliance's most important trainers of World War II, and production was in the order of 17,000 or more aircraft. The series was pioneered by the NA-16 prototype that flew in April 1935 as an all-metal cantilever low-wing monoplane with two open cockpits, fixed landing gear and the 298-kW (400-hp) Wright R-975 radial. The type was then ordered in a form with a glazed enclosure over the cockpits as the BT-9 and NJ series for the U.S. Army and U.S. Navy respectively.

Additional aircraft were produced for export to several countries including Canada, where the aircraft was known as the Yale.

This NA-18 version was then developed further with the 447-kW (600-hp) Pratt & Whitney R-1340 radial, equipment comparable with that of contemporary combat aircraft, and retractable tailwheel landing gear to serve as a combat trainer. This NA-26 variant was first ordered as the AT-6 Texan (initially BC-1) and SNJ series for the U.S. Army and Navy

respectively. Production was undertaken in many improved and specialized models up to the T-6F and SNJ-6. The USAAF's most numerous models were the AT-6C and AT-6D (2,970 and 4,388) with a revised structure that made fewer demands on strategically important light alloys, while the U.S. Navy's equivalents were the 2,400 SNJ-4s and 1,357 SNJ-5s. The British and their Commonwealth allies also operated the type in comparatively large numbers under the basic designation Harvard, which were delivered from

American and licensed Canadian production in variants up to the Harvard Mk 4. From 1949 some 2,086 American aircraft were rebuilt as T-6G multi-role trainers with the R-1340-AN-1 engine, increased fuel capacity, an improved cockpit layout, a steerable tailwheel together with many other modifications.

NORTH AMERICAN T-6D TEXAN (RAF HARVARD)
Role: Advanced trainer
Crew/Accommodation: Two
Power Plant: One 550 hp Pratt & Whitney R-1340-AN1 Wasp air-cooled radial
Dimensions: Span 12.81 m (42.02 ft); length 8.84 m (28.99 ft); wing area 23.57 m² (253.72 sq ft)
Weights: Empty 1,886 kg (4,158 lb): MTOW 2,722 kg (6,000 lb)
Performance: Maximum speed 330 km/h (205 mph) at 1,524 (5,000 ft); operational ceiling 6,553 m (21,500 ft); range 1,207 km (750 miles)
Load: Two .303 inch machine guns

The Harvard Mk IIB

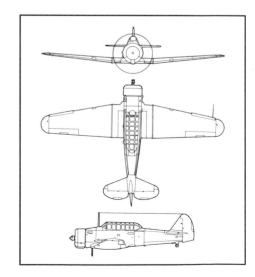

North American BC-1

149

MILES MAGISTER (United Kingdom)

Magister Mk I

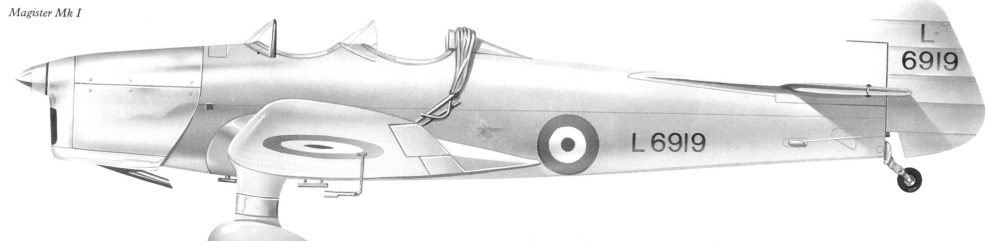

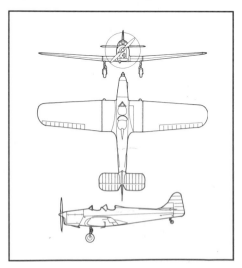

The Magister was the Royal Air Force's most important elementary trainer in the opening stages of World War II, and was also of historical importance as the service's first monoplane trainer. The type was developed to meet a 1936 requirement for a monoplane trainer to complement the monoplane combat aircraft entering Royal Air Force service in this period. It was derived as the M.14 from the Hawk Trainer, of which 25 had been built within the context of the M.2 Hawk series. Modifications from the Hawk Trainer included larger cockpits and blind-flying equipment, the latter including a hood that could be erected over the rear cockpit.

The type was a low-wing monoplane with fixed but nicely faired tailwheel landing gear and open tandem cockpits, and was unusual in reverting to the type of all-wood construction that the RAF had eschewed from the early 1920s. In addition to its monoplane configuration, trailing-edge flaps and full aerobatic capability, the Magister also offered to the pilots who trained on it the advantage of higher overall performance without any significant increase in landing speed. Production began in May 1937, and deliveries of the initial Magister Mk I to the Central Flying School started in October of the same year. The type was generally operated without its main landing gear fairings, and to improve spin recovery the Magister Mk II of 1938 introduced a slightly larger rudder.

Production lasted to 1941 and comprised 1,293 aircraft in the U.K. and another 100 licence-built in Turkey. After the end of World War II, many surplus Magisters were sold on to the civil market, and large numbers of these were adopted by civil flying schools with the designation Hawk Trainer Mk III. The Royal Air Force retired its last Magisters in 1948.

MILES MAGISTER Mk II
Role: Elementary trainer
Crew/Accommodation: Two
Power Plant: One 130 hp de Havilland Gipsy Major air-cooled inline
Dimensions: Span 10.31 m (33.83 ft); length 7.51 m (24.63 ft); wing area 16.35 m² (176 sq ft)
Weights: Empty 583 kg (1,286 lb); MTOW 862 kg (1,900 lb)
Performance: Maximum speed 225 km/h (140 mph) at sea level; operational ceiling 5,029 m (16,500 ft); range 591 km (367 miles)
Load: Up to 109 kg (240 lb) including student pilot

The Miles Magister was a simple yet highly effective trainer

BEECH T-34 MENTOR (United States)

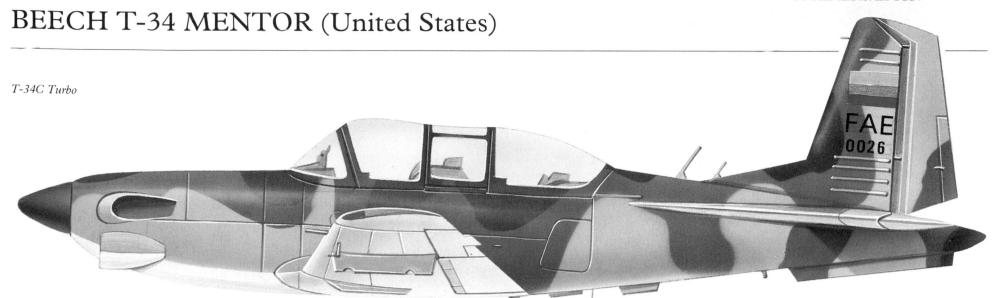

T-34C Turbo

The T-34 resulted from Beech's 1948 decision to develop a trainer derived from the Model 33 Bonanza with a conventional tail and accommodation for the pupil and instructor in tandem. The first example of the Model 45 Mentor flew in December 1948. At this time the U.S. Air Force was looking for a new primary trainer, and in 1950 evaluated three Model 45s under the designation YT-34 with two types of Continental flat-six piston engine. In March 1953 the Model 45 was selected for USAF service, and 450 T-34As were ordered with the 168-kW (225-hp) Continental O-470-13 engine. In June 1954, the U.S. Navy followed this lead with an order for 290 out of an eventual 423 T-34B trainers with the identically rated O-470-4 engine.

The basic soundness of the design is attested by further development of the airframe in the early 1970s. By this time the turboprop was seen as the better powerplant, offering engine reliability, considerable fuel economies, and the use of turbine engines right through the pupil pilot's training. Two T-34Bs were therefore converted to YT-34C standard with the Pratt & Whitney Canada PT6A-25, and the first of these flew in September 1973. The engine is provided with a torque limiter that restricts power output to some 56 per cent of the maximum, and this ensures constant performance over a wide range of altitude and temperature conditions. Successful evaluation led to orders for the T-34C Turbo-Mentor production model with a strengthened airframe. This entered service in November 1977, and the U.S. Navy currently operates about 340 of the type. For the export market, Beech developed the T-34C-1 with four underwing hardpoints for a 544-kg (1,200-lb) warload in the weapon training role, with counter-insurgency and light attack as possible operational tasks. The export civil version without hardpoints is the Turbine Mentor 34C.

Beech T-34C-1s

BEECH T-34C TURBO-MENTOR
Role: Basic trainer/light strike
Crew/Accommodation: Two
Power Plant: One 550* shp Pratt & Whitney Canada PT6A-25 turboprop (*400 shp in de-rated form as used by the US Navy)
Dimensions: Span 10.18 m (33.40 ft); length 8.76 m (28.75 ft); wing area 16.70m² (180.00 sq ft)
Weights: Empty 1,429 kg (3,150 lb); MTOW 2,495 kg (5,500 lb)
Performance: Maximum speed 396 km/h (214 knots) at 5,334 m (17,500 ft); operational ceiling 9,144 m (30,000 ft); radius 555 km (300 naut. miles)
Load: Up to 620 kg (1,369 lb) of external weapons/fuel

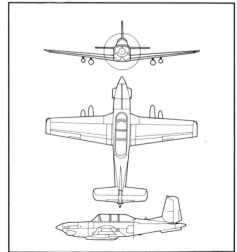

Beech T-34C Mentor

151

FOUGA CM.170 MAGISTER (France)

CM.170 Magister

The Magister was designed as the CM.170 and placed in production by Air Fouga, which later became part of the Potez corporation that was then absorbed in the Aerospatiale group. The CM.170 was evolved to meet a French Air Force requirement for a purpose-designed jet basic trainer, and in its time was one of the world's most widely used trainers and light attack aircraft. The type's characteristic

features are a high cockpit enclosure over the tandem seats, a V-tail , and mid-set wings with the two small turbojets installed in their roots. The type flew in prototype form during July 1952, and in the following year a pre-production batch of 10 aircraft was ordered for evaluation purposes. The French Air Force ordered an initial 95 aircraft in 1954, and the first of these CM.170-1 aircraft was delivered in February 1956 in a programme that eventually witnessed the delivery of 437 Magisters to the French Air Force.

The CM.170-1 is exclusively a land-based variant powered by two

400-kg (882-lb) Turboméca Marboré IIA turbojets, and overall production was 916 aircraft including major exports to West Germany, and licensed construction in both Finland and Israel. Variants produced in substantially smaller numbers were the CM.170-2 Super Magister and CM.175 Zephyr. The 137 Super Magisters are land-based aircraft powered by two 480-kg (1,058-lb)

thrust Marboré VI turbojets, while the 32 Zephyrs are naval trainers fitted with arrester hooks and powered by Marboré IIA engines. The basic type has a useful light attack capability, and this is improved in the AMIT Fouga, otherwise the Tzukit (Thrush), an upgraded version developed by Israel Aircraft Industries with Marbore VI engines in a strengthened airframe and fitted with modern avionics.

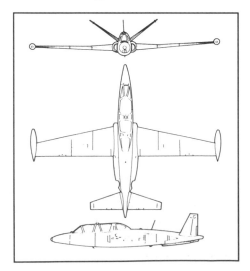

Fouga CM.170 Magister

FOUGA CM. 170 MAGISTER
Role: Basic/advanced trainer
Crew/Accommodation: Two
Power Plant: Two 440 kgp (880 lb s.t.) Turboméca Maboré IIa turbojets
Dimensions: Span 12.15 m (39. 83 ft); length 10.06 m (33 ft); wing area 17.3 m^2 (186.1 sq ft)
Weights: Empty 2,150 kg (4,740 lb); MTOW 3,200 kg (7,055 lb)
Performance: Maximum speed 700 km/h (435 knots) at sea level; operational ceiling 13,500 m (44,291 ft); range 1,250 km (775 miles)
Load: Two 7.62 mm machine guns

Fouga Magister trainers of the French Air Force

CESSNA T-37 and A-37 DRAGONFLY (United States)

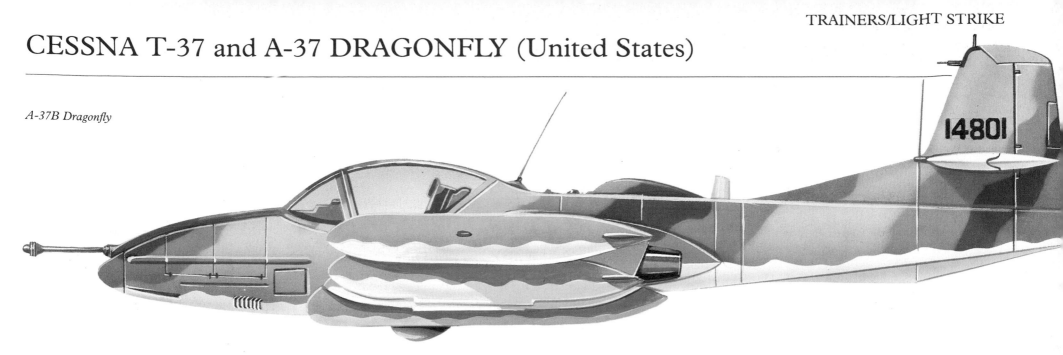

A-37B Dragonfly

In the early 1950s, the U.S. Air Force adopted a programme of all-through training using jet-powered aircraft, and issued a requirement for a new basic trainer with turbojet propulsion. Several companies responded with design proposals; in 1953 Cessna was declared winner with its Model 318. Two XT-37 prototypes were ordered. The first of these flew in October 1954 with two Turboméca Marboré turbojets licence-built in the United States as 417-kg (920-lb) thrust

Continental YJ69-T-9s. The type was ordered into production as the T-37A. Powered by J69-T-9 turbojets, these 444 aircraft entered service only in 1957 as changes were found to be necessary, most notably in the layout of the cockpit.

These aircraft were followed by 552 examples of the T-37B with 465-kg (1,025-lb) thrust J69-T-25 engines. All surviving T-37As were later brought up to T-37B standard. The last trainer was the T-37C, which

offered light armament capability on underwing hardpoints, together with the option of wingtip fuel tanks. Production totalled 198 aircraft for delivery in aid packages to eight countries. A special counter-insurgency and light attack version was developed as the YAT-37D with 1089-kg (2,400-lb) thrust General Electric J85-GE-5 turbojets. Some 39 of the type were produced as T-37B conversions, and these were evaluated from 1967. Their success with an armament of one 7.62-mm (0.3-in)

Minigun multi-barrel machine gun and disposable stores on eight underwing hardpoints led to development of the beefed-up Model 318E, which was ordered into production as the A-37B with 1293-kg (2,850-lb) thrust J85-GE-17A engines, inflight refuelling capability, and the ability to carry a warload of more than 2268 kg (5,000 lb). Production amounted to 577 aircraft.

A Cessna T-37B Tweet with the marking of the Greek Air Force

CESSNA A-37B DRAGONFLY
Role: Light strike
Crew/Accommodation: Two
Power Plant: Two, 1,293 kgp (2,850 lb s.t.) General Electric J85-GE-17A turbojets
Dimensions: Span 11.71 m (38.42 ft); length 9.69 m (31.83 ft); wing area 17.09 m² (183.9 sq ft)
Weights: Empty 1,845 kg (4,067 lb); MTOW 6,350 kg (14,000 lb)
Performance: Maximum speed 771 km/h (479 mph) at 4,724 m (15,500 ft); operational ceiling 7,620 m (25,000 ft); radius 380 km (236 miles) with 843 kg (1,858 lb) bombload
Load: One 7.62 mm multi-barrel machine gun, plus up to 2,576 kg (5,680 lb) of bombs or air-to-ground rockets carried on underwing pylons

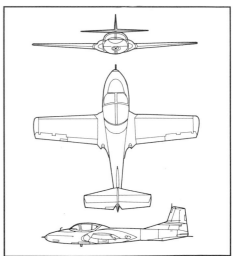

Cessna T-37B

153

AERO L-39 ALBATROS (Czechoslovakia)

L-39ZA Albatros

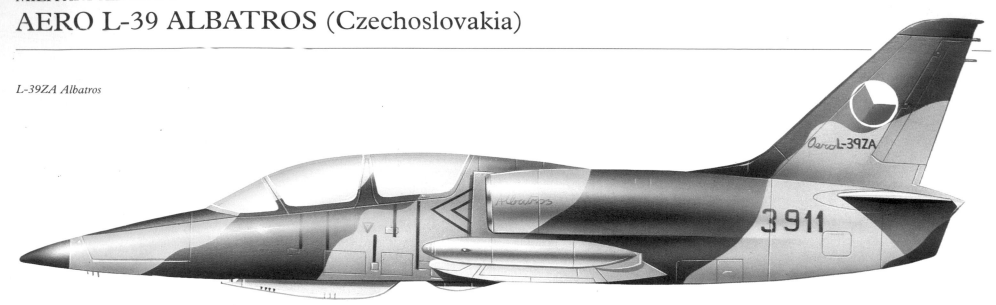

The L-39 is an attractive and effective trainer that was developed to succeed the same company's L-29 Delfin. The L-29 can be regarded as the Communist bloc's counterpart to the Aermacchi MB.326 in its use of a turbojet, straight flying surfaces, and tandem accommodation in ejector seats with very little vertical stagger. As Aermacchi later evolved the MB.339 from the MB.326, so Aero

developed the L-39 as successor to the L-29 with the same type of straight flying surfaces, but also with turbofan power and tandem seating of considerable vertical stagger.

The first of three prototypes flew in November 1968, and the only major problem was integration of the Soviet turbofan into the Czech airframe. The L-39 entered service in 1973, and since that date has become the standard basic and advanced trainer of most Communist air arms. The unswept flying surfaces curtail outright performance, but in addition to the fuel-economical turbofan

engine and staggered seating, positive features are the type's tractable handling, reliability, and easy maintenance.

Variants are the basic L-39C with two underwing hardpoints, the L-39ZO weapons trainer with four hardpoints, the L-39ZA attack/reconnaissance type with four

hardpoints and an underfuselage pack containing one 23-mm twin-barrel cannon, the L-39V target-tug, and the L-39MS updated trainer with a modernized cockpit, an improved and more easily maintained airframe, and greater power for better performance rather than greater warload.

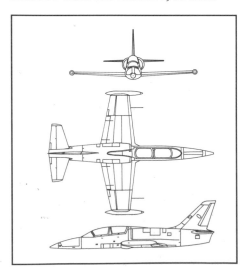

Aero L-39 Albatross

AERO L-39Z ALBATROS
Role: Light strike/advanced trainer
Crew/Accommodation: Two
Power Plant: One 1,500 kgp (3,307 lb s.t.) Walter Titan turbofan
Dimensions: Span 9.46 m (31 ft); length 12.13 m (39.76 ft); wing area 18.80 m² (202.4 sq ft)
Weights: Empty 3,565 kg (7,859 lb); MTOW 5,650 kg (12,450 lb)
Performance: Maximum speed 700 km/h (378 knots) at sea level; operational ceiling 11,000 m (36,090 ft); range 1,100 km (594 naut. miles) on internal fuel only
Load: One 23 mm cannon, plus up to 2,000 kg (3,300 lb) of externally underslung ordnance

The Aero L-39 Albatros has straight flying surfaces and turbofan power

DASSAULT-BREGUET/DORNIER ALPHA JET (France/West Germany)

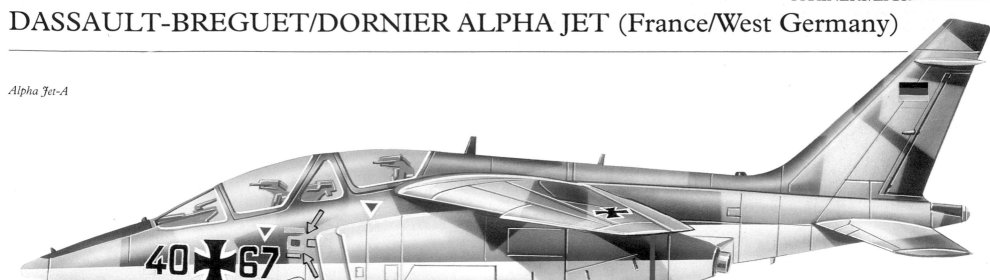

Alpha Jet-A

This Franco-West German aircraft was designed as an advanced two-seat trainer and light attack type of high subsonic performance, and was designed to replace aircraft such as the Fouga Magister trainer and Fiat G91 light attack warplane. The programme was announced as a collaborative venture in July 1969, and Dassault and Dornier each produced design proposals from which the Alpha Jet was selected in July 1970. The first of four prototypes flew during October 1973 with two specially developed

Turboméca Larzac non-afterburning turbofans, and is a nice example of the modern trainer/light attacker with swept flying surfaces including a shoulder-mounted wing and vertically staggered seating. The prototypes confirmed the type's basic capabilities, and large-scale production was authorized in March 1975. The design has since proved highly successful in the domestic and export markets.

The two main variants are the Alpha Jet-A close support/attack aircraft with a pointed nose and more

advanced sensors for its operational role used by West Germany, and the Alpha Jet-E advanced flying/weapons trainer used by France plus most export customers, and characterized by a more rounded nose and less sophisticated sensors. Derivatives of the Alpha Jet-E are the Alpha Jet MS2 trainer and light attacker with a more advanced nav/attack system, the Alpha Jet NGEA (Alpha Jet 2) with the MS2's nav/attack system, more powerful engines and air-to-air missile capability, the Lancier (Alpha Jet 3)

derived from the NGEA with radar and the capability for several advanced weapon types, and the Alpha Jet ATS (Advanced Training System) based on the Alpha Jet 3 with state-of-the-art cockpit and displays. No orders have yet been placed for the Lancier and Alpha Jet 3, but West Germany is now upgrading its Alpha Jet A (now Alpha Jet Close Support Version) fleet in a modest programme.

The Dassault-Breguet/Dornier Alpha Jet 2

DASSAULT-BREGUET/DORNIER ALPHA JET 2

Role: Light strike/advanced trainer
Crew/Accommodation: Two
Power Plant: Two 1,440 kgp (3,175 lb s.t.) SNECMA/Turboméca Larzac 04-C20 turbofans
Dimensions: Span 9.11 m (29.95 ft); length 12.29 m (40.25 ft); wing area 17.5m² (188 sq ft)
Weights: Empty 3,515 kg (7,749 lb); MTOW 8,000 kg (17,637 lb)
Performance: Maximum speed 1,038 km/h (560 knots) at sea level; operational ceiling 14,630 m (48,000 ft); radius 1,075 km (580 naut. miles)
Load: Up to 2,500 kg (5,510 lb) of externally carried armament

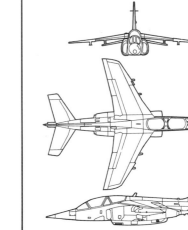

Alpha Jet-A

155

BRITISH AEROSPACE HAWK Family (United Kingdom)

Hawk 200

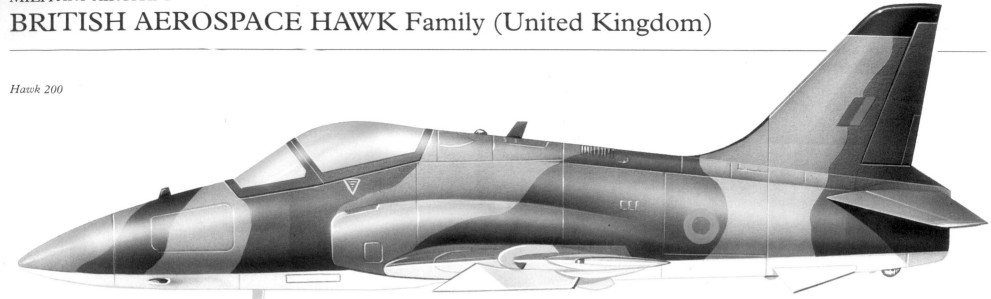

The Hawk was developed to replace the Hawker Siddeley (Folland) Gnat in the training role, and first flew during August 1974 as the P. 1182 prototype. The type is operated by the RAF as the Hawk T.Mk 1 and secondary air-defence Hawk T.Mk 1A with provision for Sidewinder air-to-air missiles on four rather than two hardpoints under the wings. There have also been several export models.

The Hawk Mk 50 series is based on the T.Mk 1, but with the 2463-kg (5,340-lb) thrust Adour Mk 851, and the Hawk Mk 60 has a slightly lengthened fuselage and the 2568-kg (5,700-lb) thrust Adour Mk 861 turbofan for improved field performance, acceleration, climb and turn rates, and payload/range. Other and more radically developed variants are the Hawk 100 two-seat dual-role trainer and light ground-attack aircraft, and the Hawk 200 single-seat attack model.

The 100 is based on the Mk 60 but has the 2651-kg (5,845-lb) thrust Adour Mk 871 and an advanced nav/attack system based on a digital databus and including a head-up display, weapon-aiming computer, radar-warning receiver, and optional sensors. The 200 is also based on the Mk 60 but has a single-seat cockpit, Adour Mk 871 engine, and advanced electronics that include radar capability and provision for state-of-the-art weaponry.

The Hawk's basic design has been adapted by McDonnell Douglas as the T-45A Goshawk carrier-capable trainer for the U.S. Navy. This has a revised cockpit, strengthened landing gear (including long-stroke main units and a twin-wheel nose unit), an arrester hook, ventral finlets, taller vertical tail surfaces, a revised wing, and the 2651-kg (5,845-lb) thrust F405-RR-401 version of the Adour Mk 871 turbofan.

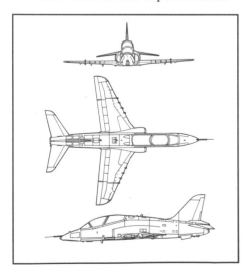

British Aerospace Hawk 60

BRITISH AEROSPACE (SIDDELEY) HAWK 60 Series
Role: Light strike/trainer
Crew/Accommodation: Two
Power Plant: One 2,585 kgp (5,700 lb s.t.) Rolls-Royce Turboméca Adour 861 turbofan
Dimensions: Span 9.4 m (30.83 ft); length 11.85 m (38.92 ft); wing area 16.69 m² (179.64 sq ft)
Weights: Empty 3,750 kg (8,270 lb); MTOW 8,500 kg (18,740 lb)
Performance: Maximum speed 1,037 km/h (560 knots) Mach 0.81 at sea level; operational ceiling 15,240 m (50,000 ft); radius 1,093 km (590 naut. miles) with 998 kg (2,000 lb) warload
Load: Up to 3,084 kg (6,800 lb) of weapons/fuel carried externally

A British Aerospace Hawk 100

AERMACCHI MB.326 and MB.339 Family (Italy)

MB.339K Veltro 2

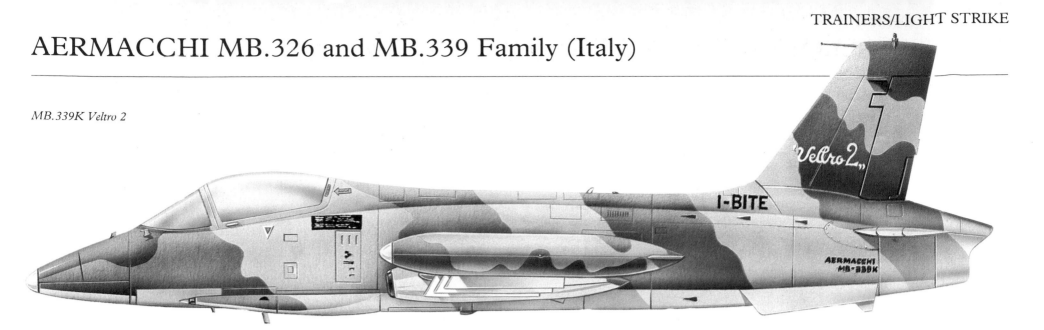

One of Macchi's most successful designs, the MB.326, was planned as a basic and advanced trainer. The type reveals its 1950s' origins in its turbojet engine, unswept flying surfaces, and vertically unstaggered seats. In its time, however, the MB.326 was an excellent aircraft that achieved considerable export success in a number of variants.

The first prototype flew in December 1957 with a 794-kg (1,750-lb) thrust Armstrong Siddeley (later Bristol Siddeley and finally Rolls-Royce) Viper 8 turbojet, and the second machine featured the 1134-kg (2,500-lb) thrust Viper 11. The first MB.326s entered Italian Air Force service in February 1962, and were immediately popular for their strength, agility, and generally good fields of vision through the large canopy over the pressurized cockpit with tandem ejector seats. The basic trainer was developed with steadily more powerful engine marks and was produced in armed variants that included the Impala Mk 1 and Xavante versions built under licence respectively in South Africa by Atlas and in Brazil by EMBRAER.

The basic design was also adapted as the commercially successful MB.326K single-seat light attack aircraft with the volume of the erstwhile rear cockpit used for more fuel, improved avionics, and the ammunition for the two inbuilt 30-mm cannon. This last was also built in South Africa as the Impala Mk 2.

Employing the same basic structure and propulsion as its predecessor, the prototype MB.339 emerged with a redesigned forward fuselage with vertically staggered seating to improve visibility for the rear occupant and first flew in 1976. The single seat MC.339 Vettro II close air support's variant's maiden flight followed in 1980.

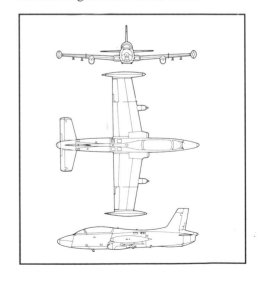

The Aermacchi MB-339K

AERMACCHI MB.326H
Role: Light/strike trainer
Crew/Accommodation: Two
Power Plant: One 1,134 kgp (2,500 lb s.t.) Rolls-Royce Viper II turbojet
Dimensions: Span 10.85 m (35.71 ft); length 10.67 m (35 ft); wing area 19.4 m² (208.3 sq ft)
Weights: Empty 2,685 kg (6,920 lb); MTOW 5,216 kg (11,500 lb)
Performance: Maximum speed 867 km/h (468 knots) at sea level; operational ceiling 14,325 m (47,000 ft); range 1,850 km (998 naut. miles)
Load: Up to 1,814 kg (4,000 lb) of externally carried armament

Aermacchi MB.326GB

CONSOLIDATED PBY CATALINA (United States)

PBY-1 Catalina

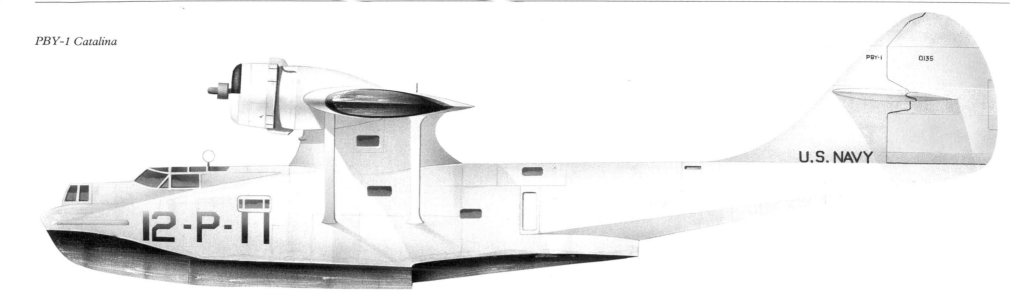

In the early 1930s, the U.S. Navy issued a requirement for a patrol flying boat that offered greater range and payload than the Consolidated P2Y and Martin P3M it than had in service. Design proposals were received from Consolidated and

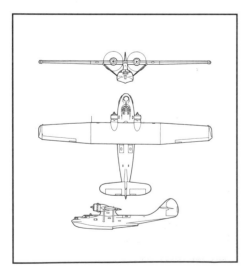

Douglas, and single prototypes of each were ordered. The Douglas type was restricted to the XP3D-1 prototype, but the Consolidated Model 28 design became one of the most important flying boats ever developed. The XP3Y-1 prototype first flew in March 1935 and was a large machine with a wide two-step

CONSOLIDATED PBY-5 (RAF CATALINA Mk IV)

Role: Long-range maritime patrol bomber flying boat

Crew/Accommodation: Nine

Power Plant: Two, 1,200 hp Pratt & Whitney R-1830-92 Twin Wasp air-cooled radials

Dimensions: Span 37.10 m (104 ft); length 19.47 m (63.88 ft); wing area 130.1 m² (1,400 sq ft)

Weights: Empty 7,809 kg (17,200 lb); MTOW 15,436 kg (34,000 lb)

Performance: Cruise speed 182 km/h (113 mph) at sea level; operational ceiling 5,517 m (18,100 ft); range 4,812 km (2,990 miles) with full warload

Load: Two .5 inch and two .303 inch machine guns, plus up to 1,816 kg (4,000 lb) of torpedoes, depth charges or bombs carried externally

hull, a strut-braced parasol wing mounted on top of a massive pylon that accommodated the flight engineer, and stabilizing floats that retracted in flight to become the wingtips and so reduce drag.

The type clearly possessed considerable potential, and after being reworked as a patrol bomber was ordered into production as the PBY-1, of which 60 were built with 671-kW (900-hp) R-1830-64 radial engines. The following PBY-2 had equipment improvements, and production totalled 50. Next came 66 PBY-3s with 746-kW (1,000-hp) R-1830-66 engines and 33 PBY-4s with 783-kW (1,050-hp) R-1830-72 engines. The generally improved PBY-5 with 895-kW (1,200-hp) R-1830-82 or -92 engines was the definitive model, but only 683 were built as it was more than complemented by the PBY-5A amphibian version, of which 803 were built. The Naval Aircraft Factory produced 155 of a PBN-1 Nomad version of the PBY-5 with

aerodynamic and hydrodynamic improvements, and 175 of a comparable amphibian model were built by Consolidated as the PBY-6A. The basic type was also produced in Canada and the U.S.S.R. as the Boeing PB2B (232 built) and GST respectively, while the U.K. adopted the aircraft in several variants with the name Catalina that has since been generally adopted for all PBY models.

The Consolidated PBY-6A Catalina

SHORT SUNDERLAND Family (United Kingdom)

Sunderland Mk I

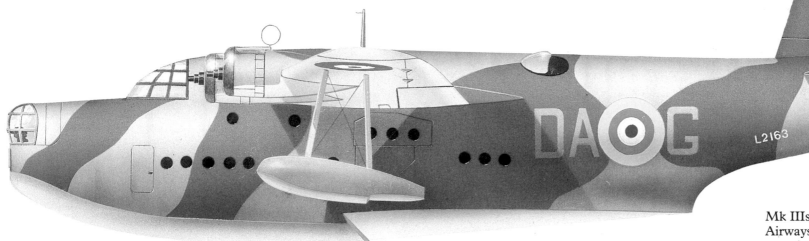

The Sunderland was the U.K.'s premier maritime reconnaissance flying boat of World War II, and derived ultimately from the S.23 class of civil 'Empire' flying boats. The prototype flew in October 1937 with 753-kW (1,010-hp) Bristol Pegasus XXII radials, and was the first British flying boat to have power-operated defensive gun turrets. The prototype proved most satisfactory, and production of this variant totalled 90

Sunderland Mk II

before it was overtaken on the lines by the Sunderland Mk II with 794-kW (1,065-hp) Pegasus XVIII radials and a power-operated dorsal turret in place of the Mk I's two 7.7-mm (0.303-in) beam guns in manually operated waist positions.

These 43 'boats were in turn succeeded by the Sunderland Mk III, which was the most extensively built variant with 456 being built. This variant had a hull revised with a faired step, and some 'boats were to the Sunderland Mk IIIA standard with ASV. Mk III surface-search radar. The Sunderland Mk IV was developed for Pacific operations and became the S.45 Seaford, of which a mere 10 examples (three prototypes and seven production 'boats) were built with 1253- and 1283-kW (1,680- and 1,720-hp) Bristol Hercules XVII and XIX radials respectively. The last Sunderland variant was the Mk V, of which 150 were built with 895-kW

(1,200-hp) Pratt & Whitney R-1830-90B radials and ASV. Mk VIC radar under the wingtips; the more powerful engines allowed the type to operate at cruising rather than maximum engine revolutions, which improved engine life and aided economical running.

Sunderlands were also used for civil transport, the first of 24 Sunderland

SHORT SUNDERLAND Mk V
Role: Anti-submarine/maritime patrol
Crew/Accommodation: Seven
Power Plant: Four 1,200 hp Pratt & Whitney R-1830-90B Twin Wasp air-cooled radials
Dimensions: Span 34.39 m (112.77 ft); length 26 m (85.33 ft); wing area 156.6 m² (1,687 sq ft)
Weights: Empty 16,783 kg (37,000 lb); MTOW 27,250 kg (60,000 lb)
Performance: Maximum speed 343 km/h (213 mph) at 1,525 m (5,000 ft); operational ceiling 5,455 m (17,900 ft); range 4,300 km (2,690 miles) with maximum fuel
Load: Six .5 inch machine guns and eight .303 inch machine guns, plus up to 908 kg (2,000 lb) of bombs/depth charges

Mk IIIs being handed over to British Airways in March 1943. The 'boats were later brought up to more comfortable standard as Hythes, and were then revised as Sandringham with R-1830-92 radials and, in addition, neat aerodynamic fairings over the erstwhile nose and tail turret positions.

Sunderland Mk V

159

ARADO Ar 196 (Germany)

Ar 196A-3

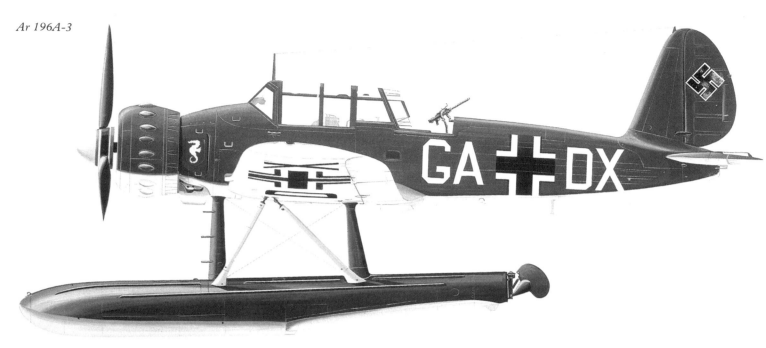

contender from the running and, after testing of the two alighting gear arrangements, the Arado type was ordered into production as the Ar 196A with twin floats. Total construction was 546 aircraft, including machines built in Dutch and French factories under German control.

The type was built in two main streams for shipboard and coastal use. The shipboard stream comprised 20 Ar 196A-1s with two wing-mounted 7.92-mm (0.312-in) machine guns and 24 strengthened Ar 196A-4s based on the Ar 196A-3. The coastal stream comprised 391 examples of the Ar 196A-2 with two 20-mm wing-mounted cannon and the strengthened Ar 196A-3 with a variable-pitch propeller, and 69 examples of the Ar 196A-5 with better radio and a twin rather than single machine-gun installation for the radio-operator/gunner. The Ar 196 was used in most of the German theatres during World War II.

The Ar 196 was designed to meet a 1936 requirement for a floatplane reconnaissance aircraft to succeed the same company's Ar 95 biplane, and was intended for catapult-launched use from German major surface warships, though a secondary coastal patrol capability was also envisaged. The type clearly had more than a passing kinship with the Ar 95, but was an all-metal monoplane and was designed for use on either twin floats or a combination of one main and two outrigger floats. Several proposals had been received in response to the requirement, and orders were placed for Arado monoplane and Focke-Wulf biplane prototypes.

Initial evaluation in the summer of 1937 removed the Focke-Wulf

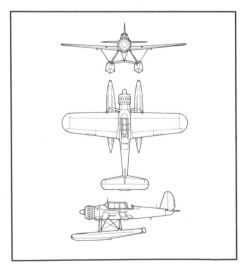

Arado Ar 196A-3

ARADO Ar 196A-3
Role: Shipborne reconnaissance floatplane
Crew/Accommodation: Two
Power Plant: One 960 hp BMW 132K air-cooled radial
Dimensions: Span 12.4 m (40.68 ft); length 11 m (36.09 ft); wing area 28.4 m² (305.6 sq ft)
Weights: Empty 2,990 kg (6,593 lb); MTOW 3,730 kg (8,225 lb)
Performance: Maximum speed 310 km/h (193 mph) at 4,000 m (13,120 ft); operational ceiling 7,000 m (22,960 ft); range 1,070 km (665 miles)
Load: Two 20 mm cannon and two 7.9 mm machine guns, plus 100 kg (210 lb) of bombs

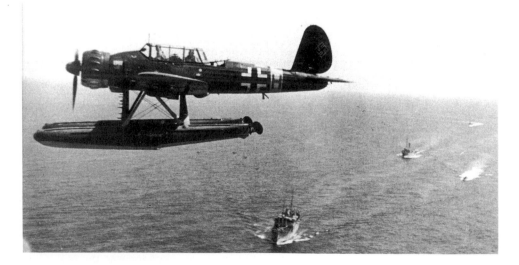

The Arado Ar 196A floatplane

VOUGHT OS2U KINGFISHER (United States)

OS2U-2 Kingfisher

To replace its O3U Corsair biplane operated by the U.S. Navy in the scouting role, Vought produced its VS.310 design with a cantilever monoplane wing in the low/mid-position, a portly fuselage with extensive glazing, and provision for fixed landing gear that could be of the tailwheel or float type, the latter based on a single central float and two stabilizing floats under the wings.

The U.S. Navy ordered a single XOS2U-1 prototype, and this first flew in March 1938 in landplane configuration with the 336-kW (450-hp) Pratt & Whitney R-985-4 Wasp Junior radial; in May of the same year the type was first flown in floatplane form. The trial programme was completed successfully, and the type was ordered into production as the OS2U-1 with the R-985-48 engine.

Production totalled 54 aircraft, and in August 1940 these became the first catapult-launched observation/scout aircraft to serve on American capital ships. Further production embraced 158 examples of the OS2U-2 with the R-985-50 engine and modified equipment, and 1,006 examples of the OS2U-3 with the R-985-AN-2 engine, self-sealing fuel tanks, armour protection, and armament comprising two 7.7-mm (0.303-in) machine guns (one fixed and the other trainable) and two 147-kg (325-lb) depth charges. The type was also operated by inshore patrol squadrons in the anti-submarine air air-sea rescue roles, proving an invaluable asset. Some aircraft were supplied to Central and South American nations, and 100 were transferred to the Royal Navy as Kingfisher Mk I trainers and catapult-launched spotters. Nothing came of the planned OS2U-4 version with a more powerful engine and revised flying surfaces that included a straight-tapered tailplane and narrow-chord wings with full-span flaps and square cut tips.

A Vought OS2U-2 Kingfisher floatplane

VOUGHT-SIKORSKY OS2U-3 KINGFISHER
Role: Shipborne (catapult-launched) reconnaissance
Crew/Accommodation: Two
Power Plant: One 450 hp Pratt & Whitney R-985-AN-2 or -8 air-cooled radial
Dimensions: Span 10.95 m (35.91 ft); length 10.31 m (33.83 ft); wing area 24.34 m² (262.00 sq ft)
Weights: Empty 1,870 kg (4,123 lb); MTOW 2,722 kg (6,000 lb)
Performance: Maximum speed 264 km/h (164 mph) at 1,676 m (5,500 ft); operational ceiling 3,962 m (13,000 ft); radius 1,296 km (805 miles)
Load: Two 0.3 in machine guns, plus up to 295 kg (650 lb) bombload

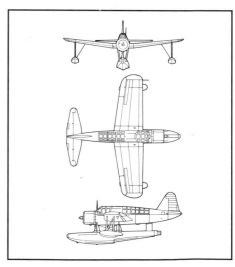

Vought OS2U Kingfisher

AVRO SHACKLETON (United Kingdom)

Shackleton AEW.Mk 2

To give the Lancaster a long-range capability at high altitude, Avro planned the Lancaster Mk IV, but this Type 694 emerged as so different an aeroplane that it was given the name Lincoln. The prototype flew in June 1944, and though plans were laid for 2,254 aircraft, British post-war production amounted to only 72 Lincoln B.Mk 1s and 465 Lincoln B.Mk 2s.

Canada completed one Lincoln B.Mk XV, but Australia built 43 Lincoln B.Mk 30s and 30 Lincoln B.Mk 30As, and 20 of these were later modified to Lincoln B.Mk 31 standard together with a longer nose accommodating search radar and two operators.

Meanwhile, experience with the Lancaster in the maritime role after World War II made the British decide to develop a specialized aeroplane as the Lincoln GR.Mk III with the wing and landing gear of the bomber married to a new fuselage, revised empennage, and Rolls-Royce Griffon engines each driving a contra-rotating propeller unit. Later renamed Shackleton, the first example of the new type flew in March 1949, leading to production of the Shackleton GR.Mk 1 (later MR.Mk 1) with two Griffon 57As and two Griffon 57s, and the Shackleton MR.Mk 1A with four Griffon 57As. The Shackelton MR.Mk 2 had revised armament and search radar with its antenna in a retractable 'dustbin' rather than a chin radome, while the definitive Shackleton MR.Mk 3 was considerably updated, lost the dorsal turret but gained underwing hardpoints, and changed to tricycle landing gear. Twelve MR.Mk 2s were converted in the 1970s into Shackleton AEW.Mk 2 airborne early warning aircraft especially equipped with specialist radar.

Avro Shackleton MR.Mk 3

AVRO SHACKLETON AEW.Mk 2
Role: Airborne early warning
Crew/Accommodation: Ten
Power Plant: Four 2,456 hp Rolls-Royce Griffon 57A water-cooled inlines
Dimensions: Span 36.52 m (119.83 ft); length 28.19 m (92.5 ft); wing area 135.45 m² (1,458 sq ft)
Weights: Empty 25,583 kg (56,400 lb); MTOW 44,452 kg (98,000 lb)
Performance: Cruise speed 322 km/h (200 mph) at 3,050 m (10,000 ft); operational ceiling 5,852 m (19,200 ft); endurance 16 hours
Load: None, other than APS 20 long-range search radar

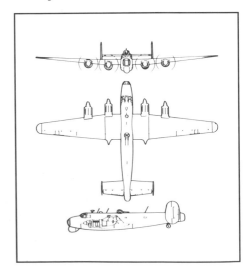

Avro Shackleton MR.Mk 1

LOCKHEED P-3 ORION (United States)

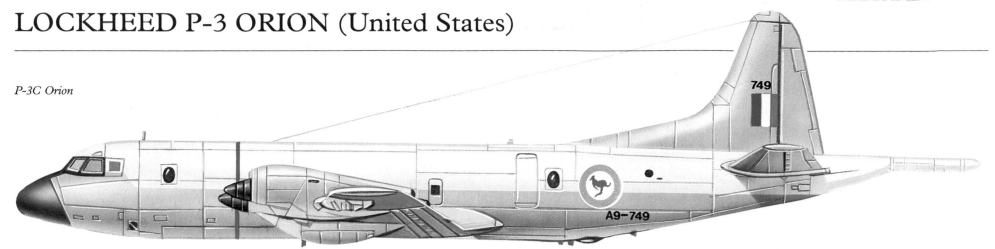

P-3C Orion

In 1957 the U.S. Navy issued a requirement for a maritime patrol type to supplant the piston-engined Lockheed P2V Neptune, and stressed the urgency it attached to the programme by agreeing to the development of the type on the basis of an existing civil airframe. Lockheed's Model 85 proposal was therefore based on the airframe/ powerplant combination of the relatively unsuccessful Model 188 Electra turboprop-powered airliner, though with the fuselage shortened by 2.24 m (7 ft 4 in) as well as modified to include a weapons bay in the lower fuselage.

The YP3V-1 prototype first flew in November 1959, and while the initial production variant was delivered from August 1962 with the designation P3V-1, it was redesignated P-3A in 1962. More than 700 Orions have been delivered in steadily improved variants. The 157 P-3As were powered by 3356-kW (4,500-shp) Allison T56-A-10W turboprops and, though the initial aircraft had the same tactical system as the P2V-7, the 109th and later aircraft had the more advanced Deltic system that was then retrofitted to the earlier machines. The 145 P-3Bs have the same Deltic system, but are powered by 3661-kW (4,910-shp) T56-A-14 engines and were delivered with provision for the launch of AGM-12 Bullpup air-to-surface missiles. The current version is the P-3C, which retains the airframe/ powerplant combination of the P-3B but carries the A-NEW avionics system with new sensors and controls to produce the Update I, Update II, Update III and forthcoming Update IV standards. There have been several export models including the P-3F for Iran, while the CP-140 Aurora for Canada has the P-3C's airframe and powerplant with the electronics of the Lockheed S-3 Viking carrierborne anti-submarine platform. As the planned P-7 successor to the P-3 has been cancelled, development may perhaps follow in the form of a new powerplant and airframe modifications.

A Lockheed P-3C Orion

LOCKHEED P-3C ORION

Role: Long-range maritime patrol and anti submarine
Crew/Accommodation: Ten
Power Plant: Four 4,910 shp Allison T56A-114 turboprops
Dimensions: Span 30.4 m (99.7 ft); length 35.6 m (116.8 ft); wing area 120.8 m² (1,300 sq ft)
Weights: Empty 27,892 kg (61,491 lb); MTOW 64.410 kg (142,000 lb)
Performance: Maximum speed 761 km/h (411 knots) at 4,572 m (15,000 ft) operational ceiling 8,625 m (28,300 ft); radius 2,494 km (1,346 miles) including 3 hours on partol
Load: Up to 8,733 kg (19,252 lb) of weapons and sonobuoys

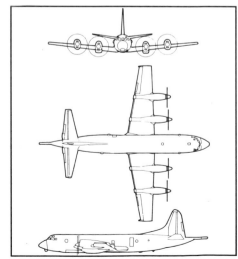

Lockheed P-3C Orion

BRITISH AEROSPACE NIMROD (United Kingdom)

Nimrod MR.Mk 2

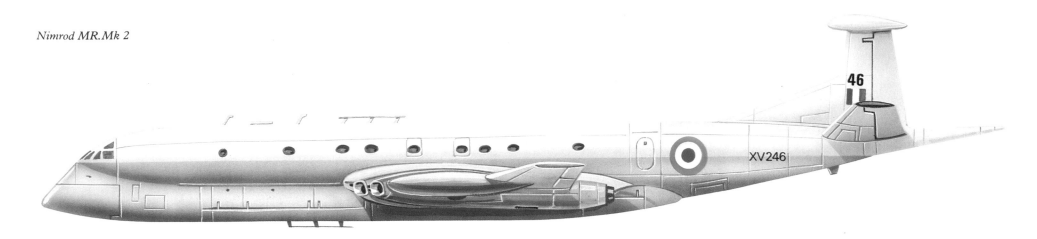

The Nimrod was developed on the aerodynamic and structural basis of the Comet 4 airliner as a jet-powered maritime patroller to replace the piston-engined Avro Shackleton. The Nimrod looks remarkably similar to the Comet 4, but features a fuselage shortened by 1.98 m (6 ft 6 in) and deepened to allow the incorporation of a weapons bay 14.78 m (48 ft 6 in) long below the wide tactical

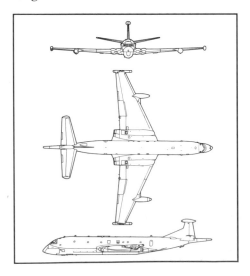

compartment, a turbofan powerplant for significantly improved reliability and range (especially in the patrol regime with two engines shut down), and highly advanced mission electronics including radar, MAD and an acoustic data-processing system using dropped sonobuoys. The wings, tailplane, and landing were basically similar to those of the Comet 4C, though the landing gear was strengthened, and the first prototype flew in May 1967 as a conversion of a Comet 4C. Successful trials led to

BRITISH AEROSPACE (HAWKER SIDDELEY) NIMROD MR. Mk 2
Role: Long-range maritime reconnaissance/anti submarine
Crew/Accommodation: Twelve
Power Plant: Four, 5,507 kgp (12,140 lb s.t.) Rolls-Royce Spey Mk 250 turbofans
Dimensions: Span 35 m (114.83 ft); length 38.63 m (126.75 ft); wing area 197 m² (2,121 sq ft)
Weights: Empty 39,000 kg (86,000 lb); MTOW 87,090 kg (192,000 lb)
Performance: Maximum speed 926 km/h (500 knots) at 610 m (2,000 ft); operational ceiling 12,802 m (42,000 ft); endurance 12 hours
Load: Up to 6,120 kg (13,500 lb) including up to nine lightweight anti-submarine torpedoes

production of 43 Nimrod MR.Mk 1s with EMI ASV-21D search radar.

A variant of this baseline version is the Nimrod R.Mk 1, a special electronic intelligence variant of which three were produced. Further development in the electronic field led to the improved Nimrod MR.Mk 2, of which 32 were produced by conversion of MR.Mk 1 airframes with EMI Searchwater radar, Loral ARI. 18240/1 ESM in wingtip pods to complement the original Thomson-CSF ESM system in a fintop fairing,

Emerson ASQ-10A magnetic anomaly detection, and a thoroughly upgraded tactical suite with a Marconi ASQ-901 acoustic data-processing and display system allowing use of many active and passive sonobuoy types.

The type is currently beginning to suffer corrosion and the first signs of fatigue problems, and may be phased out of service from the mid-1990s onward. The project to produce a Nimrod AEW.Mk 3 airborne early warning version was cancelled back in 1987.

A British Aerospace Nimrod MR.Mk 1

FIESELER Fi 156 STORCH (Germany)

Fi 156C Storch

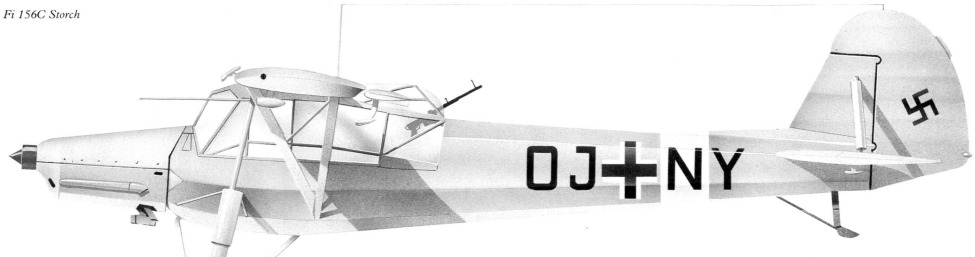

The Fi 156 Storch (Stork) was Germany's most important army co-operation and battlefield reconnaissance aircraft of World War II, and the first of four prototypes flew in the early part of 1936. The Fi 156 was a braced high-wing monoplane with an extensively glazed cockpit offering very good fields of vision and fixed tailwheel landing gear, the main units of which were of the long-stroke type to absorb landing forces at high sink rates. The prototype displayed exceptional STOL capabilities because of its wing, which combined good aerodynamic qualities with the advantages offered by fixed slats and slotted ailerons/flaps over the entire leading and trailing edges respectively. The prototypes showed that the Storch could take off in as little at

60 m (200 ft) in a light head wind, and also land in about one-third of that same distance.

The type was adopted for a wide assortment of army co-operation and associated duties in its Fi 156A-1

The Fieseler Fi 156 Vi

initial production form. The civil Fi 156B remained only a project, so the next variant was the military Fi 156C. This had improved radio equipment and a raised rear section of the cabin glazing allowing a 7.92-mm (0.312-in) machine gun to be mounted. Fi 156C variants were the Fi 156C-1 for liaison, two-seat Fi 156C-2 for tactical reconnaissance or casualty evacuation with a litter in the rear cockpit, Fi 156C-3 for light transport, and Fi 156C-5 with a ventral tank for extended range. The last production

model was the Fi 156D-1 ambulance powered by an Argus AS 10P engine and with provision for one litter loaded through a larger hatch. Production totalled about 2,900 aircraft built in Germany and, under German control, Czechoslovakia and France. Mraz and Morane-Saulnier continued production in these two countries after the war.

FIESELER Fi 156 C-1 STORCH
Role: Army co-operation/observation and communications
Crew/Accommodation: Two or one, plus one litter-carried casualty
Power Plant: One 240 hp Argus As 10C air-cooled inline
Dimensions: Span 14.25 m (46.75 ft); length 9.9 m (32.48 ft); wing area 26 m² (279.9 sq ft)
Weights: Empty 930 kg (2,051 lb); MTOW 1,320 kg (2,911 lb)
Performance: Maximum speed 145 km/h (90 mph) at sea level; operational ceiling 4,600 m (15,092 ft); range 385 km (239 miles)
Load: One 7.9 mm machine gun, plus provision to evacuate one litterborne casualty

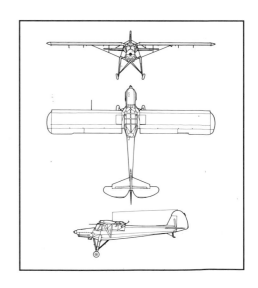

Fieseler Fi 156C-0

165

WESTLAND LYSANDER (United Kingdom)

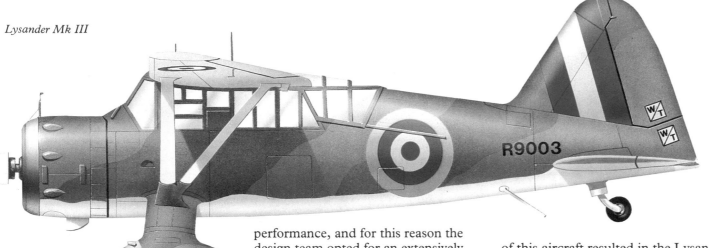

Lysander Mk III

The Lysander resulted from a 1934 British Air Ministry requirement for a two-seat army co-operation aircraft. Key features of the requirements were good fields of vision and STOL

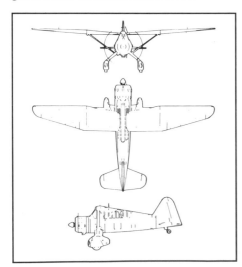

Westland Lysander Mk III

performance, and for this reason the design team opted for an extensively glazed cockpit supporting the roots of the unusually shaped high-set wing, the outer portions of which were braced by V-struts to the cantilever main legs of the fixed tailwheel landing gear. These legs were also fitted with small stub wings which could carry up to 227-kg (500-lb) of light bombs or other types of stores.

The first of two prototypes flew in June 1936 with the 664-kW (890-hp) Bristol Mercury XII radial, and after successful trials the type was ordered into production as the Lysander Mk I, of which 169 were built for service from June 1938. Further development

of this aircraft resulted in the Lysander Mk II, of which 517 were built with the 675-kW (905-hp) Bristol Perseus XII radial, the Lysander Mk III of

which 517 were built with the 649-kW (870-hp) Mercury XX, and the Lysander Mk IIIA of which 347 were built with the Mercury 30. Early operations in France revealed that the Lysander was too vulnerable for its designed role in the presence of modern fighters and anti-aircraft defences, and though the type saw further limited first-line service in the Middle East and the Far East, most aircraft were relegated to second-line duties such as target towing, air-sea rescue, radar calibration and special agent infiltration and extraction. Some 14 Mk I conversions to Lysander TT.Mk I standard validated the target tug version, and a similar process provided five TT.Mk IIs, 51 T.Mk IIIs and 100 TT.Mk IIIA aircraft.

WESTLAND LYSANDER Mk III
Role: Communications/tactical reconnaissance
Crew/Accommodation: Two
Power Plant: One 890 hp Bristol Mercury XX air-cooled radial
Dimensions: Span 15.24 m (50.00 ft); length 9.29 m (30.50 ft); wing area 24.15 m² (260.00 sq ft)
Weights: Empty 1,980 kg (4,365 lb); MTOW 2,865 kg (6,318 lb)
Performance: Maximum speed 336 km/h (209 mph) at 1,524 m (5,000 ft); operational ceiling 6,553 m (21,500 ft); range 966 km (600 miles)
Load: Four .303 in machine guns, plus up to 227 kg (500 lb) of bombs

The Westland Lysander had excellent STOL performance

166

BLOHM und VOSS BV 141 (Germany)

BV 141A

In 1937 the German air ministry issued a requirement for a short-range reconnaissance and observation aircraft with a single engine, a crew of three, and excellent all-round fields of vision. The requirement drew proposals from three companies including Hamburger Flugzeugbau (a Blohm und Voss subsidiary), whose Dr Richard Vogt produced a design of extraordinary novelty. The BV 141

was of asymmetric layout, with the 645-kW (865-hp) BMW 132N radial engine located at the front of a nacelle/boom offset to port of the wing's longitudinal centreline and balanced by the extensively glazed crew compartment, which was offset to starboard. The official preference was for the Focke-Wulf FW 189, which featured a well-glazed central nacelle and twin tail booms, but Blohm und

Voss decided to produce its prototype as a private venture.

This BV 141 V1 first flew in February 1938, and was followed by two further machines each slightly larger than the first. The third machine also featured wider-track main landing gear units, armament (two fixed and two trainable 7.92-mm/0.312-in machine guns plus provision for four 50-kg/110-lb bombs), and cameras. The BV 141 V3 was successful enough in its trials for the air ministry to order five BV 141A pre-production aircraft with a wider-span wing and a 746-kW (1,000-hp)

BMW-Bramo 323 radial. The BV 141A was again moderately successful but apparently underpowered, and production plans were cancelled. An order was nonetheless placed for five examples of the revised BV 141B with structural strengthening, an asymmetric tailplane and an engine of greater power, but the development programme was so delayed that the type was finally cancelled in 1943.

A prototype of the Blohm und Voss BV 141A model

BLOHM und VOSS BV 141B-02
Role: Tactical reconnaissance
Crew/Accommodation: Three
Power Plant: One 1,560 hp BMW 801A air-cooled radial
Dimensions: Span 17.46 m (57.28 ft); length 13.95 m (45.77 ft); wing area 53.00 m² (570.49 sq ft)
Weights: Empty 4,700 kg (10,363 lb); MTOW 5700 kg (12,568 lb)
Performance: Maximum speed 370 km/h (230 mph) at sea level; operational ceiling 10,000 m (32,808 ft); range 1,200 km (745 miles)
Load: Four 7.9 mm machine guns, plus 200 kg (441 lb) of bombs

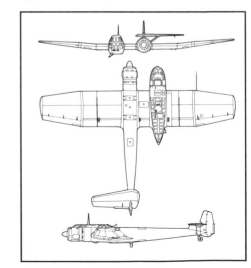

Blohm und Voss BV 141B-0

ARADO Ar 234 BLITZ (Germany)

Ar 234B-2 Blitz

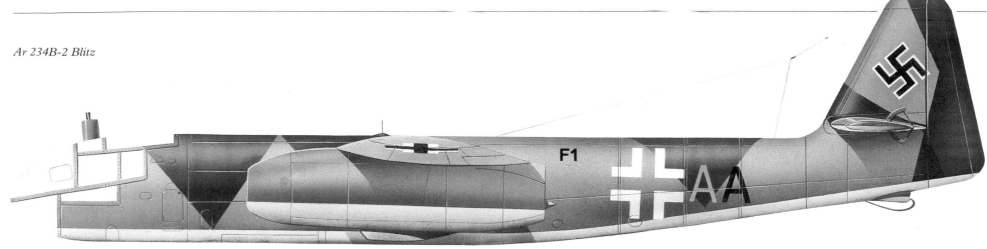

The Ar 234 Blitz (Lightning) was the world's first purpose-designed jet bomber. As first flown in June 1943, the all-metal Ar 234A had straight flying surfaces with two Junkers Jumo 004B turbojets in nacelles slung under the shoulder-mounted wings, and a fuselage too slender to accommodate retractable wheeled landing gear. As a result, the first prototypes were designed to take off from a jettisonable trolley and land on retractable skids. Some 18 prototypes were trialled with twin Jumo 004B or quadruple BMW 003A turbojets. The trolley/skid arrangement proved workable but was hardly effective, so the 20 pre-production aircraft featured a wider fuselage to make possible the installation of retractable tricycle landing gear.

These paved the way for the 210 examples of the Ar 234B production model with two engines but no pressurization or ejector seat; this series included the Ar 234B-1 reconnaissance and Ar 234B-2 bomber variants. Another 12 prototypes were used to develop the multi-role Ar 234C model, which had four engines, cabin pressurization and an ejector seat; only 14 of this late-war model were built, and the series included the Ar 234C-1 reconnaissance and Ar 234C-4 multi-role bomber and ground attack variants. The Ar 234C-4 bomber and Ar 234C-2 armed reconnaissance variants remained projects, as did several other variants. The Ar 234 entered service in July 1944, and proved itself a capable first-generation jet warplane in the hands of three operational squadrons.

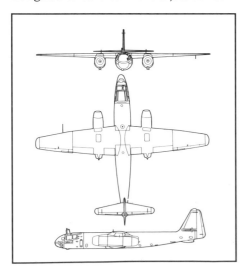

Arado Ar 234B-2 Blitz

ARADO Ar 234B-2 BLITZ
Role: High speed bomber
Crew/Accommodation: One
Power Plant: Two 900 kgp (1,980 lb s.t.) Junkers 004B Orkan turbojets
Dimensions: Span 14.44 m (47.38 ft); length 12.64 m (41.47 ft); wing area 27.3 m² (284.2 sq ft)
Weights: Empty 5,200 kg (11,464 lb); MTOW 9,800 kg (21,715 lb)
Performance: Maximum speed 742 km/h (461 mph) at 6,000 m (19,685 ft); operational ceiling 10,000 m (32,810 ft); range 1,556 km (967 miles) with 500 kg (1,102 lb) payload
Load: Two rear-firing 20 mm cannon, plus up to 2,000 kg (4,410 lb) of bombs

Arado Ar 234B Blitz

CESSNA L-19/O-1 BIRD DOG (United States)

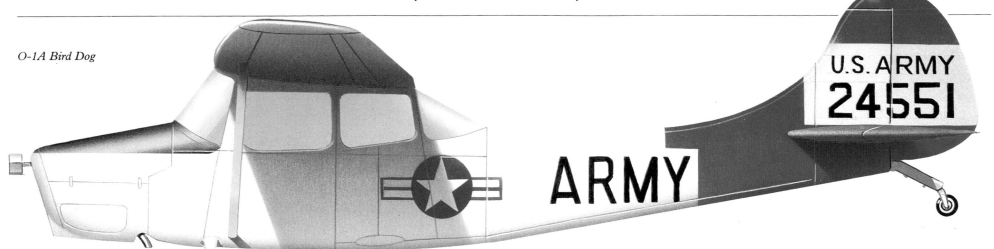

O-1A Bird Dog

This classic aircraft was designed to meet a U.S. Army requirement of the late 1940s for a purpose-designed observation type. From submissions from several companies, Cessna's Model 305A was awarded the contract for an initial 418 aircraft placed in June 1950. The design was derived from that of the Model 170 with a new powerplant, cut-down rear fuselage to offer better fields of vision (enhanced by transparencies in the wing centre section that formed the cabin roof), and a wing with trailing-edge flaps to provide better field performance. The type also featured a wider door so that a litter could be loaded into the fuselage.

Deliveries of the L-19A Bird Dog initial model began in December 1950, and by October 1954 deliveries to the U.S. Army totalled 2,486 aircraft, including 60 diverted to the U.S. Marine Corps with the designation OE-1. Trainer models were the L-19A-IT of 1953 and the TL-19D of 1956, the latter with a constant-speed propeller. Total production of the Bird Dog amounted to 3,431 aircraft, and the last variant was the L-19E able to operate at higher weights.

In 1962 the series was redesignated as the O-1, and at this time the U.S. Army's L-19A, TL-19D and L-19E were restyled the O-1A, TO-1D and O-1E respectively. The U.S. Army also operated TO-1A and TO-1E trainers derived from the basic models. The U.S. Marine Corps' OE-1 became the O-1B that was complemented by the higher-powered O-1C. Bird Dogs saw limited service in the Korean War, but were extensively flown in the Vietnam War as forward air control aircraft. When modified for this role, the TO-1D and O-1A were redesignated O-1F and O-1G respectively. The Bird Dog was also built under licence in Japan by Fuji, and large numbers were exported to American allies.

This is a machine of the Italian army aviation service

CESSNA L-19E/O-1E BIRD DOG
Role: Battlefield observation/artillery direction
Crew/Accommodation: Two
Power Plant: One 213 hp Continental 0-470-11 air-cooled flat-opposed
Dimensions: Span 10.97 m (36 ft); length 7.87 m (25.83 ft); wing area 16.17 m² (174 sq ft)
Weights: Empty 732 kg (1,614 lb); MTOW 1,089 kg (2,400 lb)
Performance: Cruise speed 167 km/h (104 mph) at 1,524 m (5,000 ft); operational ceiling 5,639 m (18,500 ft); range 835 km (530 miles)
Load: None, other than special-to-task communications equipment

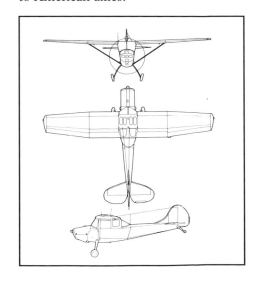

Cessna L-19A

LOCKHEED SR-71 (United States)

SR-71

17978

Until its recent retirement at the end of 1989, the SR-71 was the world's fastest and highest-flying 'conventional' aircraft, and was a truly extraordinary machine designed for the strategic reconnaissance role with a mass of classified sensors. The airframe was designed for a crew of two (pilot and systems operator) and minimum drag, and was therefore evolved with a very slender fuselage and thin wings of delta planform blended into the fuselage by large chines that generate additional lift, prevent the pitching down of the nose at higher speeds, and provide additional volume for sensors and fuel. The airframe was built largely of

titanium and stainless steel to deal with the high temperatures created by air friction at the SR-71's Mach 3+ cruising speed at heights over 21,335 m (70,000 ft). Power was provided by the two special continuous-bleed turbojets which at high speed provided only a small part of the motive power in the form of direct jet thrust from the nozzles (18 per cent), the greater part of the power being provided by inlet suction (54 per cent) and thrust from the special outlets at the rear of the multiple-flow nacelles (28 per cent). Nicknamed 'Blackbird' for its special overall colour scheme that helped dissipate heat and absorb enemy radar emissions, the SR-71 was developed via the four YF-12 interceptors (three YF-12As and one YF-12C), which reached only the

experimental stage, from the 21 A-11 drone-launching reconnaissance platforms first revealed in 1964. The SR-71A entered service in 1966 and was built to the extent of at least 29

aircraft, while training was carried out on a conversion type that was at least two SR-71Bs and one similar SR-71C converted from SR-71A standard.

Lockheed SR-14A 'Blackbird'

LOCKHEED SR-71A
Role: Long-range high supersonic
   reconnaissance
Crew/Accommodation: Two
Power Plant: Two 14,742 kgp (32,500 lb s.t.)
   Pratt & Whitney J58 turbo-ramjets
Dimensions: Span 16.94 m (55.58 ft); length
   32.74 m (107.41 ft); wing area 149.1m²
   (1,605 sq ft)
Weights: Empty 30,618 kg (67,500 lb); MTOW
   78,020 kg (172,000 lb)
Performance: Cruise speed 3,661 km/h (1,976
   knots) Mach 3.35 at 24,385 m (80,000 ft);
   operational ceiling 25,908 m (85,000 ft);
   range 5,230 km (2.822 naut. miles)
   unrefuelled
Load: Up to around 9,072 kg (20,000 lb) of
   specialized sensors

A dramatic view of a Lockheed SR-71A taking on fuel

CURTISS-WRIGHT C-46 COMMANDO (United States)

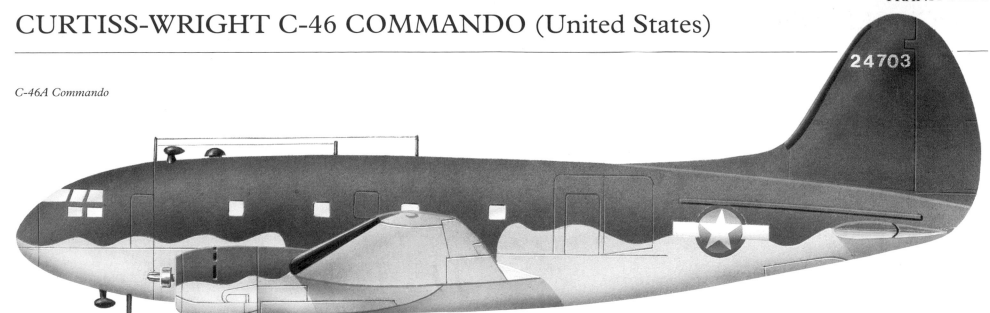

C-46A Commando

The aircraft that entered widespread production as the C-46 Commando troop and freight transport was conceived as a civil type to pick up where the Douglas DC-3 left off by offering such advantages as longer range, higher cruising speed, cabin pressurization, and a larger payload in the form of 36 passengers carried in a smooth-nosed fuselage of the double-lobe type. The twin-finned CW-20T prototype flew in March 1940 with 1268-kW (1,700-hp) Wright R-2600

radials, but soon afterwards was converted into the CW-20A with a revised tail unit featuring a single vertical surface and flat rather than dihedralled tailplane halves.

Such were the needs of the growing U.S. military establishment, however, that subsequent development was geared to the requirements of the U.S. Army Air Corps (later U.S. Army Air Forces), which evaluated the CW-20A as the C-55 and then ordered the type as the militarized CW-20B. This

version became the C-46 with 1491-kW (2,000-hp) Pratt & Whitney R-2800-51 radials and accommodation for 45 troops. Some 25 of the original C-46 troop transports entered service from July 1942 as the USAAF's largest and heaviest twin-engined aircraft. The series was used almost exclusively in the Pacific theatre during World War II.

There were several variants after the C-46, including 1,493 C-46As as the first definitive model with R-2800-51 engines and a strengthened fuselage floor that could take up to 50 troops or freight loaded through large

port-side cargo doors. Later variants such as the 1,410 C-46D troop and 234 C-46F utility transports were comparable to the C-46A apart from minor modifications and adaptations. The type was also used by the United States Navy with the designation R5C, and after the war many ex-military machines were released on to the civil market where some remain to the present.

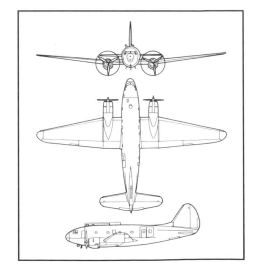

A Curtiss-Wright C-46 Commando

CURTISS-WRIGHT C-46A COMMANDO
Role: Long-range transport
Crew/Accommodation: Four, plus up to 50 troops
Power Plant: Two, 2,000 hp Pratt & Whitney R-2800-51 Double Wasp air-cooled radials
Dimensions: Span 32.91 m (108 ft); length 23.26 m (76.33 ft); wing area 126.34 m² (1,360 sq ft)
Weights: Empty 13,608 kg (30,000 lb); MTOW 25,401 kg (56,000 lb)
Performance: Cruise speed 278 km/h (173 mph) at 4,572 m (15,000 ft); operational ceiling 7,468 m (24,500 ft); range 1,931 km (1,200 miles) with full payload
Load: Up to 6,804 kg (15,000 lb)

Curtiss-Wright C-46A Commando

DOUGLAS DC-4 and C-54 SKYMASTER (United States)

Douglas DC-4

Even before the DC-3 had flown, Douglas was planning a longer-range air transport with four engines, retractable tricycle landing gear, and greater capacity. The DC-4 (later DC-4E) pressurized prototype first flew in June 1938, but was too advanced for its time and therefore suffered a number of technical problems. The DC-4E's performance and operating economics were also below

specification, and the company therefore dropped the type. As a replacement, Douglas turned to the unpressurized and otherwise simplified DC-4 with a lighter structure, a new high aspect ratio wing, and a tail unit with a single central vertical surface in place of the DC-4E's twin endplate surfaces. The type was committed to production with 1081-kW (1,450-hp) Pratt & Whitney R-2000-2SD1-G Twin Wasp radial engines even before the first example had flown.

With the United States caught up into World War II during December

1941, the type was swept into military service as the C-54 (Army) and R5D (Navy) long-range military transport, and the first aircraft flew during February 1942 in U.S. Army Air Forces markings. The main military versions were the 24 impressed C-54s with R-2000-3 radials for 26 passengers, the 207 fully militarized C54As and R5D-1s with R-2000-7s for 50 passengers, the 220 C-54Bs and R5D-2s with integral wing tanks,

the 380 C-54Ds and R5D-3s with R-2000-11s, the 125 C-54E and R5D-4 convertible freight/passenger models with revised fuel tankage, and the 162 C-54G and R5D-5 troop carriers with R-2000-9s. After military service many of these aircraft found their way on to the civil register and performed excellently in the long-range passenger and freight roles. Two civil models were produced after World War II; total production was 1,122 aircraft.

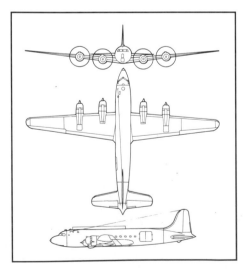

Douglas C-54D Skymaster

DOUGLAS DC-4 and C-54 SKYMASTER
Role: Long-range passenger transport
Crew/Accommodation: Four, plus three/four cabin crew, plus up to 86 passengers
Power Plant: Four 1,450 hp Pratt & Whitney R.2000 Twin Wasp air-cooled radials
Dimensions: Span 35.81 m (117.5 ft); length 28.6 m (93.83 ft); wing area 135.35 m² (1,457 sq ft)
Weights: Empty 16,783 kg (37,000 lb); MTOW 33,113 kg (73,000 lb)
Performance: Cruise speed 309 km/h (192 mph) at 3,050 m (10,000 ft); operational ceiling 6,705 m (22,000 ft) ; range 3,220 km (2,000 miles) with 9,979 kg (22,000 lb) payload
Load: Up to 14,515 kg (32,500 lb)

The Douglas R5D series was the naval counterpart of the C-54 Skymaster

ANTONOV An-2 and An-3 'COLT' (U.S.S.R.)

An-2 'Colt'

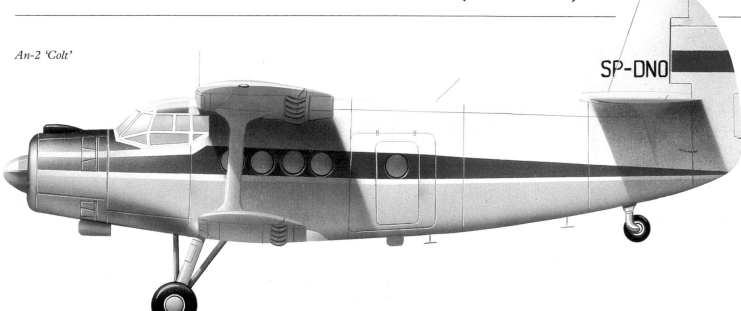

admirable field performance thanks to its combination of automatic leading-edge slots, slotted trailing-edge flaps, drooping ailerons on the upper wings, and slotted trailing-edge flaps on the lower wings. The type entered service with the 746-kW (1,000-hp) ASh-62IR radial, and though designed primarily for agricultural use, has been and still is produced in a number of variants suiting the An-2 to a variety of other roles. Typically, these are transport (12 passengers and two children or 1240-kg/2,733-lb of freight), float-equipped transport, ambulance work, fire-fighting, meteorological research, geophysical research, photogrametric survey and TV relay.

More than 15,000 examples of the An-2 have been built, about 10,000 of them in Poland since 1960. This total also includes some 1,500 examples of the licensed Chinese model, the Shijiazhuang Y-5. The An-3 is the latest model, an agricultural version powered by a 701-kW (940-shp) Glushenkov TVD-10B turboprop for 40 per cent more payload.

The An-2 first flew in August 1947 with the 567-kW (760-hp) Shvetsov ASh-21 radial engine, and was apparently an anachronism because it was a large sesquiplane with I-type interplane struts, fixed but exceptionally robust tailwheel landing gear, and a strut-braced tailplane. The An-2 has been produced in vast numbers and continues to serve most capably and usefully in both its Soviet-produced and later Polish-built variants. The type is known in the NATO system of reporting names for Soviet aircraft as the 'Colt'.

An all-metal but unpressurized type with fabric covering on the tailplane and rear portions of the wings, the An-2 is exceptionally rugged, and has

The Antonov An-2 is a modern oddity

ANTONOV An-2 'COLT'
Role: Utility transport/agricultural spraying
Crew/Accommodation: Two, plus up to 12 passengers
Power Plant: One 1,000 hp Shvetsov ASh-62M air-cooled radial
Dimensions: Span 18.18 m (59.65 ft); length 12.74 m (41.8 ft); wing area 71.1 m² (765 sq ft)
Weights: Empty 3,450 kg (7,605 lb); MTOW 5,500 kg (12,125 lb)
Performance: Cruise speed 185 km/h (100 knots) at 1,750 m (5,741 ft); range 900 km (485 naut. miles) with 500 kg (1,102 lb) payload
Load: Up to 1,500 kg (3,306 lb)

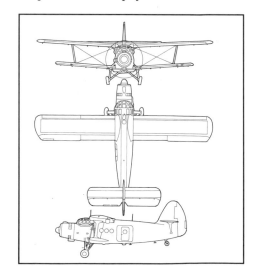

Antonov An-2

FAIRCHILD C-82 and C-119 Family (United States)

C-119C

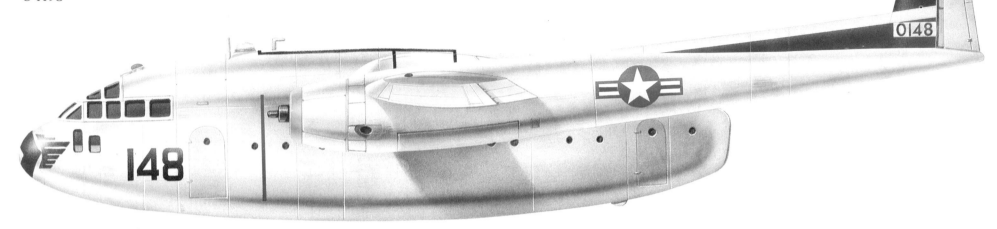

In 1941, Fairchild began work on its F-78 design to meet a U.S. Army Air Forces' requirement for a military freighter. The XC-82 prototype first flew in September 1944 as a high-wing monoplane with twin booms extending from the engine nacelles angles of the inverted gull wing to support the empennage so that clamshell rear doors could provide access to the central payload nacelle.

The payload could comprise 78 troops, or 42 paratroops, or 34 litters, or freight. The only production version was the C-82A Packet with 1566-kW (2,100-hp) Pratt & Whitney R-2800-34 radials, and delivery of 220 such aircraft was completed.

The basic concept was further developed into the C-119 Flying Boxcar with 1976-kW (2,650-hp) Pratt & Whitney R-4360-4 radial engines and the cockpit relocated into the nose of the nacelle. The XC-82B prototype of 1947 led to production of the C-119B with 2610-kW (3,500-hp) R-4360-20 engines, structural

strengthening, and the fuselage widened by 0.36 m (1 ft 2 in) for the carriage of a heavier payload that could include 62 paratroops or freight. The 55 examples of this initial model were followed by 303 C-119Cs with R-4360-20WA engines, dorsal fin extensions, and no tailplane outboard of the vertical tail surfaces, 212 examples of the C-119F with ventral fins and other detail modifications, and 480 examples of the C-119G with different propellers and equipment

changes. The 26 AC-119G aircraft were gunship conversions of C-119Gs and were later upgraded to AC-119K standard, the 62 C-119Js were C-119F/G transports revised with a flight-openable door in the rear of the central pod, the five C-119Js were C-119Gs modified with two 1293-kg (2,850-lb) thrust General Electric J85-GE-17 booster turbojets in underwing nacelles, and the 22 C-119Ls were C-119Gs updated and fitted with new propellers.

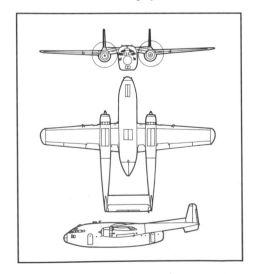

Fairchild C-119G Flying Boxcar

FAIRCHILD C-119C FLYING BOXCAR
Role: Military bulk freight/paratroop transport
Crew/Accommodation: Four, plus up to 42 paratroops
Power Plant: Two 3,500 hp Pratt & Whitney R-4360-20 Wasp Major air-cooled radials
Dimensions: Span 33.32 m (109.25 ft); length 26.37 m (86.5 ft); wing area 134.4 m² (1,447 sq ft)
Weights: Empty 18,053 kg (39,800 lb); MTOW 33,566 kg (74,000 lb)
Performance: Maximum speed 452 km/h (281 mph) at 5,486 (18,000 ft); operational ceiling 7,285 m (23,900 ft); range 805 km (500 miles) with maximum load
Load: Up to 8,346 kg (18,400 lb)

The C-119G was built in large numbers

LOCKHEED C-130 HERCULES (United States)

L-100-30 Hercules

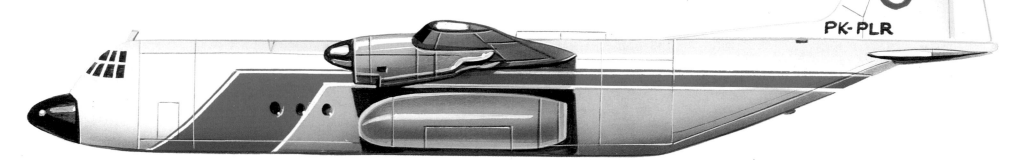

The Hercules is the airlifter against which all other turboprop tactical transports are measured. It was the type that pioneered the modern airlifter layout with a high-set wing, a capacious fuselage with a rectangular-section hold terminating at its rear in an integral ramp/door that allows the straight-in loading/unloading of bulky items under the upswept tail, and multi-wheel landing gear with its main units accommodated in external fairings. No demands are made on

hold area and volume, leaving the hold floor and opened ramp at truckbed height to help loading and unloading.

The type was designed in response to a 1951 requirement for STOL transport, and first flew in YC-130 prototype form during August 1954 with 2796-kW (3,750-shp) Allison T56-A-1A turboprops driving three-blade propellers. Over 1,700 aircraft have been delivered and the type remains in both development and

production, having been evolved in major variants from its initial C-130A form to the C-130B with more fuel and a higher maximum weight, the C-130E with 3020-kW (4,050-shp) T56-A-7a turboprops driving four-blade propellers, greater internal fuel capacity and provision for external fuel tanks, the C-130H with airframe and system improvements as well as 3362-kW (4,508-shp) T56-A-15 turboprops, and the C-130H-30 with a lengthened fuselage for the accommodation of bulkier payloads.

There is a host of variants for tasks as diverse as Arctic operations, drone and spacecraft recovery, special forces insertion and extraction, airborne command post operations, and communication with submerged submarines. It is also produced in L-100 civil form that has secured modest sales. An updated C-130J model is under development with improved engines and a modern flight deck.

The special mission EC-130H 'Compass Call'

LOCKHEED C-130H HERCULES
Role: Land-based, rough field-capable transport/tanker
Crew/Accommodation: Four crew with up to 92 troops
Power Plant: Four 4,508 shp Allison T56-A-15 turboprops
Dimensions: Span 40.4m (132.6 ft); length 29.8 m (97.75 ft); wing area 162.1 m² (1,745 sq ft)
Weights: Empty 34,397 kg (75,832 lb); MTOW 79,380 kg (175,000 lb)
Performance: Maximum speed 621 km/h (335 knots) at 3,658 m (12,000 ft); operational ceiling 10,060 m (33,000 ft); range 7,410 km (3,995 naut. miles) with 9,070 kg (20,000 lb) payload
Load: 19,850 kg (43,761 lb)

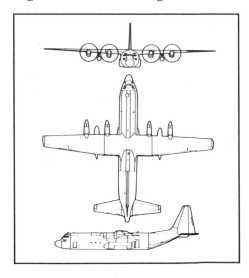

Lockheed C-130H-30 Hercules

BOEING KC-135 STRATOTANKER (United States)

KC-135A Stratotanker

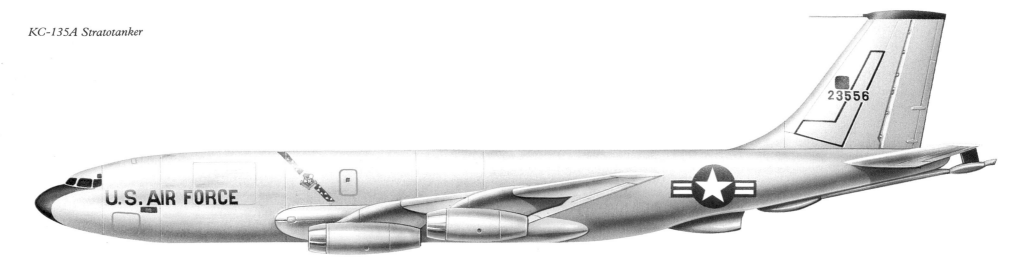

One of the provisions of Boeing's Model 367-80 prototype was for the company's patented 'flying boom' inflight refuelling system, and after this had been proved in trials, the U.S. Air Force announced in August 1956 that it was to procure the KC-135A inflight refuelling tanker based on the 'Dash 80'. The first of these flew in August 1956. Such was the priority allocated to this essential

support for the United States' strategic bombers that production built up very rapidly, and eventually more than 800 KC-135 series aircraft were produced. Some 724 of these were KC-135A tankers with 6237-kg (13,750-lb) thrust Pratt & Whitney J57-P-59W turbojets, and later aircraft were built with the taller vertical tail surfaces that were retrofitted to the earlier machines. Some 48 aircraft were completed as 18 turbojet-powered C-135A and 30 C-135B turbofan-powered transports, but as the role was better performed by the Lockheed C-130 Hercules and C-141

StarLifter, the aircraft were later converted into special-purpose machines to complement a number of KC-135As also adapted as EC-135 command post and communication relay platforms, or as RC-135 electronic reconaissance platforms.

The type remains so important that most are being upgraded for continued viability. Some 151 KC-135As operated by the Air Force Reserve and Air National Guard are being improved to KC-135E standard

with reskinned wing undersurfaces, new brakes and anti-skid units, and the Pratt & Whitney JT3D turbofans (complete with their pylons and nacelles) plus the tail units from surplus civil Model 707 transports. A similar but more extensive upgrade is being undertaken to improve 630 USAF KC-135As to KC-135R standard with better systems, a larger tailplane, greater fuel capacity, and 9979-kg (22,000-lb) thrust CFM International F108-CF-100 turbofans.

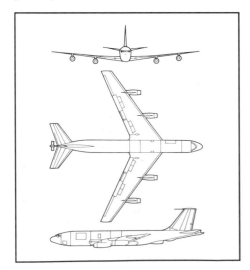

Boeing KC-135A Stratotanker

BOEING KC-135A STRATOTANKER
Role: Military tanker-transport
Crew/Accommodation: Four, including fuel boom operator
Power Plant: Four 6,237 kgp (13,750 lb s.t.) Pratt & Whitney J57P-59W turbojets
Dimensions: Span 39.88 m (130.83 ft); length 41.53 m (136.25 ft); wing area 226.03 m² (2,433 sq ft)
Weights: Empty 44,664 kg (98,466 lb); MTOW 134,718 kg (297,000 lb)
Performance: Cruise speed 888 km/h (552 mph) at 9,144 m (30,000 ft); operational ceiling 15,240 m (50,000 ft); range 1,850 m (1,150 miles) with maximum payload
Load: Up to 54,432 kg (120,000 lb)

A Boeing KC-135A Stratotanker

LOCKHEED C-5 GALAXY (United States)

C-5A Galaxy

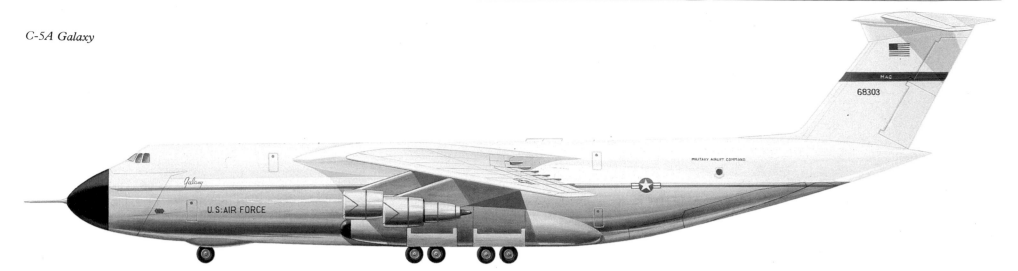

The Galaxy was produced to meet a U.S. Air Force requirement, ultimately shown to be considerably overambitious in its payload/range requirements, of the early 1960s for a long-range strategic airlifter to complement the Lockheed C-141 StarLifter logistic freighter, and as such able to operate into and out of tactical airstrips close to the front line through use of its 28-wheel landing gear that keeps ground pressure to the low figure that makes it possible for the Galaxy to use even unpaved strips.

The C-5A first flew in June 1968, and the type has many similarities to the C-141, though it is very much larger and possesses a lower deck 36.91 m (121 ft 1 in) long and 5.79 m (19 ft 0 in). This hold can accommodate up to 120,204-kg (265,000-lb) of freight, and is accessed not only by the standard type of power-operated rear ramp/door arrangement but also by a visor-type nose that hinges upward and so makes possible straight-through loading and unloading for minimim turn-round time.

Production comprised 81 aircraft with 18,597-kg (41,000-lb) thrust General Electric TF39-GE-1 turbofans, and the first operational aircraft were delivered in December 1969 as the first equipment for an eventual four squadrons. Service use revealed that the wing structure had been made too light in an effort to improve payload/range performance, so the 77 surviving aircraft were rewinged and fitted with 19,504-kg (43,000-lb) thrust TF39-GE-1C

engines to maintain their operational viability. This process also allowed an increase in maximum take-off weight from 348,809-kg (768,980-lb) to 379,633-kg (837,000-lb), allowing the carriage of a maximum 124,740-kg (275,000-lb) payload. Another 50 aircraft have been built to this standard as C-5Bs with improved systems. Production ended in February 1989.

Lockheed C-5B Galaxy

LOCKHEED C-5 GALAXY
Role: Military long-range, heavy cargo transport
Crew/Accommodation: Five, with provision for relief crew and up to 75 troops on upper decks as well as 290 troops on main deck in place of cargo
Power Plant: Four 18,643 kgp (41,100 lb s.t.) General Electric TF-39-GE-1 turbofans
Dimensions: Span 67.88 m (222.7 ft); length 75.53 m (247.8 ft); wing area 576 m² (6,200 sq ft)
Weights: Empty 145,603 kg (321,000 lb); MTOW 348,812 kg (769,000 lb)
Performance: Cruise speed 814 km/h (439 knots) at 7,620 m (25,000 ft); operational ceiling 14,540 m (47,700 ft); range 3,015 km (1,627 naut. miles) with maximum payload
Load: Up to 120,200 kg (265,000 lb)

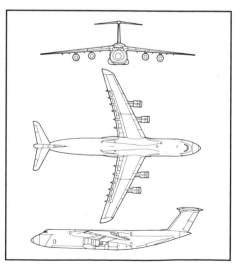

Lockheed C-5B Galaxy

WRIGHT FLYER (United States)

Flyer I

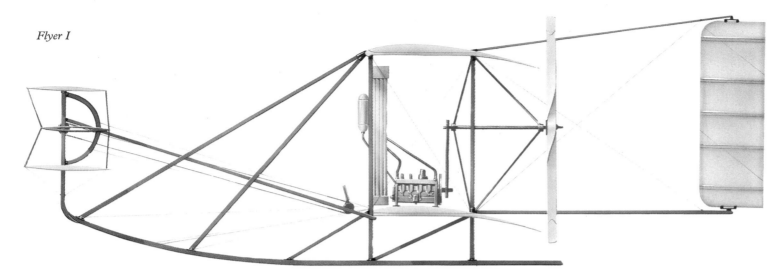

The Flyer II took off about 100 times and achieved some 80 flights as the brothers perfected the task of piloting this inherently unstable aircraft. The flights totalled about 45 minutes in the air, and the longest covered about 4.43 km (2.75 miles) in 5 minutes 4 seconds.

The machine was broken up in 1905, the year in which the brothers produced the world's first really practical aircraft as the Flyer III, with improved controls but with the engine and twin propellers of the Flyer II. This machine made more than 40 flights, and as they were now able to control the type with considerable skill, the emphasis was placed on endurance and range. Many long flights were achieved, the best of them covering some 38.6 km (24 miles) in 38 minutes 3 seconds.

With the aircraft now designated Flyer I, the Wright brothers made the world's first powered, sustained and controlled flights in a heavier-than-air craft during December 1903. The machine was a canard biplane powered by a 9-kW (12-hp) Wright engine driving two pusher propellers that turned in opposite directions as the drive chain to one was crossed, and take-off was effected with the aid of a two-wheel trolley that carried the Flyer I on a 18.3-m (60-ft) ramp.

On the historic day of December 17, 1903, the Flyer I achieved four flights: the first covered 36.6 m (120 ft) in 12 seconds, and the last achieved 260 m (852 ft) in 59 seconds. The improved Flyer II of 1904 was of the same basic configuration and dimensions as its predecessor, but its wings had revised camber and the engine was an 11-kW (15-hp) type. Take-off was aided by the use of a trolley that was boosted by a weight that was dropped from a derrick to pull the tow rope connected to the trolley.

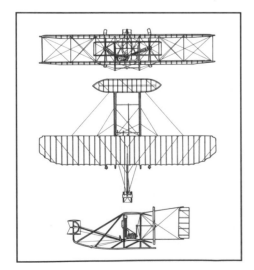

Wright Flyer III

WRIGHT FLYER I
Role: Powered flight demonstrator
Crew/Accommodation: One
Power Plant: One 12 hp Wright Brothers' water-cooled inline
Dimensions: Span 12.29 m (40.33 ft); length 6.41 m (21.03 ft); wing area 47.38 m² (510 sq ft)
Weights: Empty 256.3 kg (565 lb); MTOW 340.2 kg (750 lb)
Performance: Cruise speed 48 km/h (30 mph) at sea level; operational ceiling 9.14 m (30 ft); range 259.7 m (852 ft)
Load: None
Note: the range quoted here was the longest of four flights made by the Wright Brothers on 17 December, 1903

Wilbur Wright piloting the Wright Type A

BELL X-1 (United States)

Bell X-1A

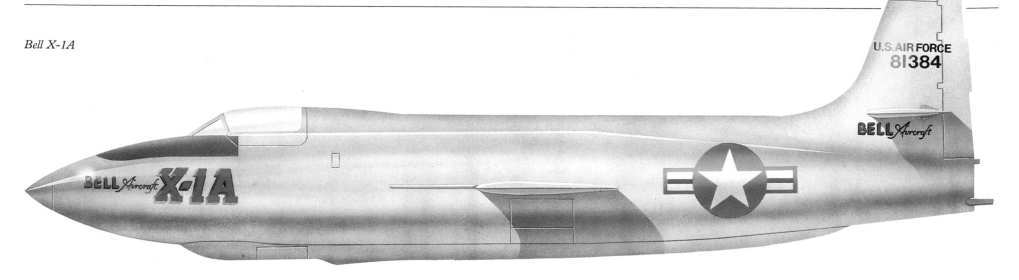

The X-1 has a distinct place in aviation history as the first aircraft to break the 'sound barrier' and achieve supersonic speed in level flight. The origins of the type lay in the February 1945 decision of the U.S. Army Air Forces and the National Advisory Committee for Aeronautics for the joint funding of an advanced research aircraft to provide data on kinetic heating at supersonic speeds. Bell had the choice of turbojet or liquid-propellant rocket power, and opted for the latter in a very purposeful design with an unstepped cockpit, mid-set wings that were unswept but very thin, unswept tail surfaces, and tricycle landing gear, the units of which all retracted into the circular fuselage. This girth of body provided the capacity for the rocket fuel and oxidizer.

The type was designed for air launch from a converted Boeing B-29 bomber, and the first of three XS-1 (later X-1) aircraft was dropped for its first gliding flight in January 1946. The first powered flight followed in December of the same year, and in October 1947 Captain Charles 'Chuck' Yeager achieved history's first supersonic flight with a speed of Mach 1.05; the type also attained an altitude of 21,372 m (70,119 ft). The third X-1 was lost in an accident on the ground. Three more airframes were ordered for the type's immensely important research programme, and these were delivered as one X-1A with a stepped cockpit and a fuselage lengthened by 1.40 m (4 ft 7 in) for the greater fuel capacity that made possible a maximum speed of Mach 2.35 and an altitude of more than 27,430 m (90,000 ft), one X-1B, which was used for thermal research, and one X-1D variant of the X-1B that was lost when it was jettisoned after a pre-launch explosion. The X-1E was the second X-1 to be reworked and it was distinctive for its stepped canopy and thinner wings.

The first Bell X-1 in flight

BELL X-1 (Initially XS-1)
Role: Trans-sonic research
Crew/Accommodation: One
Power Plant: One 2,721 kgp (6,000 lb s.t.) Reaction Motors XLR-11-RM-5 four-barrel liquid fuel rocket
Dimensions: Span 8.54 m (28.00 ft); length 9.45 m (31.00 ft); wing area 12.08 m² (130.00 sq ft)
Weights: Empty 3,674 kg (8,100 lb); MTOW 6,078 kg (13,400 lb)
Performance: Maximum speed 1,556 km/h (840 knots) Mach 1.46 at 21,379 m (70,140 ft); operational ceiling 24,384 m (80,000 ft); endurance 2.5 minutes at full power
Load: Nil, other than specific-to-mission mission test equipment

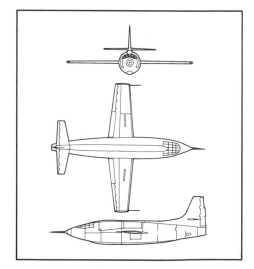

Bell X-1

DOUGLAS D-558 SKYSTREAK and SKYROCKET (United States)

D-558-II Skyrocket

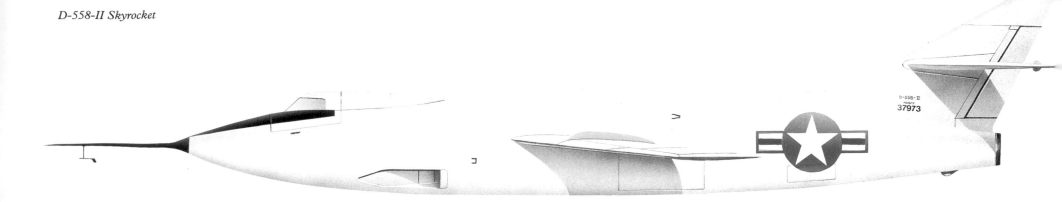

In 1945, the U.S. Navy's Bureau of Aeronautics and the National Advisory Committee for Aeronautics issued a joint requirement for a high-speed research aircraft able to generate the type of high-subsonic flight data that were unobtainable in current wind tunnels. The resulting D-558-I Skystreak was kept as simple as possible, and was based on a circular-section fuselage and straight flying surfaces. The type was powered by the 2268-kg (5,000-lb) thrust Allison J35-A-11 turbojet, and the first of three aircraft flew in May 1947. The type secured two world speed records, and also a mass of invaluable data using a pressure recording system with attachments to 400 points on the airframe, and strain gauges attached to key positions on the wings and tail unit.

It was then planned to provide higher performance by replacing the original engine with a smaller unit to allow the incorporation of a booster rocket, but this notion was then revised to a new type with swept flying surfaces. This materialized as the D-558-II Skyrocket, which had not just the mixed powerplant and swept flying surfaces, but a larger-diameter fuselage incorporating a pointed nose as the D-558-I's nose inlet was replaced by two lateral inlets. Three aircraft were again ordered, and the first of these flew in February 1948.

The orginal flush canopy offered the pilot wholly inadequate fields of vision, and was soon replaced by a more conventional raised enclosure. The Skyrocket flight programme proved successful in the extreme before it finished in December 1956, and included such milestones as an altitude of 25,370 m (83,235 ft) in August 1953 and the first 'breaking' of the Mach 2 barrier in November 1953 with a speed of Mach 2.005.

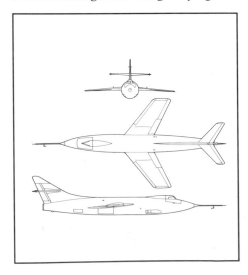

Douglas D-558-II Skyrocket

DOUGLAS D-558-II SKYROCKET
Role: Supersonic research
Crew/Accommodation: One
Power Plant: One 2,721 kgp (6,000 lb s.t.) Reaction Motors XLR-8 rocket plus one 1,360 kgp (3,000 lb s.t.) Westinghouse J34-WE-22 turbojet
Dimensions: Span 7.62 m (25.00 ft); length (13.79 m) 45.25 ft); wing area 16.26 m² (175.00 sq ft)
Weights: MTOW 7,161 kg (15,787 lb) from airborne launch
Performance: Maximum speed 2,078 km/h (1,121 knots) Mach 2.005 at 18,900 m (62,000 ft); operational ceiling 25,370 m (83,235 ft)
Load: Nil, other than specific mission test equipment

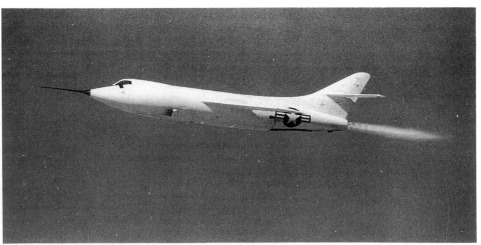

The Douglas D-558-II Skyrocket

FAIREY F.D.2 (United Kingdom)

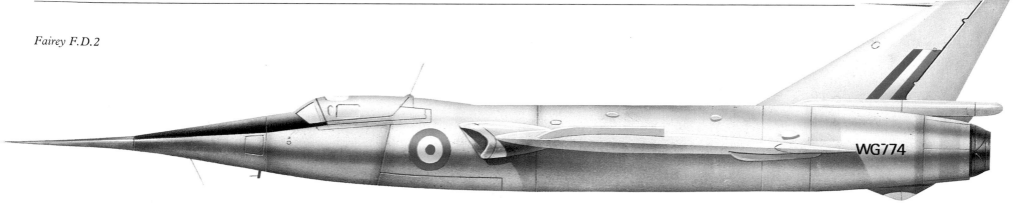

Fairey F.D.2

After a number of experiments in 1947 with vertically launched models, which confirmed the basic feasibility of the delta-winged planform, Fairey was asked to consider the possibility of supersonic delta-winged models. The company anticipated that this would eventually lead to a piloted supersonic research aircraft, and started initial work in advance of any officially promulgated requirement. When such a requirement was announced, English Electric and Fairey each secured a contract for two prototypes. The English Electric type was the P.1 that led finally to the Lightning fighter, and the Fairey design was the droop-snoot nosed Fairey Delta 2. This was designed only as a supersonic research aircraft, and was based on a pure delta wing and a slender fuselage sized to the Rolls-Royce Avon turbojet. Greater priority was given to the company's Gannet carrierborne anti-submarine warplane, so construction of the first F.D.2 began only in late 1952.

The machine first flew in October 1954, and after a delay occasioned by the need to repair damage suffered in a forced landing after engine failure, the type went supersonic for the first time in October 1955. The world absolute speed record was then held by the North American F-100A Super Sabre at 1323 km/h (822 mph), and the capabilities of the F.D.2 were revealed when it raised the speed record to 1822 km/h (1,132 mph) in March 1956. The second F.D.2 joined the programme in February 1956, and the two aircraft undertook a mass of varied and most valuable research work. The first F.D.2 was later revised as the BAC 221 with an ogival wing for test before its use on the Concorde supersonic airliner.

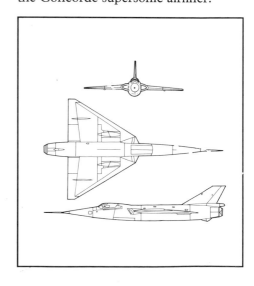

Fairey F.D.2

FAIREY F.D.2
Role: Supersonic research
Crew/Accommodation: One
Power Plant: One 4.309 kgp (9,500 lb s.t.) Rolls-Royce Avon RA14R turbojet with reheat, the use of which was limited, but gave 5,386 kgp (11,875 lb s.t.) at 11,580 m (38,000 ft)
Dimensions: Span 8.18 m (26.83 ft); length 15.74 m (51.62 ft); wing area 38.4 m² (360 sq ft)
Weights: Empty 5,000 kg (11,000 lb); MTOW 6,298 kg (13,884 lb)
Performance: Maximum speed 1,822 km/h (1,132 mph) or Mach. 1.731 at 11,582 m (38,000 ft); operational ceiling 14,021 m (46,000 ft); range 1,335 km (830 miles) without reheat
Load: Confined to specialized test equipment

The first of two Fairey F.D.2 research aircraft

NORTH AMERICAN X-15 (United States)

North American X-15

The X-15 was designed to meet a U.S. Air Force and U.S. Navy requirement for an aircraft able to reach an altitude of 72,600 m (250,000 ft) and a speed of more than 6437 km/h (4,000 mph) after air-launch from a modified Boeing B-52 bomber. Though funded by the two services, the programme was overseen at the technical level by NASA's predecessor, the National Advisory Committee on Aeronautics. In December 1954 a request for proposals was issued to 12 airframe manufacturers, and in February 1955 four companies were invited to tender for the planned machine's rocket propulsion system. Contracts eventually went to North American for the NA-240 aircraft and Reaction Motors for the XLR-99 rocket engine.

The X-15 was designed in advanced materials and comprised a long cylindrical fuselage with lateral fairings to accommodate control systems and fuel tanks, a small wing and tailplane, and wedge-shaped dorsal and ventral fins. The lower portion of the latter was jettisoned before landing to provide ground clearance for the retractable twin skids that, with a nosewheel unit, formed the landing gear. The first of three X-15As was powered by two 3629-kg (8,000-lb) thrust XLR-11 rockets, and made its initial unpowered flight in June 1959, followed by the first powered flight in September 1959. The second X-15A was fitted with the XLR-99 engine and made its first powered flight in November 1960. The three X-15As made almost 200 very important flights, and the second machine made additional contributions after being rebuilt as the X-15A-2 with heat-resistant surface treatment, a fuselage lengthened by 0.74 m (2 ft 5 in) and external auxiliary fuel tanks. In this form the machine reached 107,960 m (354,200 ft) and 7297 km/h (4,534 mph).

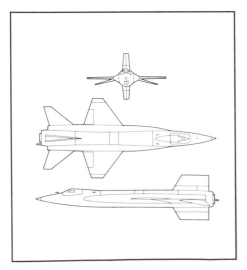

North American X-15

NORTH AMERICAN X-15A-2
Role: Hypersonic research
Crew/Accommodation: One
Power Plant: One 25,855 kgp (57,000 lb s.t.) Thiokol XLR99-RM-2 rocket motor
Dimensions: Span 6.81 m (22.33 ft); length 15.98 m (52.42 ft); wing area 18.58 m² (200 sq ft)
Weights: Empty 6,804 kg (15,000 lb); MTOW 23,095 kg (50.914 lb) air-launched
Performance: Maximum speed 7,297 km/h (3,937 knots) Mach 6.72 at 31,120 m (102,100 ft); operational ceiling 107,960 m (354,200 ft); radius 443 km (275 miles)
Load: Nil, other than dedicated mission test equipment

The X-15A-2 had great endurance and high speed

JUNKERS F 13 (Germany)

F 13

From its J 10 that saw limited service in World War I as the CL I escort fighter and close support warplane, Junkers developed Europe's single most important transport of the 1920s, the classic F 13 low-wing monoplane with a single nose-mounted engine and fixed tailwheel landing gear. This used the metal construction patented by Dr Hugo Junkers in 1910 for thick-section cantilever monoplane wings.

The F 13 first flew in June 1919, and was based on nine spars braced with welded duralumin tubes and covered in streamwise corrugated duralumin skinning to create an immensely strong and durable structure. The accommodation comprised an open cockpit for two pilots and an enclosed cabin for four passengers. The cockpit was later enclosed, and the engine of the first machine was a 119-kW (160-hp) Mercedes D.IIIa inline, which was superseded in early production aircraft by the 138-kW (185-hp) BMW IIIa inline that offered much superior performance. Production continued to 1932, and amounted to at least 320 and probably 350 aircraft in more than 60 variants with a host of modifications and different engines, the most frequent being the 156-kW (210-hp) Junkers L-5 inline.

The main operator of the type was Junkers Luftverkehr, which operated more than 60 aircraft in the period between 1921 and 1926, in the process flying some 15,000,000 km (9,300,000 miles) and carrying nearly 282,000 passengers. The airline then became part of Deutsche Luft-Hansa (later Deutsche Lufthansa) which still had 43 such aircraft in service in 1931. The other F 13s were used by civil and military operators in most parts of the world. The fact that the type was immensely strong, needed little maintenance, and could operate from wheel, ski or float landing gear, made the F 13 especially popular with operators in remoter areas.

The Junkers F 13 was a light but enduring light transport

JUNKERS F 13
Role: Light passenger transport
Crew/Accommodation: One, plus up to four passengers
Power Plant: One 185 hp BMW III A water-cooled inline
Dimensions: Span 14.47 m (47.74 ft) length 9.6 m (31.5 ft); wing area 39 m² (419.8 sq ft)
Weights: Empty 1,150 kg (2,535 lb); MTOW 1,650 kg (3,638 lb)
Performance: Cruise speed 140 km/h (75.5 mph) at sea level; operational ceiling 3,000 m (9.843 ft); range 725 km (450 miles)
Load: Up to 320 kg (705 lb) payload

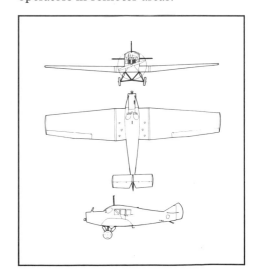

FOKKER F.VII-3m (Netherlands)

Fokker F.VIIB-3m

1985

In 1924-25, Fokker built five examples of its F.VII powered by the 268-kW (360-hp) Rolls-Royce Eagle inline engine, and then evolved the eight-passenger F.VIIA that first flew in March 1925 with a 298-kW (400-hp) Packard Liberty 12 engine and a number of aerodynamic refinements and simple three-strut rather than multi-strut main landing gear units. The type undertook a successful

demonstration tour of the United States, and orders were received there and in Europe for 42 aircraft with inline or radial engines in the class between 261 and 391 kW (350 and 525 hp); licensed production was also undertaken in several countries. The type was a typical Fokker construction, with a welded steel-tube fuselage and tail unit covered in fabric, and a high-set cantilever wing of thick section and wooden construction. For the Ford Reliability Tour of the United States, Fokker produced the first F.VIIA-3m with a powerplant of three 179-kW (240-hp) Wright Whirlwind radials mounted one on the nose and the others on the

main landing gear struts below the wing.

All subsequent production was of the three-engined type, and many F.VIIAs were converted. The F.VIIA-3m spanned 19.30 m (63 ft 3.75 in), but to meet the requirement of Sir Hubert Wilkins for a long-range polar exploration type, a version was produced as the F.VIIB-3m with wings spanning 21.70 m (71 ft 2.5 in). This also became a production type. Dutch construction of the two F. VII-

3m models was 116 aircraft, and large numbers were built under licence in seven countries. The British and American models were the Avro Ten and Atlantic F.7. The type was also adopted by the U.S. Army Air Corps and U.S. Navy as the C-2 and RA respectively. The F.VII-3m was of great importance in the development of European and third-world transport for passengers and freight, and was also used extensively for route-proving and record-breaking flights.

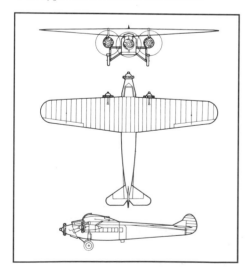

Fokker F.VIIB-3m

FOKKER F.VIIB-3m
Role: Passenger Transport
Crew/Accommodation: Two, plus up to 8 passengers
Power Plant: Three 240 hp Gnome-Rhone Titan air-cooled radials (the aircraft was equipped with various makes/powers of European and U.S. radials)
Dimensions: Span 21.70 m (71.19 ft); length 14.20 m (46.56 ft); wing area 71.20 m² (722 sq ft)
Weights: Empty 3,050 kg (6,724 lb); MTOW 5,250 kg (11,574 lb)
Performance: Maximum speed 185 km/h (115 mph) at sea level; operational ceiling 4,875 m (15,994 ft); range 837 km (520 miles) with full payload
Load: Up to 1,280 kg (2,822 lb)

Fokker F.VIIB-3m Josephine Ford

FORD TRI-MOTORS (United States)

Ford 4-AT

For its time, the Tri-Motor was an unremarkable aircraft in its layout as a high-wing monoplane with fixed landing gear, but was nonetheless notable for its corrugated all-metal construction. This resulted in the inevitable nickname 'Tin Goose' and also ensured that at least some examples are still flying. From his 2-AT Pullman powered by a single 298-kW (400-hp) Packard Liberty inline engine, William B. Stout evolved the 3-AT with three uncowled radial engines mounted two on the wings and one low on the nose. This was unsuccessful, but paved the way for the 4-AT that first flew in June 1926 with three 149-kW (200-hp) Wright Whirlwind J-4 radials located two under the wings in strut-braced nacelles and one in a neat nose installation. The 4-AT accommodated two pilots in an open cockpit and eight passengers in an enclosed cabin.

The type was produced in variants that ranged from the initial 4-AT-A to the 4-AT-E with 224-kW (300-hp) Whirlwind J-6-9 radials and provision for 12 passengers. Production totalled 81 aircraft, and was complemented from 1928 by the 5-AT with 13 passengers, span increased by 1.17 m (3 ft 10 in), and three 313-kW (420-hp) Pratt & Whitney Wasp radials. Production continued up to 1932, and these 117 aircraft included variants up to the 5-AT-D with 17 passengers in a cabin given greater headroom by raising the wing 0.203 m (8 in). Other variants were four 6-ATs based on the 5-AT but with Whirlwind J-6-9 engines, one 7-AT conversion of a 6-AT with a 313-kW Wasp, one 8-AT conversion of a 5-AT with only the nose engine, one 9-AT conversion of a 4-AT with 224-kW Pratt & Whitney Wasp Junior radials, one 11-AT conversion of a 4-AT with three 168-kW (225-hp) Packard diesel engines. Army and Navy versions were the C-3, C-4 and C-9, and the JR and RR respectively.

The legendary 'Tin Goose' is here seen as a Ford 5-AT

FORD 4-AT-E TRI-MOTOR
Role: Passenger transport
Crew/Accommodation: Two, plus up to 11 passengers
Power Plant: Three 300 hp Wright J-6 air-cooled radials
Dimensions: Span 22.56 m (74 ft); length 15.19 m (49.83 ft); wing area 72.93 m² (785 sq ft)
Weights: Empty 2,948 kg (6,500 lb); MTOW 4,595 kg (10,130 lb)
Performance: Cruise speed 172 km/h (107 mph) at sea level; operational ceiling 5,029 m (16,500 ft); range 917 km (570 miles)
Load: Up to 782 kg (1,725 lb)

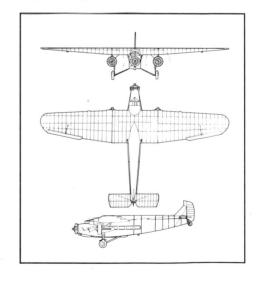

Ford 5-AT Tri-Motor

185

JUNKERS JU 52/3m (Germany)

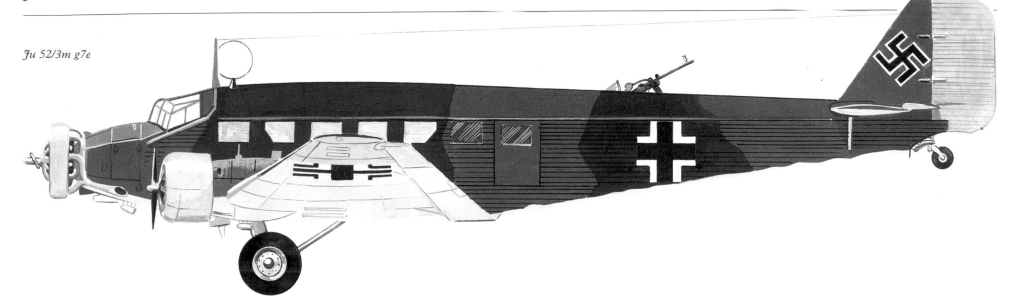

Ju 52/3m g7e

First flown in October 1930 with a single 541-kW (725-hp) BMW VII engine, the Ju 52 was produced to the extent of just six aircraft as civil transports with various engines. The type was of typical Junkers concept for the period, with corrugated alloy skinning on an angular airframe, fixed but faired tailwheel landing gear, and a low-set wing trailed by typical Junkers full-span slotted ailerons/flaps. The Ju 52 would clearly benefit from greater power, and the company therefore developed the Ju 52/3m ce tri-motor version that first flew in April 1931 with 410-kW (550-hp) Pratt & Whitney Hornet radials. The type was produced in Ju 52/3m ce, de, fe and ge civil variants, the last with accommodation for 17 passengers on the power of three 492-kW (660-hp) BMW 132A-1 radials. Development then veered to German military needs, resulting in the Ju 52/3m g3e interim bomber-transport pending the arrival of purpose-designed aircraft. Then the type was built as Germany's main transport and airborne forces aircraft of World War II.

The main variants in an overall production total of about 4,850 aircraft were the Ju 52/3m g4e bomber-transport with a heavier payload and a tailwheel in place of the original skid, the Ju 52/3m g5e with 619-kW (830-hp) BMW 132T-2 radials, the Ju 52/3m g6e improved transport, the Ju 52/3m g7e with an autopilot and a larger loading hatch, Ju 52/3m g8e multi-role transport with conversion kits for specialized roles, Ju 52/3m g9e airborne forces version with a glider-tow attachment and BMW 132Z radials, Ju 52/3m g12e civil and military transport with 596-kW (800-hp) BMW 132L radials, and Ju 52/3m g14e final transport version with improved armament and armour protection. There were also small numbers of the later Ju 252 and Ju 352 developments with more power and retractable landing gear.

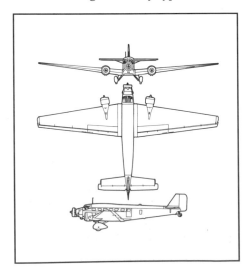

Junkers Ju 52/3m

JUNKERS Ju 52/3m g4e
Role: Military transport (land or water-based)
Crew/Accommodation: Three, plus up to 18 troops
Power Plant: Three 830 hp BMW 132T-2 air-cooled radials
Dimensions: Span 29.25 m (95.97 ft); length 18.9 m (62 ft); wing area 110.5 m² (1,189.4 sq ft)
Weights: Empty 6,510 kg (14,354 lb); MTOW 10,500 kg (23,157 lb)
Performance: Cruise speed 200 km/h (124 mph) at sea level; operational ceiling 5,000 m (18,046 ft); range 915 km (568 miles) with full payload
Load: Three 7.9 mm machine guns and up to 2,000 kg (4,409 lb) payload

BOEING 247 (United States)

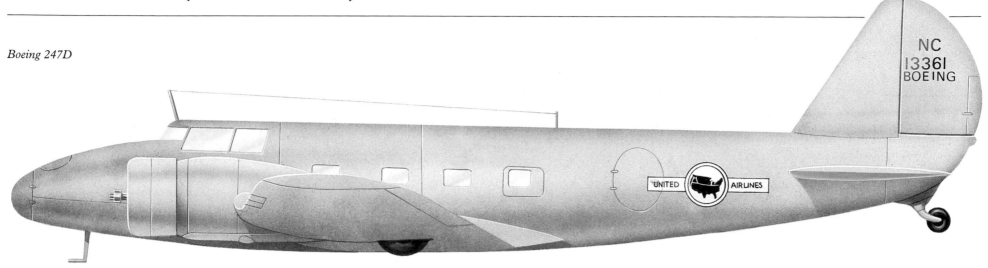

Boeing 247D

The Model 247 was the logical development of other pioneering Boeing aircraft, most notably the Model 200 Monomail and Model 215. The Model 200 was a mailplane with limited passenger capacity, and introduced the cantilever monoplane wing, semi-monocoque fuselage, and retractable landing gear. The Model 215 was an extrapolation of the Model

200's concept into the bomber category, and introduced larger size and a twin-engined powerplant. The Model 247 was slightly smaller and lighter than the Model 215, and has many claims to the title of the world's first 'modern' air transport as it had features such as all-metal construction, cantilever wings, pneumatic de-icing of the flying

surfaces, a semi-monocoque fuselage, retractable landing gear, and fully enclosed accommodation for two pilots, a stewardess, and a planned 14 passengers. Passenger capacity was in fact limited to 10, but with this load the Model 247 could in fact both climb and maintain cruising altitude on just one engine.

The type first flew in February 1933 but, despite its undoubted technical merits, was not a great commercial success. The reason for this was the exact sizing of the machine to the requirement of Boeing Air Transport. It therefore lacked the larger capacity needed by most other potential purchasers. Thus BAT's 60

aircraft were complemented by only 15 more aircraft for companies or individuals. A Model 247 ordered by Roscoe Turner and Clyde Pangborne for the 1934 England to Australia 'MacRobertson' air race introduced drag-reducing NACA engine cowlings and controllable-pitch propellers, and these features proved so successful that they were retrofitted to most aircraft, which thus became the model 247Ds.

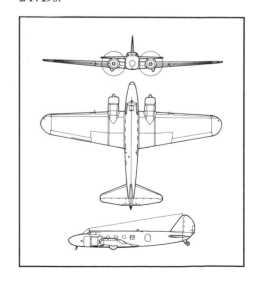

Boeing Model 247D

BOEING 247D
Role: Passenger transport
Crew/Accommodation: Two crew, one cabin crew, plus up to ten passengers
Power Plant: Two 550 hp Pratt & Whitney Wasp S1H1G air-cooled radials
Dimensions: Span 22.56 m (74 ft); length 15.72 m (51.58 ft); wing area 77.67 m² (836 sq ft)
Weights: Empty 4,148 kg (9,144 lb); MTOW 6,192 kg (13,650 lb)
Performance: Cruise speed 304 km/h (189 mph); operational ceiling 7,742 m (25,400 ft); range 1,199 km (745 miles)
Load: Up to 998 kg (2,200 lb)

A model 247D of United Air Lines

187

LOCKHEED L10 ELECTRA (United States)

XR20-1

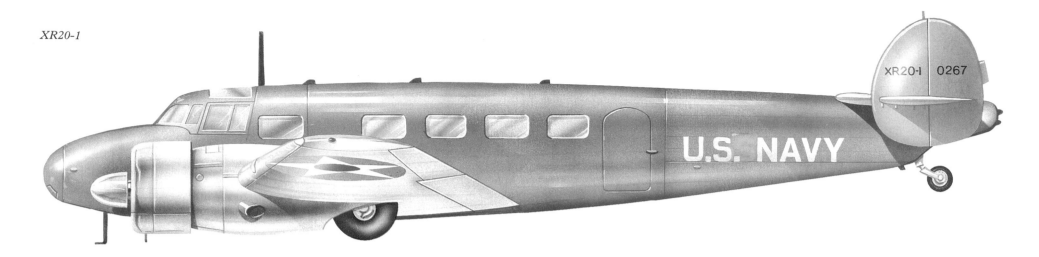

After cutting its teeth on a series of single-engined light transports that also achieved many record long-distance flights, Lockheed decided to move a step up into the potentially more lucrative twin-engined transport market with the Model 10 Electra that offered lower capacity but higher performance than contemporary Boeing and Douglas aircraft. The Electra was an advanced type of all-metal construction with endplate vertical tail surfaces, retractable tailwheel landing gear and other advanced features. The first machine flew in February 1934 with a pair of Pratt & Whitney Wasp Junior SB radials and, though the type's 10-passenger capacity was thought by many to be too small for airline operators, production totalled 148 aircraft in major variants such as 101 Electra 10-As with 336-kW (450-hp) Wasp Juniors and accommodation for 10 passengers, 18 Electra 10-Bs with 328-kW (440-hp) Wright R-975-E3 Whirlwinds, eight Electra 10-Cs with Wasp SC1s, and 15 Electra 10-Es with 447-kW (600-hp) Wasp S3H1s.

Nothing came of the projected Electra 10-D military transport, but 26 civil Electras were later impressed with the designation C-36A to C to supplement the single XC-36 high-altitude research type, three C-36s with 10-seat accommodation and the single C-37 used by the Militia Bureau. The XR2O and XR3O were single U.S. Navy and U.S. Coast Guard aircraft. The L-12 Electra Junior was a scaled-down version intended mainly for feederlines and business operators, and first flew in June 1936. Some 114 were built in Model 12 and improved Model 12-A forms with accommodation for five passengers, and many of the 73 civil aircraft were later impressed for military service. Here they shared the C-40 designation with the machines built for the U.S. Army Air Corps.

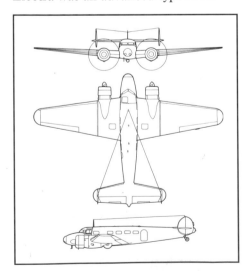

Lockheed L-10A Electra

LOCKHEED L10-A ELECTRA
Role: Passenger transport
Crew/Accommodation: Two, plus up to ten passengers
Power Plant: Two 450 hp Pratt & Whitney R-1340 Wasp Junior SB air-cooled radials
Dimensions: Span 16.76 m (55 ft); length 11.76 m (38.58 ft); wing area 42.59 m² (458.5 sq ft)
Weights: Empty 2,927 kg (6.454 lb); MTOW 4,672 kg (10,300 lb)
Performance: Maximum speed 306 km/h (190 mph) at 1,525 m (5,000 ft); operational ceiling 5,915 m (19,400 ft); range 1,305 km (810 miles)
Load: Up to 816 kg (1,800 lb)

The Lockheed L-10A Electra

SIKORSKY S-42 (United States)

S-42A

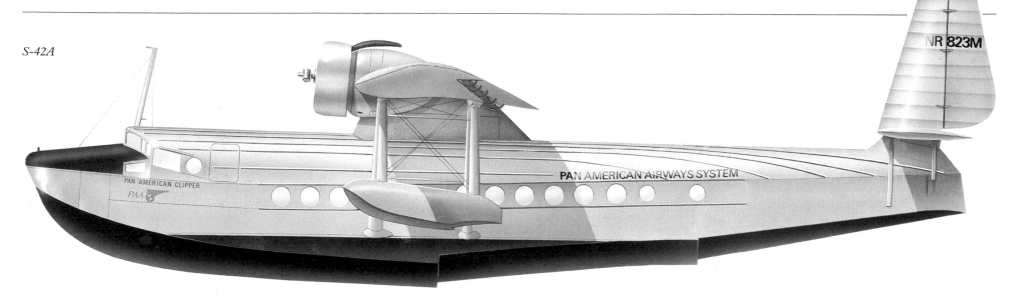

In August 1931, Pan American Airways issued a requirement for a new type of flying boat. This was needed for the transatlantic service that the airline intended to inaugurate, and called for a type carrying a crew of four and at least 12 passengers over a range of 4023 km (2,500 miles) at a cruising speed of 233 km/h (145 mph). At the end of 1932, the airline contracted with Martin for its M-130 and with Sikorsky for its S-

42. The latter was related to the S-40 amphibian to be used on Pan American's routes across the Caribbean and South America.

The S-40 had been based on the S-38 and retained the earlier design's combination of a central pod for 40 passengers and a crew of six, with a twin-boom tail and a parasol wing braced to a 'lower wing' that also supported the stabilizing floats. The

larger and more powerful S-42 was a parasol-winged flying boat with a wholly conventional boat hull, a high-set braced tailplane with twin vertical surfaces, the wing braced directly to the hull and supporting the two stabilizing floats as well as four radial engines on the leading edges. The first S-42 was delivered in August 1934, and the type flew its first service during that month between Miami and Rio de Janeiro. The type was used mainly on the airline's South American and transpacific routes (including pioneering flights across the South Pacific to New Zealand). Total

production was 10 'boats including three S-42s with the 522-kW (700-hp) Pratt & Whitney Hornet S5D1G, three S-42A 'boats with 559-kW (750-hp) Hornet S1EG radials and longer-span wings, and four S-42B 'boats with further refinements and Hamilton Standard constant-speed propellers permitting 907-kg (2,000-lb) increase in maximum take-off weight.

The Sikorsky S-42 was based on a substantial hull

SIKORSKY S-42B
Role: Intermediate/short-range passenger transport flying boat
Crew/Accommodation: Four and two cabin crew, plus up to 32 passengers
Power Plant: Four 800 hp Pratt & Whitney R-1690 Hornet air-cooled radials
Dimensions: Span 35.97 m (118.33 ft); length 20.93 m (68.66 ft); wing area 124.5 m² (1,340 sq ft)
Weights: Empty 9,491 kg (20,924 lb); MTOW 19,504 kg (43,000 lb)
Performance: Cruise speed 225 km/h (140 mph) at 610 m (2,000 ft); operational ceiling 4,878 m (16,000 ft); range 1,207 km (750 miles) with full payload
Load: Up to 3,626 kg (7,995 lb)

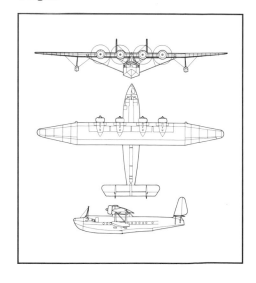

Sikorsky S-42

DOUGLAS DC-3 and Military Derivatives (United States)

DC-3

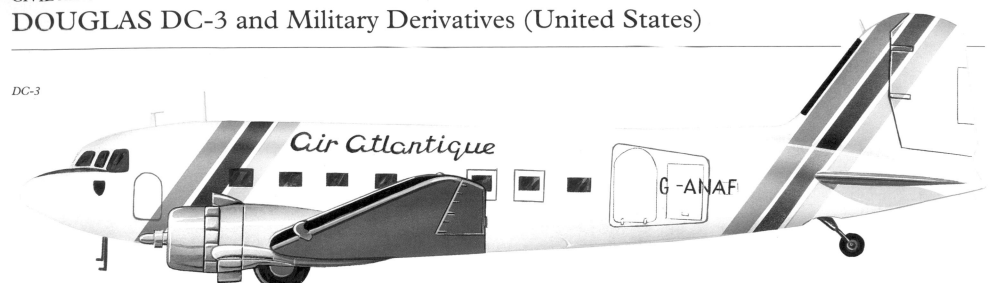

The DC-3 can truly be said to have changed history, for this type opened the era of 'modern' air travel in the mid-1930s, and became the mainstay of the Allies' air transport effort in World War II. Production of 10,349 aircraft was completed in the United States; at least another 2,000 were produced under licence in the U.S.S.R. as the Lisunov Li-2, and 485 were built in Japan as the Showa (Nakajima) L2D.

The series began with the DC-1 that first flew in July 1933 as a cantilever low-wing monoplane of all-metal construction (except fabric-covered control surfaces) with enclosed accommodation and features such as retractable landing gear and trailing-edge flaps. From this prototype was developed the 14-passenger DC-2 production model, which was built in modest numbers but paved the way for the Douglas Sleeper Transport that first flew in December 1935 as an airliner for transcontinental night flights with 16 passengers in sleeper berths. From this was evolved the 24-passenger DC-3. This latter was produced in five series with either the Wright SGR-1820 Cyclone or Pratt & Whitney R-1830 Twin Wasp radial as the standard engine. The type was ordered for the U.S. military as the C-47 Skytrain (U.S. Army) and R4D (U.S. Navy), while the British adopted the name Dakota for aircraft supplied under the terms of the Lend-Lease Act.

The type was produced in a vast number of variants within the new-build C-47, C-53, C-117 and R4D series for transport, paratrooping, and glider-towing duties, while impressed aircraft swelled numbers and also designations to a bewildering degree. After the war, large quantities of these monumentally reliable aircraft were released cheaply to civil operators, and the series can be credited with the development of air transport in most of the world's remoter regions.

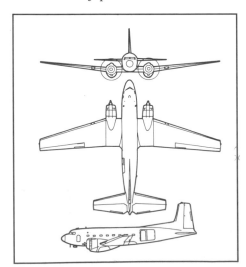

Douglas R4D-8

DOUGLAS DC-3A
Role: Passenger transport
Crew/Accommodation: Three, plus two cabin crew and up to 28 passengers
Power Plant: Two 1,200 hp Pratt & Whitney Twin Wasp S1C3-G air cooled radials
Dimensions: Span 28.96 m (95 ft); length 19.65 m (64.47 ft); wing area 91.7 m² (987 sq ft)
Weights: Empty 7,650 g (16,865 lb); MTOW 11,431 kg (25,200 lb)
Performance: Maximum speed 370 km /h (230 mph) at 2,590 m (8,500 sq ft); operational ceiling 7,070 m (23,200 ft); range 3,420 km (2,125 miles)
Load: Up to 2,350 kg (5,180 lb)

A Douglas DC-3 in service with East African Airways

FOCKE-WULF FW 200 CONDOR (Germany)

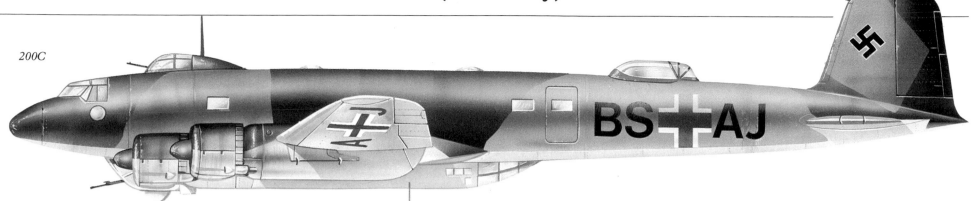

200C

The FW 200 was developed as a transatlantic passenger and mail aircraft that might appeal to Deutsche Lufthansa. The first of three prototypes flew during July 1937 with 652-kW (750-hp) Pratt & Whitney Hornet radials and room for a maximum of 26 passengers in two cabins; the next two aircraft had 537-kW (720-hp) BMW 132G-1 radials. Eight FW 200A pre-production transports were delivered to Lufthansa and single examples to Brazilian and Danish airlines. Four FW 200B airliners with 619-kW (830-hp) BMW 132H engines followed. Some of these later became the personal transports of Nazi VIPs.

The Condor's real claim to fame rests with its FW 200C series, Germany's most important maritime reconnaissance bomber of World War II. This was pioneered by maritime reconnaissance prototype ordered by Japan but never delivered. Ten FW 200C-0 pre-production aircraft were delivered as six maritime reconnaissance and four transport aircraft, and there followed a steadily more diverse sequence of specialized aircraft that were hampered by a structural weakness in the fuselage aft of the wing but nevertheless played a major part in the Atlantic and Arctic convoy campaigns. The FW 200C-1 was a reconnaissance bomber with a 1750-kg (3,757-lb) bomb load, and the FW 200C-2 was an aerodynamically refined variant. The FW 200C-3 had 895-kW (1,200-hp) BMW-Bramo 323R-2 Fafnir radials, structural strengthening, and improved defensive and offensive armament in four subvariants. The main model was the FW 200C-4 with radar, and there were two 11- and 14-passenger transport derivatives of this. The FW 200C-6 was the C-3 modified as launcher for two Henschel Hs 293 anti-ship missiles, while the FW 200C-8 was another missile carrier with improved radar. Total production was 276 aircraft.

The FW 200 V5

FOCKE-WULF FW 200C-3 CONDOR
Role: Long-range maritime reconnaissance bomber
Crew/Accommodation: Seven
Power Plant: Four 1,200 hp BMW Bramo 323 R-2 Fafnir air-cooled radials
Dimensions: Span 32.84 m (107.74 ft); length 23.85 m (78.25 ft); wing area 118 m² (1,290 sq ft)
Weights: Empty 17,000 kg (37,485 lb); MTOW 22,700 kg (50,045 lb)
Performance: Cruise speed 335 km/h (208 mph) at 4,000 m (13,124 ft); operational ceiling 6,000 m (19,685 ft); range 3,560 km (2,211 miles)
Load: One 20 mm cannon, three 13 mm and two 7.9 mm machine guns, plus up to 2,100 kg (4,630 lb) of bombs

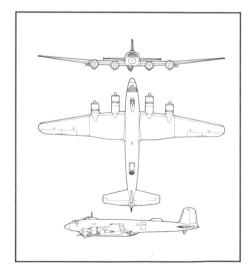

Focke-Wulf FW 200C-1 Condor

BOEING 314 (United States)

Boeing Model 314A

The Model 314 was the greatest flying boat ever built for the civil air transport role. It was designed to the requirement of Pan American Airways for the transatlantic service which the airline had requested from the U.S. Bureau of Air Commerce as early as January 1935. The airline already operated the Martin M-130 and Sikorsky S-42 flying boat airliners, but wanted a 'state-of-the-art' type for this new prestige route. Boeing designed its Model 314 on the basis of the wings and modified tailplane of the Model 294 (XB-15) experimental bomber married to a fuselage accommodating a maximum of 74 passengers in four cabins. The engines were a quartet of 1119-kW (1,500-hp) Wright GR-2600 Double Cyclone radials with fuel for a range of 5633 km (3,500 miles). Some of the fuel was stored in the two lateral sponsons that stabilized the machine on the water and also served as loading platforms.

The first aeroplane flew in June 1938, and the original single vertical tail was soon replaced by twin endplate surfaces that were then supplemented by a central fin based on the original vertical surface but without a movable rudder. The Model 314 entered service in May 1939 as a mailplane, and the first passengers were carried in June of the same year. The six Model 314s were later joined by six Model 314As (including three for the British Overseas Airways Corporation) with more fuel and 1193-kW (1,600-hp) engines driving larger-diameter propellers. Six of the aircraft were used in World War II by the American military in the form of C-98s and B-314s.

Boeing Model 314

BOEING 314A
Role: Long-range passenger flying boat
Crew/Accommodation: Three, plus seven cabin crew and up to 74 passengers
Power Plant: Four 1,600 hp Wright GR-2600 Double Cyclone air-cooled radials
Dimensions: Span 46.33 m (152 ft); length 32.31 m (106 ft); wing area 266.35 m² (2,867 sq ft)
Weights: Empty 22,801 kg (50,268 lb); MTOW 37,422 kg (82,500 lb)
Performance: Cruise speed 295 km/h (183 mph) at sea level; operational ceiling 4,084 m (13,400 ft); range 5,632 km (3,500 miles)
Load: Up to 6,713 kg (14,800 lb)

The Boeing Model 314 was undoubtedly the finest flying boat airliner ever built

DORNIER Do 26 (Germany)

Dornier Do 26

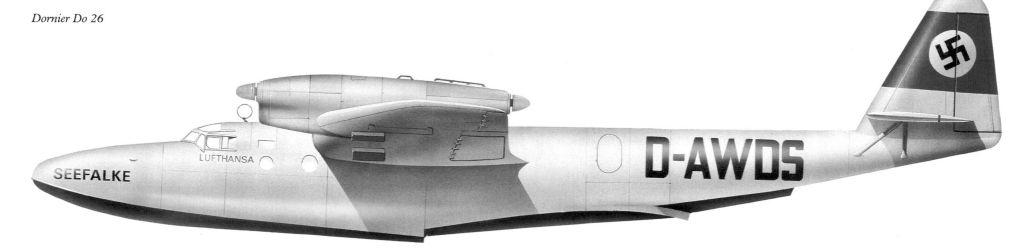

Dornier built many types of flying boat, but the type that offered the cleanest aerodynamics and the most pleasing lines was, without doubt, the Do 26. The type had its origins in the transatlantic mail services developed in the 1930s, and was designed to carry a flight crew of four and 500 kg (1,102 lb) of mail between Lisbon and New York. The all-metal design was based on a slender two-step hull carrying a shoulder-mounted gull wing

and a simple tail unit with braced tailplane halves. The four engines were located in the angles of the gull wings as push/pull tandem pairs in single nacelles that offered minimum resistance. Junkers Jumo 205C/D diesel engines each delivering 447-kW (600-hp) were chosen for their reliability and low specific fuel consumption, and the two pusher engines were installed on mountings that allowed them to be tilted up at

10° at take-off so that the three-blade propeller units were clear of the spray from the hull.

The flying boats were stressed for catapult launches from support ships, and Deutsche Lufthansa ordered three aircraft during 1937. The first of these flew in May 1938, and the two machines completed before the outbreak of World War II were delivered to the airline with the designation Do 26A. These were never used for their intended North Atlantic route, and completed just 18 crossings of the South Atlantic. The third machine was to have been the

Do 26B with provision for four passengers, but was completed as the first of an eventual four Do 26D military flying boats in the long-range reconnaissance and transport roles. These were powered by 522-kW (700-hp) Jumo 205Ea engines, and carried a bow turret armed with a single 20-mm cannon in addition to three 7.92-mm (0.312-in) machine guns in one dorsal and two waist positions.

In the air, the Dornier Do 26 had very clean lines

DORNIER Do 26A
Role: Long-range mail transport
Crew/Accommodation: Four
Power Plant: Four 700 hp Junkers Jumo 205C liquid-cooled diesels
Dimensions: Span 30.00 m (98.42 ft); length 24.60 m (80.71 ft); wing area 120 m² (1,291.67 sq ft)
Weights: Empty 10,700 kg (23,594 lb); MTOW 20,000 kg (44,100 lb)
Performance: Maximum speed 335 km/h (208 mph) at sea level; operational ceiling 4,800 m (15,748 ft); range 9,000 km (5,592 miles) with full payload
Load: Up to 500 kg (1,103 lb)

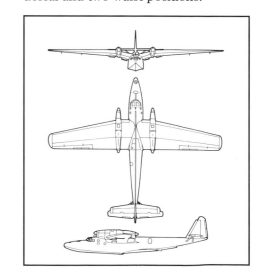

Dornier Do 26 V4

193

LOCKHEED CONSTELLATION Family (United States)

EC-121K

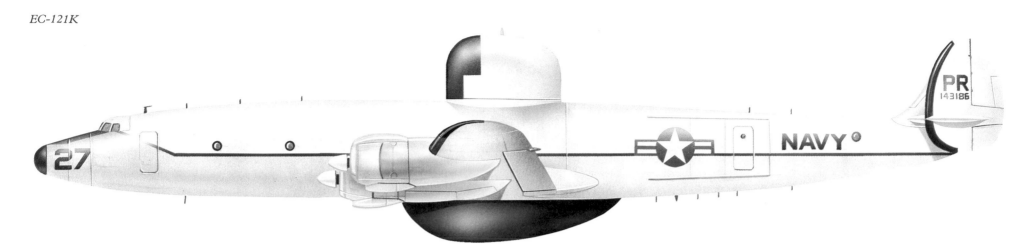

This was surely one of the classic aircraft of all time, developed as an elegant yet efficient airliner but also of great military importance as the basis of the world's first long-range airborne early warning and electronic warfare aircraft. The design was originated in 1939 to provide Pan American Airways and Transcontinental and Western Air with an advanced airliner for use on long-range domestic routes.

The Lockheed design was centred on refined aerodynamics, pressurized accommodation and high power for sustained high-altitude cruising at high speed, and tricycle landing gear was incorporated for optimum field performance and passenger comfort on the ground.

The type first flew in January 1943, and civil production was overtaken by the needs of the military during World War II; the L-49 thus became the U.S. Army's C-69, of which 22 were completed before Japan's capitulation

and the cancellation of military orders. Some aircraft then on the production line were completed as 60-seat L-049 airliners, but the first true civil version was the 81-seat L-649 with 1864-kW (2,500-hp) Wright 749C-18BD-1 radials. Further airliners were the L-749 with additional fuel, the L-1049 Super Constellation with the fuselage lengthened by 5.59 m (18 in 4 in) for the accommodation of 109 passengers, and the L-1649 Starliner with a new, longer-span wing and 2535-kW (3,500-hp) Wright 988TC-

18EA-2 radials fed from increased fuel tankage for true intercontinental range. Production of the series totalled 856 including military variants that included the C-121 transport version of the L-749, the R7O naval transport version of the L-1049, and the PO-1 and VW-2 Warning Star airborne early warning aircraft. These R7O, PO-1 and VW-2 aircraft were later redesignated in the C-121 series that expanded to include a large number of EC-121 electronic warfare aircraft.

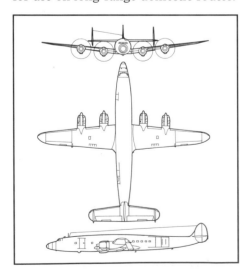

LOCKHEED L749 CONSTELLATION
Role: Long-range passenger transport
Crew/Accommodation: Four and two cabin crew, plus up to 81 passengers
Power Plant: Four 2,500 hp Wright 749C-18BD-1 Double Cyclone air-cooled radials
Dimensions: Span 37.49 m (123 ft); length 29.03 m (95.25 ft); wing area 153.3 m² (1,650 sq ft)
Weights: Empty 27,648 kg (60,954 lb); MTOW 47,627 (105,000 lb)
Performance: Cruise speed 557 km/h (346 mph) at 9,072 m (20,000 ft); operational ceiling 10,886 m (24,000 ft); range 3,219 km/h (2,000 miles) with 6,124 (13,500 lb) payload plus reserves
Load: Up to 6,690 kg (14,750 lb) with 6,124 kg (13,500 lb)

This is an L-049E named Baltimore

CONVAIR CONVAIRLINER Series (United States)

Convair 440

The CV-240 series was developed in the hope of producing a successor to the legendary Douglas DC-3, and though the type was in every respect good, with features such as pressurized accommodation and tricycle landing gear that kept the fuselage level on the ground, it failed to make a decisive impression on a market saturated by the vast number of C-47s released on to the civil market when they became surplus to

military requirements. The spur for the type's original design was a specification issued in 1945 by American Airlines for a modern airliner to supersede the DC-3 and offer superior operating economics.

The CV-110 prototype first flew in July 1946 with 1566-kW (2,100-hp) Pratt & Whitney R-2800-S1C3-G radial engines and pressurized accommodation for 30 passengers. Even before this prototype flew,

however, American Airlines had revised its specification and now demanded greater capacity. It proved a comparatively straightforward task to increase capacity to 40 passengers by lengthening the fuselage by 1.12 m (3 ft 8 in), and in this form the airliner became the CV-240. No prototype was built, the company flying its first production example in March 1947. The CV-240 entered service in June 1948, and 176 were built as airliners. There followed the 44-passenger CV-340 with 1864-kW (2,500-hp) R-2800-CB-16 or 17 engines and a

fuselage stretch of 1.37 m (4 ft 6 in), and finally the similar CV-440 with aerodynamic refinements and high-density seating for 52 passengers. Turboprop conversions were later made to produce the CV-540, 580, 600 and 640 series. Variants for the military were the T-29 USAF crew trainer, the C-131 air ambulance and transport for the USAF, and the R4Y transport for the U.S. Navy.

The CV-440 Metropolitan

CONVAAIR 440 CONVAIRLINER
Role: Short-range passenger transport
Crew/Accommodation: Two, plus up to 52 passengers
Power Plant: Two 2,500 hp Pratt & Whitney R-2800-CB16/17 Double Wasp air-cooled radials
Dimensions: Span 31.10 m (105. 33 ft); length 24.84 m (81.5 ft); wing area 85.47 m² (920 sq ft)
Weights: Empty 15,111 kg (33,314 lb); MTOW 22,544 kg (49,700 lb)
Performance: Cruise speed 465 km/h (289 mph) at 6,096 m (20,000 ft); operational ceiling 7,590 m (24,900 ft); range 459 km (285 miles) with maximum payload
Load: Up to 5,820 kg (12,836 lb)

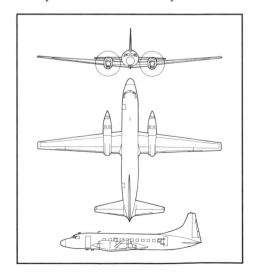

Convair CV-580

AIRSPEED AMBASSADOR (United Kingdom)

AS.57 Ambassador

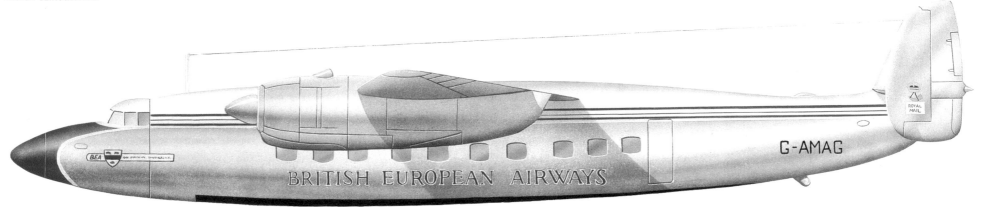

The Ambassador was one of the most elegant aircraft ever built, and resulted from the Brabazon Committee's 1943 recommendation for a 30-seat short/medium-range airliner to be built after World War II within the context of reviving the U.K.'s airline network and civil aircraft production capability. The AS.57 was designed in the closing stages of the war with a high aspect ratio wing set high on the circular-section pressurized fuselage, which ended in an upswept tail unit with triple vertical surfaces; the main units of the tricycle landing gear retracted into the rear part of the two engine nacelles slung under the inner portions of the wing.

The first Ambassador flew in July 1947 and, with two Bristol Centaurus radials, had very promising performance. Just over one year later, an order for 20 aircraft was received from BEA, but the programme was then beset by a number of technical problems during its development. This delayed the Ambassador's service entry until March 1952, and meant that the initial 20-aircraft order was the only one fulfilled as this piston-engined type had been overtaken in performance and operating economics by the turboprop-powered Vickers Viscount. Even so, the 'Elizabethan' class served BEA with great popularity for six years, and the aircraft were then acquired by five other operators. The second and third prototypes went on to important subsidiary careers as test beds for turboprops, such as the Bristol Proteus, the Napier Eland, and the Rolls-Royce Dart and Tyne.

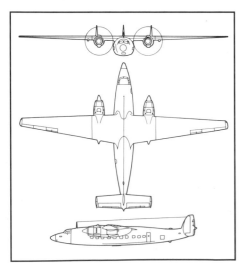

Airspeed AS.57 Ambassador

AIRSPEED AMBASSADOR
Role: Short range passenger transport
Crew/Accommodation: Three, plus three cabin crew and 47/49 passengers
Power Plant: Two 2,700 hp Bristol Centaurus 661 air-cooled radials
Dimensions: Span 35.05 m (115 ft); length 24.69 m (81 ft); wing area 111.48 m² (1,200 sq ft)
Weights: Empty 16,277 kg (35,884 lb); MTOW 23,590 kg (52,000 lb)
Performance: Cruise speed 483 km/h (300 mph) at 6,096 m (20,000 ft); range 1,159 km (720 miles) with maximum payload
Load: Up to 5,285 kg (11,650 lb)

The Airspeed Ambassador was a design of aerodynamic elegance

BOEING STRATOCRUISER and C97 Series (United States)

Stratocruiser

The Model 377 was a commercial transport developed from the C-97 military transport, which itself evolved as the Model 367 to combine the wings, engines, tail unit, landing gear and lower fuselage of the B-29 bomber with a new upper fuselage lobe of considerably larger radius and so create a pressurized 'double-bubble' fuselage. This provided considerable volume, and also provided the Model 377 with its distinctive two-deck layout. The Model 377-10-9 prototype was based on the YC-97A with Pratt & Whitney R-4360 radial engines, and first flew in July 1947.

The aircraft was later delivered to Pan American Airways, which soon became the world's largest operator of the Stratocruiser, with 27 of the 55 aircraft built. Tcn of them were fitted with additional fuel tankage as Super Stratocruisers, and these were suitable for the transatlantic route. At a later date, all Pan Am's aircraft were modified with a General Electric CH-10 turbocharger on each engine for an additional 37.3 kW (50 hp) of power for high-altitude cruise. The other major operator of the type was BOAC, which bought six new aircraft and then found this particular type so useful that it secured another 11 from other operators.

The Stratocruiser was available in Model 377-10-26, -28, -29, -30 and -32 variants with interior arrangemnts that catered for anything between 58 and 112 day passengers, or alternatively 33 night passengers accommodated in five seats as well as 28 upper- and lower-deck berths. The standard accommodation was on the upper deck, with access to the 14-person cocktail lounge on the lower deck via a spiral staircase. The strangest derivative was the Model 377-PG 'Pregnant Guppy' which was developed by Aero Spacelines for the carriage of outsize freight items.

The Aero Spacelines Guppy-201

BOEING 377 STRATOCRUISER
Role: Long range passenger transport
Crew/Accommodation: Five and five cabin crew, plus up to 95 passengers
Power Plant: Four 3,500 hp Pratt & Whitney R-4360B3 Double Wasp air-cooled radials
Dimensions: 43.03 m (141.19 ft); length 33.63 m (110.33 ft); wing area 159.79 m² (1,720 sq ft
Weights: Empty 35,797 kg (78,920 lb); MTOW 67,131 kg (148,000 lb)
Performance: Maximum speed 603 km/h (375 mph) at 7,625 m (25,000 ft); operational ceiling 9,754 m (32,000 ft); range 7,360 km (4,600 miles) with full fuel
Load: Up to 13,608 kg (30,000 lb)

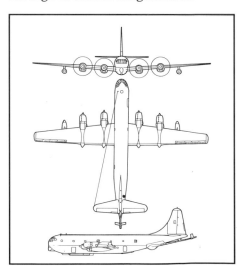

KC-97G Stratofreighter

de HAVILLAND CANADA DHC-2 BEAVER (Canada)

DHC-2 Beaver

The only model to achieve mass production was the Beaver I, of which 1,657 were produced with the ability to carry the pilot and a basic payload of seven passengers or 680 kg (1,500 lb) of freight. No fewer than 980 of these Beaver Is were bought by the U.S. Army and U.S. Air Force with the basic designation L-20 (from 1962 U-6); six were YL-20 service test aircraft, 968 were L-20A production aircraft, and six were L-20B production aircraft with different equipment. One Beaver II was produced with the 410-kW (550-hp) Alvis Leonides radial, and there were also a few Turbo-Beaver IIIs with the 431-kW (578-ehp) Pratt & Whitney Canada PT6A-6/20 turboprop and provision for 10 passengers. Production of this classic type ended in the mid-1960s as de Havilland Canada concentrated on more ambitious aircraft.

The DHC-2 Beaver was designed from 1946 specifically to meet a specification issued by the Ontario Department of Lands and Forests, and resulted in a superb aircraft that fully met the overall Canadian need for a bushplane to replace pre-World War II types such as the Noorduyn Norseman and various Fairchild aircraft. Key features of the design were the rugged reliability of the airframe and single radial engine, STOL performance, operational versatility, and the ability to carry wheels, skis, or floats on the main units of its tailwheel landing gear, whose wide track gave the type exceptional stability on the ground, snow, or water. The DHC-2 was designed round the readily available and thoroughly reliable Pratt & Whitney R-985 Wasp Junior engine, and emerged for its first flight in August 1947 as a braced high-wing monoplane together with sturdy fixed landing gear.

de Havilland Canada DHC-2 Beaver

de HAVILLAND CANADA DHC-2 BEAVER I
Role: Light utility transport
Crew/Accommodation: One, plus up to six passengers
Power Plant: One 450 hp Pratt & Whitney R-985AN-6B Wasp Junior air-cooled radial
Dimensions: 14.62 m (48.00 ft); length 9.23 m (30.25 ft); wing area 23.20 m² (250.00 sq ft)
Weights: Empty 1,294 kg (2,850 lb); MTOW 2,313 kg (5,100 lb)
Performance: Maximum speed 257 km/h (160 mph) at 1,524 m (5,000 ft); operational ceiling 5,486 m (18,000 ft); range 756 km (470 miles) with full payload
Load: Up to 613 kg (1,350 lb)

The de Havilland Canada DHC-2 Beaver

DOUGLAS DC-7 (United States)

Douglas DC-7C

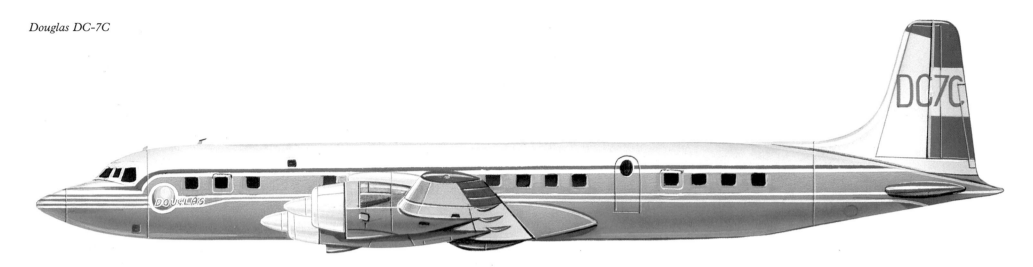

In its C-54 military guise, the DC-4 proved an invaluable long-range transport in World War II. The type's reliability is attested by the fact that only three aircraft were lost in the course of 80,000 or more oceanic crossings. Capacity was limited, however, and Douglas developed to army order the similar but pressurized XC-112A with a longer fuselage. This first flew in February 1946 and was thus too late for the war. With no military orders forthcoming, Douglas

marketed the type as the civil DC-6 that later spawned a military C-118 Liftmaster derivative. And from the DC-6B passenger transport, the company developed the DC-7 to meet an American Airlines' requirement for an airliner to compete with TWA's Lockheed Super Constellation. The DC-7 had a lengthened fuselage, beefed-up landing gear and the same 2424-kW (3,250-hp) Wright R-3350 Turbo-Compound engines as the Super Constellation.

The type first flew in May 1953 and entered production as the DC-6 transcontinental transport, of which 105 were built. To provide transatlantic range, Douglas developed the DC-7B with additional fuel capacity in longer engine nacelles. Production of this variant totalled 112 aircraft, but the model proved to possess only marginally adequate capability in its intended role, and was therefore superseded by the DC-7C, often called the Seven Seas. This became one of the definitive piston-engined airliners, and production

totalled 120. The type had 2535-kW (3,400-hp) R-3350-18EA-1 engines, a fuselage lengthened by 1.02 m (3 ft 4 in) to allow the carriage of 105 passengers and, most importantly, increased fuel capacity in parallel-chord inboard wing extensions that also possessed the additional benefit of moving the engines farther from the fuselage and so reducing cabin noise.

This was the thirtieth Douglas DC-7 to be built

DOUGLAS DC-7C
Role: Long-range passenger transport
Crew/Accommodation: Four and four/five cabin crew, plus up to 105 passengers
Power Plant: Four 3,400 hp Wright R-3350-18EA-1 Turbo-Compound air-cooled radials
Dimensions: Span 38.86 m (127.5 ft); length 34.21 m (112.25 ft); wing area 152.08 m² (1,637 sq ft)
Weights: Empty 33,005 kg (72,763 lb); MTOW 64,864 kg (143,000 lb)
Performance: Cruise speed 571 km/h (355 mph) at 5,791 m (19,000 ft); operational ceiling 6,615 m (21,700 ft); range 7,410 km (4,605 miles) with maximum payload
Load: Up to 10,591 kg (23,350 lb)

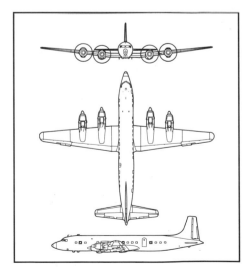

Douglas DC-7C

BRITTEN-NORMAN BN-2 ISLANDER Family (United Kingdom)

BN-2A Islander

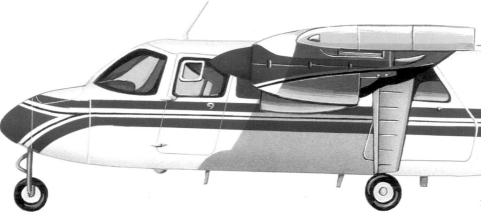

The Islander was designed as a simple feederliner for operators in remoter areas, and was schemed as a low-maintenance type of all-metal construction with fixed tricycle landing gear, a high-set wing mounting the two reliable piston engines, and a slab-sided fuselage with 'wall-to-wall' seating accessed by one door of the starboard side and two on the port side. The first Islander flew in June 1965 with two 157-kW (210-hp) Continental IO-360-B engines. The type was underpowered and had too high a wing loading. This meant the adoption of a wing spanning 1.22 m (4 ft 0 in) more, and a powerplant of two 194-kW (260-hp) Lycoming O-540-E engines. The result was the BN-2 model that entered service in August 1967.

Later variants have been the refined BN-2A and the heavier BN-2B Islander II with an interior of improved design and smaller-diameter propellers for lower cabin noise levels. Options include turbocharged engines and an extended nose providing additional baggage volume. The type has also been produced in Defender and Maritime Defender militarized models with four underwing hardpoints, and options for weapons and/or sensors that can optimize the Defender for a number of important roles in the electronic warfare arena. Turbine power became an increasingly attractive alternative during the Islander's early production career, and the result was the BN-2T Turbine Islander with two 239-kW (320-shp) Allison 250-B17C turboprops. The largest derivative is the BN-2A Mk III Trislander with a third piston engine added at the junction of the enlarged vertical tail and the mid-set tailplane. The Trislander has a lengthened fuselage for 17 passengers.

BN-2A Islander

BRITTEN-NORMAN BN-2B-26
Role: Light short-field utility/passenger transport
Crew/Accommodation: One, plus up to nine passengers
Power Plant: Two 260 hp Lycoming 0-540-E4C5 air-cooled flat-opposed
Dimensions: Span 14.94 m (49 ft); length 12.02 m (35.67 ft); wing area 30.2 m² (325 sq ft)
Weights: Empty 1,866 kg (4,114 lb); MTOW 2,993 kg (6,600 lb)
Performance: Cruise speed 257 km/h (160 mph) at 2,140 m (7,000 ft); operational ceiling 3,597 m (11,800 ft); range 1,251 km (675 naut. miles) with full payload
Load: Up to 755 kg (1,665 lb)

The Britten-Norman BN-2 Trislander

VICKERS VISCOUNT (United Kingdom)

Viscount 800

The Type 630 Viscount was the world's first turboprop-powered airliner to enter service. The aircraft originated as the VC2 to meet a requirement for a 24-seat short-medium-range airliner with a turboprop powerplant. The specification was issued during World War II by the Brabazon Committee that was charged with assessing the U.K.'s post-war civil air transport needs, and the prototype Type 630

was designed as a 32-passenger airliner of attractive design and orthodox construction based on a cantilever low-wing monoplane layout with retractable tricycle landing gear.

The first example flew in July 1948 with four 738-kW (990-shp) Rolls-Royce Dart RDa.1 Mk 502 turboprops in slim wing-mounted nacelles. The type had too low a capacity to attract any real commercial interest, but was then revised in

accordance with the requirement of British European Airways for an airliner with pressurized accommodation for between 40 and 59 passengers. This Type 700 became the first production version with a powerplant of four 1044-kW (1,400-shp) Dart Mk 506s or, in the Type 700D, four 1193-kW (1,600-shp) Dart Mk 510s. These latter engines also powered the Type 800 with a lengthened fuselage for between 65 and 71 passengers. The Type 810 was structurally strengthened for operation at higher weights, and was powered by 1566-kW (2,100-shp) Dart RDa.7/1

Mk 525s. Total production was eventually 444 aircraft, and the type made the world's first turbine-powered commercial airline flight on 29 July, 1950 at the beginning of a two-week experimental service between London and Paris. The Viscount was sold in many parts of the world, and made good though not decisive inroads into the lucrative American market.

A Vickers Viscount 785 of Alitalia

VICKERS VISCOUNT 810
Role: Short-range passenger transport
Crew/Accommodation: Three and two cabin crew, plus up to 71 passengers
Power Plant: Four 2,100 shp Rolls-Royce Dart R.Da 7/1 Mk. 525 turboprops
Dimensions: Span 28.5 m (93.76 ft); length 26.11 m (85.66 ft); wing area 89.46 m² (963 sq ft)
Weights: Empty 18,753 kg (41,565 lb); MTOW 32,886 kg (72,500 lb)
Performance: Maximum speed 563 km/h (350 mph) at 6,100 m (20,000 ft); operational ceiling 7,620 m (25,000 ft); range 2,775 km (1,725 miles) with maximum payload
Load: Up to 6,577 kg (14,500 lb)

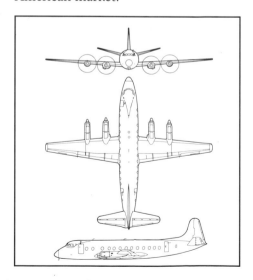

Vickers Viscount 800

201

BRISTOL BRITANNIA (United Kingdom)

Britannia

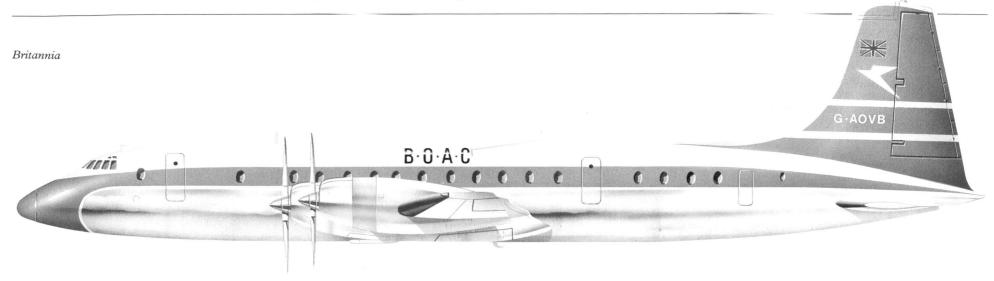

Probably the finest turboprop airliner ever built, the Britannia was so delayed by engine problems that it was overtaken by jet-powered airliners and thus failed to fulfil its great commercial promise. The type was one of eight types proposed by five companies to meet a BOAC requirement shortly after the end of World War II for a Medium-Range Empire airliner with pressurized accommodation for 36 passengers. The Type 175's proposed powerplant of four Bristol Centaurus radials was more than adequate for the specified load, so the design was enlarged to 48-passenger capacity. The Ministry of Supply ordered three prototypes, but the design was further amended and, when the first machine flew in August 1952, it had provision for 90 passengers on the power of four 2088-kW (2,800-ehp) Bristol Proteus turboprops. This paved the way for the first production model, the Britannia Series 100 which entered service in 1957 with 2819-kW (3,780-ehp) Proteus 705s; 15 of these were built for BOAC.

There followed eight Britannia Series 300s with the fuselage lengthened by 3.12 m (10 ft 3 in) for a maximum of 133 passengers carried over transatlantic routes, and 32 Britannia Series 310s with 3072-kW (4,120-ehp) Proteus 755s and greater fuel capacity. Only two were built of the final Britannia Series 320 with 3318-kW (4,450-ehp) Proteus 765s, while production of the Britannia for the civil market in total numbered just 60 aircraft. The last variant was the Britannia Series 250 modelled on the Series 310 but intended for RAF use as 20 Britannia C.Mk 1s and three C.Mk 2s. Exactly the same basic airframe was used by Canadair as the core of two aircraft, the CL-28 Argus maritime patroller with 2535-kW (3,400-hp) Wright R-3350-EA1 Turbo-Compound piston engines, together with the CL-44 long-range transport with 4273-kW (5,730-ehp) Rolls-Royce Tyne 515 Mk 10 turboprops.

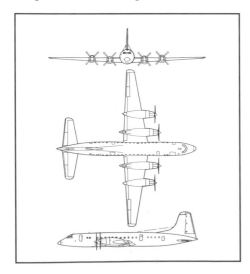

Bristol Britannia 320

BRISTOL BRITANNIA 310 Series
Role: Long-range passenger transport
Crew/Accommodation: Four, four cabin crew and up to 139 passengers
Power Plant: Four 4,120 ehp Bristol Siddeley Proteus 755 turboprops
Dimensions: Span 43.37 m (142.29 ft); length 37.87 m (124.25 ft); wing area 192.78 m² (2,075 sq ft)
Weights: Empty 37,438 kg (82,537 lb); MTOW 83,915 kg (185,000 lb)
Performance: Cruise speed 660 km/h (410 mph) at 6,401 m (21,000 ft); operational ceiling 9,200+ m (30,184 ft); range 6,869 km (4,268 miles) with maximum payload
Load: Up to 15,830 kg (34,900 lb)

A Bristol Britannia 253F

FOKKER F.27 FRIENDSHIP and 50 (Netherlands)

F.27 Mk 200 Friendship

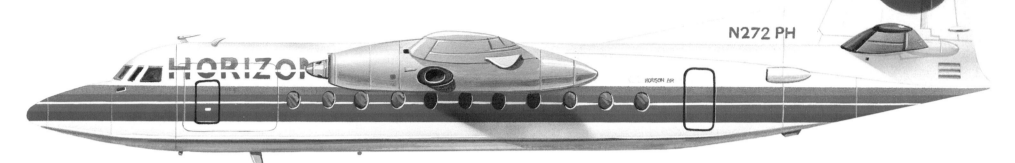

After World War II Fokker sought to recapture a slice of the airliner market with a type matching the best of its classic interwar airliners. After long deliberation, the company fixed on a short/medium-range type powered by two Rolls-Royce Dart turboprops on the high-set wing. The first of two prototypes flew in November 1955. The Friendship entered service in December 1958 as the F.27 Mk 100 with two 1279-kW (1,715-shp) Dart RDa.6 Mk 514-7 engines for the

carriage of between 40 and 52 passengers, and was followed by successively upgraded models such as the F.27 Mk 200 with 1529-kW (2,050-shp) Dart RDA.7 Mk 532-7 engines, the F.27 Mks 300 and 400 Combiplane derivatives of the Mks 100 and 200 with reinforced cabin floors and a large cargo door on the port side of the forward fuselage. The F.27 Mk 500 introduced a fuselage lengthened by 1.50 m (4 ft 11 in) for between 52 and 60 passengers. The

last variant was the F.27 Mk 600 convertible variant of the Mk 400 without the reinforced floor.

Military variants are the F.27 Mks 400M and 500M Troopship, and specialized maritime reconnaissance models are the unarmed F.27 Maritime and armed F.27 Maritime Enforcer. F.27 production ended with the 579th aircraft, which was delivered in 1987. The basic Mks 100, 200 and 300 were licence-built in the United States as the Fairchild F-27A, B and C to the extent of 128 aircraft, and the same company also produced a variant with its fuselage stretched by 1.83 m

(6 ft 0 in) as the FH-227, of which 79 were produced.

The durability of the Friendship's basic design is attested by the recent development of the Fokker 50, a thoroughly updated 58-passenger version with 1603-kW (2,150-shp) Pratt & Whitney Canada PW124 turboprops driving six-blade propellers. The type first flew in definitive form during February 1987.

A Fokker F.27 Mk 600R Friendship

FOKKER 50
Role: Short-range passenger transport
Crew/Accommodation: Two and two cabin crew, plus up to 58 passengers
Power Plant: Two 2,250 shp Pratt & Whitney PW 125B turboprops
Dimensions: Span 29 m (95.15 ft); length 25.25 m (82.83 ft); wing area 70 m² (754 sq ft)
Weights: Empty 12,741 kg (28,090 lb); MTOW 18,990 kg (41,865 lb)
Performance: Cruise speed 500 km/h (270 knots) at 6,096 m (20,000 ft); operational ceiling 7,620 m (25,000 ft); range 1,125 km (607 naut. miles) with 50 passengers
Load: Up to 5,262 kg (11,600 lb)

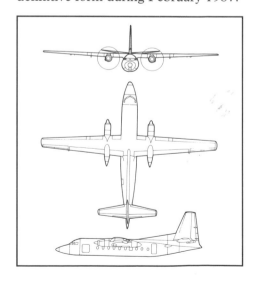

F.27 Mk 200 Friendship

203

ANTONOV An-22 ANTHEUS 'COCK' (U.S.S.R.)

AN-22 'Cock'

In its time the An-22 Antei (Antheus) was the world's largest aircraft, and was designed for the twin tasks of military heavy transport and support for the resources exploitation industry in Siberia. The specification for the type was issued in 1962, and the first example flew in February 1965. The type was first revealed in the West, where it had the NATO reporting name 'Cock' during the Paris air show of June 1965. At that time it was reported that the design could also be developed as a 724-passenger airliner, but this proposal came to nothing. Given the type's highly specialized role and size, it is not surprising that production was limited to only about 100 aircraft, all completed by 1974.

Keynotes of the design are four potent turboprops driving immense contra-rotating propeller units, and an upswept tail unit with twin vertical surfaces at about three-fifths span. The 14-wheel landing gear allows operations into and out of semi-prepared airstrips, and comprises a twin-wheel nose unit and two six-wheel units as main units; the latter are three twin-wheel units in each of the two lateral sponson fairings that provide an unobstructed hold. The upswept tail allows in the rear-fuselage a hydraulically operated ramp/door arrangement for the straight-in loading of items as large as tanks or complete missiles. The hold is 33.0 m (108 ft 3 in) long and 4.4 m (14 ft 5 in) wide and high, and has four overhead travelling gantries as well as two 2500-kg (5,511-lb) capacity winches for the handling of freight.

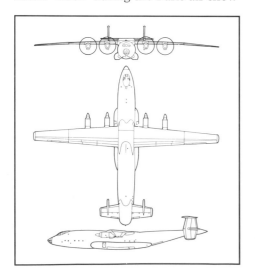

Antonov An-22 'Cock'

ANTONOV An-22 ANTHEUS 'COCK'
Role: Long-range freight transport
Crew/Accommodation: Five, plus up to 29 passengers/troops in upper cabin
Power Plant: Four 15,000 shp Kuznetsov NK 12MA turboprops
Dimensions: Span 64.4 m (211.29 ft); length 57.8 m (189.63 ft); wing area 345 m² (3,713.6 sq ft)
Weights: Empty 114,000 kg (251,327 lb); MTOW 250,000 kg (551,156 lb)
Performance: Cruise speed 679 km/h (366 knots) at 8,000 m (26,247 ft); operational ceiling 10,000 m (32,808 ft); range 5,000 km (2,698 naut. miles) with maximum payload
Load: Up to 80,000 kg (176,370 lb)

An Antonov An-22 of the Soviet civil operator Aeroflot

EMBRAER EMB-110 BANDEIRANTE (Brazil)

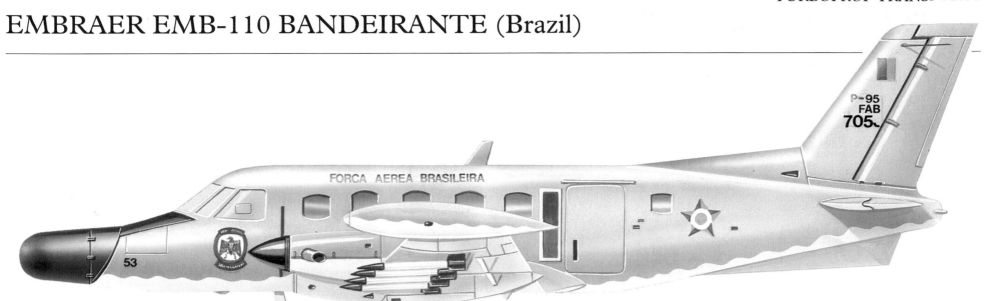

The Empresa Brasileira de Aeronautics SA was created in 1969 to promote the development of an indigenous Brazilian aircraft industry, and began operation in January 1970. The company builds Piper aircraft under licence, but has also developed and produced a number of interesting light transports. The most successful of these has been the EMB-110 Bandeirante (pioneer), whose design origins lie in the period before EMBRAER's creation. The EMB-110 was evolved under the leadership of Max Holste as a utility light transport to meet the multi-role requirement of the Brazilian ministry of aeronautics, and first flew in October 1968 in the form of a YC-95 prototype.

The Bandeirante is of all-metal construction and of typical light transport configuration with low-set cantilever wings, a conventional fuselage and tail unit, retractable tricycle landing gear, and two wing-mounted Pratt & Whitney Canada PT6A turboprop engines. The accommodation varies with model and role, but the EMB-110P2 is typical of the series with seating for 21 passengers. The type has been produced in a number of civil variants such as the 15-passenger EMB-110C feederliner, the 18-passenger EMB-110P export model, the EMB-110P higher-capacity model with a fuselage stretch of 0.85 m (2 ft 9.5 in) in EMB-110P1 mixed or all-cargo and EMB-110P2 passenger subvariants, and the EMB-110P/41 higher-weight model in EMB-110P1/41 quick-change and EMB-110P2/41 passenger subvariants. Large-scale production for the Brazilian Air Force resulted in a number of C-95 utility transport, R-95 survey, SC-95 air ambulance and EMB-110P1SAR search-and-rescue models. There is also an EMB-111 coastal patrol version operated as the P-95 with search radar, a tactical navigation system, wingtip tanks and provision for underwing weapons.

An EMBRAER EMB-110P1 Bandeirante

EMBRAER EMB-110P1A BANDEIRANTE
Role: Short-range passenger/cargo transport
Crew/Accommodation: Two, plus up to 19 passengers
Power Plant: Two 750 shp Pratt & Whitney PT6A-34 turboprops
Dimensions: Span 15.32 m (50.26 ft); length 15.08 m (49.47 ft); wing area 29.1 m² (313 sq ft)
Weights: Empty 3,630 kg (8,010 lb); MTOW 5,900 kg (13,010 lb)
Performance: Cruise speed 393 km/h (244 mph) at 2,438 m (8,000 ft); operational ceiling 5,791 m (19,000 ft); range 371 km (230 miles) with 19 passengers
Load: Up to 1,565 kg (3,450 lb) passenger version, or 1,724 kg (3,800 lb) cargo-carrier

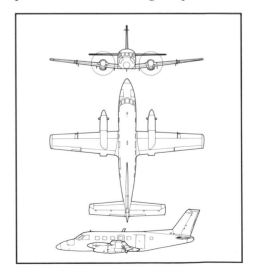

EMB-110 Bandeirante

CASA C-212 AVIOCAR (Spain)

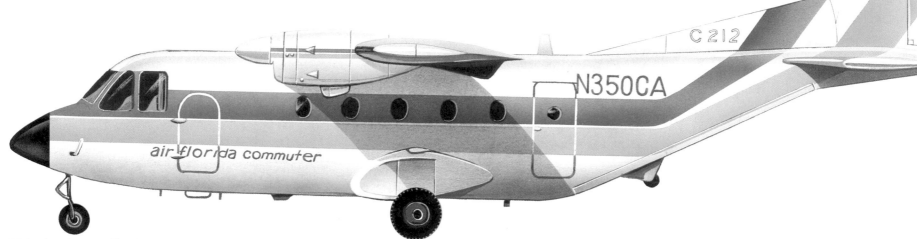

C-212 Aviocar

This simple yet effective light transport aircraft was developed to replace the Spanish air force's miscellany of obsolete transports. CASA conceived the type with the civil as well as military markets in mind, and thus schemed the type with STOL capability, highly cost-effective operation, great reliability, and simple maintenance. The resulting Aviocar is of all-metal construction and of typical airlifter configuration with an upswept tail unit above a rear ramp/door that provides straight-in access to the rectangular-section hold. This last measures 5.0 m (16 ft 5 in) in length, 2.0 m (6 ft 7 in) in width and 1.7 m (5 ft 7 in) in height. The tricycle landing gear is fixed, and the attachment of the main units to external blister fairings leaves the hold entirely unobstructed.

The first C-212 first flew in March 1971, and it soon became clear that CASA had designed the right type as orders arrived from third-world civil operators as well as air forces. Spanish production has been complemented by Indonesian construction by Nurtanio. The basic variants are the C-212A military transport with a payload of 2000 kg (4,409 lb) including 19 passengers or 15 paratroops, the C-212-5 (later C-212 Series 100) civil type with 579-kW (776-shp) Garrett TPE5331-5-251 turboprops, the heavier C-212-10 (later C-212 Series 200) with TPE331-10-501Cs and a hold increased in length to 6.5 m (21 ft 4 in) for a payload of 2770 kg (6,107 lb) including 28 passengers or 24 troops, and the still heavier C-212 Series 300 with 671-kW (900-shp) TPE331-10R-512Cs driving Dowty rather than Hartzell propellers, with the span increased to 20.4 m (66 ft 11 in), and in addition to this, a payload of 2820 kg (6,217 lb).

CASA C-212 AVIOCAR Series 200
Role: Short, rough field-going utility transport
Crew/Accommodation: Two, plus up to 24 troops
Power Plant: Two 900 shp Garrett AiResearch TPE 331-10-501C turboprops
Dimensions: Span 19 m (62.33 ft); length 15.2 m (49.75 ft); wing area 40 m² (430.6 sq ft)
Weights: Empty 4,115 kg (9,072 lb); MTOW 7,450 kg (16,424 lb)
Performance: Cruise speed 353 km/h (190 knots) at 3,048 m (10,000 ft); operational ceiling 8,534 m (28,000 ft); range 760 km (410 naut. miles) with maximum payload
Load: Up to 2,250 kg (4,960 lb)

C-212 Aviocar

A CASA C-212 Aviocar

SHORTS 360 (United Kingdom)

Shorts 360

After the success of its SC.7 Skyvan series, Shorts decided to produce a larger and more refined derivative as the SD3-30 that then became the Shorts 330 with retractable tricycle landing gear and accommodation for 30 passengers. The type entered service in August 1976, and has proved most successful. Even so, the company appreciated that a larger-capacity type would broaden the series' market appeal, and the result was the Shorts 360. Market research indicated that capacity 20 per cent greater than that of the Shorts 330 was really desirable, and it was in 36-passenger configuration that the first Shorts 360 flew in June 1981 on the power of two 990-kW (1,327-shp) Pratt & Whitney Canada PT6A-65R turboprops.

The Shorts 360 is similar to its predecessor in being a high-wing monoplane with aerofoil-section lifting struts that brace the high aspect ratio wing to the sponsons that accommodate the main units of the retractable tricycle landing gear, but differs in having a single vertical tail in place of twin endplate surfaces, the lengthening of the forward fuselage by 0.91 m (3 ft 0 in) to allow the incorporation of an extra three-seat passenger row, and revision of the rear fuselage to improve aerodynamic form and permit the addition of another extra three-seat passenger row.

The Shorts 360 entered service in December 1982, and the type's only major improvement to date has been the introduction from 1986 of 1063-kW (1,424-shp) PT6A-65AR engines to produce the Shorts 360 Advanced. The maximum passenger payload is 3184 kg (7,020 lb), but in the type's alternative freight configuration the payload is somewhat increased to 3765 kg (8,300 lb).

SHORTS 360-300

Role: Short range passenger transport/ freighter

Crew/Accommodation: Two and two cabin crew, plus up to 37 passengers

Power Plant: Two 1,424 shp Pratt & Whitney Canada PT6A-67R turboprops

Dimensions: Span 22.80 m (74.79 ft); length 21.58 m (70.94 ft); wing area 42.18 m² (454.00 sq ft)

Weights: Empty 7,870 kg (17,350 lb); MTOW 12,292 kg (27,100 lb)

Performance: Maximum speed 401 km/h (216 knots) at 3,048 m (10,000 ft); operational ceiling 3,930 m (12,900 ft); range 1,178 km (732 miles) with 36 passengers

Load: Up to 4,536 kg (10,000 lb) for freighter version.

Note: operational ceiling artificially restricted for passenger comfort

Shorts 360

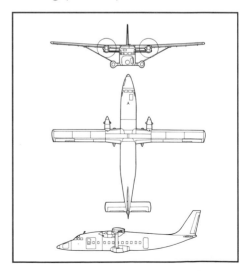

A Shorts 360-300

CESSNA CARAVAN I (United States)

Caravam I

The Model 208 Caravan can be considered as Cessna's replacement for the elderly Model 185 Skywagon in the light utility transport role. The Model 208 offers its operators considerably greater capacity and performance, combined with more advanced features such as tricycle landing gear and the turboprop powerplant that runs off fuel that can be obtained anywhere in the world and also offers great reliability and better operating economics.

The first Model 208 flew in December 1982, and the first deliveries of production aircraft followed in 1985. The type can operate on sturdy wheeled or float landing gear, and is otherwise a conventional high-wing monoplane with a fuselage of slightly odd appearance because the fuselage has been optimized for the freight role in its long parallel upper and lower lines and large loading door in the side at easy loading/unloading height.

Current versions are the Model 208 Caravan, the Model 208A Cargomaster freighter with underfuselage cargo pannier and no fuselage windows, and the Model 208B Super Cargomaster with a 1.22-m (4-ft) fuselage stretch for greater capacity. The type has proved successful in several roles. There is a U-27 military variant, and Cessna now promotes an armed model for more overt military applications.

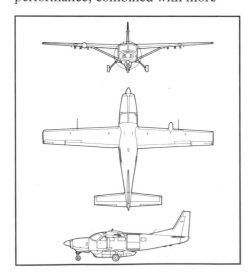

Cessna Caravan I

CESSNA 208 CARAVAN I
Role: Commercial and military short field-capable utility transport
Crew/Accommodation: One, plus up to 14 passengers
Power Plant: One 600 shp Pratt & Whitney Canada PT6A-114 turboprop
Dimensions: Span 15.88 m (52.08 ft); length 11.46 m (37.58 ft); wing area 25.96 m² (279.4 sq ft)
Weights: Empty 1,742 kg (3,800 lb); MTOW 3,311 kg (7,300 lb)
Performance: Cruise speed 341 km/h (184 knots) at 3,048 m (10,000 ft); operational ceiling 8,410 m (27,600 ft); range 2,362 km (1,275 naut. miles) with full payload
Load: Up to 1,360 kg (3,000 lb)

A Cessna Caravan I of the small-package carrier Federal Express

de HAVILLAND CANADA DHC-8 DASH 8 (Canada)

DHC-8-100 Dash 8

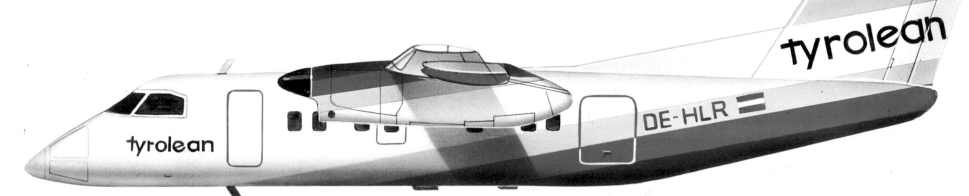

The DHC-8 was developed to the same basic operating philosophy as the 50-passenger DHC-7, but was sized for 40 passengers in the commuterliner role. As with other de Havilland Canada transports, STOL capability was a primary consideration, and the type was made attractive to potential operators by its fuel-economical turboprop engines driving propellers of large diameter, which turn slowly and so generate considerably less noise than fast-turning propellers of smaller diameter. A feature of the powerplant is the safety system that in the event of an engine failure automatically increases the output of the surviving engine to 1491 kW (2,000 shp). Other features are a large cargo-loading door in the port side of the fuselage aft of the wing, retractable tricycle landing gear with twin-wheel main units, and a T-tail keeping the tailplane well clear of the disturbed airflow behind the wings and propellers.

The first of four pre-production aircraft flew in June 1983. The type entered revenue-earning service in November 1984, and the baseline variant is the Dash 8 Series 100 with 1432-kW (1,800-shp) Pratt & Whitney Canada PW120A turboprops. In its basic commuterliner layout, this carries a crew of three (two flight crew and one cabin attendant) and between 36 and 40 passengers. An alternative layout is for between 17 and 24 passengers in the corporate transport layout. The higher-weight Dash 8 Series 200 remained a project, so the only other variant to have entered production (after Boeing's January 1986 purchase of the company) is the Dash 8 Series 300 with span increased by 1.52 m (5 ft 0 in) and length by 3.43 m (11 ft 3 in) to allow a maximum 56 passengers on two 1776-kW (2,380-shp) PW123 turboprops.

A de Havilland Canada DHC-8 Series 300

---

de HAVILLAND CANADA DHC-8 DASH 8 Series 100

Role: Short field-capable passenger transport

Crew/Accommodation: Two, plus up to 39 passengers

Power Plant: Two 1,800 shp Pratt & Whitney Canada PW 120A turboprops

Dimensions: Span 25.91 m (85 ft); length 22.25 m (73 ft); wing area 54.4 m² (585 sq ft)

Weights: Empty 9,978 kg (21,998 lb); MTOW 15,649 kg (34,500 lb)

Performance: Maximum speed 554 km/h (265 knots) at 7,620 m (25,000 ft); operational ceiling 7,620 m (25,000 ft); range 1,019 km (633 miles) with full payload

Load: Up to 4,128 kg (9,100 lb)

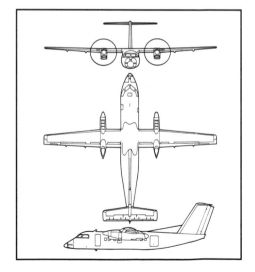

de Havilland Canada DHC-8

EMBRAER EMB-120 BRASILIA (Brazil)

EMB-120 Brasilia

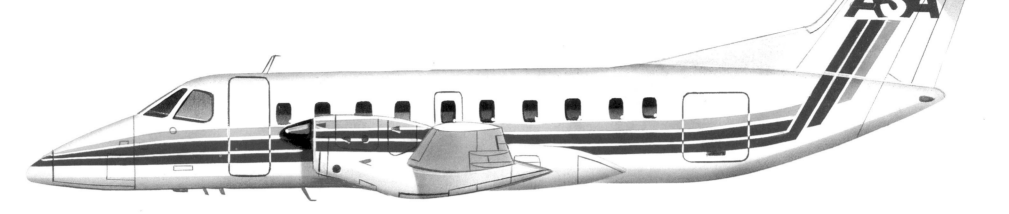

The Brazilian government and EMBRAER were both highly encouraged by the EMB-110's penetration of the world market for commuterliners and feederliners. From this success, there emerged plans for an EMB-12X series of three pressurized types sharing a fuselage of common diameter but different lengths. Of these only the EMB-121 Xingu business transport actually entered production. In September 1979 EMBRAER decided to move a step further up the size ladder with a pressurized 30-seat regional airliner, and this retained the overall configuration of the earlier 20-passenger EMB-120 Araguaia.

The type was designated EMB-120 and later named Brasilia, and metal was cut for the first aircraft in May 1981. Six aircraft were produced for the test and certification programmes, and the first machine flew in July 1983 as a low-wing monoplane with a circular-section fuselage, a T-tail, retractable tricycle landing gear, and a powerplant of two wing-mounted 1118-kW (1,500-shp) Pratt & Whitney Canada PW115 turboprop engines. Though designed as a regional airliner with 30 seats, the Brasilia has a large cargo door in the port side of the rear fuselage, and is also available in freight and mixed-traffic versions, the former offering a payload of 3470-kg (7,650-lb) and the latter the capacity for 26 passengers and 900-kg (1,984-lb) of cargo. The Brasilia has an airstair door on the port side of the forward fuselage to reduce demand on external support at small airports, and for the same reason is also offered with a Garrett auxiliary power unit in the tail cone as an option. Later aircraft are powered by a pair of 1343-kW (1,800-shp) PW118 turboprops for improved performance at higher weights.

EMBRAER EMB-120 BRASILIA
Role: Short range passenger transport
Crew/Accommodation: Two and one cabin crew, plus up to 30 passengers
Power Plant: Two 1,600 shp Pratt & Whitney PW115 turboprops
Dimensions: Span 19.78 m (64.90 ft); length 20.00 m (65.62 ft); wing area 39.43 m² (424.42 sq ft)
Weights: Empty 6,878 kg (15,163 lb); MTOW 11,500 kg (25,353 lb)
Performance: Maximum speed 556 km/h (300 knots) at 7,620 m (25,000 ft); operational ceiling 9,083 m (29,800 ft); range 1,751 km (945 naut. miles) with 30 passengers
Load: Up to 3,470 kg (7,650 lb)

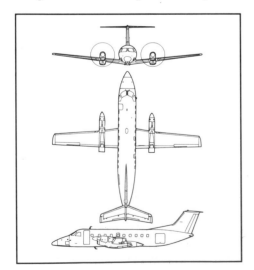

EMB-120 Brasilia

An EMBRAER EMB-120 Brasilia of the German carrier DLT

SAAB 340 (Sweden)

Saab 340

In January 1980, Saab and Fairchild agreed to undertake the collaborative design and development of a turboprop-powered small transport for the civil market. This was initially known as the Saab-Fairchild SF-340 and planned in the form of a low-wing monoplane featuring a wing of high aspect ratio with long-span slotted flaps and retractable tricycle landing gear with twin wheels on each unit. Construction is of the all-metal type, with selective use of composite materials in some areas, and while Saab was responsible for the fuselage, assembly and flight testing, Fairchild built the wings, tail unit and nacelles. The type was planned as a passenger transport with provision for 34 passengers in addition to a flight crew of two or three plus one flight attendant, but the cabin was schemed from the beginning for easy completion in the passenger/freight or alternative 16-passenger executive/corporate transport roles.

The first machine flew in January 1983 with 1215-kW (1,630-hp) General Electric CT7-5A turboprops, and the certification programme was undertaken by the first production machine in addition to the two prototypes. Certification was achieved in May 1984, and the type entered service in the following month. In November 1985, Fairchild indicated its unwillingness to continue with the programme, which thereupon became a Saab responsibility. Fairchild continued as a subcontractor until 1987, giving Saab time to complete additional construction facilities in Sweden. Early aircraft are limited to a maximum take-off weight off 11,794 kg (26,000 lb). Later machines have CT7-5A2 turboprops driving larger-diameter propellers, and are cleared for maximum take-off weight of 12,371 kg (27,275 lb) with a maximum payload of 3531 kg (7,785 lb).

A Saab 340 of the American operator Northwest Airlines

SAAB 340
Role: Short range passenger transport
Crew/Accommodation: Two and one cabin crew, plus up to 37 passengers
Power Plant: Two 1,870 shp General Electric CT7-9B turboprops
Dimensions: Span 21.44 m (70.33 ft); length 19.73 m (64.75 ft); wing area 41.81 m² (450.00 sq ft)
Weights: Empty 8,035 kg (17,715 lb); MTOW 12,927 kg (28,500 lb)
Performance: Maximum speed 527 km/h (285 knots) at 5,486 m (18,000 ft); operational ceiling 7,620 m (25,000 ft); range 1,813 km (980 naut. miles) with 35 passengers
Load: Up to 3,758 kg (8,285 lb)

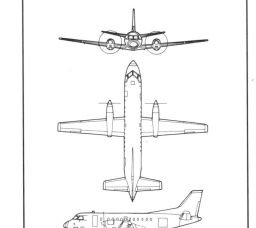

Saab 340

de HAVILLAND D.H.106 COMET (United Kingdom)

D.H.106 Comet 4

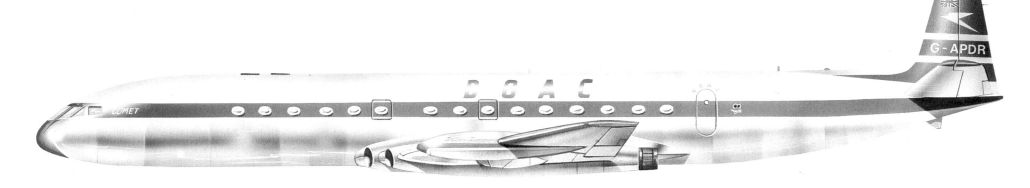

The Comet was the world's first turbojet-powered airliner, but failed to secure the financial advantages of this potentially world-beating lead because of technical problems. The type was planned from 1944 in response to the far-sighted Type IV specification resulting from the Brabazon Committee's wartime deliberations into the shape of British air transport needs after the end of World War II. It

first flew in July 1949 with four de Havilland Ghost 50 centrifugal-flow turbojets. The type entered service in January 1952 as the Comet 1 with multi-wheel bogies rather than the two prototypes' single wheels on the main landing gear units. The Comet 1 was used initially as a freighter, and only later as a passenger-carrying airliner, and deliveries to the British Overseas Airways Corporation totalled nine between January 1951 and September 1952; there followed 10 Comet 1As with greater fuel capacity.

One crash in 1953 and two in 1954 resulted in the type's grounding, and it

was then established that fatigue failures at the corners of the rectangular window frames were to blame. Rounded windows were introduced on the 44-passenger Comet 2, of which 12 were built with a 0.91-m (3-ft) fuselage stretch and axial-flow Rolls-Royce Avon 503 engines, but these BOAC aircraft were diverted to the RAF as 70-passenger Comet C.Mk 2s. The Comet 3 was precursor to a transatlantic version

that entered service as the 78-seat Comet 4 with Avon 524 engines in May 1958, when the conceptually more advanced Boeing Model 707 and Douglas DC-8 were already coming to the fore of the market. Some 27 were built. Derivatives were the 18 shorter-range Comet 4Bs with a shorter wing but longer fuselage for 99 passengers, and the 29 Comet 4Cs combining the wing of the Comet 4 with the Comet 4B's fuselage.

de Havilland D.H.106 Comet 4

de HAVILLAND D.H.106 COMET 4
Role: Intermediate range passenger transport
Crew/Accommodation: Three, plus four cabin crew and up to 78 passengers
Power Plant: Four 4,649 kgp (10,250 lb s.t.) Rolls-Royce Avon RA29 turbojets
Dimensions: Span 35 m (114.83 ft); length 33.99 m (111.5 ft); wing area 197 m² (2,121 sq ft)
Weights: Empty 34,200 kg (75,400 lb); MTOW 72,575 kg (160,000 lb)
Performance: Cruise speed 809 km/h (503 mph) at 12,802 m (42,000 ft); operational ceiling 13,411+ m (44,000+ ft); range 5,190 km (3,225 miles) with full load
Load: Up to 9,206 kg (20,286 lb)

This is a Comet 4B of British European Airways

BOEING 707 and 720 (United States)

Boeing 707-300C

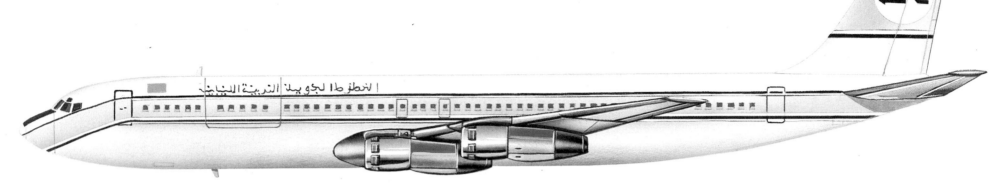

Though preceded into service by the de Havilland Comet, the Model 707 must rightly be regarded as the world's first effective long-range jet transport. In an exceptionally bold technical and commercial move, Boeing decided duirng August 1952 to develop, as a private venture, the prototype of an advanced transport with military as well as civil applications. This Model 367-80 prototype first flew in July 1954 with 4309-kg (9,500-lb) thrust Pratt &

Whitney JT3P turbojets, and in October of the same year the company's faith in its capabilities was rewarded by the first of many orders for the KC-135A inflight refuelling tanker dervied from the 'Dash 80'. Once the U.S. Air Force had given clearance, the company then started marketing this type as a civil transport with a slightly wider fuselage, and in October 1955 Pan American took the bold step of ordering the type for its long-haul domestic network in the

United States.

Some 844 examples of the Model 707 were eventually built, and the major variants were the Model 707-120 transcontinental airliner with 6123-kg (13,500-lb) thrust Pratt & Whitney JT3C turbojets, the Model 707-120B with JT3D turbofans, the Model 707-220 with 7938-kg (17,500-lb) thrust JT4A turbojets, the Model 707-320 intercontinetal airliner with longer wing and fuselage plus 7938-kg (17,500-lb) thrust JT4A turbojets, the Model 707-320B with aerodynamic refinements and turbofans, the Model 707-320C

convertible or freighter variants with turbofans, and the Model 707-420 with 7983-kg (17,600-lb) thrust Rolls-Royce Conway turbofans. The Model 720 is aerodynamically similar to the Model 707-120 but has a shorter fuselage plus a new and lighter structure optimizcd for the intermediate-range role. There is also a Model 720B turbofan-powered variant, and production was 154.

A Boeing 707-320 of Air India

BOEING 707-320C
Role: Long-range passenger/cargo transport
Crew/Accommodation: Three, plus five/six cabin crew, plus up to 189 passengers
Power Plant: Four 8,618 kgp (19,000 lb s.t.) Pratt & Whitney JT3D-7 turbofans
Dimensions: Span 44.42 m (145.71 ft); length 45.6 m (152.92 ft); wing area 283.4 m² (3050 sq ft)
Weights: Empty 66,224 kg (146,000 lb); MTOW 151,315 kg (333,600 lb)
Performance: Cruise speed 886 km/h (550 mph) at 8,534 m (28,000 ft); operational ceiling 11,885 m (39,000 ft); range 6,920 km (4,300 miles) with maximum payload
Load: Up to 41,453 kg (91,390 lb)

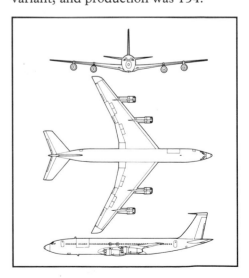

Boeing 707-300C

213

SUD-EST CARAVELLE (France)

Caravelle VI-N

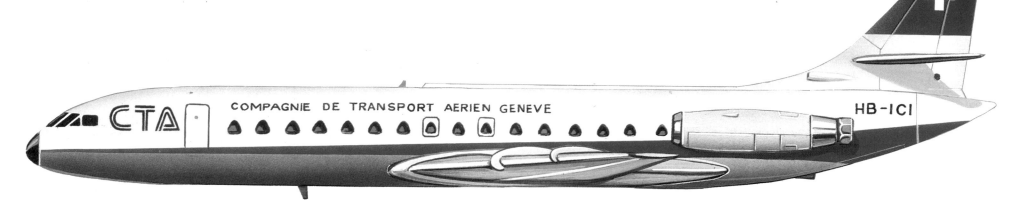

The Caravelle was France's first jet-powered airliner, the world's first short/medium-range jet airliner, and also the world's first airliner with its engines pod-mounted on the sides of the rear fuselage. The type resulted from a 1951 French civil aviation ministry requirement, and out of submissions from six manufacturers the S.E.210 was selected for hardware development in the form of two prototypes. The first of these flew in May 1955 with two 4536-kg (10,000-lb) thrust Rolls-Royce Avon RA.26 turbojets and had accommodation for 52 passengers.

Successful evaluation paved the way for the Caravelle I with its fuselage lengthened by 1.41 m (4 ft 7.5 in) for 64 passengers. The 19 Caravelle Is had 4763-kg (10,500-lb) Avon RA. 29 Mk 522s, while the 13 Caravelle IAs had Avon RA.29/1 Mk 526s. Next came 78 Caravelle IIIs with 5307-kg (11,700-lb) thrust Avon RA.29/3 Mk 527s, and all but one of the Mk I aircraft were upgraded to this standard. The Caravelle VI followed in two forms: the 53 VI-Ns had 5534-kg (12,200-lb) Avon RA.29/6 Mk 531s and the 56 VI-Rs had thrust-reversing 5715-kg (12,600-lb) thrust Avon Mk 532R or 533R engines.

Considerable refinement went into the Super Caravelle 10B, of which 22 were built. This first flew in March 1964 with extended wing roots, double-slotted flaps, a larger tailplane, a lengthened fuselage for 104 passengers, and 6350-kg (14,000-lb) thrust Pratt & Whitney JT8D-7 turbofans. The 20 Super Caravelle 10Rs used the Mk VI airframe with JT8D-7 engines, and 20 were built. The final models were the six Caravelle IIRs for mixed freight and passenger operations, and the 12 Caravelle 12s lengthened for 140-passenger accommodation and powered by 6577-kg (14,500-lb) thrust JT8D-9s.

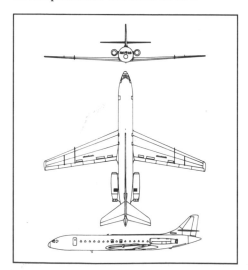

Aerospatiale Caravelle

AEROSPATIALE (SUD AVIATION) CARAVELLE 12
Role: Short-range passenger transport
Crew/Accommodation: Two, four cabin crew, plus up to 140 passengers
Power Plant: Two 6,577 kgp (14,500 lb s.t.) Pratt & Whitney JT8D-9 turbofans
Dimensions: Span 34.30 m (112.5 ft); length 36.24 m (118.75 ft); wing area 146.7 m² (1,579 sq ft)
Weights: Empty 31,800 kg (70,107 lb); MTOW 56,699 kg (125,000 lb)
Performance: Maximum speed 785 km/h (424 knots) at 7,620 m (25,000 ft); operational ceiling 12,192 m (40,000+ ft); range 1,870 km (1,162 miles) with full payload
Load: Up to 13,200 kg (29,101 lb)

A Sud-Aviation Caravelle VI-N

DOUGLAS DC-8 (United States)

Douglas DC-8-50

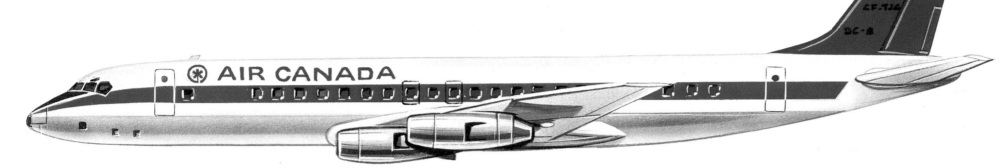

After planning the DC-7D with four 4273-kW (5,730-shp) Rolls-Royce Tyne turboprop engines, Douglas decided instead to challenge the Boeing Model 707 in the market for turbojet-powered airliners. The result was the DC-8, a worthy type that nevertheless trailed the Model 707 because of its later start and the availability of only a single fuselage length. In an effort to catch up with the Model 707, Douglas produced nine test aircraft with three different types of engine, and the first of these

flew in May 1958. Total production of the initial five series was 294 built over a period of nine years. These series were the DC-8-10 domestic model with 6123-kg (13,500-lb) thrust Pratt & Whitney JT3C-6 turbojets, the similar DC-8-20 with uprated engines for 'hot-and-high' routes, the DC-8-30 intercontinental model typically with 7620-kg (16,800-lb) thrust JT4A-9 turbojets, the similar DC-8-40 with 7938-kg (17,500-lb) thrust Rolls-Royce Conway Mk 509 turbofans, and the DC-8-50 with Pratt &

Whitney JT3D turbofans and a rearranged cabin for 189 passengers. The DC-8F Jet Trader was based on the DC-8-50 but available in all-freight or convertible freight/passenger layouts.

From 1967 production was of the JT3D-powered Super Sixty series, of which 262 were produced. This series comprised the DC-8 Super 61 with the fuselage stretched by 11.18 m (36 ft 8 in) for 259 passengers, the DC-8 Super 62 with span increased by 1.83 m (6 ft 0 in) and length by 2.03 m (6 ft 8 in) for 189 passengers carried over very long range, and the DC-8 Super

63 combining the Super 61's fuselage and Super 62's wing. These models could be delivered in all-passenger, all-freight, or convertible freight/passenger configurations. Finally came the Super Seventy series, which comprised Super 61, 62, and 63 aircraft converted with General Electric/SNECMA CFM56 turbofans with the designations DC-8 Super 71, 72, and 73 respectively.

A Douglas DC-8-50 of Japan Air Lines

DOUGLAS DC-8-63
Role: Long-range passenger transport
Crew/Accommodation: Four and four cabin crew, plus up to 251 passengers
Power Plant: Four 8,618 kgp (19,000 lb s.t.) Pratt & Whitney JT3D-7 turbofans
Dimensions: Span 45.24 m (148.42 ft); length 57.1 m (187 ft); wing area 271.93 m² (2,927 sq ft)
Weights: Empty 71,401 kg (157,409 lb); MTOW 158,760 kg (350,000 lb)
Performance: Cruise speed 959 km/h (517 knots) at 10,973 m (36,000 ft); operational ceiling 12,802 m (42,000 ft); range 6,301 km (3,400 naut. miles) with full payload
Load: Up to 30,126 kg (55,415 lb)

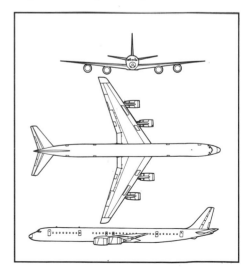

Douglas DC-8 Series 70

VICKERS VC10 (United Kingdom)

Vickers VC10

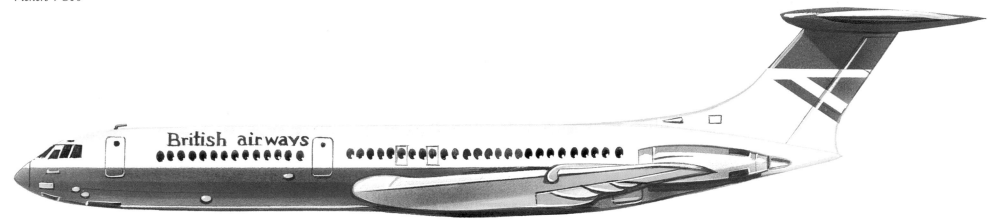

In 1957, the British Overseas Airways Corporation issued a requirement for an airliner able to carry a 15,422-kg (34,000-lb) payload over a range of 6437 km (4,000 miles) on the operator's Commonwealth routes. Vickers responded with its Type 1100 design. This was optimized for BOAC's route network, which included many 'hot-and-high' airports with short runways, with a large wing left uncluttered for its primary lifting task by the location of the four engines in paired pods on the sides of the rear fuselage below the tall T-tail. Other features were the retractable tricycle landing gear and six-abreast seating in the pressurized circular-section fuselage.

The first VC10 flew in June 1962, and the type entered service with BOAC in April 1964 with 9525-kg (21,000-lb) thrust Rolls-Royce Conway RCo.42 turbofans, a crew of 10 and a payload of between 115 and 135 passengers. BOAC took 12 such aircraft, and other customers were Ghana Airways (two), British United Airways (three), and the Royal Air Force (14 VC10 C.Mk 1s with a revised wing, greater fuel capacity and Conway RCo.43 engines). The prototype was also revised to production standard and was then sold to Laker Airways.

Development evolved the Type 1150 that entered production as the Super VC10 with Conway RCo.43 engines, greater fuel capacity and a fuselage lengthened by 3.96 m (13 ft 0 in). BOAC took 17 such aircraft and East African Airways another five. Because of its large wing, the VC10 had inferior operating economics to the Boeing Model 707, and most airports upgraded their facilities to cater for the Model 707 and Douglas DC-8.

The RAF bought from airlines five VC10s and 10 Super VC10s for conversion as VC10 K.Mks 2 and 3 three-point inflight refuelling tankers. The VC10 C.Mk 1s are also being adapted as two-point tanker transports with the designation VC10 C.Mk 1(K).

Vickers VC10 K.Mk 3

VICKERS/BRITISH AIRCRAFT CORPORATION SUPER VC-10

Role: Long range passenger transport
Crew/Accommodation: Five and seven cabin crew, plus up to 180 passengers
Power Plant: Four 9,888 kgp (21,800 lb) Rolls-Royce Conway RC0.43D Mk 550 turbofans
Dimensions: Span 44.55 m (146.17 ft); length 52.32 m (171.66 ft); wing area 272.40 m² (2,932 sq ft)
Weights: Empty 71,940 kg (158,594 lb); MTOW 151,950 kg (335,000 lb)
Performance: Maximum speed 935 km/h (505 knots) at 9,449 m (31,000 ft); operational ceiling 11,582 m (38,000 ft); range 7,596 km (4,720 miles) with full payload
Load: Up to 27,360 kg (60,321 lb)

A Vickers Super VC10 of East African Airways

BOEING 727 (United States)

Boeing Model 727-100

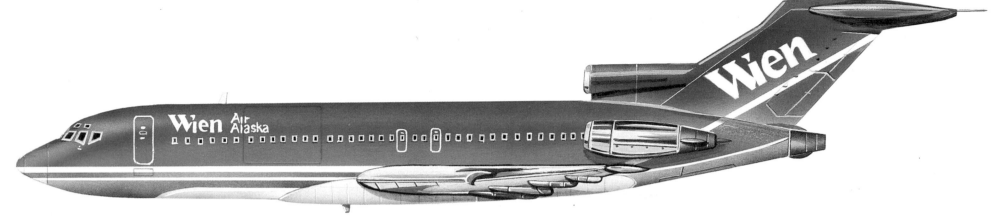

The Model 727 was conceived as a short/medium-range partner to the Model 707, with the primary task of bringing passengers to the larger airports used by the long-range type. The type was designed for as much construction commonality as possible with the Model 707, and among other features was designed to use the same fuselage cross-section. The design team considered 70 concepts before finalizing its concept for the Model

727 as a fairly radical type able to meet the apparently conflicting requirements for high cruising speed at the lowest possible altitude and minimum seat/mile costs. Other factors that had to be taken into account were frequent take-off/landing cycles, the need for fast 'turn-round' time, and the need for low take-off noise so that the type could use airports close to urban areas. The Model 727 emerged with three rear-

mounted engines, a T-tail and an uncluttered wing with triple-slotted flaps along its trailing edges. Independence of airport services was ensured by an auxiliary power unit and a ventral airstair/door.

The Model 727 first flew in February 1963, and production has reached 1,831 in two main variants. The basic variant is the Model 727-100, which was also produced in convertible and quick-change convertible derivatives. Then came the Model 727-200 lengthened by 6.1 m (20 ft) and featuring the structural modifications required for operation

at higher weights; the latest version is the Advanced 727-200 with a performance data computer system to improve operating economy and safety. Also operational in smaller numbers is the Model 727F, which was produced to the special order of small-package operator Federal Express; this variant has no fuselage windows and can carry 26,649-kg (58,750-lb) of freight.

A Boeing 727-200 of Pan American World Airways

BOEING 727-200
Role: Intermediate-range passenger transport
Crew/Accommodation: Three and four cabin crew, plus up to 189 passengers
Power Plant: Three 7,257 kgp (16,000 lb s.t.) Pratt & Whitney JT8D-17 turbofans
Dimensions: Span 32.9 m (108 ft); length 46.7 m (153.17 ft); wing area 153.3 m² (1,650 sq ft)
Weights: Empty 46,164 kg (101,773 lb); MTOW 95,028 kg (209,500 lb)
Performance: Cruise speed 982 km/h (530 knots) at 7,620 m (25,000 ft); operational ceiling 11,582+ m (38,000+ ft); range 5,371 km (2,900 naut. miles)
Load: Up to 18,597 kg (41,000 lb)

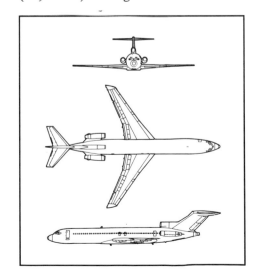

Boeing Model 727-200

BRITISH AIRCRAFT CORPORATION ONE-ELEVEN (United Kingdom)

BAC One-Eleven 500

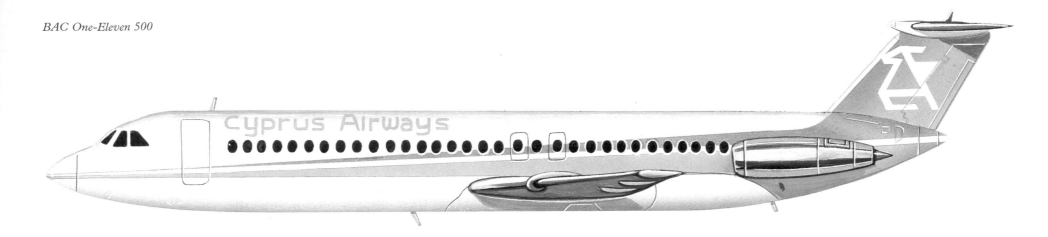

This pioneering airliner was conceived as the Hunting H.107 short-range airliner with accommodation for 59 passengers, and to provide the type with excellent field performance and low cabin noise levels it was decided to use aft-mounted engines; this left the wing uncluttered and therefore better able to perform its primary function, and dictated the use of a T-tail to lift the tailplane well clear of the

jet exhausts. Hunting was bought by BAC and the H.107 became the BAC 107. There was little airline enthusiasm for an airliner with so small a passenger payload, and the basic concept was therefore enlarged to provide 79-passenger capacity. This was redesignated the BAC 111, and later the One-Eleven. The design was finalized with a circular-section pressuized fuselage with a ventral airstair let into the underside of the fuselage under the tail unit, a low-set wing of modest sweep with Fowler trailing-edge flaps, and a variable-

incidence tailplane at the very top of the vertical tail surfaces.

The prototype flew in August 1963 with two 4722-kg (10,410-lb) thrust Rolls-Royce Spey Mk 506 turbofans, and was lost in a fatal crash some two months later as a result of a 'deep stall' occasioned by the aft engine/T-tail configuration. After this problem had been cured, useful sales were secured for the basic One-Eleven Series 200 with Spey Mk 506s, the

One-Eleven Mk 300 with 5171-kg (11,400-lb) thrust Spey Mk 511s, the generally similar but higher-weight One-Eleven Mk 400 for U.S. airlines, the stretched One-Eleven Series 500 for 119 passengers, and the 'hot and high' One-Eleven Series 475 with the fuselage of the Series 400 plus the wings and powerplant of the Series 500. The One-Eleven production line was bought by Rombac in Romania, where One-Elevens are still built.

British Aircraft Corporation One-Eleven 675

BRITISH AIRCRAFT CORPORATION ONE-ELEVEN 500

Role: Short-range passenger transport
Crew/Accommodation: Two and three/four cabin crew, plus up to 119 passengers
Power Plant: Two 5,692 kgp (12,500 lb s.t.) Rolls-Royce Spey 512-DW turbofans
Dimensions: Span 28.5 m (92.5 ft); length 32.61 m (107 ft); wing area 95.78 m² (1,031 sq ft)
Weights: Empty 24,758 kg (54,582 lb); MTOW 47,000 kg (104,500 lb)
Performance: Maximum speed 871 km/h (470 knots) at 6,400 m (21,000 ft); range 2,380 km (1,480 miles) with full passenger load
Load: Up to 11,983 kg (26,418 lb) including belly cargo

The BAC One-Eleven pioneered the aft engine/T-tail combination

ILYUSHIN Il-62 (U.S.S.R.)

Il-62M

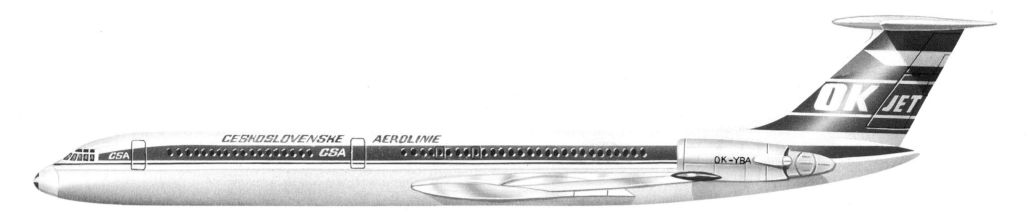

The Il-62 was developed as a long-range airliner to complement and then to supplant the Tupolev Tu-114 on domestic and international routes. The Soviets specified high levels of comfort and performance in the hope that this would result in a type that would gain a measure of the export success that had eluded earlier Soviet airliners, which in no way matched their Western opponent's sales in terms of operating economics. The first Il-62 flew in January 1963 with four 7500-kg (16,535-lb) thrust Lyul'ka AL-7 turbojets as the planned 10,500-kg (23,150-lb) thrust Kuznetsov NK-8-4 turbofans were not yet ready for flight. Clearly the design had been influenced by that of the Vickers VC10 in its configuration with a large wing, a T-tail, rear-mounted engines, and retractable tricycle landing gear. This similarity was also carried over into the flight test programme for, like the VC10, the Il-62 required lengthy development for the problem of its deep-stall tendency to be overcome. The NK-4 turbofans were introduced later in the test programme, which involved two prototypes and three pre-production aircraft.

The initial Il-62 production version entered service in September 1967 with accommodation for between 168 and 186 passengers, and cascade-type thrust reversers were fitted only on the outer engines. In 1971 there appeared the Il-62M with 11,000-kg (24,250-lb) thrust Soloviev D-30KU turbofans with clamshell-type thrust reversers, and the improved specific fuel consumption of this more advanced engine type combined with additional fuel capacity (a fuel tank in the fin) to improve the payload/range performance to a marked degree over that of the Il-62. Other improvements were a revised flight deck, new avionics, and wing spoilers that could be operated differentially for roll control. The Il-62MK of 1978 introduced structure, landing gear and control system modifications to permit operations at higher weights.

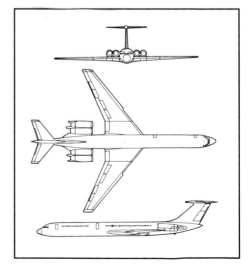

Ilyushin Il-62M

ILYUSHIN Il-62M 'CLASSIC'
Role: Long-range passenger transport
Crew/Accommodation: Five, four cabin crew, plus up to 186 passengers
Power Plant: Four 11,500 kgp (25,350 lb s.t.) Soloviev D-30KU turbofans
Dimensions: Span 43.2 m (141.75 ft); length 53.12 m (174.28 ft); wing area 279.6 m² (3,010 sq ft)
Weights: Empty 69,400 kg (153,000 lb); MTOW 165,000 kg (363,760 lb)
Performance: Cruise speed 900 km/h (485 knots) at 12,000 m (39,370 ft); operational ceiling 13,000+ m (42,650+ ft); range 8,000 km (4,317 naut. miles) with full payload
Load: Up to 23,000 kg (50,700 lb)

An Ilyushin Il-62 long-range airliner of Aeroflot

DOUGLAS DC-9 and McDONNELL DOUGLAS MD-80 Series (United States)

McDonnell Douglas MD-80

Planned as a medium-range partner to the DC-8, the DC-9 was then recast as a short-range type to compete with the BAC One-Eleven. Having learned the sales disadvantages of a single-length fuselage with the DC-8, Douglas planned the DC-9 with length options, and decided to optimize the efficiency of the wing by pod-mounting engines on the fuselage sides under a T-tail. The type first flew in February 1965 and built up an excellent sales record based on low operating costs and fuselage length tailored to customer requirements.

The success of the type also demanded so high a level of production investment, however, that Douglas was forced to merge with McDonnell Douglas.

The variants of the initial production series were the DC-9-10 with Pratt & Whitney JT8D turbofans and 90 passengers, the DC-9-15 with uprated engines, the DC-9-20 for 'hot-and-high' operations with more power and span increased by 1.22 m (4 ft 0 in), the DC-9-30 with the fuselage stretched by 4.54 m (14 ft 10.75 in) for 119 passengers, the DC-9-40 with a further stretch of 1.92 m (6 ft 3.5 in) for 132 passengers, and the DC-9-50 with more power and a further stretch of 2.44 m (8 ft 0 in) for

139 passengers. Developments for the military were the C-9A Nightingale aeromedical transport based on the DC-9-30, and the C-9B Skytrain II fleet logistic transport combining features of the DC-9-30 and -40. Production totalled 976, and from 1975 McDonnell Douglas offered the DC-9 Super Eighty series with a longer fuselage and the refanned JT8D (-200 series) turbofan. This first flew in October 1979, and variants are the DC-9 Super 81 (now MD-81) with JT8D-209s and a fuselage stretched by 4.34 m (14 ft 3 in) for 172 passengers, the DC-9 Super 82

(now MD-82) with JT8D-217s, the DC-9 Super 83 (now MD-83) with JT8D-219s and extra fuel, the DC-9 Super 87 (now MD-87) with JT8D-217Bs and a fuselage shortened by 5.0 m (16 ft 5 in), and the DC-9 Super 88 (now MD-88) development of the MD-82 with JT8D-217Cs and an electronic flight instruments system combined with a flight-management computer and inertial navigation system. McDonnell Douglas is now considering a further updated MD-90 series with the latest electronic flight systems and IAE V2500 turbofans or a propfan powerplant.

McDonnell Douglas DC-9 Super 80

DOUGLAS DC-9-10
Role: Short-range passenger transport
Crew/Accommodation: Two and three cabin crew, plus up to 90 passengers
Power Plant: Two 6,580 kgp (14,500 lb s.t.) Pratt & Whitney JT8D-9 turbofans
Dimensions: Span 27.2 m (89.42 ft); length 31.8 m (104.42 ft); wing area 86.8 m² (934.3 sq ft)
Weights: Empty 23,060 kg (50,848 lb); MTOW 41,142 kg (90,700 lb)
Performance: Cruise speed 874 km/h (471 knots) at 9,144 m (30,000 ft); operational ceiling 12,497 m (41,000 ft); range 2,038 km (1,100 naut. miles) with maximum payload
Load: Up to 8,707 kg (19,200 lb)

A McDonnell Douglas MD-83

BOEING 737 (United States)

Boeing 737-200

The short-range Model 737 is the small brother of the Models 707 and 727, and completed the Boeing family of airliners covering the full spectrum of commercial operations at the time of the company's November 1964 decision to design such a type. The Model 737 is currently the world's best-selling airliner, with more than 2,200 ordered. Intended for short sectors, the Model 737 first flew in April 1967 and is distinguished by a fuselage cross-section similar to that of

the Models 707 and 727, JT8D turbofans pod-mounted directly on to the under surfaces of the wings, main wheel units that are left uncovered when retracted into the under surfaces of the wing root/fuselage interface, and a tail unit reminiscent of the Model 707. Despite the somewhat different appearance of the two aircraft, there is about 60 per cent commonality of structure and systems between the Models 727 and 737. The wing of the Model 737 draws

heavily on that of the Model 727, and combines both the attributes required for economical operation during high-speed cruise at moderately low levels and for good lift and excellent low-speed handling for short-field operations.

First flown in April 1967, the initial variant was the Model 737-100 for 100 passengers, but only a few were built before production switched to

the larger Model 737-200 for 130 passengers. This first flew in August 1967, and there are also convertible, quick-change convertible, and advanced derivatives. Later came the Model 737-300 with 9072-kg (20,000-lb) thrust CFM56-3 turbofans and further lengthening for 148 passengers, the further stretched Model 737-400 for 156 passengers, and the considerably updated Model 737-500 with more power.

BOEING 737-300
Role: Intermediate/short-range passenger transport
Crew/Accommodation: Two and four cabin crew, plus up to 149 passengers
Power Plant: Two 9,072 kgp (20,000 lb s.t.) General Electric/SNECMA CFM56-3-BI turbofans
Dimensions: Span 28.9 m (94.75 ft); length 33.4 m (109.58 ft); wing area 91 m² (980 sq ft)
Weights: Empty 31,630 kg (69,730 lb); MTOW 56,470 kg (124,500 lb)
Performance: Cruise speed 908 km/h (491 knots) at 7,925 m (26,000 ft); operational ceiling 11,278 m (37,000 ft); range 2,923 km (1,580 miles) with maximum payload
Load: Up to 16,030 kg (35,270 lb)

Boeing 737-300s

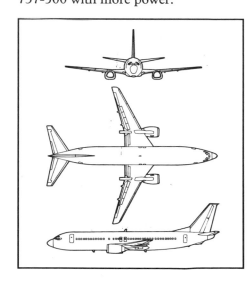

Boeing 737-400

AEROSPATIALE/BAC CONCORDE (France/United Kingdom)

Concorde

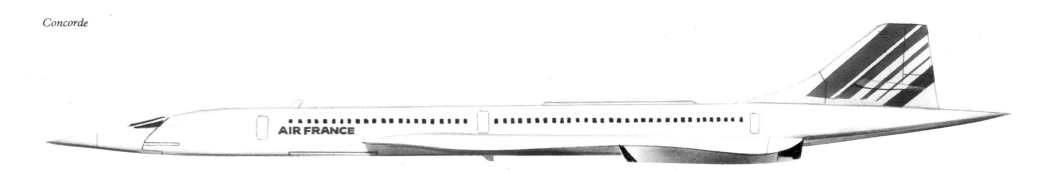

Currently the world's only supersonic air transport, the Concorde originated from separate French and British projects which were considered too expensive for single-nation development. The two efforts were therefore amalgamated in 1962 by an inter-governmental agreement. The French and British airframe contractors were Sud-Aviation and the British Aircraft Corporation, which eventually became parts of Aérospatiale and British Aerospace respectively. The project matured as a medium-sized type with a delta wing and a slender fuselage; the wing has an ogival leading edge, and the aerodynamically clean forward section of the fuselage has a 'droop snoot' arrangement to provide the crew with an adequate field of vision for take-off and landing.

The French were responsible for the wings, the rear cabin section, the flying controls, and the air-conditioning, hydraulic, navigation and radio systems; the British were tasked with the three forward fuselage sections, the rear fuselage and vertical tail, the engine nacelles and ducts, the engine installation, the electrical, fuel and oxygen systems, and the noise and thermal insulation. A similar collaborative arrangement was organized between Rolls-Royce and SNECMA for the design and construction of the engines.

The first of two prototypes, one from each country, flew in March 1969, and these two machines had slightly shorter nose and tail sections than later aircraft. The type has proved an outstanding technical success, but political and environmental opposition meant that only two pre-production and 14 production aircraft were built.

AEROSPATIALE/BAC CONCORDE
Role: Supersonic passenger transport
Crew/Accommodation: Three and four cabin crew, plus up to 144 passengers
Power Plant: Four 17,260 kgp (38,050 lb s.t.) Rolls-Royce/SNECMA Olympus 593 Mk610 turbojets with reheat
Dimensions: Span 25.6 m (84 ft); length 67.17 m (203.96 ft); wing area 358.25 m² (3,856 sq ft)
Weights: Empty 77,110 kg (170,000 lb); MTOW 181,400 kg (400,000 lb)
Performance: Maximum speed 2,333 km/h (1,260 knots) Mach 2.05 at 16,600 m (54,500 ft); operational ceiling 18,288 m (60,000 ft); range 7,215 km (3,893 naut. miles)
Load: Typically 11,340 kg (25,000 lb)

Concorde

A British Aerospace/Aerospatiale Concorde of British Airways

BOEING 747 (United States)

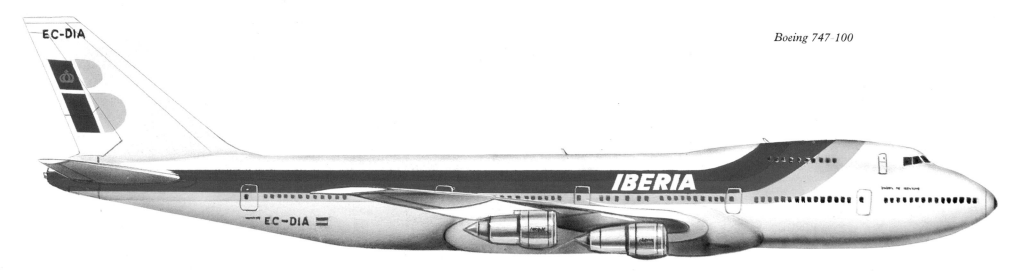

Boeing 747-100

Known universally as the 'Jumbo', the Model 747 introduced the 'wide-body' airliner concept. It is the world's largest airliner, and is the mainstay of the Western world's long-range high-capacity routes. After failing to win the U.S. Air Force's CX-HLS competition for a long-range logistic freighter, Boeing decided to capitalize on its work by developing the basic concept into a civil transport. Initial thoughts centred on a 430-seat type with a 'double bubble' fuselage configuration in which each lobe would be about 4.57m (15 ft) wide. This failed to secure major airline interest, so Boeing finally opted for a 'big brother' to the Model 707 using basically the same layout but with a fuselage large enough to accommodate a cabin 6.13 m (20 ft 1.5 in) wide and 56.39 m (185 ft 0 in) long. The type first flew in February 1969 and, with more than 900 aircraft ordered, the Model 747 is still in development and production with a choice of General Electric, Pratt & Whitney and Rolls-Royce turbofans.

The main variants have been the initial Model 747-100 with a maximum weight of 322,051-kg (710,000-lb) and strengthened Model 747-100B, the Model 747-200 (also available in convertible and freighter versions) with further structural strengthening, greater fuel capacity and uprated engines for a maximum weight of 377,842-kg (833,000-lb), the Model 747SP long-range version with the fuselage reduced in length by 14.35 m (47 ft 1 in) for a maximum of 440 passengers, the Model 747SR short-range version of the Model 747-100B with features to cater for the higher frequency of take-off/landing cycles, the Model 747-300 with a stretched upper deck increasing this area's accommodation from 16 first-class to 69 economy-class passengers, and the Model 747-400 with a revised and modernized structure, a two-crew flightdeck with the latest cockpit displays and instrumentation, extended wings with drag-reducing winglets, and lean-burn turbofans.

BOEING 747-400

Role: Long-range passenger/cargo transport

Crew/Accommodation: Two, pus up to 412 passengers and cabin crew in 3-class configuration

Power Plant: Four 26,263 kg (57,900 lb s.t.) General Electric CF6-80C2 or 25,741 kgp (56,750 lb s.t.) Pratt & Whitney PW 4000 or 26, 308 kg (58,000 lb s.t.) Rolls-Royce RB211-524G turbofans

Dimensions: Span 64.8 m (213 ft); length 70.7 m (231.87 ft); wing area 525 m² (5,650 sq ft)

Weights: Empty 178,262 kg (393,000 lb); MTOW 324,625 kg (870,000 lb)

Performance: Cruise speed 939 km/h (507 knots) at 10,670 m (35,000 ft); operational ceiling 13,000+ m (42,650+ ft); range 13,658 km (7,370 naut. miles) with maximum fuel

Load: Up to 65,230 kg (143,800 lb) including belly cargo

Boeing 747-400

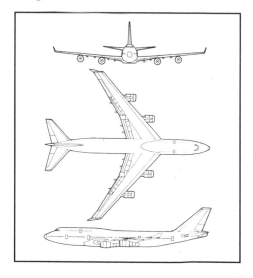

Boeing 747-400

FOKKER F.28 FELLOWSHIP and 100 (Netherlands)

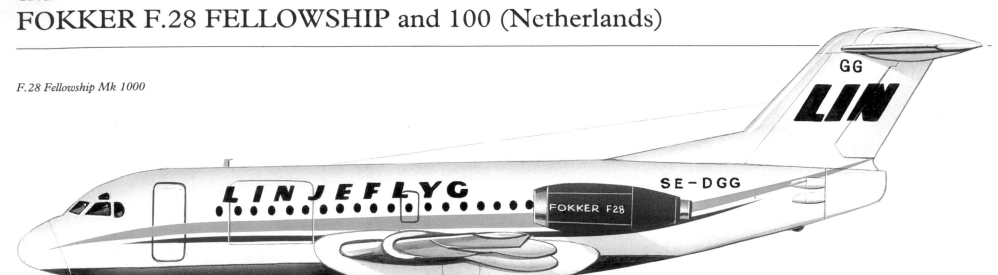

F.28 Fellowship Mk 1000

The F.28 Fellowship was designed as a complement to the turboprop-powered F.27 with slightly higher passenger capacity and considerably improved performance through the use of a twin-turbofan powerplant. Initial design work began in 1960, and Fokker opted for a T-tail configuration and rear-mounted Rolls-Royce Spey engines to provide an uncluttered wing. The first of three

F.28 prototypes flew in May 1967, and the certification and delivery of the initial production machine were achieved at the same time in February 1969.

The first production version was the F.28 Mk 1000 for 65 passengers on two 4468-kg (9,850-lb) thrust Spey Mk 555-15s, and a subvariant was the F.28 Mk 1000C with a large cargo door on the port side of the forward fuselage for all-freight or mixed freight/passenger services. Subsequent models have been the F.28 Mk 2000 with its fuselage stretched by 2.21 m (7 ft 3 in) for 79 passengers, and the

F.28 Mks 3000 and 4000 with the fuselages of the Mks 1000 and 2000 respectively, span increased by 1.57 m (6 ft 11.5 in), and two 4491-kg (9,900-lb) thrust Spey Mk 555-15Ps.

In order to keep the type matched to current airline demands, in November 1983 Fokker announced an updated and stretched Fokker 100 version. This has a revised wing of greater efficiency and spanning 3.00 m (9 ft 9.5 in) more than that of

the F.28, a larger tailplane, a fuselage stretched by 5.74 m (18 ft 10 in) by plugs forward and aft of the wing to increase capacity to 107 passengers, and 6042-kg (13,320-lb) thrust Rolls-Royce Tay Mk 620-15 turbofans. At the same time, the interior was completely remodelled, composite materials were introduced, and an electronic flight instrument system was introduced. The first Fokker 100 flew in November 1986, and the type has built up a useful order book.

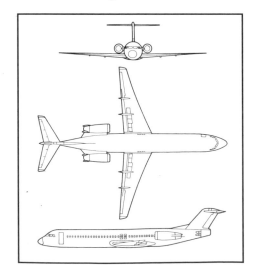

Fokker 100

FOKKER 100
Role: Short-range jet passenger transport
Crew/Accommodation: Two and four cabin crew, plus up to 119 passengers
Power Plant: Two 6,282 kgp (13,850 lb s.t.) Rolls-Royce Tay 620-15 turbofans
Dimensions: Span 28.08 m (92.13 ft); length 35.53 m (116.57 ft); wing area 93.5 m² (1,006.5 sq ft)
Weights: Empty 24,355 kg (53,695 lb); MTOW 43,090 kg (95,000 lb)
Performance: Cruise speed 765 km/h (413 knots) at 8,534 m (28,000 ft); operational ceiling 10,668 m (35,000 ft); range 2,298 km (1,240 naut. miles) with 107 passengers
Load: Up to 12,385 kg (27,305 lb)

A Fokker 100 of Swissair

LOCKHEED L-1011 TRISTAR (United States)

L-1011-1 TriStar

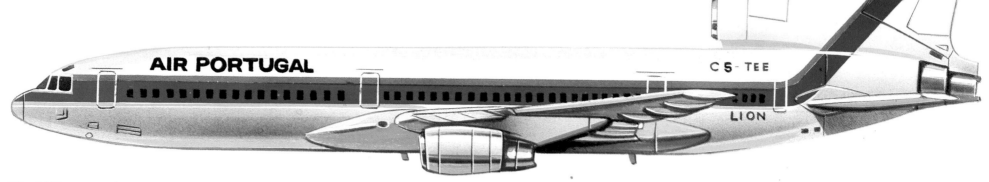

The TriStar was planned to meet an Eastern Airlines' requirement for a wide-body airliner optimized for short- and medium-range operations with a large number of passengers, and was planned in parallel with its engine, the Rolls-Royce RB.211 turbofan initially offered at a 19,051-kg (42,000-lb) thrust rating. Development problems with the engine broke Rolls-Royce and nearly broke Lockheed, both companies having to be rescued by their respective governments. Construction began in 1968, and the first TriStar flew in November 1970.

Certification was delayed until April 1972 by the two companies' financial problems, and the L-1101-1 variant entered service in the same month with RB.211-22B engines and provision for up to 400 passengers at a maximum take-off weight of 195,045-kg (430,000-lb). The L-1011-100, which was the same basic airliner with RB.211-22B engines but the fuel capacity and weights of the L-1011-200, which first flew in 1976 with 21,772-kg (48,000-lb) thrust RB.211-524 engines and a maximum take-off weight of up to 216,363-kg (477,000-lb) depending on the fuel load. The final production model was the L-1011-500 for very long-range operations, with 22,680-kg (50,000-lb) thrust RB.211-524B engines, increased fuel capacity, the fuselage shortened by 4.11 m (13 ft 6 in) for the accommodation of between 246 and 330 passengers, and the wings increased in span by 2.74 m (9 ft 0 in) as part of the new active control system that also saw a reduction in tailplane size. Sales failed to match Lockheed's marketing forecasts, and production ended in 1984 with the delivery of the 247th aircraft. L-1011-1s modified with the L-1011-500's engines are designated L-1011-250. Several ex-airline machines were converted as TriStar K.Mk 1 tankers for the RAF.

A Lockheed L-1011-1 TriStar of Air Canada

LOCKHEED L-1011 TRISTAR
Role: Intermediate-range passenger transport
Crew/Accommodation: Three, six cabin crew, plus up to 400 passengers (charter)
Power Plant: Three 19,051 kgp (42,000 lb s.t.) Rolls-Royce RB211-22 turbofans
Dimensions: Span 47.35 m (155,33 ft); length 54.46 m (178.66 ft); wing area 321.1m² (3,456 sq ft)
Weights: Empty 106,265 kg (234,275 lb); MTOW 195,045 kg (430,000 lb)
Performance: Cruise speed 796 km/h (495 mph) at 9,140 m (30,000 ft); operational ceiling 12,800 m (42,000 ft); range 4,635 km (2,880 miles) with maximum payload
Load: Up to 41,152 kg (90,725 lb)

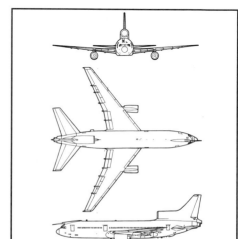

Lockheed TriStar K.Mk 1

225

DOUGLAS DC-10 and McDONNELL MD-11(United States)

DC-10-10

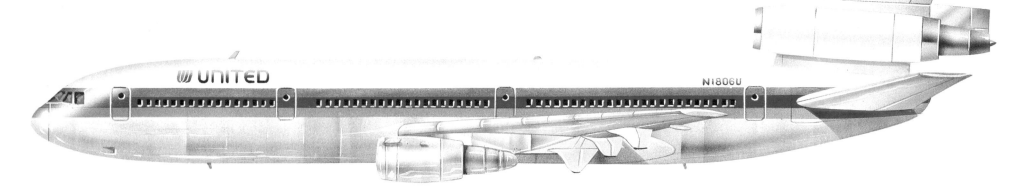

Douglas began work on the design of the DC-10 in 1966 in response to a requirement of American Airlines for a wide-body airliner offering the same sort of range as the Boeing Model 747 with a smaller payload. With orders for 55 aircraft and options for another 55 received, Douglas launched production in April 1968. The design matured as a basically conventional low-wing monoplane with swept flying surfaces, tricycle landing gear and three turbofan engines (one under each wing and the third on a vertical pylon above the rear fuselage with the vertical tail above it).

The first example flew in August 1970, by which time Douglas had amalgamated with McDonnell. Production totalled 427, and the main variants were the 122 DC-10-10s with 18,144-kg (40,000-lb) thrust General Electric CF-6 turbofans for 380 passengers, the nine DC-10-10CF convertible freight/passenger transports, the seven DC-10-15s with 21,092-kg (46,500-lb) thrust CF6-50 engines and higher weights, the 161 DC-10-30 intercontinental transports with the span increased by 3.05 m (10 ft 0 in), 22,226-kg (49,000-lb) thrust CF6-50A/C engines, extra fuel and a two-wheel additional main landing gear unit between the two standard units, the 26 DC-10-30-CF convertible transports, the three or four DC-10-40 intercontinental version of the 30 with 24,040-kg (53,000-lb) thrust Pratt & Whitney JT9D turbofans, and the 60 KC-10A Extender transport/tankers for the U.S. Air Force. The MD-11 is an updated version for the 1990s with drag-reducing winglets on wings extended in span by 3.05 m (10 ft 0 in), a fuselage lengthened by 5.66 m (18 ft 7 in) for 405 passengers, a smaller fuel-filled tailplane, advanced avionics and a choice of CF6-80, PW4358 or RB211-524L turbofans.

McDonnell Douglas DC-10-30

McDONNELL DOUGLAS MD-11
Role: Long-intermediate-range passenger/cargo transport
Crew/Accommodation: Two, eight cabin crew and up to 323 passengers (2-class, high density seating)
Power Plant: Three 27,896 kgp (61,500 lb s.t.) General Electric CF6-80C2-D1F or 27,216 kgp (60,000 lb s.t.) Pratt & Whitney PW 4358 or 29,484 kgp (65,000 lb s.t.) Rolls-Royce RB211-524L turbofans
Dimensions: Span 51.76 m (169.83 ft); length 61.37 m (201.33 ft); wing area 342.64^2 (3,688 sq ft)
Weights: Empty 128,462 kg (283,131 lb); MTOW 273,290 kg (602,500 lb)
Performance: Cruise speed 876 km/h (473 knots) at 10,668 m (35,000 ft) operational ceiling 12,802 m (42,000 ft); range 9,266 km (5,000 naut. miles) with 55,792 kg (123,000 lb) payload
Load: Up to 70,080 kg (154,500 lb) for the Combi version

A McDonnell Douglas DC-10-30

AIRBUS INDUSTRIE A300 (France/Netherlands/Spain/U.K./W. Germany)

Airbus Industrie A300 B4

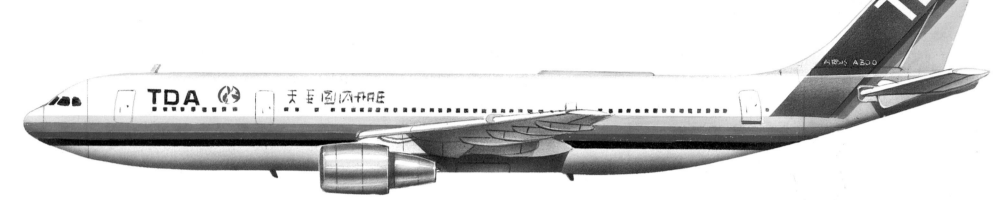

The Airbus consortium was established in 1967 to co-ordinate a European challenge to the American 'big three' of airliner production - Boeing, Lockheed, and later McDonnell Douglas. A number of national designs had already been studied before the consortium was created to design, develop, and build a

250-seat airliner powered by two British or American turbofans. The political and economic infighting as the programme got underway was considerable, and the two sponsoring countries were France and West Germany, later joined by industrial partners in the United Kingdom, the Netherlands and Spain.

The first prototype A300B1 flew in 1972, and this was lengthened by 2.65 m (8 ft 8 in) to create the initial production model, the A300B2-100 with General Electric CF6-50 engines; variants are the A300B2-200 with leading-edge flaps, the A300B2-220 with Pratt & Whitney JT9D-59A turbofans, and the A300B2-320 with higher take-off and landing weights. Then came the A300B4-100 long-range version with CF6 engines, the A300B4-200 with higher weights and the A300B4-200FF with a two-crew

cockpit. The A300C4 is a convertible freighter based on the A300B4, and in 1980 Airbus launched the A300-600 as an advanced version of the A30B4 including a rear fuselage with the profile pioneered in the A310 and a choice of General Electric CF6, Pratt & Whitney JT9D or Rolls-Royce RB.211 turbofans. The A300-600R improved version has wingtip fences and other modifications.

An Airbus Industrie A300-600R

AIRBUS A300-600R
Role: Intermediate-range passenger transport
Crew/Accommodation: Three and six cabin crew, plus up to 344 passengers
Power Plant: Two 27,307 kgp (60,200 lb s.t.) General Electric CF6-80C2A3 or 26,310 kgp (58,000 lb s.t.) Pratt & Whitney PW4158 turbofans
Dimensions: Span 44.84 m (147.1 ft); length 54.08 m (177.4 ft); wing area 260 m² (2,799 sq ft)
Weights: Empty 87,728 kg (193,410 lb); MTOW 165,000 kg (363,760 lb)
Performance: Maximum speed 891 km/h (554 mph) at 9,450 m (31,000 ft); operational ceiling 13,000+ m (42,650+ ft); range 5,200 km (3,430 miles) with maximum payload
Load: Up to 41,504 kg (91,500 lb) including belly cargo

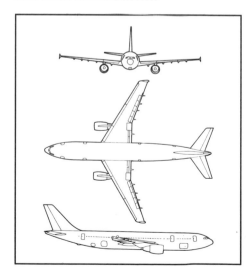

Airbus Industrie A300-600

227

BOEING 767 (United States)

767-200

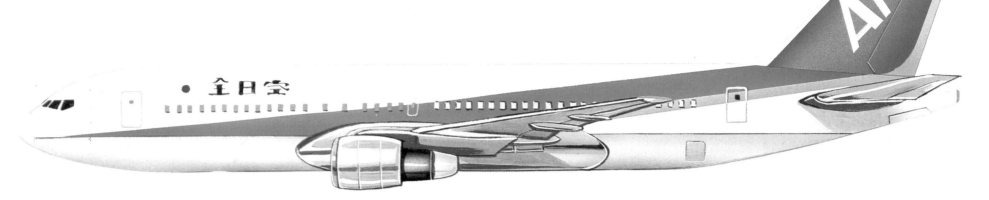

Planned in concert with the Model 757, the Model 767 is a wide-body transport with a fuselage width about mid-way between those of the Models 727 and 747, and therefore about 1.24 m (4 ft 1 in) wider than that of the Model 757. Even so, the Models 757 and 767 have so much in common that pilots can secure a single rating for both types. The type was schemed as a high-capacity airliner for medium-range routes, with accommodation for between 211 and 230 passengers, and is offered with a choice of General Electric CF6 or Pratt & Whitney JT9D turbofans, later joined by the Rolls-Royce RB.211 turbofan. Drafting was undertaken with the aid of computer-aided design techniques, and production of much of the Model 767's components and assemblies (about 45 per cent of the value of each plane) is undertaken by 28 companies spread round the world. The Model 767 differs from the Model 757 in

having larger wings of increased sweep, but similar features are the tail unit, landing gear and engine pods.

The first Model 767 flew in September 1981 and, with the cancellation of the planned Model 767-100 with a shorter fuselage for the carriage of a maximum 180 passengers, the Model 767-200 became the standard variant in three forms with maximum weights varying between 127,913 and 142,884-kg

(282,000 and 315,000-lb). There is also the extended-range Model 767-200ER with additional fuel in a second centre section tank for greater range. This comes in two forms with maximum weights of 156,489 and 159,211-kg (345,000 and 351,000-lb). The Model 767-300 provides greater capacity, and has its fuselage stretched by 6.42 m (21ft 1 in); it is also available in an extended-range variant.

BOEING 767-300
Role: Intermediate-range passenger transport
Crew/Accommodation: Two/three, six cabin crew plus up to 290 passengers (charter)
Power Plant: Two 23,814 kgp (52,500 lb s.t.) General Electric CF6-80C2B2 or 22,770 kgp (50,200 lb s.t.) Pratt & Whitney PW4050 turbofans
Dimensions: Span 47.57 m (156.08 ft); length 54.94 m (180,25 ft); wing area 283.4 m² (3,050 sq ft)
Weights: Empty 86,954 kg (191,700 lb); MTOW 159,211 kg (351,000 lb)
Performance: Maximum speed 906 km/h 489 knots) at 11,887 m (39,000 ft); operational ceiling 13,000+ m (42,650+ ft); range 5,965 km (3,220 naut. miles) with maximum payload
Load: Up to 39,145 kg (86,300 lb)

Boeing 767-300

A Boeing 767-200

BOEING 757 (United States)

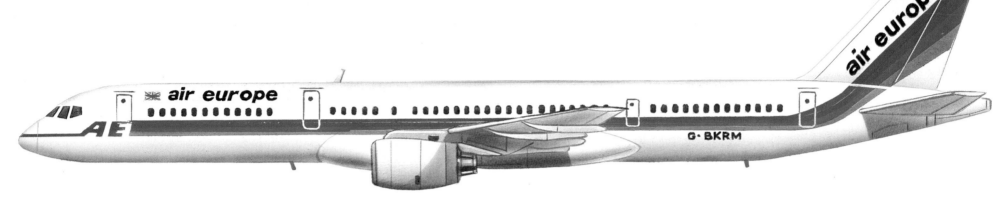

Boeing 757-200

In the later part of 1978, Boeing announced its intention of developing a new generation of advanced-technology airliners. The two definitive members of this family were the Models 757 and 767, while the Model 777 was less certain. The Model 757 retained the same fuselage cross-section as the Model 727, and could be regarded as the Model 727's potential successor in the carriage of between 178 and 224 passengers over short- and medium-range routes. Where Boeing offered considerable improvement, however, was in a new standard of fuel efficiency expected to offer 45 per cent fuel savings per passenger/mile by comparison with contemporary types. The Model 757 is therefore a narrow-body type (with the same fuselage diameter as the Models 707, 727 and 737) and was at first offered with Rolls-Royce RB.211-535 or General Electric CF6-32C1 turbofans in underwing pods; General Electric then dropped the CF6-32 engine, and Pratt & Whitney entered the lists with the PW2037.

The type was originally planned in Model 757-100 short-fuselage and Model 757-200 long-fuselage variants; launch customers all opted for the latter with RB.211 engines, and the shorter variant was then dropped. The Model 757-200 first flew in February 1982, and is now offered in versions at three maximum weights (99,792, 104,328 and 108,864-kg/220,000, 230,000 and 240,000-lb) with steadily increasing fuel loads and therefore ranges. The Model 757PF is the package freighter version without cabin windows but with a freight door at the forward end of the port fuselage side. The same loading door is used in the Model 757 Combi, which was introduced in 1986 as the convertible passenger/freight version.

A Boeing 757-200

BOEING 757-200
Role: Intermediate/short-range passenger transport
Crew/Accommodation: Two, four cabin crew, plus up to 239 passengers (charter)
Power Plant: Two 18,189 kgp (40,100 lb s.t.) Rolls-Royce RB211-535E4 or 17,327 kgp (38,200 lb s.t.) Pratt & Whitney PW2037 turbofans
Dimensions: Span 38.05 m (124.83 ft); length 47.32 m (155.25 ft); wing area 181.3 m² (1,951 sq ft)
Weights: Empty 58,264 kg (128,450 lb); MTOW 108,862 kg (240,000 lb)
Performance: Cruise speed 850 km/h (459 knots) at 11,887 m (39,000 ft); operational ceiling 13,000+ m (42,650 + ft); range 6,150 km (3,320 naut. miles) with maximum payload
Load: Up to 26,349 kg (58,090 lb)

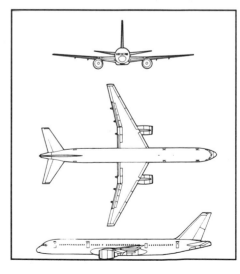

Boeing 757-200

AIRBUS INDUSTRIE A310 (France/Netherlands/Spain/U.K./W.Germany)

Airbus Industrie A310

A major problem facing the design team of the Airbus family of airliners was the lack of clear signals from potential purchasers both in Europe and elsewhere in the world. The A310 resulted from an Airbus programme designed to produce a large-capacity airliner for the short-haul market. At one time, the programme encompassed no fewer than 11 proposals designed to attract the widest possible spectrum of possible buyers. The final A310 was designed to satisfy the emerging market for a 200-seater offering the same type of fuel economy as the A300, and was indeed designed for the highest possible commonality with the A300. Thus the A310 may be regarded as a short-fuselage derivative of the A300, and the powerplant comprises lower-rated versions of the A300's CF6 and JT9D engines, with the RB.211 available as an option. Different features are the engine pylons, landing gear and low-drag wing. This last was designed initially by VFW-Fokker but completed by British Aerospace as an advanced item offering a lift coefficient usefully higher than that of the A300.

The type was first flown in 1982, entering service in 1983. It was proposed in A310-100 short-range and A310-200 medium-range versions, but the former was dropped in favour of different-weight versions of the A310-200 optimized for the two roles. The A310-300 is a longer-range version with drag-reducing wingtip fences (retrospectively applied to the A310-200) and a tailplane trim tank, available in the weight options for the A310-200. Convertible and freight versions are designated A310C and A310F.

Airbus Industrie A310

AIRBUS 310-300
Role: Intermediate-range passenger transport
Crew/Accommodation: Three and six cabin crew, plus up to 280 passengers
Power Plant: Two 22,680 kgp (50,000 lb s.t.) General Electric CF6-80C2-A2 or Pratt & Whitney JT9D-7R4E turbofans
Dimensions: Span 43.9 m (144.0 ft); length 44.66 m (153.08 ft); wing area 219 m² (2,357 sq ft)
Weights: Empty 77,040 kg (169,840 lb), MTOW 150,000 kg (330,693 lb)
Performance: Maximum speed 903 km/h (561 mph) at 10,670 m (35,000 ft); operational ceiling 13,000+ m (42,650+ ft); range 6,950 km (4,318 miles) with maximum payload
Load: Up to 35,108 kg (77,400 lb) including belly cargo

An Airbus Industrie A310-300

AIRBUS INDUSTRIE A320 (France/Netherlands/Spain/U.K./W. Germany)

Airbus Industrie A320

One of the fastest-selling airliners in recent times, the A320 is powered by CFM56-6 or International Aero Engines V2500 turbofans. It was conceived as a 150-seat short/medium-range partner to the A310, and, despite its longer fuselage, bears a strong external resemblance to its larger brother. The decision to develop such a type was taken in June 1981, and the new design was initially marketed in 154- and 172-seat A320-100 and A320-200 versions with fuselages of different lengths. These designations were altered to versions of a single-fuselage variant (for 162 passengers) with low and high fuel capacities optimizing the model for short- and medium-range routes.

In detail the A320 is a wholly new design using a large percentage of composite materials and advanced electronic features, such as a quadruplex digital fly-by-wire control system with sidestick controllers, an electronic flight instrument system, and an electronic centralized aircraft monitor. Aerospatiale has 34 per cent of the programme and is responsible for the nose and forward fuselage; Deutsche Airbus has 35 per cent and handles the centre and rear fuselage; British Aerospace has 24 per cent and is tasked with the wing; and the final 7 per cent is allocated to CASA (5 per cent for the rear fuselage panels and tailplane) and Belairbus (2 per cent for the wing leading edge).

The first A320 flew in February 1987 and entered service in March 1988 after accelerated flight test and certification programmes. The type offers very low operating costs.

An Airbus Industrie A320-200

AIRBUS A320-200

Role: Intermediate/short-range passenger transport

Crew/Accommodation: Two and four/five cabin crew, plus up to 164 passengers (single class cabin)

Power Plant: Two 11,340 kgp (25,000 lb s.t.) General Electric/SNECMA CFM56-5 or IAE V2500 turbofans

Dimensions: Span 33.91 m (111.25 ft); length 37.58 m (123.25 ft); wing area 122.4 m² (1,318 sq ft)

Weights: Empty 39,268 kg (86,570 lb); MTOW 71,986 kg (158,700 lb)

Performance: Maximum speed 903 km/h (560 mph) at 8,535 m (28,000 ft); operational ceiling 13,000+ m (42,650+ ft); range 4,730 km (2,940 miles) with maximum payload

Load: Up to 19,142 kg (42,200 lb) including belly cargo

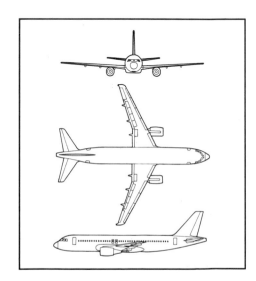

Airbus Industrie A320

231

ANTONOV An-225 MRIYA (U.S.S.R.)

An-225 Mriya

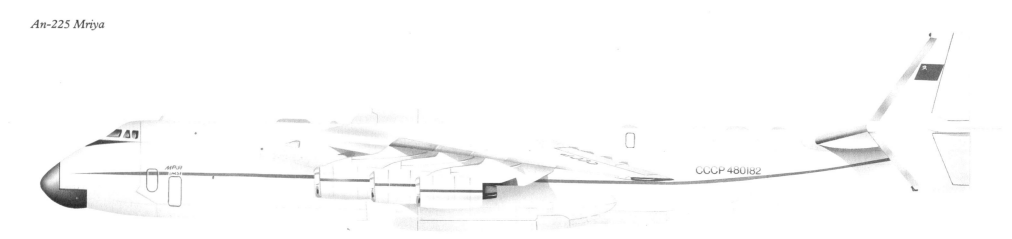

The An-225 Mriya (Dream) first flew in December 1988 and should enter service in the early 1990s as successor to the same design bureau's An-124, taking over from this machine as the world's largest aircraft. The type appears to be based on the outer wings and four-turbofan powerplant of the An-124, these being married to a new centre section (with an additional pair of engines) and massive fuselage ending in an empennage with endplate vertical surfaces. This allows the 'piggy-back' carriage above the fuselage of outsize loads (including the new Soviet space shuttle) weighing up to 70,000-kg (154,321-lb) and too large to fit into the cavernous hold, which is accessed by a rear ramp/door arrangement. In common with other Soviet strategic logistical and resources-exploitation support airlifters, the An-225 has the type of multi-wheel landing gear that bestows the ability to use semi-prepared airstrips.

The An-225 is a truly prodigious heavy-lift type designed to carry massive loads in the fuselage hold or, as noted above, over the fuselage. This latter consideration led to the design of the tailplane with its widely separated endplate vertical surfaces. The hold is approximately 43.0 m (141 ft 1 in) long, 6.4 m (21ft 0 in) wide and 4.4 m (14 ft 5 in) high. The landing gear comprises two 14-wheel main gear units and two twin-wheel nose units, the multi-wheel arrangement being designed to spread the load and so prevent damage to standard runways.

One of the An-225's most significant capabilities is the ability to operate from 1000-m (1,095-yard) runways.

ANTONOV An-225 MRIYA
Role: Heavy-lift cargo transport
Crew/Accommodation: Three
Power Plant: Six 24,400 kgp (53,800 lb s.t.) Lotarev D-18 turbofans
Dimensions: Span 84.4 m (290 ft); length 84 m (275.6 ft)
Weights: MTOW 600,000 kg (1,322,772 lb)
Performance: Cruise speed 700 km/h (378 knots); range 4,500 km (2,428 naut. miles) with 200,000 kg (440,920 lb) payload
Load: Up to 250,000 kg (551,145 lb)

An-225 Mriya

The Antonov An-225 Mriya is the world's largest aeroplane

BRITISH AEROSPACE BAe 125 Family (United Kingdom)

BAe 125-700

The H.S. 125 was initially schemed by de Havilland as a long-range executive transport with a crew of two and accommodation for six to eight passengers. The type was designed as a low-wing monoplane of all-metal construction with a pressurized fuselage of the fail-safe type and modestly swept flying surfaces that included a tailplane set high on the vertical tail surfaces. The first example flew in 1962 with two 1361-kg (3,000-lb) thrust Armstrong Siddeley (later Bristol Siddeley and finally Rolls-Royce) Viper 20 turbojets, replaced by identically rated Viper 520s in the D.H. 125 Series 1 production aircraft, which had span and length increased by 0.91 and 1.19 m (3 ft 0 in and 3 ft 11 in).

Successive variants have been the D.H. 125 Series 1A/1B with higher weights and 140-6-kg (3,100-lb) thrust Viper 521 and 522 engines, the H.S. 125 Series 2 operated by the RAF as the Dominie T.Mk 1 navigation trainer (the same name was also used for the Dominie CC.Mks 1 and 2 communications aircraft of later series), the H.S. 125 Series 3 and H.S. 125 Series 400 with more powerful Viper 522s, the H.S. 125 Series 600 with a 0.94-m (37-in) fuselage stretch for 14 passengers in a high-density layout, the H.S. 125 Series 700 which switched to turbofan power, in the form of two 1678-kg (3,700-lb) thrust Garrett TFE731-3-1Hs, for markedly improved range with a considerable decrease in noise as a means of improving the type's saleability in sensitive areas such as the American west coast, and the improved H.S. 125 Series 800 with a revised wing and 1950-kg (4,300-lb) thrust TFE731-5R-1Hs.

Latest in the lineage is the BAe 1000, equipped with fuel thrifty Pratt/Whitney Canada PW300 turbofans to provide yet further range extension.

The BAe 125-1000

BRITISH AEROSPACE BAe 125 Series 800
Role: Executive Jet transport
Crew/Accommodation: Two and one cabin crew, plus up to 14 passengers
Power Plant: Two 1,950 kgp (4,300 lb s.t.) Garrett ÀiResearch TFE731-5R-1H turbofans
Dimensions: Span 15.66 m (51.38 ft); length 15.6 m (51.17 ft); wing area 34.75 m² (374 sq ft)
Weights: Empty 6,858 kg (15,120 lb); MTOW 12,430 kg (27,400 lb)
Performance: Cruise speed 741 km/h (400 knots) at 11,887 m (39,000 ft); operational ceiling 13,100 m (49,000 ft); range 5,318 km (2,870 naut. miles) with maximum payload
Load: Up to 1,088 kg (2,400 lb)

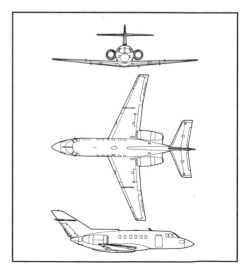

BAe 125-800

BEECH KING AIR AND SUPER KING AIR (United States)

C-12A

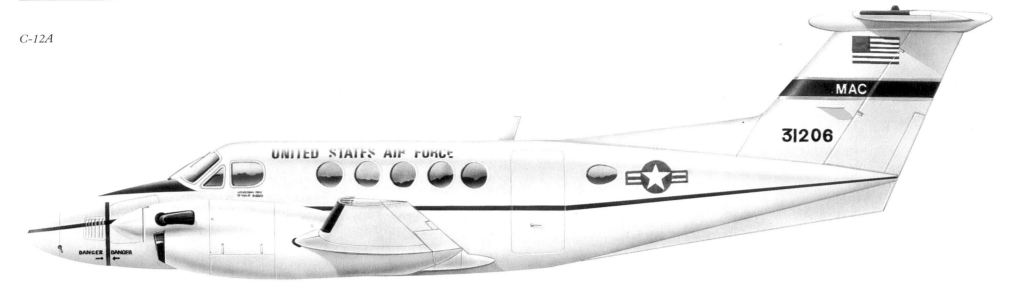

The King Air was developed as a turboprop-powered derivative of the Model 65 Queen Air, and first flew in 1963 as the Model 65-80 conversion with two 373-kW (500-shp) Pratt & Whitney Canada PT6A engines. The type entered production as the unpressurized Model 65-90T King Air to meet initial orders from the military for what became the U-21

Ute utility and special mission series, the first examples of which were delivered in 1967. This family was in fact preceded into service by the initial civil version, the pressurized Model A90.

The type has gone through many variants to culminate in the Model F90 King Air, which is a hybrid model with the fuselage of the Model 90, the wings and powerplant of the Model 100, and the tail unit of the Model 200. Delivered from August 1969, the Model 100 King Air introduced a

reduced-span wing based on that of the Model 99 Airliner, larger elevator and rudder areas, and a fuselage lengthened for 15 persons (including the pilot) rather than the 10 carried by the Model 90. Powered by 507-kW (680-shp) PT6A-28 turboprops, the Model 100 was followed in 1971 by the improved Model A100 (military U-21F), and from 1975 by the Model B100 with 533-kW (715-shp) Garrett TPE331-6-252B turboprops. In October 1972 the company flew the

first Model 200 Super King Air with a T-tail, an increased-span wing, and greater fuel capacity for its more powerful PT6A-41 turboprops.

The type is used by the U.S. military as the C-12 Huron communications and special mission series with a number of engine marks, while civil models include the Model B200 with PT6A-42 engines for improved cruise performance. This can be delivered in freighter or maritime surveillance configurations.

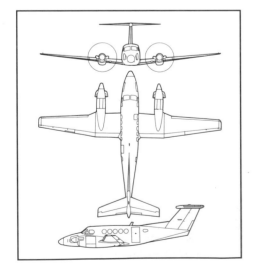

Beech Model 200 Super King Air

BEECH SUPER KING AIR 300
Role: Executive transport
Crew/Accommodation: Two plus up to 13 passengers (normally 6)
Power Plant: Two 1,030 shp Pratt & Whitney of Canada PT6A-60A turboprops
Dimensions: Span 16.61m (54.5 ft); length 13.34 m (43.75 ft); wing area 28.15 m² (303 sq ft)
Weights: Empty 3,715 kg (8,190 lb); MTOW 6,350 kg (14,000 lb)
Performance: Maximum speed 583 km/h (315 knots) at 7,315 m (24,000 ft); operational ceiling 10,670 m (35,000 ft); range 2,593 km (1,400 naut. miles) with 8 passengers and baggage
Load: Up to 1,660 kg (3,600 lb)

A Beech King Air 100

CESSNA CITATION (United States)

Citation I

With its Citation family, Cessna moved into the market for high-performance 'bizjets' offering its purchasers the combination of performance and fuel economy they wanted for commercial reasons, together with the low noise 'footprint' that avoided the vociferous complaints of the growing environmental lobby. The company's investment in the project was very considerable, and when the prototype, at that time called the Fanjet 500, first flew in September 1969, it became clear that Cessna had a type that offered serious competition to market leaders such as the BAe HS 125, Dassault Falcon 20, and Gates Learjet. The type was typical of Cessna twin-engined aircraft in many features other than its aft-mounted podded engines, and was renamed Citation shortly after its first flight. Test flights revealed the need for several important modifications before certification could be secured, so this straight-winged type entered service only in 1971 with Pratt & Whitney Canada JT15D-1 turbofans.

Later developments have been the Citation I of 1976 with greater span, the Citation I/SP for single-pilot operation, the Citation II of 1978 with greater span, a lengthened fuselage and 1134-kg (2,500-lb) thrust JT15D-4 engines, the single-pilot Citation II/SP, the completely revised Citation III of 1982 with swept wings of supercritical section, a lengthened fuselage for two crew and 13 passengers, a T-tail and 1656-kg (3,650-lb) thrust Garrett TFE731-3B-100S turbofans, and the most recent Citation V, which combines the short-field performance of the Citation II with a larger cabin and the speed and cruising altitude of the Citation III.

Cessna Citation II

CESSNA CITATION S/II (T-47A)
Role: Executive transport and military trainer
Crew/Accommodation: Two, plus up to eight passengers
Power Plant: Two, 1,134 kgp (2,500 lb s.t.) Pratt & Whitney JT15D-4B turbofans
Dimensions: Span 15.90 m (52.21 ft); length 14.39 m (47.21 ft); wing area 31.83 m² (342.6 sq ft)
Weights: Empty 3,655 kg (8,059 lb); MTOW 6,849 kg (15,100 lb)
Performance: Cruise speed 746 km/h (403 knots) Mach 0.70 at 10,670 m (35,000 ft); operational ceiling 13,105 m (43,000 ft); range 3,223 km (1,739 naut. miles) with four passengers
Load: Up to 871 kg (1,920 lb)

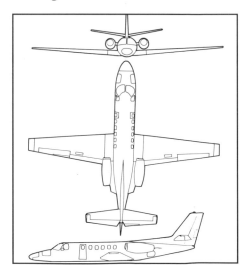

The Citation II/SP

BEECH STARSHIP (United States)

Starship 1

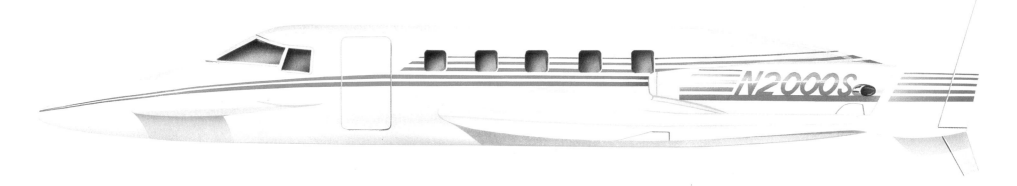

The Starship marks a radical departure from previous aircraft in the Beech line, being a futuristic canard design with swept flying surfaces and two turboprops located in the rear-mounted wing to drive pusher propellers. The engines are located as close to the rear fuselage as possible to reduce thrust asymmetry problems in the event of an engine failure. The type is also notable for the high

percentage of composite materials used in the airframe: this offers an extremely attractive combination of low weight with great strength. The Starship's wings are monocoque structures with composite wingtip stabilizers, and terminate in endplate surfaces that provide directional stability as well as serving as drag-reducing winglets. The foreplanes are of the variable-geometry design that contribute to the Starship's good field performance before being swept back to improve maximum cruise speed.

In overall terms, the Starship reflects the design concepts of the

adventurous Burt Rutan, and the type was first flown during August 1983 in the form of an 85 per cent scale version developed by Rutan's Scaled Composites Inc. Full-scale flight trials began in February 1986 with the first of six pre-production Starships. The type received Federal Aviation Administration certification in 1989,

with deliveries beginning later in the same year, despite the fact that payload/range performance is lower than guaranteed because of unexpected drag and weight problems. A number of fixes are being developed, and it is expected that these shortfalls will be eliminated in the early 1990s.

Beech Starship

BEECH STARSHIP 1
Role: Executive transport
Crew/Accommodation: Two, plus up to ten passengers
Power Plant: Two 1,100 shp Pratt & Whitney Canada PT6A-67 turboprops
Dimensions: Span 16.46 m (54 ft); length 14.05 m (46.08 ft); wing area 26.09 m² (280.9 sq ft)
Weights: Empty 4,044 kg (8,916 lb); MTOW 6,350 kg (14,000 lb)
Performance: Cruise speed 652 km/h (405 mph) at 7,620 m (25,000 ft); operational ceiling 12,495 m (41,000 ft); range 2,089 km (1,298 miles) with maximum payload
Load: Up to 1,264 kg (2,884 lb)

The Starship and the Model 17 'Staggerwing'

BELLANCA PACEMAKER (United States)

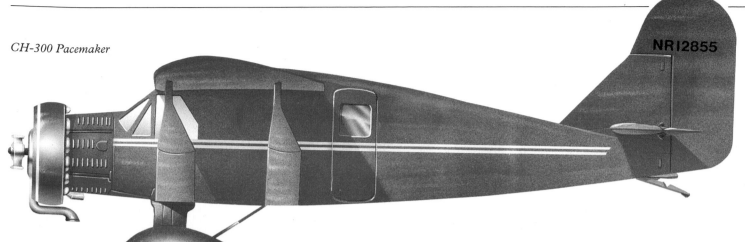
CH-300 Pacemaker

The Pacemaker was a logical development of the CH-300 utility transport, and the first model was the PM-300 Pacemaker Freighter. This was certificated in September 1929, and the cabin was laid out for four passengers and 386 kg (850 lb) of freight in its forward and aft sections respectively; three of the seats could be removed to allow a 714-kg (1,575-lb) freight load. For its time the Pacemaker was a remarkable transport, for on the power of a single 224-kW (300-hp) Wright J-6 it could carry a payload greater than its own empty weight. The type could be used on wheels, skis or floats, and though not many Pacemaker Freighters were built, some CH-300s were in fact modified to this standard. In May 1931 a Pacemaker Freighter with a 168-kW (225-hp) Packard diesel engine set a world unrefuelled endurance record of 84 hours 33 minutes.

The basic Pacemaker design was refined during its six-year production life. The Model E Senior Pacemaker of 1932 had a 246-kW (330-hp) Wright engine that was soon replaced by the 313-kW (425-hp) Wright R-975-E2. In concert with a larger wing and spatted landing gear, this offered improved performance with a payload of six passengers; this model also had chair-pack parachutes that formed part of the upholstery until needed. Another variant was the Senior Pacemaker Series 8, which was a pure freighter that could carry a 907-kg (2,000-lb) payload over a range of 805 km (500 miles) in wheeled configuration, or a 811-kg (1,787-lb) payload over the same range in floatplane configuration. As an alternative to the R-975, Bellanca offered the Pacemaker with the Pratt & Whitney Wasp Junior radial of the same power. While the only known U.S. military Pacemaker was a single JE-1 operated by the U.S. Navy as a nine-seat communications type, the Royal Canadian Air Force used 13 CH-300 in all, the type being operated by the RCAF between 1929 and 1940.

BELLANCA CH-300 PACEMAKER
Role: Utility transport
Crew/Accommodation: One, plus up to five passengers
Power Plant: One 300 hp Wright J-6E Whirlwind air-cooled radial
Dimensions: 14.12 m (46.33 ft); length 8.46 m (27.75 ft); wing area 25.36 m² (273 sq ft)
Weights: Empty 1,201 kg (2,647 lb); MTOW 1,952 kg (4,300 lb)
Performance: Maximum speed 230 km/h (143 mph) at sea level; operational ceiling 5,181 m (17,000 ft); radius 2,189 km (1,360 miles with full fuel)
Load: Up to 408 kg (900 kg)

A Bellanca Senior Skyrocket

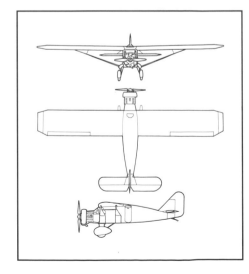
Bellanca Skyrocket

FAIRCHILD 24 (United States)

Fairchild 24R

In 1931, Sherman Fairchild bought the American Aviation Corporation's Kreider-Reisner subsidiary, and with this new Fairchild Aircraft Corporation came the rights to a two-seat sport and training aircraft of braced parasol-wing layout. This was marketed as the Fairchild 22 Model

C7 that survived slow initial sales to become a commercially successful and popular type. The success of the Model C7A variant persuaded Fairchild to produce a version with enclosed accommodation for two seated side-by-side in a higher fuselage that turned the parasol-wing Model C7A into the high-wing Fairchild 24 Model C8. The type was certificated in April 1932 with the 71-kW (95-hp) A.C.E. Cirrus Hi-Ace inline engine and though only 10 of this variant were produced, the type paved the

way for extensive development and production.

The main developments (with approximate production total) were the Model C8A (25) with the 93-kW (125-hp) Warner Scarab radial, the Model C8C (130) with slightly greater size and the 108-kW (145-hp) Warner

Super Scarab, the Model C8D (14) with three seats and the 108-kW Ranger 6-390B inline, the Model C8E (50) version of the Model C8C with improved equipment, and the Model C8F (40) version of the Model C8D with improved equipment. The designation then changed to Model 24, and this series ran to some 200 aircraft in four Model 24-G to Model 24-K three/four-seat variants. The final civil models were the two Model 24R (60) and four Model 24W (165) variants with Ranger inline and Warner radial engines. Another 981 inline- and radial-engined aircraft were built to military order as the U.S. Army Air Forces' UC-61 Forwarder, including large numbers supplied to the Royal Air Force with the name Argus. Additional aircraft were impressed for the American forces, the U.S. Navy and U.S. Coast Guard models being the GK and J2K.

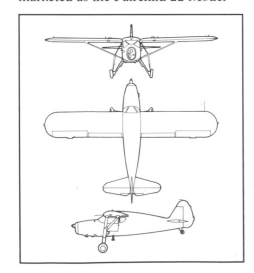

Fairchild 24

FAIRCHILD MODEL 24W-9
Role: Touring
Crew/Accommodation: One, plus up to three passengers
Power Plant: One 165 hp Warner Super Scarab 175 air-cooled radial
Dimensions: Span 11.07 m (36.33 ft); length 8.79 m (25.85 ft); wing area 17.96 m² (193.30 sq ft)
Weights: Empty 732 kg (1,613 lb); MTOW 1,162 kg (2,562 lb)
Performance: Maximum speed 212 km/h (132 mph) at sea level ; operational ceiling 4,267 m (14,000 ft); range 1,028 km (639 miles)
Load: Up to 245 kg (540 lb)

The Fairchild Model 24

BEECH 18 (United States)

Beech C-45G

In 1935, Beech began the development of an advanced light transport of monoplane layout to supersede its Model 17 biplane transport, whose reverse-staggered wings had earned the soubriquet 'Staggerwing'. The Model 18A was an all-metal type with a semi-monocoque fuselage, cantilever wings, electrically retracted tailwheel landing gear, and endplate vertical tail surfaces. The first example of this celebrated aeroplane flew in January 1937 with two 239-kW (320-hp) Wright R-760-E2 radial engines, and the type then entered manufacture for 32 years.

The initial civil models were powered by a number of radial engine types, and reached an early peak as the Model 18D of 1939, which was powered by two 246-kW (330-hp) Jacobs L-6 engines that combined the Model 18A's economy of operation with higher performance. The American military acquired an interest in the type during 1940, and during World War II the type was produced to the extent of 4,000 or more aircraft in various roles. The staff transport in several variants had the American designations C-45 (army) and JRB (navy), and the British name Expediter. In 1941 Beech introduced the AT-7 Navigator and AT-11 Kansan (or naval SNB) navigation and bombing/gunnery trainers.

After the war improved civil models appeared. From 1953 the Super 18 appeared as the definitive civil model with drag-reducing features, cross-wind landing gear, and a separate flightdeck, and from 1963 retractable tricycle landing gear was an option. Substantial numbers were converted to turboprop power by several specialist companies, these variants including the Volpar Turbo 18 and Turboliner, the Dumod Liner, the PAC Turbo Tradewind, and the Hamilton Westwind.

The Model 18 was a superlative light transport

BEECH D18S
Role: Light passenger/executive transport
Crew/Accommodation: Two/one, plus up to seven passengers
Power Plant: Two 450 hp Pratt & Whitney R.985-AN14B Wasp Junior air-cooled radials
Dimensions: Span 14.50 m (47.58 ft); length 10.35 m (33.96 ft); wing area 32.4 m² (349 sq ft)
Weights: Empty 2,558 kg (5,635 lb); MTOW 3,980 kg (8,750 lb)
Performance: Cruise speed 338 km/h (211 mph) at 3,050 m (10,000 ft); operational ceiling 6,250 m (20,500 ft); range 1,200 km (750 miles)
Load: Up to 587 kg (1,295 lb)

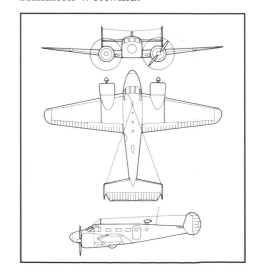

Beech Model 18

BÜCKER Bü 131 JUNGMANN and Bü 133 JUNGMEISTER (Germany)

Bü 133 Jungmeister

Bü 131B spanned 7.40 m (24 ft 3.25 in) and had a maximum take-off weight of 680 kg (1,499 lb).

To meet production for its Bü 131, Bücker opened a second factory and here the company's design team evolved for the advanced training role the basically similar Jungmeister (Young Champion). This had smaller dimensions than the Bü 131, had single-seat accommodation, and was stressed for full aerobatic capability. The first example flew with the 101-kW (135-hp) HM 6 inline engine and revealed excellent performance. The type was ordered in large numbers by the German air force, and the major variants were the Bü 133A with the 101-kW (135-hp) HM 6 inline, the Bü 133B with the 119-kW (160-hp) HM 506 inline and the Bü 133C main production model with the 119-kW Siemens Sh 14 radial.

The Jungmann (Young Man, or Youth) was the first product of Bücker Flugzeugbau, and first flew in April 1934 as a compact trainer of the classic single-bay biplane formula with tandem open cockpits in a fabric-covered airframe comprising wooden wings and a steel-tube fuselage and empennage. The type entered production as the Bü 131A with the same 60-kW (80-hp) Hirth HM 60R air-cooled inline engine that had powered the prototype, while the improved Bü 131B had the 78-kW (105-hp) HM 504A-2. The type was built in Japan as the Watanabe Ki-86 and K9W, of which more than 1,250 were produced, and was also widely exported by the parent factory. The

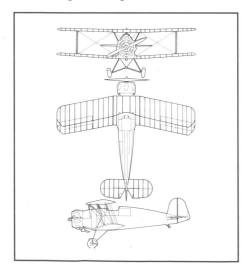

Bücker Bü 133 Jungmeister

BÜCKER Bü 131B JUNGMANN
Role: Trainer
Crew/Accommodation: Two
Power Plant: One 105 hp Hirth HM 504A-2 air-cooled inline
Dimensions: Span 7.4 m (24.28 ft); length 6.62 m (21.72 ft); wing area 13.5 m² (145.3 sq ft)
Weights: Empty 390 kg (860 lb); MTOW 680 kg (1,500 lb)
Performance: Maximum speed 183 km/h (114 mph) at sea level; operational ceiling 3,000 m (9,843 ft); range 650 km (404 miles)
Load: None

This is a Bücker Bü 131

PIPER J-3 CUB and L-4 GRASSHOPPER (United States)

L-4 Grasshopper

In 1929, C. Gilbert Taylor and his brother created the Taylor Brothers Aircraft Corporation, reorganized as the Taylor Aircraft Company in 1931.

A Piper L-4 Grasshopper

When the company ran into financial problems, the rights to the Taylor Cub were bought by W.T. Piper Snr, the company's secretary and treasurer. In 1937, Piper bought out the Taylor brothers and renamed the company the Piper Aircraft Corporation in order to continue production of the Cub, which had first flown in September 1930.

The Cub was a classic braced high-wing monoplane of mixed construction with fabric covering, and could be powered by any of several types of flat-four piston engine. The initial J-3 Cub was powered by the 30-kW (40-hp) Continental A40-4, but production soon switched to the J-3C-50 with the 37-kW (50-hp) A50-4, the suffix to the aircraft's basic designation

indicating the make of engine and its horsepower. Further development produced the Continental-engined J-3C-65 and then variants with Franklin and Lycoming engines as the J-3F-50 and F-65 and the J-3L-50 and L-65, while a radial-engined model was the J-3P-50 with the Lenape Papoose. Some 14,125 Cubs were built in these series for the civil market, and another 5,703 military liaison and observation aircraft expanded this number. The U.S. Army evaluated several types of civil lightplane in these roles during 1941, and the four J-3Cs evaluated as YO-59s with the 48-kW (65-hp) Continental O-170-3 paved the way for 140 O-59s and 948 O-59As that were later redesignated L-4 and L-4A in a sequence that ran to L-4J and included training gliders; the U.S. Marine Corps also adopted the type as the NE. Such has been the abiding popularity of the type that it was reinstated in production during 1988 with a number of more refined features that, however, fail to obscure the essentially simple nature of the basic aircraft.

PIPER L-4 GRASSHOPPER
Role: Observation/communications
Crew/Accommodation: Two
Power Plant: One 65 hp Continental 0-170-3 air-cooled flat-opposed
Dimensions: Span 10.47 m (32.25 ft); length 6.71 m (22 ft); wing area 16.63 m² (179 sq ft)
Weights: Empty 331 kg (730 lb); MTOW 553 kg (1,220 lb)
Performance: Maximum speed 137 km/h (85 mph) at sea level; operational ceiling 2,835 m (9,300 ft); range 306 km (190 miles)
Load: Up to 86 kg (190 lb)

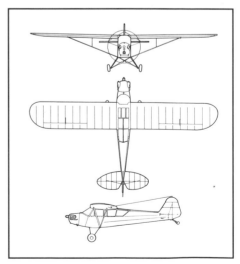

Piper L-4A Grasshopper

BEECH BONANZA (United States)

V35B Bonanza

Another long-lived Beech design, the four/five-seat Bonanza first flew in December 1945 as the V-tailed Model 35 with the 138-kW (185-hp) Continental E-185-1 piston engine, though later aircraft have the 213-kW (285-hp) Continental I0-520 flat-six engine. The type was an immediate success, for, even before the first production Bonanza had been delivered, the company had orders for some 1,500 aircraft, many of them for pilots who had learned to fly with the ever-expanding military forces during World War II. Large-scale production of the Bonanza was undertaken in a number of forms with normally aspirated or turbocharged engines, the use of the latter being indicated by the suffix TC after the model number. From the beginning, the Model 35 had retractable tricycle landing gear, but from 1949 the original castoring nosewheel was replaced by a steerable unit to create the model A35.

In 1959 the company introduced the Beech 33 Debonair with a conventional tail and lower-powered engine for those worried about the 'gimmickry' of the V-tail. The lower-powered engine dictated that passenger accommodation was reduced from four to three, and in 1967 this variant was taken into the designation mainstream as the Model E33 Bonanza.

The third Bonanza type is the Model 36 Bonanza. This was intoduced in 1968 as a utility six-seater. This is based on the Model V35B with its fuselage lengthened by 0.25 m (10 in), and fitted with the tail unit of the Model 33 as well as the strengthened landing gear of the Model 55 Baron. The fuselage is accessed by double doors so that the type can double as a light freight transport. Many variants were in fact produced.

Beech Bonanza V35

BEECH BONANZA
Role: Tourer
Crew/Accommodation: One, plus up to three passengers
Power Plant: One 196 hp Continental E185-8 air-cooled flat-opposed
Dimensions: Span 10.01 m (32.83 ft); length 7.67 m (25.16 ft); wing area 16.49 m² (177.6 sq ft)
Weights: Empty 715 kg (1,575 lb); MTOW 1,203 kg (2,650 lb)
Performance: Cruise speed 272 km/h (170 mph) at 2,440 m (8,000 ft); operational ceiling 5,485 m (17,100 ft); range 1,207 km (750 miles)
Load: Up to 373 kg (822 lb)

Beech Bonanza V35A

de HAVILLAND CANADA DHC-1 CHIPMUNK (Canada)

Chipmunk T.Mk 10

The DHC-1 Chipmunk was the first aircraft designed by de Havilland's Canadian subsidiary, and was evolved as a successor to the legendary D.H.82 Tiger Moth, of which a special version had been built in Canada. The type was therefore designed as a primary trainer, and despite its low performance and fixed tailwheel landing gear, the DHC-1 was a thoroughly modern type with enclosed tandem accommodation, stressed-skin construction of light alloy, a low-set wing with trailing-edge flaps, and attractive lines highlighted by the typically de Havilland tail unit. The first example flew in May 1946 with a 108-kW (145-hp) de Havilland Gipsy Major 1C inline engine. Production of the Chipmunk in Canada lasted to 1951 and accounted for 218 aircraft, most of which had a bubble canopy.

Aircraft suffixed -1 and -2 were powered by the Gipsy Major 1 and Gipsy Major 10 engines respectively, and the main variants were the semi-aerobatic DHC-1A and the fully aerobatic DHC-1B in a total of nine subvariants including the Royal Canadian Air Force's DHC-1A-1 and DHC-1B-2-S3 used as the Chipmunk T.Mk 1 and T.Mk 2 respectively, the latter for refresher training at civil clubs. In its fully aerobatic form, the type also found favour with the Royal Air Force, and this resulted in British manufacture of 1,014 Chipmunks, of which 735 Gipsy Major 8-powered examples went to the RAF as Chipmunk T.Mk 10 *ab initio* trainers for use by all 17 university air squadrons and many RAF Volunteer Reserve flying units.

Aircraft of the Chipmunk T.Mk 20 were produced for the military export market (217 Chipmunk T.Mk 20s with the Gipsy Major 10-2) and for the civil market (28 basically similar Chipmunk T.Mk 21s). Another 60 Chipmunks were built under licence in Portugal by OGMA.

---

de HAVILLAND CANADA DHC-1 CHIPMUNK T.MK 10
Role: Primary trainer
Crew/Accommodation: Two
Power Plant: One 145 hp de Havilland Major 8 air-cooled inline
Dimensions: Span 10.46 m (34.33 ft); length 7.82 m (25.66 ft); wing area 15.98 m² (172.00 sq ft)
Weights: Empty 643 kg (1,417 lb); MTOW 908 kg (2,000 lb)
Performance: Maximum speed 223 km/h (138 mph) at sea level; operational ceiling 4,876 m (16,000 ft); radius 483 km (300 miles)
Load: Nil

de Havilland Chipmunk T.Mk 10

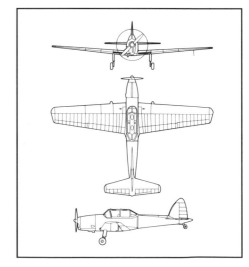

de Havilland Canada DHC-1 Chipmunk

243

CESSNA 170, 172, 175 and 182 Series (United States)

Cessna 172 Skyhawk

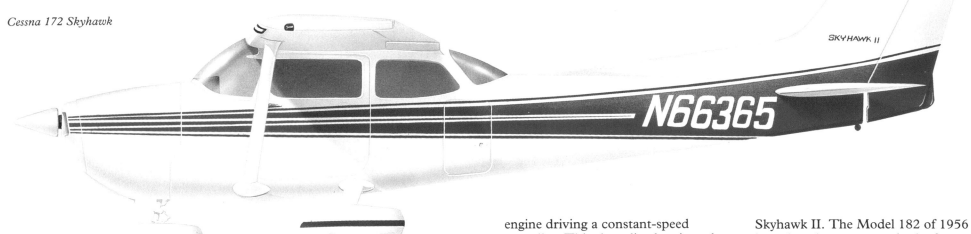

This series enjoys the distinction of being the most successful lightplane of all time. The Model 170 first flew in 1948 as the two-seat Model 120 with the 108-kW (145-hp) Continental C-145-2 engine and its fuselage re-engineered to four-seat configuration. Good sales were later boosted by the advent of the Model 170B with improved field performance as a result

of the Fowler slotted trailing-edge flaps, a type pioneered in the Cessna range by the Model 305. In 1955, the company introduced the Model 172, which was basically the Model 170B with the original fixed tailwheel landing gear replaced by fixed tricycle landing gear.

In 1958, Cessna placed into production the Model 175, which was in essence the Model 172 with a number of refinements (including a free-blown windscreen and speed fairings), as well as the more powerful 131-kW (175-hp) GO-300-C geared

engine driving a constant-speed propeller. This short-lived variant also appeared in upgraded Model 175A and de luxe Skylark forms.

A comparable de luxe version of the Model 172 was also produced as the Skyhawk, and this was later revised with a swept vertical tail of the type which market research had shown to be desirable as a means of keeping the model's appearance fully up to date. From 1980, a new and slimmer rear fuselage with rear windows was introduced on the Skylark II and

Skyhawk II. The Model 182 of 1956 introduced more power in the form of the 172-kW (230-hp) Continental O-470-S engine, and was also produced in upgraded Skylane versions.

Further development of the Models 172 and 182 has produced a host of versions with improved furnishing, better instrumentation, retractable landing gear, and turbocharged engines. The Model 172 has additionally been produced in T-41 Mescalero trainer form.

Cessna Model 172

CESSNA 172 SKYHAWK (T-41A)
Role: Light touring (and military basic trainer)
Crew/Accommodation: One, plus up to three passengers
Power Plant: One 160 hp Lycoming 0-320 air-cooled flat-opposed
Dimensions: Span 10.92 m (35.83 ft); length 8.20 m (26 ft); wing area 16.16 m² (174 sq ft)
Weights: Empty 636 kg (1,402 lb); MTOW 1,043 kg (2,300 lb)
Performance: Cruise speed 226 km/h (122 knots) at 2,438 m (8,000 ft); operational ceiling 4,328 m (14,200 ft); range 1,065 km (575 naut. miles) with full payload
Load: Up to 299 kg (660 lb)

A Cessna Model 172

CESSNA 310, 320, 335 and 340 Series (United States)

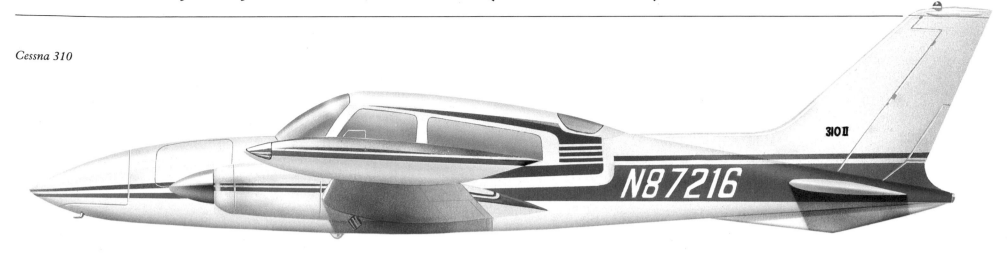

Cessna 310

The design of the Model 310 was started in 1952, the company's desire being to develop a five/six-seat competitor in the market that was emerging for what was to become known as an executive transport, with comparatively high performance and the reliability offered by two engines. The Model 310 emerged as a low-wing monoplane of all-metal construction with retractable tricycle landing gear, two wing-mounted engines and, as a very distinctive identification feature, two wingtip tanks that accommodated the Model 310's entire fuel capacity.

The prototype flew in January 1953 with 168-kW (225 hp) Continental O-470 engines, though early production examples switched to the more powerful 194-kW (260-hp) IO-470 version of the same engine type when deliveries began in 1954. As production continued, the company introduced a number of refinements as part of a product-improvement programme that culminated during 1966 in the introduction of a de luxe version with turbocharged engines, air conditioning and an oxygen system. This Turbo-System Executive Skynight was designated as the Model 320 for a short time, and then became the Turbo T310. Later versions are the Model 310 II and Turbo T310 II.

In 1971 there appeared the Model 340 which is basically as Model 310 with pressurized accommodation together with the wing and landing gear of the Model 414. Upgraded versions are the Models 340A and 340A II, the former with 231-kW (310-hp) TSIO-520-NB engines and the latter with a more sophisticated avionics and equipment package. An unpressurized and lighter variant is the Model 335, also produced as the improved Model 335 II. Military aircraft of the Model 310 type were originally designated L-27, but were redesignated in the U-3 series from 1962.

A Cessna Model 310 II

CESSNA 310L (USAF U-3)
Role: Light twin passenger/utility transport
Crew/Accommodation: Two
Power Plant: Two 260 hp Continental 10-47 0V0 air-cooled flat-opposed
Dimensions: Span 11.25 m (36.92 ft); length 8.99 m (29.5 ft); wing area 16.63 m² (179 sq ft)
Weights: Empty 1,418 kg (3,125 lb); MTOW 2,360 kg (5,200 lb)
Performance: Maximum speed 357 km/h (222 mph) at 1,981 m (6,500 ft); operational ceiling 6,065 m (19,900 ft); range 1,554 km (966 miles) with full payload
Load: Up to 420 kg (925 lb)

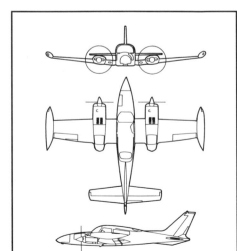

Cessna Turbo T310R

CESSNA 150 and 152 Series (United States)

Cessna 152

In September 1957 Cessna flew the first Model 150, and thereby re-entered the potentially lucrative market for two-seaters in which its earlier competitors had been the highly successful Models 120 and 140. The Model 150 was similar to the

Model 140 in its basic layout as a braced high-wing monoplane of all-metal construction, but differed in having fixed tricycle landing gear in place of the Model 140's fixed tailwheel landing gear. Production started in August 1958 with the 75-kW (100-hp) Continental O-200 flat-four piston engine, and options included dual controls.

The type went through a number of steadily improving variants, and the last of these were the Model 150

Standard, Model 150 Commuter, improved Model 150 Commuter II, and Model 152 Aerobat. This last was a strengthened aerobatic type capable of chandelles, loops, vertical reverses, and rolls of the aileron, barrel and snap types.

The Model 150's production career ended in 1977 after the delivery of

23,836 aircraft, this total including 1,754 French-built Reims F150 aircraft. The Model 150's successor is the Model 152, which entered production late in 1977 with an 82-kW (110-hp) Lycoming O-235-L2C engine in place of the earlier model's O-200. The Model 152 was also delivered in a number of versions.

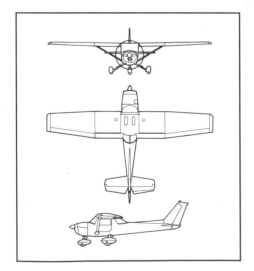

Cessna Model 150

CESSNA 150K
Role: Light tourer/trainer
Crew/Accommodation: Two
Power Plant: One 100 hp Continental O-200A air-cooled flat-opposed
Dimensions: Span 9.97 m (32.71 ft); length 7.24 m (23.75 ft); wing area 14.57 m² (156.86 sq ft)
Weights: Empty 456 kg (1,005 lb); MTOW 726 kg (1,600 lb)
Performance: Cruise speed 188 km/h (117 mph) at 2,134 m (7,000 ft); operational ceiling 3,856 m (12,650 ft); range 909 km (565 miles) with no reserves
Load: Up to 111 kg (245 lb)

A Cessna Model 150

PIPER CHEROKEE (United States)

Cherokee 140

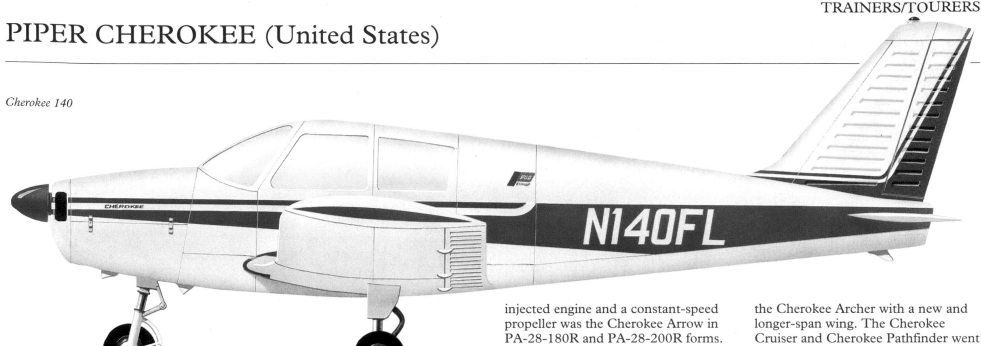

First flown in prototype form during January 1960, the four-seat Cherokee and its successors have been a remarkable success story for Piper. This all-metal cantilever low-wing type has gone through a large number of developments and variants with engine horsepower indicated by the numerical suffix appended to the basic designation; thus the initial PA-28-150 with the 112-kW (150-hp) Lycoming O-320 engine and fixed tricycle landing gear was followed in chronological sequence by the PA-28-160, PA-28-180, PA-28-235, and PA-28-140. An upgraded series introduced in June 1967 with retractable landing gear, a fuel-injected engine and a constant-speed propeller was the Cherokee Arrow in PA-28-180R and PA-28-200R forms. The first series was then redesignated, the PA-29-140 becoming the Cherokee Flite Liner and, in de luxe form, the Cherokee Cruiser 2 Plus 2, the PA-28-180 becoming the Cherokee Challenger with a slightly lengthened fuselage and increased-span wings, and the PA-28-235 becoming the Cherokee Charger. In 1974 further changes in name were made: the Cherokee 2 Plus 2 became the Cherokee Cruiser, the Cherokee Challenger became the Cherokee Archer, and the Cherokee Charger became the Cherokee Pathfinder.

A new type introduced was the PA-28-151 Cherokee Warrior based on the Cherokee Archer with a new and longer-span wing. The Cherokee Cruiser and Cherokee Pathfinder went out of production in 1977, when the PA-28-236 Dakota was introduced with the longer-span wing and the 175-kW (235-hp) O-540 engine. In 1978 there appeared the PA-28-201T Turbo Dakota that went out of production in 1980 to leave in production aircraft now designated PA-28-161 Warrior II, PA-28-181 Archer II and PA-28RT-201T Turbo Arrow IV.

A Piper Cherokee Six

PIPER PA 28-161 CHEROKEE WARRIOR II
Role: Tourer
Crew/Accommodation: One, plus up to three passengers
Power Plant: One 150 hp Lycoming 0-320-E3D air-cooled flat-opposed
Dimensions: Span 10.65 m (35 ft); length 7.2 m (23.8 ft); wing area 15.8 m² (170 sq ft)
Weights: Empty 590 kg (1,301 lb); MTOW 1,065 kg (2,325 lb)
Performance: Cruise speed 213 km/h (133 mph) at 2,438 m (8,000 ft); operational ceiling 3,930 m (12,700 ft); range 1,660 km (720 miles) with full payload
Load: Up to 342 kg (775 lb)

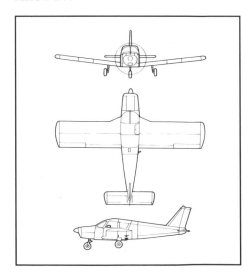

Piper PA-28 Cherokee

BLÉRIOT MONOPLANES (France)

Bleriot XI

Louis Blériot was one of the true pioneers of aviation, and secured his place in history during 1911 as the first man to fly a heavier-than-air craft across the English Channel. The machine involved in this epoch-making flight was a Blériot XI with an 18.7-kW (25-hp) Anzani engine, the culmination of a series of monoplanes that had started with the unsuccessful Blériot V of 1906. This was Blériot's first design after he had ended his association with Gabriel Voisin, and was a canard type that made a few hopping flights, then crashed and was scrapped. Next came the tandem-wing Blériot VI that achieved a few hops during 1907. The Blériot VII was a modestly successful tractor monoplane, and this layout was used in the fabric-covered Blériot VIII that was later rebuilt as the Blériot VIIIbis with flap-type ailerons and Blériot VIIIter with pivoting wingtip ailerons. The Blériot IX had paper-covered wings of short span and a fuselage partially covered in fabrics, but never flew, while the Blériot X pusher biplane was never completed.

The Blériot XI was initially powered by a 21-kW (28-hp) R.E.P. engine, but its lack of success with this engine led to its modification as the Blériot XI (Mod) with the 18.7-kW (25-hp) Anzani. The Blériot XI (Mod)'s cross-Channel triumph secured a comparative flood of orders for his aircraft, which was steadily upgraded with more powerful engines. The type was also developed for the military as a reconnaissance machine in Blériot XI-2 and -3 two- and three-seat forms.

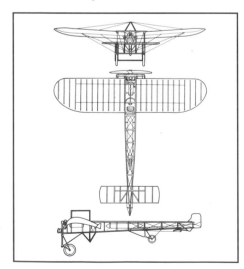

Bleriot XI

BLERIOT XI-2
Role: Reconnaissance/training
Crew/Accommodation: Two
Power Plant: One 80 hp Gnome air-cooled rotary
Dimensions: Span 10.35 m (33.96 ft); length 8.4 m (27.56 ft); wing area 19 m² (205 sq ft)
Weights: Empty 335 kg (786 lb); MTOW 585 kg (1,290 lb)
Performance: Maximum speed 120 km/h (75 mph) at sea level; endurance 3.5 hours
Load: None other than crew

The Bleriot XI monoplane was highly successful

MACCHI MC.72 (Italy)

Macchi MC.72

dimensions but powered by the 746-kW (1,000-hp) AS.3. Technical problems knocked all three out of the race, but one machine later raised the speed record to 479.29 km/h (297.818 mph) and another was fitted with a smaller wing to become the M.52R that raised the record to 512.776 km/h (318.625 mph).

For the 1929 race, Castoldi designed the M.69 of which three were built with the 1342-kW (1,800-hp) Isotta-Fraschini 2-800 with coolant radiators on the wing surfaces, underside of the nose, sides of the rear fuselage, float legs, and upper sides of the floats! Neither of the entered aircraft finished the race.

The MC.72 was designed for the 1931 race, and was powered by a Fiat AS.6 engine (two 1119-kW/1,500-hp AS.5 units mounted front to back and driving contra-rotating propellers). Five aircraft were built, but problems prevented any of them from taking part in this last Schneider Trophy race. Two of the machines later set world speed records, the latter at 709.209 km/h (440.683 mph).

The MC.72 was the culmination of a long series of racing floatplanes designed by Mario Castoldi for the Schneider Trophy races, and despite the fact that it never won such a race,

the MC.72 was without doubt the finest machine of its type ever produced. The starting point for this family was the M.39, which pioneered the twin-float layout with a low-set

wing wire-braced to the floats and the upper part of a slim fuselage tailored to the frontal area of the inline engine.

The first of six M.39s flew in July 1926 as a trainer with the 447-kW (600-hp) Fiat AS.2 engine, and a racer powered by a 597-kW (800-hp) version of the same engine won the 1926 race; the type also raised the world speed record to 416.68 km/h (258.875 mph). For the 1927 race, the company produced three examples of the M.52 with slightly smaller

The Macchi MC.72 drove contra-rotating propeller units

MACCHI MC.72
Role: Racing
Crew/Accommodation: One
Power Plant: One 3,100 hp Fiat AS.6 liquid-cooled inline
Dimensions: Span 9.48 m (31.10 ft); length 8.32 m (27.29 ft) wing area 15.00 m² (161.46 sq ft)
Weights: Empty 2,500 kg (5,511 lb) MTOW 2,907 kg (6,409 lb)
Performance: Maximum speed 709.209 km/h (440.681 mph) at 500 m (1,640 ft)
Load: Nil

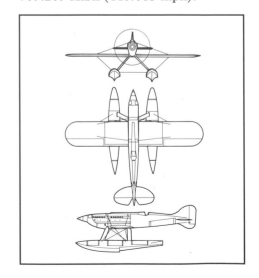

Macchi MC.72

GEE BEE SPORTSTER SERIES (United States)

Sportster R-1

The period between 1925 and 1935 saw the development of many fascinating aircraft specifically for racing, especially in the United States, where the philosophy of cramming maximum engine into minimum airframe approached extraordinary levels. One of the main protagonists of the philosophy was the team of five brothers running Granville Brothers Aircraft. Gee Bee's first type was the Model 'A' side-by-side two-seater, but the brothers then graduated to a low-cost sporting machine, the Model 'X' Sportster single-seater of 1930, that developed into the Model 'Y' Senior Sportster two-seater.

A number of racing successes followed, so the brothers decided to produce a pure racer as the Model 'Z' Super Sportster that introduced the distinctive barrel-shaped fuselage tailored to the diameter of its 399-kW (535-hp) Pratt & Whitney Wasp Junior, and featured a diminutive vertical surface that projected only marginally above the enclosed cockpit, a wire-braced low/mid-set monoplane wing, and fixed but nicely faired tailwheel landing gear. The type enjoyed some racing success, but broke up in an attempt on the world air speed record in December 1931.

For the 1932 season there followed two Model 'R' Super Sporters: the Model R-1 with a 597-kW (800-hp) Pratt & Whitney Wasp and the Model R-2 with a 410-kW (550-hp) Wasp Junior. The first flew in August 1932, and won the Thomson Trophy race as well as setting a landplane record of 476.815 km/h (296.287 mph). Both aircraft were entered for the 1933 Bendix Trophy race, the Model R-1 with a 671-kW (900-hp) Pratt & Whitney Hornet and the Model R-2 with the R-1's original Wasp. The R-1 was later damaged and the R-2 virtually destroyed, but components of both were used to create the Model R-1/R-2.

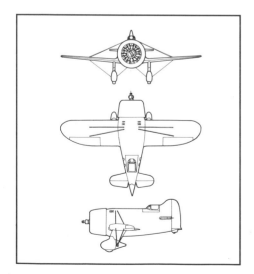

Super Sportster Model R-1

GEE BEE SUPER SPORTSTER R-1
Role: Racing
Crew/Accommodation: One
Power Plant: One 730 hp Pratt & Whitney Wasp TD3-1 air-cooled radial
Dimensions: Span 7.62 m (25.00 ft); length 5.41 m (17.66 ft); wing area 9.29 m² (100.00 sq ft)
Weights: Empty 835 kg (1,840 lb); MTOW 1,095 kg (2,415 kg)
Performance: Maximum speed 473.82 km/h (294.418 mph) at sea level
Load: Nil

Gee Bee Super Sportster Model R-1/R-2 hybrid

de HAVILLAND D.H.88 COMET (United Kingdom)

D.H.88 Comet

The Comet was planned specifically as a competitor for the October 1934 Victorian Centenary Air Race between Mildenhall in England and Melbourne in the Australian state of Victoria. Prize money was donated by Sir MacPherson Robertson, and de Havilland received three orders before the expiry of its February 1934 deadline. The design was very clean by the aerodynamic standards of the day, and based on an all-wood structure as a low-wing monoplane with two wing-mounted engines. The fuselage accommodated three large fuel tanks in the nose immediately ahead of the two crew members, who were seated in tandem under a canopy faired into the tail unit by a dorsal decking. The engines were 172-kW (230-hp) de Havilland Gipsy Six R inlines driving two-position propellers which used the air pressure of 240-km/h (150-mph) speed for the shift from take-off fine pitch to cruising coarse pitch. Other notable features were split trailing-edge flaps and manually retractable main units for the tailwheel landing gear. The first Comet flew in September 1934, and all three machines had received their required certificates of airworthiness before the start of the race on 20 October. The speed section of the race was won by *Grosvenor House* in 70 hours 54 minutes, and is now preserved at the Shuttleworth Trust. *Black Magic* was forced to retire at Baghdad, and G-ACSR finished fourth but then set an out-and-back record of 13.5 days when it came straight back to England with film and mail. Two other Comets were later built, one as a mailplane to French government order and the other for two unsuccessful attempts on the London to Cape Town record.

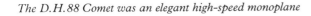

The D.H.88 Comet was an elegant high-speed monoplane

de HAVILLAND D.H.88 COMET
Role: Long range racing
Crew/Accommodation: Two
Power Plant: Two 230 hp de Havilland Gipsy Six R air-cooled inlines
Dimensions: Span 13.41 m (44.00 ft); length 8.84 m (29.00 ft); wing area 19.74 m² (212.50 sq ft)
Weights: Empty 1,329 kg (2,930 lb); MTOW 2,517 kg (5,550 lb)
Performance: Maximum speed 381 km/h (237 mph) at sea level; operational ceiling 5,791 m (19,000 ft); range 4,707 km (2,925 miles)
Load: Nil

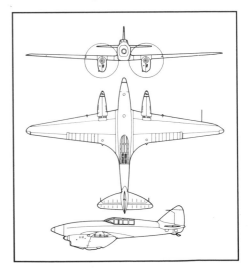

de Havilland D.H.88 Comet

PERCIVAL P.6 MEW GULL (United Kingdom)

Mew Gull

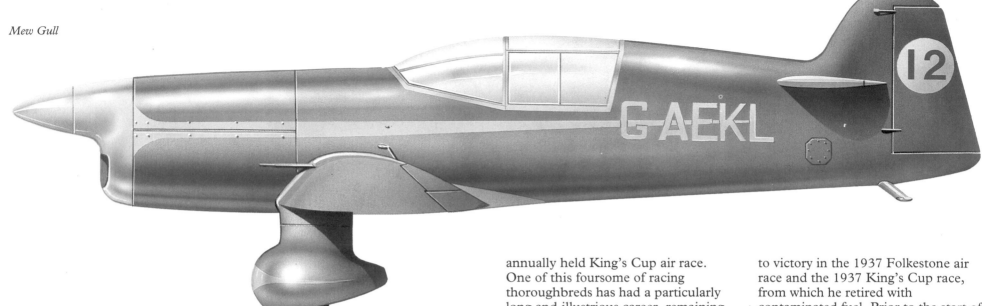

First flown in March 1934, the P.2 prototype was of angular and somewhat austere appearance that gave little hint of the beautiful P.6 Mew Gull to follow. Altogether, five examples of the P.6 were to be built,

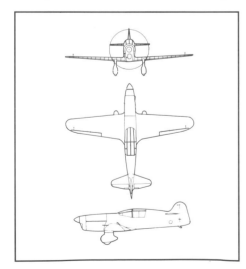

Percival Type E Mew Gull

including the converted P.2 and these subsequently dominated the British air racing scene during the three years prior to September 1939 and the outset of World War II. Of exceptionally well-proportioned shape, the P.6 Mew Gulls were constantly in the headlines, frequently being flown by the aircraft's designer/pilot Captain Edgar Percival in such events as the

PERCIVAL P.6 MEW GULL
Role: Racer
Crew/Accommodation: One
Power Plant: One 205 hp de Havilland Gipsy Six Series II air-cooled inline
Dimensions: Span 7.54 m (24.75 ft); length 6.88 m (21.92 ft); wing area 8.18 m² (88 sq ft)
Weights: Empty 562 kg (1,240 lb); MTOW 1,066 kg (2,350 lb)
Performance: Maximum speed 398 km/h (247 mph) at sea level; range 3,219 km (2,000 miles) with 386 l (85 Imp gal) tankage
Note: figures are for Alex Henshaw's modified G-AEXF as configured for his February 1939, record-breaking England-Cape Town return flight

annually held King's Cup air race. One of this foursome of racing thoroughbreds has had a particularly long and illustrious career, remaining airworthy into the 1990s. Initially built for the South African pilot A. H. Miller and carrying the appropriate ZS-AHM registration, this machine took part in the September 1936 Schlesinger England-South Africa air race, having to retire at Athens as a result of a fuel-feed problem. Shortly thereafter, this machine passed into the hands of Alex Henshaw, receiving the British registration G-AEXF. Initially acquired by the extremely youthful, but capable Henshaw, G-AEXF was powered by a DH Gipsy Six I, in which form Henshaw flew it

to victory in the 1937 Folkestone air race and the 1937 King's Cup race, from which he retired with contaminated fuel. Prior to the start of the 1938 racing season, Henshaw had his aircraft re-engined with the higher-powered Gipsy Six R, simultaneously fitting a Ratier variable pitch propeller to better utilize the extra 30 hp (23 kW) engine output. In this form, G-AEXF achieved 398.3 kph (247.5 mph) in both the Hatfield-Isle of Man and Manx Air Derby races of 1938. Later that year, by now sporting a new DH propeller, Henshaw romped home to win the King's Cup with a record-setting speed of 380 kph (236 mph).

This is the fifth of the six Percival Mew Gulls built

PITTS SPECIAL (United States)

S-1 Special

Designed and built by Curtis Pitts for the celebrated aerobatic display pilot Betty Skelton, the Pitts 190 Special first flew in September 1944 with a 67-kW (90-hp) Continental engine and single-seat accommodation in an open cockpit. The type was of mixed construction, with a covering of fabric over the wooden wings and the steel-tube fuselage and tail unit. The result was a diminutive braced biplane with fixed tailwheel landing gear, and from the very beginning the design revealed exceptional aerobatic capabilities. Pitts then developed the design for homebuilders as the Special Biplane with engines in a range between 48 and 71 kW (65 and 90 hp) and ailerons on the lower wings only. The type's aerobatic qualities meant that an increasing number were built for competition purposes with airframes stressed to higher levels, ailerons on the upper as well as lower wings, and engines of up to 134 kW (180 hp).

In the mid-1960s Pitts developed a two-seat model, and this first flew in 1967 as the S-2 Special to complement what now became the S-1 Special. The S-2 was somewhat larger than the S-1 and powered by the 134-kW (180 hp) Lycoming O-360-A1A, while aerodynamic refinements made it stable in rough air and also enhanced manoeuvrability. This model reintroduced factory production with Pitts Aviation Enterprises (later Pitts Aerobatic Company), and definitive models were the S-1S with the 134-kW (180 hp) IO-360-B4A engine, the S-1T with the 149-kW (200-hp) AEIO-360-A1E driving a constant speed propeller, the S-2A with the same engine, and the S-2B with the 194-kW (260-hp) AEIO-540-D4A5.

In 1983 Christen Industries bought Pitts, continuing production of current models and introducing the S-2S single-seat version of the S-2B.

Pitts Special S-1

PITTS S-1 SPECIAL
Role: Aerobatic sportsplane
Crew/Accommodation: One
Power Plant: One 180 hp Lycoming 10-360-B4A air-cooled flat-opposed
Dimensions: Span 5.28 m (17.33 ft); length 4.72 m (15.5 ft); wing area 9.15 m² (98.5 sq ft)
Weights: Empty 327 kg (720 lb); MTOW 522 kg (1,150 lb)
Performance: Maximum speed 285 km/h (177 mph) at sea level; operational ceiling 6,795 m (22,300 ft); range 507 km (315 miles)
Load: None

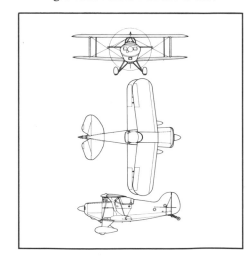

Pitts S Special

INDEX